"A great th . . ."

Nation

THE MAN ON A DONKEY spans three decades and reaches into every corner of England in the reign of Henry VIII to show how great noblemen, rich abbots, knights and commoners lived and played their roles in a vast and tragic drama.

It is the time of the Reformation in England, when the King's men are despoiling the monasteries and dividing church wealth among the royal favorites—"the new men"—and a rebellion is rising in the North Country.

Principally, this is the story of Christabel Cowper, the able and imposing prioress of Marrick Priory; Thomas, Lord Darcy, who loves honor and would fight for it; the girl Julian, who will pledge her life for her one love; Gilbert Dawe, the heretical priest, burdened with a fiery hatred; and Robert Aske, leader of the rebellion, who is judged a traitor and hanged in chains.

"There are besides," Miss Prescott says in her preface, "the king and three who were his queens, and many others, men and women, gentle and simple, good and bad, false and true, who served God or their own ends, who made prosperous voyages or came to shipwreck. . . ."

A rich, absorbing, deeply moving work of fiction, *The Man on a Donkey* is the finest achievement of a superb scholar and ranks as one of the three or four greatest historical novels written in this century.

From the reviews of this book:

"A unique achievement. It blends fine scholarship with great literary imagination. . . . It is undoubtedly one of the finest historical novels written in this century." —John Raymond, *New Statesman and Nation*

"A towering accomplishment, bold in design, meticulous in detail . . . a total recreation of Tudor England." —*Washington (D.C.) Sunday Star*

"Packed with characters . . . great suspense . . . as good as a historical novel can be—fresh, imaginative, sensitively written, bringing back alive a violent period." —*New York Post*

"The English have always excelled in historical novels and this is one of the best. Miss Prescott has brought the crowded years to life as though she had lived them herself." —Marchette Chute
New York Herald Tribune Book Review

H.F.M. PRESCOTT is an English historian and novelist, and former lecturer in Modern History at Oxford. *Mary Tudor*, Miss Prescott's biography of the eldest daughter of Henry VIII, was awarded the James Tait Black Historical Prize, and her novels— *Son of Dust, The Unhurrying Chase*—are distinguished by a fusion of literary and scholarly excellence. *The Man on a Donkey*, which was the product of eight years spent in research and writing, is considered her finest book.

THE MAN ON A DONKEY

A Chronicle

❦

H. F. M. Prescott

BALLANTINE BOOKS • NEW YORK

This edition published by arrangement with The Macmillan Company.

First Printing: February, 1967

Printed in the United States of America

BALLANTINE BOOKS, INC.
101 Fifth Avenue, New York, New York 10003

To DOROTHY MACK

Because it is her book

AUTHOR'S NOTE

The book is cast in the form of a chronicle. This form, which requires space to develop itself, has been used in an attempt to introduce the reader into a world, rather than at first to present him with a narrative. In that world he must for a while move like a stranger, as in real life picking up, from seemingly trifling episodes, understanding of those about him, and learning to know them without knowing that he learns. Only later, when the characters should by this means have become familiar, does the theme of the whole book emerge, as the different stories which it contains run together and are swallowed up in the tragic history of the Pilgrimage of Grace. And throughout, over against the world of sixteenth-century England, is set that other world, whose light is focused, as through a burning glass, in the half crazy mind of Malle, the serving-woman, and in the three cycles of her visions is brought to bear successively upon the stories of the chief characters of the Chronicle.

CONTENTS

THE BEGINNING AND THE END

SIR JOHN UVEDALE had business at Coverham Abbey in Wensleydale, lately suppressed, so he sent his people on before him to Marrick, to make ready for him, and to take over possession of the Priory of St. Andrew from the Nuns, who should all be gone by noon or thereabouts. Sir John's steward had been there for a week already, making sure that the Ladies carried away nothing but what was their own, and having the best of the silver and gold ornaments of the Church packed up in canvas, then in barrels, ready to be sent to the King. The lesser stuff was pushed, all anyhow, into big wicker baskets; since it would be melted down, scratches and dints did not matter.

Sir John's people left Coverham before it was daylight, because the November days were short. They had reached the top and were going down towards Marrick when the sun looked over the edge of the fells in a flare of wintry white gold. It was about ten o'clock in the morning that they came down into Swaledale and through the meadows towards Marrick stepping-stones; the Priory stood opposite them across the river, at the top of a pleasant sloping meadow whose lower edge thrust away the quick running Swale in a great sickle-shaped curve. The cluster of buildings and the tall tower of the Church took the sunshine of a morning mild and sweet as spring. Behind the Priory, with hardly more than the width of a cartway between, the dale side went up steeply, covered for the most part with ash, beech and oak; the mossed trunks of the trees showed sharply green in the open sunlit woods. There was one piece of hillside just behind the Priory where there were no trees, but only turf nibbled close by the nuns' neat black-stockinged Swaledale sheep; in the summertime the Ladies had used sometimes to sit here with their spinning and embroidery, and here in spring the Priory washing was always spread out; now, on this winter morning, the slope was empty.

They crossed the stream, climbed the meadow by the cart-track, and turned the corner of the long Priory wall. Sir John's steward stood in the sunshine that struck through the gate-house arch; he swung a big key from his finger—the key of the Priory gate, which the Prioress herself had a moment ago put into his hand.

And now he watched the Prioress and the last two of the Ladies who went with her, and a couple of servants, as they rode alongside the churchyard on their way to Richmond and into the world. Of the three middle-aged women, one, plump and plain, was crying helplessly and without conceal-ment; she kept her face turned to look back on the Priory, for all that her tears drowned the sight of it. Another, a hand-some woman yet, who had flashed her dark eyes at the steward, glanced once over her shoulder; her mouth shook, but she tossed her head and rode on.

The Prioress herself did not look back, nor was her face in any way discomposed. Down at the core of her heart she was angry, though not with the King for turning away all the monks and nuns in England and taking the abbeys into his hand—surely he had a right to them if any had. She was not indeed angry with any man at all, but with God, who had tricked her into thirty years of a nun's life, and suffered her to be Prioress, and to rule, and now had struck power out of her hand.

But that anger lay beneath, so that she did not even know it was there. Her mind was set on the future as she considered and tried to estimate what her position would be in the house of her married sister. She would have her pension—but suppose it were not paid regularly—? On what foothold could she stand so as to make her will felt? Her thoughts were so closely engaged that she did not notice when they crossed the muddy lane which was the boundary of the Priory lands, and so left Marrick quite behind.

The steward stood where he was until the Ladies were out of sight. Now, for the first time for close on four hundred years, there were no nuns at Marrick. But he was not thinking of that as he turned back into the gate. Before Sir John arrived there was much to be done; he gave his orders curtly, and even before dinner was ready the servants were all about the place, sweeping up stale rushes, scrubbing, unpacking trussing-beds and coffers that they had brought on the baggage animals, shaking out hangings, lighting fires.

Most of Sir John's men were of the new persuasion, and glad to see the houses of religion pulled down. One or two of them opened the aumbry in the cloister, and there came upon a few books which the Ladies had left behind. They found great cause for satisfaction, as for laughter, in tearing out the pages of these books and scattering them in the cloister garth; one of the books was very old and beautiful, gay with colours and sumptuous with plumped-up burnished gold; another had initial letters of a dusky red like drying blood; when the pages were strewn about the garth it looked as if flowers were blooming in November.

Two only, out of those who had come this morning from Coverham, took no part at all in this business of setting the House to rights for its new owner. One of these was Sir John's old priest, the other was the woman Malle, who was the priest's servant now, and had therefore, with him, so strangely come back to Marrick.

The old man sat down on the horseblock for some time in the sun, then wandered out and down to the river, to pace the level bank there just below the stepping-stones, telling his beads, and letting the unceasing hushing of the water fill his mind with peace. There was nothing for him to do but wait. His stuff was among the rest that had been unloaded in the Great Court of the Priory, but he knew that the steward would have no time to think of sending it to the parsonage till all was ready for Sir John's coming.

Even before he came down to the river Malle left him, to drift about looking here and there, more as if she were searching for something or someone than merely revisiting places that had once been familiar. After going to the edge of the woods and staring up over the little wooden gate at the foot of the Nuns' Steps, she came back into the kitchen, then into the Great Court and climbed the outside stair that led up to the door of what had been the Prioress's chamber. It was quite empty now; all the goods of Christabel Cowper, last Prioress of Marrick, had been taken away; there were no rushes on the floor nor wainscot on the walls; only cobwebs, and the marks where the wainscot had been. Over the hearth the old painted letters, which had been hidden by a small but specially fine piece of arras, showed once more—

I.H.S. Malle could not read but she knew that the symbols meant, somehow, God, so she curtseyed and crossed herself.

From the Prioress's chamber she wandered over to the guest-house, and stood inside the door of the upper chamber, just where she had stood when my Lord Darcy had sat on the bed, with his hands on the cross of his walking staff, questioning about her visions. She did not remember him nor his questions because something in her that had been a restlessness was strengthening into belief; she began to know that if now she sought, she would find.

So she went quickly once more across the Great Court and into the cloister. The crumpled pages of the books were sidling about the grass, the flower beds, and the cloister walks as a light fresh wind shifted them. She stooped to pick up some that moved just before her, because they were pretty to look at; from between two of the red-lettered pages a pressed flower fell, the bell of a wild foxglove, pale purple, frail, and half transparent; she did not know that Julian Savage had put it there one day, because Robert Aske had worn it on his finger, like the finger-tip of a glove, while he talked to her. She had put it there for a charm to shield him from hurt.

Two men coming down the day-stairs shouted at Malle; They knew that she was at least three parts fool, and they laughed loudly as she bolted out of the cloister and into the Great Court again. She had meant to go into the Church, but, since she did not dare until the two men had gone away again, she began peeping into the stables on the opposite side of the Great Court. In them some of the beasts stood, patient and idle, only their mouths working; there were empty stalls too, for some had been led out to the fields; this morning the Priory servants had each done as seemed best to himself now the bailiff was gone already, and the Prioress to go by noon.

After the stables she looked into the dove-house; the sleepy crooning there had a summer sound, which made it seem that time had turned back. She went next into the guest-house stable. Leaning in one corner among some pea-sticks was the fishing rod that Master Aske had put there on the afternoon when Malle had sat here peeling rushes for lights, while the rain poured down outside. She did not now think of Master Aske, or of that day, nor of any time since, because all the sorrows of the world were clean washed from her mind by the shining certainty that was growing in it.

So she would wait no longer for the men, but went back, hurrying, into the cloister, and so into the Nuns' Church.

But He was not in the Nuns' Church. The door in the wall that separated the Nuns' from the Parish Church was open to-day; so she went through. Here Gilbert Dawe had told her that He was dead, and now lived, and was alive for ever-more. But He was not in the Parish Church either.

She did not know where else to look, and it was without thought or intention that she came to the Frater and opened the door; there was no supposing that He would have come to that room. No one ever used it except at great feasts like Christmas, since for a long time the Nuns had eaten by Messes, each Mess in its own chamber.

Yet to-day the Frater had been used. To-day, instead of eating in their chambers, all stripped of furnishing, the Ladies had breakfasted together, according to the ancient Rule of their Order, but hastily and in confusion of mind. The dis-array of that hurried meal lay upon the table, and the sun, shining through the painted glass of the windows in the south wall, spilled faint flakes of colour, rose, green, gold, upon the white board-cloth.

There were eleven wooden trenchers set on the table, with crumbled bread and bits of eggshell on them. There were eleven horn drinking-pots too, and several big platters, all empty, except that there was upon one a piece of broiled fish, and on the other half a honeycomb.

The Chronicle is mainly of five:—of Christabel Cowper, Prioress; Thomas, Lord Darcy; Julian Savage, Gentlewoman; Robert Aske, Squire; Gilbert Dawe, Priest.

There are besides, the King and three who were his Queens, and many others, men and women, gentle and simple, good and bad, false and true, who served God or their own ends, who made prosperous voyage or came to shipwreck.

There is also Malle, the Serving-woman.

Elevaverunt Flumina Fluctus Suos: A Vocibus Aquarum Multarum. Mirabiles Elationes Maris: Maribilis in Altis Dominus.

The Floods arise, O Lord: The floods lift up their noise, The floods lift up their waves. The waves of the sea are mighty and rage horribly: but yet The Lord that dwelleth on high is mightier.

CHRISTABEL COWPER, PRIORESS

SHE WAS BORN in 1495 at Richmond in Yorkshire. Her father's house stood looking up at the barbican, and at the proud head of the great keep above the barbican, across the wide and steep square. Her father's father had built the house of stone, very solid: very small as his son came to think it. But the warehouse behind where the wool was kept, was large; for that, to Christabel's grandfather's mind, was far more important than the place where he ate and slept.

Christabel's father, Andrew Cowper, was not so good a man of business as old Andrew; but then, he had a better start, for when the old man died there was gold money, mostly in coin of Flanders and Spain, in leather bags, hidden in the recess behind the red and white curtains of the great bed. Only Christabel's father, as well as old Andrew, knew the secret of that hiding place, and he was not told of it till he was a grown man of twenty-five, married, and with four children of his own.

As well as the hidden gold there were silver gilt cups on the livery cupboard in the great chamber downstairs, and in the chest at the foot of the old man's bed there were six bags of silver, and a standing cup made of polished cokernut enclosed in roped bands of silver gilt, which he drank out of during all the Christmas Feast, and at Easter, Whitsun, and upon St. Andrew's Day. The name of the great cup was Edward.

When old Andrew knew that he was dying he sent for one of the Grey Friars, an old man too. They had birds'-nested and played at marbles together in the old days, and snowballed in the square below the window that very day that the snowy field of Towton was dabbled red with blood.

Andrew Cowper told Brother William that he wanted him

to make a will, so the other old man sat down by the fire, and taking on his knee one of the square scrubbed chopping-boards from the kitchen, spread his parchment on it and wrote down what he was told.

It took long to do, for it was a stormy day in November and the wind brought the smoke swirling out from the chimney till it filled the room and the air was blue; the smoke caught old Andrew's chest, and sent him off into long fits of coughing that left him panting and speechless.

The beginning of the will was all in Latin, for it was about the money that was to be spent on the old man's obit, and on mass every year on St. Andrew's Day, and on wax candles for the rood-loft in the Friars' Church, and on a cow to give milk to the poor of Richmond; and besides the money for these pious purposes old Cowper's best velvet gown was to be given to the Friars to make a cope.

After these things they came to the rest of the old man's clothes, and the beds, and kitchen pots and pans, the hangings, a golden chain, silver spoons, and all the household stuff that was to go to son Andrew and his two brothers and sisters, and to son Andrew's sons and daughters. Here Brother William gave up the Latin, fetched a deep sigh, relaxed his toes which had been crimped upwards with the effort—for his Latin was rusty—and wrote the rest in English.

Andrew got most, which was natural, for he was to be a merchant and freeman of Richmond as his father had been. But the other two sons had money, or a bit of land here and there which old Cowper had bought, and the daughters had money too, though much less than the men, and enough to buy themselves a mourning gown each. Andrew's sons came off almost as well as their uncles, but his daughters, grown women now except for Christabel, had no more than a silver spoon of the Apostles each. Except, again, for Christabel; to her the old man left his great cup Edward—the cup made out of a nut.

There was a great quarrel over that when the old man was dead and buried. But Christabel got the cup and held it, while the quarrel raged, and her two married sisters, and the one not yet married, and her brothers all said what they thought of a bequest so outrageous. They had known, they said, that Christabel was the favourite of their grandfather, but their father, or their mother, or the old friar should not have permitted him to do anything so foolish and unfair. The eldest married sister, who was of an excitable disposition, was even heard to murmur something about sorcery, though when pressed she only mumbled, "Well, how could he have done it else? No, I don't say it was—but—" They all agreed however that it was as absurd as it was wrong of the old man, knowing quite well that Christabel was to be a nun, to leave her the cup. What did nuns want with a cokernut cup which had come from Flanders, and was a rarity, and very costly, and his favourite cup into the bargain?

Christabel was twelve at the time, a square-built, solemn girl. She sat clutching the cup, pressing it into her lap, really afraid sometimes that they would try to wrench it out of her hands. If they had she would have struggled with them, but they kept to words, and with words she met them. It was hers by will, she told them, and why should not a nun have a cup, and the old man had always promised it to her (which was not true, for the gift had surprised her very much), and she could not see that being the youngest made her any worse than the rest of them, and—going back again to the beginning—it was hers by her grandfather's will.

She was only a child, but while they lost their tempers she kept hers, and in the long run she kept the cup. What was more, being puffed up by her success, she asked to have it to drink out of the very next Sunday, being the Feast of St. Andrew, as her grandfather had done. Her mother refused, and was so put out by the request that she beat Christabel handsomely, and recommended her to learn to be of a meek stomach or she'd come to ill some day.

Her father, however, only laughed when he heard of it, and said she'd be prioress at Marrick before she'd done. He was a very easy-going man, little like his father except in his size and big bones. He dressed always like a gentleman, everything not only very trim and good but also gay. Quite a lot of the gold from behind the tester bed was spent on a gold belt buckle, and a brooch for his cap which had a naked woman in a circle of leaves, holding a pearl in her hand. Perhaps it was right that he should dress so much more fine than his father, seeing that his wife's mother was a second cousin of my Lord of Westmorland. Certainly Christabel thought it was right; she liked to watch him amongst the other merchants of Richmond; he looked well, he made a good show, though she knew inwardly even at this early age that he was not the man his father had been, and worried herself sometimes lest he should make some disastrous mistake that would lose money, and besides that make them all look fools before the more provident merchants of Richmond. She tried once to tell her mother of her anxiety, but only got her ears boxed for speaking so undutifully of her father.

As time went on Christabel thought less of her father, who was kind and careless, with now and again a fit of temper when he had drunk too much. And at the same time she grew into a feeling of kinship with her mother. Christabel believed that though her mother had boxed her ears, yet she also watched Andrew Cowper with anxiety and irritation. Christabel's eyes would go from one to another at table, reading or guessing by the signs in her mother's hard, pale face, at the hidden but embittered disagreement between them when Andrew came in with a new jewel or talked large before friends of the arras he would buy for the hall. Christabel approved of her mother, though she got no tenderness, and indeed, barely kindness, from her. Only one thing she must disapprove of—"If I'd come of such a house," she decided when she was not quite thirteen years old, "I'd not have married so low." She felt, because she had her mother's blood in her, that she could despise her father. And always a thought rankled—"He has no right to waste that which my grandfather had laid up, which is for us."

Christabel had not been able to despise her grandfather, in spite of his plain merchant blood, even when she began to grow up and count these things as important. When very small she had been his pet, to be carried round Richmond, tossed up on his shoulder, and fed with cakes, wafers or strawberries. When she was a little bigger than that she would trail after him, stumping along on sturdy fat legs, hanging on to the long metal-studded tongue of his belt, or tugging at his gown as she grew tired, to ask him for a pick-aback.

But as she grew older Andrew had occasion more than once to box her ears for impudence, and once he took his stick to her and beat her. She never forgot that, and always would behave herself very meekly while he was in the house, but she never loved him after, nor went willingly near him; and when they told her that he had left her his great cup Edward, privately, deep down in her own mind, she thought the less of him, as if it had been a weakness in him not to know that she did not love him.

It was when she was eleven that her elders told her that she was to be a nun, and Christabel, having been taken a little while before by her mother to her eldest sister's second lying-in, decided that it was on the whole better to be a nun than a married woman, even though the clothes nuns wore were not near so fine as her sister's grey velvet night-gown with the white fur. However, she had noticed that the Prioress of Nun-Appleton, who was the sister of Christabel's sister's husband, and who came to the christening, wore a silk, and not a linen, veil, and that her girdle was of silk too, and that the skirt of her habit opened up at the front over a damask petticoat which, though black, was very rich. As she rode home pillion behind her mother, with her cheek jolting against Elizabeth Cowper's shoulder blades, she announced that when she was a nun she would wear a silk veil, and a silk girdle, and a gold pin; she threw that in as an extra flourish. Her mother, who had been too busy to notice what the lady prioress wore, and who was now running over in her mind all the things which she would send from Richmond for the new baby, only said: "That you will not. For nuns must not wear such things."

"I shall. I shall. I shall," Christabel whispered, and because she could not stamp her foot she thumped Grey Hodson's flank with one heel. Her mother did not hear; Grey Hodson was old and too staid to show resentment; and reflecting afterwards Christabel came to the conclusion that it was well her declaration had gone unnoticed. "I shall not tell them what I shall do," she thought. "But when they have made me a nun I shall do it. *And* I shall drink from the cokernut cup whenever I please."

A year after old Andrew Cowper's death Christabel's father and mother took her to Marrick, where she was to be a nun. It was more than ten miles up the dale, and to reach it you had to leave Swaleside and go up and over the fells. That, since they would take a mule laden with all Christabel's stuff, meant a whole day's ride, and an early start.

The night before they set out Christabel was sent to bed specially early, and not to her own bed in the little attic but to her parents' bed in the great chamber. Her mother came and fussed about the room a bit while Christabel undressed, and even when she had slipped into bed and lay, naked as a fish, between the sheets. It was as if Mistress Elizabeth Cowper felt that she had forgotten something, or left something undone—"and yet that," thought Christabel, listening to her movements, "is not possible." She knew that her mother was a most methodical person and that everything was sure to be completely ready for to-morrow.

Dame Elizabeth stood for a moment at the door, looking across the thin slit of light that came between the shutters, to the blank curtains of the bed in the dusky corner of the room. Not a sound nor stir of movement came from the child behind them.

"Go to sleep."

"Yes, Madame."

"We shall start at sunrise."

"Yes, Madame."

Mistress Elizabeth lifted the latch, and Christabel held her breath, waiting for the sound of the door closing which would tell her that she was alone. But her mother still lingered.

"You must be a good girl and heed what you're told."

"Yes, Madame."

She heard her mother sigh sharply, as if with exasperation.

"Well," said Elizabeth Cowper rather loudly, but more to herself than to Christabel. "Well. It's the best for you. I've done what I can for you all. Go to sleep." The door shut sharply even before Christabel had time to reply "Yes, Madame."

So she waited a little, listening to her mother's deliberate, heavy tread. A stair creaked, that was the sixth one down; another creaked with quite a different note, that was the last but one; then she heard the parlour door shut. She waited till she had counted over her fingers twice, then she pulled her feet from under the sheet and the green counterpane, and slid out of bed. But still she stood listening.

There was no sound in the house. From the yard outside came a steady burr, which she knew for the noise of Marget's wheel. Old Marget always sat out in the yard spinning on warm evenings, following the sun from the edge of the wall to the mounting block, then to the hay-loft steps, and last of all, when the sunshine was no more than a narrow wedge, to the corner by the pigstyes.

Christabel slunk across the room meaning to ease up the latch of the shutters and look down on Marget, but thought better of it, because Marget might look up. A knife-blade of sunshine still slit through the dusk from the joint in the shutters. She turned about in it, like a joint on a spit, twitching her shoulders, and enjoying the delicate warmth on her naked back. Then, with a sudden skip, she made for the bundles that lay alongside the wall at the far side of the room. Her purpose in stealing out of bed had not been any thought of taking a last look at the yard, the wool-store, or Marget, but to feel and finger and prod the bundles.

The biggest of them was bulgy and soft, and swelled up between the cords that bound it; that was the feather-bed and the fustian blankets, and the two pairs of sheets. The second was not so billowy, but it was heavier and had a hard core to it, for in between the bolster and pillow there was a little square chest of ashwood that held, wrapped up in a tester of painted cloth for the bed, a silver spoon and two candlesticks, two pewter plates and a little brass pot. The two other bundles were quite small. In one was a pair of tongs, a frying-pan and a skillet. In the other, which was the smallest of all, were her three new shifts, two pairs of shoes, and the habit of a novice of the Order of St. Benedict —white woollen gown, white linen coif and veil, with enough woollen cloth to make hosen for the next two years, and the great cup Edward—all these things packed up in a coverlet of striped say, red, white and green.

Christabel hung over the bundles, wriggling her fingers into the folds in the hope of touching what was inside, poking them, thumping them gently with her fist, feeling them softly all over. She did not envy her eldest sister, even though she had married a knight, and he was just now building a new house which would have glass in all the windows of the Hall, and of the summer and winter parlours—and carved wainscot too. If Christabel could have had the house without the husband it would have been different. But as that couldn't be, she thought, "This is better. He tore Meg's best sheets tumbling into bed drunk with his boots on. No one can tear my sheets. They're mine."

She punched the big bundle again, possessively and defiantly, and then, hearing a door open downstairs, scuttled across the room and dived between the curtains of the bed.

Next morning the dale was still full of mist when they turned up the road which led to the fells, but here the sun was warm on their backs, the larks were up, and the sky blue without a cloud. Their shadows, jerking along the road before them, were absurd pointed shapes; the two big bundles corded on the mule's pack saddle showed in the dust like shadows of another and huger pair of ears. Christabel, riding pillion behind her mother, kept looking back—not to see the shadows, nor to see the last of Richmond, where the smoke was going up as the mist cleared, thin and steady and blue as hyacinths, against the woods beyond the town; but to see her goods coming safely after her.

There were, as well as the mule laden with her gear, two others going light. On the way home all three would be almost hidden below the great sarplers of wool, for Christabel's father would be buying wool up and down the dale—wool from the Manor and Priory at Marrick, wool from the little House of Cistercian Nuns a mile down the river, and from the Manor at Grinton and the Manor at Marske. The two seven-pound leaden wool-weights, bearing the King's leopards and lilies and joined by a strap like a stirrup leather, hung down on either side of his horse in front of the saddle.

They stopped about noon to dine, and sat down on a bank beside the road. The turf was short, crisp and wiry, and meddled with bright pink thyme, and yellow crow's-foot. A shepherd came near as they sat eating, and crossed the road, his flock going before him. They were fresh from the shearing, very trim in their black and white, small black faces, neat black stockings, and some spotted with black; when the sun shone through their ears it made them rose-red. On the wool of every sheep the shear-marks showed like ripple-marks.

The shepherd knew Master Cowper quite well, and stopped to talk. The Wool-man gave him a pull of ale out of the leather bottle, and a bit of brawn between two tranches of white bread; when the shepherd saw the white bread the look came into his eyes that a dog has when it is begging, rapt and exalted. While he ate, with his crooked staff leaning on his shoulder, Master Cowper talked to him about wool, and the condition of the dale sheep, and the good weather they had had—praise the Saints—for washing and shearing. And the shepherd, his mouth very full, nodded or shook his head in answer, and only when necessary tucked as much of the victuals as he could into his cheek, and spoke indistinctly through the crumbs.

Christabel watched first the shepherd and then her father, for once approving of him. Master Cowper looked well, with his long legs stuck out before him in leathern riding hosen, and his doublet of fine holly green Flanders cloth. He sat leaning back on his hands, very much at ease, and his beard jigged as he talked.

"The shepherd thinks my father to be some very great man," Christabel decided to herself, forgetting that the shepherd knew every Wool-man who went up the dale.

He moved on at last over the fell top, into the great silence of blue air above green turf, and even the sound of his piping died—for he had laid his pipe to his lips when he parted. In the noon heat Andrew Cowper and his wife and the servant drowsed; Christabel sat looking along the road, where it dipped and rose again and vanished over the long lift of the fells, going towards Marrick.

They reached Marrick Manor in the early evening, and the bailiff came out, a great fat pleasant man who shouted for ale and cakes, and a dish of strawberries. So they all sat down on the benches inside the Hall, and Andrew Cowper talked again of wool. When Christabel had drunk dry her cup of wine and water, and shaken the crumbs from her lap, and licked as much of the pink of the strawberries from her fingers as she could, she stole out and stood on the steps looking about her. Across the dale there were woods; below her were woods; looking back towards Richmond there were woods too, with crags of stone sometimes breaking through, steep as the walls of the castle at Richmond. Only behind the Manor, in the direction from which they had come, there were the open fells, while farther up the dale a great crouching hill, spined like a beast, and dark with heather, split the wide dale into two narrow valleys; beyond that hill were fells and more fells, higher and higher, melting now into colourless disembodied shapes as the sun stood low over them.

When her parents were ready they all left the Manor; the bailiff kissed Christabel, and pinched her ear, which she resented silently; and called her his pretty little sweetheart, which pleased her. Perkin, with the laden mule, was to go down by the longer way, but the others by the steps. So, when they had gone through some little stone-walled closes, they came to a flagged walk of stone that ran down the steep slope, dived into the woods, became steeper, and turned into great slabbed steps of stone. Christabel went bouncing down them at a run, bunching up her skirts with both hands. Sometimes she would stop, and look back at her parents, but mostly she looked forward, peering through the trees for a sight of the Church and the Priory. The trees however were too close, and the slope too steep; only now and then she caught a glimpse of the spined, sleeping hill at the head of the dale, or far down on the left, the quick, shallow Swale, running clear brown, and flashing white sparkles of light from its ripples.

Then, quite suddenly, they were out of the woods, and upon

a steep slope of clean turf, and there, just below, was the Priory; you could have thrown a stone down into its Court. The chief thing among the buildings was, of course, the Church, with its tall bell tower, but all round that there were stone-slatted roofs, and lower and smaller roofs of thatch. Christabel, searching the buildings with her eyes, saw an orchard, and there were Ladies in it, walking about in twos and threes under the trees. They were every one in black and white. One of them stopped and pointed upwards and spoke, and they all stood looking towards Christabel; she heard an exclamation go up from them, and, though she could distinguish no words, she said to herself, "They were watching for me to come," and she felt important. She did not know how little important a thing need be, and yet the Ladies would be watching for it.

When the parents had sat talking a little while with the Prioress they said good-bye to Christabel, refusing an invitation to supper but accepting one to dine to-morrow at the Priory. They bade Christabel be a good girl, and serve God truly, and learn what she was taught, and do what she was told. She was to be sure and mind her manners, and not wipe her fingers, if they were greasy, on the table-cloth, and certainly not on the hangings—that from her father—and to keep her clothes neatly mended, "not cobbled, mind you" —this from her mother.

Then they both kissed her, and her father put her hand into that of the Prioress. The Prioress's hand was hot and damp, as was natural with such a large fat woman on a warm evening, but Christabel did not like it, so she wriggled her hand free, and then waved it to her parents as though that was why she had wanted to get it away.

She stood beside the Prioress on the top step of the outside stairway of stone that led up to the Prioress's Chamber, where they had all been sitting. Her father and mother went along the Court below, turned at the gateway and waved their hands to her; then they were gone.

"Oh!" cried Christabel sharply.

"There! There!" the Prioress comforted her. "Thy mother will be here again to-morrow."

Christabel said, "Yes, Madame." The dog which had certainly intended to make a convenience of one of her two bundles, dumped down by Perkin in the Court, had changed its mind and preferred the leg of a wheelbarrow. But she hoped the bundles would not long be left where they were.

"I will show you the Cloister," said the Prioress, and they went down, Christabel alongside the sweeping bulk of the Lady, through the narrow Great Court, where hens followed hopefully, and an old grey pony looked out kindly at them from over a half-door. They turned under an arch just beyond the bell tower, and found themselves in the Cloister, which, after the open Court, seemed very dark. It was very small too, small and somehow countrified; mustard was laid out to dry upon a trestle table along one wall, and there was a bunch of teazles hanging from a nail beside the door into the Church.

At the far end of the west walk, in which Christabel and the Prioress stood, there were two children, a boy a couple of years or so younger than Christabel, in a brown coat and with brown curls, and a girl who looked to be about her age. The boy was whipping a top and took no notice of them; the girl jumped off the low wall, between the Cloister arches crying—

"Look, John! She's come."

John said, "I care not," and gave a great slash at his top, but so unskilfully that it scuttered across the stone flags on its side, bounced off the wall and lay still.

"Come, John! Come, Margery!" the Prioress called them, and they came, staring all the time at Christabel.

The Prioress told Christabel that Margery Conyers was a novice; this Christabel could see for herself, since Margery wore a white woolen gown just like the one in Christabel's own pack. "And John is her cousin." Christabel would not have known that, for Margery was a thin child with a large nose and a little proud mouth, whereas John's face was round, snub-nosed and merry.

"Lout down, knave, lout down!" said the Prioress, tapping him on the shoulder, so that he bowed to Christabel. He did it awkwardly and looked at her with a pouting face, but then smiled at her suddenly, a bright, sunshiny smile.

Behind and above them the bell in the tower began to ring, and several of the Ladies came into the Cloisters from one side and another, arranging their veils and pulling up their black hoods which had lain on their shoulders.

"After Compline," the Prioress said, moving towards the Church door, "you shall have supper."

"Yes, Madame."

It was a strange thing, but till that minute Christabel had never thought that, of course, nuns were nuns in order to go to church over and over during the day and night.

She looked back over her shoulder and was sorry to see that John had returned to his top, though Margery was coming after them into the Church.

"You shall lay off these to-morrow," the Prioress said, touching Christabel's blue hood as they curtseyed before the Rood.

"I have my habit in my packs, Madame," Christabel answered sedately, and she thought, "There is supper to look forward to."

NOW THE CHRONICLE BEGINS

1509

July 20

The last loads of the hay-harvest were bumping and bounding along the rough track homeward to the Priory. The sun, low down over Mount Calva, filled all the dale with gold, and shot long shadows before them. Those of the Nuns who had come out to help stood while the wain moved off, flapping their hot faces with the big straw hats they had tied on over close coifs; no one wore veils in the hayfield. Some of them had taken off their black gowns and worked with the white woolen undergown—more yellow than white from repeated washings—tucked up over their girdles.

"Where," said one of them, "are those children?" and they turned to look back across Applecote Ing, where the mown grass was all rough from the scythes, and smudged with small grey strewings of hay which the rakes had missed. The Ing, which had been so full all day with horses and wains, and men and women raking and pitching the hay, was empty now.

Margery Conyers said, looking at her feet, that "they two had gone up towards Briary Bank," so the Ladies stood staring up and calling "John! Christie!" and telling each other to shout louder.

But they must have cried loud enough, for now they

heard John's shrill hail, and down the slope the two young things came pelting, hand in hand.

"Truly," said one of the younger Nuns, "it's as well that the boy's going away."

An elder, smiling to see the two, told her, "Lord, there's no harm. Christie's a little mother with him. I love to watch them."

They came near and stood panting.

"John made me this garland." Christabel pointed at the honeysuckle garland aslant on her hair. She shot a quick glance at Margery Conyers, who stood in the background, and gave her a triumphing smile; then she looked at John, and smiled very differently.

He said, "It's all awry with running down the bank," and he straightened it for her. The two young faces were grave and happy, and close together, for John, though he was nearly three years younger than Christabel, was grown so tall that they stood the same height.

"Go along with you, go along," the Ladies told him, and, "Go you with them, Margery." So Margery went on alongside the others, but as they were hand in hand again she walked a little apart.

By the time the hay had been tossed up on the new rick the sun had set; only the top of the bell tower was still bright, and when the pigeons, which had been disturbed by the shouting and stir, floated down again, wings raised and spread, they dropped out of the sunshine into shadowed air.

But if the Great Court was in shadow the Cloisters seemed almost dark; and more than dark, for after the long day in the sunny, sweltering field, the familiar, small sheltered house suddenly seemed strange. It was as though, while they had gone from it, it had also slipped away from them; as though, empty since dawn, it had been engaged upon some business of its own, and was not quite the same, and never would be quite the same again.

It was the children who felt it most, though they only stood still, looking round with quick, searching glances, and then looked at one another.

One of the older Nuns said, "How strange—yet it's only this morning we went out."

Then all of them went towards the laver beside the Frater door, where there were twelve little wainscot cupboards—one for each of the Nuns to keep her towel in.

Someone turned on the watercock, and the water tumbled

out in a shining glassy curve; even the sound of it seemed cooling, and the older Nuns were already splashing their hot faces, and bathing hands and wrists with exclamations of satisfaction.

John, to while away the time, kicked the end of a bench, then, lifting up his brown paw began to sniff at it. The palm smelt of all sorts of things; of the horses' sticky, dusty coats; of hay, of earth, of dirt. The back smelt different, and rather pleasant; he did not know what the smell was, and then realized that it was the smell of John. He put his tongue to it, and it tasted slightly of salt.

Margery Conyers was standing near.

"Smell my hand," he said, shoving it under her nose. She struck it away.

"It's not foul. Not the back." He was angry, and punched her with his fist before he turned away to find Christabel.

"Smell my hand, Christie," said he. She smelt it and then her own, and then he must smell hers, holding it in both of his, while Margery watched them.

Christabel slept in the very last room of what had once been the open dorter, but had for a long time now been divided up into a series of little chambers. This one, which they called the Richmond Chamber because of the blue and yellow chequers painted on the ceiling, was shared by three of the Nuns and Christabel. Here they slept and ate, as all the other Ladies, three or four to a Mess and each Mess in its own particular chamber, fetching its food away from the kitchen. So the old Frater on the Cloister was hardly ever used, except at the great feasts.

It was just on midnight, but not dark because of the full moon that shone through the two little windows. The Ladies had gone down to the Church for Matins and Lauds, but Christabel had not wakened either at the candlelight or the shuffling about in the room as they pulled on hosen and shifts and gowns, or at their sleepy, yawning conversation. She only woke when John laid a hand on her.

"Christie! Christie!"

She woke up then with a start.

"Oh! John!" She put out a hand and felt his—yawned, stretched and whispered, "How did you come?" She made room for him on the bed, and he curled up by her inside the curtains.

"Up the pear-tree."

"And through the Sacrist's chamber? Did Margery hear you?"

"No—she was snoring." He began to fumble in his shirt, and then put something into her hand in the dark.

"It's cherries and some comfits."

"Oh, knave!" Christabel said, putting a comfit into her mouth.

"I'm not. Maudlin gave them me," he said, and they ate them together merrily.

But when they were finished he sighed.

"I came to tell you something. When I was in the kitchen with Maudlin, the Lady"—that was what they called the Prioress—"the Lady went by in the Great Court, and I heard her say that she had writ to my father that I must go from here, now that I am so big." He put his arm round her neck and said, "Oh, Christie!" and kissed her. She kissed him as readily, and put her arms about him.

"But you'll come back to see me, John."

"It won't be the same. I can't come often. Christie, come with me."

"You silly boy," she said, "how can I?" She felt much older than he; he was only a child.

He pulled himself away from her. "You don't love me."

She said again, "How can I?" because, though she knew it was silly, yet she was setting two things up against each other. The one was life at Marrick—it was made up of solid, sensible things—meals, lessons, her own gear in this little room. The other was nothing to be seen or touched—it was loving John.

"Oh!" she cried, "I do. I do love you." It was true, and she had never loved anyone before, except her grandfather, long ago, before he had beaten her. But John was so easy to love. John was her little boy, and her lover, and the child she played with, all in one. Being yet children they could have it so, without even knowing that it was so.

She took a deep breath. She couldn't go away with him; she was old enough to know that. But at that moment for Christabel foolishness was wiser than wisdom, and things that are not, brought to nought things that are. She caught him again in her arms. She must do something to show him that she loved him; she must somehow break and hurt the things that are, for the sake of the things that are not.

"I know. I shall give you my great cup Edward."

"Oh! Christie!" he said, in such a voice that she felt warmth and light all through her, and glad to be giving away the great cup Edward. Tears came into her eyes, and were running down her cheeks when he kissed her, and when Dame Anne Ladyman, stepping softly, suddenly twitched the curtains of the bed open, and stood looking in, shining a candle upon the two of them.

"Jesu!" said Dame Anne, "it's as well I slugged abed and did not rise to Matins."

Margery Conyers crept away, quiet as a mouse. She had seen them, but they had not seen her. Yet she had done right to waken Dame Anne. John had no business to be out of his bed at this time of night, a little boy like that. And he was her cousin, not Christie's. He should have loved and followed her. She hated Christie.

1511

March 11

The Bishop had arrived last night and lay in the guest-house; Christabel's father and mother, her eldest brother, the sister who had married a knight, and her husband too, were all staying at Master Christopher Thornaby's up at Marrick village; and any time now, for it had been light for a couple of hours, Margery Conyers' father and mother might ride in from Marske. None of Bess Dalton's people would be coming; her nearest kinsman was a cousin, a cross-grained, ill-conditioned fellow, who was only too ready to be rid of the girl, but who did not mean to spend any more on the settling of her than he need.

For at Chapter Mass the three of them, Christabel, Margery, and Bess, were to be made nuns by the Bishop, and afterwards the Conyers and the Cowpers would feast the new nuns and all the rest of the House. It would be a great dinner, served in the old Frater, which had been scrubbed, and cleaned, and strawed fresh with rushes, and with whatever little tufts of greenery the young year provided.

Christabel and Margery were at it now, scattering the pansy leaves they had gathered, which would smell sweet, though faint, of violets. As was fitting they spread them thickest at the table set crosswise at the dais end, for there the Bishop, the Prioress, and the guests would sit.

"My ring," said Christabel, because she knew that Margery's

father and mother would sit above her own at the board—"my ring has a ruby in it." She knew also that Margery Conyers' ring was of plain gold. Margery had said that nuns should not have precious stones set in their espousal rings, but that was only to make the best of it.

"My cousin John, who is page to my lord my uncle, is coming to the feast," said Margery.

Christabel had not known this before and wondered if it were true. She said nothing for a minute, scrabbling in the basket for the last of the leaves, and dropping them carefully where they would best show.

"My sister's husband, who is a knight," she said, "has offered a gold piece to St. Andrew. And my father has brought a whole bolt of cloth for gowns for the House, and last night he sent a servant down from Marrick with pounds and pounds of spices to the kitchen here."

"My father has sent a heron and two cranes, and partridges, I know not how many."

"Huh! Those cost nothing." Christabel tossed the last of the pansy leaves disdainfully out on the rushes.

"Last time I went home," Margery said, "I saw my cousin John, and I asked him if he would be sorry that you should be a nun, Christabel. But he said he cared not, whether or no, and when I said that you would be fain to see him at the feast he pulled an ugly face and made a scream like a peacock."

"Little boys," said Christabel, "that lack the rod, grow up unmannerly."

But Margery Conyers, in order to have the last word, had gone out into the Cloister, leaving the door open. The snowdrops in the garth were almost over and here and there the daffodils had pushed up a green mace among the leaves. A delicate sunshine, shining through thin cloud, made the Cloister light, but threw no shadows. The big pear-tree, up which John had climbed, was covered with large buds; they had been caught and blackened at the tips by the late frosts, and every day now, since the weather had become warm, one of the Nuns would wonder if the frost had really spoiled the blossom. Across the other side of the Closter Bess Dalton stood, looking up into the air. On an ordinary day the Ladies would have been sitting there, sewing and reading in the sun, but to-day they were far too busy preparing for the feast, or entertaining the Bishop, to have time to sit in the Cloister, and Bess should not have had time either, to stand there, only staring.

She began to throw handfuls of corn out into the Cloister garth, and down came the pigeons. Bess watched them, and then saw Christabel and came round the Cloister to her. She was a fat, cheerful, stupid girl, never out of temper. To-day she looked happier than usual.

"They should have their feast too," she said, tipping her head back towards the birds.

Christabel answered, thinking of the good corn: "The Cellaress will be angry."

"Oh! Not to-day."

"Your cousin," said Christabel, not looking at Bess, but fiddling with the empty basket on her arm—"your cousin—hath he sent aught towards our feast?"

Bess laughed. "Perdy! Not he! He's a mean old snudge. But there's plenty. Oh! it will be a rare feast!" She went off quite happy, though everyone knew that her cousin had paid no more than her bare dower, and that what household stuff she had brought with her was poor and old.

Christabel was thinking about this when she found that Bess Dalton had come back, and all, so it turned out, to tell Christabel that she was so happy she could jump out of her skin, because to-day she was to be made a Nun at Marrick, where all the Ladies were so good and kind, every one of them. And if her cousin had not paid her dower, and she had had to leave Marrick, "I should have broken my heart, Christie, for I love them all here, they are so kind to me."

When she had gone away, crying a little and smiling, and wiping the tears off with the back of her hand, Christabel went again into the Frater. She had been pleased this morning at the thought that she would be made a Nun to-day, but what Margery Conyers had said seemed to have overcast the pleasure. And there was Bess Dalton, so happy about nothing. Christabel thought, "The Ladies are not so bad." If Margery Conyers were gone, and Dame Eleanor Maxwell who was so deaf, yet always wanted to be talked to, and Dame Anne Ladyman—"then I would like them well enough." It was Dame Anne who had found John and her together in the middle of the night, so it was Dame Anne who was responsible for the beating that Christie got, and the days on bread and water, locked up in the closet beyond the Prioress's room. John had been beaten too, and sent off the very next day. Christabel had not seen him since, and did not want to see him now. Loving

John had been pleasant and sweet. But they had made her smart for it, and had made her ashamed of it, so that now it was an offence to her.

The serving-woman came in from the kitchen and began to set out the wooden platters on the Nuns' table, with here and there a small silver cup. They brought them from the latticed aumbries beside the Cloister door. Christabel cheered up at this, and watched them now in pleased anticipation. Yes. There it was. One of the women took off the shelf a tall hand-some cup, the bowl made of a cokernut, cunningly borne in worked bands of silver gilt. It was Christabel's great cup, Edward. She watched the woman set it on the table, right down at the lower end of the Frater. But none of the Ladies had one fit to match with it, not even the Prioress. The Bishop to-day would drink from the Prioress's best, which was an old small silver cup. Christabel would drink from Edward.

She sidled up to the table and began to run her fingers about the rim. "Supposing," she thought, "I had given John the cup, and he had gone away with it." She felt that she had been spared a great loss. Now she would always be pleased when she used the great cup. It was unlikely anyone at Mar-rick would ever have one so fine. She felt secure again, and content. If she could only avoid having to speak to John to-day, she could enjoy these solid, real, dependable things— her great cup, the new coverlet her mother had brought for her, the gold pin her father sent her last New Year, the ring with the ruby which the Bishop would put on her finger to-day. And in the future there would be other things to look for-ward to, and to scheme for.

As it turned out she did not have to speak to John. She did not see him in the Church until the very last of the long Mass. She and the other novices had laid their new habits at the foot of the altar, and the gowns had been blessed and sprin-kled with holy water, and taken up again. They had put them on in the vestry, and come in with their lit candles, and knelt before the Bishop, received the veils, and had been espoused to Christ by the rings—wet and difficult to get on because they too had been sprinkled. At the very end of the office, with Bess Dalton crying happily, Margery shivering with excitement, and Christabel very proud and demure, they had come once more to the Bishop, their hands covered in a linen cloth, bear-ing the bread and wine with which he should communicate them. As Christabel knelt she heard a scuffling noise behind. She turned and saw John: he and another page-boy were trying to stamp on each other's feet. Then a tall man behind cuffed them each soundly, and they were still, with crimson faces. Christabel turned back and received the bread.

She saw John serve, of course, at the feast, but he served only at the table where the Bishop sat. When her own folk had taken leave and ridden away she saw him again. She was going along the Cloister towards the door leading up to the Richmond Chamber. There was a shout and a scuttering of feet, and three boys, John the smallest of them, came out from the Parlour, and went by her at the rate of a hunt. She had to jump out of the way, and they raised loud and jeering shouts as they passed her; she thought they jeered at her, and went on up to the Richmond Chamber with her cheeks burning. But they were jeering at the Cook's man, whom they had braved, stealing wafers from the kitchen.

By evening they were gone, and now she sat at table with the other nuns, and the great cup Edward was before her, and nothing would take it from her, nor uproot her from the comfortable security of her possessions in this House at Marrick.

1515

December 3

On a fine and bright winter morning the Ladies at Marrick were always pleased to be able to walk for a while in the or-chard. They grew very tired of the Cloister during the winter and, "Really," said Dame Anne Ladyman, holding up her bare palm to feel the sunshine on it, "it's as warm to-day as if it were spring."

To-day there was news to listen to, and talk over, for Dame Anne and Dame Bess Dalton had been away at Dame Anne's sister's house at Topcliffe on Swale, for the christening of a first child. Just a year ago they had been given leave by the Prioress to go there for the wedding, so the Ladies knew about the house, and the family, almost as much as could be known by those who had never seen any of the places and people. That made this second visit all the more interesting in the hearing. There were younger sisters of last year's bride, who might by now have had marriages arranged for them. And last year half the bees at Topcliffe had died of disease; how had they sped this year? And had Dame Anne's sister finished the embroidery for the chair that she was working last year? And did the parlour chimney still smoke? And the babe? He, of course, was new, and as a subject of conversation, inexhaustible.

Last year Bess Dalton and Dame Anne had talked so fast, prompting, and correcting, and supplementing each other, that hardly a question had to be asked; but this time Bess seemed heavy and dumpish, and Dame Anne would stop in her talk, when she was speaking of the guests, or the games they played, or songs that were sung, and purse her lips, looking sly and saying, "Well! Well! least said soonest mended," or, "Lord! you must ask Bess to tell you who sang the sweetest." The Nuns, knowing Dame Anne, and seeing Bess's crimson cheeks, could guess what all that meant, but little Margaret Lovechild, the youngest of the novices, who walked hanging on with both hands to Bess Dalton's arm, was too simple to guess.

"And the babe," said Bess, brightening up a little at a question from one of the older Nuns who wished to stop Dame Anne's tongue—"the babe is the prettiest little gentleman, with the bluest eyes."

"Ah!" Dame Anne cried, "but there was a prettier little gentleman yet, whose eyes were brown."

"Were there twins?" piped little Margaret, and Dame Anne let out a squeak of laughter.

Bess grew crimson, tried to answer Margaret, stammered, and burst into tears. When she had gone away, hurrying off with her head bent, Margaret began to cry too.

The others stood silent. The air here was never perfectly quiet, for always there was the sound of the rushing Swale below, and almost as constant as that the sleepy meditation of the wood pigeons in the bare bright woods high above the Priory.

"Run away, child!" Dame Anne bade Margaret, and she went, with a scowl at Dame Anne, because she loved Bess Dalton dearly. Dame Anne tittered again.

"Now I can tell you all about poor Bess and her—"

"No one wants to hear it," the old Cellaress interrupted heavily, and pushed past her. Most of the others followed, so Dame Anne had not much of an audience.

Christabel was in the Richmond Chamber when Bess came in; but Bess did not see her, and flopped down on her bed and sobbed aloud.

"Jesus!" said Christabel. "What's amiss?"

Bess cried for awhile and then told her. The priest at Top-cliffe was a young man, comely and gentle. "So gentle and so good," Bess said, lifting a hot, wet face for a moment. "Anyone must see it who but looks at him." Bess had seen him at the wedding a year ago. "He lives in the house, for he's chaplain to Sir Wat, in a little bare room. I looked within once—only from the door, Christie; there was but a bed and a crucifix and some books. And such a torn coverlet upon the bed. A blue coverlet."

Christabel had to wait till Bess had snuffled a little before she could go on.

"He said my eyes were like a dove's. And he said—But then—No, Christie, I can't tell you what he said, for it is sacred. But I know that he will go wretched all his days for want of me—as I for want of him." At that she broke down again, and wept desolately.

Christabel laid a hand on her shoulder and shook her.

"Fiddlesticks!" she said, and again, loudly and clearly, "Fiddlesticks!"

"What's fiddlesticks?" Bess sniffed.

"That either of you'll be wretched all your life long. In a twelve-month he'll have forgot, and you too."

"I'll not," cried Bess.

"You'll see you will."

Bess gave a great sob. "I must try to forget. It's sin to love him."

"You'll forget sooner if you don't try," Christabel told her, with greater wisdom than her years.

Bess only shook her head, and drooped in silence for a while. Then she started up—"A twelvemonth! I can't endure not to see him for a twelvemonth. Oh! Jesu-Mary! I can't stay here."

"You!" said Christabel bluntly. "You, that was glad that always you should live at Marrick."

"It's different now. You can't understand."

"Tush!" said Christabel.

1516

March 19

The first of the pedlars to come up the dale every year was a lean, leather-faced, elderly man with a grey donkey, which he called Paul of Derby. The pedlar's name was Jake, but the Ladies always called him "The Lent Pedlar," because of the season of his visits.

There were other pedlars with better wares, for this man bought only in Richmond, to sell up the dales, whereas some others went to York and even further. But Jake was one of the most popular because he came after the long winter, and brought news of the world from which the Ladies had been cut off perhaps for months when the snow blocked the road over the fells.

This year there had been snow lying from Christmas to Carle Sunday only ten days ago. But since then the spring had come with a rush, and from the dale the snow had vanished almost overnight. The Marrick Manor shepherd was reported to have said that the road was clear to Richmond, but they could not be sure of that till Jake actually came into the gate-house late one afternoon.

Then, when the Prioress had had him up to her chamber, to choose, with the Sacrist, a length of fine linen for a new alb for the Church; and the Cellaress had had him into her office to buy whipcord, and cheesecloth for the summer ewes-milk cheeses, he was allowed to come into the Cloister, where the dusk was falling, and spread out the pack that contained more frivolous things: pins for veils, carved wooden combs, purses and girdles of leather or of silk. The Ladies came round him, fingering and turning things over, and he doled out his news little by little, knowing pretty well how much they could be persuaded to buy, and never parting with his last titbits of information till he had given up hope of any more sales.

So to-night, it was not till Dame Elizabeth Close had at last made up her mind to lay out a shilling upon two bobbins of red and green silk that he sat back on his heels, rubbed his hands together, and said:

"Marry, if I bain't a fool not to tell your Ladyships the biggest bit of news of all."

"What, Jake? What is it?"

"Why none else but that the Queen was brought to bed of a fair child."

"Knave or girl?"

"Girl."

"Will she be our queen? What is her name?" Bess Dalton had bought nothing, for she never had money to spend. Yet she could not help watching and wishing—not cheerfully in these days, as she had used to watch, but with a long face. However, now that the buying was over she could join in the talking.

"Silly!" said Christabel Cowper, "it's a prince we want to be our king."

"Aye. There'll be a knave child soon. King Harry's a lusty gentleman. They say he—" Jake gave a bit of high-spiced gossip, which embarrassed some of the Ladies, amused others, and interested all.

"What is her name called?" Bess Dalton asked again.

"The little lady is the Princess Mary."

"Queen Mary," Bess said, trying the name. "I should like it well if there were a queen."

"There never hath been a queen to rule in England," Christabel maintained, and none of them knew enough to contradict her.

At the King's Palace of Greenwich that same day was sweet and mild. The gardens, bare of flowers and leaf but for primroses, and here and there a company of daffodils, were almost as full of ladies and gentlemen, strolling or sitting, as they would have been on any summer day. And all, except perhaps the oldest, felt the exquisite exhilaration of the spring, so that a waft of scent, a snatch of a blackbird's song, or only the warmth of the sun on the cheek, brought longing, promise, and rapture, all in one. Below the garden the river ran, glittering, and beyond the river lay the green Essex shore.

Someone had spread a tawny velvet cloak on one of the benches under the south wall where the sun was warmest, and the King sat on it, a young man in green and white satin, with a complexion like a rose, a small, soft mouth, but a nose fine-boned and imperial. A crowd of gentlemen stood about him, some close enough to join in the talk, others only listening and looking.

What those said who were talking with the King none but themselves could have understood anything more than the bare words, for their jokes and their teasings were those of men who know each other well, and who play and drink and hunt together. So such a remark as, "Mass, *he* would. Trust him. We all know about his stirrup-irons," or, "And where was your lute-string that time?" or, "Not the points of his hosen! Oh, Mass! Not again," provoked long gusts of laughter, though it was not so much the shared jokes that made them laugh, as their own well-being, and the sweet white wine of the day.

"Look," cried one, "a bee!" and pointed to the flower bed below the wall where, above the soft fresh turned earth, and the small leaves of plants just pushing up towards the light, a worker bee was hovering uncertainly.

"I'll have him!" cried the King, and snatching off his velvet cap with its jewelled brooch, flung it towards the passaging glitter of tiny wings and golden brown velvet. "I have him. No, Tray! Tray!"

Others now, laughing and shouting, flung their caps till the flower bed was gay as summer with scarlet, green, blue and carnation colour; then the bee, finding no flowers for its rifling, rose in the air, and went away into the shining blue while they cried after him, "Hue! Hue!"

As they were laughing and picking up their caps, someone said: "The Queen's Grace," and the outer parts of the group about the King—those who merely watched and listened—opened a way, by which came into the midst the Queen and her ladies.

Queen Katherine was five years older than her husband, and to-day, six weeks after the pains of childbirth, she looked older even than her years. So, when she came and stood beside the King and asked, "What do you? I heard laughter even within," it was more as if an indulgent mother had spoken the question than a wife.

But when the King told her, "Hunting of a bee," and proclaimed it a new sport that he would, one day, write a book on, so that every young gentleman should know the courteous terms of that quarry, she laughed as merrily as any of them, and laughed again, softly, looking down into the King's face as he looked up at her, with the sun making the red gold of his fine, closely curling hair glitter as if it burned. "And his teeth," she thought to herself with a weakening pang of delight, "are like a little boy's."

The King put up his hands and pushed her, gently but masterfully, so that she stood between him and the sun, and then, lowering his eyes, which had been dazzled by the glare, he began to play with the long gold lace of her girdle from which hung an enamel of Paris and his three goddesses.

"But what," said he, and dropped the pretty jewel, "what's this?" and he pulled at the end of a ribbon that strayed from beneath the parted skirts of her crimson velvet gown, and trailed across the gold brocaded petticoat. Quite a lot more came out as he pulled, and he began to laugh, while the Queen snatched at his hand and tucked the ribbon away in a painful embarrassment.

"Oh, Madame!" cried the King, still laughing. "Fie on your women!"

"No. It was my fault. They had no time to make me ready for Mass, because I slept so long."

"So long? I know how long you lie abed, sweetheart. Charles!" He looked up at the big, good-humoured Duke of Suffolk who stood close by, his fine legs in their white hosen straddled wide. "Charles, what should you do with a wife that steals from her lord's bed before it's light, to hear Masses?"

Suffolk laughed, and made no other answer, not being one of the quickest witted, but Katherine cried out:

"Sir, Sir, I pray you! These gentlemen—"

But the King interrupted.

"No, Madame, these gentlemen are all on my side. So I shall kiss you now, this once, for all the kisses I've lost when you go gadding after holiness betimes in the morning."

He had her by the wrist and pulled her to him, though she put her hands first upon his, to pull them away, and then upon his breast.

"No, no, my dear!" she cried. "No, Sir!"

"Why not? A' God's Name, whom but thou should I kiss this fair morning, and whom but me shouldst thou?"

She muttered, "No—for it is uncomely behaviour."

"What?" said he, catching her now by the arms, and drawing her down towards him. "To kiss? Or for a king to kiss? Or to kiss openly in the sunshine? There!"

But she had turned her face away so that he could only kiss her cheek.

"It is not so done in Spain," she whispered, at which he cried "Fie on her!" for she was a Spanish woman no longer.

"No," she said. He had loosed her, but now she seemed unwilling to move away. She touched his cheek with the back of her hand, and withdrew it sharply; it was the advance and retreat of a young girl, unpractised and shamefaced. "No. I am English now. But in Spain I was bred, and what a child learns early, that she cannot forget."

He was looking up at her, but, because of the brightness of the sky behind her head, he could not see the tenderness of her look as she added in lower tones, "So it will be with our little maid." But because he himself was fascinated and amused by the smallness and perfectness of that ridiculous puppet their daughter, a new human being, a microcosm, like a mirror to catch and reflect the universe and the Maker of the universe; and because besides he was a man who loved scholars and loved learning, he answered eagerly—

"It is true. And I have been thinking—" and, drawing her down beside him on the bench, began to talk of how the child should be taught—first letters, then music and the ancient tongues, then French and Italian.

"Already!" she teased him, "at six weeks old!" But soon she became as absorbed as he. Some of the gentlemen who stood about gave their opinions on this and that, and the group about the King shifted and settled into a different arrangement, as Suffolk and those of the younger men who cared more for the tilt-yard than the study fell back, and others took their place.

On the outskirts of the little crowd Suffolk found himself beside one of the Queen's ladies—a very young lady, gawky and self-conscious, "yet," he thought, "she has the skin of a peach," and so he began to be pleasant with her, but found it heavy going. Growing nettled he rebuked her. "My child, you're a fool if you take a lesson from your good mistress in how to deal with men. For if a woman wears always her virtue about her, like the boards of her stays, it wearies a husband, and—there are other women more comfortable to a man's liking."

He left her then, nodding to her in a friendly way, for he was rarely put out for long. But the girl stood, twisting her hands together and hating the things he had said, both those about herself and about the Queen.

"She is too good," she said to herself, and wished that she had been in time to say it to him—"she is too good to think of such things."

That would not have disconcerted Suffolk, being exactly what he himself thought; but, for the Queen's sake, he considered that it was a pity.

1519

July 15

Chapter began in the murk and hush that goes with thunder weather. All week a storm had threatened, and had not

[43]

broken, but to-day, by all the signs, it must break. When the Prioress came to the lectern, to read the daily chapter of the Rule, it was so dark that she had to send Christabel to the kitchen for a taper, and while she went there was silence, without wind, without stir, in the small Chapter House, so that if someone moved her feet upon the hassock of sedges, or if someone's inside gurgled, all heard. Christabel came back from the kitchen with a burning taper. She lit the two fat candles of the lectern, blew out the taper and went back to her seat. The Prioress opened the book and at that movement the spiry flames of the two candles, which had just steadied and lengthened, flinched aside, and flared out, so that the embossed golden letters and the blue and green and scarlet decorations seemed to crawl and quiver. The Prioress found her place and began to read, following along the lines with her finger. No one listened to the Rule. They knew it too well; and to-day, irritated by the heat and oppression of thunder, most of the Ladies were thinking rather of those sins of omission and commission in their fellows, which it was their solemn duty to bring to light, when the time came for confession and accusation.

The Prioress finished reading, went back to her chair, and murmured the words which would set tongues free. There was hardly a pause long enough to give any penitent the chance to confess her own faults before the Cellaress coughed behind her fingers, stood up, and accused the Chambress of having more fried eggs from the kitchen, last evening at supper-time, than she and the other Ladies of her Mess should have had—more eggs by three, the cook had said.

That brought in not only the Chambress but the other two Ladies of her Mess. The Chambress grew shrill in her indignation, the Cellaress's voice was as loud as it was deep, and old Dame Joan, who was one of the Chambress's Mess, though she could hardly make her thin piping heard, did what she could to add to the din by clattering the iron end of her stick upon the stone floor. Even Dame Elizabeth Close grew ruffled, and no wonder, for the Chambress, losing her head and striking a sidelong blow at one of her own side, hinted that if too many eggs had been eaten last night it was Dame Elizabeth who had eaten them. This, however, was only a glance at Dame Elizabeth's known reputation as a trencher woman, and did not, in the eyes of the affronted Mess, mean that they for one moment admitted the charge, either corporately or singly.

The Chambress, who had just denied having ever asked for more than the just share of three devout and hungry women, was soon hard pressed by the Cellaress. For the cook had said —("God be his judge," cried the Chambress)—that he could not help it if some went short when others would not be content with their portion. Dame Elizabeth, whose anger never lasted long, threw in a suggestion that perhaps the eggs were double-yolked. The Chambress would have no such appeasement, and retaliated upon the Cellaress by a general condemnation of her management of the Priory hens. How could such poor starved bags of bones lay anything but eggs that would shame a sparrow. And where hens were poor scrags what wonder if the Nuns pined. Christabel Cowper looked from the soft bulk of the Chambress to the hard bulk of the Cellaress, and put her hand over her mouth so that she could smile.

"And," concluded the Chambress, "did the Cellaress think that the Priory would take their frumenty this Founder's Day without a word gainsaying? If so, she was mistook."

That sudden diversion, from eggs to frumenty, was too sudden for the Ladies. They needed a moment to work from eggs to hens, from hens to corn, from corn to the Cellaress's known unwillingness to feed corn to hens in the winter, and from that small meanness to the mouldy corn in the frumenty last year.

In the short silence which resulted from this pre-occupation Dame Anne Ladyman stood up, and accused the Cellaress of talking for a long time—a very long time—through the kitchen window to the miller's wife of Grinton.

The Cellaress, turning on her like an angry bull, retorted by a long account of the burdens which lay upon the bowed but faithful shoulders of any hard-driven Cellaress. From that, somehow, the dispute broadened out so as to include the character of the miller's wife, thence to the honesty of the miller, and so to that of other millers scattered throughout Yorkshire and known to the Nuns before they came to Marrick. In this stage the argument dwindled, since not one of these other millers was known to any but the Lady who happened to cite him as an example of depravity or rectitude.

Christabel Cowper waited for a pause, and when it came stood up. It was the first time that she had made an accusation, and they all turned and looked at her. More than one face could be seen to fall when she said that she spoke not in accusation, but for the good of the House.

"For there are," she went on, looking down at her clasped hands, "moths in the vestment press."

"Moths!" cried one or two in shocked tones.

"No. Never!" cried Dame Anne Ladyman who was the Sacrist.

Those whose faces had fallen brightened again. If this was not an acccusation it was as like one as pea to pea in the cod.

Christabel said, with her eyes on the worried, sagging face of the old Prioress, "I fear it is so, Madame; I found one yesterday."

"Found a moth! Found a night-moppet . . ." Dame Anne scoffed—and so on. "There's lavender laid in every fold," and more to this effect. "Do you think I know nought of embroidery?" They did not think so. All knew that the Sacrist was the best embroidress that had been in the Priory for long enough.

When she paused Christabel spoke again, and this time she looked Dame Anne in the eyes: "Madame," she said, "I saw moths yesterday. I killed one and one flew away."

All this time the Prioress had said nothing. These days she would rarely speak in Chapter except to mumble the well-known forms, to read, or, when she was forced, to give a decision. Now, as so often, she sat, pressing her white plump hands together, never lifting her head lest she should catch the glances thrown at her, and read in them the reproach that she was past her work.

The Cellaress heaved up her great bulk.

"I think we should look," she declared.

They all rose, the Prioress too, as if the Cellaress had pulled them up from their seats, and went out into the Cloister. The novices there, whose heads had been very close together, drew them quickly apart, and bent them studiously over their books.

The Church was darker even than the Chapter House or Cloister, for the painted windows made the dull light outside little better than twilight, even though the Ladies left both doors standing open.

The Sacrist had lifted up the lid of the big press, and was ferreting among gold fringes and silk fringes.

"Moths!" she says, "Show me the moths!"

As though all had expected moths to rise in clouds when once the press was opened, the Ladies stood dumb till Christabel Cowper said that the vestments should be lifted out, one by one.

Someone murmured then, "If they have got at the great white cope!"

Even that faintly whispered suggestion was enough to harden the determination of the Ladies, for the cope, though very old—some said it was as old as the Priory itself—was the loveliest thing they had. It was of white velvet which had changed with age, as ivory changes and deepens in colour, but the wheat-ears which were worked all over it were still of a rich, lustrous gold.

"We must look," said the Cellaress, and laid hold of one end of the topmost vestment—it was of blue velvet sprinkled with white stars, and had been given to the Priory two hundred years ago by one of the Askes. The Sacrist took the other end and they lifted it out. The Chambress puffed with her breath to clear the dust from the top of an old alms chest, and they spread it out over that.

Under the blue velvet there was a dun and green silk, worked with true lovers' knots, and under that a crimson banner powdered with harts and butterflies, and then a very old black sarcenet cope with roses and stars on it. And as they lifted it out the Cellaress dropped the edge she held, and began to clap her hands together in the air.

"Oh!" cried the Ladies. The Cellaress opened her hands and showed them on her palm a little smear of dulled silver-gold dust, and shattered wings. "Oh!" they cried again.

In the silence that followed, while they watched the Sacrist's face grow red and begin to work, there came suddenly from outside the Church a sound as though someone had breathed a long, harsh sigh, and the rain began.

That evening when everything lay drenched and still, except that the gutters still ran and eaves dripped, Christabel was walking with Bess Dalton in the little garden.

Bess said that the Prioress's cushion was nigh done now, and very fine.

"If I were the Prioress . . ." Christabel began.

They were just passing the Parlour door as she said it, and a shrill laugh came from within, which they knew for Dame Anne Ladyman's, and next minute she came to the door with her embroidery frame in her hand, and the white damask trailing, which she was embroidering for a new banner.

"Ah!" said she, "it's Dame Christabel who is to be Prioress, is it? God-a-mercy! and which of us does she think will want to make her so. D'you hear that?" she cried to someone behind her in the room, and turned back. As the two girls passed on they heard her begin to retail the story, and heard Margery Conyers laugh.

Christabel had grown red, but not so red as poor Bess.

"Oh, Christie!" Bess could not speak till they had reached the first of the beehives along the west wall. "That she should say such a thing! You did not mean that at all."

"No. I was going to say that if I were the Prioress I should have worked the buck's horns in gold."

"How absurd to say you think to be Prioress."

"I do not think of it. I shall not be old enough when the Lady dies, for anyone can see she will last but a year or two longer."

"Oh, no!" cried Bess.

"Unless the Cellaress—but no. I do not think of it."

1520

June 30

Sir William Aske came rarely to the little Manor house at Marrick, partly because it was so little a house, and partly because he was so old a man. He had survived his only son Sir Roger, and when he died there would be two little girls to inherit all the lands that belonged to Askes of Aske.

But now, at the end of June, word had come to the bailiff at Marrick to set all things ready for Sir William's coming, and there had been a great business of scouring and cleaning and strawing, and fetching in of beasts and cheeses, of flour and spices from York: there had also been much to-ing and fro-ing between the Priory and the Manor, for the bailiff, being taken by surprise, had borrowed soap and scrubbing brushes and goose-wings for dusting, and the Prioress, who remembered Sir William when he was a young man and she a little girl, sent up her best coverlet—the one with the white hart standing on a green hill between lilies—and two great candlesticks. She knew that Sir William would bring all necessary household stuff with him, but these would help to furbish up the old, deserted house for an old and lonely man.

To-night Sir William had to come down to sup with the Prioress, and, as it was Christabel Cowper's week to eat and sleep in the Prioress's lodging, she came to supper with them. The Prioress had tried to hint that perhaps it would be fitting

[48]

for the Cellaress or another of the older Ladies to sup with Sir William instead of Christabel, but Christabel had not taken the hint.

Old Sir William, very lean and bent, sat in the Prioress's own chair, and his big knotty hands were laid upon the arms of the chair which ended each in the carved head of an angel. The heads were worn smooth as silk and pale as straw by the hands of Prioress after Prioress, since the chair had been carved very long ago in the third King Henry's time.

The Lady's servant came in with a dish of veal, served in a sauce of mulberry juice and eggs and spices. She set it down on the table, and stood back a moment looking proudly at it, because it was a special dish at the Priory; no one else round about knew how to make it, and it was only made on very great occasions. It was called "Red Murrey" or sometimes "King's Murrey," because thirty years ago or so a cook of King Richard's kitchen had told the Nuns' cook of those days how to make it. The King's cook was all for King Richard, though it was that Richard who was nicknamed Crouchback and had such an evil reputation. But when the old man who had been his cook had drunk too much ale he would tell tales to show what a good master Crouchback had been, and call him Duke Dick, because he had been in his household long before Richard murdered his nephews and made himself king. Duke Dick had once given the cook a ring for making this very same "Red Murrey"; he showed it to the Nun's cook—a dark ground sapphire set loose in gold claws, so loose that you could turn it about, but safe as the world hung in the midst of all the turning stars; it was, the cook said, a ring that had been made in Italy.

So the Lady's servant set down the dish and looked at it proudly. She was very hot with helping in the kitchen, and she wiped her face with the loose end of the kerchief that covered her head, bobbed her curtsey and began to serve forth.

Christabel sat eating, and taking no part in the talk, which was all of old days, and old people, of whom she had heard sometimes barely the names and sometimes nothing at all. She was so discreetly silent that they seemed to forget her, and Sir William spoke of his dead son Roger, and the Prioress cried a little, and then the old man spoke of his own death— "which won't be long," said he—and of Masses to be sung for him in the Founder's Chapel in the Church, and wax for lights on the Roodloft. The Founder's Chapel, or the Aske

Chapel, was part of the parish church, which lay to the east of the Nuns' Church, all under one roof, but separated by a wall taller than a man, and, above the wall, a wrought-iron grille twined in curves like a briar. There was one door only in the wall, and the Prioress had the key of it, and the Priest.

All this did not interest Christabel much, but when Sir William said he'd found a husband for little Nan she pricked up her ears, because she knew that little Nan was Mistress Anne Aske, his grandchild, and, with her sister Elizabeth, heir to all the Aske lands. "It's Nan," said Sir William, "shall have Marrick and all that goes with it. Oh—a good enough match," he told the Prioress, who asked who was to be the groom, "Rafe Bulmer, Will Bulmer's second son." The Prioress only knew the Bulmers by name—a family with lands in Cleveland and farther north in Durham. What age was Sir Rafe? Sir William told her and then went on to tell her of the bargain he had struck with Rafe's father. "Oh, yes, a towardly young gentleman enough," he said, when she pressed him for more. But he clearly cared little what sort of man the young man was, and soon went back to the question of his own death, and how he would provide at Aske for a Chantry Priest. "My Lord Darcy," he said, "showed me a while ago the book of his foundation. He had builded a hospital and free school, where Masses shall be sung for ever for him."

"But," the Prioress objected, wrinkling up her face, "he is not old." The Prioress's mother had been a Tempest of the Dale, so she was connected with Lord Darcy, though distantly, through his first wife. Besides, there was little she did not know about the great families of Yorkshire.

Sir William agreed with her that Tom Darcy was not old. Indeed to him to be fifty-five years old seemed to be young. "But you know that rupture he got at Thérouanne; it is for that reason he thinks of his soul." He stopped and sighed heavily, for it was of the same disease that his son Roger had died, suddenly and in great pain. "I told him that he need not fear to die, since many live long ruptured. He said he did not fear it, but would have all in order. So the hospital and chapel are built already, and his friends send to him singing-men and boys from all the North Country. I cannot do so much, but what I can I will, for Roger's soul and for my own."

He sighed again and they sank into silence. The candles had been lit, and now the sky darkened outside the windows, and grew gloriously blue.

Now the Chronicle is broken

to speak of

THOMAS, LORD DARCY

THIS Lord Darcy, though, as Sir William said, a devout man, was also a great fighter, and as well used to Courts as to camps; a man too with as many friends as enemies, because, while he could use on occasion guile or violence, he stood by his given word, and by his friends and his men in all things.

Nine years ago he had gone to Spain as a Crusader. The thought to do so had come to him when he was, by chance, in company with a Venetian merchant at the table of the King's Chaplain, Master Thomas Wolsey. After supper talk turned somehow upon doctors, and the Venetian said that the Saracens were the best doctors he knew, and began to tell how, at the place where the Saracens bathed, there were those who would so stroke, rub, yca, and strongly pummel a man that he would get up cured. "I have seen," said he, "how they would wrench a man's neck, till I thought he was dead; but dead he was not, and when he rose up, from being bent and in pain, he could instead go strongly and at ease."

"You have seen this?" Darcy leaned to him across the man that sat between them. The Venetian nodded.

"In Jerusalem."

"You have been to the Holy Places?"

"It was when I was a lad. But I remember that Saracen, and how great a crack the man's neck made."

"Tell me," said Darcy, "of the Holy Sepulchre."

But the Venetian could not tell much, though by now those around were listening. Ten days only he had been in the Holy Land, for the galleys that brought the pilgrims from Italy would not stay longer for them than that. "So we ran from place to place," he said, and blew out his cheeks and fanned his face with his hand. "Oh! I was weary!"

"But you saw Jerusalem? Bethlehem?"

"Jerusalem. But Bethlehem, no. For to Bethlehem we went by night, when it was dark, and all I remember of it was the hard-boiled eggs and bread we ate sitting on some steps. But as for the Holy Sepulchre,"—he pulled a ring off his finger—"my father laid that ring upon the Holy Sepulchre."

They stared at it. When Master Wolsey, from farther along the table, asked what it was, Lord Darcy answered him, but without taking his eyes off the ring where it lay between the paring of a red-skinned apple and some crumbled bread.

"A precious ring indeed," said Master Wolsey, and reached out his hand as if he expected that someone would take up the ring and give it to him. When no one did that he turned back to the French Ambassador who sat on the farther side, and went on talking about the King of Spain.

Those near the Venetian asked him questions, and he told them quite a lot about the oranges and grapes that the pilgrims had of the pedlars in the Church of Calvary, and how fine the two galleys were which brought them all from Venice, with their painted banners, and the trumpets, drums and fifes which played every time they set out from any port. Darcy listened but he spoke no more; only when the Venetian reached out his hand and took the ring again, he gave a start and a sigh, as if something had been taken away from him.

That night in bed beside his wife, Lord Darcy told her of the Italian: how fine a dark sanguine silk his coat had been, and of the silver spoon and prongs of silver which he brought out from a little leather case, the colour of raspberries, which he carried at his belt; he had used those things at supper and afterwards had wiped them and put them back. And he talked about the way Italian faces seem to have been made with greater care and skill than English faces. By that time she began to snore, and he had told her nothing about the ring.

He spoke about it to no one else till next Christmastime, and then only to the priest who houselled him. It was in the chapel in his house at Templehurst, and beyond the shut door they could hear voices, footsteps, and laughter, and sometimes the scratch and hiss of the boughs the servants were bringing in to deck the house for the feast.

"And," said the priest, "you will go on pilgrimage to the Holy Places?"

"No. On Crusade. Against the infidels in Spain. King Ferdinand has asked for fifteen hundred English archers, and will need some nobleman, besides captains, to lead them."

The priest sat silent, and Lord Darcy let his eyes rest upon the crucifix in his hands. It was a little thing of bone, old and smooth.

"Since," he said, "there is peace in the realm in these days, and peace with the French—" But he stopped there, because though there was restlessness in his mind, it was not that which was at the root of it. At last he pointed with his finger at the little bone crucifix. "Because I am a worldly man and a sinner I would be glad to strike a blow for God who was killed for me, and if He will have it, to be killed for Him."

The priest blessed him then, and after they had talked a little about how my Lord would raise men to go to Spain, Darcy went out. As he crossed the court he looked up at the blue sky, for it was a day like spring, and then about at the roofs of the house where the pigeons were sidling up and down. It was a great house, Templehurst, great and fair, and now he knew that it was most dear to him, and that it would be hard to leave it, if that meant that he must never come back. He was glad it was so, that Templehurst was a thing worthy to give to God, and his own life precious to him. That afternoon he wrote a letter to the King.

Lord Darcy, and the gentlemen who were captains under him, and the English archers, landed at Cades on the first day of June in the next year. All that blazing afternoon they were at it, bringing ashore their gear and finding lodgings: the dust lay thick, and blinding white, and there were flies everywhere. It was difficult to make anyone understand them when they spoke, but by the time that the sun was setting in a golden pomp beyond the infinite extent of the sea the archers were housed in the town, and my Lord and his captains in an Abbey outside the walls.

When Vespers were over Darcy and the others sat drinking the Abbot's wine in a vine arbour in the Monastery garden. The garden was quiet, and cool in the failing light, but the town, where the archers were drinking, was not quiet at all.

"There'll be heads broken before night," said Sir Robert Constable, and laughed. He, like most of the other captains, was a Yorkshireman, a dozen years younger than Darcy, short, broad, red-haired, and with green eyes.

The others laughed, and began to brag how the English archers would come off the best. Darcy thought so too, for he was proud of the men, but he took no part in the talk. Instead he drew back, drinking and saying nothing, but feeling to his very bones the strangeness of this strange country, where bread, wine, people, smells, and even the very sun itself seemed new. That strangeness had worked so strongly as to make these friends of his, and the big, ruddy, upstanding archers strange also; he could see them now as he had never seen them before, set over against the dark Spaniards; he saw Templehurst too, as clearly as if he were there, and yet as he had never seen it before, because he saw it from this warm, shadowed garden, where the dark trees stood up, straight as spears. When he tried to realize the purpose with which he had come here, it seemed to have become as unfamiliar as the rest, as if God had been left behind in England, or lost overboard upon the seas. He sighed sharply, and then straightened his shoulders. Thank God he need not think now, or only of the things about which a soldier must think in the way of his trade. But this time, when he fought, he would fight for God, so that it did not matter that his mind was like a boat drifted from its moorings; thoughts did not matter now, since it was by acts that he would serve God.

Three days later, in the hottest of the afternoon, he came to where his captains, sick of doing nothing, had rigged up some butts, and were shooting with the bow. They had a couple of the archers with them—"For to shoot against 'em will keep us up to the mark," said one of the gentlemen. So it did, but the two big silent men, who seemed to draw the six-foot bow as easily as if it were a willow withy, and loose off the clothyard shaft with hardly a pause to take aim, were on the mark itself every time, and the gentlemen could not match them.

"Death of God!" Sir Robert Constable stamped his foot. "Again!" His shaft had scudded off to the left.

"It was prettily shot, Sir," said one of the archers soothingly, "well knocked and well loosed. But you feared to draw the shaft through the bow, and so you looked at the shaft and not at the mark."

Sir Robert groaned. The archer glanced at him with a twinkle, "We've a saying, Sir—'Shoot like a gentleman, fair and far off.'"

They saw my Lord then, coming to them, and the archers drew away, and moved off towards the butts, while the captains went to meet Darcy. He came quickly, with a very red face, but they saw at once that he was not only hot but very angry.

"This King!" said he—and wished a pox on him, and on all Spaniards. He did it so loud that any might have heard; the archers must have heard, but that did not matter since they were English, and at this hour of the day there were no Spaniards about and awake except a few ragged children watching the shooting.

It was a little time before they got from him, so angry was he, the cause of his anger. When they had it they were angry too, for the news that the Duke of Alva had brought from King Ferdinand was that he had made peace with the infidels, so that having come they might now go away again.

Lord Darcy was thinking of that day, and the time that followed it, as he lay in his bed at Templehurst, ill and in pain, more than two years later, while the October gale swept the rain past the windows with the last of the leaves. He was angry still; if it had not been for King Ferdinand's yea and nay ways this rupture that he had got fighting at Thérouanne last summer against Christian Frenchmen might have come on him in war against the infidel. Then, if he had died of it, God would have looked gently on his sins; and if he had lived, as he was now likely to live, it would have been easier to endure a life crippled by a hurt taken in God's service. He turned over in bed carefully, and groaned, not for the pain, but because he would have to live and move with care.

This morning Sir Robert Constable and two other gentlemen had been with him; in fact they had not been long gone. Sir Robert had grumbled fiercely at the rain. "It'll beat in our faces the whole way," he said, and to Darcy, when they left, "Lie you snug there, my Lord, and think of us as wet as drowned rats." Darcy thought of them now, but he was not glad to be snug.

"I must," he said to himself, "learn how to live as an old man," and he knew that it would be hard to do so, although he was now past fifty.

Yet even an old man, if he have a stout heart and a busy, working head, may play a part, and next summer Lord Darcy was again Captain of Berwick, and going about the ramparts of the castle with Tom Strangways, the master porter, or walking along the river strand to see what the catch of salmon had been, though now, wherever he went it was with a cross-handled stick to lean on. He must not ride, except at a soft pace, and for a little while, but must go in a litter; yet that did not mean that he had forgotten how to pick a good man-at-arms when he saw him, nor how to command the men whom he had chosen. And when Parliament was called, in the late autumn, my Lord went to it, traveling by easy stages, and took the same house at Stepney that he had hired before, and sat with his peers to give counsel to the King.

In these days Master Thomas Wolsey, who had been the King's Chaplain when Darcy first knew him, then Dean of Windsor, then Bishop of Lincoln, then this, then that, was become more things than a man could easily remember, and Cardinal into the bargain. Six years after Darcy had got his rupture, that is, in July 1518, the Papal Legate landed at Sandwich, and came by way of Canterbury to London. My Lord was with the other lords in the great cloth of gold pavilion that was pitched in a meadow beside the road from Blackheath, to welcome the Legate. Though July, it was a chilly, gusty morning, and the cloth of gold flapped and bellied out in the wind, and by the time the Legate arrived, the Lords, in their efforts to keep out the cold, had well drunken of the wine that was to regale him. So when the cry rose that he was coming there was some scurrying to have the gilt cups swilled out and set again on the rere-table in the pavilion, and some covert laughter among the Lords, though the welcome they gave him was as stately as it should be.

With the rest my Lord Darcy came into London at the head of the great procession, and by that time the sun was out and the day fair, so that the gold and silver crosses of the clergy, friars, and monks, who welcomed them beyond London Bridge, and the copes of cloth of gold that they wore, made a most brave show.

That afternoon he was among those who waited upon Thomas Wolsey, Cardinal of York, to announce the Legate's arrival, and wait they did indeed. He and some other lords sat in a window, and played cards for an hour and more before the door of the chamber was opened and they were bidden through seven other rooms, each one hung with tapestry of Arras, to the chamber where Wolsey was. And even then they had little of his attention, for he was busy with the choir-master of his Chapel, choosing the music that should be sung at next morning's solemn Mass.

So they went away more than a little chafed, and in a mood to carp at everything. One of them said, as they looked across the street from the Cardinal's gate, "All this mighty show, but look you there at that!" and he pointed at where a handful of hay hung out over the door of a house; they all knew what that meant—the Sweating Sickness, and most likely Death, were in the house that showed that sign, and they crossed themselves and held up a lap of their coats before their mouths, and went on quickly.

"And what," said another, "of this Crusade?" The Legate had come to get the King's promise for a great Crusade against the Turk.

"Mass!" said Darcy, in a loud reckless voice. "I think the Soldan must laugh to hear of it. For the Cardinal will spend on painted pictures from Flanders, and clocks—such as are must cunningly and artificially made—and tapestries, so that they may hang a fresh set every week in every one of those great chambers of his. And the King will spend on jousts and revels. But if they will spend money on men-at-arms, and shipping for them to go against the Turk, then . . . then I'll . . . I'll eat my hat!"

"Say you'll eat my Lord Cardinal's," one of the others cried; and they all laughed, thinking of the great scarlet hat with its hanging cords and tassels.

"Aye, so I will, and his scarlet satin gown, and his tippet of sables," Darcy declared. At one time he and Thomas Wolsey, the King's Chaplain, had been familiar together, when they shared a room and a bed in the Palace of Westminster; but now the Cardinal of York only gave my Lord Darcy his ring to kiss; so my Lord was free to make game of him with his fellows if he chose.

1520

July 2

On this morning Thomas, Lord Darcy, prepared himself to accompany the gentlemen who were the French King's envoys on a visit to Princess Mary, King Harry's only heir, four and a half years old this month, and betrothed since last year to the little French Dauphin. She was at Richmond just now, and they would go there by river after they had dined—early because of the tide—with the Lord Mayor.

My Lord Darcy was in his bed-chamber at the house at Stepney; one of the young gentlemen of his household was with him, and a servant, and the servant's head was inside a great standing press where my Lord's best gowns hung on perches. He was searching for a black silk doublet with cloth of gold sleeves, while my Lord stood in the middle of the room in his shirt, breeches and hosen. The young gentleman knelt beside him, tying up the points that held his hosen to his short breeches.

My Lord looked every bit of his fifty-five years, but he looked, too, a remarkably handsome man. Very tall, very lean, he had curling hair which might have been as easily silver as gold. With that hair went a fair complexion, and blue eyes, that had a keen, or laughing or blazing look in them, but which were never dull.

"Then," said he, "if it's not there, Will, give me the cloth of silver!" He laughed. "It'll do no harm if it makes the Frenchmen think that all is as loving between their master and King Harry as it was when I wore it at Guisnes!"

At Guisnes the two kings had met in the great splendour which had got that little valley and small decayed town the name of "The Field of the Cloth of Gold."

Darcy, wandering over to the window while the servant ferreted still in the press, thought of that day four weeks, when he and all the King's company had ridden from Calais to Guisnes, reaching there just before sunset. Guisnes castle and town took the low light, but it was not that half ruinous keep, nor the moat, grown thick with weeds, at which they stared and marvelled. Beyond the moat, upon the castle green, a palace had been built of carpenter's work, larger than the King's great house at Eltham. When Darcy and the other nobles passed inside the embattled gate of this mushroom palace there were fresh marvels, for the roofs of the galleries under which they went were covered with white silk, fluted and adorned with gold, and all the hangings were tapestry of silk or gold, while the red Tudor rose was set on every ceiling upon a ground of fine gold.

"Come on, Will, come on," he said, without turning, "give me the cloth of silver."

"My Lord, let me try the trussing coffer," said Will; so Darcy shrugged. He was not eager to show these Frenchmen more courtesy than was needful. He did not think he was meant to do so, though it was hard even for a clever man to read the purposes of the King and the Cardinal.

His thoughts ran on to a night in his tent outside Guisnes, when the flaps were tied up to let in the cool air, which was refreshing after the long heat of the day. He and the Duke of Buckingham had sat together there, with candles lit, talking over their wine; laughing talk mostly of the day's jousting. His Grace of Buckingham was a great talker, and a great mimic. He had aped one by one the knights that rode that day, French as well as English, and then he aped another whose name he did not mention, but Darcy knew well enough it was the French King himself, by the habit he had of tossing up his head sideways like a fidgety horse. He and Buckingham laughed, and heard the gentlemen, sitting a little apart from them in the tent, laugh too, and whisper together.

And then the Duke leaned towards Darcy; a little man, he was as quick and graceful in his movements as a fish, and he murmured in Darcy's ear—

"But we'll taste the wines of Spain again after these light French wines, and I think we'll be content thereof, every man of us."

Darcy, who was older than the Duke, and wiser, only nodded. He knew well enough what was meant. After all this show of friendship between France and England there was to be a meeting between King Harry and the sober young Emperor at Gravelines, and that meeting, though less splendid, might make a truer story than this fairy-tale of gilded palaces, and jewelled doublets, and burning cardboard dragons drawn through the air for a wonder and a show.

"Perdy! and here it is!" Will cried, and Darcy turned back into the room.

Will drew out the black and gold doublet and held it up. The young gentleman took it from him, and put it on my Lord, while Will laid back the rest of the clothes that he had taken out of the coffer, and shut the lid, and set on it again the silver basin still full of warm soapy water from my Lord's shaving.

After dinner the French gentlemen, and Lord Darcy and Lord Berners who were to conduct them to the Princess, went down to the Mayor's barge, and so by river to Richmond. It was a grey afternoon, so that the silk awning of the barge was not needed, but as it was warm the motion and the air were pleasant. The gentlemen sat together under the awning, and if there was little conversation between them there was sufficient for courtesy, especially after so plentiful a dinner and on so warm an afternoon. The country people were cutting and carrying their hay in the meadows on either side of the river, so there was plenty to watch, and merry sounds to hear of shouting and laughter, or of some old man piping a tune to cheer on the workers. If, for a space, the wide reaches of the river were solitary, with no laden barges going up or down, and no one in sight in the meadows, there were always the long glassy ripples to watch, which the barge pushed out before it, spreading smoothly till they were caught by the churned water the oars tossed up, which, spreading in the wake, became smooth again and only lapped softly at the pale mud of the banks, just stirring the drooping comfrey and water-mints and small forget-me-nots there. The French gentlemen were so content that they shut their eyes, and one of them even made a little snoring noise through his nose.

In the Presence Chamber at Richmond they were all wide awake again. The Countess of Salisbury was there, and the Duke of Norfolk's daughters. And then the gentleman usher opened the door and the Princess came in, very solemn and flushed in cloth of gold with pearls in her hair. She stood while the French gentlemen and English lords knelt and bent down to kiss her little perfect dimpled hands. She said that they were "vewy welcome," and then looked at the Countess.

"Ask for the Dauphin's Grace that is to be your husband."

"How does my husband?" said the little girl.

One of the Frenchmen, who had little girls of his own at home, told her that His Grace was well, "and playing merrily at ball when I saw him last."

"Is he as big as me?" the Princess wished to know, and quite a lot of other things. When the Countess suggested that my Lady's Grace should play upon the virginals, so that the gentlemen could tell the Dauphin how good and clever a girl she was, the Princess was not at all shy. One of the ladies set a cushion on the stool and lifted her up on it, and she played, very earnest, and biting the tip of her tongue over the trills and runs.

After that the servants brought in a big silver-gilt platter of honey-wafers and strawberries, and poured wine for all. The pages carried these round, and the Princess kept on calling to the page with the platter of strawberries to bring her more, until the Countess forbade it, "for we shall have you all out in spots if you do eat more."

Lord Berners laughed aloud at that, and at the way the Princess pouted, though she obeyed. But Lord Darcy turned to the French gentlemen and said now they had seen Her

Grace—"not only how fitly taught in music and deportment, but how meek of spirit, as a maid should be to make a good wife."

"*Sang de Dieu!*" they cried, "she will be a very worthy lady, worthy both for her noble parentage and for her own excellencies. Well may we pray that such a lady shall be Queen of France."

"And Queen of England too," said Darcy, a trifle acid.

That, they said, was not to the matter in hand. They had heard their master say that if King Harry had ten children and all sons but this lady, King Francis would rather have her for his son's wife than any other—"Yea, than the Princess of Portugal with all the spices that her father hath," they said.

That remark had a shrewd point, for it was pretty well known to all there, except the little girl, that the Emperor was even now hesitating whether to ask for her hand, or for that of the Portuguese Princess. Darcy got up and went to the open window which looked out towards the river. When he came back he said that the tide had turned and was fair for their departure.

December 6

The tawny velvet gown that Sir William Aske had left to make a vestment to the Priory, when he died last August, had all been unpicked, and now lay spread out, yards and yards of it, on one of the long tables in the old Frater. Several of the Ladies had come in to look and talk about it, and advise Dame Anne Ladyman, the Sacrist, how best it should be cut up into a cope. The seamstress with the shears stood respectfully waiting for their decision.

Dame Anne had asked them to come. She wanted advice; she had been scheming and planning, turning the stuff this way and that. There was so much of it, surely it would make more than one cope. Yet there were places in it worn and rubbed, and try as she would she could not devise how to avoid these, unless she cut wastefully and were content that it should make one cope and no more.

So she had asked the Cellaress to come, and the Chambress, because they were the two Ladies most used to dealing with such practical matters. But she regretted that she had asked anyone when she saw Dame Christabel Cowper come in with the others. She remembered then what she

[61]

ought to have remembered before—that the old Cellaress leaned much on Dame Christabel in these days.

However, it was too late now to do anything more than put up her eyebrows in surprise when she caught Christabel's glance.

The Cellaress saw the lifted eyebrows, and she explained Christabel. "I brought her because she's the best head for contriving of all of us." That did not improve matters, nor did the account the Cellaress gave, after she had sunk heavily down in the bench, of how Christabel had detected the trickery of the miller. They had all heard it before anyway; Dame Anne barely let the Cellaress finish before she began explaining to them the difficulty about the tawny velvet. While she did so she managed to edge in between Christabel and the others, and then, quite naturally, and as it might have been unconsciously, turning her face towards the older women she was able fairly to turn her back on Christabel.

Christabel smiled, and made no effort to regain a place in the conclave. She put out her hand and stroked the smooth bloom of the velvet. What had been the lower edges of the gown and of the huge hanging sleeves was most cunningly dagged into a pattern of leaves in the fashion of half a generation ago. She stooped and sniffed at the stuff. The faintest scent still clung to it, a scent of musk; a rich, worldly, seductive scent, though now dwindled to a ghostly fragrance. She thought, "It's known some brave doings at Court," and she was right, for Sir William had worn it the year the dead Prince Arthur was born, this King Harry's elder brother, and it had seen pageants and water-parties and masqueings, much gaiety and some gallantry.

The Sacrist explained her problem, more than once. She asked each one, except Christabel, what her advice would be, and got nothing very clear from them. The Chambress hesitated, the Cellaress weighed one advantage against the other.

"What do you think?" said the Cellaress, craning her big dark face round Dame Anne, so that she could speak to Christabel.

"Why"—Christabel was always prompt and always confident —"it's a fair piece of stuff. Let's have one cope that'll be fine and seemly and rich. Not two that are worn in patches like a scabbed sheep."

She knew directly she had said it that the matter was decided. The Sacrist would cut her velvet as thriftily as she knew how, and the rubbed parts would be an eye-sore to all who liked things trim and neat, for many years to come.

When the unpleasantness which followed had been somehow smoothed over by the Chambress, the Ladies went away leaving Dame Anne and the seamstress standing over the velvet with the shears.

"A cope and a chasuble," Dame Anne said, before they had gone out of hearing.

1521

May 11

The primroses in the woods above Marrick Priory were almost over, and the bluebells well begun, but the skies were heavy, and a bitter wind blew off the fells. The young leaves shivered in it and cuckoo was dumb. "Miserere!" said the Nuns, as they splashed their hands in the cold water of the laver, "Christmas was more kindly than this."

The Prioress and the new Cellaress had gone up the hill to Marrick Manor, because Sir Rafe Bulmer and his bride, who had been Anne Aske, were come home there. The Prioress rode the little mule because it had the easiest pace; the Nuns called it Francis. The new Cellaress walked, and of the two servants one led the mule and the other carried the Priory gifts—an embroidered cushion, cut from what had been left over from Sir William Aske's gown, after the tawny velvet cope and chasuble had been made, and, in a little pannier, a pot of the Ladies' rose-leaf conserve.

It was much colder in the village, for here there was no shelter from the wind. The Prioress was very glad when they got inside the Manor House; she always had a bad cough in winter time and this winter weather had brought it on again.

But the parlour was gratefully warm, and from the fireside old Dame Felicia Aske, Sir William's widow, got up to welcome her. They knew each other from a great many years back, and were soon deep in recollections and inquiry, while the Cellaress stood with one foot on the edge of the raised hearth, listening for the approach of Sir Rafe and his wife.

"For," said the old lady, "there they are, both of them, outside in the stable, as though she were no gentlewoman but a lad. Alas! I know not what's come to the girls of this day. Ever since she could walk it hath been horses, horses—nothing but horses."

The two came in just then, both of them wind-blown, Sir Rafe with muddy boots, and the girl with mud round the hem of her draggled gown, and wispy, light-brown hair blown out from under her hood. Sir Rafe was a big man, like all the Bulmers, but thinner than most of them, with a big craggy nose. Dame Nan's face was still childishly round and soft, for she was only fifteen, but she had bones in it that would make her handsome when puppy thinned out to hound.

They stayed just long enough for courtesy, and then went back to the stable-yard, for Sir Rafe was buying a horse, sired by the Jervaulx breed, which is the best in the North Country. The new Cellaress went with them; she did not ask leave of the Prioress, but simply went. The two old ladies were pleased to be left alone; the waiting gentlewoman who sat apart did not count as company unless the mistress chose.

Dame Felicia asked after Clemence; Clemence had been the name of the old Cellaress.

"Ah!" cried the Prioress, " 'Deus miseratur animae suae.' She died at Christmastide, suddenly, like an elm bough falling. I thought always it should have been I to go first." She wiped her pale eyes, and her lips shook a little. Dame Felicia murmured something of sympathy, and then asked who was now Cellaress at the Priory.

"That gentlewoman." The Prioress nodded towards the door by which Christabel had gone out.

"She's young."

"It's a grey head though the shoulders be green. And for the last two years she did much for Clemence. Clemence needed help; she must have been ill and we knew it not, for when she died Christabel found out how the bailiff had wronged us at Downholm, and at Topcliffe too, taking our rents—Oh! I can't tell you what we lost by him."

"What is her name?"

"Christabel Cowper," said the Prioress. "And her father's a worthy Woolman of Richmond. At least—" She began to tell Dame Felicia something of the gossip about Andrew Cowper's doings that had filtered through from Richmond.

May 19

My Lord Darcy sat in the little closet beyond the Chequer Chamber at Templehurst. It was here that were kept all his evidences, the old, butter-yellow parchments, sealed by kings long dead, which had granted lands or offices, rights of warren or fishing or wood, to Darcy's forefathers; and there were other writings, newer, larger, and more floridly written in the present style of the Chancery, for lands and offices which had been granted to himself.

He sat wrapped in a long, fur-lined gown, for there was no fire in the room, making up a list of stuff that his steward should buy in London and have sent up here. He had put down already—

"Three bonnets. One choice butt of Malmsey of the best that can be chosen. Sixty of the greatest Spanish onions, the whitest and greatest that can be found."

He stopped to nibble at the end of the quill, and stare out through the little barred window. Then he looked down again at the list, and added, "John Trumpet and Roye my brewer's wife can help therein."

He stopped again, drew inky patterns on the table and wiped them out with his thumb.

"And 2s. in nutmegs," he scrawled, "and 12d. in citron."

He stopped there and called out "Come in!" because someone had knocked at the door.

A man came in whose face was pinched by cold and weariness. He had on Darcy's green livery with the Buck's, Head, and his leather hosen were splashed with mud. He shut the door, and stood against it.

"Well?" Darcy said, and when the man made no answer, "It is done?"

"I saw it done."

Darcy looked harder at him, because of something in the tone of the man's voice.

"You mean you saw him tried?"

"No. I saw the execution of the sentence."

"God's Death!" Darcy muttered, and crossed himself. "What was the sentence?"

"He died by the axe."

After a silence Darcy said, "Well, go away and get them to give you to eat and drink. You shall tell me more after."

When the man had gone he sat there thinking of the Duke of Buckingham whose head had fallen by the axe. "This," said Darcy to himself, "is because he was of the blood royal." He himself had half expected it, since he had heard that the Duke was brought to trial, yet it was strange to him to think of so great a nobleman, and so confident and imperious a man, thus quickly and easily brought down.

"This House of Tudor," he thought to himself, "will be masters, by guile or by plain force. They will be kings indeed." He was not too sure if this new way pleased him. Here in the North many men had liked their Lancastrian kings, between whom and the nobility a hard bargain had been struck, and who had been sworn to rule by Law.

Well! The Duke was dead. The King lived, and the Cardinal. Not that Darcy was of those who believed that the King went hither and thither as the Cardinal's hand guided him.

He returned to the papers before him, and wrote down instructions as to how the stuff should be sent—"by an honest sure carrier, and the wine with an honest man by sea."

But as he wrote it the thought of the Duke hung over his mind. He remembered a bastard daughter. "I'll wager Thomas Fitzgerald will never wed her now." But that was nothing to him. He only remembered the girl—her name was Margaret—because she was very well favoured, a lovely young creature.

September 30

The Cellaress, Christabel Cowper (and now she was Treasuress too), sat in her office, which looked out on the Great Court, and, across the Great Court and the stone-slatted roofs of the stables and dove-house, to Calva, the hill that was like a great beast crouching, red russet now in the morning light, with heath and bracken turning for the autumn.

She sat on the bench-stool with carved ends, on which her predecessors had sat for the past fifty years, and the account roll of the Priory was laid out upon the desk which they had used. In the corner of the room by the door there was another bench, heavier, larger, and plainer. On it the Priory tenants sat when they waited to pay their rents. The only other furniture in the little low room was a great iron-bound chest with three locks; the Prioress, the Cellaress and the Chambress had the keys for these locks, and inside the chest were all the evidences of the Priory, from the Foundation Charter, a strip of parchment yellow now as honey and with a dark green seal dangling, to the Injunctions which the Bishop had written to the House after the last Visitation.

The Cellaress had her eyes on the Priory roll; but when she heard the door shut she knew that Jake Cowton had gone out. She looked up and found that the bailiff was still in front of her; he was an elderly man with a watery eye and thin grey hair; his pursed lips made him look a fool, but the Cellaress knew that he was no fool.

"The man can't pay more," he said, "and he's a good tenant. He's held that yard-land for twenty years."

"He'll have to pay more if he wants to hold it again. All landlords are taking bigger gressums when the leases fall in."

"We'll lose him. He'll go elsewhere. And maybe we'll get worse in his room." He waited between each remark for the Cellaress to answer but she listened in a silence which disconcerted him. "We all know Jake's a good tenant," he said.

"We all know he's your cousin." The Cellaress let the roll run itself up with a rattling sound. She tied it with the little strip of parchment. The bailiff realized that she had said the last word.

"I'll speak again with Jake," he said.

"He must make up his mind quick. He's had three months to think of it; and now it's past Michaelmas."

The bailiff went out. The Cellaress tossed the big sheepskin roll on to the top of the chest, and went out after him, locking the door behind her.

1522

March 24

From the Round Tower to the Piper and Gascoigne Towers, thence by the stables, bake-house, kitchens, and Hall, with its cellars, then on by Queen's Tower, King's Tower, and so, back by the gate towers to the great Round Tower again—that was how my Lord Darcy went about Pomfret Castle, taking view of the defences, and of munitions and stores, as the King's Constable for the Castle and Honour.

He stopped quite a while on top of the Queen's Tower so that the two sergeants who went with him could count the quilted leather jacks and the pikes stored in the room below, while the clerk, who followed after, wrote all down in his roll. As Darcy waited, with the fresh wind whipping the long skirts of his gown and the clouds racing by overhead, he looked about him, estimating, with a satisfied eye, the great strength of this castle of the King's Grace. From the Piper Tower round to the King's Tower (that is a full half-circle from west to east through north) walls and towers were built on the crest of a deep and steep fall, naked rock in places and perpendicular as the walls themselves, in other places a sharp slope of broken sandstone jutting out of the tough clay. To the south where the slope was gentler a barbican guarded the gate, and on the west, below the huge Round Tower which was the old keep, the Norman builders had carved out a deep and wide moat. Not that the Round Tower looked to need much strengthening, because the sandstone bluff on which the castle was built rose highest here, and if part of the keep were built of ashlar, part was the rock itself.

"Blood of God!" Darcy muttered to himself, thinking of the builders of such a hold. "They found a right place for their castle." For though the western windows of the Round Tower looked up a long wide street to Pomfret town high above it, yet the castle stood apart, secure and orgulous, upon that huge isolated outcrop of rock.

"Fifty, fifty-one, fifty-two—no, the shaft's sprung—fifty-one; cast it aside, Sim." The elder sergeant was counting the pikes; the shafts rattled together and the blades clashed. Lord Darcy stamped his feet because the morning was early yet, and chill. Far below, on low ground, through which a brook went rambling, stood the Abbey of St. John. As he looked the bell in the tower of the Monks' Church began to ring, and he could see how from the out-buildings and orchard, from garden and from offices, the Brothers came, like hens at feeding time, all making for the Cloister and the Church door. For a moment the knowledge that they would soon be singing Mass made a quiet in his mind.

"One hundred and thirty-four," said the sergeant in the room just below.

"The full tally?" asked the clerk.

"Aye, the full tally."

Darcy turned and went down the stairs. "Bows and arrow sheaves in King's Tower, you said?"

"Aye, my Lord."

They went on towards the King's Tower.

October 30

Dame Christabel, the Cellaress, was making a new little garden where before there had been only a tangle of rose bushes, no one knew how old. The best of them she kept, and in the spring they would be cut back and trimmed. But when the others had been grubbed up there was room to plant the gooseberry bushes that Sir Rafe Bulmer had given her, and raspberry canes from her brother at Richmond. She stood watching the gardener now. It was a perfect day for setting, for the rain fell, steady, mild and gentle, steeping air and earth. The gardener's leather coat was dark with wet, and, as he stooped over the gooseberry bush that he was planting, heavy drops fell from the edge of the hood above his eyes. Christabel went near to him.

"Leave space enough between for the strawberries."

"Aye, Lady." He did not look up, but went on treading in the wet soft earth round about the roots.

"And send out one of the lads to-morrow to dig up roots from the wood. I saw plenty beside the steps where we felled that beech last year."

"Them's no use." He had filled in the hole and made all fair and smooth, and now he turned away and picked up his spade. "The best always grow among thorns. I'll get 'em myself. A lad don't know how to choose and pick them."

"And see that you dung them well," said Christabel, and went out of the garden and through the Nuns' Court, thinking of her rows of raspberries, gooseberries and strawberries, all in bearing next summer, and of the neat rows of pottles on the shelves of the still-room, when the conserves were all made and ranged in order.

"Tell me to dung 'em well!" said the gardener to the haft of his spade.

November 20

A month and a day ago Andrew Cowper had died; everyone at the Priory knew that it was drinking that had killed him, but his Month's Mind had been celebrated yesterday with great solemnity, so too had his burial been, for by his will he had been buried in the Church of St. Andrew of Marrick. The Nuns, and Christabel, passed the slab of stone under which he lay every time they went into the Church. There was to be a fine brass upon it later, bearing the figure of a merchant in a long furred gown, with a dagger hanging from one side of his belt, and a laced pouch at the other, and his children kneeling in two rows below, girls to the left, boys to the right. There was room upon the stone for a brass of his wife.

To-day those things which he had left by will to the Church, and to Christabel, had come up the dale by the pack-horse carrier. There was one small pannier for the Church, and a much bigger bundle for Christabel.

She had opened both, the little one in the presence of the Prioress and Sacrist and as many Ladies as could find excuses for not being in the Cloister at that moment. The pannier contained a pair of silver-gilt candlesticks—"Not the best pair," Christabel said, preferring that the Ladies should think Andrew deficient in piety rather than in goods; then there was a yard or so of lace of gold of Venice, set with pearls. The Ladies said "Lord!" and "Jesu! Mercy!" at the sight of such a pretty gaud. The last thing in the pannier was a tiny silver flagon; Christabel remembered it well; she took out the stopper and sniffed, and remembered a dozen other things, and happenings, and feelings, that she had forgotten; or rather she did not remember them but they were present with her again at the faint scent of rose-water that still lingered in the little flagon.

Altogether, she thought, she need not feel ashamed of her father's gifts to St. Andrew. He might have nigh ruined the fine inheritance of trade that his father had left him, but these relics of his extravagance were respectable enough. "And," thought Christabel, "Will will soon have the trade again." Will, even when she was a child at home, had been a close and saving young man, and very industrious.

The big bundle Christabel unpacked in the room which she shared with two others. She found that the great bulk of it consisted in a roll of hangings of painted cloth. As she spread them out they brought back as many memories as the scent of the rose-water, for these had hung around the parlour when she was a child. For the last two years, so her eldest sister had told her, there had been fine hangings of Arras in their place, but she had not seen them, and as she opened the roll she was back in the parlour at home. The dusty, dry, yet oily smell of the stuff was the same, and there was the place where a fool of a serving woman had scorched it; the scorched part had worn into a hole and been mended, so that a winged child standing by a fountain of water in a garden had no feet, but stood up to his ankles in a patch of green say. Besides the hangings there were Andrew's mother's beads of white jasper; and two pewter pots.

Christabel was standing in the midst of the room looking down at the painted cloth and the pewter pots at her feet, and swinging the beads from her hand when Dame Elizabeth Close came in. She and Dame Bess Dalton were the other two

Ladies of Christabel's mess. Dame Elizabeth looked down at the floor, and then at Christabel. She was excited to see the hangings—they would make the chamber look very well; but she felt it would be as unbecoming to rejoice as to allow it to appear that the death of Andrew Cowper was anything but a sad loss to his family.

Christabel looked round at her, and murmured that these things used to be in the parlour when she was a little girl.

"Ah!" said Dame Elizabeth, feeling sure that sympathetic regret was her cue. "To see things you remember brings old time again."

"Yes," Christabel answered her vaguely. "Yes, it is so." Her mind was concentrated on the problem as to whether her brother could possibly have held back anything which was due to her by her father's will. "If he did," she thought, "Mother would stand by him. But there are the others. He couldn't be sure that they wouldn't tell me."

She decided with relief, and at the same time with a feeling of disappointment, that it would have been too risky a thing for him to try. Then a new idea struck her. Supposing Andrew's will had said only, "the hangings of my parlour." Would Will have substituted these old hangings for new fine Arras cloth ones? Did he think that she did not know of the others?

She said to Dame Elizabeth, "There are new hangings in the parlour now."

"Ah! But your father knew it was the old that you would best like to have."

"I wonder," said Christabel. It was not a reply to Dame Elizabeth, but the expression of her own thoughts.

Last evening, under a glum sky that brought the dusk early, Lord Darcy and his household had come to Temple Newsam. Templehurst, which was the house he liked best, would be empty for a month or so, of any but servants and a steward to see that they scrubbed and swept the house, cleansed the privies and made all ready for my Lord to return and keep his Christmas there.

This morning, because it was a saint's day, and he at leisure, and his thoughts turning that way, he went to Mass as soon as he got up. There was a little old chapel, dark and rather damp, so that the painted frescoes had stains on them and in some places the plaster had flaked away. But the vessels on the altar were of gold, and the candles lit sparkles in the jewels of the great cross, and the priest wore a magnificent cope of blood-red damask; blood-red because this was the Feast of St. Edmund, the King whom the heathen Danes had made a martyr.

"A brave man," Lord Darcy thought, as the priest moved here and there, "and now in bliss." He thought, "I'd die for the faith!" It was true; he had been ready to die for it in Spain. And yet he thought again, "I'm a worldly man. To die would not make me a saint," and he began to feel shame and to wonder. "What would God have of us then?" but his eye caught sight of a painted hawk sitting on the fist of one of the three Kings, upon the wall, and his thoughts went off to his falconer here at Temple Newsam, and though he kept calling them back he missed the meaning of most of the rest of the Office.

1523

July 15

Four of the Ladies and the singing man from Richmond were in the orchard; the Ladies sat on cushions on the grass with the music spread upon their knees; the singing man stood in the midst beating time and sometimes singing with them. When he did so the deep voice that came so strangely from such a thin shrimp of a man made beautiful and solemn harmony with the fluting notes of the women.

They were singing antiphons and responses, practising them over and over with great earnestness. The idea that they should do so, and the more daring idea that they should have a teacher, had been Dame Christabel's. The Prioress had not been difficult to persuade; it was an attractive prospect—to have such singing in choir that St. Bernard's Ladies down the river, White Nuns, neighbours and therefore perpetual rivals, should fall into the sin of envy at the thought of it. The idea that the lesson should take place in the orchard and not in the Church was Christabel's too, but she did not take that to the Prioress; she thought it enough to persuade away the faint objections of Bess Dalton, Margaret Lovechild and Bessy Singleton.

And then, when they had perfected their chants, it was Dame Christabel who asked the singing man, "What songs are they singing nowadays?" So he sang a song about the mutability of fortune—very moral, and with a most cunning melody; and then he paused, and looked at them and cleared his throat, and gave them two pretty merry love-songs. When he had done Dame Christabel cried, "O! those we must learn! Jesu! what sweet airs."

So they did learn them, taking no notice of the expression of disapproval on the faces of two of the older Nuns who looked out of the window of one of the upper rooms. The bell for Compline began to ring before they had fully mastered both songs. They went on till after it had finished, and only then, with a good deal of smothered laughter, smuggled the singing man through the Cloister into the kitchen, and afterwards, composing their faces, tiptoed to their places in Church.

"We'll hear of this in Chapter," Dame Christabel whispered behind her hand to Bess Dalton. Bess looked startled and apprehensive at that, as though she regretted what they had done; but Christabel met Dame Anne Ladyman's accusing eye across the choir with a faint but sufficient hint of a smile.

November 3

Lord Darcy and his eldest son, Sir George, came out of the parlour on their way to the stables, and found one of the old women servants and Mistress Bess Constable—Bess Darcy before her marriage, and my Lord's only child by his second wife—kneeling in front of an open coffer, out of which trailed old gowns, and testers, and hangings, and unmade lengths of stuff: purple velvet, tawny velvet, crimson damask, black satin.

Bess was holding up a gown of yellow velvet; it was old-fashioned, but for that reason easier to cut up into a gown such as ladies were wearing at present. Bess waved it at her father. "See what I've found."

Lord Darcy did not take it from her, but he laid his hand on the soft, crushed pile, and looked at it, and not at Bess, and she saw that his face was serious. Then he smiled.

"Well, if fine feathers'll make a fine bird—" he said, and brushed her cheek with the back of his hand and then went on with Sir George.

They had gone down the steps before either of them spoke.

"It was my mother's gown," said Sir George.

"I know," Darcy turned and looked at him, but saw only George's severely handsome profile, and thin mouth as always set hard. "You remember it?"

"My lady my mother wore it one Christmas—the year the Lord of Misrule got his coat set on fire."

Darcy smiled. "By the Rood! Yes. How he skipped. And they put him out with the ale they were drinking." He looked at George again sharply, but again could learn nothing from his face.

"Your mother," he said, with some hesitation. "Do you think on her often?"

"I paid for 'de Profundis' daily for a year. And every year ten gallons of oil for the lamps before Our Lady." Sir George faced his father for the first time. "But I do not see, Sir, why Bess should help herself to what she will of my mother's gowns. There is Doll too." Doll was his wife.

1524

April 12

The Cellaress came down from the Prioress's chamber with her lips pursed up and her cheeks pink. She hurried into the Cloister, shut the door behind her, and began to laugh. All the Ladies sitting there in the pleasant sunshine looked up. "What is it?" they cried. "Tell us what it is."

She told them. "Here's the Sacrist from St. Cross"—that was the little Priory of St. Bernard's Ladies down the river—"and she says they have a precious relic, the girdle of St. Maura. They found it in the Church—just like the Holy Lance, she says. For that fat old thing their Cellaress dreamt of it, and then they found it."

"But what is it?" The Ladies were querulous. They did not want the Nuns of St. Bernard to have a holy relic, and if they all disbelieved in it perhaps it would work no miracles. But if someone had dreamt of it and then it had been found! Things looked bad. Could it be that it was indeed the girdle of St. Maura? "What is it? It can't be," they cried again.

"A bit of old horse harness!" Christabel began to laugh again. "The buckle's on it still."

They all began to giggle then, relieved of their anxiety, and enjoying the gullibility of the Nuns of St. Bernard.

"What will they do with it?" they asked her.

"There is a girdle of the holy St. Maura at Paris, and another at Worms. And the Sacrist says that both these are a most sovereign help to all women in childbirth."

"And how useful that will be then to the Ladies of St. Bernard!" cried someone shrilly, and they all laughed again till their sides ached.

September 28

The Cellaress was getting ready to ride to Richmond. It was yet early, and the morning sharply cold since the sun had not yet risen above the top of the fells.

She came down into the Cloister holding tight the fringed purse in which was money for those things which she must buy. The list was in it too, written on a scrap of paper torn from the bottom of a letter:

A rundle for the roller towel.
Wooden spoons.
A new meal shovel.
Two dozen hoops for the swans' necks—Spanish
latten if it may be had.

She and Dame Margery Conyers, who was to ride with her, drank each a pot of mulled ale, standing in the Cloister, and chatting with Dame Bess Dalton. "Oh! that I were coming too!" said Bess, who now found many things to wish for that she did not have. The lack of them was pulling down the corners of her mouth which had used to turn up in a pleasant silliness. Dame Margery made some effort to comfort her, but Christabel's head was too busy with the thought of what she must see to in Richmond that day, and what she would not be able to see to in Marrick. Presently the bell began to ring for Terce. Bess said, "That bell!" and went away from them. Christabel swilled the dregs of her ale about the bottom of the pot as she watched the Ladies go into Church. She was glad not to be going in with them.

Outside in the Great Court a servant was holding the horses, and another sat already in the saddle. As they rode out of the gate behind the two men, they heard the sound of singing from the Church, and a great squawking as someone chased a hen out of the dairy.

November 19

The Court was at Greenwich, and Lord Darcy went there two days after he had come to London. He landed at the steps and stood with Sir Robert Constable waiting for their people to get ashore. A little farther along half a dozen men were

[75]

heaving and straining to lift into a barge a great erection of beams and painted cloths, battlemented, and with towers, made to represent a castle. Already the effigy of a unicorn stood in the barge, its brown paper side torn in places and fluttering in the wind, a forlorn sight, except that its painted horn was still gay and fresh. The staging and properties for the last jousts were being taken back to the Wardrobe in London.

They found the King coming away from dinner, and when they had kissed his hand they followed him to the Queen's apartments. There, not being noticed any more by His Grace, they withdrew to a window, and watched the group by the fire, where the King stood, his feet wide apart, swinging a big jewel which hung by a gold lace round his neck, and talking and laughing with a cluster of gentlemen and ladies.

"His Grace," Darcy murmured in Constable's ear, "is thickening," and Constable, looking at the round bulge of the King's jowl above the fine shirt collar worked in gold with a pattern of roses and pomegranates, nodded his head.

"Yet he rides, hunts and plays at tennis."

Darcy's eyes had left the group at the fire, and looked beyond Constable's head. He said. "Yea. Yea," but not as though he heard what was being said to him.

Constable gave a little laugh under his breath, "And His Grace's father was as lean and little as a smoked herring."

Darcy said, in a voice as low but with no laughter in it, "I can remember His Grace's grandfather, Kind Edward. His Grace is a man much like to him."

"What are you looking at?" said Constable, and turned, craning his neck to see what it was.

Darcy told him, "Nothing. Nothing," and brought his eyes back to the group round the King. But he had been looking to the place where the Queen stood, pleasant and smiling, and with people about her. And yet he thought that she seemed ill at ease, as if she would have come where the King was, and yet, again, would not.

"And the why she would not," thought Darcy to himself, "is that young maid in sanguine red," and he took a good look at the girl who stood up, slim and glowing in her velvet gown, with black hair falling loose over her shoulders. He could see that she had a marvellous pretty throat and neck, and thought that she knew it too, and young though she was, knew how to show it, for she would let her head droop, now this way, now that, and then she would lift her chin till all the whiteness of her throat was displayed, and then would dip her head again, as graceful as a swan.

Yet she was no languishing beauty who trusted only in her looks to bring down the game. When she turned herself about Darcy saw that her dark eyes were alive and alight with mockery, and her voice as well as her laughter sounded often and merrily. By and by indeed it was her voice and the King's which answered each other, while the rest of those about spoke less and less, as though they found it more absorbingly interesting to listen.

So now Darcy and Constable could catch most of what was being said by the fire. Just what it was about they could not tell, but the girl was certainly asking His Grace for something, now imperious, now wheedling, now saucily feigning a timorous humility.

"Well, then," said the King at last, "you shall have it. And if wives are more importunate than maids, God help me!"

"Oh! Sir, Your Grace is the noblest Prince in Christendom. I humbly thank Your Grace," and she gave him a very low curtsey, and caught his hand and kissed it; Darcy was not the only one who could see how the King seemed to wish to prevent her lips touching his hand. "And when?" said she, standing before him again, palm laid to palm under her chin—"And when?"

The King swore then, by God's Blood, that she was the most insolent beggar of them all, and when she only laughed at him, he swore again, and walked a few paces from her, but came back, and stood close to her. "Some day," he said, "some day."

"Lord!" she cried, "what a promise! As they say in France— *'Faictes moi une chandelle quand je suis morte.'* For I fear the fashion may have changed by then."

His Grace still stood very close to her, looking down at her laughing face. But he was not laughing.

"Some day. And it may not be as long time hence as you think."

He turned from her then and went away down the room. The group at the fire broke up, and several passed close to the window where Darcy and Constable stood. Darcy called to one of them, "Sir Thomas! Sir Thomas Wyatt!"

The tall bearded man would have gone by if Darcy had not caught him by the arm. He paused then unwillingly, while his eyes followed the girl in the blood-red gown. Only when he saw her join those about the Queen he shrugged his shoulders, and seemed content to linger.

They talked for a while about the Duke of Suffolk, and last year's campaign in France, and Sir Thomas was very caustically witty at the Duke's expense. Then Darcy asked him—"Who was that merry, free-spoken maiden?"

Wyatt looked at him sharply. "She that was asking the King to give her a husband?"

"A husband?" said Darcy with his eyebrows up, and Sir Robert Constable muttered something about a whipping.

"Yes. Mistress Anne's a mad lass. She says she wants to have one of those billements of pearls, those new things that women are wearing. And since maids must wear their hair loose, so that without a husband she cannot have a billement, she says forsooth that she will have both."

Sir Thomas Wyatt shook his head smiling indulgently, and Darcy had to remind him that he had not told them who the young gentlewoman was.

"Why!" said he, "she is Mistress Anne Boleyn."

Darcy whistled. "Sister to her that is now Lady Carew and that was the King's minion a year or two—"

Wyatt interrupted him. "You North-country men talk too free."

"Well," said Darcy, very much the nobleman, yet with a spice of mockery in his voice, "perhaps you'll give me leave to say, Sir Thomas, that the King seems to like well that family. But how is your good lady and your bairns?"

Sir Thomas seemed to care for that subject as little as the other. He muttered a hasty answer and moved away. The two watched him pushing through the crowd till he stood beside Mistress Anne Boleyn.

"That manner lass," said Constable, "is born to make trouble among men."

Darcy agreed, and suggested that such should be drowned, like kittens, when young.

It was dusk when Lord Darcy parted from Sir Robert Constable near St. Laurence Pountney, and went on towards the Pope's Head Tavern where he was staying. His way took him past the long wall of the house which had been the Duke of Buckingham's and was called the Red Rose. The gates were shut now, and no smoke rose from the chimneys behind the mean tenements that bordered the road on either side of the gatehouse. But though the great house was deserted the tenements swarmed. Men were sitting on the doorsteps, and within, by the light of the fires, women were cooking supper. Children ran out and in and screamed and laughed at their play in the road.

Just as he came abreast of the gate itself it opened a little and carefully. A man in a sober plain gown of good cloth came out, and after him an old woman in a red kerchief, and a very lovely young girl. She was so lovely that Darcy could not but stare at her. Between them squeezed out also a little maid of perhaps four years old, who stumped across the road and began to ferret about among the rubbish that lay there.

"To-morrow, then," said the man to the elder of the two children. "And now a kiss, sweetheart."

He had his arm half about her but she drew back with a twist as strong and graceful as the motion of a fish turning about in a running river. He looked angry and muttered to her: "You wait till to-morrow."

"And so do you," said she, and dipped him a curtsey that did not accord with her company. Then she went back into the gates. The man went on just in front of Darcy; the old woman picked the child up from the kennel, and carried her, kicking, and clutching to her a trampled cabbage leaf, back into the great house.

It was not till Darcy had passed the garden of the Red Rose that he remembered who the elder of the two young girls must be. She was, he was sure, that bastard daughter of the Duke of Buckingham, who, had her father lived, would have been the wife of young Fitzgerald. And now, Darcy supposed, she was to marry the man who had wanted a kiss from her, a comfortable worthy London merchant by his look.

Her beauty was such a rare thing, in tint so delicate, in contour so rich, and in spirit so quick and keen, that Darcy was still thinking of her when he reached the Pope's Head. He wondered how she came to be living still in the great deserted house. To the other little girl he did not give a thought, supposing her to be some neighbour's child.

Now the Chronicle is broken
to speak of

JULIAN SAVAGE, GENTLEWOMAN

YET little Julian was, as well as Margaret, the bastard daughter of the Duke, by Agnes Savage, the priest's niece at Southampton, whom Edward Stafford had first seen one evening in the summer of the year young King Harry became King—that is, in 1509. She was down by the sea, shrimping at low water, when he and some others came riding back from trying their horses, one against the other, along the shore. She had on a coarse gown of soiled white woolen, and it was kilted up about her legs, as she stood almost to her thighs in the water. The sun, which was low and golden, lit her white and her gold to a lovely rose, and Edward Stafford knew that he had never seen so beautiful a creature. He rode on with the others, and as soon as he could rode wildly back to the shore again, and caught her up, pulling his horse back on its haunches with a long slither that cast the sand up all about like gouts of water. Then he sat, looking down into her face, and at the wet gown where it clung to her.

The sun had dropped below the horizon, but all the sky towards the west was warm, and in the east a full moon hung. The tide ran whispering in, with only the laziest small tumbling waves at the edges, that broke and spread forward, and then lapsed back. She stood quite still, meeting his eyes, until slowly, for in everything she did she was slow, she flushed as rosy as when the sunset light had painted her with rose. He took the wet sack of shrimps out of her hands, and rode back beside her, through the dunes, not even knowing that the salt water from the shrimps was soaking his hosen and spoiling his long green riding-boots of Spanish leather.

He had her to Thornbury that autumn, caring nothing for what his wife said or thought about it, and Margaret was born almost a year to the day after that on which Edward Stafford first saw her mother. Then the Duke married her to the Miller of Rendecombe, giving her a good portion, a gown of green sarcenet and some fine shifts, and a chain of gold for little Margaret when she grew up; the Stafford knot set with garnets and pearls hung from the chain.

He did not see her again for nine years, and then only by one of those seemingly casual decisions which can bring life or death as their consequences. He was in the West Country, and, in the summer of 1519, found himself one day alone in a great wood, having lost the rest of the hunt. He followed a track that brought him to the fall of the hillside and thence, through the tree-tops, he saw far below a valley, a river, and a mill. A hind passing up into the wood with an axe on his shoulder told him that it was Rendecombe. When the hind had gone by, the Duke sat looking down at the quiet and sheltered place. But for some red and white cows in the closes down by the river it seemed deserted. And then he saw a thin feather of smoke, blue as wood bluebells, go up from the chimney of the mill.

Between him and that distant quiet place the woods were dressed in all the colours of autumn's arrogant, mortal beauty, but the valley seemed still to be green with an unfading summer. He put his horse to the downward track with something of the impatience and the despair that had made him separate himself from the rest of the hunt. He was come, early in his years, to that time in his life when a man asks himself what he has been seeking? Whether he has found it? Whether it has been worth finding?

He said to himself that he was a fool to turn out of his way to see her, that by now she would have grown fat; and once he pulled up and half swung the horse round. Yet he went on.

He found her standing in the hazy autumn sunshine among the beehives, spinning. If she had been lovely before, now she was glorious.

Yet it was not her beauty which this time gave him happiness, because now what he needed, and what she brought him, was security, quiet, and rest. She chose, and he would in nothing gainsay her, to go back to the old priest at Southampton. "Then," he said speaking lightly, but clinging to her hands as if she were saving him from drowning, "then I shall come to you whenever the King goes to war with France." She said, "I shall be there."

She went back, and at Southampton, during the next sum-

[81]

mer, when the Duke was in France with the King, she bore him another female child, and died. He learnt it when he came again to find her, and found only the priest, a wailing infant, and Margaret, a little girl in a ragged gown and barefoot, but already beautiful.

So she and the baby, Julian, came up to London with the Duke, and with a country woman whom he had hired to suckle the baby, and Julian had swaddling bands of the finest, and a little cap worked with gold, and a fine carved cradle, for the Duke was unmeasured in his desire to care for Agnes' children; and in the autumn of the year he betrothed Margaret to young Fitzgerald, of whom he had the wardship.

But before Agnes had been dead a year the Duke himself had gone the same way, by the axe, and for a week the two little bastards remained in a strangely quiet house, whose ordinary inhabitants were almost all gone, being replaced by men in the King's or the Cardinal's livery, who went round into every room, making lists of all that was there, even of the cradle in which Julian Savage lay.

Soon after that the two were fetched away by the late Duke's brother, Henry Stafford, Earl of Wiltshire. The little caps stitched with gold, which Julian had worn, were now replaced, when she had outgrown them, by plain ones of linen, and Margaret was no longer the betrothed of young Fitzgerald, but one of the serving gentlewomen to Earl Henry's Countess; that was a change of fortune which grieved only Margaret, since the little one cared nothing for gold upon her caps, so long as she was wrapped warmly and had her posset regular.

And as she grew, and began to blunder about the house, the Earl took note of her, because of the almost absurd and increasing likeness that there was between them. Unless she changed very much Julian would be no beauty, like her sister, for the Earl, who was a thin man and lightly built as his brother the Duke had been, lacked his fine features; Henry Stafford's jaw was so heavy as to make him almost seem undershot; his colouring was indeterminate and sandy, and the little lass was a small copy of him.

Afterwards, when she was a grown girl, Julian could not remember her uncle's face, but only the jewelled buttons of his doublet, and a great pearl with some emeralds round it that he sometimes wore, and, clearer than all these, the velvet or damask pouches that hung at his belt and out of which came comfits, or money to buy them, or sometimes a gift of greater value, such as a ring for her finger, or a brooch to pin her gown. She remembered too the roughness of his cheek and chin as he kissed her; a salutation which she much disliked; and apart from these tangible things he remained in her mind as a person who was always kind. Not everyone in that house, which was the first place she remembered, was kind, but he was, and another man, an old priest who never kissed her but once, because he saw how she turned her baby face away, but who would let her climb over him, and make her cat's cradles, or show her the painted pictures in his books when her hands were clean.

But he died before her uncle, when she was not three years old, and Julian took good care not to remember him, except sometimes when she was going to sleep, and then would waken screaming, because she remembered something else (unless it was a nightmare) which made her stop her ears and dive under the bed-clothes. There had been a dog that ran about slavering, and people had screamed and shouted. The old priest had tried to catch hold of the dog; some of the men had come running out with bows and shot it, but not before it had bitten the old man. And afterwards—he—he— had died. For long after when the memory stirred, Julian, cowering in bed, would drive her thumbs into her ears, saying to herself: "It did not happen. I am awake. It is not true."

Two years after his brother, the Earl died, and after that Julian got no more kisses and no more comfits. But though she did not know it, her uncle had set a charge upon his manor of Shute in Devon to give her a marriage portion, or, if she went into religion, a dower. It was no great thing, but more than Margaret got, for she got nothing. That, to Henry Stafford's mind, was fair enough; Margaret had her beauty; Julian had nothing but her likeness to himself, and it was right she should profit by it.

As for Margaret, her beauty was unfolding like the young leaves in spring, as fresh, as vivid, and as delicate. Once, after the Earl died, Julian let out to the Countess that Master John Bulmer had kissed her sister, a lot of times, behind the screens in the Hall. She never was so indiscreet again, whether it were Master John who kissed, or any other, for Margaret was well beaten, and from the beating came away, without a tear on her cheeks, but flushed and dishevelled, and beat Julian, telling her not to be such a little silly, not ever again. Julian never was; whatever she saw, she kept to herself.

One noon in November, a year after the Earl's death, Julian was playing by herself inside the well-house with some coloured pebbles which she had collected. She was cold, but she blew on her fingers and spat once more on the pebbles to brighten their colours. Margaret came in wearing her cloak and hood. She said nothing but, "Hush! Quiet!" and when the horns blew for dinner would not let Julian go in, but after waiting a little took her hand and led her, by way of the stables and privies, to the little gate of the house that let out on Gracechurch Street. A bundle and a very small trussing coffer lay on the ground by the gate. Margaret picked them up, bade Julian, "Keep hold of my gown, and don't let go or the Blackamoors'll get you," and then they both went out into the street.

The house they came to Julian did not at all remember, though Meg said that they had lived there with their father, and it frightened her because it was so empty and so quiet. Only an old woman and her husband lived there now in one small room beside the gate. But Margaret insisted on going about, opening doors upon empty echoing chambers where rats scuttled away, and great clogged spiders' webs hung across every corner. Julian began to cry, and hung back, but Margaret would have her come on, and up the narrow turning staircase—"For," said she, "you shall see the great chamber where my Lord Duke slept." And when they came into a long room, lighted dimly now by three windows in which the coloured glass was all thickly clouded with dirt, she said: "Here my father slept. He was your father too," she added, but rather as though he had been so only in some indirect, secondary way. Then she told Julian where the bed had stood, and told her of the sparver and tester, damask cloth of gold with the Stafford arms, and here a great painted chest, and just here a little coffer of ivory, very precious. "And all round the walls there were hangings of arras. One was of the tale of King Arthur, and it was woven with gold in the woof." The walls were bare now, and only the pegs for the hangings showed below the carved timbers of the ceiling.

Julian was glad to come back to the fire and the untidy huddle of the little room by the gate, though she was not glad to find Master William Cheyne there. Margaret did not seem to welcome him either. "Well, Sir," she cried, "did you give him my message; and will he or no?" She looked at him with her chin up, very haughty but lovely as a thorny rose.

Master Cheyne looked away from her, and at the fire.

"He will, in a manner."

Margaret gave Julian a push from her, and went to the hearth, moving with her light step, that was almost dancing even when she walked. "What manner?" she asked, and Julian, knowing by her voice that she was angry, got herself away into a corner.

Master Cheyne was a pale young man with a pink and white complexion, fair hair, and a thin face with full lips; he had a side-long glance that seemed to wait its opportunity for a stabbing look when others should be off their guard. Now his eyes came no higher than Margaret's knee.

"He says he cannot put away his wife."

"He told me he would."

"She has borne him five children, he says."

"Not since this day fortnight."

Master Cheyne looked as though he felt himself to blame. He rubbed his chin and mumbled something about it being best that Margaret should go back to her kinswoman.

"She's none of mine." And Margaret, forgetting for a moment the matter in hand, told Master Cheyne of all she had suffered at the hands of her uncle's widow, the Countess. "And now she would have had me married to that creature with a hump on his back, and no more than a merchant; not one drop of gentle blood, let alone noble, in all his miserable body." As she ran on, Cheyne continued to shake his head and to murmur what might have been sympathy or advice.

"She would have been glad to disparage me by such a marriage," cried Margaret at last, "but she shall not."

Cheyne became audible then. He said that bastards could suffer no disparagement.

Margaret looked at him as if he were a sheep that had roared like a lion.

"I'm a Stafford," she said, after a minute, and he let that go by with a shake of his head. But he had managed to remind her that though not noble, and in trade, he was true and not base-born, and also of a gentle house. She spoke to him now in a different tone, quick and broken, almost as if she asked his help—

"I cannot go back."

He looked at her then with one of his sharp looks, and she

dropped her eyes. "You said that in a manner he would . . ." she muttered, turning her face from him.

"Why surely," Master Cheyne laughed. "Any man would, and most gladly."

Margaret was, as her father had been, a creature of swift movement. She sprang at him, struck his face with her open palm, and was away again. "I'll be no man's drab." she cried at him, and then broke into an astonishing storm of tears.

He watched her, and after a little went near her and took one of her hands. She turned to him then, suddenly childish, for she was still in years a child. "Oh! what shall I do? What shall I do?" she cried, and clung to him.

"Be my wife," he told her, so quiet and almost casual about it that she did not take it in at first.

When she did she drew away from him. "No. No."

But just then the old woman came back followed by her husband. She carried a pie, and he a big pot of ale. "Come now," they cried, full of good humour, "fall to! Fall to!" And when Cheyne turned to the old woman, telling her what had passed, and bidding her counsel her lady, the old woman made no bones about it, but was all for a wedding.

Margaret looked from one to another, and then at Julian, who watched, and listened, from her corner. "Well," said she at last, "let's eat," so they all went to table.

At the end of it, and it was not a merry meal, Margaret spoke to Cheyne, as if they two were alone.

"I cannot stay here. I will not go back. How quick can it be done?"

He answered her, in the same curt tone, that it could be done as soon as she pleased. "And soonest will please me," he added, but she took no notice of that.

"Without they cry it at the Church door," she objected, "it will not be lawful."

"Trust me. It shall be lawful," he said; but she took him up.

"I'll trust you if I see cause."

Yet she did not really distrust him, and did not guess for some time after—not until he told her indeed—that he had never taken her message to John Bulmer, but had come there that evening determined to have her himself if he might.

When it grew dusk they took him to the gate, and she refused him a kiss, and so laid up trouble for herself. Next day, very early in the morning, they were married at St.

Martin's, Vintry, for Master Cheyne was a Vintner and lived in the parish. Afterwards there was a feast, not a great affair, but there was plenty of wine to drink, and they kept it up, both friends and servants, long after the bride had been put to bed.

Nobody remembered about Julian, so she slept on some cushions in a window, cold, unhappy, and frightened at all the strange people.

1525

February 20

The Cellaress was coming back from Grinton where she had been buying winnowing fans at the market. Dame Elizabeth Close was with her, and after them a Grinton man carrying the big wicker fans.

It was a pleasant walk back along the river side, for though the sun did not shine the clouds were high and thin, dove-coloured, except where a gleam of blue deepened them. It was dirty underfoot, but that did not matter for the two Ladies were country shod. Dame Christabel was gay as she swung along, humming a tune, and feeling pleasure in everything, in the fair soft day, the business well accomplished at Grinton market, and in herself.

She stopped for a moment to look down at a pair of swans, softly oaring their way up the river, with silken ripples rising before them and streaming out, traced with fine lines like waving hair. One of the birds paused, turning her head to stroke the plumage of her side with a stretched snake-like head; with her nobbed brow she ruffled, and with her bill she smoothed the soft feathers. Her wings, slightly lifted, made a heart-shaped, shadowed hollow among the lovely white of her plumage.

The fellow from Grinton caught the two Ladies up, and stood beside the Cellaress as they watched the birds, which now sailed on past them.

"Good eating they be," says he, watching them wistfully. "I tasted their meat once. It was at Sir Rafe's marriage, and some was left, and came out to us that were eating in the great garner."

"Tcha!" said the Cellaress, and moved sharply away from him. "These fellows think of nothing but their bellies. And

[87]

how he stinks of garlic and I don't know what else!" She fanned the air under her nose, and walked quickly on. Dame Elizabeth agreed breathlessly; she found it difficult to keep up with the Cellaress.

Behind them, at a good distance, trailed the man from Grinton. He was indeed a dirty creature, with foul teeth and a look of a hungry stable cat. But then he had eight children and a thriftless wife. That also was perhaps his own fault.

February 28

Lord Hussey had just gone away from the house which my Lord Darcy had hired at Stepney, when Lady Elizabeth came to her husband in the upper privy chamber, beyond the great chamber, where the two lords had been alone together. She looked about it, and could see no one, but, "Bet! Bet!" Lord Darcy called to her, and she found that he was standing in the deep window, looking down at the road, where in the early twilight the last of Hussey's gentlemen was turning the corner beyond the orchard wall. She said nothing for a minute, and, after the first quick glance, did not look at him. But that had been enough to tell her that my Lord was angry.

She said at last, not beating about the bush as many wives might, but going to the heart of the matter because she was a great lady and her husband's trusted friend, "Tell me, Sir, what my Lord has said."

Darcy turned to her. "That fellow Banks will have a writ against us."

He was silent again, and, because she dreaded his silent anger, knowing him, old man as he was, capable of some wild doing if he brooded on a wrong, she prompted him. "It is this business of my Lord Monteagle's will?"

He told her "Yea," and she thought he would say no more, but suddenly he began to talk and to stride up and down the room, whacking at the table and the cupboards with his staff. "Was not Monteagle my friend? Did he not leave his son in my charge? Am I a man to waste the boy's heritage as this villain says?" She heard him grind his teeth as he came near her. "And he says—this Banks—that Hussey and I crept into poor Monteagle's friendship when he was ill, by feigned talk of holy things. Am I such a man? Am I, Bet?"

He came and stood staring down at her. She shook her head.

"But he will have a writ against us, and hath procured a fellow in the Cardinal's house to be his friend."

"But who? But what can he do?"

"You won't know him. Thomas Cromwell is his name. An apt servant of his master, and they say, hath his master's ear. And much justice I'm like to get from that same Cardinal who voided me from my office at Berwick, as if I were. . . ." Lady Elizabeth had heard it all before, and heard it patiently again. "But," she tried to soothe him when he had finished. "He cannot prevail so manifestly against justice."

"Who? Banks? The Cardinal can. There's nothing in England he cannot."

She watched him as he stared out of the window. She was very well content with this second marriage of hers, and now she suddenly slipped her hand through his arm and pressed it, meaning to show him that she was angry with them that could believe such a charge against him. By all she knew of him he was not one to cheat the son of a friend who was dead, and that son left in his charge.

He took her hand and smiled at her, but stared out of the window again, and she saw him gnaw his lower lip, and the pressure of his fingers grew hard so that she was sure he had forgotten her.

He said: "His servants' servants will bear rule over us nobles soon," and after he had brooded a while she heard him mutter, "If fair won't serve, then must foul. But some means we shall find to tumble him down."

"Ah! Sir!" she cried out, because it seemed so hopeless a thing, and dangerous, to work against the Cardinal. He turned on her angrily.

"You don't understand, being a woman. No man can meddle in things of governance and keep his hands quite clean. If the honest men should try always to deal honestly, then they would leave the field to the knaves, and they should rule all."

She saw that they were at cross purposes, and let it be so. After a silence she said:

"That fur on the sleeve of your gown is worn quite away. You must use your red say for a while and the wenches and I will see to this. There's a marten fur on an old gown of mine that will . . ."

"Mass!" he cried impatiently, interrupting her, but then he laughed. "Never, you tyrant, will you suffer me to wear the old stuff that I like. What does it matter if the budge is rubbed?"

She told him, as she had told him fifty times before, why such a thing should matter.

Master Cheyne came into the solar where Margaret was sitting by the fire with a heap of his shirts on the floor beside her, and a lute on her knee.

He looked at the shirts and at the lute, and then turned away and threw down in the window the birch that he had been using. He said that if that brat didn't learn her manners he'd not keep her. He did not say it blusteringly but rather in a flat, casual way, as if he had said that it would rain before night. But Margaret had learnt to know him well enough to fear that tone more than she would have feared another man's bawling. She put down the lute, though she knew that it was too late, and picked up a shirt. As she stooped over it she was deciding that if he turned July out, she would go too. It was not that she had any tenderness for the little plain sister. Yet it would be worse than ever to be alone here. And they two were Staffords, she and July. He should not—she felt the heartening glow of pride rise—he should not wrong that blood.

"I'd be loath we should lose the profit of her marriage." She did not look up, but she knew that she had his attention. "My Lord our uncle left her a portion for her marriage, or to dower her in religion."

He came then and sat beside her and began to question her closely. When she had told him all she knew he was silent, rubbing his chin. She knew that he was angry, both because she herself had no portion, and because Julian's was so small a thing. But she did not think that he would now send Julian away.

August 14

"But she will live?" said Sir Rafe Bulmer.

Dame Christabel, holding the veil under her chin to keep the wind from flapping it across her face, answered that, thank God, the Lady would live, and soon after that Sir Rafe Bulmer and his wife rode away from the Priory.

As they passed the East Close on the way home, Sir Rafe heard Nan give a little giggle, and turned, and cocked an eyebrow at her.

"So there won't be a new Prioress yet," she said, and he laughed out loud, though he told her not to be a ribald. "And cannot she be content," he said, "to be Cellaress, and Treasuress also?"

"All the same," she told him, "I like Dame Christabel."

"I like a woman to be gentle and meek spoken . . . woman-like," he argued, forgetting how little the young wild thing riding by him in a shabby green gown, stained with the cast of her hawks, was like the women he thought he approved of. "And," he said, speaking almost to himself, "if Dame Christabel were Prioress we should never get those closes up at Owlands from the Nuns."

Dame Nan knew all about those few closes of good grazing up among the sheep-walks of Owlands; they had been granted to the Nuns by her ancestor, that Roger Aske who had founded the Priory, and every Aske after him had wished them back in the Manor. Sir Rafe, though no Aske, wished for them most vehemently, and meant to get them if he might.

They turned up the hill and the track grew very steep; she, riding feather-light on her big horse, took the lead. Halfway up she turned to say over her shoulder:

"I think we might get them from her."

"Never," he said, and then, because he greatly respected this girl's shrewdness, "How?" and he drove his horse up alongside her to hear the better.

But Nan shook her head and was vague. She was thinking, she told him, that if ever there came a time of great need at the Priory, then, "She wouldn't be afraid to sell them, if there were need. The others would be afraid."

He admitted the truth of that. "But what sort of great need?"

She could not tell him.

September 18

Lord Darcy sat in the closet that led off from the Council Chamber in the Castle of Pomfret. It was chilly there, so they had set a brazier of coals near his chair, and, since the day was gloomy, candles burnt on the table among the scatter of papers that he and the steward, Tom Grice, were busy with.

They had talked of Darcy's Manor of Torkesey in Lincoln-shire, looking through old parchments, and a copy of the Lincoln Doomsday to trace out my Lord's rights, and had come now to the matter of the Prioress of Fosse, whose predecessor had cut down thirteen oak saplings in the waste of my Lord's Manor there, claiming that they grew in her freehold. But she had lost her case, and now this new Prioress must pay to my Lord 117s.

"They were but little saplings," said Tom Grice, biting on

his knuckles, and looking at his master under his big rough eyebrows.

"Well?" Darcy's tone was not encouraging.

"The Bishop of Lincoln thinks the fine very grievous."

"I've no doubt." Darcy was stiff. It was clear that Tom Grice agreed with the Bishop.

"Look you, Tom," said Darcy, with that sudden comradely tone that made men love him, "you think that because these ladies are in religion I should deal softly with them. But I'll not. If it is a grievous fine, yet they shall pay it. They have land and rents of their own, and for what? To serve God?" He gave an angry laugh. "Snug in their beds perhaps. Oh! no, it's not only of the Nuns of Fosse I'm thinking. It may be a well-ordered House. But all these religious live easy and lie soft. I tell you, Tom, there's no state of the realm so meet to be reformed as the religious, and the clergy."

He shifted his papers about on the table impatiently, and said: "Now, what of the woods in Knaith Park? How much can we fell?"

Tom Grice, having in mind Lord Darcy's debts, understood that he must choose between the Prioress of Fosse and the woods of Knaith Park. My Lord would not, and could not, spare both. Tom abandoned the Prioress. "It were pity to fell at Knaith," he said; and they began to argue that out.

November 20

Julian wakened up at a sound, but too late to know what it was that had wakened her, so she was frightened, and her heart was pounding before she was fairly awake. And then the light from the torches, carried before the merry party of gentlemen just going by, cut like a knife through the shutters, and began to slide, silent and furtive, across the unceiled timbers of the floor above, rippling over the big cross beams like a snake. Last of all it ran down the wall in a long pencil of brightness, and then was eaten by the dark. Julian began to scream, and then buried herself in the bed lest Master Cheyne had heard her.

1526

July 8

The Cellaress and Dame Bess Dalton came slowly along the side of the wood from the home of the parish priest.

"Poor soul!" said Bess, and sighed.

"He can blame none but himself," Christabel told her. "For years he has soaked himself in ale."

They had been to visit the old priest in the parsonage which was just beyond East Close. He lay sick in bed, with his face still twisted, but had not got again both his speech and the use of his hands, and, so far as Christabel could see, was likely to live.

They stood for a moment at the gate of Kid Close before going out into the heat of the open field.

Christabel thought—"How these old people live on!" The Prioress was in her mind, as well as the priest, and down at the bottom of her mind, in a place nearly dark, even to herself, was the thought that it would be well if there were a way by which they could be made to yield place to others, younger, more able.

October 3

Although there was a moon outside the window, inside the curtains of the bed it was quite dark. Lord Darcy, wide awake, and restless because of the unseasonable warmth of the night, shifted uneasily, and, because he had a troubled mind, he sighed.

"Sir?" his wife whispered, and, "Tom?"

"Go to sleep, Sweet."

"What's amiss, Tom?"

"It's too hot for October," he told her, but the obvious truth did not put her off. He felt her hand grope for his, and when she had found him she said again, "What's amiss?"

He broke out, and it was with a great sigh—"By God's Death! I think all the world's amiss."

"Is it," she asked, "this great battle in the East that the infidels have won?" It was only a little more than a month since the King of Hungary and most of his chivalry had fallen at Mohacz, and the Turk was pouring into the eastern parts of Europe.

He told her it was that, but she asked, "And what else?"

He said nothing for a moment, and she felt him move in the darkness, and knew that he had shaken his head.

"If you were not a woman who is as secret as any man," said Darcy, "I could not tell you. Come near that I can speak low."

When her head was close to his mouth he told her, in a whisper.

At first she could not believe him.

"The King put away his wife? Divorce the Queen? After all these years? How many? Fifteen or more. He cannot. Why should he wish?"

She was silent, and then murmured, "How do you know this thing?"

"Never mind how, but I know. There's the Bishop of Bath in Rome treating with the Holy Father of it."

"Shame on him then—the Bishop I mean."

"Oh! He likes it as little as any. *'Istud benedictum divorcium,'* they say is what he calls it."

She took him up. " 'As little as any?' You like it little?"

He moved restlessly. "God knows—" he began again. "If it's the King's will—"

"Fie on you, Tom," she cried, "it can't be God's."

He stiffened at her rebuke. "The King needs an heir."

"The Princess Mary."

"She's a girl."

"She's lawful. But there's the bastard boy as well."

"Hush!" he told her, but she said she was not afraid to speak the truth, and Henry Fitzroy might be Duke of Richmond but certainly he was a bastard.

"And why else," she persisted scornfully, "does the King wish it? There was great talk about that niece of Norfolk's, the Boleyn girl. Ah!" She read his silence. "It's that, is it?"

After a long time she turned suddenly towards him.

"Tom, why will you suffer this as if it would be well?"

He told her, hesitating, at first, but then in a hard tone— "For an heir for one thing. And for another because, in so great a business as this will be, we may find means to pull down the Cardinal."

She drew away from him, but he could hear what she muttered to herself. "God forgive you men!" she said.

November 1

When Julian heard one of Master Cheyne's men say that

he was going down to Asselyn's Wharf to find the Master of a ship unloading there, she waited till he had gone out of the house, and then ran after him, and asked if she might go too.

He looked a little doubtful, but made no trouble. She could come if she would, but she must be a good lass, and hold on to his coat, and not go roving off nowhere alone. So she went with him, one hand clutching the skirts of his brown coat, and the other pressed tight to her thin, flat chest to keep the precious scraps of silken stuff from slipping down inside, out of reach.

Those precious bits she had found in the yard a week ago, and swept up in her hand, and hidden, meaning to keep them for always. They were bits thrown aside from the making of a gown for Meg, of a scarlet silk so brilliant, rich, and lustrous, that the stuff seemed to hold in it a light and life of its own.

But just after she had found and hidden the pieces, she had seen, when at Billingsgate with one of the women who had gone to buy fish, the Ship. The Ship had been quite a long way off down the river, but near enough for Julian to see great yellow and green sails, and pennons of all colours straining out upon the wind. Among all the shouting and stir of the fishermen and the housewives and the servants on the wharf, the voice of the Ship's trumpets had come across the water, sharp, eager, and confident, as she moved off down the river towards the sea. The Ship was a lovely thing, and more, she was free and was going away.

All the way home Julian had tried to find out where the Ship was going, but the woman could not tell her. However, it did not matter very much. That night in bed Julian suddenly saw a way of following the Ship, a way of belonging to the Ship, or else of possessing the Ship; she was not sure which.

So, to-day, when Master Cheyne's man was talking to the little wizened Master of the *Trinity* of Calais, which was to Julian's eyes a small and wretched craft, she let go his coat, and slunk off to the edge of the wharf, till she was looking down into the restless green water that sidled by, slapping at the wooden piers of the wharf, and then dipping past, sleek and shining.

Julian took out the little bundle from inside her gown, clutched it once as hard as her hand could close, so as to say it good-bye, and threw it down into the water. It spread out, a brilliant spatter of scarlet, for one instant, then darkened sadly as the water soaked through it. That shocked Julian so that she cried out, for she had thought of it sailing on after the Ship in all its bravery. But still, it did begin to sail. She followed it with her eyes, leaning over till she began to be dizzy, and then went stumbling backwards just as Master Cheyne's servant found and snatched her. He took her home, holding her not very gently by the arm the whole way, and all the way Julian wept for the lovely silk which she had thrown from her.

December 31

The Cellaress had gone into the kitchen to make wafers for the New Year Feast. She would trust no one else to make them. She guessed that if she left it to the cook much of the cream and some of the rosewater would go into dainties that would never come to the Nuns' tables.

The cook was very busy to-day preparing for to-morrow's dinner that all the Priory servants would eat. There was a big cauldron of souse steaming over the fire, and on the table a row of pots where the brawn was just setting in a rich jelly, and five great pies. Two women were plucking poultry and in the yard outside one of the men was singeing off the bristles of the pig that had been killed. He passed the flame over the carcase, shielding his eyes from the smoke as well as he could, while some of the carter's brats watched him, absorbed. Now and again he would flourish the burning straw towards them to make them jump back, and then the sparks dripped, and the flame curled back on itself like a horse's tail in the wind.

The cook went by the Cellaress towards the big bake-oven. He paused a moment, leaning on the long wooden shovel for lifting out the loaves.

"They'll have a rare feast and right good cheer," said he, wagging his head about at all the food. The Cellaress was just breaking her eggs. She tipped the oozy yolk of one backwards and forwards from one half of the shell to another, and let the white drain sluggishly down. She tossed the yolk into the bowl of finest white wheat flour, before she answered.

"Give 'em good cheer, and they'll work the better. I'll not grudge it them, nuts and apples, carols and all."

The cook went on and opened the bake-oven, letting out a tide of warmth, and an exquisite sweet smell of bread. When he had got out the loaves he shovelled them on to a wooden tray, and carried them out on his shoulder. The Cellaress glanced at them as they passed her, and stopped sprinkling cinnamon into her batter. "What are those?" she asked him sharply.

"Loaves," he told her, a little saucily, but dropped his eyes when she looked at him.

"Of wheat flour? I thought you had baked enough for the Ladies' tables, and for the servants."

"These," he said, "are for the poor men's dole," and he went on with them, hurrying, as if they were too heavy to linger with. She did not speak again till he came back, and then she told him that the poor did not have wheaten bread, but maslin, "and see that you put in a fit amount of rye, not just a handful to say it's maslin."

If it had not been Christmas-time, and he had not already drunk a good pot of mulled ale, he might not have tried to argue. But now he said, "It's Christmas. The poor's fed for Christ his sake—"

"Not on white wheat flour," she told him. "Poor man means idle man. If they'll eat let them work. If you kindle more faggots in the oven at once you can bake the maslin after the pies."

He went off mumbling inaudibly, while she continued to beat the creaming batter in which the long, sluggish bubbles were rising.

1527

February 13

Margaret Cheyne kept the door of the solar open long enough for her husband and all the company drinking there to hear her mocking laughter. Then she slammed it and went off, still laughing, down the stairs and into the kitchen. Yet she was afraid. "But—No!" she told herself, pausing outside the door of the kitchen, and hearing the din inside there. "I'll not fear him," and she tossed up her chin. She was beginning to learn that she could, almost, make William Cheyne fear her. But to do that she must be herself reckless and fearless. She thought, loitering in the darkness, and thinking of his anger, "I must goad him, and goad him, until—" But she did not know whether it would be until he was goaded into a killing cruelty, or into fear of nothing more

[97]

substantial than her spirit. "I'm a Stafford!" she cried out to that spirit, to hearten it. "He shall smart for all."

She opened the door of the kitchen, and stood still. At the sight of her the babel died down, and it was not because she was the mistress, but because even the most fuddled of the men drinking there saw her beauty in that moment glowing like a blade before the smith seethes it.

"Where is my sister?" she asked them, looking about for July.

She was not there, but one said this, and another that, and then one of the men said he'd seen her at the stable door. Margaret knew now where she would be, and left them to drink.

But though she knew Julian's bolt-holes she had much trouble in laying her hands on the child in the darkness of the hay-loft, and before she succeeded she caught her foot in her new gown and heard the damask rip. So when she had Julian by the arm she twisted it with even more intent to hurt than she would have meant otherwise, and Julian kicked and screamed, and so got a crueller wrench yet.

"You're not to lie, you hear, you little jade," Margaret cried, shaking the child.

Julian screamed at her. "You lie. You do. You said that chain was your own that Sir Bulmer gave—Ow! Stop it! Don't!"

"Hold your tongue then. It was my own since it was given me. And if you tell him that Sir John . . ."

"I'll not. I'll not. Oh! Meg, do stop."

"Very well. But you're not to tell lies."

Julian, dropping on the hay, mumbled that she had to tell lies.

"Then don't tell such as he must know are lies. Saying it was one of the cats that ate the marchpane off that subtlety, and then being sick of it all over the place when he beat you."

"I wasn't sick of it till he beat me."

"Well," said Meg, "if he beats you I shall twist your arm, because when he's beaten you he's as likely as not to beat me."

May 6

The King, passing through the gallery that looked onto the orchard at Greenwich Palace, stopped to speak to this one or that. When he came to where Lord Darcy and the Marquess of Exeter leaned beside a window, sunning themselves, he stayed quite a long time talking and was very gracious. Darcy had been speaking to the Marquess of the hospital and free school that he had been building, and the King asked questions about it, and spoke nobly and gravely of the value of such foundations, "so many in old time, and so few, alas, in ours," said he. And then he must give Darcy something for the Chapel of the Hospital; "Go to the Keeper of the Great Wardrobe. Ask him for something of the chapel stuff he has: a Mass Book or a cope, or what you will. Here—I'll write an order." He called, then blew on a little golden whistle that hung on a chain round his neck, and when someone had fetched a clerk an order was written, and Darcy put it in his pouch.

But while the clerk wrote, and while Darcy was speaking his thanks, the King began to fidget, and to glance towards the open window beyond Darcy's shoulder, and at last he pushed past him, put Exeter by with his hand, and leaned out of the window. A girl's voice was singing down below in the orchard while someone thrummed on a lute. Darcy caught the eye of the Marquess, and each looked to the ground. They knew what it was that the King wished to see, for they had been watching before he came a group of young men and women sitting together on the grass, the women all gabbling like ducks. Mistress Anne Boleyn was among them, and she it was who was singing.

The King turned at last from the window. He had a look as of a man who has opened a box to feed his eyes on the sight of a very rare jewel; now he had closed the box, but the glow and softness of delight were still on his face and a little private smile that faded quickly. He went away, and they saw the crowd open for him, and in the empty space he met the Cardinal, and the French Ambassadors.

When the King and these others had gone, many people left the gallery, but the Marquess and Darcy stayed at the window. The young things below had begun to play Hoodman Blind, and had scattered among the trees, with laughter, screams and shouting.

The Marquess turned his long, serious, irresolute face to Darcy, and he was frowning.

"My Lord of Norfolk," said he, "swears that niece of his to be a very virtuous and chaste lady. But—"

Darcy could have laughed to see this great nobleman blushing for a girl who had, Darcy thought, forgotten how to blush before she was well out of the schoolroom.

"They say her sister—" he began, but the Marquess did not

let him finish, muttering hastily, "Nay, my Lord, nay. Let be!"

Darcy let it be, and asked what else Norfolk had said.

"It was all in praise of Mistress Anne. How she would leave the Court and away to Hever, though her father was angry."

"He would be," said Darcy. "Some fathers would be sorry that a daughter should be a minion, even if it were a King's, but not Sir Thomas Boleyn."

The Marquess shook his head, though not in disagreement, for he cared as little for the Boleyns as Darcy did.

"And who," Darcy persisted, "are this virtuous, chaste lady's friends? Sir William Compton that's an open adulterer; Bryan—Bryan. By the Rood! he's made the name enough common in the stews. And, if it comes to a point, who is my Lord of Norfolk to talk of virtue, who keeps that drab Bess Holland in the same house as—"

Exeter hushed him again. "And," says he, "surely a wench is virtuous that will resist a king's desires. Grant her that."

"Or grant her a clever, scheming jade that dares to play for a high stake."

"What can she win? God's Body, my Lord, not that! She cannot think to be Queen." She had whispered the word, but still he looked back into the almost empty room behind them.

Darcy raised his eyebrows and shrugged his shoulders. "If it is that she aims at, she plays well. Three years ago His Grace began to affect her, and now he looks at her as if he were a boy in love."

The Marquess, remembering the King's face as he turned from the window, fell into a very troubled silence.

Meg had let Julian come out with her when she went to buy a pair of gloves, a sugar loaf, and some saffron. Meg walked ahead, leading a black and white dog on a leash of green ribbon, and Julian came behind with old Cecily who was to carry home in her basket the sugar loaf and the saffron.

In Lombard Street they came on Sir John Bulmer. He was talking to another young man, or rather, the other was talking to him, very merrily, in a voice that had in it a ringing note like that of a finely cast bell, and with a broad North Country touch in his speech like Sir John's own.

Sir John saw Meg, and said something hastily to the other, and left him to come to her.

"Who was that?" Meg asked, looking after the young man

who had waved his hand to Sir John and gone off down the street; as he went they could see him turn his head this way and that, alert and quick.

"He looks a merry gentleman," Meg persisted, knowing that Sir John, if he could, would have emptied the streets of men when she came out. "And comely too, though it's a pity he hath not another foot to his height."

"And another eye to his face!" Sir John cried derisively.

"God 'a mercy! Hath he but one eye? How did he lose the other?"

"How do I know? I never asked him."

"But tell me his name."

Sir John told her very crossly that his name was Aske—Robin Aske. "And I don't know why you care to know," said he.

"I don't care. But I like to see you chafe." She looked up at him sidelong, laughing, and then became serious and drew near to him as they walked. By the time they reached the glover's shop he was in a very good humour, and bought Meg two pairs of Louvain gloves.

*Now the Chronicle is broken
to speak of*

ROBERT ASKE, SQUIRE

The Askes, the younger branch of the Askes of Aske, had been at Aughton for about a hundred years—since the time when an Aske had married an heiress of the de la Hayes. For much more than a hundred years the old castle on the mound above the fen had been deserted and left to crumble; cows and goats had browsed over it, and down to the low-lying ings beside the river, for longer than anyone could remember to have heard tell, even by the oldest grandfathers. Instead, the lords of the Manor of Aughton, de la Hayes first, and Askes after them, had lived in the moated house a little to the south-east of the castle mound, and exactly east of the chancel of the parish church, so that they went to Mass through the orchard, and across a little bridge over the moat, and so into the churchyard.

Mound and church and moated house all stood at the tip of a tongue of land jutting out from a sort of low, flat-topped island in the fen; east of them on the same island as Aughton village, and to the north Ellerton, where the Gilbertine Canons were; but between Aughton church and the Derwent was nothing in summer but the green ings where the cattle grazed and grew fat, and pools and twisting channels where the rushes whispered, and marshy land with tussocks of reed; in the winter, when Derwent was in flood, the river came up, filling all the pools and waterways, drowning the reed-beds and black quaking paths which only a man born in Aughton would dare to use, so that the feet of the churchyard wall were in the flood, and the squat Norman tower looked out, west and south, over nothing but water.

The house, at first cramped up within its moat, had now straggled over it towards the village, letting the ditch on this side silt up with farm refuse, so that when you came to the Manor from the village you passed first all the huddle of barns and stables, the stack-yard, the carpenter's shop, and the long thatched shippens. Only after these you came to the corner of the old dairy where the moat began again, and so to the little gate-house, stone below, and timber and daub above, for stone was scarce in these parts.

Inside the gate-house lay the court-yard: the new dairy to the right, the brew-house to the left, and opposite you the Hall, its roof as high as the upper storeys of the rest. Partly to please his wife, and partly because so many were doing it in these days, Sir Robert Aske had pulled down the old buildings at the further end of the Hall from the screens, and built a fine winter parlour there looking out on the stack-yard, and also southward over the fen; above it were two new bedchambers, in one of which all the younger children, from Robin downwards had been born. That older chamber, at the other end of the Hall, above the kitchen, in which Sir Robert himself had been born, and in which his father had died, was now divided into several smaller rooms where the older children slept, joined every now and then by the newest and youngest, just promoted from the cradle to share a bed with an elder sister or brother.

Dame Elizabeth Aske was proud of her winter parlour

when it was new, and spent much of her spare time embroidering cushions and stitching at hangings for it; but Sir Robert never took to it. He would go there if she asked him, for he was a good-tempered man, though not an easy one, and was, besides, fond almost to weakness of his wife. But habit kept him to the Hall, and he would, if not prompted, potter about in the big bay just inside the screens which had been built out on the foundation of what had once been a tower, where the bows stood in their racks, and his favourite hawk sat humped on her perch.

And so, except sometimes when there were guests of great honour, the family never ate in the parlour, but had their meals in the old manner in the Hall, and Sir Robert would carry on conversations with the ploughman, or the stockman, down half the length of the room, and then turn to tease Dame Elizabeth in a boyish way that never left him, or to cuff the lads for quarrelling or for bad manners at table.

Of these lads John did not quarrel with Kit, for John, though the eldest son, was always a gentle child, and a delicate, reserved youth. Nor did Richard, for he died when he was five, and was, for two years before that, a poor little shrimp, more often ill in bed than running about; but as soon as Robin was old enough to quarrel with anyone he and Kit were rarely at peace. Kit was five years old when Robin was born, and even from the first he resented the fuss that his elder sisters, Julian and Bet, made of the new baby. For they being only too delighted to have such a creature to pet, certainly spoilt him outrageously, the more because Robin was a towardly child, sturdy and merry, and adorably ticklish; at any moment, just by feeling for his well covered ribs, they could draw from him shrieks and gurgles of laughter. Kit therefore conceived it his duty to supply some discipline to counterpoise their petting.

This, being five years the elder, he could at first do easily, either by tongue or hand, and even in those early days Kit's tongue had a sting in it, and ran nimbly. As for physical correction, Kit supplied that too, when the elders were not looking, and Robin got many a buffet, at which, if he could not dodge it, he would howl lustily, till one day Jack told him that no man of worship would cry like that for a blow, but only cowards and those of villain blood. After this Robin did his best to behave like a man of worship, or at least to cry quietly and in secret.

But by the time that he was eight, and Kit thirteen, he did

not try to dodge Kit's fist, nor passively to endure, but instead gave blow for blow. The difference in their ages did not count for so much now, and was to count for less as time went on, for Robin, always a stout and healthy child, was now a big boy for his age, not slim and graceful as both Kit and Jack had been, but stocky and sturdy, resembling in this, as in much else, his father, Sir Robert. Kit, on the other hand, Kit, with his mouth already twisted and tightly compressed by the habit of enduring the intermittent pain in his back, went always lame of one leg—nothing very much, but enough to make him slow on his feet in a fight. Because of that slowness, and the lameness, and the pain, of all of which he was miserably ashamed and which he concealed as much as he could, Kit set out to make sure of a foothold for his pride. If he could not run, then he would ride; if he could not fight on foot because of his dragging leg, then at least he would shoot with the bow so that none could match him. He heard his father one day telling Tom Portington, who was to marry Kit's sister Julian, how Kit had ridden the bay stallion, and jumped Hogman's Pool—the mad knave. "Of course I beat him for it, for he might have killed the beast and himself in that black bit of bog down there. I've known a horse go under there in five minutes, and no one would have seen him, for we were all the other way, busy with the barley." Sir Robert laughed. "Mass! I beat him soundly, but I liked him for it. I think he fears nothing, and he's got a good horseman's seat, and hands you couldn't better. Robin's nothing to him." Young Portington said that Robin would come on when he was a bit older, perhaps, and Sir Robert agreed, but Kit had slunk away by then without them knowing that he had been there. He had heard enough to warm his heart for him, and he went off to the stable and petted the bay stallion; he even shed some tears on the smooth, warm and shining coat, because he was so glad. He took care, too, not to come away till there was one of the stable boys there to see him, walking out of the bay's stall, with the beast nuzzling his ear. He knew that most people, even Sir Robert himself, were chary of going too near the stallion's hoofs and teeth.

But, though Kit might be happy at such praise for a while, he was always too conscious that Robin was coming on hard at his heels ever to be really content. Robin was never tired, never ill, never, except when he fought with Kit, out of temper; and even the fighting he seemed to enjoy, and only to wish to knock Kit down for the fun of it. If he missed the mark with his arrow, he laughed; if he hit in the midst, he laughed. It was not that he was contented to do a thing badly; when he failed he would go on trying always harder, but cheerfully, and without any shame of his failure. Kit knew very well, that soon, though Robin would never equal him as a horseman, in everything else his younger brother would pass him, and the knowledge was bitter.

Things were always happening which made it clear how quickly Kit was being overhauled by the youngster. Though Kit was a very pretty bowman he had not the plain strength for a man's bow till he was close on seventeen. Then he got his first bow of full force, a lovely one with a fine long grain from one end to the other. He was immensely proud of it, though it was as much, even now, as he could manage, and for a while his shooting fell off, and Robin beat him at every match. All Kit could do was to mock the boy unmercifully for the way he had, when he had loosed, of standing on one foot and curling the other round his leg till he saw the arrow strike.

But as he came into his new bow Kit began to go ahead again. They were at the butts one still evening in summer, just after hay harvest. The light was beginning to fail a little, and Sir Robert, who had been shooting with them, had gone in. Their mother had left the place long ago to see that the little girls had been put to bed, so only the Aske boys and some village lads were there. Jack said it was time to go in; what use in shooting when you could not see, and to hit was all luck. But Kit, who was shooting beautifully, would not give up, nor would Robin, simply because he knew that when they went into the house it would be supper and then bed.

So, at last, it was Kit and Robin shooting against each other, the one from the men's distance, and the other from farther forward, because children's bows, being cut from the branch and not the bole, are weaker in their cast.

Then Robin, drawing strongly, snapped his bow; the arrow went wreathing aside, with everyone yelling ,"Fast! Fast!" to warn each other out of the way. But it lit, with no harm done, in a patch of thistles.

"You little fool!" cried Kit, "you might do hurt to anyone that way."

"How could I help it? It's that bow. It's all knotty and weak." Robin slipped the string out of the notch, chucked away the splintered pieces of the bow, and went off to get his arrow. He was not put out, being used to Kit's tongue, and being indeed rather pleased with himself for breaking his bow. When he came back he said, again, "It was all knotty and weak. I'll ask if I can have a man's bow."

"You!" cried Kit, but Robin had gone to Jack and was crouching down by him. "Lend me yours, Jack," he said. "Let me try how I can shoot with it."

"No!" Kit shouted, in such a strange voice that Jack turned and stared at him.

"I pray you, do," Robin wheedled, and Jack pushed the bow into his hands.

Kit got up and went away as quickly as he could, but not quickly enough. He did not hear the thrum of the string as Robin loosed, but heard him shout, "Ouch!" as the shaft flew wide and everyone laughed; Kit caught the sound of Robin's laughter among the rest. Then Robin must have loosed again, for he cried, with triumph in his voice, "There! That was better. I like this bow. I like the way he pulls so strong against the hand."

It was Robin who brought Kit's bow up from the butts where he had left it. He found Kit reading in the tower corner in the Hall. Kit only glanced up from the book, and then held out his hand for the bow, without a word.

"Shall I wax him for you?" Robin asked, and stooping over the bow he rubbed his cheek on the wood, as if he loved it.

"No." Kit wrenched it out of his hand, and Robin went away whistling, to snatch as he passed at a dish of pasties that one of the women was carrying in for supper. She let out a blow at him, and he dodged it, laughing, his mouth full, and spluttering crumbs. Kit thought him insufferable.

Next morning, which was the morning before Jack's wedding day, he and Kit got up as soon as it was light, and dressed quietly. But Robin woke as Kit was getting into his hosen. "Where are you going?" he asked, and without waiting for an answer, bounced out of bed.

Jack told him, "A-fishing," and Kit said, "We don't want you," but he cried, "Ah! Let me come," and Jack, too weak, thought Kit, allowed it. It had been Kit's idea to have Jack to himself this time. Now Robin had spoiled it.

The sun was not yet up as they went out from under the gate-house, but the sky was delicately and serenely blue. Some of the men were just going by from the village to mow their own hay, now that the Askes' hay was cut and carried. One of them hailed, "Master Robin! Master Robin!" and Robin ran off to him, and came back waving a pipe in his hand, such as shepherds play on. "See what Mat has made for me. Thank you, Mat," he yelled shrilly after the men; Mat's red hood jerked in acknowledgement.

They went down past the churchyard, across the ings, and on among the pools; the waters seemed as still as the air above them; they were bright with the sky, though a thin mist steamed up from them. The mist would be gone before noon, to gather again towards evening.

"It's as still as glass," said Kit, looking down into one of the pools and speaking low because of the silence and stillness of the unsullied day. ·

"No," said Robin, pointing at the shadows of the alders on the far side; "look how the leaves shiver in it." It was true that the reflection trembled ceaselessly in the water, perfect and unbroken, while the trees themselves were still. But, "God's Blood!" Kit muttered crossly, and went on after Jack with his rod jigging over his shoulder. Robin came behind; he began to tootle on the pipe; then he ran forward and said that he was the minstrel from York, playing before Jack at his wedding, and so preceded them, posturing and blowing on his pipe. Even Jack was angry with him and Kit hated him. When they came to the place where they meant to fish they turned their backs on him and told him to go to the devil.

He did not go, and soon, one way or another, he tried Kit beyond endurance. Kit struck him, and the blow sent Robin off into one of his brief rages. He skipped back, and fishing out a big handful of weed from the water's edge he slung it at Kit's face, yelling with triumph when he saw how lucky his aim had been. Kit, half blinded by the dripping, stinking stuff, ran at him, the long rod held like a lance.

And then Robin gave one scream, and went backwards; for a moment he wriggled about on the dewy grass as wildly as if he had been a fish they had landed, but he got up again to his knees, and knelt bowed and with his hands over his face.

They both ran to him, Jack scared, and Kit scared and angry, crying, "What's the matter? What's the matter?"

He did not answer, and Kit wrenched at one of his hands and managed to drag it away. He let it go very quickly.

"His eye!" he said. "His eye!"

Because Kit was no good at running, it was Jack who went back to the house, and burst into his father's and mother's bed-chamber, shuttered and dark still, to tell them what had happened. Kit came after, leading Robin, who stumbled along with his hands over his face, and blood running down his chin on the right side, and blood sopping the breast of his shirt.

Kit wanted to be the one to ride to York for the surgeon, but Sir Robert sent off one of the men with a led horse. There was nothing for Kit to do but to go down to the river bank and bring back his fishing rod, and Jack's; he found Robin's pipe there, and brought that too.

This happened in July, and it was early September before Robin was out again. He had grown while he was in bed; he was pale now, instead of brown as a nut; and, for a while at least, he was rather quiet. Kit, whose heart had been wrung by fear, shame and compassion, was uncommonly gentle to him, and for a few months there was peace between them.

By this time Jack's young wife was getting used to her new estate. Nell was fifteen, a little fair thing, with a finished prettiness which time might harden and sharpen. After being very meek at first, she was now beginning to show off. Sir Robert laughed at and petted her, Dame Elizabeth was too gentle to give her more than a mild rebuke. It was Robin only who infuriated her with his teasing. In return she would jeer at him for lacking an eye, and then he would threaten to lift the empty eyelid, and would chase her about the house on that threat. They were never good friends, and it was still worse between them when, in the New Year after Robin lost his eye, Dame Elizabeth died. Robin stopped teasing Nell; that had been done not out of unfriendliness, but because, being a boy, tease he must. Now he left her alone, except to scowl at her under his heavy brows, and sometimes to go out of his way to cross her. But Kit came on him one day, hammering at a bent arrow-barb on the anvil in the workshop as if it were a thing he meant to kill, and with tears running down his face.

He smudged them away with a dirty hand when he saw Kit, and said, "I hate her. She is glad that our mother is dead."

Kit had seen that too. They talked about Nell, then about their mother for a time, and afterwards for a while Kit was quite warm towards Robin.

By the time spring came, and Robin had passed his thirteenth birthday, he was strong again, but he had found out that there were things that could not be well done by someone who was short of an eye. He could not now aim sure with the bow, nor play at quarterstaff. At first he tried, harder and harder, then suddenly gave it up, and after that would sit watching the others, calling out now and again, "Oh! well shot!" or "Well laid on!" At home he would keep his bow most carefully waxed, so that it glittered like gold—it was a good bow, full strength, which Sir Robert had brought from York while he was in bed—but he rarely took it out, except sometimes to go fowling among the pools by himself.

One blustering evening that April, the young men were again at the butts. Kit was shooting most cunningly, so that the shifty wind hardly balked him at all. Robin sat watching among the rest, but when the groups broke and reformed, as one after another went to take his turn at the mark, he was left alone. And now he did not watch. Kit, glancing that way more than once, saw him digging his hands into the new grass, tugging at it, and frowning. After a while he got up and went away; Kit noticed that too, and grew angry, knowing whose doing it was that Robin did not now take his turn with the rest. Their brief accord was over. Kit could not forget what he had done to his brother, and besides that, since Robin had been ill he seemed to have grown up in his mind; whereas before he had fought Kit with his fists, now it was with his tongue, and he was as resolute, and was becoming as quick in argument, as he had been in the other kind of fighting.

Robin set off to go to Ellerton, through the great open Mill Field, in which two ploughs were still at work, breaking up the fallow for next autumn's wheat. He walked with his head down, kicking at the clods that lay loose on the trodden path. Before him Ellerton was half buried in pear-blossom and the bright budded apple-trees, but he did not glance about, nor, hardly, at the men trudging back from the fields or the women at their doors when they gave him good evening. The gate of the monastery was open; he did not trouble to knock, but went in, and straight to the kitchen. When he came near he could hear the sound of scrubbing. He looked in and saw Dom Henry stand in the midst; one of the lay brothers was scrubbing wooden bowls; he had those that were already done set out in a long row at the window to dry in the evening sun; another, with his gown hitched up, kneeled on a folded sack and swabbed the floor from a wooden pail.

Dom Henry turned, saw Robin and said, "It is nearly done." To the lay brother with the scrubbing brush he said, "Are all the towels dry in the press?" and to another monk who came in beside Robin, "There. All's ready for your week's serving. And I have come to the end of mine, and to-day shall eat my meat with a conscience as clean as a well scoured bowl." Then he laid his hand on Robin's shoulder, gave him a push and bade him, "Get out of this. I'm weary of cooking pots and sauce ladles. I would the brethren might live holily on manna, as Moses."

"Beginning to-day?" asked Robin saucily, and the monk chuckled and said no—beginning last Saturday night, and ending to-day. He reached down two horn cups from a shelf, went out of the kitchen and came back with them full of ale. "My brewing," he told Robin, giving him one, and together they went outside, walking with care so as not to spill the ale. The horse-block in the outer courts still had the sun, and was sheltered from the wind, so they sat down there, Robin on the top step and the monk below him.

Dom Henry raised the horn cup. "Ah!" he said, after a silence. "That's better."

He glanced up at the boy. Robin was twisting his cup about; a little of the ale slopped over onto his hosen; he shifted his leg and struck the drops off with his hand, but he did it absently. Dom Henry had taught all the Aske boys, and knew them as well as any man did, but he knew that Robin was changing, and he did not know what he would change into. "Not so sharp and eager a wit as Kit's," he thought to himself, "but it grips, and there may be more than wit in him."

"Well?" he said at last; but Robin, who was generally very ready, gave him no answer for a long time.

"If you'll not drink that ale, give it to me," Dom Henry prompted him.

Robin shook his head, and began to drink, then he put the cup down on the stone beside him, and said, "Sir, if I tell my father that I would be a monk, will you stand by me?"

Afterwards, thinking it over, Dom Henry wondered why he had received the suggestion so unfavourably, pouring scorn on it as if it must be only a boyish notion. "All because you can't hit the middle of a painted mark with your arrow!"

Robin said, stiffly and angrily, that that was not all, and when the monk asked what else, he would not say, only he looked both resentful and unhappy. In the end Dom Henry made him promise to do nothing in the matter for a year. "And you shall say no word of it to anyone."

"Why should I? But why should I not?" Robin asked shrewdly.

"Because if you have told it to any, you're of that stubborn humour that you may hold yourself to it for very pride. And an unfit monk is a misery to himself, and a hair shirt upon the backs of his brethren. I know."

Robin flung off the horse-block then and went home. He told himself that he had been a fool to speak of it to Dom Henry, worldly and witty, who read more in Plautus than in any of the Fathers, even if he were a distant kinsman, and his schoolmaster.

Dom Henry, mechanically singing the responses which he knew so well, was able to reflect upon the conversation throughout Compline. He understood, better than the boy himself, he thought, why Robin, halting between longing and dread, had come to him, and not to the Prior, who would have rehearsed for him all the old arguments why it was good for every man to be a monk, arguments so old that all the truth seemed to have been worn off them, like the pile on the old velvet copes. "Robin knows," Dom Henry thought, "that he'll get the truth from me, as I think it." That it was not the whole, nor the only truth, the monk was well aware. Men became monks for many reasons; leisure and comfort were his own. But if Robin were to be a monk, it would not be for these, but because for him the Prior's old worn reasons were still harsh and fiery with truth.

He shut the Office book with a clap. Compline was over. As they went out into the windy chill of the Cloister he thought, "In the old days—yes, perhaps. But not now. Monks should be quiet men." He was sure of one thing, that Robin Aske, either in the world or in the Cloister, would not be a quiet man, contented, easy, amused and comfortable. And he did not want his own quiet disturbed with something that would be too like shame to be pleasant. He went into the little room beside the Chapter House where the books were kept. For a moment he hesitated over Origen. Origen had a piercing subtle wit that Henry could relish, but though he drew half out the big book in its yellowing sheepskin binding, he drove it back again with his fist, and took to read instead the companionable Horatius Flaccus. "Man," he thought, "isn't all soul." He did not confess to himself that he could have wished to be entirely without that troublesome and hungry flame.

Before Dom Henry's stipulated year was out Kit had gone to Skipton, to be one of the gentlemen in the household of the Askes' Clifford kinsman, the Earl of Cumberland, and Robin to the Household of the Earl of Northumberland. When his father had first told him that he was to go there he had come, rather shame-faced, to Dom Henry, asking, "What shall I do?"

But the monk, who was in the grip of one of his great and sore winter colds, had little patience for him this time.

"Do? Go," he answered.

"But—"

"Do you suppose that you cannot as well choose to become a monk, if you do so choose, at Wressel as at Aughton?"

"No," said Robin with an obstinate look, and went home.

When he came to say good-bye Dom Henry was kinder. He kissed Robin, blessed him, clapped him on the back, told him not to forget his latinity, and gave him a little gold brooch with a crucifix upon it. He was really sorry to part, but having always made a semblance of finding boys even more ridiculous creatures than men, he could not well show it.

So Robin set off to Wressel Castle with his father, in a new doublet of the Percy colours, crimson and black, and crimson hosen under his long riding boots. Will Wall, who was to be his servant, rode behind with the two men who would go back to Aughton with Sir Robert. Will was fifteen, but saucy enough to teach monkeys, the two men said, as they were riding home again. Sir Robert replied that to live in so great a household would teach him sense and a meekness proper to his age and station. He did not say that it should do the same for Robin, who, though not exactly saucy, was in his opinion too positive and pragmatical a lad; but that was what he was thinking when he rode under the gate-house at Aughton, and the three little girls, Nan, Moll and Doll, ran out to welcome him. Mistress Nell, Jack's wife, came out more slowly, and rebuked them, telling Nan to pick up the spindle she had dropped, before everyone had caught their feet in the wool and fouled it. Nell was seventeen now, and very pleased to rule the household and the little girls.

But that same evening Sir Robert found Nan and Moll, the two who came after Robin in age, sitting together on the top step of the stairs going up to their bedroom. Nan was sniffing and gulping after tears, and Moll was helping her to wipe them from her face with the hanging lappet of her coif. Nan said that she was crying because Robin had gone away.

"Silly little goose!" Sir Robert told her, but not unkindly. "Look at Moll. She does not cry."

Moll answered for Nan that though she did not cry, yet she

was sad for it. "But," said she, "it is Nan loves him best," and then she screwed up her face and began to whimper too.

Sir Robert, thinking of the way that Robin teased and tyrannized over the girls, more than either of his elder brothers had ever done, hoped that there was something good in the lad that made them now cry for his going.

He did not come home for close on three years, and by then he was for his sisters a young man, and a stranger, with already a dark shaven chin, and lips that pricked when he kissed them.

Yet to Dom Henry it seemed at first that the young man held out a hand, as it were, to the very young Robin, the careless, good-humoured boy, over the head of that lad who had begun to appear before he went away. Dom Henry was down near the river among the fish-ponds when Robin came to him. It was a day in late October with a steady wind, and the sky looming blue through grey cloud. Some of the willows had already turned yellow, while others kept their grey-green, but all had been thinned out by last night's storm. Now the wind, flowing through their branches as strongly as the swollen Derwent in his course, streaked all the tiny sharp leaves one way.

Dom Henry had been in a mood of chilly melancholy, but he brightened up when he saw Robin. He was pleased that Robin had sought him out, and at the new grace with which he went down on his knee for a blessing; he had not grown much taller, but had broadened, and wore his livery well—a thought carelessly, as a gentleman should. They walked together towards the Priory gate. At first the young man seemed to think that the last two months which he had spent with his master, young Henry Percy, in the Household of the Cardinal of York, qualified him to correct Dom Henry when they spoke of a book by Erasmus of Rotterdam which the monk had read and he had not. It did not take his old schoolmaster long to put him right on that point, and then he became just an eager boy, talking of all the strange things and people that were to be seen in London; ships from Spain, Italy, the Levant; Venetian merchants in silks that noblemen envied them; French gentlemen that came and went with the Ambassador, all chattering like monkeys; the wonderful things, gold plate, clocks, pictures to be seen in the Cardinal's house.

"By St. James!" said Dom Henry, "though Kit has his books—did you know that he is copying a great book on hunting with his own hand?—and Jack his wife and those three stout knave children of his, I think you have better than either."

Robin made no answer for a minute. His face was lifted and he seemed to be intent upon a couple of wild duck flying fast down the wind; his blind eye was towards Dom Henry, but the monk could see the new hard line of the jaw where before had been a boyish softness.

Then Robin said, "If he—if my master were another manner man! But he's sick, and he's silly. Oh! you know not how many hours we kick our heels, waiting on him, while he's slugging abed, or biting at his nails in his chair. If I could but have some work to set my hand to now I am a man—some good work."

He stopped, then muttered, "for Christendom," and turned his face full on Dom Henry, looking at him with an eye that was hard and ready to be angry.

But Dom Henry did not wish to laugh at the great solemnity of the young. He was thinking that the other Robin was there, and had just looked out; Jack had sweetness, and Kit was clever, but here was strength. He was silent, and by his side Robin soon rattled on again with one tale after another.

"Well," says Dom Henry at last, stopping and looking at him with his odd quirk of a smile, "they haven't cured you of talking, nor you've not grown out of it for yourself."

The lad stopped, flushed, then laughed.

"They say I could talk the hind leg off my Lord Cardinal's mule, did I set my mind to it."

This was in the autumn. After Christmas Day Henry caught one of his colds; it went to his lungs, and, being a man of a full habit of body and no longer young, his heart could not stand it, and he died on Twelfth Night in the year 1519, so that he and Robin did not see each other again.

1527

May 12

Master Robert Aske sat on a stool in a small room in the lodgings of Sir Henry Percy, son of the Earl of Northumberland, in the village of Westminster. It was a small room, dark even on this bright day, and the hangings were old and faded. Aske sat with his legs stuck stiffly out in front of him, staring under his heavy brows at the woven picture of a woman in a gown of the fashion of eighty years ago. She knelt and put a black shoe on the foot of a man sitting on a flowery mount in the garden. Aske turned his head and looked round at the other walls of the room.

"What's it all about?" he muttered. "There's a man kneeling on his cap and sticking a duck's bill into the ground. Why? And look at that king in his crown, taking up the harvest man by his middle. Why? There's no sense in it, that I can see."

Another young man, tall, slim, and pale, who perched on a trestle table dangling his legs, asked, in the same low voice, what did it matter whether there were sense in it or not.

"I like to know," said Aske; and he got up and began to rove softly round the room staring at the hangings, his tongue running on, bidding look here, at this king crowning another king, and this woman with a banner and a helmet. "Well," said he at last, "either the folk of old time were mad as geese or the servants have got these pieces all mixed up like Christmas Pie," and he came back to his stool, and sat down. Then they both looked over their shoulders to where, in a deep window, a third young man sat lumping on cushions. His back was against the wall, his chin on his chest, and he snored gently from time to time. Henry Percy slept after his dinner. He was not dressed with any greater show than either of the other two, and indeed they were all three a little shabby, but upon Henry Percy's slack hand a great emerald caught the sunlight and sent up a fuzz of light.

The young man on the table said, speaking quietly, "When the Earl, his father, dies, what'll *he* do?" and he jerked his head towards the sleeper.

"Do?" Aske grinned. "What he's doing now. Unless the Cardinal chivvies him up North again to the Border."

"Would you be glad of that?"

Aske did not answer at once. Then he said, "Whether he goes or no, I'll not be there."

"Mass," the other cried, then slapped himself across the mouth, looked anxiously at Henry Percy, and whispered, "You'll leave his Household? For my Lord of Cumberland?"

Aske pulled down the corners of his mouth and shook his head.

"You could. For your mother was a Clifford."

Aske thanked him politely. "But have me excused," said he.

"My brother Kit's with the Earl. One Household isn't big enough for Kit and me. We always fall out. Kit thinks I'm too cocket."

The other turned his face away to smile because that was so exactly what others thought of Robert Aske. "Well," he concluded, "I suppose I shall stay with this Earl Henry when Henry the Magnificent is dead."

"That, my good fellow," Aske told him, "is what you will not do."

"Won't?"

"Won't. The Cardinal will see to it."

"God's Death! But the Cardinal has nothing to do with it. He can't turn off Lord Henry's gentlemen, more especially when he's Earl."

"Can and will—all of them but one or two and a groom or so. The old Earl's deep in debt. I know. And the Cardinal will see that till his debts are paid this Earl shan't have two groats in his pouch to jingle together."

The tall young man rubbed his chin. "Mass!" he murmured, "are you sure?" He knew that Aske always was sure, but remembered with some dismay that he was often, though not always, right. Besides, as Comptroller of the young lord's Household he must see better than the others what was going on. His long pale face was dismal as he asked, "What'll I do?" Then he brightened a little. "What'll you do?"

"Take to the law," Aske told him promptly.

"God's Soul! But how old are you? Four and twenty? And you've learnt none."

"But I can learn. I'm not a fool."

The other threw his head back to laugh, then, remembering the sleeping man, clapped his hand again over his mouth. Henry Percy stirred but did not wake, so he said, "No, Robin, no one would take you for that."

Aske, who had begun to frown, laughed softly instead. The other slid off the table.

"Get your bow," said he, "and I'll take you on at the butts."

"But you always beat me."

"I do. Of course we all know that you'd beat me if you had your two eyes. But pride's a deadly sin, so I'll beat you soundly to save you from damnation."

Aske got up. "Forward then to the good work," he said and both went out laughing quietly, and stepping gingerly so as not to wake their master.

Darcy was just leaving the Chamber of Presence at Greenwich Palace when he found the Duke of Norfolk at his elbow —not the old Duke, who had died three years ago, but his son Thomas Howard, who had been Earl of Surrey and got himself much honour at the Battle of Flodden. Darcy had never liked him, and liked him no more now that he was Duke, and High Treasurer of England, but Norfolk greeted him with particular courtesy, walked on with him and after a minute or two edged him away into a little closet of painted wainscot. Darcy thought he looked very pleased over something.

"Sit, my Lord, sit," said Norfolk. "I saw you lean heavily on your stick while we waited for the King." There was only a stool and a pair of virginals in the closet, but the Duke would have Darcy sit on the stool, while he tucked his own backside on to the virginals, jangling all the keys once in painful discord. Then he inquired with great kindness about my Lord's old disease.

But after a little of this he was silent, and pulled a comical face and laughed.

"Indeed we can see that it is May-time; yea, even in London and at Court," he said.

Darcy did not pretend to misunderstand him.

"How long will it last? May's but thirty-one days, and then?"

Norfolk shook his head, still smiling, then he narrowed his eyes and looked crafty.

"My niece is a most virtuous and chaste lady. You know the King—how set he is to have his will. Yet here he can have it not. I promise you I could weep for him, to read the letters he writes to her when she has crossed him, or runs away home from Court to be done with the importunities of his suit. 'H.R.' he will sign himself at the foot, and '*Aultre ne cherche*' between the letters, and right in the midst of all a heart drawn, and inscribed with A. B."

"Very pretty," said Darcy sourly. "But if she will have none of him, and he will not tire, what will be the end of it?"

"Ah!" Norfolk leaned closer. "She will none of him except lawfully. Yet—if the Queen should become a nun—" He broke off there as if he had said too much. "A little while ago," he went on, "she sent him a jewel, representing in diamonds a maid solitary in a ship, and the posy, '*Aut illic aut nullibi.*' To which he replied somewhat to this end, for she showed me the letter—'My heart is dedicated to you alone, wishing that my body were so too, as God can make it if it pleases Him.' "

"Ah!" Darcy remarked, not without malice, "God?"

The Duke got up and the strings of the virginals whined. "My Lord, I can see God's hand here, if you cannot. The realm lacks an heir. The Princess? Pooh! We lack a Prince. And one other we have with us that we could well lack." He came close to Darcy and whispered, "You and I think alike of the King's prepotent subject, my Lord Cardinal. We should be friends."

Darcy considered that for a minute, and with it the rest of what the Duke had told him. Then he said:

"You tell me that the King means marriage with your niece?"

Norfolk was looking at the floor. He did not raise his eyes but rustled the strawing with one foot and answered softly that he believed no less.

Darcy also looked down at the Duke's foot, and at a faded head of clover that Norfolk was shifting this way and that; it was as if neither wished to meet the other's eyes. The Duke moved away again, but paused at the virginals, and leaning one hand that held his blue velvet cap upon the painted case of the instrument, with the fingers of the other picked out a shivering sweet chord or two. Then he looked round at Darcy.

"And your niece, Mistress Anne, is of the same mind as yourself, my Lord, towards the Cardinal?" Darcy inquired.

"I promise you," Norfolk chuckled. "Sometimes I think a woman can outdo any man when it comes to pure, piercing hatred."

When the Duke had gone Darcy sat a while alone, turning over what he had heard. Then he shrugged his shoulders and got up. He did not think it likely, on the one hand, that Mistress Anne's virtue would prove as impregnable as Norfolk rated it; nor, on the other, if it did, that even that lively bold slip of a girl was an adversary whom the great Cardinal should fear. She might dance like a dark flame through the maskings at Court in her cloth of gold and with rubies about her neck which Darcy was sure her father had never given her, but the King must go from masking to the Council Table, and there the Cardinal would rule.

June 4

Master Robert Aske pushed his hair behind his ears, stuffed

his thumbs into them, and bent over the law book again. But Will Wall's snores could not be kept out. He shut the book at last, got up, and stretched himself, for he was stiff with long sitting, having been at work from four in the morning. This business of learning the law needed time, and he had, he felt, lost several years in Henry Percy's Household. It was useless to try to waken Will; he was more than usually sodden with drink. "Miserable swillbowl!" Aske called him as he passed him, sprawling on the straw pallet, and gave him a gentle kick. It was the second time this week that Will had come home drunk as a rat.

Hunting in the cupboard for something to eat Aske found a piece of mutton pie at which he sniffed suspiciously, and then tipped out of the window. Besides that there was only a heel of cheese, the flabby remains of a salad, and half a loaf. Well, he must make do, for he had sworn to himself that he would read so much in Bracton every day, and that left no time for going out to taverns to dine. "But what," he asked himself angrily, "do I keep such a servant for?" as if he could have brought himself to send Will away from him, or persuaded Will to go.

When he had eaten a little he felt more kindly towards everyone.

"While I read he has nothing to do," he argued, on Will's behalf, "and so runs into mischief."

June 8

This day Christabel Cowper's younger brother was married for the second time, and she was at the wedding. She wore, as she ought not to have worn, a girdle woven with silver, and a silk purse hanging from it. Her veil, as it ought not to have been, was of silk, and the pins in it were of silver; she considered that this show was for the credit of the House. Besides, she was not as others, who wore such things in Cloister, thus causing temptation to assail the younger Ladies. When she was at Marrick these adornments lay in a chest, so now she could wear them heartily.

And over dinner, where the wine was good, she struck a most advantageous bargain with Master John Cocks, the Tanner. To herself she said, "He'll be sorry for this to-morrow," but to him:

"It's good cheap for you, and a loss for us. But we poor Nuns must take what we can get for our ox-hides."

Lord Darcy did not take the King's order to the Keeper of the Great Wardrobe till this day. He had been too much occupied with business to do it before. This business was disagreeable, and sent him to the Law Courts in Westminster Hall to answer feigned bills of that villain Banks, accusing him and Lord Hussey of wasting the goods of poor Monteagle. It cost my Lord well over a hundred pounds before all was finished, what with the presents, at Court, and to certain of the King's Council, the hire of the house at Stepney, and all the letters, messages, writings, and rewards to the men of law. But at the end of it he and Hussey, Banks and young Lord Monteagle signed an accord in the house of Master Cromwell, a servant of the Cardinal's, and very deep in his confidence; Hussey had always said that there was no hope of coming lightly out of the business when he had heard that Banks had managed, by hook or crook, to get this man for his friend. "Half lawyer, half money-lender," Hussey said, who knew more about him than Darcy.

"Then whole damned," Darcy muttered, who had suffered from both.

And this day, as he passed through one of the chambers in the Great Wardrobe beside Blackfriars, there was Master Cromwell, crouching over some rolls of silk and cloth of gold that lay on the floor. Gibson, porter and yeoman tailor of the Wardrobe, was just slitting open the canvas cover of the last roll, and all about the two lay folds of the rich lustrous stuffs.

"Italian," Cromwell told Darcy, getting up from the floor. "There's none in Christendom can weave better such things." He was inclined to be friendly with Darcy, had Darcy allowed it. He was certainly very friendly with Gibson, calling him "Dick," and "gossip."

"And," said he aloud at the door, when he had taken his leave, "forget not, my good Dick, the clavichord wire." He smiled at Darcy, and said, "I confess I aim at defrauding the King's Grace to the tune of some yards of clavichord wire."

Then he was gone, a fat, cheerful, small man, with a ready laugh and a pleasant voice. His eyes were twinkling too, and merry, but Darcy had noticed, that day they had had to do with him and Banks, that every now and then he shot out of them a sharp, pricking look. And Darcy was nearly sure, that whether Master Cromwell was to have some of the King's clavichord wire or no, the roll of grey damask cloth of silver, which lay rather apart from the other silks, would go to Master Cromwell's house at the Austin Friars, and that it would never appear on the Accounts of the King's Great Wardrobe.

When Cromwell had gone away, and the clerk of the Wardrobe had been found, my Lord showed him the King's order. He took Darcy to a closet where the spare chapel stuff was kept and my Lord chose a vestment, of black silk powdered with roses and columbines, for the Chapel of his Hospital.

September 26

Robert Aske was sitting on the step of the horse-block beside the Hall door at Aughton, with a book on his lap, his elbows on his knees and his head between his fists. The women were clearing out the rushes from the floors to-day, so as to straw new for the winter, and there was no peace for any man indoors. A dog or two lay in the sun near his feet; for the most part of the time they dozed, waking up suddenly to snap at flies or to scratch. From the further yard beyond the old dairy there came the sound of someone chopping wood; a servant was drawing water from the well in the corner by the door into the kitchens; the rope creaked with a note higher than the whine of the winch, and now and again water slopped over the swinging bucket, and fell back into the well with a splash. From beyond the court came the tinkle of goat-bells.

Aske took one hand from his head to scratch his thigh. Then he let out with his foot at a spaniel that had come too close.

"Keep your fleas on your own hide," says he, and the spaniel wagged, yawned, and lay down again a little further away; Aske went back to his book.

When a shadow fell across the page he did not look up, but seeing Nan's gown he groaned, and, as if in anger, cried out on "You women who will never leave a man in quiet, but hound him out of doors with your brooms, and then come and deafen him with your clacking tongues."

Nan giggled. If Kit had said that she would not have known whether to laugh or go quietly away; but though she had found Robin rather alarming when he came home a month ago, she did not so now.

"Well?" he asked.

"Will you come and help to gather blackberries?"

"Nay, I will not."

"Then will you hold your godson for me?"

"I'll do so much. He'll mark my place as well as a straw."

He took the stiffly swaddled child from her and laid it down upon the book. "Perdy!" cried he, "he's wet!"

"They always are," she told him; and when he cried fie on her she laughed at him. "Keep him the right way up," she said, and went away.

He shifted the baby to the crook of his arm, and looked down into its unblinking eyes for a moment before he went on with his reading. Nan had been married to Will Monkton, eldest son of a man half way between yeoman and gentleman. Will was a fat young fellow, slow-speaking and grave. Robert Aske was pleased to have him for a brother-in-law, though he guessed from something Jack had said that Kit did not approve of the marriage. "But if Nan likes him—" he thought. Nan was little, pale and plain, and would always be, but Robert thought that her eyes looked happy.

"Sir," said he to the baby, "you stare too long for courtesy; and why you should bubble from your mouth when you are already so wet at t'other end—!"

October 1

Lord Darcy was returning out of London to the house at Stepney, when the Duke of Norfolk caught him up, going to try a new hawk in the fields beyond the village. The Duke sent his gentlemen on, and rode softly beside Darcy's horse-litter, talking of the North Country, and of the young Duke of Richmond, the King's son, who had been sent there with a Council and a great Household to learn the trade of a ruler, though he was barely ten years old. "But," said Norfolk, "a singular gracious and wise child as all agree," and he waited a minute for Darcy to answer, and, when he did not, added that it was a pity his mother had not been the King's lawful wife.

Darcy said rather he thought it was a pity that the boy was not Queen Katherine's child.

"That is what I would say," Norfolk assured him, but Darcy had an idea that he had put it the other way to try what answer he would get. He wondered what the Duke would be at, and wondered still more when they came to the end of the lane along which Darcy must turn. For the Duke pulled up there, and began to ask about the house. Was it big enough, in good repair, were there stables and grazing in plenty? And every now and then as he talked he would nod and tip his head towards the roof and chimneys that showed above the orchard trees, and he frowned, and then winked one eye, so that Darcy knew that he wanted to be asked to turn in for a while, and see the house, though he could not think why the Duke should want it, nor why he should make such a secret of it. But he said, "If you will turn in, my Lord, to drink a cup of wine?" and he told his footboy to go on and fetch Norfolk's gentlemen back.

The Duke would gladly turn in, he said, adding that it was as warm as summer, which was true, for, after a wet and windy September, October had come in with a light mist and still blue skies. So, at the Duke's own suggestion, they drank their wine in the garden that smelt pleasantly of box, and apples, and sweet-briar warmed in the sun.

After they had finished their wine the Duke brushed the crumbs of wafer from his knee and got up, but he waved his hand to his gentlemen, and taking Darcy's arm shoved him gently in the direction of the orchard. "Now," thought Darcy, "we're coming at it," and he was right. After a turn taken together, in which Norfolk spoke loudly of his own new grafted apple-trees at Framlingham, he dropped his voice and asked Darcy did he know that the Cardinal's Grace had returned.

"Yea, I heard."

Norfolk looked down at the hooded hawk, restless, on his hand. "Everywhere in France he was shown great honour."

As he seemed to wait for a reply Darcy said that he supposed that was but natural, seeing he was the servant of so great a master.

"And so great a servant," Norfolk suggested, to which Darcy said nothing.

"Yet I have heard say, '*Non est Propheta inhonoratus nisi in patria sua,*'" and the Duke looked sharply up at Darcy.

"How can that fit here, my Lord, unless the Cardinal thinks his honours—which, God knows, are many and great—are not enough for his services?"

"He did not think himself honoured when he came to the King at Richmond," said Norfolk softly.

"Ah!" said Darcy. "This I have not heard."

Norfolk chuckled. "I shall tell you. He came there in the evening, having landed from Calais that morning, straight to give account to his master, as a dutiful servant should, and supposing that he should be joyfully received at his home-coming, as one who has made this new treaty with France. And coming to the palace he sent one of his people to the King announcing his return, and asking where and at what hour he should visit His Grace. I was with the Cardinal, and I saw his gentleman go to the King, and I saw him return."

He chuckled again, and Darcy, not seeing why, said, "Well?"

"The Cardinal's gentleman, when he came back, was as red as those apples on the tree. Yet he only said to the Cardinal that the King would see him at once. 'Where?' says he. 'I will bring you to the King,' says the gentleman, and they went out, and I saw the Cardinal turn to him, in going, and ask again, 'Where is His Grace?' but I did not hear the answer—not then. I waited, and I saw the Cardinal come out of the palace and ride away. I asked one of his gentlemen how the King had received his master, 'Right thankfully, I'll wager,' says I. And he looked at me as awkwardly as if he'd stolen a purse, and said—'Right thankfully; very honourably,' and got himself away from me as quick as he could."

Darcy stopped walking, and they stood together under one of the trees, feeling the sun's warmth spatter through the leaves upon their heads.

"It's a long tale, but I come near to the end," the Duke assured him. "It was from my niece—" "Mistress Anne?" put in Darcy; and, "Mistress Anne," Norfolk repeated. "From her that I heard the rest. For she came to me after supper in the gallery, and showed me a new jewel she was wearing, a table emerald with three hanging pearls, very pretty, very costly. She'd had it, she said, of the King's Grace that evening, and many gracious words with it. 'And kisses not a few,' says I, whereat she laughed, and did not deny it.

"'And then,' says she, 'one came in from my Lord Cardinal and asked where and when he might wait on His Grace.' I told her I knew what he had asked; but what had the King answered?

"'It was not the King that answered,' says she. 'It was I. I said to the Cardinal's gentleman, "Where else but here should the Cardinal come? Tell him he may come here, where the King is."'

"'Mass!' quod I, 'was not the King angry?' She laughed at that and told me, no, not angry at all, but very merry, asking her if she would be one of his Privy Council."

"She is a very bold lady," Darcy said, not too cordially; but then, remembering how she had discomfited the Cardinal, he laughed. "No other would have dared."

"Bold she is," Norfolk said, "and of a marvellous ready wit, and that the King loves her for. And," he turned to Darcy, "as I told you before, she loves not the Cardinal." He held out his hand then, to say farewell. "You and I think alike over one matter; we should be friends," he said, and added, "Though not too openly."

Darcy gave an angry laugh. "Thomas Wolsey knows that I love him little, and with great reason."

"Secret is best," said Norfolk, and went on to his hawking.

November 18

Master Cheyne had gone away into Kent to the death-bed of an uncle. He wanted to be sure that the executors did not cheat him of any inheritance that might be due to him. So Julian went up into the parlour after supper, and at bed-time with Meg into her chamber. Meg was in a kind mood, and let her sister take from an iron-bound box the precious and pretty things she kept there. Julian knelt before the big chest at the foot of the bed, and laid them out, one by one, on the lid, while Meg sat in her shift on the edge of the bed, combing her hair and humming a song. The shadow of her hand, and the comb, and her hair, went up and down the painted wall.

Julian bent over the trinkets, touching those she liked best with her finger, very gently. There was a girdle enamelled white, red and black in the Spanish fashion; she had taken it half out of the soft leather that wrapped it. Besides that there were gold buttons, each set with a tiny ruby, and beyond the buttons two rings, one with a hand gripping a cat's-eye stone, and the other plain gold with a rocky pearl.

Meg laid down her comb and began braiding her hair. July knew that she had not much longer till she would be sent away to bed. She fumbled down at the bottom of the box for a thing that she knew was there, and found it—half a gold rose noble, with a hole near the broken edge, and a thin gold chain through the hole. She knew that it was the token the Duke of Buckingham had given to the girl he had met on the shore at Southampton, before Meg was born—the girl that had become their mother.

She laid the coin in her palm and let the chain hang over her hand. For a minute it was cold on her skin, then grew warm with the warmth of her flesh.

"Meg," she said, not looking up from the thing in her hand, "what was our mother like?"

Meg's quick fingers moved among her hair so that the three tails leapt and shook as she braided it.

"She was only a simple creature, of no gentle blood."

"But—" Julian began.

"But she was very beautiful." Meg tied her hair with a rose-coloured ribbon and looped the heavy rope so that it framed her face; she leaned forward and picked up the mirror, and smiled into it. She thought that she was more beautiful than ever her mother had been.

"Was—was she—good?" Julian asked.

Meg turned and stared at her, then laughed.

"Good? She bore us two bastards."

"Then," July persisted, "was she bad?"

"Oh!" said Meg lightly, and let the shift slip from her shoulders and stood up naked beside the bed, "I'd not say she was bad. But does it matter?"

July could not answer that. She began to put the things back in the box even before Meg told her to.

January 1

This morning Will Wall came into the room at Gray's Inn that his master shared with two others. He had Aske's red velvet coat over his arm, for the Christmas Feast was not half over, and to-day was a high day. Hal Hatfield was not awake yet, and Ned Bangham lay with his hands clasped behind his head, but Aske was half dressed, and was just fastening the points that tied his grey hosen to his doublet; Will put down the coat on the bench near the dead fire, and began to tie the points at his master's back.

Hal wakened, yawned, stretched and turned over.

"Well, Robin," he asked, "how did you get on with the young gentlewoman?"

Aske laughed. He sat down on the edge of his own bed, and stuck out his feet so that Will could lace the gussets of the hosen inside each ankle. "Not on—off," said he. "Last night was wine and candle to my wooing."

"Jesu Mary!" Hal rolled over the better to see him. "The end of it? My poor Robin! Is the heart broken?"

"To pieces!" Aske told him cheerfully; yet Hal thought he looked a little crestfallen.

"To pieces!"

"I never supposed," put in Ned Bangham from the other bed, "that wenches had so much sense."

"Now, Master!" Will protested, "it's not sense to refuse a likely bachelor."

Aske winked at Hal over Will Wall's head.

[126]

"I'm best out of it," he told Hal. "Mating with such a merry gentlewoman would be too much for a quiet man like me. She told me roundly she did not care how many men loved her, and wooed, and went empty away, but she had not thought of marrying for another two years." He pulled a face, and spread out his hands, making a jest of it, but his pride was sore and Will knew it. He muttered to Aske's boots, which he was pulling on, that if he'd had a daughter spoke so, he'd think that she had not been enough beaten in her upbringing.

"At least," said Aske, "she sent me packing before New Year's Day, so I've saved the gift I bought her. See here, Will —you go out and buy wine for us to the cost of it, and then you'll have no quarrel with Mistress Clare."

"Ho!" cried Hal. "Me too, Robin," and he heaved himself out of bed. "How much have we to turn on? I've a costly thirst."

"He spent 12s. 8d. on a comb for her," Will answered disapprovingly.

Ned Bangham sat up and began to pull on his shirt.

"May you never prosper in love, Robin," said he, "if your friends can drink what your ladies refuse."

March 3

The Nuns were in the choir, and Mass was almost at an end, while the wind whistled and moaned in the tower, and draughts tugged at the candle-flames. Dame Christabel knelt with her eyelids lowered and her hands folded seemly under her chin. Yet she was aware that Dame Margaret Lovechild was occupied in quieting the little dog she had brought in on his yellow ribbon leash; that the Prioress was frankly asleep; and that Bet and Grace, the two little novices, were whispering together though hardly moving their lips; it was an accomplishment they had learned since they came to Marrick.

The old priest stopped for quite a long time in order to cough; and then to hiccup because his digestion was now very bad. Christabel opened her eyes and looked at him as if she would goad him on by looking. She shut her eyes again and went back to her thoughts. She was wondering whether indeed she had done well to choose to be a Nun. If she had married— She thought of a house—perhaps even of a Manor House—with new fine glass windows, comfortable, with jolly comings and goings; there would have been many servants to rule, her own children, a husband. Perhaps she could not have ruled him, but at the worst most men could be managed. She sighed, sharply and impatiently, and then with relief took up her part in the singing. They were almost at an end now.

April 10

After dinner Lord Darcy had Lord Hussey's messenger into his chamber for half an hour or so, and when the man had gone down again to the Hall, sent for his eldest son, Sir George. But Sir George was out, and did not return till after dark when his father was getting ready for bed and Lady Elizabeth already lay within the drawn curtains asleep. My Lord's gentleman had spread the footsheet beside the fire, because the night was cold and windy. He had taken off my Lord's coat and doublet, his shoes and black hosen, his shirt with the black Spanish work about the neck, and his breeches. For a moment Darcy stood naked, lean and bony, with the curled, grizzled hair pricking on his breast at the cold; then the gentleman slipped over his head the fine night-shirt and put on him a long night-gown of green velvet, furred with red fox. He was just going away with my Lord's clothes thrown over his shoulder when Sir George came in and sat down on a stool by the hearth.

While the waiting gentleman combed my Lord's hair nothing was spoken of except a horse which Sir George had just bought, and of that they spoke quietly because of my Lady, asleep in bed. "Luttrell has broken and half trained him already," said Sir George. "A right good stallion." My Lord agreed that Luttrell had a way with horses.

"And in a week's time I shall sell him for twice that I gave. Lutrell's a fool at a bargain."

Darcy frowned at his son and tipped his head towards the gentleman, now beginning to slide the curtains softly apart along the cords of the bed.

"Let the curtains be, James," said Darcy, while George tossed up his chin and shrugged his shoulders at the rebuke. But he was silent till the fat yellow Paris candle had been lit and set at the bed-head for the night, and the dogs and an old tom-cat that was a favourite of my Lord's turned out. The gentleman paused at the door, bowed to my Lord and his son and went out. Darcy bade, "Good night to you, James," and George nodded. Then there was silence in the room.

"You sent for me, Sir," says George at last.

His father stretched out the iron-shod staff he walked with and struck roughly at a log that was out of reach of the flames.

"Will you not learn," he said, "if you must cheat one of our own people, not to brag of it? James and all my other gentlemen hold together as they hold with me, and Luttrell is one of them. Moreover I think it a wretched thing that any man should be glad to trick one of his own folk, that look to him rather for help than for such ill-natured doings."

George "pished" impatiently and muttered something about fools and their money, as if he did not care. Yet it was only a pretence; he took no account at all of his step-mother, disliked his half-sister, was jealous of his younger brother Arthur, because my Lord loved him; but my Lord he greatly admired, and almost as much hated.

"Well," said Darcy, after another silence, "I sent for you. Here's news of how the King's matter speeds in Rome, and it speeds not at all. The Cardinal has sent out Master Stephen Gardiner, and he hath threatened His Holiness with most unseemly freedom. But threaten he never so, he'll get no good, for the Pope fears the Emperor too nearly to sing but as he calls the tune," and my Lord chuckled and slapped his hands down on his thigh.

George did not so much as smile. He said, with his eyes on the fire, that he thought no loyal subject should rejoice that his Prince was thwarted in a matter so near his heart as the breaking of this ill-made marriage of his.

Darcy seized on one word, "Loyal? You say, or you think, I'm not loyal?"

"And you chide me because I profit by a fool's folly—"

"Now by God's Death, George," Darcy interrupted him, "I wonder sometimes that you are son of mine. My father taught me as I have taught you, that a man that is a lord stands by his friends and his men through flood and through fire."

"And not by his Prince?"

Darcy turned and looked at him, and answered after a while in a different voice, thoughtfully.

"You and some others have a new idea of a Prince. You think he must have his way, whatsoever it be, with the law or maugre the law. That was not the way of it in England when I was a lad."

"And a right merry England you made of it with wars and bickerings, and making and unmaking of kings." George got up and went over to the door and wrenched it open.

"Give you good night, Sir," said he, and went out.

"Is that you, Tom?" my Lady called sleepily from the bed, and Darcy said it was, and got slowly to his feet and to bed. But it was a long time before he slept, thinking as he did of old days when there was war between two Kings in England, and of his son, and of matters at Court and in Rome.

May 3

"It's ten o'clock, and my Lord Cardinal in bed this half-hour." The Cardinal's gentleman fingered his chin doubtfully, looking Mr. Foxe up and down, and seeing, in the dust on the boots and shoulders of the King's Almoner, evidence of his travels, and of his haste—and haste means always tidings of weight.

Mr. Foxe had sat stiffly down on a bench. He had come from Sandwich this morning. For more than a fortnight, since he had left the Papal Court at Orvieto, he had not slept twice in the same bed. He yawned, and said behind his hand—

"His Grace will be glad to see me."

The Gentleman looked hard at him for another second, said, "I'll tell him," and went away with the servant bearing a candle before him. Master Foxe dozed with his head back against the arras, and thought that he had fallen off his horse upon a stony road, and that the horse looked round at him with the Pope's face instead of the face of a horse. When the Cardinal's gentleman tapped him on the shoulder he sprang up all amazed.

Two servants were lighting the candles in the Cardinal's bed-chamber, and as each new-lit flame spired up the light caught here a glow of colour from the arras, and there a gleam of gold from the damask cloth of gold of the bed curtains. Master Foxe blinked in the swimming, trembling light, then he looked into the shadow between the half-drawn curtains of the bed, and went down on one knee. He could see the Cardinal's head in its lawn night-cap, embroidered with black silk and gold thread; the Cardinal's face was turned towards the room, one heavy cheek with the pouch under the eye socket plumped up by the soft down of the pillow upon which it pressed; the Cardinal's eyes were open and gleamed in the candlelight. Master Foxe kissed the warm, soft hand, which came from between the sheets and was held out to him. Then His Grace wallowed up from the bedclothes like a whale out of the sea, and sat up against the pillows. "Bring me a lignt-gown," he said, and they brought him one of crimson damask and white fur.

When the gentleman and the servants had gone and Master Foxe sat on a stool by the bed, the Cardinal said, "Well?"

Master Foxe had drawn out, and now laid on the bed, divers sealed letters. The Cardinal flicked them over. "And letters to the King's Grace?" he asked.

"I have delivered them to His Highness." The Cardinal's eyebrows went up. "I went at once to Greenwich," Master Foxe explained, "thinking to find Your Grace there, but you had been gone two hours."

"Ah! Well?" the Cardinal asked sharply.

"The Pope hath signed the dispensation without a word altered, and the commission; though *that* we strove for long, before they would consent. But at last, we, differing in two words only, demanded that *omnem* should be added to *potestatem,* and *nolente* to *impedito,* and so it was determined, Your Grace and Cardinal Campeggio being joined in the commission to try the cause of the King's marriage."

The Cardinal stirred in bed and Master Foxe paused and then went on with his tale.

"But here began a new tragedy, for now the night being far past, and the Pope sending to the Cardinals' houses, they replied that they would look up their books to-morrow.

"Then after much spoken hotly on our side, Master Gardiner saith that when this dealing of theirs should be known, the favour of that Prince, our King, who is their only friend, should be taken away. and that the Apostolic See should fall to pieces with the consent and applause of every man. At these words the Pope's Holiness, casting his arms abroad so—" and Master Foxe threw his arms wide and clapped them on his thighs, "bade us put in the words we varied for, and therewith walked up and down the chamber, casting now and then his arms abroad, we standing in a great silence. After a while—"

He paused, stumbled, and lost the eloquence which was that of an overwearied man. The Cardinal had moved again. He leaned forward in the bed.

"Master Foxe, tell me now this one thing. In this commission is it written that the Pope shall confirm the sentence, and may, if he will, revoke the cause to Rome?"

Foxe said it was so written. "But except for those clauses we thought it as good as can be devised, though not in all so open as—"

"Then," said the Cardinal, "it is nothing. Nothing."

"Sir, the King's Grace and Mistress Anne are right well pleased. His Highness sent for her that I should tell her the news, saying again and again, 'Here is that good news we have waited for' "

The Cardinal began to move his big head slowly from side to side, so that the heavy dewlap trembled a little.

Master Foxe grew more eager to reassure him of success. "I told His Highness how strongly Your Grace's letters had worked upon the Pope's Holiness, yea, and that without them we could have done nothing, at which His Highness and Mistress Anne were marvellous thankful, she saying—"

The Cardinal raised a hand.

"Is the commission decretal or general?"

"It is general. The Pope would in no wise—"

"Then I tell you that it is nothing."

"But—"

"Master Foxe," the Cardinal leaned from the bed till his big face was close to Foxe's face; "it is nothing. If Queen Katherine appeal—and she will appeal—the cause will be revoked to Rome. Will the Pope then break the marriage, if now he dare not sign a decretal commission giving full and final power to the Commissioners to break it? No, by Christ's Passion."

He drew back, and for a long time said nothing, except that Foxe heard him mutter to himself, "It is useless. It is what I feared," and now he bit his fingers and now he fiddled with the gold buttons of the pillow-beres.

Foxe roused with a jerk to hear his own name, and realized that the Cardinal was talking to him. "We must press His Holiness," he was saying, "with all possible persuasions to grant the commission decretal. For indeed, Master Foxe, it is for the very sake of His Holiness and the stability of the Holy See that I should be of such authority and estimation with the King that whatever I advise His Grace should assent to. His Holiness doth not know how matters stand here, in how perilous a state, and how tottering. For on the one hand the King, if he think the Pope his enemy, may be wrought to some desperate course, and on the other the Church is so eaten into and inwardly devoured of heretics—yea, like maggots in cheese, Mr. Foxe—that I fear—I fear—"

He bit his nails again, and began to devise arguments, one after another, to lay before the Pope, and questions to lay before the jurisconsults of the Papal Court, so that Master

Foxe, in a confused way, as his eyes blinked and burned for sleep, heard "confirmation of the sentence *per superiorem judicem* . . . the parties may *redire ad nova vota*. . . ." and the like, as the Cardinal out of his deep and subtle wit spun a new thread which might at last draw the Pope to satisfy the King's demands.

May 16

When Sim, who was clerk to Master Cheyne, got drunk, he would sit in the kitchen singing and beating time to his own singing with a wooden spoon or a rolling pin or anything handy. Mostly he sang merry songs, about young lovers or railing wives, but to-night he was in a melancholy mood—

> The life of this world
> Is ruled with wind,
> Weeping, darkness
> And hurting:
> With wind we bloomen,
> With wind we lassen,
> With weeping we comen,
> With weeping we passen,
> With hurting we beginnen,
> With hurting we enden,
> With dread we dwellen,
> With dread we wenden.

He was so affected by the words and by his own voice, which was a plaintive tenor, that he put his head down on the table and cried.

July was in the kitchen; she spent most of her time there those days; Master Cheyne thought it fittest for her, and she liked it better than those parts of the house to which he came more commonly.

She was pounding spices in a mortar but she stopped to listen to the song, with her hands lying slack in the lap of her shabby brown gown, which was now much too short for her, both in the skirt and sleeves. The words and the tune she had never heard before, but they met something that had been in her mind, she could not tell how long—it seemed to her for as long as she could remember. The song met that something that had been below the surface of her mind, as a leaf spinning down from the tree in autumn calls up in the water its own reflection; they rush together, faster and faster, touch, and are one. That was how it was with Julian.

Someone clapped Sim on the back, and they filled his cup. That cheered him and he soon was singing again; this time it was "The bailey beareth the bell away."

July pounded steadily away at the spices.

> The lily, the lily, the rose I lay,

Sim sang, but she did not stop to listen to that song.

June 5

In the evening the rain took off, and after so many wet days the younger Ladies at least were glad to be able to go out into the garden. Heavy purple clouds lay yet below the sun, but the air above was bright, and the blue of it lay in the pools which the rain had left. So they walked to and fro, lifting their gowns from the wet paths and the grass in the two little walled gardens, while the elders sat in the parlour with door and windows set wide.

Dame Christabel walked with Dame Bet Singleton, and behind came Dame Bess Dalton and Dame Margery Conyers. The garden was small, but they regulated their pace with a nice care, so that each couple walked separate until Dame Margery stooped to tighten the lacing of her shoe, and the other two Nuns must either turn back or pause with her. They paused, and just then there came from within the parlour the sound of a door slammed and a raised excited voice; Dame Anne Ladyman was crying out upon the serving-woman, Cecily a' Wood, and now they caught the words. "A thief—a thief—a murrain on her! No, I will have justice. I'll see her in the stocks. They shall whip her at a cart's tail."

Someone answered. They could not hear the words, but the voice was Dame Margaret Lovechild's, and the tone was soothing.

It did not, however, soothe Dame Anne. "Why should I forbear?" she cried more shrilly. "They are mine. The gold hand holding the pearl my mother gave me, and the other—" She paused, and her voice dropped to a note they all knew well. "The other, the brooch with a heart and a ruby, it was a love-gage given me—ah! me!—before I entered religion."

Dame Margaret spoke again. "But, Madame, she has four or five children, little ones all—"

"And bastards all," cried Dame Anne.

[134]

"And who will tend them if the constables take her?"

"Let them fend. One of them's a big lass."

"Madame!"

But Dame Anne stamped her foot and cried, "I'll not forbear. A shameless hussy and a thief!" and came flouncing out into the garden and saw the four Ladies standing there listening.

"Christ's Cross!" she said, still very shrill, "and will you also bid me let this baggage, this light-fingered trull, go free?" and she looked from one to another with her big black eyes snapping sparks.

Margery Conyers grew crimson and tears came up into her eyes; that was how it was with her always when she grew angry, and she was angry now because Cecily a' Wood was a Marske woman, and so it was the duty of any Conyers to defend her. For a few minutes she and Dame Anne raged at each other, then Dame Margery, whose position was weak seeing that she knew more of Cecily's misdemeanours than Dame Anne had ever heard, burst utterly into tears and went away, sobbing that here was a pretty way of keeping St. Benet's Rule, that talked always of holy poverty and Nuns who owned nothing, no not so much as a shift nor shoes nor a pen to write with.

"St. Benet quotha!" Dame Anne cried, looking from one to other of those that remained, challenging them also to battle.

"Madame," said Christabel, "I hold you are right. A thief's a thief, whether it's a Nun's goods she takes or another's."

They all looked at her, quite taken aback, for not one of them but had expected that if she spoke at all it would be to thwart Dame Anne, for the sake of the old quarrel between them.

"For," Christabel continued, too earnest, even to be aware of their looks, "if she thieves here she'll thieve there and everywhere. And how can any order be if the poor may idle, not caring to earn their honest living, but getting their bread by thieving from them that have, by God's will or by the industry and providence of their own kin, goods, whether cattle or corn, gold, jewels or whatsoever may be?"

"Mass!" cried Dame Bet and Dame Bess breathlessly. "How she speaks like a book! Like a book!" But it was not her eloquence that had taken away their breath.

"Mass!" cried Dame Anne too, "but it is sense she speaks, and the first I've heard. Then tell me, Madame," she

[135]

addressed herself to Christabel as amongst paynims one Christian to another, "tell me what you think I shall do."

Dame Bet and Dame Bess stood still; the two others drew together and moved off down the path towards the bee-hives.

"Holy Virgin!" said Dame Bet to Dame Bess, and turned and went into the parlour to tell anyone there, who did not know it, that Dame Christabel and Dame Anne Ladyman were walking together in the garden.

They walked there for some time. Dame Anne told Christabel all her suspicions, the traps she had laid, and at last the certainty of Cecily's guilt. She also told the whole story of the brooch with a heart and a ruby; this part of the discourse did not much interest Christabel. They did not go in till a drop of rain, heavy and chill, struck Christabel's face. More drops began to rattle on the leaves and as they reached the parlour door the shower broke full.

"After you, Madame!"

"After you!" each told the other with great courtesy, and all the Ladies within stopped talking to watch them enter.

August 18

Julian heard Master Cheyne ride out early, and some time later Meg went to Mass. Julian supposed that he would be out the whole day, and perhaps Meg too, but Meg came back quite soon with Sir John Bulmer and one or two other gentlemen, so Julian knew she must not go up to the parlour. As there was strife in the kitchen just now, on account of the cook's pursuit of one of the young serving women and the jealousy of his wife, she did not go to the kitchen. The Hall was neutral ground, so she stayed in the window there till they came in to set up the boards on the trestles for dinner. Then she went out into the yard, and tried to make friends with one of the lank stable cats. It would not come near, so she threw a stone at it and fled. She was sorry then, because she knew that it never would be friends now, whatever she did. Yet there had been satisfaction in the hollow rap that the stone had made on the creature's ribs.

It was afternoon when Sir John and the others went away and Margaret, a little flown with wine, called to them and mocked them from the parlour window. July saw that she had on her very best gown, of green damask with a lace of little pearls. One of the young gentlemen called her "Diana," and July wondered why the others let out such a shout of laughter, and why Meg pelted them fiercely with comfits, though she was laughing too.

November 10

Aske, Hatfield and Bangham went up into their room, taking with them Wat Clifton, to mull some wine and to talk. It was a chill evening and Aske slammed the shutters to, and barred them, so they were in the dark, except for the glow of a charcoal brazier, until one of the servants came back with their livery of candles. But there was light enough for Aske to begin rummaging in the elm hutch at the foot of his bed for the three horn cups rimmed with silver, a silver spoon, and a little box clasped with silver in which were spices. Hal plumped down on a stool by the wall, the guest sat on Aske's bed, and Ned perched himself on the desk by the window and set his feet on the other stool. Presently in came Will Wall and Hatfield's servant with the candles, and Will stuck two prickets on the branch and lit them; but the gentlemen hardly knew that the room was light now, so deep were they already in one of their everlasting disputations.

"You're wrong, Robin," Hatfield said.

Aske, searching now in the hutch for the sugar, grunted, and then, because he would not let an argument go by default, sat back on his heels and gave Hatfield his whole attention.

"Find me then a case, Hal," said he. "As I told you before, find me a case."

"Ask one of the Benchers," Clifton suggested. He always avoided unnecessary effort, though his fellows warned him that men of such a humour and of such a build as he, run early to fat.

Hatfield, who liked law less than music and verse, was aware that in knowledge he was no match for Aske, but he trusted in luck and said, well, and he would find a case, so he got up and went over to the shelf where Aske kept his books and took one down at random.

"No use looking there. I've searched."

"Oh! but you would!"

"There's a new one. A Year Book. Thirteen Richard II. I bought it yesterday. Where a plague is it?"

They discovered at last that Clifton was sitting on it. "I thought you slept on a mighty hard pallet," said he, giving it up without regret.

Hatfield took the manuscript in its white sheepskin boards, remarking that Aske spent some money on books. He opened it at random, looked at the morass of closely written, fantastically abbreviated pages, and drew back like a swimmer hesitating before a dive.

"Let's get it clear. You say disclaimer by parole should be enough. No need to disclaim feofment in a court of record."

"Disclaimer by parole," Aske answered, "is enough."

"Ready to aver it," Clifton chanted, and they all laughed at the consecrated phrase of the Courts.

"Ready to aver it," Aske declared, and clapped the sugar-box down on the end of the bench.

"Oh! Mass!" Hal groaned. "Pray for me!" He bent over the book, complaining that it was a sin that the printers should never clearly print these wicked old manuscripts for us poor lawmen!

He might have searched for hours or for days, but he had been right to trust in his luck.

"I have it!" he shouted. "Robin's wrong."

"Am I?" Aske's surprise made them all laugh. "Read it," said he, but then he laid an arm across Hal's shoulders and leaned over the book to read it for himself as Hal read it aloud.

" 'Et nota,' " Hatfield intoned triumphantly. " ' Et nota tenuz fuit par touz les justices'—it was held by all the justices, mark you," and he dug Aske in the ribs, " 'que tel desagreer par parol saunz estre en court de record ne vaut riens.' Couldn't be clearer. Disclaimer by parole is worthless."

Aske was bending closer over the book, and he laughed softly.

"Have you read the writing in the margin? Another good lawyer thought like me and wrote it down—'Vide mirabile judicium.' And 'Here's a marvellous judgement!' I say too."

The others looked at each other; Hal shrugged, Ned raised his eyebrows and Clifton groaned aloud.

"Not against all the justices!" cried Hal.

"Against as many justices as you like."

Hal shut the book with a clap and spoke with solemnity, as if he were giving sentence.

"Never, Robert Aske, did I know a man so set as you be in your own opinion. If you hold a thing, you sink your teeth in it and grip like a boar-hound."

"So do all men."

"Not all. But you do. It will get you into trouble one day."

It had been a green Christmas, and on this morning Dame Margaret Lovechild gathered two small pink roses from the big bush in the northeast corner of the Cloister; she put them in an earthen pot and set it on the low wall of the Cloister, where they should catch the sun. Someone even claimed to have seen a bee, but this was not generally believed, though the Ladies inclined always towards faith rather than incredulity. Certainly after Chapter the Cloister was so nearly warm that most of them preferred it to the Parlour.

Only the old Prioress, Dame Christabel and Dame Anne Ladyman sat within by the Parlour fire. The two Ladies who had so long been at enmity were now quite reconciled and often together in company. The Prioress dozed and nodded, muttering now and then, and feeling for her staff; when her fingers found it she would set it now on this side of her chair, now on that, and at once forget on which side she had put it.

Christabel caught Dame Anne's eye, and in a glance they understood each other.

"Poor Lady," said Dame Anne with propriety, but their eyes had spoken the dread each had of the ruin time makes of defeated human nature, and the hatred each bore to the Prioress as the trophy and exemplar of that defeat. They drew their stools closer together and began to talk in low voices so as not to wake her. They spoke, not as any other of the Ladies would have spoken, of Marrick doings, or of their own families in the world, but of great matters at Court, such as had filtered through to this quiet place, and chiefly of the King's divorce. Each of them found the subject interesting in her own way. "They say," Dame Anne whispered, "that this Mistress Anne is a marvellous fair lady, but also marvellous free. They say that Sir Thomas Wyatt . . . they say that Mr. Norris . . . and of her sister too . . . they say that the King . . ." So, she went on, throwing up her hands in horror and greatly enjoying herself. Dame Christabel spoke of the Cardinal's part in it all; she doubted he was no true man; she wished the King might have honest, faithful servants to send to the Pope so that his case might be truly known. Neither listened with any attention to what the other said, but as they took turn and turn about, fairly enough, the conversation contented each.

Once Christabel got up to toss another log on to the fire, and before she sat down she peeped through the little window that opened on the Cloister.

"The Ladies are all sitting with their hands tucked into their sleeves, and I swear that they are rubbing their fingers to warm them."

"And each telling other," said Dame Anne, "how warm and pleasant the day."

"I heard two of them tell the rest that to-day is the Fourth Day of Christmas. 'Jesu!' said they, 'just think of it, the Fourth Day of Christmas, and here we sit out in the sun!' "

"They are very simple," said Dame Anne.

In the afternoon the sun went in behind what had been light flecks of cloud, fine and white as lambs' wool, but now had thickened and darkened into a muddy brown curtain hung across all the western half of the sky. It was time for the Ladies to leave the Cloister and come into the Frater, which was warmed by braziers and decked with holly and bay, box and ivy, like any lord's Hall. And they danced there to the rebek and flute of the minstrels who had been hired from Richmond. When they had danced enough they sang songs and carols of God, of Adam, of Our Lady and the Little Christ.

That same afternoon Julian was shaking out and brushing Meg's clothes that lay in the great chest in her sister's bed-chamber. There were sleeves lined with fur or embroidered all over with little flowers, bees, butterflies, and running stags; there were coats of velvet, there were petticoats of damask and tinsel satin. July laid all out on the bed, lingering over them, touching them with her fingers, loving and wishing for them.

She had one hand on a white damask gown when she heard Master Cheyne's voice in the room beyond; at that she snatched her hand back and skipped away from the bed, and stood listening.

Master Cheyne was not shouting at her but at Meg and at Sir John Bulmer. He must, July supposed, at last have caught them kissing.

That did not make it much better, so great a terror to her was Master Cheyne. If it was Meg and Sir John now, it would be July after, and his temper would be sharpened because they had angered him. "O! O! O!" she whispered under her breath.

Now Sir John was shouting as well as Master Cheyne. There was a crash as if someone had overturned the big carved chair by the hearth. Then feet pounded heavily, and a door slammed.

After a long minute the door of the bed-chamber opened. Meg came in, shut the door, leaned against it and began to laugh.

"Jesu Mercy!" she cried, "I shall die of laughing. He has thrown him clean downstairs. I doubt not he has broken a leg at least. They are picking him up now."

"Downstairs!" July gaped. It did not seem strange, though it was terrible, that the terrifying Master Cheyne had thrown Sir John Bulmer down the stairs. It did seem strange, however, that Margaret should laugh.

"Aye. And then out of the house and away, before any of our knaves could be after him. I knew not Jack Bulmer could be so quick. Oh! I love him for it."

July understood then, yet she could not laugh. "But, Meg," she whispered, "what will he do to us—after." The thought of Cheyne's hoarded malice made her shrink.

Meg tossed her head and laughed again, so that July saw her white teeth in her red, open mouth. She was laughing like a fish-wife, yet whatever she did she was beautiful.

"He may do what he will," she cried. "This has paid for all."

1529

January 4

Robert Aske came out of the Monks' Church at Westminster. Mass was just over, and he was bidden to dinner with them by Dom Richard Pickering who was a Yorkshireman and a friend of his father's. Dom Richard had told him to wait outside the Church, for he himself must to-day give the great dole to the poor, which was given every day during the Christmas Feast.

So Aske stood in the rare winter sunshine in the empty Court, feeling clean within, and happy and rich, since those things which he had heard at Mass he believed, and was possessed of. Yet, for all that, he did not know exactly what it was that he possessed, but prized it as a man who keeps a treasure in a locked box that he has never opened, because he has never needed to open it.

Dom Richard came out from the Cellarer's door, and servants with him, bearing the dole; he was eating an orange and he rolled in his walk, an immensely fat man, whose bulk the Abbey's moderate fasts could not at all reduce.

Just then the porter opened the gate, and in came the crowd of poor folk who had waited outside. In a minute the Court was full. Dom Richard and the servants were surrounded, and even Aske was pushed this way and that by the poor wretches—cripples and blind, hungry, dirty and foul-smelling—they were all about him.

When the crowd was in he found himself shoulder to shoulder with a tall man in a shabby scholar's or priest's gown; marvellous thin he was, unshaved with deep harsh lines running down on either side of his huge mouth and bony nose.

Aske's hand had been in his purse already, and now something in the man's look moved him to hold out a silver mark. "Take an alms, Master Scholar," he said.

The man turned, stared at him, shook his head fiercely, and rather struck than pushed Aske's hand away. Then he wrenched round and slunk away into the crowd.

Aske lost sight of him; but when Dom Richard came back, wiping his hands and then his brow with the edge of his sleeve, he asked, "D'you know the tall thin fellow that looks like a scholar, Father, thin as a maypole and hungry looking as a tinker's cur?"

Dom Richard remembered him well, since he came often to the dole, but knew nothing of him.

"And I remember him," said Aske, "or think I do, yet cannot think how."

"Well, to dinner, to dinner," the monk said, and as they went back into the Cloister he cried, "Mass! where is my orange? I must have dropped it." But hearing the trumpets blow he forgot about the orange. "St. Joseph! there goes the boar's head and the brawn!"

*Now the Chronicle is broken
to speak of*

GILBERT DAWE, PRIEST

THE name of the man whose face Aske half remembered was Gib Dawe, and he was the fifth son of Mat Dawe, the Marrick Manor Carter. Of those five boys he was the only one that lived beyond eight years old, so Mat was very angry, and Gib got many a beating, when he began to steal away from the village and down to the Priory to learn his letters from the Nuns' old priest, who, in those days, was not so old, so deaf nor so stupid as he grew to be later.

Before that time came the boy had learnt all he could teach, and being of a sharp and impatient temper he began to grow discontented, and scornful of the old priest. His father had given up beating him; the lad was grown too big for that, and besides Mat could see that he would never shape for a carter. But neither would he, if he continued by turns so pert and so surly with his betters, get his clerkhood; and so he told Gib often, and as often got saucy replies.

It was a better chance that Gib deserved that he ever was priested. The Archbishop of York came to Marrick Priory to make his visitation of the Nuns. He had brought two clerks with him, but one slipped on a slimy stone and put his thumb out, and the other was busy with the Archbishop's Injunctions to the Houses of Religious which he had lately visited. So Gib was sent for to write letters for the Archbishop. The work kept him at the full stretch both of his penmanship and latinity, and therefore, happy, and because happy, well-mannered and serviceable. The Archbishop took such a liking to the long lad with his bright, eager eyes, that when he left, to the wonder of all the village and of Gib's family in especial, he took Gib with him, to be a clerk in his household, and to get his priesthood.

Gib did not come home to Marrick till just after he had been made priest. By that time the Archbishop thought less well of him. Able he was, but never at peace with his fellows, nor for long civil to his betters. Therefore instead of keeping Gib in his household he offered to set him to serve, with two other priests, St. Mary's Church at Richmond.

So Gib came home after great perturbation of soul, for the priesting had raised him to the height of heaven, and the Archbishop's malice (so he thought it) had flung him down headlong. It was May when he came home, and he stayed till hay-time in the summer when the weather was the fairest that could be. Gib helped with the mowing, but always a little apart from the other young people, for they, both men and maids, sheered off from him, excepting one only maid, the Miller's third girl, Joan. She, at first for kindness, and after for the stir and unquietness of her heart which drew her to him, would pause in her raking to speak, or sit near him in the noonday rest under the trees, or linger with him in the evening when everyone went slowly home from the hay fields. One evening they lingered longer than ever before—so long that the late twilight came down on them, and the dark with bright stars but no moon.

Gib, when he woke next morning to the grey light before dawn, and felt his arm stiff under the weight of her head, knew that the pillars of Heaven had failed, and that he lay broken in the ruins. That very day, before noon, he had fled from Marrick, as a man flees from a pestilence which he is aware of bearing within him.

Late in the next January Joan the Miller's girl knocked at the door of the Priest's House at Richmond. It was not that her father would have refused to keep her, though with hard words in plenty, but that she had loved Gib so well, and was (so he came to feel it) of a blind and mulish constancy. So again Gib fled, taking with him the unhappy partner in his sin, and, in her body, its fruit.

They went South; no one at home in the Dale knew where, and few would have cared to know.

1529

Further of January 4

Gib Dawe passed out under the gate of the Abbey of Westminster with a cheat loaf, two herrings, a lump of cheese and the remains of Dom Richard's orange, which he had picked up from the ground. He would not go empty to-day, nor cold, so mild was the air, but he was thankful for neither of these mercies. As he and the rest of the poor trailed away, some already munching their bread and cheese, rich and succulent smells tormented their empty bellies, as the Monks' dinner was carried, to the sound of trumpets, from the kitchen to the Great Frater. Gib thought of the vast bulk of the monk who had brought out the dole; he hated him for his round paunch and for the fine rolls of fat that lapped his jowl like that of a well-fed porker. He hated Master Robin Aske too for his careless, indifferent good humour; he would not for the world that Aske should have known him for Dawe the Carter's son of Marrick; and yet, since he well remembered the boy that he had used to see fishing in the Swale, or riding the Manor horses back from watering, he rated Aske's forgetfulness as a kind of contempt.

So he called up contempt to answer it. He despised Aske for being a friend of the Monks; for being a gentleman; for having but one eye. Having thus written him off, he felt better, and seeing that he had got as far as Ludgate he went on a bit and then turned down Creed Lane to find a quiet place in which to eat his dole, for he had not the heart to go back to his lodging, where, even before he had set out, the other men were already sodden with drink.

He found a good place at Puddle Wharf and sat down on the edge of the wooden staithes, with his feet dangling over the first widely lapping tongues of the incoming tide. The sun was warm, the river bright, and what wherries passed him were full of holiday-makers; but there were few people about since most were keeping their Christmas indoors. Just opposite him, a little way out, a barge was moored; a sailor in a red hood sat eating bread and onions in the stern; as he ate he hummed, monotonously and out of tune.

Gib for a few minutes took comfort from the sun's warmth, from the gaiety of the shining river, from the thought of the bread and cheese he would presently eat, and even from the feeling of companionship which the presence of the sailor —apart, yet not so far away—gave to him. But before long the man's humming began to annoy him. Once or twice, when the fellow was forced to be silent because his mouth was full, Gib whistled the tune correctly, but the sailor could not or would not learn it.

At last Gib lost patience.

"Sing in tune, fellow," he cried, "or sing not at all."

The sailor stopped humming and seemed to consider. "I sing for mine own pleasure," said he, and turned his back, taking up his tune again, but singing a little louder.

Gib, under his breath, wished a murrain on the fellow, who, as so many now, had no godly humility, no reverence, even for the priesthood. That rankled, though Gib knew quite well that few would recognize the priest in him under his ragged, greasy gown. "But," he thought, "so is the world these days—naughty men in honourable places, and righteousness a mock and a scorn." Whose the blame was he knew very well, and in his mind he ran over the sins of the rich—prelates, nobles, monks. "No wonder," said he to himself, "that heretics abound," and he groaned in spirit, both over the heretics, whom he hated, and over the rulers of the Church, whom he hated more.

And all the time the sailor went on singing, so that Gib at last could not endure it. He snatched up the bread and cheese to eat it hastily, and to be gone from here.

He broke the bread and found that it was green with mould within. He threw it as far as he could into the river, and then was sorry, because the crust had been good enough to eat, but now only the cheese was left, since he could not eat the herrings raw.

He looked down at the water, where the two halves of the loaf were wallowing. If he waded in he might reach it, but again, if he did he would be wet, and the loaf was by now sodden and salt.

Watching it blackly, and eating his cheese to the very rind, his mind tumbled back into its discontents. And now that mouldy loaf seemed to sum up and set a seal on all.

"To this," thought he, "is Christian charity come; to this the hospitality of monks; and to that fat paunch of the Westminster Almoner the simplicity and austerity of St. Benedict." He was empty as ever, though all the cheese was gone, and he saw the whole world, and more especially Christ's Holy Church in these latter days, in desperate case. Hunger and the distress of his mind pricked him like a goad, so that he sprang up and made his way towards Ludgate, going fast yet aimlessly, his thoughts distracted between his own need of begging or earning a meal, and the world's need of repentance and return to the virtue of the older times. *"Deus misereatur nobis,"* he kept muttering, and the few he met in the streets glanced at him, and stepped aside, so wild and fierce was his look.

He came to the wall of the Black Friars' House, and passed a little group at the gate, but then he swung about and went back. There were two comfortable, broad-shouldered, soberly clad men there, just getting down from horseback; they looked like yeomen or merchants in a small way, in from the country.

"Sirs," said Gib, pulling off his cap, and trying to look serviceable, "I will hold and walk your horses for a penny."

They gazed at him with the slow suspicion of the country-bred, and he thought they would refuse; but just then a Friar came out of the gate and they referred the matter to him. He was a quick restless man with glancing eyes that seemed to take in more than lay on the surface of things. He said surely they must leave the horses in charge of this—worthy man—he summed up Gib with a searching glance and hardly a pause, and then he was gone inside with his two guests, and Gib paced up and down the street beside the heavy beasts or stood and leaned against their barrel-like girth.

At the end of a weary hour out came the two, and Gib got his penny and no more. Still, it would buy a dish of eggs at an ordinary if he made haste, for dinner-time was almost over. He was turning away when the same Friar who had welcomed in the two countrymen put a hand on his arm.

"Have you dined, Master . . . Scholar? Or is it 'Sir Priest'?"

Gib answered only the first question: No, but he was about to dine even now.

"Upon a penny," said the other, and before Gib could be angry—"If you come within you shall dine, and yet save your penny. Come, come in!"

He left Gib to follow or no, and Gib followed, wondering what the Frair did it for. He could not know that Brother Laurence was one of those who like to interfere, kindly sometimes, and sometimes of malice, in the affairs of others.

To Gib he seemed incredibly, even, for a time, suspiciously, kind. But when a hunk of brawn, and a big piece of mutton pie, and close on a quart of ale had gone down Gib's throat he ceased to suspect, and to resent, and even to notice the sharp glances that Brother Laurence gave him, when, every now and then, the Friar would raise his eyes from his lap where his fingers were fretting his beads up and down upon the string. Feeling himself at ease Gib flung one leg along the bench and leaning an elbow on the table began to talk, with the help of an occasional question from the Friar, as he had not talked since he left Oxford behind.

He was, he told the Friar, a man of Swaledale in the north parts, of Marrick on Swale, and son of a carter. A priest he was right enough, and scholar too, for after he was priested— he stumbled there, grew vague, and passed on to the time when he served in the Queen's College at Oxford, earning his keep and getting his learning as best he could. "And then," said Gib, taking another stride to cover another awkward part of his story, "I came here to London, since when I have none well sped."

"So you have studied at Oxford?"

"Seven years. To no end." Gib brooded, and the feeling of well-being waned within him. "To no good end, for how could learning serve in these days, but if I were willing to creep into favour of some rich priest as other men do? For in these decaying times—"

He jumped at the force and suddenness with which the Friar banged his fist on the table.

"Master Priest, you have spoken the fit word. Decaying the times are, yea, decayed, corrupt, rotten."

At an opinion so congruous with his own Gib's eyes began to burn with their sombre fire. For a little while he and the Friar told each other what was amiss with the Church, and the Churchmen—Bishops, priests, monks, and nuns. Then Gib held forth alone and the other listened.

"And who shall reform the whole of the Spiritual Estate?" he concluded at last, and brooded over his own question, adding after a little, "No wonder heretics are many among us."

He was startled out of his thoughts by the Friar asking, and asking him again, what were these heretics. It seemed to him a foolish question. Everyone knew what heretics were —Lollards, those who would have no priesthood, no sacrament, no Church; those who read books that were forbidden. So he answered stiffly, not understanding the reason of the question.

The Friar sat silent a moment. It was quiet in the big, high, vaulted Frater. The sunshine had waned now, and the light came dully through coloured windows, five great traceried windows down each side. There was a smell of clean rushes, underfoot, and of wood smoke, of tallow candles, and of many meals.

"Friend," said the Friar at last, looking very hard and piercing at Gib, "wot you what those two good men, whose horses you held, came to me for?" Gib shook his head. "They came to buy from me books of the Scriptures, Englished, and other books such as are forbidden to be read." Then he said, "Come up to my chamber. It seems to me you do not yet know rightly what are heretics."

The room to which he led Gib was small, but pleasant and warm, for it had a glass window, and a little charcoal brazier was burning there. There was a bed with a red say coverlet, a big chest at the foot of the bed, a stool, a bench, and a shelf with books; Gib went to the books, like a fish to a may-fly. There was a mass book, the whole of Chrysostom and Gregory, a *Summa Angelica,* Gregory's *Moralia,* and a breviary. He sighed as he paused before turning back to the Friar, as much with pleasure as with envy, and let his hand slip lovingly over the bindings.

The Friar was smiling. "Those are not the books I would show you, and talk with you of." He took a key from his neck and unlocked the great chest, letting the lid fall back on the bed.

Gib knelt, and began to look at the books that lay within, together with an old sparver cloth, and some sheets, two or three linen shirts, and a lute. *The Burying of the Mass, The Psalter in English, An A. B. C. against the Clergy, The Practice of Prelates,* he read.

"All proclaimed against, whether to sell, buy or read," said the Friar.

Gib sat back on his heels. Yesterday he would have been horrified, but to-day it was different. As though his mind had been full of gunpowder, which it needed but a trifle to touch off, the tuneless singing of a sailorman and a mouldy loaf had caused an explosion which had unbolted doors and window shutters. And now he would listen without fear to this Friar who had fed him, and who spoke his own thoughts of the corruption of the Church, and of the greed of rich men.

So, while the Friar talked, he listened. At first it made his skin creep to hear the holy mystery of the Bread called "Round Robin," or "Jack in the Box." When the Friar blamed much of the ills in the Church upon the Pope's Court of Rome and said, "Yea, and the Hollow Father himself must shoulder it too," Gib crossed himself and blinked. But he grew used to such outrageous words, and was able to smile when the Friar read aloud to him from *A dialogue betwixt the Gentleman and the Plowman.*

"So," the Friar came to his conclusion, "these are your

heresies, and I, no doubt, one of your heretics, but what do I hold but you hold it too, though maybe you know it not? And what is it that I would do to cleanse and reform the Church, but you would do the very same?"

They were sitting now on either side of the brazier, Gib on the bench and the Friar on the stool. Gib drew a deep breath. "By God's Soul!" he cried. "It is the truth," and he brought his fist down on the seat beside him.

"Let us," said the Friar, "root out from the Church all these proud prelates with their jewelled rings, and their tippets of satin, and their scarlet hats from Rome. And with them let us root out also all these fat, lascivious abbots that keep paramours, two or three, in their lodgings, and these ignorant and beastly priests that haunt brothels. . . ."

He ran on quite a time, but Gib lost him, because those words of the Friar had thrown him back into his own past, and into the darkness of the old sore shame. So he sat, hearing nothing, but going hot and cold, and feeling the sweat start on his back, knowing he would speak, and telling himself there was no need to speak. Then, as if someone had jolted it out of him without his will, he cried, not in his own voice, which was strong and harsh, but in a wavering voice that sounded strange in his ears, though he had heard the like of it from the lips of others in the confessional, "Listen to me. Stop! I am one of them. I am a fornicator; I committed fornication with a woman, not once but often and for years, so that she bore me four children."

When he had said that he turned away upon the bench and let his head hang down so that the Friar could not see his face.

Brother Laurence had pulled up short. The thread of his discourse, which had been at that moment of the feigned miracles of St. Thomas of Canterbury, was broken off, and he needed a moment to collect himself. During the silence Gib seemed to himself to live again through all those years with Joan, the Miller of Marrick's girl, from the evening they first met under the hawthorn, with all the air heavy-sweet with the scent of the blossom and the milky scent of the cows that were swinging slowly by them—from that evening to the moonless night among the haycocks, and the winter day she came to him at Richmond, and their journey to the South.

All that was eight years ago, yet the same pang of shame went through him now, fresh as the memory of that time was fresh. What came after was more dim, more dully aching. The years of servitorship at Oxford were confused in his mind: he could remember the birth of his first son, and of the daughter that died; but when the second boy had been born he could not be sure. Joan was a servant at the Blue Anchor Inn in Ship Lane, and there the children were born, and there they had died, of the sweating sickness, just as Joan was brought to bed of a fourth child, a puny boy.

And suddenly he found himself telling all this to the Friar, who, though a good talker, knew also how to listen, and let Gib stumble on halting, returning, now mumbling indistinctly, now shamelessly candid.

"And three years ago, when the three elder brats were dead, and the other weaned, she went away. I think it was with one of those gentlemen scholars; perhaps the children also were his, or another's. Nay. Nay. They were mine. But," he cried sharply, coming back to the heart of the matter, "never for one instant, no, not when I first sinned, never did I take joy in it, but always shame. Shame," he repeated, as if he savoured the word and the thing once more.

"Tell me!" said the Friar at his side. "Did you keep yourself wholly to this woman, or did you have commerce with others?"

"With her only."

"Then I count you as it were married unto her."

"I, a priest, married!" Gib gave a sharp bray of laughter, but the Friar was grave.

"'Let the Bishop be the husband of one wife,'" he said. "And if the Bishop, then why not the priest, or senior?"

Gib stared so that a smile went over the Friar's quickly changing face. "Friend," said he, "read you in the Scriptures, and you shall know shame no longer."

"But—priests—to marry!"

The Friar laughed outright at that.

"You shall read the Scriptures new Englished." He got up and went to the great chest that still stood open.

"I cannot buy," Gib muttered hastily.

"No; but I can lend."

Gib passed out of the Black Friar's gate in the early twilight with the New Testament in English clutched close to his side. As he went through the empty and darkening streets he was like a man newly come out of prison. Now he need not think of all the years when he had lived, the Friar said, as a married priest. For it was not wrong to be a married priest, still less, he thought to himself, when he had never taken joy in it. Joan had not had much more joy than he, so greatly had she suffered from his bitter, tormented temper; but that, though he knew it well enough, did not seem to be a thing which he needed to consider.

May 1

A number of the gentlemen of Gray's Inn got up before dawn and rode out to the fields towards Islington to bring in Summer. They found and picked little tufts of budding may, for not much was in flower yet, and decked their horses' head stalls with them, and their own caps. Then they came on some young maidens sitting in a ring under a beech tree that was here and there splashed pale shining green with the young leaves, as if it had been with sea spray. The girls were making garlands of primroses, and purple orchis, and a few early cowslips. Four of the young gentlemen who were still together in company bought garlands, paying for each garland a groat and a kiss. After that they would not let the maids remain under the beech tree, but had them away, not unwilling, to Islington village to eat cakes, and cream, and brawn, mutton pie and water cresses. By the time that they had drunk their ale each young gentleman had his lass on his knee, and there was a great deal of laughter and not a little kissing.

But May morning passes, and at last Robert Aske gave his tankard into his maid's hands, bidding her sup the rest for he must be going. The others cried fie upon him, for the day was early yet. But said he, no, look at the church clock, and that he must be at Westminster Hall before the Courts closed.

"Oh," Hal groaned, "why did we bring this spoil sport in our company?" But he did not mean what he said, because Aske was always a merry companion.

They took their horses again, and the young maids went down the road with them a little way and then parted. They were all very good friends, and the men promised to come again soon, though but half meaning it, for May morning was one morning different from all others of the year, when gentle and simple, learned and unlearned, met in pleasant comradeship.

The other three young gentlemen, being not so willing as Robert Aske to return to the collar, said they would come with him as far as Westminster, and then lead his horse back with them; so they went merrily, lengthening out the holiday with teasing and talking. At Charing Cross they had to stop, because a great number of horsemen and footmen were going by; there were gentlemen and serving-men all in scarlet, and after them a number of priests, and crosses that flickered and blazed when they passed the southward-leading streets where the sun touched them. After these went the two Cardinals, the English on a white mule and the Italian Campeggio on a black.

When the gentlemen from Gray's Inn could move on again Robert Aske was silent, so that Hal asked, "What's amiss?"

Aske turned his head. "Do you like this business of the King's divorce?" He gave Hal no time for answer but said, "I tell you I do not."

"Well," said Ned Bangham, "it's the King's matter, and the Cardinal's, the two of them, but certainly not ours." And Wat Clifton, who was a cautious man, asked whether it were not better for a wise man to keep his mouth shut.

"Ah!" cried Aske. "Wise!" in an angry voice, but all the same he did shut his mouth, and kept it shut, till they came to Westminster and parted.

May 12

Gib Dawe lived now in Thames Street at the house of a pastry-cook, who had for his sign King David with his harp. Brother Laurence had brought him here from the very wretched hovel outside Ludgate where he had used to lodge, saying it was not fitting he should be there, but among friends, and honest, good folk.

Gib's new landlord was one of those called among themselves "known men" or "brothers in Christ." He longed as greatly as Gib to change things in the Church, and indeed some he wanted to change which Gib would have retained, so they had great arguments in the evening when work was done and they sat on the doorstep in the twilight. They grew very hot in their disputes sometimes, for though Gib could have borne that people should go to Church on any day of the week but Sunday (which alteration the pastry-cook believed would bring with it a notable minishing of superstitions); and though he now thought it well that all holy water, and candles, and crosses should be done away, yet he could not agree that every man was priest as truly as those who had been anointed as he had been.

So they were arguing it this evening, about and about, looking down the street to the apple blossom in the orchards of the great merchants on the other side of Thames Street, and growing hotter and hotter. Then the cook, a lean man and irascible, drew his knife, but Gib caught his wrist and prayed over him so eloquently that the cook wept, and fell on Gib's neck. Gib was satisfied that he had demonstrated the potency of priesthood, but he did not say so to the cook. Brother Laurence, when he came to bring Gib more copying of forbidden books to do, was pleased to see the two men so friendly. From each of them he had heard complaints, and feared that Gib and his host would soon part. But this evening, a fair and mild one, dying gently in a clear sky, they talked amicably of the great iniquities of the rich, about which they all agreed, till you could hardly see the colour of the apple blossom in the Thames Street gardens, and till the cook's wife called them in to supper.

July 1

When William Cheyne came out of his chamber this morning he locked the door behind him, and dropped the key of it into his pouch. Then he called down the stairs to the servants who were setting the tables for breakfast in the Hall below that they should bring his meals upstairs that day. They came up with plates and cups and food for two, but he sent down all but what he needed for himself.

The servants, of course, talked. One of them had heard the mistress calling out, very angry, from the bed-chamber, and beating on the door. But the master had only laughed, and cried out to her that if she fasted to-day, fasting would make continence more easy. "And as for me, Sweet," he said, "it comes of you that I am a lame man now, and only able to have an eye on you if I keep you under lock and key."

But if he was cheerful in the morning by the time it was dusk he had sunk into a sour, self-pitying mood. Julian had been able to keep out of his way all day, but at supper-time the maids told her that since it was her sister's carryings on that were the cause of them having to bring up the master's food, wine, and candles, she should bear her share. So they pushed the candles into her hands, and sent her before them into the upper room.

Master Cheyne sat with his chin sunk on his chest, and the staff, on which he leaned ever since his fall downstairs, between his knees.

He looked up at July, and his lips moved so that she saw his teeth, as if a dog were snarling.

She came near and put down the candles where he pointed, but before she could get away he caught one of her wrists and held her, so she stood still, with her heart beating right up into her throat, because she was so frightened of him.

"You're her sister," he said, and then let her go, and spoke as if July were not there. "God forgive me," he cried, "and have mercy on me that ever I married a whore."

When July found herself free she got away from him to the wall beside the door, and stood there clutching the painted hangings with both her hands behind her back. When the maids had set down the dishes she scuttled away after them.

August 25

There had been no train of mourners at the burial, no file of poor folk bearing candles, no singing men and boys to bring music to the very threshold of silence. The body had not lain last night under a herse stuck over with many lighted candles, and to-day, now it was laid by, there would be no great dinner, no great dole for the crowds that should have come to such a burial. All had been done quietly, quickly, almost in a secret huddled way, because, in a time of pestilence, Lady Elizabeth Nevill, second wife of Thomas, Lord Darcy of Templehurst, had died, suddenly and with the marks of the sickness upon her.

So now only my Lord himself and Lord Sandys of the Vine, Lady Elizabeth's brother, stood together in the Friars' Church at Greenwich looking down at the green and silver pall that covered the hole in the paving into which the coffin had been lowered. One or two of the Friars moved and stood further off, and unostentatiously beside a pillar, a couple of masons waited with their bags of tools, for the grave would be closed at once. At the door of the Church my Lord's gentlemen and servants hung about; they stood sadly, for Lady Elizabeth had been a good mistress and a great lady, and besides they were conscious of a lurking fear that dogged any household where one had died of the pestilence; yet there was upon them a sense of relief; it was grievous that a life was finished; it was well that the empty shell which had held the life was put away. When they saw my Lord move and come slowly down the Church towards them, they turned their faces, almost with eagerness, to the open air, the grey light and whirling dust of a dry but blustering and threatening day.

Back in the house at Stepney the two lords sat together in

my Lord Darcy's Privy Chamber, and heard the twigs of a wind-thrashed tree outside tap and whine upon the glass. For a long time they sat almost in silence. Then Darcy said, "I always thought to be buried with my father and his father at Templehurst. But now I shall choose to be laid beside her."

And after a while, in which he had looked about the room as if he were learning it, like a strange room, he said, "I see now why the dead are commonly buried with such state. It is to make the living think that death is—something." He met Sandys' eyes, and then again looked about the room from which she had gone, and from which the careful servants had removed all traces of her—the bits of embroidery, a book she had read, her lute—so that her husband's heart should not be wrung. "Whereas," said Darcy, "it is far worse than anything. It is . . . it is the nothing of it that . . ."

He did not try further to put into words the plain desolation of that one absolute negative, but Sandys understood, and nodded, and they sat again in silence, letting the knowledge of loss flow over all that was in their memory and find its way down every passage of their thought.

At last Lord Darcy stood up.

"I shall walk in the garden," he said, and they went out together into the restless tumult of the wind, on which now and again came a spitting rain. There in the orchard they walked up and down, clutching their hats to them, and with the wind flapping and tugging the skirts of their coats and beating back the breath into their mouths. But each felt better, nearer to life, and nearer too, in a strange way, to the dead, so that they began to talk about her, and even laughed, gently and lovingly, over things which Sandys now remembered of his sister when she was a little girl.

Yet, in the end, it was the knowledge of loss that must triumph. Darcy stopped and faced his brother-in-law, and let him see the tears on his cheeks.

"As long as I live I shall mourn her. She was—" He paused to choose his words. "She was my truest friend, and has left me now alone."

"You have two sons, and Bess."

"And Bess is her mother's lass, every inch. But she's a Constable now, since she's wife to Robert Constable's son."

"George," said Sandys, in a voice that did not ring true, "George is a dutiful son."

Darcy looked up into the tossing branches. Some of the

leaves, torn away by the wind, went spinning by as though it were already autumn.

"George? If there were a time when George could compass his own profit by my loss, he'd do me a shrewd turn, and rejoice in it, and call it by a fine name."

Sandys spoke no more of George, since he thought that saying only too true. Nor could he bring himself to mention Arthur Darcy, so lightly did he regard my Lord's younger son. But Darcy himself went on: "And Arthur—he means no harm nor would do none so long as to be true to his friends and his kin is as easy as playing on his virginals and his clavichords and his regals. But if it were to be a matter of strife, and blood, and danger—"

He broke off and moved away, and Sandys heard him mutter that God should forgive him for speaking so of his own sons. "But it's the truth," he said, and after that there was nothing more spoken between them till the horns sounded for dinner inside the house.

October 24

It was a day of drizzling rain and a grey murk from dawn to dusk, so that no one remarked the small closely curtained barge that brought two gentlemen and two ladies, all muffled up in fustian cloaks, to the steps of York Palace, the new great house built by the Cardinal, beautified and furnished by him, and now left empty, but for a few of the King's officers and servants.

The four who had come by water from Greenwich climbed the river-stairs, crossed the privy garden and went into the Palace by the small door that side. By this very door not a week ago the Cardinal had come out, and stood, hesitating, dazed yet by the fall from the height of his precarious greatness. "Which way? Which way?" he had murmured, like a man lost, and it had needed a servant's touch on his arm to direct him to the barge that lay waiting. Then he had gone towards it, carrying, himself, a small trussing coffer, since only few of his household came with him to carry other of his stuff. He had not once looked back at the great Palace with its gables and many gilded weather vanes catching the light, but had gone away and down to the barge walking with the cautious unsteady flat-footed pace of a very old man.

To-day, once inside the Palace, the King and the others cast down their cloaks.

"Now, Sweet," said the King to Mistress Anne, "we shall see what goods this false servant of mine hath laid by."

"There is an inventory written?" she asked sharply.

"He was bidden write it with his own hand, that nothing should be forgot."

They came on the inventory in a little closet of my Lord Cardinal's own, very richly furnished, but desolate now, with the ashes of a dead fire on the hearth, and dust of the last days on the black velvet close chairs, and the cushions velvet figury still crumpled in disorder in the window.

The King and Mistress Anne bent over the many pages of the book; he had his arm about her and his hand over hers at her waist. With his other hand he turned the pages so that their eyes caught out, from here or there, the record of something rich and lovely.

New hangings . . . 6 pieces of triumphs, counterfeit arras . . . the arms of England and Spain, roses and daisies.

Three blue velvet figury hangings . . .

Beds, one of rich tissue.

Quilts sarcenet, paned, with my Lord's arms and a crown of thorn in the midst.

Pillow beres of black silk with fleur de lys of gold; of white silk with red fleur de lys.

Mrs. Anne seemed to purr like a cat.

Cloth of silver and green satin sometime the lining of two gowns . . .

Blue and crimson velvet and it with green scallop shells of silver embossed with needlework and S S of gold on each of them . . .

But the King grew impatient and let the pages go with a run.

"Where is the plate of gold and silver?"

He found the page.

A gold cup of assay . . . a crystal glass garnished with gold . . . a gold salt garnished with pearls and stones and a white daisy on the knop.

He shut the book, and, turning, shouted for one of the royal officers who had charge of the stuff. The man's voice answered him hollowly in the great empty house.

"The keys! The keys!" the King cried, and when the keys were brought they went away with them to the chamber where all this most precious stuff had been stored.

There it was, set upon benches and cupboards, and overflowing to the floor, the dim light gleaming on the bellies of gold cups, gold salts, silver cups, silver salts, and catching the facets of jewels.

"Jesu!" cried Mrs. Anne, and the King said, "Passion of Christ!" at the sight of that sumptuous spectacle. Then they moved about, touching and lifting, here a gilt charger, there a gold cup with a cover and the top-castle of a ship on the knop.

"Ah! the pretty thing," cried Mrs. Anne, and pointed her finger at a bowl of gold with a cover, garnished with rubies, diamonds, pearls, and a sapphire set in a collet upon it.

The King stooped to look at it. Just near, upon the bench end, stood a tall gold salt with twined green branches enamelled upon the gold, and scrolled letters enlaced together; the letters were K. and H. He gave the salt a shove with the back of his hand and it fell from the bench and clattered to the ground.

Mrs. Anne tittered, because she knew that K. stood for Katherine, but the King's face had reddened with anger. He caught her by the wrist and kissed her roughly and went on kissing. As his mouth lifted from her throat or from her lips he was muttering—

"Laugh? You may laugh. And she. And the Pope. But none will laugh when it is seen what I shall do."

October 27

On this day the mermaid, (if she really was a mermaid), came to St. Andrew's, Marrick, just as the Ladies were sitting down to their Mixtum, which to-day was of fried eggs, and salt herrings soused, because it was a Friday. There was a strong wind blowing from the West, so the sound of the pack-mules' bells did not reach even those Messes whose chamber windows looked down the Dale, until the mules were quite close. But as soon as any of the Ladies heard the bells they knew them for those on the harness of the two Priory mules, Black Thomas and the Bishop, and they knew therefore that Dame Margery Conyers the Chambress, and Dame Bess Dalton and the three servants were returning from York, where the Chambress had been to buy cloth for the Ladies' gowns.

Knowing this, more than one of the Ladies clapped a fried egg or a piece of herring between tranches of bread, and bearing these in one hand and a cup of ale in the other, made for the Great Court, to greet the arrival of the returning Ladies; those who had been to York had been, they considered, into the world, and brought back news of miracles, of fashions of gowns and coifs, of the Sweating Sickness, of the Scots, of the prices of cloth; and besides news on these important subjects, other news which might be called little better than tittle-tattle, but the Ladies loved it not less than any of the rest.

Dame Christabel was eating her Mixtum with the Prioress, and the Prioress's chamber faced up the Dale, towards Calva, humped and spined like a great beast under its brown heather and red-brown bracken. For this reason, and because of the great wind that was blowing, Christabel did not hear the mule bells; the Prioress did not hear them either, but that was because she was growing very deaf.

The first thing which Christabel heard above the noises of the wind, which rattled the casement, and made strange whistlings among the rushes on the floor, was the clack of the latch. Then the door burst open, dry bits of rush rose and flew about, the fire swirled out from the chimney, and Christabel had to catch the edge of the boadcloth to prevent it flapping back across the dishes on the table. Dame Elizabeth Close came in, like a great ship before the wind, wind in her skirts, wind in her veil. For a moment she looked far too big. Then she caught the door and forced it shut behind her, and in the restored quiet of the room became her normal size again; which was big enough, Dame Christabel thought, for Dame Elizabeth was a very large woman.

"Our Lady!" cried she, casting up her hands. "Our Lady! A marvel! Here's a marvel. Jesu! it is a marvel indeed!"

She went across to the old Prioress who was tremblingly trying to get up from her chair, for if she had not heard she had seen Dame Elizabeth's gesture.

"What is it?" she cried in her shaking old voice. "Is it the Scots?"

"No, no. Not the Scots. Lord! no. It's a mermaid!"

"Where?" The Prioress looked vaguely round as if there might be one under the table.

"Here, in Marrick."

The Prioress sank down again. She was not able to deal with such a situation. It was Christabel who asked, "How did she come?"

"Dame Margery hath brought her from York."

"She would!" Christabel murmured, but under her breath; and to herself she thought, "At least if any of them would, she would." But she had not expected that any of the Ladies should have had the opportunity of committing such a rare foolishness.

She said to the Prioress, "Shall I go down and see?" And the Prioress nodded more vehemently than her ordinary ceaseless nodding, so Dame Christabel went.

The Great Court, as she went down the outer staircase from the Prioress's room, looked as if to-day were the great spring washing day, so full was it of the flapping white of the Ladies' veils. But besides the Ladies there were a great many of the serving women, and even some of the farm-men, and of course Jankin the porter in his green hood. And from the centre of the crowd came now and then the chime of the mule bells, or the ring of a hoof on stone as the beasts fidgeted.

None of them, not even the youngest girl that tended the hens, took notice of anything but what was in the centre of the mob, so, though Dame Christabel came to the outskirts of the crowd, she could see nothing, nor make any way in. "Perdy!" and, "Marry!" cried the wenches, and, "By cock!" the men. But beyond them Dame Christabel could hear Dame Margery's taut, excited voice declaring that, "Yea, truly she is a very mermaid and the Skinner's wife of York would never have sold her to us but because of the great reverence her husband and she have for St. Andrew. Two pounds I paid, and we are to pray for them both every St. Andrew's Day."

"Two pounds," thought the Treasuress, "for a mermaid!" She did not think that Dame Margery was one to have obtained at such a price a very mermaid. That would have cost far more, so the two pounds were sheer loss.

"Where," cried Dame Anne Ladyman, "shall we put her?"

"In the big fish-pond," someone suggested.

"But she'll eat all the fish," young Grace Rutherford piped up, forgetting in her excitement that it was no novice's place to speak aloud among the Ladies, still less so when there were men about.

"Little fool!" Dame Margery chid her, but not for the fault of speaking. "It's pike, not mermaids, that eat fish."

"Mass!" cried Dame Joan Barningham, with triumph in her voice. "What will the Ladies of St. Bernard say when they know that we have a mermaid in our House?"

Dame Christabel was now, by dint of shoving and some

determined elbowing, in the thick of the group, though she still could not see what the Ladies in the midst were staring at, for their great veils flapped and flew up in the wind, and thrashed like washing on a line.

That remark of Dame Joan's came to her just as she had her hands on the shoulders of two of the hinds, meaning to thrust them apart. It made her pause.

Could this thing be true? Could this be the very mermaid that Dame Margery claimed? Then what a triumph for the Chambress, though doubtless also a triumph for the whole House, as regards the Ladies of St. Bernard.

Christabel's mind—usually so prompt at a decision—for an instant wavered. Suppose the Chambress had somehow transported in a tub of water, balanced against the Nuns' bales of cloth across Black Thomas's pack saddle, a mermaid, even now lazily combing her hair over naked shoulders with a golden comb, while in the depths of the tub her tail moved with the easy grace of a fish keeping itself head on to the quietly running waters of Swale. If so, the triumph of the Chambress was complete. If, on the other hand, it were some creature, human in shape, which the Chambress's enthusiastic imagination had taken for a mermaid, would it be possible to rig it up somehow to impress the Ladies of St. Bernard, and yet within the House of St. Andrew make it clear that the Chambress had been soundly taken in. Certainly a fair young girl dimly seen in a tub in the Warming House, and reputed a mermaid, would cause the Ladies of St. Bernard to grow green with jealousy.

Dame Christabel pushed the hinds asunder with a tart, "Make way, fellows!" and, "Where's your plough to-day?" The Ladies saw her then, and made way too, and at last she came to the space in the midst of the group.

She stood there a moment, looking down at the creature sitting on the grass. Then she laughed.

"A mermaid!" she said. "And why should you think that is a mermaid?" The creature, a woman with a broad flat face, pale blue eyes and a mouth half open, raised her head, and shrank away.

"Because—the Skinner's wife was assured of it. She had her of a ship master of Bridlington, who took her at sea, swimming in a storm."

Dame Christabel had, however, infected with doubt some of the Ladies. Dame Joan, leaning forward over the creature, adjured her to say whether she was truly a mermaid and lived in the sea.

She got no answer, except that the mermaid shrank still more into herself.

"There," said Dame Margery, as if the proof lay before them. "She can no English."

"Ask," someone suggested, "if she cometh from the middle of the sea or from near the edge of England, for then she might understand something like English—perhaps French or Low German."

No one knew any Low German, but old Dame Euphemia Tempest remembered that she knew the motto of the King's Lady Mother, and that it was in French. She did not know what it meant, but perhaps the mermaid would.

"Souvent me souvient," Dame Euphemia repeated several times, but without any response.

They tried Latin next, reciting the Paternoster to her, several of them at once, which cannot have made it easier to understand. At all events she gave no sign that she had ever heard it before.

"There!" said Dame Margery again, "you see."

"And what," Christabel challenged her, "do we see, but that the creature's a heathen? There are many such in Muscovy, or the parts that lie beyond the Emperor's lands."

"Fie!" cried some, and, "That's true," said others; but there was no time for them to debate it at length, because the bell in the tower just behind them began to ring, and it was time to go in to Lady Mass. Afterwards there would be Chapter, and there they would fight it out.

By Compline that night the blustering wind of the morning had dropped, and the evening was very still, though gloomy and overcast. The storm which had raged among the Ladies had also spent itself: Dame Margery had been defeated; Dame Christabel had won; and most of the Ladies were ready to laugh, though rather regretfully, over the absurd idea of calling the creature from York a mermaid.

Yet their incredulity had not spread beyond the walls of the House, and all that day little knots of people kept coming to the gate, some with fowls to sell, some with nuts, some with gifts of warden apples, or a piece of home-spun—anything that would get them past the gate-house, and give them the chance of seeing the marvel.

At Vespers the old parish priest came hobbling down from the parsonage. It was not often now that he troubled the parish church with his mumbled and garbled Latin. But to-night he went right through the service, as loud as he could, so that the Ladies, singing their own Vespers beyond the great screen, should hear him. When both they and he had finished he went round to the gate-house, and, after a word with Jankin, into the Great Court. Along the line of windows the lights were already pricking out, so heavy were the clouds. From the kitchen came the clatter of wooden bowls and plates; the servants were fetching away supper from the kitchen to the various Messes. Then Jankin, who had gone up to the Prioress's chamber, beckoned to him and he went up.

He was not glad to see that it was Dame Christabel Cowper who tonight supped with the Prioress, because she always made him feel what he was indeed—an illiterate and doddering old man. As he blessed them both, hurriedly, and stumbling over the words, his eyes were on the Prioress. He and she had known each other for many years; there had been disagreements between them, and disapproval on the Prioress's side; but in the presence of Dame Christabel they felt that there was an alliance between them. Neither of them was very bold, but together they were just a little bolder against her than either would have been alone.

And then the door opened and the Ladies' servants brought in bowls of pottage from which a scented steam wreathed up. The old man's nose told him, "Hare!" as he sat down, and for a little time he forgot what had brought him down to Vespers.

It was the Prioress, who, with an apprehensive eye upon Dame Christabel, told him that, "Dame Margery to-day brought back a creature from York who, 'twas said there, was a mermaid. But now she hath legs."

"Christ's Cross!" said the old man. He had heard enough from Jankin as he passed to know that he must go warily. Yet he very greatly desired to see the creature. Even if she were no mermaid, even though, as the Prioress seemed to imply, she had grown legs between York and Marrick, yet still there was something marvellous in one who had been thought to be a mermaid. But his slow wits could hit on no way of asking to see her that would not draw upon him the scorn and anger of Dame Christabel.

It was Christabel herself who gave him his excuse, for she spoke to him, though she looked at an apple that she was peeling.

"She's a heathen. She does not know the Paternoster."

"God's Bread!" The old man took a bite out of his apple.

"It's for you, since our priest is away at York," said Christabel, "to make her a Christian soul."

"God's Bread!" he mumbled again, and then hastily swallowing the mouthful, "Then I must see her. I must be sure she is not christened already."

"You shall." Dame Christabel's eyes glinted with a smile at his simplicity. "You shall see this marvel."

So the creature was sent for, and came. She stood with her back to the door, where the servant had pushed her, and hung her head. The priest's hopes dwindled and died, but he began, though unwillingly because of the presence of Dame Christabel, to question the woman. "Are you christened, daughter? Can you say your Credo?" and so on. To all of it she gave no answer, only watched him through her matted hair.

"She can no English," he said at last.

"Or is an idiot."

Even a worm will turn. The old man was afraid of Dame Christabel but her scorn of him was so manifest that it pricked him into a moment's courage.

"She's no idiot," he told her quite firmly. Indeed the poor thing's eyes, though vague, had not the untenanted look of the idiot's. "But if she's a Christian soul she'll know this," and he crossed himself, which none of them had thought to do.

The woman was watching him but she did not move. It was almost conclusive. But yet he tried one thing more. On the beam across the chimney breast a little ivory crucifix hung. There was a touch of gold on the head of the cross where the monogram had been written, and red paint showed on the hands and feet. It was the work of a craftsman of old time, harsh and terrible, no King reigning, but a tortured man hanging on the tree. The old priest and the Ladies knew it too well to see it for what it was.

He came close to the woman and put it into her hand. She bent her head, peering at it, then suddenly she gave a cry, and threw it down among the rushes.

The two Ladies sprang up, and the old priest stepped back a pace.

"Jesu Mercy!" the Prioress cried, and began to cross herself.

Retro me Sathanas!" said Dame Christabel. She had not much Latin, but if she ever used it, it was with effect.

[165]

"Oh! why did she come here?" the Prioress mourned. "What shall we do with her?"

For once it was the old priest who took charge. "I'll christen her now," he said, "and so shall the devil be driven out of her."

They christened her there and then, with water in Christabel's great cup Edward, and with Christabel and Dame Margery, fetched in haste, as godmothers, and Jankin as her godfather. Dame Margery tried to have her christened Melusine, after the mermaid lady in the story, but her position was too weak; the creature had not only a devil, but legs. When therefore Christabel said that her name was Malle, so she was named. No one asked why she should be Malle, but Christabel was thinking of the sheep in Chaucer's story, which belonged to the widow whose cock was called Chauntecleer and his wife Pertelote.

When she was a Christian woman they turned Malle out. She had no idea what had been done to her.

1530

January 15

My Lord of Norfolk's long nose was still blue after his ride to Esher on the drab, raw January morning, but now the horn had blown to dinner, and he and the Cardinal went up together. All the way up the stairs and the length of the Great Chamber (which indeed was not so very great), the Cardinal was thanking the Duke for his good will, kind offices and merciful mind, in that, like the lion in his coat armour, he spared those he had pulled down. "For," said the Cardinal, "of all other noblemen, I have most cause to thank you for your noble and gentle heart, the which you have showed me behind my back, as my servant well hath reported unto me."

The Duke heard it all in a courteous silence, and if he rejoiced at so great humility in a man lately of such haut and proud stomach, or if he found it tragic, he gave no sign either way.

Then Master Cavendish, one of the Cardinal's gentlemen, came near with water warmed and perfumed for them to wash their hands. The Duke drew away, and though the Cardinal beckoned that he should come and dip his hands together with his, he would not, for, said he, it became him no more to presume to wash with my Lord Cardinal now than it did before.

"Yes," said the Cardinal, "for my legateship is gone, wherein stood all my high honour."

"A straw for your legacy," cried my Lord. "I never esteemed your honour the higher for that," and he looked about as if he wished all present to take note that he had said it, so that perhaps one might carry it to the King, saying that "my Lord of Norfolk lightly regards the Pope and his Legate in this realm." But certainly he would not wash with the Cardinal, declaring that "as Archbishop of York and Cardinal your honour surmounteth any Duke in this realm."

Nor would he sit beside Wolsey at dinner, but on the less honourable side of the table, and there not opposite to him but a little beneath. And while they dined, all this talk, as he warmed and flushed with the wine they drank, was of how highly thought of were those servants of the Cardinal who were faithful to their master, and how those were blamed who had forsaken him.

Altogether, though the day was so dark that the candles were lit all along the board, and torches here and there down the Chamber, the Cardinal and the Duke dined very cheerfully, for the Cardinal, receiving such honour from the Duke, repaid by an eager, humble courtesy, bidding the gentlemen bring the Duke always the best, whether of fish or eggs, since it was Friday, or of the wine.

But that night, when Master Cavendish came to the Cardinal to make him ready for bed, he found him very shaken and uncertain in spirits, now up, now down, now declaring that the King's mind towards him must be good, or never would such a true, plain-dealing nobleman as the Duke have spoken so honourably, giving him courage—yea—and hope that he should come again to the King's good grace and be as well as ever he had been; and now silent, plucking at his underlip with hasty fingers, shaking his head and knotting his brows.

When Master Cavendish had put upon him his fine linen nightshirt, the Cardinal sat down so that he could draw off his hosen, and then as Cavendish knelt before him, the Cardinal gave a great sigh—

"George," said he, "you know not why I am so sad."

Cavendish did not know, but he could well guess that it was due to something which had passed between his master and Mr. Shelley, Judge of the Common Pleas, who had come to

Esher even before the Duke had left, with yet another message from the King, who, when he asked the Duke to tarry and assist him in his message, the Duke denied, saying, "I have nothing to do with your message, in which I will not meddle."

And so it was, as he guessed, for now the Cardinal, having broken silence, told him all; all that Mr. Shelley had said from the King, and all that he had himself replied. The King's message was not very long but had a sharp sting. He sent to say that it was his pleasure to have my Lord Cardinal's house, called York Palace, or more commonly White Hall, near Westminster. And the judge said that all the judges and learned counsel of the realm had told the King that he had the right to it.

"Fie!" cried Cavendish roundly, "right he hath never to it."

"Ah, George." the Cardinal looked down at his bare feet upon the foot-cloth, curling and uncurling his toes much as he had done when they were new and he a baby on his mother's lap, but now with no pleasure in his skill in making the ten little pigs move. "Ah, George, so said I too. Or rather I drew a distinction, for it may be law, yet it is not conscience, and so Mr. Shelley himself admitted, that I should give away that which is none of mine, from me and my successors."

He fell silent again and motioned Cavendish away with his hand, who went about the room, laying by my Lord's clothing and preparing for the night. It seemed that the Cardinal would say no more, but just as Cavendish slid the curtains back along the rail of the bed, his master spoke again.

"So I said at the last, 'Master Shelley, I charge your conscience to discharge mine. Shew His Highness from me that I most humbly desire His Majesty to call to his most gracious remembrance that there is both a heaven and a hell.' "

"Aye!" thought Cavendish, "and that there is!" and he ground his teeth together, thinking of his master's enemies.

When the curtains were drawn again, and all lights but the great Paris candle beside the bed put out, Master Cavendish laid off his clothes and went to his trussing bed in the corner of the room. He could hear the Cardinal often stirring and turning in bed, and once he groaned and muttered, and once beat with his hand on the pillow.

Cavendish lay waking long too, watching the candle flame swing in the draught, for the wind had risen now and sang thinly round the chimneys of the house. He tried in his simple, faithful mind to resolve his master's perplexities, and know those friends on whom he could rely; but where so much was treachery how could an honest man tell who was true? He could see that the Cardinal trusted now in the Duke of Norfolk. Sometimes Cavendish trusted in him too, and sometimes, as the wind grew more boisterous and began to move the hangings and the curtains of the Cardinal's bed, he thought that there was no man in the world save himself that his master could trust.

February 2

Dame Christabel knelt in her stall. The old priest elevated the Host, and the Ladies bowed their heads.

"And she," thought Dame Christabel, who had been reviewing in her mind the episode of Dame Margery Conyers and her mermaid of three months ago, "*she* would have liked to cut up the old green cope of St. James, because of the cockle shells on it, to make a gown for the creature." She turned her head, slowly and only slightly, so that none should notice, and looked through her fingers to where, among the servants, close to the lower door, Malle knelt. Malle was not decked out in the sea green satin but in an old brown homespun gown, a worn out shift belonging to one of the Ladies, and a length of patched linen for a headkerchief. They had found her an old pair of shoes too; there was a hole in each sole, but Perkin the Carter had patched them.

The bell rang in the tower to tell the Dale that God, the Omnipotent, was in this place, this very place.

Dame Christabel smiled to herself, remembering Dame Margery's discomfiture.

March 16

Gib had been paid to sing Mass that day in the Chantry of John Chamber in the Church of Holy Trinity, Knightrider Street. The Church was small, old and ruinous, sheared up with props of timber, and the tower covered with ivy and full of noisy jackdaws. Jackdaws built inside too, so that sticks rolled and snapped under his feet as he moved about, making ready for his Mass in the Chantry, which, like all the rest of the Church, was dusty and decayed, with the paint chipping off the carved angels and little figures of mourners about the tomb.

Gib had been glad to take the money for singing the Mass, but now the dirt and disrepair of the Church affected him to a gloom more savage than melancholy. He stood and knelt, did reverence and raised the Host, all without thinking of what he did, having wilfully, though blindly, barred God out. For that morning he had quarrelled again with the Cook, his landlord, and he hated him yet. He hated him, he hated all men, and himself he hated most.

June 10

July shut the door very softly, and tiptoed away and downstairs. She did not know if Sir John and Meg knew that she had seen them, but she had seen, and now she shrank away, sick and soiled, and frightened lest something that was horrible should reach out and touch her. All that morning she lurked in the shed where the empty wine casks were stored, so that she did not know when Sir John went away, nor when William Cheyne came back, nor that there was a guest to dinner. But when she slunk in, a little late, but not enough to be noticeable, there, beside William Cheyne at the table, sat an Abbess, whose plump face looked very pink against the white of the Cistercian habit.

"Jesu!" thought July, scared, yet with a feeling of relief, "*he* knows" ("he" always meant Cheyne for her) "and he has brought this Abbess to chide Meg and persuade her to do no more of—those things—with Sir John—or other."

So she fastened her eyes on the Lady, but soon came to the conclusion that such chiding and persuasion were not to be hoped for from her, since she was a very merry, free-tongued lady, and also a little drunk.

Upstairs, when July was sent for to find a piece of music that Meg wanted, Meg and the Abbess were laughing together over a story which the Abbess told of a lusty, gallant Prior, "not twenty miles," cried the Abbess with a giggle and a wink, "from a house of religious women that I know of," and then an account of his carryings on, at which Meg laughed till she cried. But William Cheyne sat apart, watching them with a sour, thin look on his face that July knew, and her attention was more on him, wondering always, "Does he know? What will he do?" than upon the Abbess. She only wanted to find the music quickly and get away before he would come out from his silence and stillness.

But when she had found the music at the bottom of the small painted chest, Meg wanted her box regals, and when July had brought those, and pulled up a stool to set them on, Meg told her to lay hold of the bellows and blow. And then, worse still, for it made her conspicuous, Meg bade July sing the song with her. July had a voice as small as a wren's tiny pipe, but as true and clear; it was her one grace, and of no pleasure to her, because she dreaded to be noticed for any reason, seeing that to be ignored was so much safer.

She sang with her eyes lowered and did not therefore have time to draw back before she found herself drawn by the Abbess into her arms, hugged to a warm, soft breast, and kissed with moist, lingering kisses that July detested. "Nay," cried the lady, "I must kiss that sweet little mouth. Marry! and by Our Lady! But the voice is the voice of a bird."

She held July off, staring at her, while July looked only at a little chain of gold with enamel flowers of blue and white which the Abbess wore; it heaved up and down with the Lady's breathing in a way that disgusted July.

"And this is your little sister, Madame? By the Mass, little gentlewoman, I would I had you among my Ladies to sing. Such a high, sweet note! It puts me in mind . . . Ah! me!" She did not tell them of what it put her in mind, but still holding July firmly she shed a few tears, murmuring, "Alas. I was young. I was young."

July stood very still, knowing that it would be unmannerly to pull herself away, but as stiff as a poker. The Abbess loosed her at last, in order to wipe her eyes, and July drew back a little and felt enormous relief, but not for long. For the next thing was that the Abbess leaned over to Meg, and put one of her plump hands on Meg's fine small one, and said, sighingly, that there was nothing would make her gladder than to take the young gentlewoman back with her and receive her into religion. "For I doubt she's not portionless, seeing, as ye say, ye come of such high blood," and at that she turned from Meg to William Cheyne, as though he were the one to deal with that side of the matter. But he said nothing, nor gave any sign that he had heard her, though his eyes were on the three of them, cold and unwinking as a snake's eye.

Meg looked at the Abbess, then at July, and laughed.

"There!" said she to July. "You hear that? There are you provided for," and she began to thank the Abbess and praise July more than July had ever thought to be praised. But when the two of them were making all arrangements—of how and when the child's dower should be paid, and what stuff she should bring with her, and whether it would go on one of the Abbess's pack beasts or need a hired mule to carry it—July suddenly broke in on them.

"No!" she cried. "No! I will not go." She stopped because they turned and stared at her. But she cried again with a shrill, breaking voice, "No, I will not. I will not. I will never go with her."

Meg was angry, but the Abbess said, no, no, not to chide her, and put an arm once more about July, promising her that she'd find it no harsh life: "For you shall have a rabbit to keep or a little dog, and when you are grown perhaps a gay scholar of Oxford for your true love, for we must have our pleasures, we religious, being for all our vows but women, and therefore weak, as all the Fathers knew, God wot, nor would Our Saviour, who . . . but what was I saying?" She laughed a little emptily, for the wine was mounting ever more potently to her head. And then she said, very solemnly, "Even though it comes to a babe, that is no matter. And it has so come, more than once among us. For we're women, we religious, women . . . God forgive us."

July wrenched herself away. "I will not go. I will not go," she cried again, and then ducked her head because Meg had sprung up, and her eyes were flaming with anger.

But before Meg could catch her William Cheyne spoke, and his man's voice, coming so suddenly and so sharply, startled them all to stillness.

"No," said he, "she shall not go. But for you, Mistress," he spoke to the Abbess as though she were a person of no importance, "you shall be gone from my house."

Then there was a great to-do. The Abbess was dignified, then wept. Meg raged till her voice cracked. But it was the Abbess who went, July who stayed. In the charged silence after the guest had gone William Cheyne told his wife why he had refused to let July go. "For it is not right," said he, "that nuns should be so lewd, nor that such a jig as yonder Abbess should bear rule." Those were the reasons he gave, but they were not the true ones. He had refused to let July go chiefly to thwart Meg, but partly also to have the opportunity to use words of the Abbess and her wantonness that he dared not these days use of his wife; yet they both knew at whom he cast the ugly words.

Meg answered him that she would have let the child go for a Religious, "because," said she, "well I can see that her being here irks you, and for her sake I would set her beyond reach of your ill tongue and your unkindly handling." But neither was the truth. She had jumped at the offer partly because she thought if July were not there a few of Cheyne's eastwind angers might be scaped, but mostly because that morning she had seen the girl's face at the open door, though she was sure Jack Bulmer had not. But the girl had peeped in, and drawn back with such a white, sick face that she might even do so mad a thing as to tell William Cheyne what she had seen. "But Jesu!" thought Meg, tossing up her chin, "let her tell him."

They neither of them asked why July had refused to go, and she went away quietly, having realised as soon as Cheyne had spoken for her that if she had escaped the Abbess she had condemned herself to prison with him for her jailer.

Yet she would have done the same again. For while she stayed with Meg that thing which she had feared this morning would, at most, reach to her and touch, and leave a slimy trail on her mind, like that of a garden slug. But if she went with the pink-faced Abbess the thing might wind round her, catch hold and hug her close. Down in the yard she pumped water into a bowl and splashed and scrubbed her face from the touch of the Abbess's lips. Then she went and played hop-scotch with a neighbour's child, and forgot, or covered over, what had happened. But one thing remained. She would have nothing to do with that to which Meg and the Abbess took so kindly.

July 28

In the evening the New Prioress, elected, and now duly confirmed by the Bishop's letter, set about moving her belongings from the chamber she had shared with Dame Bess Dalton and Dame Elizabeth Close to the Prioress's chamber overlooking the Great Court. Jankin had been called from the gatehouse, and two of the men from the stable, and between them they carried down, and through the Cloister, and up the outside stair to the Prioress's chamber, all the stuff which Dame Christabel Cowper had brought with her from Richmond, or had since received as gifts from her family.

The meditations of the Ladies who sat in the Cloister were much disturbed by the tramping back and forth. First Jankin and the two men bore out the new Prioress's bed, which had carved oak panels, and an oak tester above; after these came the new Prioress and Dame Anne, one with a pair of tongs and a fire pan, and the other with a couple of candlesticks. And so it went on: there was the feather bed, the big silver cokernut cup, red and blue curtains, the painted hangings that Andrew Cowper had left his daughter, and irons, a pewter basin, sheets and blankets, two stools, and three worked cushions. Of course everyone knew the things by heart but to see them moved created a stir of interest in the Cloister.

At supper-time Dame Anne ate with the new Prioress. They were tired, but Dame Christabel was, and with reason, elated. After supper they sat looking about the room. It was strange and interesting to see Dame Christabel's painted hangings in place of the old Prioress's red and yellow say, and to see the carved cupboard set up beside the window which looked out towards Calva, instead of the old square coffer of ash, with its faded paintings of the life of St. George, which was now pushed to the foot of the bed. On the carved cupboard the pewter plates, a little salt of silver, and the great cup Edward made a worthy show. It was a pity that there had to be a gap in the painted hangings above the fire-place, but the old hanging for the chimney breast had been so worn it was not worth putting up again. So the raw stone showed there, and upon it in large old letters of dark red paint the monogram—I.H.S.

Dame Anne nodded in that direction. "You'll be needing new hangings." She could not keep a spice of malice from her tone. These two were now friends, or allies, but the old unkindness still ran below like a spring underground.

Dame Christabel smiled. She had not missed the tone. "I think to wainscot the room one day," she said.

"Wainscot!"

"And above the hearth, work in plaster, painted, such as I hear is done by these foreign craftsmen of Italy."

"And when," Dame Anne scoffed openly, "will such a craftsman come to Marrick?"

"But till I may find my man," Christabel continued calmly, "I shall hang between the wainscot a piece of arras, very choice."

She knew that she had triumphed. Dame Anne could not better a flight of fancy so daring. The new Prioress had pity on her.

"Let us drink a cup of wine together," she said; and when Dame Anne had poured it out, waiting upon her who was now Lady of Marrick Priory, they drank and were accorded, each reminding herself that the other must be very tired after the excitements of the day, and that weariness sharpened the temper.

The King had been shooting at the mark with the Duke of Suffolk, Sir George Boleyn and Sir Henry Norris. Lord Darcy was one of those bidden to watch the match, and when it was over—the King and Norris had won it—the King fell into conversation with Darcy of horses, and in particular of a stallion he had bought. So with Norris and Boleyn carrying the bows and quivers, for the King had sent the gentlemen and pages away, they all went in by the little gate into the Privy Garden, and that way to the stables.

Some of the grooms were leading out horses ready saddled. A very lively grey came sliding out with two grooms skipping along beside him, and all the gold fringes and tassels on the black velvet harness dancing and swinging. It was a very rich harness; besides the fringes and tassels it was studded with gilt buttons, shaped like pears, and all the buckles and pendants were gilt.

The King had been speaking to one of the yeomen grooms, an old grey fellow in a leather coat, with the cold eye and slit mouth of a man brought up among horses. But when he saw the dapple grey go bucking by he turned and cried—

"Ho! Who bade you put that harness upon that brute?"

The grooms pulled up, with some difficulty. It was Madame Anne, they said, had commanded the grey to be harnessed with one of the new harnesses sent from the Great Wardrobe, or else they had not thought to use it without his Grace's own commandment.

The King swore by God's Wounds that it wasn't the harness he cared for. "But it's not fitting she should ride that beast. I'll not have her on him. He's killed two stable boys—God's Death! Would she drive me mad?" He seemed suddenly to realize how the attention of all was fastened upon him, the gentlemen watching covertly, the grooms with a gaping curiosity. "Take the grey back and saddle the little bay with the white blaze. I'll tell my Lady why." He was half way across the stable yard, and called back over his shoulder to the yeoman groom to show my Lords the stallion. He waved his hand and was gone into the Palace by the Ewery passage.

The Lords looked at and discussed the stallion; they were shown, and admired, other sets of harness which had come from the Great Wardrobe for Mistress Anne, while Sir George, her brother, stood demurely by. Afterwards the Duke, Sir George and Norris turned back into the Palace, and Darcy and Sandys went out by the tiltyard, to take a boat at the next stairs, and so across the river to Lambeth, where Sandys went to see a couple of hounds, my Lord Darcy going with him for the pleasure of so fair an evening.

Not till they sat among the box bushes and hollyhocks of the yeoman's garden at Lambeth, waiting for the dogs to be brought out, did either speak of anything they had seen at the King's Palace of Westminster. But then Sandys said, putting down his ale can, and squinting into it, "The Black Crow goes very fine these days," and they talked a little of Mistress Anne, speculating as to whether she still kept the King off. Darcy thought yes, and Sandys no. "For," said he, "she's been openly in the Palace close on a year now, and with the King when he hunts, and how could she?"

Darcy shrugged, and said in a low voice, his eyes narrowed against the light from the golden west, that he did not like these Boleyns. "Although," said he, "at least the Black Crow helped to bring down the Cardinal."

Sandys was still frowning. "They talk, and openly, of spoiling the goods of the Church. Look how they favour Lutherans and heretics. Sometimes——" he hesitated, and then said it with a half laugh to excuse the improbability of it—— "Sometimes I think they mean to pull down the Church with the Cardinal."

He turned to Darcy for reassuring derision but Darcy was looking at the holes he was prodding in the mossed path with his iron-shod walking staff. He did not answer Sandys for a minute.

"And if they so intend," said he at last, "let them but try."

September 13

Gib was sitting at his copying, in shirt and breeches only, because the day was hot, and the upper room at the sign of King David was close under the rafters and above the big fires where the cooking was done. So he set the door open, and the window shutters as wide as they would. Downstairs he heard people coming in and out, for the roast ribs of beef and hot pies were ready, and if he had listened he could have heard what they asked for and how much they paid, but he did not, for he was busy writing.

Dinner-time was past when he laid by his pen and thought of going down to eat with the Master Cook and his wife. But as he heard the voices of two men below who had entered the shop, he waited till they should have got what they wanted and gone.

They were, he heard them say, church wardens of St. Botolph's, and come to ask for the Cook's charity for the Church, for, said they, money was needed for furnishing the rood lights.

"Ha!" Gib thought, hearing the Cook clearing his throat unnecessarily, "now will he give alms to their superstitious uses, or will he openly refuse?" And he guessed that the Master Cook would, in fact, hedge.

Hedge he did, pleading poverty; a dishonest servant had of late run away with a bag of silver. "Therefore, look you," said he, "I have nothing to give to-day, but come within and drink." So they went into the inner room and Gib heard the Cook go down the steps to the cellar and heard the cans clink in his hand.

But when he came back to the inner room and bade them drink, Gib heard one of the visitors say, "Master, what book is this lies in your window? For I read in it strange things."

Gib could guess what book it must be, since the Master Cook had, before dinner-time, been disputing with him over one of Friar Laurence's books. So now he sat very still upstairs, and leaned forward listening, but he could not hear what words the Master Cook mumbled, and Gib was angry and scornful. He said to himself that he had always known that such a prating fellow as the Cook would not hold his ground.

"There are strange things in this Prologue," said one of the two visitors. "Tell us, Master, what think you of Baptism?"

"Now," thought Gig, "he will be silent or speak humbly of the sacrament."

He heard the Cook give a kind of scraping cough, and then, in a wavering voice, say that no water, though superstitiously called holy, could save a human soul.

"Jesu Mary!" and "God's Bread!" they cried, and began to ask him of Transubstantiation, which he denied, speaking louder and in a shrill tone, and after that they said they need ask him no further, and Gib heard them go away.

After a few minutes he went down. The Master Cook sat at table drumming with his fingers on the board. There were three cans of ale beside him, untouched. At the fireside his wife was beating eggs, and as she beat tears fell down her cheeks and into the bowl.

They ate dinner very silently. The Cook drank the three

cans of ale one after the other. His wife wept without any sound. Gib was ashamed because he could not be glad that the Cook had done valiantly. He said to himself that the Bishop would not care that such a poor, ignorant fellow should talk heresy.

September 16

Gib came back to the sign of King David in time for supper; but he found no supper, and the place in confusion. Two of the servants had run away, and the wife and a serving woman were trying to do the work of those that had fled, and of the Master Cook too.

"But where's he?" Gib asked.

The Cook's wife did not lift her eyes from the pastry she was rolling.

"They've taken him away, the Bishop's officers have."

"Why?" asked Gib stupidly, knowing well why.

"For heresy."

If the woman had wept Gib would have thought less heavily of the business, but her hard flat voice, and her hands that never stopped their hurried dealings with the pastry, affected him unpleasantly. He mumbled something about returning soon, hardly knowing if it were his or the Cook's return he promised, and then went out, to roam round the streets in a sort of aimless haste, which never outran the blank fact that the Cook had been taken for a heretic.

November 8

The new Nuns' Priest had hardly been in the Priory for half an hour before he sent word to the Prioress that he would be ready to sing Lady Mass, thereby showing, as he intended, a commendable zeal.

The Ladies had heard no Mass since their old priest died a month ago, save what was mumbled through for them by the toothless, ancient Parish Priest, drunk too, most of the time. They were therefore very ready to come into Church. Besides they all wanted to have a look at their new Priest.

They saw a round, cheerful, fresh-faced man, with a small, pursed mouth, which let out a loud and tuneful voice. His demeanour was most proper, but more than one caught a glance of his eyes, full of bright, friendly curiosity. When the Mass was over and they back again in the Cloister, the Ladies were able to tell each other, with confidence, that they were pleased, and would be pleased, with their new priest.

[178]

They stayed rather longer in the Cloister than they would otherwise have stayed on such a raw, drenched day, feeling that the presence of a new priest in the House called for a stricter observance of the Rule; but the mist closing in drove them into the Parlour where they continued, in greater comfort, to discuss the new arrival.

Meanwhile the priest was exploring his two small rooms, with something of a dog's eager, prying interest. He did not sniff in the corners, or at the bed hangings, but being short-sighted, he brought his nose very close to everything he looked at, so that he did indeed seem a little like a brisk, cheerful mongrel dog. When he had examined everything he sat down by the fire and took out from his baggage his recorder and a music book. He played to himself till it was dinnertime, and one of the Ladies, hearing faintly the sweet, musing, warbling notes, reported his occupation to the others, importantly and as a discovery. Soon the sound of his recorder would be nothing to them, but to-day everything about him was news.

When it was time for dinner he went across the Great Court and to the Prioress's Chamber, and they two, Dame Joan Barningham, and Dame Eleanor Maxwell dined together. The Prioress, though more critical than most of the Ladies, was very well satisfied with her brother's choosing. The little fat priest was of Easby just beyond Richmond, brother of a good worthy yeoman; his manner was attentive; his disposition obviously cheerful. She felt she had done well for the House.

November 30

Norris said, "What an if he gains the King's ear once more? God knows he has the craft of the very serpent."

The Duke of Norfolk cried out, "Blood of God!" and wagged his hand at Norris to bid him be silent. He did not wish to hear put into words the fear that had gnawed at his mind since the King had sent for the Earl of Northumberland to arrest Cardinal Wolsey and bring him again to London. He was not going to tell Norris of the scene in the Privy Council yesterday; it would be common knowledge soon enough, such running tongues as most men had. But now, as he remembered it, he felt his face grow cold again, and stiffen, as it had done when the King thumped the board with his fist, leapt up scattering the quills and sand-box and paper all over the place, and then had stormed away from the room, crying: "Not one of you is worth what the Cardinal was worth to me.

Not one of you! Not one of you!" He had slammed the door of the Council Chamber behind him so fiercely that it had bounced open again, and in the silence that followed they had heard the King's quick footsteps go down the four stairs beyond, then along the gallery passage where the windows looked out to-day on nothing but the blank, drab fog. On the side of the gallery passage, facing those windows, was the door leading to the apartments of Mistress Anne Boleyn. Norfolk had listened—had guessed too that every other man listened—for the sound of the King's hand rapping on the door, and for the click of the latch. But the footsteps had not paused. The sound of them died away, and after a moment more of silence and a few moments of murmured, wary talk, His Grace's honourable Privy Council had broken up. Once again, as yesterday, Norfolk thought, "If she lose her power over the King and the Cardinal again wins his ear—"

He got out of his chair and went round to the fire. He heard Norris murmur that they said that "My Lady, your niece, swears she will leave the King. And shall all then be for naught, and the Cardinal rule again?"

Norfolk muttered, "When last I saw him he was much changed—aged. He's not the man now to recover that place he had." But there was confidence neither in his mind nor in his tone, and he stood staring moodily into the fire for a long time before he said, "There is the Italian's information to be used against the Cardinal. The King will not take it lightly that his own subject and servant begged the King of France to intercede for him. We can raise that nigh hand to treason itself." He let out an impatient kick at a log, which, falling inwards, sent a scatter of sparks up the chimney, and tattered flames leaping after the sparks. "I shall try the Italian again," he said, and leaving Norris hunched on his cushion in the window, went off to his own apartments.

There they presently brought in the Italian, Master Agostino de Agostinis, who had been my Lord Cardinal's doctor. He was a small, fragile man, fair in colouring, with yellow hair, and a quiet benign face; his looks, and his long, patient discretion were now turning profitable, for the Cardinal had trusted him as a man trusts his confessor, so that he had much secret knowledge to sell.

The Duke received him coldly, merely waving him to a small table where there was everything necessary for writing, and a candle set and lit, because of the gloom of the day within doors.

"Sit there, Master Augustine," said he; and no more for several minutes. Then he asked, bluntly, for information which would set the King against the Cardinal.

"Shall it be true?" The Italian's soft tone was demure, but Norfolk caught a hint of a smile on the man's face.

He stared it down. "True?" he repeated.

"You prefer it true?"

"I pay for the truth," said the Duke with a look and tone that would have quelled most Englishmen of Master Augustine's station; but then he was an alien, and more than that, an Italian, so that these lords, even the greatest of them, were to him more than half barbarian.

"I remember," said the Italian, after a silence in which the Duke twirled a big ruby on his finger and Master Augustine sat at ease, in calm consideration, "I remember the Cardinal's words to me when he first went on embassy to France."

"Write them."

The Duke picked up a book, and Master Augustine bent over the small table, writing down in careful English, and his elegant Italian hand, what the Cardinal had said to him. He remembered accurately, not only the words, but the Cardinal's hand on his shoulder, even the warmth of the Cardinal's breath on his ear as my Lord leaned close to whisper so that no one else, less trusty, should hear. But those things it was unnecessary to put down, only the words.

They were interrupted by a knock at the door, and the entrance of a gentleman in haste who began, "My Lord Duke—" and checked dead when he saw Master Augustine with his pen poised and face turned to watch.

The Duke said, "Take your paper and candle into the little closet," so Master Augustine gathered up all from the table, and went within to a cold little room where the hangings smelt of dust, and there were many dead flies on the window-sill. He was still arranging his papers and preparing to write when the Duke threw open the door and stood looking in. Beyond him, in the brighter light of the outer room, was the gentleman, also looking that way. Both had an air as of men, who, without any warning of an approaching storm, had been startled by a sudden thunder-clap.

"You can spare your writing," said the Duke; and while Master Augustine still stared, he added, "He is dead."

"The Cardinal of York!" The Italian said it, not to be sure, but to realize what the news meant.

[181]

The Duke said, "The Cardinal. At Leicester." He turned away from the other two and stood by the fire. They heard him let out a long breath. Then he bade the Italian to go, and the other to, "Send me Bowman to make me ready to go to the King."

"My Lord!" The Italian paused at the door. The Duke leaned and looked into the fire, with one hand laid against the wall above the hearth; the fingers of that hand tapped restlessly upon the hangings. "My Lord!" Norfolk only answered by a jerk of the head that meant dismissal. Master Augustine's voice rose several tones. "My Lord, I shall be paid—I shall be paid notwithstanding?"

"Yes. Yes," said the Duke, but in a manner so absent that the Italian got no assurance from it.

When both he and the gentleman were gone, and the door shut, the Duke turned and looked about the room, seeing not those four walls, hung with the tapestries of the Quest of the Fleece, but the world itself over which brooded no more the fear of the Cardinal's return. In spite of the dark day his world seemed bright as spring.

1531

February 11

The Queen was embroidering a green cape with white lilies and butterflies. Her ladies sat about on cushions; most of them were sewing, but a lute was passed round, and now one, now another, would sing. When there was no singing they talked of gowns, of sweethearts or husbands, of the weather; or else someone would tell a story.

The Queen listened, talked, and smiled, cheerful and pleasant as she was always; the Princess sat at her feet, nursing a small brown dog with flop ears. The Queen bent now and again to speak to the girl, and teased her, much as she was teasing the dog. Yet some of the older women, who knew the Queen well, thought that she had not her mind on anything that was said, but was listening. When the Countess of Salisbury came in, her eyes and the Queen's met.

"Madame," the Countess curtseyed, "have you that pattern for a cushion I asked of you—that with the beast, and a tree, and a huntsman blowing on his horn?"

"I will give it to you." The Queen got up. "No. No," she

said to the Princess, "stay here, and read in this book to the Ladies." She picked up a book from the floor, and gave it to the girl, then she and the Countess went into the inner room, and shutting the door of it, away to the further side; it was but a small room and hardly more than a closet.

"They will not hear," the Queen said. Only the low murmur of a voice sounded through the door. "Not that it matters. All will hear soon."

The Countess faced the Queen. She said:

"They have consented."

"Merciful God! It cannot be true."

The Countess laughed sharply. "It is true. The Convocation of Canterbury hath acknowledged His Grace to be 'Sole Protector and Supreme Head of the Church and Clergy of England.' "

Katherine raised her hands and laid them to her cheeks in a gesture of horror. "But it is not possible."

" 'So far as the law of God allows,' " the Countess added, and laughed again; but the Queen caught at the phrase.

"Then—then is all well and this means—nothing."

"It means—so far as the will of the King intends."

The Queen turned away and looked out of the window. The privy garden of the Palace lay below, covered deep and soft with snow. Not a foot had trodden it since the last fall, except the little dainty feet of birds; just then the big flakes began to spin downwards again, a few at first, then myriads. Away in the garden they blew with the wind, sailing by in the opposite direction, slow, giddy and uncertain.

"Meg," said the Queen, "Meg, what does it all mean? What is coming to us? Is he—is his Grace mad?"

"I do not know." The Countess let that answer all for a minute, then she said, "What anyone may know is that hard times are coming to us. You and I, Madame, though we are women, we shall have to fight."

Katherine turned then, and they looked at each other—the Countess too spare, too rare for beauty, but exquisite as carved ivory; the Queen plain, plump and heavy. The Countess was of the blood of Kings and of the King Maker; the Queen came of the royal and fighting House of Spain.

"So I will," said the Queen, "when the time comes."

February 24

Dame Christabel came to the gate of Marrick Manor; old Dame Eleanor Maxwell was with her, and behind them a servant carrying a basket of warden pears. The porter at the gate yelled to the dogs to stop barking, and to a lad to take the Ladies to my Lady in the winter parlour.

They crossed the court, and went into the Hall where a few boys were idling and squabbling on one of the benches. At the far end there was a short dark passage, and then the servant opened the door of the winter parlour, which was warm and bright with a log fire, and with sunshine.

Several women were there, sewing or spinning, but Dame Nan was busy making a hawk's lure, and a book on falconry lay open on the rushes at her feet. Her hands were stained with the medicines and ointments which she made for the horses, dogs, or hawks, and her skirts with hawks' droppings; but she did not care. When she got up, however, and greeted the Ladies, you could see that she was the daughter of a great house.

There was a cradle beyond the fireplace, and Dame Eleanor went to it at once; she bent over it making those sounds which are traditionally held to be agreeable to infants. Little Doll, however, began to cry. Dame Eleanor could not hear, but she saw the child's face crumple and redden, and she drew back. "It's my black gown," she explained as one of the women lifted the baby to comfort her, and from a more discreet distance she smiled and beckoned, twiddling her fingers and crying, "Ah! the poppet! The poppet!"

The Prioress sat down beside Dame Nan, and came at once to the point of her business. Did Sir Rafe know of any priest for the parish? Such a search she had had but a few months ago for a priest for the Priory, and now here's all to do again for the parish. Yes, it was early days, she admitted, seeing that the old priest had died only yesterday, but she did not want the Archbishop—who had no right—to put his finger into the pie. "The benefice is ours," she declared. "I have searched all the writings and it is ours to bestow."

Just then Sir Rafe came in; he was very cold for he had been up on the brew-house roof watching the men mending the chimney. So the Prioress had to wait till mulled wine had been brought, and wafers, while Sir Rafe stamped about warming himself at the fire. Then he was ready to listen.

But he knew of no priest. He seemed to think that it would be well to leave it to the Archbishop; when the Prioress was insistent, he offered to write to his brother Sir John, who, if he was not now in London, on business of a lawsuit, as he had said he should be, knew many in London who would be able to find a man.

"London? That's a far cry," the Prioress objected.

"Have it as you will then. The Archbishop——"

The Prioress thought that perhaps she had not done well to ask Sir Rafe's help. But she must choose between him and the Archbishop. So she capitulated. "I pray you ask Sir John to find us a man."

"And you'll have whom he finds?" Sir Rafe could be a close man at a bargain, and he knew that with the Prioress there was need to be close.

"We will."

Sir Rafe and his lady saw the two away from the gate-house, and both returned to the brew-house to see that the work there was well done. The two Ladies from the Priory went down the hill in the sunshine; all about were the pure lucent colours of February; there was still snow on the northern side of walls and banks, which the shadow painted with lavender.

March 2

"Woman," said Gib to the Cook's wife, "what can I do? Will you have me persuade your husband to recant and deny the truth?"

"No. Yes," she mumbled, being by now almost dumb with weeping: and then she said other words disjointedly and so low that he could not hear them.

"God's Bread!" cried Gib. "Let me alone. I will do nothing."

Yet when she had gone, fumbling for the door latch, and he had heard her shut herself into the kitchen, he went quietly out of the house and to Newgate, where the Cook lay, having been handed over by the Bishop to the secular arm. Tomorrow he was to be burned.

It cost Gib an angel, which he could ill spare, to be taken down to the dungeon of the prison, and the parting with so great a sum, and the foul air, the fear of the prison, and his old dislike of the Cook all made him very resentful.

They had gone down a good flight of steps; it was quite dark when the warder took out a key and, while Gib held the torch, set it in the lock. It was very quiet down here, damp, and horribly cold; as the key turned and Gib moved he saw a rat's eyes burn green in the light; it scuttered away as the door opened.

Gib went in, and the warder shut the door on him and locked

[185]

it. Gib's spine grew cold at the sound. The Cook was sitting with his back to one of the old squat pillars, and upon a bed of straw. He had a tallow candle in his hand and a book on his knee. He got up, looking doubtful and not altogether pleased, but Gib greeted him as "brother" and took his hand; so they sat down together on the straw. Gib could not think now, any more than he had been able to think on the way here, how he would begin; but the Cook did not wait for him to speak and asked eagerly if his wife had sent him meat or drink or something warm for to put on his back.

Gib had to say, "No," that she had not known he was coming, and at that the Cook grew angry, because it would have been so easy for Gib to tell her, "And then," said he, "I'll be bound she would have sent me something to comfort me."

Gib resented the criticsm, both because he knew the Cook's wife had been fretting to send her husband a pottle of old Malmsey and a sleeveless coat of rabbit skins, and also because he thought that a man who was to be burned to-morrow for the truth's sake should not have his mind on such things.

So when he opened his business it was not in the friendly tone he had intended, but harshly.

"Tell me," said he, "the articles for which you are condemned, for no man should consent to death unless he has just cause to die in, and it were better to submit to the ordinances of men than rashly to finish your life without good ground."

"The first article," replied the Cook stiffly, "is that I hold Thomas à Becket a traitor, and damned if he repented not; for he was in arms against his Prince, and had provoked other princes to invade the realm."

"Where," cried Gib, furious at the man's wrong-headed foolishness, "where read you that?"

"In an old history," the Cook told him with his usual stubborn, downward look.

"And it may be a lie. So it were madness for a man to jeopard his life for such a doubtful matter."

"It's no lie." The Cook breathed hard through his nose, and Gib cracked his finger joints as he did when he was angry; but in a minute he was able to command himself and asked, "What else?"

"I spoke," said the Cook in no friendly tone, "against purgatory—that it is a word the priests use to pick men's purses withal; and against masses to make satisfaction for sin."

"Hm!" Gib muttered, and again, "Hm!" because these were matters in which he also believed that a man might stay his soul so that he would die rather than recant. "But," he warned the Cook, "beware of vain-glory with which the devil will try to infect you when you come into the multitude of people and see the high stake set up in the midst, where you are to die, and all watching you."

"God's Body!" cried the Cook very loud, and he jumped up from the straw and rushed to the door and began to beat upon it. When the warder opened it he begged him to take this man away and leave him in peace.

Gib was ashamed then and tried to find something to say. "The good woman your wife——" he began, but the warder pushed him towards the door.

Then it seemed that the Cook was sorry too, for he tried to catch Gib back.

"Tell her——" said he, but the warder cried that he had no patience with either of them, and he showed Gib out into the passage and shut the door. Before it was quite shut Gib had a glimpse of the Cook standing there, holding out his hands, the candle in one of them, and the light of the candle glittering on the tears that were running down his cheeks.

As fast as Gib could he went from Newgate to the House of the Black Friars, and there found Friar Laurence reading over his charcoal brazier, nibbling raisins of the sun and spitting the pips into the fire. Gib plumped down on the bed and told him all that he had said to the Cook, and the Cook to him, while Friar Laurence murmured from time to time, "Do not speak so wildly, man," or, "Do not weep so." But Gib could not control himself, and in the midst of all his talk he would stop to knock his breast, crying loudly, "Who will deliver me from the body of this death?" meaning not only his own body but his own self that sickened him.

In the end he quieted down, and saw that the Friar was weary of him, for, though Brother Laurence had a long patience, Gib had tried him too much and too often.

"I will go," said Gib, getting up from the bed. Then it came to him that if he could go far away perhaps he might somehow leave his self behind. "Where can I go?" he cried sharply. "Is there any place I can go to?" and burst out of the Friar's room to roam about the streets till nightfall.

When he went back to the Cook's house he found that a letter from the Friar was waiting him.

Here but now was Sir John Bulmer praying me, for his brother, to find a priest for that very parish called Marrick, that you come of. Therefore, friend, if you will, you shall have this benefice, and bring the true light of the gospel into those parts which all men say are very superstitious.

Gib said to himself, "He would be glad to have me gone where I can no longer trouble him." And he could well understand that the Friar should feel so. He wrote a letter at once, saying he would willingly go back to Marrick as priest of the parish, and finding a neighbour's boy, playing with his top in the street, gave him a penny to take the letter to the Black Friars' House in the Strand.

March 20

It was Master Cheyne's birthday, so he had to supper other Master Vintners and their wives. After supper, while the older men sat longer to drink, the women went upstairs, and Master Cheyne could not prevent two of the younger husbands, whose wives were merry and fair, going up with them, although he would have preferred that his own wife should have no man's company.

Up in the solar the wives sat down to sew and to talk; one of the young men found Meg's lute in the corner by the hearth, and so, while he played, they sang songs. Julian, who acted now as her sister's waiting woman, since that saved Master Cheyne a woman's wage, was sitting on her heels in front of Meg holding a skein of dark red silk which Meg was winding.

In a pause between the songs one of the Vintner's wives began talking about the Queen. She was a fair fat woman who was embroidering a fine width of white silk for a petticoat, with little flowers of every colour, and snails stitched in gold thread sitting on the flowers. As she bent over the work to snap off a thread of green with her strong teeth, she said: "That black-eyed whore of the King's came by the other day, from the royal barge, going with as much state as if she were Queen. But I and my maids, and a neighbour or two who were standing in the street, cried out on her, 'Fie! Fie on you, Mistress, for a brazen hussy!' "

The others exclaimed at such daring, and the young men thought it a foolish thing to do, and one that might get the women's husbands into trouble. But all the wives there were for the Queen; and some thought the King was tiring of Mistress Anne and would put her away; and some said that the Holy Father would never let the Queen's cause fail.

"And what do you say, Mistress?" one of them asked Meg, just as the door opened and the elder men came in.

"Marry, I think here's a coil the Queen makes to be the King's wife still. There are some women would do as much to be unwed."

She spoke very high so that all heard, and then there was silence till she laughed and said, "Goodman husband, you'll not spend money to have a divorce of the Holy Father. But if some man will buy me, will you sell?" She laughed as if it were a jest, but they all knew that there was no jesting in it. Master Cheyne ground his teeth, and said, sell her? Yea, that he would, and in a great hurry another of the men began to talk about the repair of Galley's Key, where the Venice galleys unloaded their wine, and no one said any more about the King or Queen or divorce. But Meg caught July a sound box on the ear because the child's hands were shaking so that it was difficult for Meg to wind the silk. July knew that at night, when the guests had gone, Master Cheyne would take it out of Meg for her words, and out of July too for being Meg's sister.

March 30

In the Church of the Black Friars, where the lords sat in Parliament, it was so dark that they had lit the candles; but even now those on the one side could hardly see the faces of those on the other. Above the high, painted vaulting, blue as blue heaven and scattered with golden stars, rain drummed on the roof.

The Chancellor stood up, and the lords became silent and kept their eyes on him, but as Sir Thomas More spoke he looked neither to right nor left but only at the high altar and the steady light that hung in the shadows above it.

He spoke, as the King's mouth, and as the King had commanded him, declaring there were some who had put it forth that the King pursued this divorce out of love for some lady, and not out of any scruple of conscience. "But these," said he in a grave, steady voice, "these are lies, for His Grace is moved thereto only in discharge of his conscience, which, by means of all that he has read and discovered from doctors and from the Universities, is sorely pained by his living with the Queen. And this will appear by the seals of the Universities which I shall show you, and of which ye shall understand the tenor and substance by what Sir Bryan Tuke shall presently read unto you."

When Sir Thomas sat down Sir Bryan stood up and read loudly, in English, that which doctors in the universities of France, and of some other nations, had written of the King's divorce, declaring that his first marriage was incestuous and void. As he read the rain took off, and the sky so lightened that a fleeting gleam of watery sunshine swept through the Church, dulling the candle flames. By the greater light many looked more narrowly at Sir Thomas, but could read nothing in his face.

"Ah! watch now, Talbot!" my Lord Darcy murmured in the ear of the Earl of Shrewsbury, sitting in front of him. "Soon will come in chiming other hounds of the King's pack!" For the Bishop of Lincoln had stood up and began to speak.

"And now London," Darcy muttered as Lincoln sat down. Shrewsbury made no answer, and shifted his shoulders uncomfortably. He, no less than Darcy, disliked all these doings, but he wished to be discreet, for he was a man who loved peace. Therefore he took no more notice of the other lord's mutterings than if it had been a fly pestering him.

"Those two," Darcy chuckled, "those two trust that as Bishop Fisher is not here to answer, none else will dare." Darcy did not think much of Bishops, regarding their part in this controversy rather as the play of children. It would not be the Bishops, he thought, who would check the King. Yet, when first the Bishop of St. Asaph, and then he of Bath, stood up and spoke against the other two, he grunted approval, especially as they spoke both manfully and with subtle reasoning.

Bath, however, was not allowed to finish, for the Duke of Norfolk got up, so hastily that he knocked down the walking staff of an old lord beside him, which fell clattering; the little sharp echoes ran into the aisles and chapels and died there. The Duke said that it was not the King's purpose that they should debate the sentence of the learned doctors of Christendom. "But," said he, "you have heard the King's mind by the mouth of the Lord Chancellor."

It seemed then as though no other would speak; Sir Thomas stood up as though to conclude the business, when someone said:

"My Lord Chancellor, you have declared the King's mind. What is your mind in the matter?"

Sir Thomas More turned about.

"My Lord, I have many times declared it to the King's Grace."

They waited, but they got no more of him, and then someone behind Norfolk asked what my Lord of Shrewsbury thought, because they all knew that he and the Chancellor agreed together on this. But Talbot would say no more than that it was not for him to give an opinion in such a matter.

Then, after a little uneasy silence, the Chancellor went away down the Church to declare the King's words to the Commons. Norfolk, Suffolk, the Bishops of Lincoln and London, Sir Bryan Tuke, and many others went with him.

The rest of the lords sat waiting, without much talking, and heard the rain begin again to mutter on the roof.

April 1

In the evening Gib Dawe came home to Marrick. It was one of those days when a cold and winterly spring is, at one stride, overtaken by the heat of summer. The new chestnut leaves hung limp and very green. Roads were deep in dust, and for the first time the sweet smell of grass breathed in the air.

It was nearly a month since Gib had left London, and to-day he had walked from Richmond. He came from the open fells to the first of the village fields where the oats were pricking up. The sun had just dropped below the opposite side of the dale but the sky that way was of a flushed gold, like an apricot. All the way across the fells the air had been full of the crystal singing of the larks; now that he came near the big chestnut trees behind the Manor he could hear a blackbird lazily spilling notes that were rich as honey.

He passed two little girls, naked, with water pots hugged to them, on their way to the well; they shied off the road at the sight of a stranger, and one of them threw a stone after him. He came to the green opposite the ale-shop; the ale-shop bench was full; he recognized more than one sitting there, but he hurried by, so that they should not know him, or should not greet him. The road now ran between cottages on one side and a stone-walled orchard on the other. At the town end, the very last cottage before the way went steeply down to the Priory was the one in which he had been born. There were a couple of lambs under the tree, and a sow rooted by the wall. In the garden beyond the cottage he could see rows of onions, kale and cabbages. He came abreast of the door and looked in. Smoke from the fire swam out, hot and blue in the bright warm air. His mother, small and very bent, stood over the fire. She stirred something with one hand, and with the other held up a lappet of her kerchief to shield her eyes from the heat of the flames. He went inside and greeted her.

They ate their supper sitting on the door step; there was pottage in wooden bowls, and black bread and cheese. Hankin, the old dog, sat opposite them, moving his eyes from one to another as Gib or his mother lifted hand to mouth. The brown and speckled hens picked at crumbs in the dust at their feet, moving with jerky nods that shook the fringes of their feathered hoods about their shoulders.

After supper the old woman brought out her spindle. Gib bent and pulled off his shoes. His leather hosen were of the kind that has no foot; he waggled his toes, and began to shift his feet softly to and fro in the warm dust, pleased to think that to-morrow he would not have to take his staff and wallet and trudge off again.

"That wench that you went off with——" said his mother behind him, and tittered. Gib jumped as though a flea had bitten him.

"How did you know?"

"She told me when she came back. But you needn't fear. She's told no one else."

"She has come back?"

"She came. Then she died. Last Martinmas."

Gib knew that he was very glad of that. Though now he believed that it was well for a priest to be married, he did not wish ever to see the miller's Joan again.

"And," his mother went on, "the little knave won't tell neither, for he's dumb, and a fool too. And moreover the miller sells him, if he hath not yet sold him, to the lead miners up beyond Owlands."

"The little knave——" Gib repeated as though the words were news to him. But indeed he had only forgotten. Then he asked, "How old is he?"

She cackled at that. "You should know." But Gib could not remember. "A four or five years child, by his looks," his mother told him.

A little while after she left him to milk the cow, and he sat there, his body at ease, but not his mind.

May 31

The ladies who were to undress the Queen had taken off the

billement of pearls and sapphires that surrounded her neck and was tucked into the bosom of her gown, and it lay beside the rings from her fingers, and the collar of gold with the great table sapphire and three hanging pearls, upon the velvet cushion which another held, kneeling. Then someone knocked, and when the door was opened word came that, late as it was, a great company of lords were asking audience of the Queen.

"What lords?" she asked. They had taken off her velvet head-dress and her hair, pale silver-gold now, was bare; she looked older so, and less stately.

They told her—"My lords of Norfolk, Suffolk, Shrewsbury, Northumberland, Wiltshire—"

"That is enough. Friends, a few—and unfriends," she said, and broke off, to sit frowning for a minute. Then she motioned to them to put on again her headgear, but when they would have added the pearls she said, "No. Not those," and so went out to the lords, who, thirty or more of them, waited in her chamber of presence. She would have none of her own people to follow her, except two or three of her elder ladies.

The lords had come, as she knew well, from the King, and, as she might guess, with reproaches against her, for being the occasion of His Grace being cited to appear before the Pope at Rome. They delivered their message, and she answered the reproaches patiently, having learnt patience in a hard school.

But at last Doctor Lee, the Archbishop-elect of York, spoke, saying that since her first husband, Prince Arthur, the King's brother, had had carnal knowledge of her, therefore the marriage between her and the King was very detestable and abominable before God and the world, as learned doctors and the universities had declared. At that the Queen flushed crimson, and then went white. Her hands closed on the carved arms of the chair she sat on, until her knuckles too showed white. Yet she let him finish.

Then she told him, in a voice not one of them all had heard before, so hard and sharp it was, that he could talk to others so, but not to her. "Nor are you my counsellor, nor are you my judge," said she, "that I should believe you. Prince Arthur knew me not." She stopped there because her breath was short. "This," she cried, though her voice shook, "this is not the place to set forth such things. Go you to Rome, Doctor, if you will, and there you will find other than women to answer you; aye, men be there who will show you, Master

Doctor, that you know not, nor have not read, everything."

After that they spoke more bitterly, and bitterly she answered them; telling them one by one to go to Rome, to go to Rome, and at last when all that wished had spoken, she reproached them all, so many and so great, for taking her by surprise, at night, and unfurnished of Counsel.

Norfolk spoke up then, saying *that* she could not complain of, seeing she had the most complete Counsel in England—as Archbishop Warham of Canterbury, the Bishop of Durham, Fisher, Bishop of Rochester, and others.

"Jesu!" cried the Queen, "fine counsellors! for when I asked counsel of the Archbishop he answered that he would not meddle in such affairs, saying often, '*Ira principis mors est.*' The Bishop of Durham said that meddle he dared not, being the King's subject. The Bishop of Rochester bade me keep up my courage, and *that*," the Queen concluded, "was all the counsel I had from them."

After this, and some argument about her appeal, they asked leave to withdraw, which she gave them curtly. When they had gone, for a long while she sat in the Chamber of Presence, where the candles had been lighted. It was dark now outside, and from the garden moths swung in and whisked about, blundering into the flames and making them dip, sizzle and flare.

At last the Queen got up, and went back into her Privy Chamber. Her head was up and her countenance serene, for all that anyone could see, but she moved slowly because of the heavy knocking of her heart, and as her heart knocked, so it seemed to her to ache.

July 25

The Duke of Norfolk, coming into the gallery that led to the King's Privy Chamber, recognized the voice of his niece, Mistress Anne Boleyn. It was raised and shrill, but he was certain it was hers, though he did not catch the words. And then, from a doorway at the far end of the great room she bounced out, cried, "I will not! I will not! I will not!" on a rising note that ended as high as a peacock's scream, and slammed the door behind her.

The Duke made as if there were nothing strange in all this. As she swept by him with a whistling of silk, he saluted her gravely, though unnoticed; and rebuked, by a long hard look, the stares of the gentlemen and pages who had got to their feet from games of dice or cards.

He went the long length of the room slowly and with dignity, but in his mind he was wishing that the elderly and rheumatic gentleman who followed him had not arrived in time to see that bit of business, since he came as a messenger from Queen Katherine. As for his niece, the Duke thought, "Mass! The girl's out of her wits. She'll lose all by this manner."

"Wait here, Sir," he said to the elderly gentleman, and knocking gently on the door, went into the Privy Chamber.

The King stood looking out of the window. He did not turn, and the sunshine, streaming past him, threw his broad shadow across the strewn rushes on the floor.

"Your Grace," said Norfolk, down on one knee, "here is a gentleman come with greetings and a letter from the Queen, who—"

Then he saw that the King had his dagger out in his hand, and was stabbing with it at the wooden sill of the open window. The silent violence of that repeated gesture was like a blow across Norfolk's mouth. He gasped and was silent.

"By God's Death!" The King plunged in the dagger and wrenched it out again. "She will not. Will she not?" He swung round suddenly on Norfolk. "This girl's your niece. Yours! Did you teach her this manner duty? The Queen never spoke to me so. I've made—I can unmake her."

Norfolk's eyes flinched from the King's face. He muttered something about "love" and "loyalty" and held out the Queen's letter. When the King whipped it out of his hand and flung back to the window Norfolk told himself that soldiers, aye, brave men, men that feared nothing, were afraid of their Prince, so great is the majesty of kings. Yet he felt the flush on his cheekbones, and was glad that none had been there to see and to hear.

The King said "Tchah!" and crumpled the letter into a ball. "A very dutiful letter. She asks how I do, laments that I left her at Windsor without the consolation of bidding farewell. Very dutiful!" He dropped the crumpled paper on the floor and set his foot on it. "And it's she that will have me cited to Rome, and thinks I'll forgive. God's Blood! I'll not see her face again."

He sent Norfolk away and remained alone in the small sunny room where still lay a scatter of bright silks and a piece of embroidery that Mistress Anne had thrown down when their quarrel had begun. The King tramped to and fro, rolling a little in his walk, concocting in his mind the cruellest answer to the Queen's letter that he could devise. There were two women who crossed him, and he would make one pay for both. For already an uneasiness was growing in his mind and a restless craving. Supposing that other should—mad wench—leave him after all? He could not endure the thought.

October 30

Julian had been sent out to buy lemons and therefore was not present when Master Cheyne sold Meg to Sir John Bulmer. Nor was Meg herself in the room when the business was transacted, but only Master Cheyne, Sir John, and Gregory Cheyne. Gregory, who drew up the deed, was a notary and second cousin to Master Cheyne, and therefore, he considered, privileged to titter as he wrote out so strange a document, and to mutter pleasantries which he took care Sir John should not quite hear.

William Cheyne, who felt the cold sadly since his leg was broken, sat hunched in his chair beside the fire. His head was sunk deep into the warm fur of his collar, and fur lined the wide sleeves of his dark red cloth coat. Sir John was dressed no more richly than he, for Master Cheyne, whose ships went to and fro between London and Bordeaux, could have put down gold for gold against the knight. But Sir John was far gayer; in green, with a yellow hood and scarlet hosen.

Gregory giggled to see how neither of those two faced the other, nor seemed to be concerned in the business afoot; for Master Cheyne sat with his back to the room and his hands held out to the fire, and Sir John was astride the bench by the window, with his long thick legs stretched out; he looked, and meant to look, insolent and disdainful as he turned his big heavy head this way and that, staring about the room, and then through the window again. The room was on an upper floor and you could see, over the scanty yellowing leaves of an orchard opposite, a glimpse of the river. There were ships lying there, swung one way by the tide, and now and again a wherry went by.

Gregory Cheyne finished the writing, and paused, his pen still poised over it as he looked aslant along the lines. The tip of his tongue had been showing between his teeth as he wrote, but now he drew it in and pursed his lips, and opened his eyes very wide, as if he were astonished or shocked at what he had written. Then he giggled.

Sir John turned on him, but he was serious again, and intent on sanding the ink. He had sprinkled sand over the page, and now he tilted it neatly back into the pounce box, and snapped the lid shut. Next he began to root in his pouch, and brought out, and laid on the table, a medley of those things which notaries carry always with them—a twist of plaited threads and some ribbon for scales to hang on; a tinder box; two or three lumps of wax, scarlet, green and yellowish white. But he wanted none of those just now—only a pair of scissors. He found them and then began to snip the parchment across the middle in pointed jags, exactly where he had written in large, fanciful, flourished letters, the word "Chirographia," so that fragments of the letters remained on one half and fragments also on the other.

There was no sound in the room except the snip of the scissors and the soft fluttering of flames on the hearth, till Master Gregory said, "There!" and, "God's Bread! Never till to-day have I drawn up such a deed."

He got up and handed them each a half of the paper. Sir John seemed for a moment to intend to cram it into his pouch unread, but he thought better of that and spread it out on the table. Gregory bent over his cousin's shoulder, his pen pointing along the lines till William Cheyne struck his hand away, and then he went back to his stool.

Sir John nodded. "That is good enough."

"Now pay for the trull you're buying," William Cheyne said.

Sir John took a bag from the bench between his knees, and opening the throat of it let the gold pieces, marks and rose nobles with occasionally an old angel of the last King's time, slide out on to the table.

"Count it, Greg," Master Cheyne bade, turning in his chair.

Gregory had put a foot down on one gold piece that had rolled over the table edge and fallen into the rushes; but Sir John, who was neither so slow nor so careless as he looked, said unpleasantly, "Under your foot. A rose noble." William Cheyne smiled for the first time.

The money was counted and stood in piles on the table. "Now," said Sir John, and stood up, "send for her, and I'll take her away."

"Fetch her, Greg. She'll be listening at the door," and he pointed to the door of the inner room. As Gregory went to do as he was told, William Cheyne said, "And you'll take her away in her shift."

Sir John was very angry at that, and so was Meg, who had been busy decking herself in the rose-coloured velvet with a cloth of silver petticoat, which was her best gown, and with jewels about her neck and hidden in her bosom. She was so angry when she knew that it must be so, and that William Cheyne would not yield, that she began to tear at her clothes, as if to strip herself before the three men.

"God's Teeth!" she cried shrilly, "then I'll go out naked and shame you."

That drove Sir John wild, what with Gregory's chirrups of delight and Cheyne's cold smile. He pushed her back into the bed-chamber, throwing his own cloak after her and bidding her roughly, "Take off your clothes and wrap you in that."

"You see betimes," said William Cheyne, "what you have bought. God give you grace to be glad of your bargain."

Julian did not know till supper-time that Meg had gone, for she had dallied over the buying of the lemons till it was nearly dusk. But when she came in the kitchen was humming with the news, and supper not near ready. She listened, at first struck into a sort of blind and dark helplessness by the news. Meg was gone, and here she was, alone. It was long, black minutes before she thought, "I'll go after her. I'll find her." But that only brought her heart into her throat for haste and fear. She came to the group of men and maids who were all talking it over, and clawed at this girl's elbow, and the skirts of that man's coat, crying, "Where does he live? Where does he live?"

Only after a time one turned and thrust her off, but told her, "In Yorkshire."

"Where is that?"

"In the North Country."

"But when he is in London?" They did not know or would not tell, and so Julian left them, and went into the empty Hall where the trestles were set up, but nothing on them. Master Cheyne was limping down the stairs; Gregory Cheyne came after him. In an ordinary way Julian would have bolted back into the kitchen at the sight of him, but to-day she went straight forward and dropped a curtsey.

"Sir," she said, "where is he in London? Sir John Bulmer?"

She got less help from William Cheyne than from the servants, since the sound of Sir John's name drove him into a fury. After he had managed to lay his stick across her shoulders once or twice he shouted at her to go, to go to the devil with her sister.

When she saw the way clear to the street door, beyond the screens, Julian ran for it; she got the door open somehow and shut it behind her with a slam. Then she ran on till she could run no more, thinking that Master Cheyne was after her.

So there she was, out in the streets in the owl-light, knowing only that Meg was with Sir John Bulmer, but not where to find him.

She began by asking here and there, where he lived, but no one could tell her, and some were angry, shoving her out of the way, and some did not seem to hear her, and others frightened her more by trying to catch hold of her. A fat, wheezy fellow did that, and so she ran again, and apprentices shouted after her and threw dirt picked up from the kennel. Then she met a monk and asked him to tell her, catching at his sleeve, but he pushed her away and shook his head and told her she was a bad wench—so young and all. He was deaf, but July did not know that.

Once she knocked at a door because the candles were lit inside and the shutters not yet barred, and she could see a pleasant painted room with a couple of apprentices and journeymen, and maids, two or three, and the mistress of the house sitting by the hearth, while the master, a jolly merchant with a curly beard, drank his wine standing astraddle, with his back to the fire.

When she knocked, the boy who answered the door said he'd ask, and went in, and after a minute out came the merchant, and seemed surprised, and as though he had expected to see someone else. But she told him whom she was looking for, and why, at which he laughed and said, "Yes, yes," he'd take her to Sir John, but just now—he turned his head over his shoulder and seemed to listen, and then whispered, "Slip in, and through that door, and up the stairs and stay still as a mouse. I'll come as soon as I can."

But just then out came the mistress, and the merchant gave July a push in the chest, and shut the door on her. So when she had picked herself up she knocked at no more doors, and inquired of no more folk, but went on, because she must go on till she could go no further.

After a long time, seeing the steps and the dark shape of the great Cross in Cheap, all its niches and images hidden by the dusk, but the gilded cross at the top just showing a shadowy pale gleam against the deepening blue of the night sky, she sat down on the top step and made herself as small as she could, and thought that perhaps in her grey gown she might not be noticed there.

But she had forgotten her white headkerchief, and how it would show up, and hardly had she sat down when one of two men going by glanced aside, and he told the other, and they both stood, looking at her. All July could do was to turn her face towards the stone of the Cross, and then hide it in her hands. But she knew that one of them was coming towards her, and now stood over her, and she knew somehow that his hand was stretched out to touch her.

He did not touch her though, because he saw how she shrank. He only said, "Little maid, where's your home? What do you here alone at this hour of the night?"

She took her hands softly from her face and peered up at him, catching her breath when she saw he had only one eye. But she did not care for that; his voice was what mattered, which she thought was the most beautiful she had ever heard. Even though he spoke so gently it had a ringing note in it like a well-tuned bell.

"Oh! Sir!" she clutched his fingers, and then, with her other hand, his arm. "Tell me where is Sir John Bulmer?"

"Mass!" said he, "and you have asked one that *can* tell, being myself a man of the North Country. And in a manner, though distant, a kinsman, for my name's Aske, and my grandfather married Elizabeth Bigod, who was Sir John's wife's aunt," and he went on a little about the Bigods, Askes and Bulmers, not because he conceived that the child would be interested in such an excursion into genealogy, but having himself young sisters he guessed that it would be well to give the little thing time to stop shaking so.

"There now," he said after a minute, "now let us go softly over to Sir John's lodging, and as we go you shall tell, if you will, how you come to be seeking him."

She told him, all in a rush, and he gave a soundless whistle in the dark. He could not now, being kinsman to Sir John's wife, like the business, nor feel quite so sorry as he had felt for the little girl; but when Will muttered that they might well leave Sir John's drab's sister to find her own way, Aske told him to hold his tongue, and spoke gently to July, telling her that the place was not far off.

So they went out through Newgate, and along Holborne. Here there were fields, and houses with gardens, and here gentlemen would take lodgings who preferred to be out of the noise of the city, and free from the bustle of taverns, or who for some reason wished to be private.

It was nearly dark when they stopped at one of these houses, and Will knocked on the door.

July caught Aske's wrist. She had just remembered again to be frightened.

"Suppose they will not let me stay."

Aske said, "I'll come in and see they do."

He had not intended to come in, saying to himself, "Let the fellow keep his whore, but for my kinswoman's sake I'll have nothing to do with him or her." All the same, since he must go in out of pity for the child, he was not a little curious to see this wench that Sir John had bought. He was ashamed of the curiosity, but it was there.

An hour or so later he got up from the bench beside the fire in the room upstairs, and said he must be going. Sir John at once set Margaret down from his knee; he did not seem to be very sorry to part with Aske, but Margaret said he must come again, and soon.

At the door Aske paused. "Where's little Mistress Julian?"

Meg laughed. "To bed this hour ago. She was all eyes for you, and you never looked her way."

Aske grew a little red, because he knew where he had been looking; but he sent his duty to July, and kissed Meg on the cheek with Sir John standing close at her shoulder, and then went away.

As he and Will walked back through a night as black as the inside of a bag, he did not exactly reckon up whether by mortgaging his Manor at Empshott in Hampshire, and selling the farms his father had given him at home, he could have raised the price which Sir John had paid for Meg, and which Meg had told him, laughing. But he did feel suddenly sorry for himself, a younger son of no great house, and not yet even a barrister. Also he felt considerable dislike for Sir John Bulmer, yet intended to cultivate his acquaintance.

November 3

Gib came back with the flour from the Nuns' mill. He drove the donkey on very fiercely, and reached home breathless and red though it was a chill evening with a raw wind from the east. Yet when he had dumped the sack into the big flour bin, and turned the donkey out to graze, there seemed to have been no need for hurry at all, for he sat down on a stool by the fire, with his fingers idle and no book on his knee.

When his mother came in and asked had he got the flour, and good weight, and no mixing of rye-flour like that naughty fellow the miller was like to make, Gib only grunted. But when she was just going off with the pail to milk he said, "Miller said he's sold the brat to the miners."

"Did you ask?"

"No. I heard him say."

She went away then, nodding her head, and muttering, but to herself, that it was good hearing, for now there'll be no talking. Gib sat still by the fire, scraping out the dirt from under his nails with a thorn, and with thorns pricking into his mind so that he shrugged his shoulders and wagged his head to be rid of them and could not.

At last he gave a sort of groan, pulled on his shoes again, and picked up his staff from the corner of the room. Just then his mother came back with the full pails, and "Where are you going?" she asked him.

"To fetch the brat," he told her.

She slopped the milk over, she was so surprised, and that angered her as well as the anger she might well feel at such foolishness. So she railed at him: Would he have all the village and the Ladies know that he had taken that trull from Marrick, and got children on her? And see how he had made her spill the good milk. And if the miners had taken the child, what then? Would he to Jingle Pot mine this night, with the dark coming on, and the miners naughty men that cared for none, neither priest nor layman.

Gib, as answer to all that, told her that it was right for a priest to have a wife, and she laughed at him, and asked whether the miller's wench had been his wife. He said no, and let her talk on. But at last he shouted at her, "I'm going. And I shall bring him back," and went away, as angry as she was, and more unhappy. He did not want the little knave. He did not want it to be known that he had taken the miller's girl with him when he went. But he knew that this thing was laid upon him, and he must do it.

He came back by star-light, dragging after him a boy of five who whimpered and moaned, but who could speak no word, and whose voice was not like a human voice. Gib had paid a price for him, and all the way from Jingle Pot the child had struggled and cried. Gib's patience was out long before they got to the cottage, where all was dark and the fire dead. He shut the boy into the lean-to beside the house with the donkey and the sow; there was no window and he barred the door so that he could not break out and run away.

Sir John's men, and the maids he had hired to serve Meg in the hired house, had been busy in every corner and on every stairway making garlands and swags of holly, bays, ivy, box and yew. Now these hung from the row of wooden pegs at the top of the walls on which the painted cloths and the tapestries were stretched, so that the gods and goddesses, the virtues and vices, the huntsmen, wood-cutters, falconers and hunting dogs looked out from under real instead of pictured branches.

The kitchen had been furnace hot for a week past, and there was still, every day, a great business of baking. July, slinking about the house in the quiet way she had learned, came there, and stood beside one of the maids who was beating batter for a cake, full of raisins of the sun and spices. Her plump fingers showed pink through the batter, which was richly yellow, sticky with honey, and spotted with plump raisins and the black eyes of currants. About the wooden bowl lay the broken shells of a score or so of eggs. The woman bade July hold out her palm, and slapped into it a lump of sweet dough. July drifted off again, licking it with her tongue.

In the Hall they were laying places for dinner, so she did not stay there. In the solar, she could tell by the noise that came from it, there was a merry company. She meant to slip by the door, but it opened just too soon, and Meg burst out, laughing and running. After her Master Aske came, his hands stretched out, his face muffled in a hood, for he was Hoodman Blind. After him the other guests crowded the narrow passage, laughing and calling on him to catch Meg, or on Meg to give him the slip. ·

Aske caught Meg just beside July and threw his arms about her. For a second Meg tried to drag away, but could not; then she turned and drove her fist at his covered face.

He let her go, stepped back against the wall of the passage and stood there so long that July thought, "Oh! She has hurt him!" and for a minute she thought to strike Meg. But just then he pulled off the hood, and he was laughing.

Meg and he went back into the solar, and the door was shut, but July knew that he was angry (though he laughed); very angry, as if he had wanted to hurt Meg. July was not surprised at that, because Meg had hit out hard, yet somehow she was frightened. And as for Meg, her sister knew very well that warm shining look she gave to a man, and the way she leaned towards Aske as they went back into the solar together.

January 1

The clerks of the Great Wardrobe were busy already setting down in fair copy the gifts which had been sent that day to the King, by nobles, gentlemen and commoners. They had their rough lists, made out when the servants brought the gifts from their masters, but now they must go through all again, weighing, counting, and carefully describing the stuff before it was carted away to the Great Wardrobe. Some of the gifts were not in the gallery at all: "A pair of geldings, grey and a black bay," had been led off to the stables; "a beast called a civet" and a leopard were jolting away in their cages to the menagerie at the Tower.

But in the gallery, all over the floor, on the window-sills, upon chests and benches lay the King's New Year gifts, and amongst them moved certain of the clerks, while others sat with their lists and their pens ready; these last would call out the name of a giver, and the other clerks would answer with the gift. The names were first those of royal persons, for the lists went strictly in order of precedence.

"By the Queen," the list began, but there they must leave a blank, and a blank also for the Princess's gift, for the King would accept nothing from either of them. After that there were the Bishops' gifts.

"Carlisle?" "Two rings with a ruby and a diamond."

"Winchester?" "A gold candlestick," and so on.

Next came the Dukes and Earls, and first among these, though he was neither, Sir Thomas More. "The Lord Chancellor?" said one old clerk, and another answered, "A walking staff wrought with gold." These, the noblemen's gifts, were mostly of gold—gold tables and chessmen, a gold flagon for rose-water—"The weight?" asked the old clerk who was writing the list—and they weighed it and told him.

"Ten sovereigns in a glove." "Have you counted?" The old clerk checked his pen till the sovereigns were tipped out and counted.

Then there came the gifts of lords.

"The Lord Chamberlain?" "A pair of silver-gilt candlesticks."

"Lord Darcy?" "Gold in a crimson satin purse."

"How much?" "Six pounds, thirteen shillings and four pence."

"Lord Lisle?"

Again there was a pause, a long pause, for the clerk counted twice.

"Twenty pounds lacking six pence," he said, "in a blue satin purse."

"Lord Audley?" "A very pretty gift. A goodly sword, the hilt and pommel gilt and garnished."

"Tchk!" says the old clerk, "I have writ as you said, 'A goodly sword.' But no matter." He peered at the sword in the other's hands. "It is, as you say, a goodly sword."

After the lords came the Duchesses and the Countesses.

"The old Duchess of Norfolk?"

The clerk had opened a little gilt and enamelled box, very curious work. " 'The birth of Our Lord in a box' is what I have writ here," the old clerk prompted him, and they left it at that.

And so they went on, through the Ladies, the Chaplains, the gentlewomen, Knights and gentlemen, down to "A dumb man that brought the jowl of a sturgeon."

Master Aske came in with another gentleman from Gray's Inn. Those two and Meg, and one of Sir John's boys who had a sweet voice, sat by the fire singing while Meg played on the box regals Sir John had bought for her. Sir John sat by her, toying with her neck, or arm, or the gilt ball of her girdle. Now and again the servants brought wine, and spiced ale, which they drank till they were pretty merry, and very well pleased with the world.

Just before the candles were lighted July came in and sat down beside Meg's woman, away from the fire, but below a branch candlestick so that they could see to sew.

Meg saw her, and called out to her that here was kind Master Aske who had brought her a New Year's gift. Master Aske was singing just then; he smiled at Meg, and with his hand that was beating time he made a little gesture towards July.

At the end of that song they began another, and after that talked, and then asked riddles. When it was quite dark outside Master Aske and the other gentleman got up and said good-bye. Master Aske stood looking down at Meg, one hand on his hip; he was telling Meg about a masking there was that night at Gray's Inn; July bent her head and kept her eyes on the shift she was sewing, because she knew that he had forgotten the New Year's gift, and she would not remind him, not by so much as a look. As he went out she sat as still as a stone and a stone seemed to her to be sticking in her throat.

January 6

As Sir John and his household sat down to dine on Twelfth Night Master Aske came in. He had been invited, and now made his excuses for being late. "And it's not," said he, "that I stayed to see whether I could have a better dinner at Gray's, but my man did, and drank himself to sleep, so that I had to dress myself." He was dressed in crimson cloth, and crimson satin, under a black coat—all pretty well worn and carelessly put on, but his shirt was very fresh and fine with black Spanish work round the collar.

All that July saw, and then kept her eyes on her platter, because Master Aske's eye was looking about the room as though he sought someone.

"Sit down then. Sit down," Sir John Bulmer cried.

"A moment, pardon me. Ah—there she is."

July knew that he was coming towards her. He stretched out his hand over her shoulder, and there were a dozen gilded sugar plums in it.

"See, Mistress, a New Year's gift that a careless fellow brought, and then forgot."

July raised her head. He had been looking down at her with a smile, but now he was looking away, and July knew that his eye was upon Meg.

"I do not like sugar plums," she said, in a voice that was not her own.

"What! you do not like—"

He stood behind her still, and his hand was still stretched out with the sugar plums in it. He began to toss them up and down on his palm as if he were wondering what to do. "My niece Julian would give her soul for sugar plums," he said; and then, "See, I'll set them here, and you shall do as you will with them."

He tipped them out on the table and they rolled between a dish of stewed eels and a big mutton pasty.

Then he went away, and sat down where Meg made room for him beside her.

When dinner was over July found a place where she could be alone. There she laid the sugar plums in her lap and wept over them silently and steadily, till a good deal of the gilding was washed off them. Now and again she ate one, but that only made her more miserable, because they tasted of tears, made her throat ache, and gave her hiccups as well. Altogether her misery was extreme. Either she had hurt Master Aske or made him angry; probably the latter. She imagined him telling Meg, or his friends at the Inn, of the girl who behaved herself so unmannerly. Next time he came he would look at her with cold disapproval, or else speak a hard word. Yet the worst he could say was better than that she should have hurt him. The catastrophe of her wickedness loomed over her, darkness without a star, unbearable and irremediable.

January 8

There was snow on the wind, but sunshine in between the squalls, and the Prioress chose a sunny interval to go across the orchard to the workhouse to look over the new flails which the carpenter had been making. One of them hung ready on the wall, and the willow hand-staves for two more, peeled, and dried in the oven, lay beside the holly swingles on the bench. They waited only for the cap and thong of oxhide which would join swingle and stave. The Prioress, who liked to oversee these things herself, picked up each stave and swingle, one after the other, and turning towards the doorway looked along it to see that it was duly straight.

It was so that she saw Gib Dawe, who was passing the door. He had come to ask the Nuns' bailiff for some of the Priory dung for his garden, and he was not pleased to see the Prioress, because he knew that she did not like those who asked for Priory stuff, even for dung. "And of that same grudging humour," thought Gib, "are all the rich of the earth."

He had almost got by, but heard her call his name, so he came back and stood in the doorway, peering into the brown, dusty twilight of the shed where the sunshine struck in, smoke blue, and where there hung always a pleasant mingled smell of sawdust, oil and leather.

"Sir Gilbert," said the Prioress, "what is this I hear of you?"

Gib wondered what it was; she might have heard more than one thing that would not please her.

"How can I tell, Madame?"

"For a priest to stumble into fornication," the Prioress told him, with her cold grey eyes narrowed against the sun, "is one thing. And it is long ago and all but forgotten. Yet it's another matter that he should make an open scandal of it."

Gib knew now that she had heard the talk about him taking into his house the dumb child. He had his answer ready.

"Madame," said he, "I count it no scandalous thing, but meetly right for priests to marry and beget, even as other men. For if you read in the Scriptures—"

"And what," cried the Prioress, "have the Scriptures to do with it? Priests do not marry."

"That is in these latter times. But in the first, most holiest ages of the Church, as we may read in the Scriptures—"

The Prioress took fire at his schoolmastering tone, and tossed the hand-stave clattering down on the bench.

"What is your Scriptures against the Fathers and Doctors of the Church? Yea, and if that were not enough, Popes of old time and every time, that are successors of our lord St. Peter."

"Ha!" Gib was triumphant. "Peter Bar-Jona was himself a married man."

He thought that would end it, but the Prioress was stouter of heart and quicker witted than he knew. It took her a second to realize of whom he spoke so lightly, as if he spoke of Jankin the porter. But then she answered like a flash: "Was he then Pope of Rome when he had a wife? Was he priest at all?"

A man might have given him time to find a retort, but not a woman—certainly not the Prioress. She laughed in his face, and waved her hand as if to brush him and his argument away. Her sleeve was lined with fur, and as she moved a smell of musk came to him.

"The Scriptures—" he began, in a voice that should have frightened her, but she laughed again.

"Lord! You and your Scriptures! You've but the one word, like my brother's talking popinjay bird. And will you tell me that your Scriptures say the blessed St. Peter was a fornicator like you?" She looked up into his face quite unperturbed by his glance of smouldering fury, and now she spoke in a tone casual, reasonable, almost friendly, that galled him more than any other could have done.

"Go your ways, Master Priest, and hold your tongue about your sin, and the fruit of your sin. If the miller put force on you to take the brat (though what they say is that you sought him out wilfully), then keep the lad, but keep your mouth shut as to who begot him. Say that you needed a boy in the house to help the old wife, your mother. Say what you will that's not the truth. But how will you curse me the young maids and men when they fall into incontinence, when you declare yourself, unashamed, a fornicator?"

She stepped forward then, and Gib must move aside to get out of her way. He stood awhile after she had left him, biting at his nails, and then went home, still raging. "It's easy," he thought, "for a woman's tongue to outrun a man's." But that comforted him little. "She would not let me speak the truth, being a woman benighted in the old ways," he told himself, but that only spread salt on his raw self-respect. And truly the grudge he had against her was deeper. He told himself, "It is for mine honest dealing in taking charge of the lad, and for avowing the true pure knowledge of the New Learning that I am rebuked."

He should have rejoiced so to suffer for righteousness. He had brought the lad home, laying on himself that penance for the old sin, that he might be at peace with himself. A little also he had taken pleasure in braving, as one having the New Learning and new light, the censure of the ignorant. But the presence of the dumb brat in the house nagged at him like a toothache, and for a toothache few men would endure to be chidden.

January 30

Meg had gone out with Sir John to buy stuff for yet another gown. She had already, hanging from the perches in her chamber, gowns of green velvet and carnation satin, of white silk and blue silk, of black cut velvet with cloth of silver, and now she must have a gown of cloth of gold of Lucca. Sir John had pledged a gilt cup and a collar of enamel, and they had gone off to buy the stuff for it.

Master Aske, when he heard they were from home, said, "No matter, no matter," he would sit and wait awhile, and went into the Hall. July was there in the sunshine of one of the windows, with a piece of sewing, and old Mother Judde sat spinning by the hearth; she had a tuneless sort of song which she sang to the buzz and rattle of the wheel, and her attention was divided between the thread and a twelve-months infant belonging to one of the women, which was crawling about by the hearth.

Master Aske went over to the fire. Mother Judde looked up at him, but her head went on nodding to the working of her treadle, and she did not interrupt her crooning. He stood for a few minutes, warming his hands, and looking about the room, before he saw July. He took off his cap to her, hesitated, and then came across the room towards the window. July, her face burning with embarrassment and distress, scrambled off the seat and curtseyed to him. It seemed to her that there was nothing she could, and nothing he would, say to heal the unforgivable slight she had put upon him.

He said, "Good morning to you, Mistress July," and pushed aside July's thread and scissors from one of the cushions in the window-seat. When he had sat down she still stood in front of him, looking only at his shoes, her sewing hanging from her clasped hands. He took up the hem of it.

"Do you like sewing?" he asked.

July shook her head, but could not speak, so he asked her again, did she like sewing, and then, glancing up, saw her with her cheeks burning and tears in her eyes, and thought that she was a strange child, and was sorry for her because she was such a skinny little thing and her eyes so big.

"My niece July," he said, "loves to sew."

"I know."

"How do you know?"

"You said so."

He laughed. He remembered now that he had said so, talking to Meg, quietly, by the fire, a few nights ago.

"Then," he said, "you are a good girl to sit sewing, and with such neat small stitches that a man with one eye can hardly see them." He did not know what pains July had taken since she had heard of his July, to shorten and straighten the great staggering stitches she generally made. But as if he knew he put his arm about her and drew her to his knee, and spread out the shift, smoothing it over his leg.

To July it was as if a miracle had been performed. In a breath, and without a word said, all was forgiven. She began to grow bold.

"Sir—" she whispered, staring at the thick springy hair that fell across his cheek as he stooped over the piece of linen.

"Anon?" He glanced up at her, half smiling.

"Why have you only one eye?"

"Because someone came for me with a fishing rod and stuck out the other."

"Who?"

"One of my brothers. Kit. The second one."

"Oh!" July twisted her hands together. "Did it hurt?"

Master Aske, glancing up, saw her face, and his arm tightened about her for a second. "Oh yes," he told her lightly. "But never mind. It was a long time ago."

"Was he sorry?"

"Kit? He was. And the more when my father beat him."

"Is that—" July asked, having no sorrow to spare for Kit. "Is that why you are not a knight?" To her mind he was like that Sir Lancelot whose pre-eminence among all knights she had learned by listening to a book from which Meg sometimes read aloud.

"No," Master Aske explained. "But I am the third son, and that is why."

July gave up the mythical Sir Lancelot without a pang. "What are you?"

He told her, "A barrister—utter barrister, and I hope one day inner barrister." And then, without knowing why, he said what lurked in his thoughts these days, pricking him with uneasy shame. "Once I thought to have been a monk." He had not long intended that, and only years ago, but he could not rid it from his mind just now, seeing that now his desire was for a thing so different. And after he had spoken he sat silent, frowning.

It took July a little while to make up her mind that his frown did not mean that he was angry with her. Then she wriggled in his arm, and put a finger on the haft of the small knife that hung at his belt, so as to recall him from his thoughts.

"That's what I sharpen my pens with," he told her, but it was not the knife she was interested in.

"How many brothers have you?" she asked, "and sisters?"

"D'you want to know?"

She nodded fiercely, so he stuck out one hand with all the fingers spread, and bent a finger for each one he told her.

"There's Jack—he's the eldest, and my little July's father. Then my big sisters, Bet and July, who are dead." He paused to cross himself, and bowed his head, saying something in Latin. July crossed herself too.

"Then there's Kit, then me, then—"

"What is your name?"

"Mine?" He seemed surprised that she did not know it, as if it were written all over him. "Why! Robert. And then—"

"Do they call you Robert?"

"Sundays and Saints' Days," he told her, "but working days it's Robin."

"Silly!" she cried delightedly, loving him very much, and

having quite forgotten her awe of him. She began to laugh and dabbed her nose against his, and put her arms round his neck meaning to kiss him.

She did not, because just then Sir John came in, and Meg. Meg made very merry over July's lover, and said that they'd have a wedding before Lent began. It was not July she was teasing, for the three of them went on together to the solar, leaving July alone. Aske, who was hardly ever at a loss, was now a little put out, but he answered Meg's sallies as best he could, as they went up.

February 12

The lords whom the Duke of Norfolk had bidden to his house stood about the fireplace in the gallery, waiting for him to come to them. Their waiting should not have been tedious because there were many rarities to look at in the gallery: enamelled clocks, carved gems, some books most exquisitely printed by a press in Venice, and the arras hangings themselves, which showed the story of Ulysses, with gods and goddesses, ships, and many strange sea beasts. Though it was a dark day the room was bright with candle-flame and firelight and the Duke's gentlemen served his guests with cakes and plenty of very good wine.

But the lords, who knew pretty well for what kind of business they had been summoned, talked only in low voices, and not at all when the Duke's gentlemen were near, unless they spoke of trivial things.

At the end of about half an hour the Duke came in. He looked smaller than ever, with his face peering out of deep furs that faced and lined his long coat of purple and crimson velvet. He greeted them all with a sort of plain, blunt courtesy that made those who did not know him well think him to be the simple, honest soldier. Those that knew him better were aware that there were in his head too many schemes, and too great, for a man of that humour. Yet, whether they knew him or no, his manner always worked on others. The lords disposed themselves to listen patiently to business which, they could well guess, would be unpleasing to them.

And unpleasing it was, for the Duke, standing in the midst and stretching out his fine, small hands to the fire, set before them how ill the Pope had treated the King in not remitting to judgement in England this cause of the King's divorce, since here at home it should be judged according to the privileges of the kingdom. "And," said he, turning a ring with a great sapphire round and round on his finger, "even without those same privileges the cause should be judged here, for there are Doctors, learned and many, that say matrimonial causes belong to the temporal jurisdiction, so that the King, as Emperor in his kingdom, hath the judgement of them, and not the Pope. But come," said he, looking round at them again with the same candid air, "give me your advice, for well I believe there is no man here but would spend life and goods maintaining the King's rights."

After that there was a silence, so complete that they could hear the tick-tock of the German clock measuring time away. Someone coughed; someone shifted his feet in the rushes and stirred a sweet scent of rosemary, strawed along with other sweet herbs. When Lord Darcy spoke they all turned quickly towards him, and each man was glad that another had spoken before himself.

And what Darcy said pleased them too, for he promised the Duke that for his part life and goods were at the King's service. "But on the other part," he said, and met the Duke's eyes, "I have heard tell, and in divers books read, that matrimonial causes are spiritual and under the Church's jurisdiction. And, my Lord," said he—and now the Duke turned his glance away—"surely the King and his honourable Privy Council know what is right in this matter without coming to us to—" Darcy paused and laughed, "to pull the chestnuts out of the fire for them."

Many of those there murmured that yea, that was their counsel also, and none spoke against it, for the cunning old lord had shifted back the burden which the Duke had hoped might be shogged off on to the shoulders of the noblemen. The Duke was put out and showed it. He had thought by this device to threaten the Pope with the word that the Lords of England were in agreement with the King's Grace in this matter. It would have set him high in the King's favour had he succeeded where all others had failed; besides, if he had succeeded, his niece would have been Queen.

February 13

Meg lay late in bed, so Sir John sent up July and one of the women to bring her the bread and fish and ale that other people were breakfasting on this first morning of Lent. When the woman had gone down July stayed, laying Meg's cloth of gold petticoat in the big hutch at the foot of the bed, and hanging up her carnation satin gown, all of which had been cast down anyhow when Meg and Sir John came back, late last night, from the masking at Gray's Inn.

While July was busy Meg began again to tease her about Master Aske. July, as usual, took it in silence, because she knew well enough that if she answered, Meg would strike harder and probe deeper with words. But she heard how Master Aske, "your lover," was dressed last night, all in tags and tails and skins. "Cyclops he was. I asked him what Cyclops were, but he would only laugh at me. He said that was his part since he had one eye."

Meg stopped talking to drink some of the ale and July took the opportunity to curtsey and get to the door. "May I go now, Madame?"

"No—no—stay a little. Come here, sister."

When July came to the bed Meg surprised her very much by taking her in her arms. July stood very still while Meg held her cheek to cheek.

"Nay, sister," Meg whispered, "listen and I'll tell you a secret. It's your lover that I love much more than I love that great ox downstairs. Oh, he's a witty man, not a block of wood. And though he's but a third son, yet by the Mass I think he will be greater than Sir John one day, for there's—there's a power in him." Meg sat with her proud, lovely face lifted as though she looked into the future and saw fame there and heard horns blowing.

July tried to draw away and Meg let her, except that she still held her by the wrist.

"I think," said Meg, with one of her bright wild smiles, "I think—nay by Cupid! I know he loves me. Shall I tell you what he said? "You're too bright, Mistress Meg," he said, "for a man with but one eye. You'll make me blind." "Then, Sir," I answered him, "you'll have to go tapping along the roads with a stick; 'tis pity, but the maids will be the safer." "It's not the maids I'm after," says he, and then he laughed and said right under Sir John's nose, "A word in your ear. When *he's* out of the way one fine night, send me a token, and I'll come." "Holy Virgin! I will," I told him; and when he asked, "What will you send?" "A whetstone," I said, and because we laughed, and because I said "A whetstone," that fat ox thought I was promising Robin the prize for a lie."

And she began to sing, sawing July's hand up and down in time with the tune—

I saw a dog seething a souse,
And an ape thatching a house,
And a pudding eating a mouse.
I saw an egg eating a pie,
Give me a drink, my mouth is dry.
It is not long since I told a lie.
And I will have the whetstone if I may.

"But," she said, and suddenly flung July's hand away to cross her arms over her own breast and hug herself tight, "But he—Robin—when there was dancing caught my fingers hard—aye, cruel hard—and whispered to me that he meant it all." She laughed softly. "The dear fool! His voice was angry and his face as red as fire. 'I mean it, you bawd!' he said, as though he hated to mean it. But I'll make him love to mean it. He shall love me better than he loves Our Lady and all the Saints. Aye, even the prettiest little she-saint in the Calendar."

July was at the door. "You're jealous, sister," Meg cried. She did not mean what she said, because July was a child, but July had a scowling way with her, and Meg loved to tease. As the girl went out Meg began to sing, very softly, to herself—

A! Robin, gentle Robin—

March 8

Will Wall came bustling into the room at Gray's Inn, waving a letter and crying that here was the York carrier in, "and news for us, Master, from home."

Robert Aske took it; "Less noise, fellow," he bade Will, and slipped the letter under his thigh on the bench, and, though Will hung about, would not read it, but went on with his law book. Hatfield and Wat Clifton, who had looked up, returned to their occupations. Will, giving it up at last, crept away, shaking his head and pursing his lips. Master Hatfield and Master Clifton might guess what ailed his master that he was so surly these days, but Will knew.

After a time Aske took up the letter and broke the seal. He read it through twice, and then laid it on his knee, and opened the book again. But now he did not follow the learned arguments of Justice and Counsel long dead and gone, but instead he saw the house at Aughton and the fields about, and his father, on a hundred chance and trivial occasions: cracking nuts in his teeth by the fire; kneeling in church; drinking with the reapers at the harvest home. He could hear his voice too.

Presently he got up and went out. Will was in the little closet half-way down the stairs, where he slept; he was polishing the silver studs on his master's best belt. Aske went in, shut the door, and laid his hand on Will's shoulder from behind.

"The news is—my father's dead."

"Master Robin!" said Will turning to him, and then away. So they stood in silence, neither looking at the other, but Aske's hand hard on Will's shoulder.

"My mother," Aske said, in a stifled voice, "will be glad of his coming there where she is." And that made Will weep too, and they sat down together, as if they had been boys again, on Will's pallet, and spoke of Sir Robert, and of Aughton, with the long silences of old friendship.

But after a time Will began to fidget and grow uneasy, and at last said, "Master, may I speak?"

Aske turned to him, stared, frowned, and said, "No." But Will did speak.

"Master Robin," said he, "what the master leaves is all good—good name, good memory, good sons to carry on the name."

"Hush!" Aske told him but he would not.

"It's for you to leave sons as good," Will said, and then Aske sprang up, and went away from him to walk about the streets till dusk. Will was an unaccountable fellow, a sloven, a drunkard, and quarrelsome too sometimes, but he had spoken the truth. Marriage and sons—that was the right, sound, clean way for a man. But for Aske there was Margaret Cheyne, Sir John Bulmer's minion, and there was nothing else but her. He was in as great shame as he was in pain that it was so.

March 25

It was the last Sunday in Lent, but the fast had not enabled Robert Aske to call back his thoughts and desires from rushing, like flames on a wind, always towards Meg Cheyne. And in the evening, as he and another man had come back in the twilight to the gate of Gray's Inn, a boy was waiting for him, in a patched green coat, with cheeks as red as a strawberry and eyes as bright as a bird's.

"Who sent you?" said Aske, who had never seen the lad before.

"She told me not to say."

That set the other man laughing and he went away mocking and railing at Aske over his shoulder.

Then the boy took out of his pouch a thing wrapped in a scrap of carnation satin. It was heavy in Aske's hand, and he knew without opening it that it was the whetstone which is the prize for the greatest liar, and the token which Meg had promised.

"She bade me say 'to-night,' and she said you'd give me a groat, or more maybe."

Aske gave him two groats, and went up to his room; he was glad that neither of his fellows was there, and that he could cast the whetstone unseen into the coffer, still wrapped in the bright satin. He was glad also that they should not see him begin to dress himself hastily, without calling Will Wall, in his best clothes.

It was while he searched in the bigger coffer for his silver-studded belt that he came on the old sword which had belonged to his great grandfather, Sir Richard Aske, and which his father had given him when he was between boy and man. His fingers met the hilt, and he drew them away quickly, and sat back on his heels. He had not till this moment contemplated anything but to go to Meg. Now he remembered that he had sent no word at all by the boy. He need not go. He thought, "I'll not go," and then, "O! God forgive me!" He reached out his hand again and searched for the silver-studded belt till he found it.

March 26

Before it was light old Mother Judde came into the dark chamber, shielding with her hand the flame of the wax taper she carried. She lit with it all the candles in the room, and then pulled back the curtains of the bed, but softly so that the rings did not knock together.

"Come now," she said, and tittered as she looked down at the tumbled bed. "Come, my turtle-doves, you must part."

Aske started up. He neither felt nor looked like a turtle-dove, but like a young man who has a bad taste in his mouth from drinking too much wine last night, and a worse taste in his mind.

He did not glance at Meg, but flung out of bed and began to drag on his clothes. The room was at once cold and stuffy, and as the candles began to gutter and smoke the air grew worse.

"Dear heart," said Meg from the bed, "let me be your servant to tie your points," and she held out her arms.

"No," Aske told her. He managed to knot one pair of points, then, in tugging at it, broke it.

"I'll call Mother Judde," Meg said.

"No." Aske hated Mother Judde as much as anyone in the whole business. He finished dressing somehow, and then stood hesitating.

Meg held out her arms again, and he looked at her once and turned his head away, yet he went unwillingly to the bed, and let her take his hand.

"Kiss good-bye," she murmured, trying to draw him towards her. "No, nor it's not good-bye, for do not fear but I'll send again when I may, Robin. But not a whetstone this time. What shall it be?"

She was playing with his fingers, and now lifted his hand towards her lips. He snatched it away.

"Nothing. You shall not send, for I will not come."

When Mother Judde came back from letting him out by way of the brew-house door she found Meg in tears.

"Nay, nay," she tried to pat Meg's shoulder. "What a pair of true lovers. Here's one crying her eyes out, and the other gone off like a man to his hanging, as glum as a death's head. But heart up! There'll be other times."

Meg lifted her face. "No. He says no. And I love him. He doesn't know how I love him."

"Tchk! Tchk!" Mother Judde sat down on the bed and began to expound the ways of men, about which she knew a great deal. She promised Meg that the sweet gentleman should come again. She herself would be sorry if he did not, for Meg had paid her well, and Aske had crammed a gold piece into her hand as he went off.

March 29

In the afternoon, which was the afternoon of Good Friday, many of the Marrick people came, by custom, into the Nuns' Church. On that day the door in the screen between it and the Parish Church was set open, so that all who chose should come in with their baskets and bunches of wild violets and primroses, to straw on the Easter Sepulchre. So there was quite a crowd there to watch the Nuns' little brisk, round priest, as he washed the Rood from the Rood Screen in wine and water, wrapped it in a pall of green silk, and laid it, together with the Host in its gilt Pyx, in the Easter Sepulchre.

The Nuns' Priest moved about nimbly, bowing and prostrating himself very properly, but, every now and then, as he came near to the place where the Prioress sat, he spoke to her, though in a low voice, for he was a very cheerful and garrulous man.

Gib came to the door in the screen and watched for a while; the Marrick smith was with him who, like Gib, was one who called himself one of the "known men."

"Ha! See!" said the smith, speaking behind his hand, when the Nuns' Priest laid the Pyx beside the hidden crucifix, "there goes little Jack into the box."

Gib smiled at the joke, but sternly. Here in the Dale, where folk were so ignorant and superstitious, he was fortunate, and knew it, to find even one who had seen the light of the New Learning. Yet the smith's bludgeoning wit did not please him, nor did it please him that the fellow, because he could slowly spell out the English Scriptures—at least if they were fairly printed—thought himself sufficient to debate points of doctrine with Gib.

The women and children were now about the Sepulchre, casting on their flowers. Among them was the Priory servant Malle. She had a round basket full of violets, white and blue, and now she was throwing great handfuls among the rest, jumping up and down on her feet and laughing, with squawks like a hen.

"Tchah!" said Gib, and turned back into the Parish Church; but the smith stayed, and began to call out to one or other of the crowd in the Nuns' Church, jesting with them, since the Prioress had gone away now, and the Priest was never one to spoil other folks' enjoyment.

April 12

Dame Anne Ladyman came back from a visit to her brother's house, where his youngest girl had been married. Her brother lived beyond York, so she had spent some hours in the city, and came back therefore not only with news, but laden with stuff from the York shops.

This she produced first in the Parlour for all to see: a little frail of figs, some spices, a jar of green ginger, three bobbins of silver thread to work the new black satin cover for the Gospel Book, half a pound of pins, and a fine large new book of paper for the Cellaress's accounts.

The news she kept back, at least most and the best of it, till she and the Prioress sat down to supper together with the priest. Then Dame Anne had much to say of the wedding, of this one's surly husband who beat her, or that one's unfaithful husband who kept his whore in the house, or that other's undutiful son who wasted his money on harlots. She had, in a short time, acquired an amazing knowledge of such happenings. The little priest crowed with laughter, or clucked with the correct amount of horror, at her tales. The Prioress listened with half an ear. Nowadays, since this kind of thing had ceased in any way to interest her, it had ceased also to shock her. She let Dame Anne have her head; they two understood each other now.

By the time they sat round the fire, eating walnuts kept fresh all winter in salt under damp hay, Dame Anne had disposed of scandals among her acquaintances, and was touching on the King's affairs. For at her brother's house had been a man of the Bishop of Durham, a very courteous gentleman but of a free tongue. "Oh! Jesu Mercy!" Dame Anne threw up her hands, "I would I could tell you some of the words he said. But I could not for shame. I promise you I chid him more than once. 'For remember I'm a Religious,' I told him, and he said—" She whispered what he had said, which did not amount, the Prioress thought, to very much, unless it had a meaning which she could not be bothered to seek out.

"But I would tell you," Dame Anne ran on, "how he spoke against this lady of the King's, calling her no better than a common stewed whore. 'Fie, Sir,' says I, 'not in my hearing!' But he would have it she was a common stewed whore that ruled the King, and made all the spiritualty to be beggared, and the temporalty too. 'But,' says he, 'when the great wind shall rise in the West we shall have news afterwards.'"

"What news?" the priest asked, but Dame Anne did not know, and now clapped her hands together and said: "And should I forget to tell you what that same servant of the Bishop told me?" The Prioress yawned discreetly behind her hand. Dame Anne, she thought, was sometimes hardly to be borne. She began to wonder why she did indeed bear with her so frequently.

Then she found herself listening. For among all his gallantries the Bishop of Durham's gentleman had spoken at least one piece of sense. He had told Dame Anne that if any in England be converted from any erroneous faith and misbelief in the Christian and Catholic faith, then will the King pay yearly, for and towards his or her relief and finding, during her life natural, three half-pence every day. So Dame Anne reported the Bishop's gentleman, and the Prioress had no doubt but that those were the very words he had used, for she knew Dame Anne to be possessed of a most remarkably accurate memory.

"Malle!" said the Prioress, and Dame Anne nodded, "Malle!"

The Prioress stood up, shaking the walnut shells from her lap into the fire where they crackled sharply.

"Let us write now to the King's Grace," she said.

The priest sighed and drank up his wine hastily. He knew that he would have to write the letter, for the Prioress's penmanship was crabbed. So the servants were sent for to clear the table, and Malle was sent for to tell what her name was before she was christened, since the Bishop's gentleman had instructed Dame Anne that it would be necessary to write this in the letter.

Yet when they had questioned Malle, bidding her repeat her old name over and over, and had at last sent her away, the priest hesitated with the pen in his hand.

"It is no name at all," he objected. "I cannot write it."

"Do as well as you may," the Prioress urged.

He wrote, scored it out, wrote, altered it, and shoved the paper over.

"I cannot say it," the Prioress confessed, after she had tried once or twice. "It is, as you say, no name at all, yet it has a most heathenish look," and she passed the paper back to the priest.

"I never thought," she said softly to Dame Anne as he bent over his writing, "that the Priory should be the better for the creature Malle."

May 20

M. de Montfalconnet, the Emperor's messenger, was brought through the base-court, where some hens were picking, to a little inner court, and so into the house, which was small and dark, having been built in the old days when windows were few because all houses must be defensible.

The Queen got up from among a few of her ladies, and came towards him. She had been at prayer half the night, and her eyes were red; never careful about dress, she now looked no finer than any citizen's wife, and not so neat. Indeed she made a jest of her disarray at the sight of the Emperor's messenger and said that he found them like busy house-wives at their sewing and spinning. But when she had laughed her lips shook because it was so seldom now that she saw a friend. M. de Montfalconnet, angry and sorry (and he did not know whether one more than the other), went down on both knees and kissed her hand.

When she had sent the ladies away she asked him many questions about the Emperor, her nephew, for Monsieur was the Master of the Imperial Household. And then she sat smiling, her eyes distant, her hands idle in her lap and her mind far away in the past. Only after some time did either of them mention that which lay at the core of the unhappy present—namely, the business of the King's divorce. Then Monsieur listened while the Queen urged on him arguments, appeals and encouragements. If the Pope would only give sentence, she said, twisting her hands together, the matter would be settled, "and I do assure you that the sentence, what-ever it is, will increase and re-establish the friendship be-tween—my—between the King's Grace and the Emperor."

Montfalconnet was silent. He could not think it, but he in-clined his head, torn once more between anger and pity, and answered only that he would surely do all he could to explain her advice to the Emperor.

But the Queen seemed hardly to hear him, so eagerly did she continue to pour out her arguments. "You see," she interrupted herself with a half apology, "I have so long time to think of all these matters. My nephew—the Emperor—has many other cares, but I have none but this. So I think I see clearest."

Yet with very little of all that she told him could Montfalcon-net agree. She would have it that if once the sentence were given the King would obey. ("Not now. Not now, whatever might have been once," he thought.)

"The Pope," she said, lifting her chin, and showing him for an instant the face of an indomitable woman, "the Pope does very wrong so long to delay. And if the decision goes against me I'll bear it for the honour of God, for Monsieur, I have not deserved it."

After she had sat brooding for a while she began to say: "If I could but speak once to the King, if—" but on that she had to get up from her chair and go to the window so that he could not see her face. "If I could speak to him," she said, with her back to Montfalconnet, "all that has happened would be as nought—because he is so—good." Montfalconnet turned away at the sound of her voice. She said, with difficulty, "He would be kinder to me than ever. But they will not let me see him."

Montfalconnet would have been glad to get himself out of the room at once, and in silence, but ceremony forbade it. He could only go down on his knee and keep his eyes strictly upon the cap in his hand till she came back to her chair and he could take his leave.

June 20

Gib found the door of the Marrick Church standing open. "God's Body!" he muttered, thinking that as likely as not he would find the sheep in the sanctuary, dropping their dung everywhere. But when he went in there was no scurry and stampede of small hoofs; only a sudden quiet, after the living air outside, and a twilight that kept him standing for a moment till his eyes were used to it.

The Parish Church at Marrick had been painted round about the walls at the same time as the Nuns' Church, that is to say nearly two hundred years ago. But whereas the pictures in the Nuns' Church were all of the life of St. Benedict on the one side, and on the other the Prophets, here, for the instruction of the people, were shown the Precursors of Christ, two on the North and two on the South wall, on either side of the iron grille which divided the two parts of the Church, and from these, coming East towards the Chancel, were pictures of the birth, life and death of Christ, and of His rising from the dead. Of the Precursors, Isaac unfortunately was almost swallowed up now with creeping stains of damp; only his father's curved, menacing knife showed above the fringes of the mould, and in the corner a very large ram in a very small thornbush. David too had suffered, though not so much as his neighbour, but his fine kingly blue mantle had deadened to pale grey, because the damp of the wall had caught the lime with which the paint had been laid on.

The two Precursors on the South wall were however both of them in good fettle. There was Joseph, as Master of the Household to the King of Egypt, neat as a grasshopper in a green surcoat of the old fashion, with a heavy jewelled belt round his hips, and his yellow hair rolled up in a curl on each side of his face. And next to him stood Solomon, with the Temple on a hill behind him, but it was very like the Friar's Church at Richmond. Solomon was bearded and handsome in a purple robe sewn with golden bees.

At the feet of Solomon knelt Malle, the serving woman. She crossed herself many times, and then held out her clasped hands, and bent her head before the picture.

Gib went down the aisle towards her. She did not notice him till he was quite near and then she jumped up and backed away a little, because she could see that he was angry.

"What," he said, "is this idolatry?"

She shook her head.

"What are you doing?"

"I pray to this Saint," she told him.

That made him angrier, but now he was not angry with her but with the Prioress, the Ladies, and their Priest—with all those who wore warm, fine clothing, and lived delicately, who were proud, who despised the poor, who worshipped the painted images of Saints, who left this christened soul so deep in ignorance that she worshipped King Solomon.

"Did they not teach you the Faith?" he asked her.

"Oh! yes," she said, "they did indeed. The priest, the old man, brought me in here and told me. He told me of those—" and she pointed up the Church to the Rood Screen. The Screen and the paintings on it were much newer than the pictures on the walls, having been set there not much more than thirty years ago by old Sir Roger Aske. The colours were much fresher, and, as they were painted with oil and resin in the paints, more deep and glorious than the frescoes, and besides that picked out with much gold leaf, so that the burnished haloes of the Apostles, who stood in rank along the Screen, shone darkly, even in the dim light of the Church; and their robes were scarlet, green, azure, purple, and rose colour.

Gib looked at them and snorted. "You shall not make to you gods of silver, neither shall you make to you gods of gold," he said, but Malle had left him, and was moving towards the Screen. She stopped before the picture of St. Philip who stood against a background of scarlet patterned with gold. His prettily tousled hair showed up in curls against his halo; his cloak was green as new beech leaves, and under it was a sumptuous gown of brocade, the colour of ripe corn, with the pattern of a huge vine growing all over it, curved and notched stock, leaves, tendrils, heavy grape bunches and all.

"These," said Malle, as Gib came up behind her, "are the Holy Apostles, that sit on thrones in heaven." And she began to recite their names, but when she had pointed at St. James she faltered. "The priest was called to dinner and could not stay," she said, "so I do not know them all."

Gib looked at her. Her face was dirty, her kerchief torn, and her toes were coming through one of her shoes. He looked at the row of splendid and pompous figures that stretched across the Church, glowing with colour and gold. Then he raised his arm, and pointed to where the tortured Christ hung, half naked between the blue, starred mantle of the Virgin, and St. John's crimson cloak.

"*He* said, 'How hard it is for a rich man to enter into the Kingdom of Heaven.' And *He* said, 'Woe be to you that are rich.' And again *He* said, 'The rich man also died and was buried in Hell.' " Gib was thinking of the Prioress and the Nuns' Priest, the Bishops and great Abbots, and his voice grated. "For these," he told Malle, sweeping his hand along the length of the screen, "were fishermen, he, and he, and those two. And the Lord" (he pointed again at the great Rood), "He was a carpenter's son, and a carpenter."

She looked at him with her mouth open, foolish, but most intent.

"God." He jabbed his finger towards the Christ. "A poor man, a carpenter!" And warmed by his triumphant indignation against all the great and the rich, he seized her by the wrist and dragged her towards the font, where, painted on the wall, the angels told the news to the poor shepherds, first of all men.

So he began to instruct her, going from picture to picture, and she listened with strained attention, for the sake of which he bore with her foolishness, though now and again he must chide her. For when he was telling her of the child in the manger she laid a finger on the brown dog, which sat, upright and very respectful behind the youngest shepherd's feet, calling him "Trusty," which was the name of one of the convent's sheep dogs. "Listen to what I tell you," he bade her sharply. Again, when they stood before the picture through which Christ rode, in the midst of a crowd of folk in mushroom coloured hoods, upon a donkey not much bigger than a dog, she wanted to know whether that was the miller's donkey. This time he was less patient, and struck her with the flat of his hand between the shoulder blades, and bade her hold her tongue.

In the end they came again to the Rood Screen, and stood below the Rood. Gib had had enough, and was for leaving her, but she caught at his gown and he waited.

"Who is—that one—and that one?" she asked and nodded

her head to the picture of the baby in the hay, and then lifted her wide, vague eyes towards the Rood.

He cried "Mass!" angrily, and told her, "God," but when she murmured after him "God?" he was not so much angry as amazed at the vacancy of her simplicity. It was not even, he thought, like pouring knowledge into the little cup of a child's understanding, but into a pail that had holes in it. How could such a one learn to know the incomprehensible? What in her twilight mind was God?

"The living God," he said, and he spoke aloud, but more to himself than to her, the words that came into his mind. " 'I am the first and the last, and am alive and was dead, and behold I am alive for ever more.' "

She stared at him, with something of light in her look that was usually as vague and dim as the colourless, half transparent jelly fishes that bob about in the clear fringes of the tide as it slides in over a sandy shore.

"Sir," she mumbled, "what for did he this thing? What for?"

Of course she could not understand, and he pushed past her as he said, "To shew us the face of God. To brast the chain of sin. To be the glory of his people Israel."

But at the door she was beside him.

"Where is he—now?"

He lifted his arm and pointed up to the sky beyond the steep woods, and beyond the edge of the fells where a huge white cloud stood in the blue, leaning its head towards the Dale.

She did not follow him any further, but when he looked back from the gate of the churchyard she was staring up under her hand towards Gawnless Wood where a woodcutter was working. The ringing of the axe on the tree came faint but clear in the summer silence.

July 15

Master William Cowper had come to Marrick Priory to buy wool. Last night he had supped with the Prioress and been pleasant with her and those Nuns that were her guests; but to-day was for business; he must weigh the Priory wool-clip and be off to the next seller up the Dale.

He had begun the day by a brief, and, he had reason to believe, a private interview, with the Priory bailiff. At nine, just as the bell began to ring for Chapter Mass, he came into the wool-barn where the scale-beam hung from the roof and the wool fells lay in piles ready for weighing. His man came after him with the two seven-pound weights slung over his shoulder by a leathern strap, and the other odd weights in a bag. The inevitable knot of little boys closed in from the wide open doors; a grey goose approached, stared about with haughty disapproval and went away into the sunshine.

"Now," said Will Cowper, speaking very short and brisk, "to work, Master Bailiff. Where's your stone for the weighing?"

But the bailiff had forgotten to bring his book in which to write the tally of the convent's wool, so his man had to be sent to fetch it, and consequently only Will and the bailiff were at the weighing of the big fourteen-pound block of stone against Will Cowper's two weights; the stone was that same which had been used in wool weighing for longer than any could remember. It was but a form to weigh it, so they two did it while the two Priory servants went to fetch the fleeces to the scales.

When the bailiff's man came back Will and the bailiff stood opposite each other, watching the scales swing under the first tod. The wool scale dipped, so Will put into the weight-pan a two-pound weight from those in the bag, and—

"Two to the wool," said he as the scales steadied; the bailiff nodded, and they went on with the next lot of fleeces.

The bell in the church tower rang faster, so they knew it was nearly time for Mass, and that all the Ladies would soon be piously occupied in church. The bell rang on. Will sang out, "Five pounds less three due to the wool leaves two pounds to the weights."

Just then the Prioress came into the barn. She had on a riding hat above her hood, and gloves on her hands.

Will and the bailiff turned. They stood so still that the two men loading fleeces on the scales turned too, and stood, and stared. There was a short but pregnant silence, during which they heard the after-song of the last stroke of the bell hum through the sunny air and die away.

Will Cowper stammered, "Not—not at Mass, sister?"

The Prioress looked from one to the other of them; she smiled.

"I thought this morning when I saw your heads so close laid together that it were well I came to the weighing."

"You saw—" Will looked at his sister in dismay and dislike; but there was respect in his glance too.

"Well, no—I should not say I saw you. But I saw your shadows on the stable wall, and your chins wagging. So I said to myself—"It is time my father's wool weights were brought to the sheriff for assay, seeing that they are old.' "

No one said anything, until the Prioress asked Will would he not go with her. Then he began to bluster, asking her did she think the weights were loaded?

"Why," said she, "whether loaded to my loss, or overlight to yours, brother, neither thou nor I would be willing to defraud other."

"No!" cried Will. "No!" and swore it by Cock's Bones. "Well then—"

"Well then," Will wiped his brow, "a God's Name, if you have other weights—"

"There's weights in the kitchen."

"Then we'll use those for this time. It's true that these are old, and may be not—not—" He picked up the seven-pound weights by their strap, and slung them away into a dark place beside the wall. When weights had been fetched from the kitchen they settled again to the weighing. The Prioress sat at one end of the bench by the door, Will at the other; each had a book to enter in the number of fleeces weighed. Will's man stood by the scale calling the weights; the bailiff sweated carrying the fleeces from the pile to the scale, and away again. No one said that he should do his man's job, but he did it. No one spoke all through the weighing except the necessary words, as when Will's man would call, perhaps, "Two to the wool," if the fleeces weighed heavier than the 28 pounds of a tod, or "Three to the weights," if the three-pound weight was needed to bring the fleeces down to the level. When they had weighed this year's wool clip the bailiff began to bring out last year's, and, when that was weighed, yellowed fleeces from the year before. Will fidgeted with his feet and scowled over his book, but he said nothing. When the Prioress said, "All at one price," he said, "Aye."

Will and his man went away, after they had all, the bailiff as well, drunk a cup of ale together. The Prioress turned back from the gate. The bailiff's man and the two servants, still goggle-eyed from the events of the morning, took themselves off; the Prioress nodded her head cheerfully to the bailiff.

"All the old wool sold, and at the price of this year's clip. That was good."

The bailiff, crimson from heat already, managed to colour deeper.

"Madame—I—I—"

The Prioress went on as if he had not spoken.

"Since we have sold so well I look to do a thing I have some while intended. Know you of a good craftsman who could wainscot my chamber fairly?"

The bailiff, though unable at once to credit and understand so strange an oblivion, could tell the Prioress of a good Richmond craftsman, a right worthy man.

"An honest workman?"

The bailiff choked, and said, "Yea, honest," and would have said more but that he realized in time that the Prioress was that rare woman, one who will let facts work in silence. She did not even tell him what he knew very well, that she would watch him like a hawk, and the next trick he tried to play her, if ever he should try, would be the last. She only bade him look to the scythes in good time for the harvesting, and then went up to her chamber with the wool-book, which he had used to keep, under her arm.

The story of the bailiff's excursion into double dealing leaked out, but not through the Prioress. It spread like damp on a wall, upwards, from the bailiff's man. So it was the Ladies who last heard it, and more than a week after Will Cowper had gone. Among them, when the topic had been privately but exhaustively discussed, there were two schools of thought. The more timorous were shaken to their very souls by the knowledge that such wolves as Master Cowper and their own bailiff wore doublet and hosen and walked the earth on two legs, but ravening. One or two even said, but erroneously, that they would not sleep easy in their beds, knowing that wickedness prowled so near. The others, more adventurous, triumphed in the triumph of their Prioress. "Mass! If we could but have seen the bailiff's face!" they cried, "down on his knees clutching at the Lady's habit, praying for mercy!" "And Master Cowper, he wept they say."

So they relished the affair, each after her own manner. But there was about it something not one of them could understand. Neither soon nor late did their Prioress speak a word of blame, either of her brother or of the bailiff. Indeed, to deepen their incomprehension, it was whispered, on the authority of Dame Anne Ladyman, that Dame Christabel had said, Perdy! she loved Will for it, the rascal! That was beyond them.

August 3

Robert Aske had just parted from a client after walking and talking with him a while in Paul's, when he came up against Sir John Bulmer, whom he had not seen since April, and who was the last man on earth he wanted to see. He regretted now that he had stayed for the summer vacation lectures at Gray's; Hal had gone off weeks ago; Clifton last Thursday. However, he neither would nor could run away from Sir John, so they turned and walked together out of the Cathedral into the sunshine of a day of heavy, thundery heat.

"One told me that I should find you here," Sir John began. "Often I have meant to seek you out, but never—"

Aske interrupted him by standing still.

"Well, you've found me. What would you have of me?"

Sir John, facing him but not looking at him at all, pulled off his cap and began to fidget with the brooch in it, a pretty thing of Europa riding on a golden bull. He began to talk in starts, jerks and half sentences. "None of the servants will tell, but maybe—not even Mother Judde, not a word, and she, if any of them—by God's Death, I don't trust her. Only the boy spoke clear enough, yet he's only a child." He put up a hand to tug at his hair, and then cried, "Did you come to the house and lie with her that night I rid to Dorking the first time?" and he looked Aske in the face at last.

Aske did not pretend he did not know who "she" was, but he was by no means so simple as to answer such a question either with yea or nay.

"And what night was that?"

"Lady Day night."

"And other times you rid to Dorking, you say. What of them?"

"The lad—he says you ever said nay but that first time he was sent. Besides, I had set watch."

"And what," Aske fenced, playing for time as he wondered whether, if put to it, he could speak a flat lie, "and what did I say to the lad that one time?"

"He says you gave him a groat."

"I see," said Aske, "that I must beware how I give groats to boys," and he began to walk again; for a moment he thought he had shaken off Sir John, but he came up behind and caught him by the elbow.

"Wait a minute, for I need counsel. I must go home northwards soon. I have thought much of how my wife will bear the matter of a bawd. So I consider whether to take her with me or fairly turn her off here in London."

Aske could have laughed aloud at such a simple cunning,

though indeed laughter, in this nasty business, was a dismal thing.

He said: "I'm a bachelor. I've neither wife nor bawd. Go you to others for counsel."

"Well," Sir John watched him narrowly, "I think I shall turn her off."

"Since," said Aske steadily, "I am kinsman to your wife, though distantly, I think you would do well."

It was a comfort to be able to speak the exact truth, and he could see that whatever answer he had expected, Sir John had not expected that, and was now at a loss, for he put up his hand again to tug at his hair, dropped his cap, stooped for it and came up very red.

"No, by God's Blood," he cried, "I'll not believe it of you," and he caught Aske's hand and wrung it, crying, "Forgive me, but I think I'm crazed with loving her. You do not understand, she—" and he ran on, doing his best to make Aske understand.

When he could escape from those undesired confidences Aske set off alone, and at a great pace, for the river, though not with any other purpose than to keep moving. It was noon, and the dogs lay panting in the shade; Aske felt the sweat run down his back and his shoulders prick at the touch of the hair shirt he had worn since Lady Day.

October 14

Sir John and his household started for the North early in the morning in a cold downpour of rain. They came along Holborne towards Newgate because they must strike the road for Highgate and the North, and so they passed the end of Gray's Inn Lane.

July, riding behind one of the servants, peered through the driving shower; she could see the tops of the trees tossing in the garden of the Inn; she could see the smoke of the kitchen chimneys driven aside by the rain. Master Aske was there, asleep yet perhaps; or drinking his ale and eating his breakfast before going off to the Courts at Westminster. But she was being taken away to the North Country, and she supposed she should never see him again. He had not been to the house for months now; no one had told her why, but July knew: it was because Master Aske had at last found out the things that Meg did. She thought, as they rode out from the gate into the slanting cold rain and the drowned countryside, that she could not endure to be so unhappy. All the same she had to endure it.

October 18

Sir John Bulmer held the Manor of Pinchinthorpe, eight miles or so from his house at Wilton. There was a little house at Pinchinthorpe, but old and in disrepair, for it had not been used for some time. However it was a convenient distance from Wilton; neither too far for Sir John to ride easily between one and the other, nor yet scandalously close. Meg mocked at him, but angrily, when he told her why he would leave her at Pinchinthorpe. She could not move him though in this; he said that it should be so. "My son is at Wilton," he told her.

"Lord! and what of that?"

"I will not put him to shame," he said, and scowled at her.

They came to Pinchinthorpe at dusk and rode into the little grassy courtyard where brambles sprawled in the corners. The Hall itself was opposite them; they could see winking lights in all the windows, for the servants whom Sir John had sent forward had got the fire lit there.

Yet when they went in the Hall was very cold. There was no furniture but trestle tables and a few benches, and in a corner a heap of teazles and some sickles and a little painted cupboard, in which they found two cracked earthen pots.

Sir John was surly, because now that he was so nearly home he could not but be thinking what he would say to his wife, Dame Anne, when he saw her; whether to tell of Meg or leave her to find out he could not decide. Meg was angry because she was tired, and because Pinchinthorpe was such a poor and rustic place. "Goodman John," she called Sir John, as if he were a farmer, jeering at him. "Shall I brew and bake and milk the kine?" she asked him. "Jesu! had I known before I came with you I'd have gone—"

He struck her then and she snatched at his dagger and tried to draw it against him. July left them, creeping out quietly into the chill and now dark night. She was hungry, but it was better to be quiet than to eat. She felt her way up the outside stair to the room where they would sleep, and found that the servants had set up the beds, though not the sparvers and curtains to them. She crept into one in the further small chamber where she supposed she would lie with Meg's woman. She was too tired and too cold to sleep at once, and the strange nakedness of sleeping without curtains kept her waking long, watching the slant of moonlight that edged across the floor. To all her old and usual fears of Meg, of Sir John, of the devil, had been added a new one—the fear of Sir John's wife. Meg laughed at Sir John's discomfort, but July could not laugh, being herself in the grip of a shame more disabling than Sir John's own. As she lay cowering in bed she said over and over, "Oh! we should not be here. We should not be here." For Dame Anne was kinswoman to Master Aske; he had told her so on that evening when he had found her at the Cross in Cheap; and if Dame Anne was angry and all her kinsfolk angry, July was undone. She could not distinguish in blame, and did not expect any other to distinguish, between herself and Meg.

1533

February 24

Lord Darcy sat in the house at Stepney reading a book of devotion by the light of the branch of wax candles which stood behind his chair. He kept his eyes on the page faithfully enough, but his mind wandered. Thoughts about Templehurst mingled with his meditations on mortality: the roof of the great chamber that needed mending, the young fawns that should be fed in the lower close; or there would come clear and near before the eye of his mind a glance of the Chequer Chamber window, of the steps going down to the Chapel, of the trees beyond the distant river, sleeping on a summer evening with the light dying behind them.

At last he dropped the book beside the chair and went over to the window. Outside the rain fell, steady and dark; it leaked through the casements, running in heavy drops along the iron bars of the windows and splashing down on the sill. In places it bubbled and spat upwards from the corner of the window frames. The gentlemen who were with him in the room watched him, then turned back to their occupations.

"By the Rood!" said Darcy, half aloud, "I would I were at home in the North Country."

He did not turn when someone knocked at the door, supposing it to be the servants with more lights; but as well as the lights they brought in his brother-in-law, Lord Sandys of the Vine, who slung off his heavy red felt coat which was dark across the shoulders where the rain had soaked in, and below that all silvery with the standing drops. He shook it before he tossed it to one of the gentlemen, and the wet flew off it and spattered the dogs that had run forward to greet him, so that they backed away.

He kissed Darcy, and said, holding him hard by the shoulder and looking him in the eye, "I'm soaked to the bone. Will you lend me a dry gown to put on?"

"That I will. Come within." Darcy led him towards the door of his bed-chamber, then over his shoulder, bade one of the gentlemen, "Bring light, James."

In the bed-chamber, when James had lit the fire, and set candles, Darcy took Sandys by the arm and brought him to the high-backed bench in front of the hearth where two green cushions were set, worked with the Buck's Head in silver.

"Now, tell me your news," said he.

Sandys leaned towards him so that their shoulders touched, and said in a low voice, "She is with child."

"You mean the King's—"

"Sh!" Sandys looked over his shoulder at the gentleman, leaning against the door, and paring his nails with a little knife.

"Keep me the door, James," said Darcy, and when the young gentleman had gone out—"Well then, the Marchioness of Pembroke."

Sandys nodded, and spat in the fire. "Nan Boleyn," he said.

"Who told you it?"

"She did."

"She? Told *you*?"

"She told us all—all that were waiting outside the King's Chamber."

"Who?"

"God's Body! a dozen or so—Exeter, Huntingdon, Norfolk, Wyatt too."

"Who was her lover once."

"They say so."

"Well I can believe it. And it's not *credo quia impossibile est.*" Sandys shrugged and went on.

"I was talking with Wyatt as we warmed our hands at a brazier, when the door of the King's Chamber opens, and out prances my Lady Marchioness, the Queen's jewels all over her, aye, even some I can remember to have seen Her Grace wear when first she came from Spain. And this one had more too; they say the King gives her jewels every day. She'd as many as the Virgin of Conques.

[234]

"So out she comes, twisting her hands together like this," and he wrung his hands daintily together.

"She looks round at us all, and then cries out to Wyatt, naming him by name—'Sir Thomas! Sir Thomas! By the Holy Virgin you'll not guess what the King says.' Wyatt began to stroke his beard like he does when he's thinking out one of his pretty sayings, but she didn't give him time.

"'You know what I told you yesterday, how sharply I long for apples? I told His Grace, and he says it means I am with child,' and back she skipped into the Privy Chamber, cackling like a hen."

"God's Soul!" said Darcy, "and did she clap her hands to her belly like that?"

"She did, Tom."

They sat together in silence for quite a long time before Sandys murmured, "Will he marry her?" and then answered his own question. "But he cannot, unless the Pope at last should give sentence against the Queen."

Darcy leaned his head near and spoke with his lips close to Sandys' ear.

"I was told—but did not then believe it—"

"Tell me first who told you."

"No, never mind. I was told that about a month ago now this new Archbishop, Cranmer, married them. It was very secret, but folks will talk."

"But," persisted Sandys, "no Archbishop can, while the appeal lies at Rome."

Darcy looked at him with his head tipped back and angry dancing lights in his eyes.

"You may say he cannot, but this Cranmer will do it. And will declare the King's first marriage void, if he is set up to judge in the cause."

"I know," said Sandys, "that he was Nan Boleyn's father's chaplain. But he cannot. It is not possible."

Darcy laughed at him, but grimly.

"You shall see what he can do, and what the King can do now that this child is begotten."

May 17

Thomas Cranmer, Archbishop of Canterbury, walked in the fields, for it was evening, and Saturday, and all day he had sat in the Court at Dunstable, trying the matter of the King's first marriage. Now he took the air with one of his gentlemen. They walked at the foot of a gentle slope that ran up to a small oak wood. The little hill was a hill of gold, so thick the buttercups grew, and the oak trees themselves were greenish gold. A black puppy went with them, flopping and galloping, making parade of having to attend to affairs of great weight, with mischief shining in its eyes; when it came back to them, blundering against their legs, its muzzle was golden green from the gold pollen of the buttercups. On the fringe of the wood the milkmaids were busy among the kine; their voices and laughter came pleasantly, and one of them began to sing. All the birds were singing too, so many and so merry that there was never an instant's silence; single amongst all their flutings cuckoo called, and called again from the distance.

"Would," said the Archbishop, pinching his lower lip between his fingers, as he did when he was troubled, "would that I could have pronounced the King's first marriage incestuous this day, before the Court closed."

"But, my Lord, you have brought it to a final sentence which—"

"Which I cannot give till Friday next, seeing all the days between are ferial; so that the Court cannot sit."

"But," the gentleman objected again, "on Friday—" and again the Archbishop interrupted him irritably.

"Supposing *she* hears the bruit of it—Queen Katherine. She hath not appeared to answer her summons—but if she should—"

He brooded over that, teasing his lip.

"I have written to the King," he said. "I must write to Master Cromwell. But I shall pray either of them to make no relation of the matter lest she should be stirred to appear afore me in the time, or afore the time, of sentence. For if she came I should be greatly stayed and let in the process, and you know time runs on, and this marriage must be broken before our gracious Queen Anne is crowned."

He started forward, going towards the house.

"I shall write now. See to a messenger for me," he cried over his shoulder, and went in to write to Master Cromwell of how nearly the process of the King's divorce was accomplished, and how fearful he was lest Katherine of Spain should appear in the Court to answer in her own cause, in place of that docile and complaisant counsel whom the King had appointed to answer for her.

As well as the house at Mortlake, which Lord Darcy now rented instead of the one at Stepney, he had hired a small house at Westminster to use when Parliament was sitting. The house was old and crushed in between one of the tall kitchen offices of the new Palace of Whitehall, and a house that belonged to the Abbot of Westminster. It had no garden at all, which was strange for Westminster, a countrified place where the Palace sat among greenery, like Richard Crookback's crown on a thornbush, but the Cardinal had bought and built upon the little garden which it had possessed, thus almost choking the house on one side of light and air. Because Lord Darcy did not care to be without a garden he hired one that lay at the end of the lane, and nearer the river; it was called the Vine Garden, because there was a very old vine in it, fantastically and harshly knotted, but still fertile, and now breaking out with exquisitely innocent and gay young leaves.

On this day, which was the Friday before Whitsuntide, my Lord came in from Mortlake in his litter. The servants had been sent on hours earlier, so as to have the house ready, but when my Lord came it was all hugger-mugger; in the room beyond the Hall, where the ancient windows had pointed arches, and stone seats under them in the thickness of the wall, the hearth had not yet been cleared of the pale ash of the last fire, nor filled with green boughs for summer. When my Lord sat down on a cushion on the seat below the window, he could hear feet scurrying overhead, and heavy bumps now and again, as the servants set up the beds in haste.

Presently Lord Hussey came in, so the two lords and several of their gentlemen chose to repair out of the confusion of the house to the little Vine Garden at the end of the lane.

The Vine Garden, though small, was a pleasant place. As well as the old vine on the wall there were trim hedges of thorn and box, and a trellis where the first monthly roses were pink and white like raspberries drenched in cream. Close to the gate by which they entered there was a cherry tree, whose fruit, plump, polished, and yellow, was already flushing with scarlet; a blackbird scrambled noisily from among the leaves, and flew away, shouting with fright and proprietary anger as they came in. At the other end of the walk a honeysuckle hedge and arbour were backed by a low wall, and as Darcy and Hussey sat together in the arbour they could hear the slap of the Thames' tide upon the stones behind them. A salt smell mingled with the scent of the honey-suckle, and seagulls drifted by, golden white against the blue, turning their heads from side to side as they spied about for garbage.

While the gentlemen sat, or strolled about the garden, the two lords talked, securely private in the honeysuckle arbour. Hussey could tell Darcy all the news there was of Princess Mary, for he was Chamberlain of her Household; he could also tell much of the Queen, for letters had been passing between Katherine and her daughter, even though they were forbidden.

"The Princess"— Hussey said, and checked himself, not for the first time; that title was forbidden. "The Lady Mary," he began again, and then struck one palm with the other fist. "Blood of God," he cried, but keeping his voice low, "if you knew how I live now between my wife, whose sweetest name for me is "coward," and these lords who come from the Court to bid me call the—call my Lady—this or that or t'other! She," he explained, and Darcy knew that he meant Lady Hussey, "she is passionate for the Queen. Oh God! the Princess Dowager I mean, and for—her daughter. But what can a man do other than obey his Prince?"

Darcy prodded the ground at their feet with his walking staff. He murmured, "Women are like that," remembering how his dead Elizabeth had, from the beginning, taken this same business of the King's new marriage. How many years ago was that beginning? Why, the thing had hung over them for close on six years. And now it was come to an end, but to a different end, and by very different paths than any which he or others had dreamed of then.

For a breath Darcy could have believed that his wife had been right, and all was as simple as women saw it. "Here's a man married. What if he be a king? Here's his wife and his true-born child. What if she be a lass instead of a lad? There's a whore. What if she be crowned queen and wear a collar of pearls about her neck as big as chick peas?"

He sighed, and Hussey beside him swore softly again and went on complaining of how his wife goaded and reproached him. Darcy only half listened. He was thinking that this "great matter" of the King's, so long ago begun, was perhaps not yet ended. It had spread so far as a flood spreads, that none could say now where it would cease to undermine, to bring down, to efface. No. Certainly the women's simple way was not for a man to take when all known paths were hidden, and he must feel about for foothold. "But," he comforted himself, "all will return into place one day," and when he thought—"If it does not—?" he answered the doubt promptly. "Aye—but it must."

In the evening he was promised to supper with the Marquess of Exeter at that same Manor of the Rose which had once been Buckingham's. Just past Temple Bar the preparations for shows began. The streets too were gravelled, and along one side a railing had been set up, so that the Londoners would not be hurt by scared horses trampling in on them. The conduit in Fleet Street was freshly coloured, as bright as a Book of Hours; the shields of arms were sticky with paint—scarlet, blue, green—and the angels all new gilded. A sort of gallery had been built out above, like a little walled town with a turret at each corner, and the sound of instruments of music and the voices of singing boys came from it and mingled with the noises of the street. A few men of the city stood below, listening and looking up, with the script of the music in their hands, for it was their pageant.

A dray unloading hogsheads at the conduit held up Darcy's litter for a while, so he leaned out to watch while he waited. The instruments and voices sounded pleasantly here, and the setting sun made the conduit and its fanciful adornments like a picture of the New Jerusalem. But now something had gone wrong; the music faltered, the viols and recorders played a phrase alone, then played it again, but raggedly. Someone from below cried out in anger, and, when a boy put his head over the rail above, complained, "You there, Justice! We don't want you. That's Temperance his part."

The boy glanced back over his shoulder: "Well, Sir, Temperance is—Temperance—Marry! Sir, one of the casks of the conduit to run wine to-morrow was stove in, and Temperance—he's very sick, Sir."

Darcy let out a laugh, and someone else beside him laughed too. When Darcy looked round to see who it was, he found a gentleman on horseback close beside the litter, with many in livery following him; and then he saw that it was not a gentleman at all, but Master Cromwell, Keeper of the King's Jewels.

"Temperance," said Cromwell, "will have not only a sore head tomorrow, but a sore backside," and he nodded at the enraged citizen, already climbing the narrow ladder, with such a pleasant puckering of the eyes in his laughter that Darcy could not, for the moment, dislike him.

So they rode up the Strand together, talking pleasantly, and indeed Master Cromwell was a good talker, ranging easily from praise of the great arch the Venetians were busy setting up, to the whole city of Venice itself, thence to speak of the more ancient Italy, with talk of the Cave of Scylla, "which," said he, "I have with mine own eyes seen, but no monster therein, only a row of sea birds sitting and looking out, very solemn and wise, like Justices on the Bench." By the time the Keeper of the King's Jewels pulled up his horse in Candlewick Street and said that here must he take his leave, Darcy had decided that this was a much pleasanter rogue than he had thought.

And Master Cromwell lingered after dismounting, as if unwilling to part with my Lord. He stood talking, shading his eyes with one hand against the great flood of swimming dusty gold that the sun poured down the street, leaning an elbow on the side of Darcy's litter, and idly flicking to and fro a pair of new and costly Louvain gloves, dove grey, like his dove grey satin coat, and stitched with silver.

The streets were still very full, though it was past suppertime for merchants and working folk; everyone was about, staring at the decorations, though not, Darcy noticed, with that free hilarity that such shows usually brought. People moved slowly, and spoke low to each other. But the shows were plentiful, and every house along the way had hung out lengths of coloured stuffs, or painted cloths or devices. Below the windows of the house opposite, almost hiding the twined roses and pomegranates carved along the timbers, hung damask velvet of crimson red. And even now some wenches and an apprentice or two were leaning out from the windows, to better it with painted shields, white and green, each with two letters interlaced—an H. and an A.

Master Cromwell twinkled at Darcy, said farewell, and moved away. Darcy told the boy on the leading horse to "Get on!" and he looped up the reins in his hand ready to obey. Just then among the crowd there came three young gentlemen, arm in arm, going towards Westminster, with the sun on their faces. They were opposite the litter when the midmost of the three suddenly stopped and pulled the others up. "Look you!" he cried, and freed one arm to point at the lettered shields that hung a little drunkenly. "Look you there!" He had a notable voice, deep, but with a clear note in it that rang above the noises of the street, so that people looked round at him. "Why! That's what we all say of this coronation, and now they write it for us to read—H and A. That spells Ha!" and he let out a great, derisive "Ha! Ha!" Someone in the street laughed, and then more than one, and a shrill boy's voice echoed the "Ha! Ha!" and there were cat-calls and more laughter.

The litter stopped and Darcy found that Master Cromwell was beside him again. "Wait!" said he to Darcy. "Who said that? Which way did he go? What manner of man?"

Darcy leaned out and peered eastward towards the Tower, and then westward towards St. Paul's. In that direction he could see the red cap of the young gentleman who had said, "Ha! Ha!" Then it was hidden by the stiff white coifs of a couple of citizens' wives who had gone by with an apprentice boy following them. "By the Rood!" he answered slowly, "I could not say who. Nor could I not say which way. Nor what manner of man."

"Ah!" said Cromwell, after a silence. "I see. And it mat-ters—but little."

His eyes, sharp and small and full of consideration, seemed to be looking through Darcy's head, as if he were adding up a sum that was written on the green and tawny curtains of the litter behind it. He said farewell again with no less courtesy and sweetness than before, though without a smile.

Darcy went on to the Rose, and chuckled more than once as he went. The trumpet was blowing for supper when he got there, and he had time only to wash his hands and join them at the board. But after supper, when the candles were lit, he and the Marquess stood together in a window, in a shadow that lay between the cold turquoise of the sky and the warm light of the fluttering candle flames. The Marquess asked for news, but when Darcy began to tell him what Hussey had said he knew it already.

Then Darcy told him of the young man in the street, and of Master Cromwell's concern. The Marquess laughed, but at once his face fell again into its expression of tired and fas-tidious melancholy. He had royal blood in him, and he looked royal, but as if an exiled and weary king.

"Who was he—this young man? Did you see him?" he asked with so little interest that it was enough for Darcy merely to shake his head.

"I fear that Master Cromwell has notched a tally against me in that working brain of his," said he, and at that the Marquess exclaimed with disgust upon Cromwell. "A petty usurer," he called him in such a tone as one would speak of a louse. "Never fear for him."

"Fear?" Darcy had not thought of fear, and something made him turn his eyes from the Marquess for kindness' sake, as from the face of one who has betrayed himself without knowing it. And, because that other, the saucy young man, was so different, he remembered again his face, which indeed he had seen well, and not forgotten. For if a man has but one eye it is easy to remember him; and easier yet if the eye is sharp with scorn, and bright with laughter. Darcy had caught its glance for an instant, and his lips twitched now as he remembered the liveliness and mockery of that single eye. "By the Rood!" he thought to himself, hearing again in recollection the northern broadness of speech, "By the Rood! he's a Yorkshireman I'll swear, and that's a bold, true man." And he thought with warm love of the North Country, and the men that were bred there.

June 8

This Sunday, the next after the Queen's coronation, almost everybody went to Court, and Lord Darcy one of them. As he paused on the landing of a stairway, Master Cromwell came out from a door which he locked carefully behind him. He seemed greatly pleased to see Darcy, and urged him to "Come up, my Lord, come up," as though he spoke for the King. They went on up the stairs together, and Darcy saw that Cromwell had a little crimson velvet casket in his hand, a pretty thing with gilt hinges and a tiny gilt key.

"A jewel for Her Grace," said Cromwell. "The King sent for it, and it came but yesterday." He stopped at the next window, and opened the box in the sunshine. Darcy bent his head and saw a great emerald flash back the light and hold it in depths of under-sea green that glowed as if with fire. There were three pearls hanging from it, large and elongated, the shape of plovers' eggs.

"Hm!" he said, though not much interested, "pretty."

"And of great price." Cromwell prodded it with a forefinger. He had fat hands, with dimples at the knuckle joints, yet they looked strong too. "It was the Princess Dowager's. She brought it from Spain. It was a jewel, perhaps, of those Kings of the Indies. Now His Grace will give it to Queen Anne."

He shut the box, and they went on together. Darcy guessed that Cromwell expected him to say something, either to approve or deplore, or discreetly to turn the conversation. He did none of these, being too honest to approve, too wary to deplore, and at once too practised and too bold to fear a silence.

He had thought that when they reached the Presence Chamber Cromwell would leave him, but instead the Master of the Jewels laid a hand lightly on his arm, and twinkling at him with the smile that Darcy could not dislike, said that he would he were of the number of my Lord's friends, few men of these days being so stout and honest. "And," said he, "as I would earn your love I will essay a small thing thereto. I will bring you, without pain of waiting, at once to His Grace." And he began to push his way, not roughly yet with determination, between the wide puffed shoulders of the men, and the spreading stiff gowns of the women, crowded into the long room and all looking towards the far end, where hung the cloth of estate above the King's chair. Darcy followed him, but not now liking either him or the times in which such an upstart could lead a nobleman to his Prince's presence.

When they reached it the chair of estate was empty, and Cromwell, catching the eye of a gentleman in silver and green who stood on guard at a closed door, led Darcy there, knocked, and went in.

The room was small, hot with sunshine, and fragrant with strewn flowers and perfumes of musk, ambergris, and orris. There were two small chairs, covered with purple velvet and fringed with silver, set below one of the windows, and the King's Grace and the Queen sat on them. The King's hand with its rings was laid on hers or touching or toying with her all the time, whether he greeted Darcy or spoke to the French Ambassador or argued with her father about the voice of one of the singing boys of the Children of the King's Chapel.

Cromwell knelt, and presented the jewel to the Queen. "It is," said he, "a gift from His Grace."

"For me," she cried, and turning her head tipped up her face to the King who hung over her. Darcy thought, "She knows what will prick a man to desire."

The King lifted the jewel out of the box. He leaned closer and set the chain about her neck. Then he must settle the jewel so that the midmost pearl hung plump above the cleft between her breasts, which showed where the jewelled edge of her gown ended. His fingers lingered on her flesh; she let herself droop towards him.

"A born harlot!" Darcy thought, and guessed that Crom-

[243]

well thought no other, though the Master of the Jewels kissed her hand and took leave with due humility.

But he had to acknowledge that she had wit, for she began to talk about her coronation in the Abbey of Westminster, and had them all laughing because she so pricked through the splendours and solemnities that she pierced to the folk behind them, and as she talked these were no more reverend than a rout of villagers at a May Game.

When she finished, ". . . And so we came away to dinner," the King wiped his eyes, though his bulk still shook with diminishing gusts of laughter. He flung his arm across her shoulders and bade her tell them more. "What of the dinner?" he pressed her.

She let herself be pulled towards him, then put both hands on his breast and pushed him away.

"No, but I'll tell you what I saw at the Abbey. But you'll be angry."

"Not with you, Sweetheart."

"Faith! but you will. You'll say, 'To the Tower with her.' "

"Madcap!" The King looked about at them all, and then again at the Queen's father, a mass of slashed green velvet and cloth of gold, set upon a pair of thin legs.

"This daughter of yours!" he cried dotingly, and then to her, "Well, you little rebel? I shall not be angry. Or you shall have a pardon."

"Shall I? But you will be angry. See. I will wager you a prince to a collar of rubies that you are angry."

"A prince? How will you pay with a prince?"

"The prince I bear in my belly."

"Ho!" the King laughed. "You'll pay with him at your time, will you, nill you?"

"And isn't he enough to wager against a collar of rubies?"

The King swore by St. Edward that he would be enough, and then asked again, "Sweet, what did you see? Tell us now."

"I saw jewels."

"God's body! so you should. Here have I been writing orders to Master Cromwell for this, that and t'other for you. And now today I have given you the emerald. My Lord," said the King to Darcy, in high good humour, "should these not be enough?"

"Sir," Darcy answered, "if women be as insatiate as the sea, it is that they know our weakness, and their own worth," and on the last he bowed to the Queen. She inclined her head but he had seen her eye snap at his guarded courtliness.

The King however was growing impatient.

"Jewels?" he urged. "Are there not some few on the crown and the sceptre?"

She pouted her lips, and blew all those away with scorn.

"Jewels! Not those. But the jewels on the shrine. Jewels in the Lord Abbot's mitre. Jewels in his staff. And there was a great ruby in the cross on the altar. I saw none in the crown nor in sceptre like to these."

The King had withdrawn his arm from her neck.

"I think, Madame," he said, "that you forget."

She flashed a look at Darcy that said, "You would be glad to hear me rebuked," and then turned her eyes, sparkling and reckless, upon the King.

"You owe me a ruby collar, for indeed you are angry."

"The Devil I do!" The King got up quickly, but she did not move. He turned back. "One day, Madame, you'll go too far."

"And then," she smiled at him, "you will send to Ampthill and bring Dame Katherine back."

The King had been angry, but now it was as if he had been hit with a stone between the eyes. He looked at her, but if he hoped to beat down her glance he failed. Darcy thought, "She can stare like any cat." And it was with the same bland sweetness of malice.

The King went back to his chair.

"I believe you would not fear the devil."

"Not if he wore a beard. And shall I have my rubies?"

"Ask the Keeper of the Jewels."

"Not the Abbot of Westminster?"

The Queen's father cried, in an agony, "Peace, girl! Madame, I pray you, peace!" but the Queen did not so much as look at him.

"You'll get none of my Lord Abbot." The King's tone was gruff.

"These monks," the Queen murmured softly, "have all, and give nought. And the King can't take. Yet the Cardinal took."

"Body of God!" the King turned on her. "The Cardinal took only a few little Priories, some of an ill name. But to speak of Westminster! By the Blood of Hales!" he cried, "I won't have this talk." He got up and went out of the room with his arrogant walk, swinging his wide, white satin shoulders.

When Darcy stood waiting for his litter and looking at all

the coming and going in the Great Courtyard between the Palace and Master Holbein's new gallery and gate, he found Cromwell at his elbow, and thought as he greeted him, "How the man sticks!"

"How sweet is the sunshine," Cromwell said, as though in idlest talk. "Truly I think this fair summer shows that God's favour is upon this marriage. That, and already so blessed a hope of issue."

"Already," Darcy repeated drily.

"Ah! my Lord, how I love the bluntness of you men of the North Country. But at least," he murmured, "at least, even you, my Lord, will confess we have a Queen now, young, witty, beautiful, and, let us hope, fruitful."

"And bold," said Darcy. "She wants the King to do with the Abbey of Westminster what the Cardinal did with the Priories."

"She said that, did she?" Cromwell remarked, in a tone almost innocent of meaning, and yet something in Darcy's brain pricked an ear, and he thought, "It's not the first time that same has been said, nor was she the first to say it." He was just thinking that this man was perhaps more dangerous, though not greater, than the Cardinal, when Cromwell spoke again.

"But, my Lord, there's a thing I'd ask of you. That young gentleman in Candlewick Street the other day, did you see his face?"

When Darcy did not answer he went on, "I thought I had heard his voice before. I'm sure I have heard it." He rapped with his knuckles on his forehead, and then bit at them angrily. "It was a voice that one should remember, and I cannot."

He waited, and then ran on again, begging pardon for keeping my Lord when his litter waited, "But it would be well I should know of any young gentleman so quick, bold, forward, as that one seemed to be. It was a young gentleman, you said?"

"*You* said," Darcy corrected him; and then with a sharp smile, "Master Cromwell, if I tell you, shall I have the reward proclaimed for those who informed against any that speak evil of this marriage?" He looked at Cromwell, and laughed; the Keeper of the Jewels was not often out of countenance, but now he was quite taken aback. He began to justify himself; it was necessary, he said, that quiet should be kept.

"Therefore I keep watch. People murmur at this marriage. Her Grace was displeased that so few caps came off, and there was so little shouting when she passed through the city. And there's a nun in Kent sees visions—foretells the King's death —" He paused and seemed to recollect himself, and laughed. "So perhaps I make too much of the idle jest of a saucy young man."

Darcy said, "Perhaps," in a tone that made Cromwell glance at him sharply, and then they parted. As Darcy looked back from below the new Gateway arch, he stood there, still sunning himself on the steps, a sober, quiet figure, in his grey silk and black fur. Darcy thought he was like one of those floating spots which trouble a distempered vision, and which the eye can neither quite catch, nor yet be rid of.

June 30

The Nuns' shepherd had come down from Owlands for goose grease, or butter, or swine's grease to mix with pitch and tar for sores upon his beasts, but before he went back to the lonely hut on the fells he turned into the kitchen where the cook and his man and the maids all greeted him well. The cook sent off at once to draw ale for him and he sat down on the bench with a great heap of lettuces on the floor between his feet, and his dog at his heels.

Beside him on the bench were two strangers; one grey-haired, with a weather-beaten pleasant face; the other younger and clearly of less importance. The elder of the two was stirring a white treacly mess in a pail beside him; at intervals he tipped down his throat deep draughts of priory ale.

For a long time Shepherd said nothing, for his way of life had made him more ready to listen than to talk. But at last, in a pause in the talk, he nudged the strange man, and pointed at the stuff in the pail. "What's yon, goodman?"

The stranger turned his broad, red face.

"Yon's lime, and a heel of old, poor cheese."

Shepherd looked at the stuff in the pail, and from one to another in the kitchen. "What beasts," he asked in his slow way, "will you feed or physic with such?"

They all laughed at that, but the stranger answered seriously.

"It's for no beast, seeing I'm a Master Carpenter; but 'tis to glue wainscoting. For there's no glue like lime and cheese and spring water to hold wood together. It'll last you from now till Doomsday morrow."

"Lord!" said Shepherd, and stared at it long before he asked, "And is it in Frater, or Cloister, or maybe in Church, that y're sitting up wainscoting?"

The cook answered that, telling him that it was for the Lady's own chamber. "Painted hangings nor yet arras aren't good enough for *her*." He stood up and scratched himself inside his doublet. "Time to get dinner," said he, and sweeping the flies from a piece of meat on the table began to pare off a long dark red sliver, that flopped back over the fingers of his left hand as the knife moved. A boy came into the kitchen and squatted down on the floor in the corner with a basket of peas between his heels; he shelled them into a wooden bowl; pop went the pods and the peas rattled against the sides of the bowl.

"And it's time you and I got back to work," the Master Carpenter said to his mate, "or the Lady will be wroth to find us idling." So they went away, back to the Prioress's Chamber, not too soon, for she came in and found them there five minutes after.

The furniture in the room had been moved into the middle of the floor and shrouded in sacking. Everywhere sawdust lay, soft to touch, and fresh smelling. But already except for one corner the wainscoting was in place upon the walls, clean pale golden wood, cunningly carved in the panels with softly flowing, scroll-like curves. Nor was that the whole of its beauty. All over the carved undulations of the pattern as well as over the firm uprights and horizontals of the panelling, the wood was alive with the living pattern of its own grain. Here swam, it seemed, a shoal of little fishes; there shining blotches floated like tiny clouds in the sunset; there you could trace wavering tongues like flames, or like the soft sleek trails of water weeds, swayed by a slow river; and there the wood was dappled as if it were shallow running water. It was beautiful wood and beautiful work.

That was what the Prioress thought of it when she came in, and having shut the door stood looking about at the strange and fine new clothing of the familiar walls.

The carpenter, when he saw her, stopped whistling between his teeth, and laid down his T square and charcoal. He came forward with a sort of rough and breezy gallantry, not disrespectful, yet with a spice in it of laughter. He had had many dealings with women Religious, being known for an honest fellow and not given to too much drinking. He was wont to declare that there were but two kinds of such women; the fools he overawed by a frowning look, and talk that none but a carpenter could understand; the masterful women he courted in the same manner in which he now set himself to court the Prioress.

Certainly it went well here, but then the two already had a respect for each other. He did good work, and she knew and acknowledged good work when she saw it. So now he moved confidently beside her, as she let her hand slide over the smooth, sleek curves, and cast a penetrating eye on the joints to see that all were close.

As they went he talked, giving her news of folk in Richmond and the Dale; she heard him, raising her brows or faintly smiling, but never letting herself be distracted by his talking from her examination of the work.

"And have you heard," said he, "of mighty great doings down at Easby?"

"That peg stands too high. I can feel its head."

He moved his fingers over the surface. "You'll not feel him when we've taken the oil and sand over all. . . . I hear there's them that say Master Oldbarrow won't last the summer out."

"That joint," the Prioress said, "could be tighter," and then though they were alone in the room she brought her mouth close to the Master Carpenter's ear. "Show me the hidden place you have made."

He showed her the panel low down in the darkest corner of the chamber, where there was a lock cunningly concealed by a fold of the carving. When you knew where to look for the lock you could see that there were also hinges, and a little door. He opened the door, and showed the small secret cupboard.

"That is good," said the Prioress.

July 11

Lord Mountjoy, Queen Katherine's Chamberlain, her Almoner, and others of the Household, paused with one consent at the door of her chamber. None looked at another, but each knew that his neighbour squared his shoulders, or took a deeper breath than usual, or clenched his teeth, before Lord Mountjoy lifted his hand and knocked, and they must go in to do a business that they hated.

She lay on a bed in the vaulted room which was a sombre

place in the dull light of an overcast and stormy morning. A few days ago she had pricked her foot with a pin as she had got out of bed, and gone barefoot, in the middle of the night, to pray before the crucifix in her chamber; now the foot was inflamed so that she could not put on a shoe. When the gentlemen came in she cast the hem of her heavy skirts over it, and tried to pull herself up on the bed. Yet it did not need those small attempts at dignity to make them go down on their knees, as much in reverence of her sorrows, as of her birth and station. But for all the propriety of their behaviour, her ladies, drawn away together to the empty hearth, some of them clutching embroidery, book, or instrument with which they had been employed, gave angry and grudging looks to the gentlemen; in this pass to which their Queen was come, they, as women, stood by her, a woman wronged by men. So a fundamental and eternal cleavage split in two that unhappy household.

Mountjoy spoke. They had, he said, come to her as she had yesterday commanded them, to read to her their report of that interview, before they sent it to His Grace's honourable Privy Council, to give account of the performance of the commission enjoined on them by the same honourable Council.

"Shameful commission!" cried one of the younger ladies, then flushed crimson, and nearly burst into tears when the Queen rebuked her with a frown.

Yet the faces of the gentlemen seemed to give colour to her words; yesterday they had felt shame in declaring to their mistress that her marriage with the King, in which she had lived blameless, honourable, and honoured, as a thing "detestable, abominable, execrable, and directly against the laws of God and nature." And to-day they looked as hangdog as any collection of respectable and well-intentioned persons might look.

"To whom," asked Queen Katherine of Mountjoy, "do you say in your Report that you have discharged your commission?"

He told her, looking on the ground, "To the Princess Dowager."

Queen Katherine drew herself up on the bed till she sat upright.

"Bring me the Report!" she said to the gentlemen, and to the ladies, "Bring me pen and paper."

She was obeyed by both, though all in that room knew what

she would do. When one of the ladies knelt by her, holding the ink, she set the Report on her knee and scribbled out the words, "Princess Dowager," wherever they came. As she did it the sharp complaint of the driven quill and the Queen's harsh coughing were the only sounds in the room.

The gentlemen received again the Report and asked leave to depart. But before they went the Queen spoke, while they stood twisting their caps and looking more like schoolboys in disgrace than any of them had looked for many years.

As she spoke she was shaken more and more by her cough, and inwardly by the thought of all the injustice she suffered, so that in the end she was crying out almost incoherently, that if she agreed to their persuasions to call herself anything but Queen she would be a slanderer of herself, she would thereby confess to have been the King's harlot for twenty-four years. She stopped a moment because she must, and when she could speak again it was in a whisper. The King had said that her case should be heard in some place indifferent, "but now it is determined by a man of the King's own making, the Archbishop of Canterbury. And how much impartial he be," she cried, "God He knows. Nor is the place impartial, since the King has taken upon himself to be *supremum caput ecclesiae,* with greater authority than our Lord the Pope himself."

They waited for a while when she was silent, but she waved her hand to them to be gone, only to beckon them again to stay.

"I am," she said, in a voice whose bitterness pierced them, "I am, you know, no Englishwoman but a Spaniard, and having no counsel may err in my words. But you shall say that if anything else there is in the Report prejudicial to my cause I protest against it."

They went away then, and the Queen bade that one of her ladies who had been reading aloud find her place again and read on.

So it would have seemed that nothing had happened in the dull room, except the failing and increase of light, as the wind outside gathered or drove away the clouds. But none of the ladies heard much of what was being read, and none of them could look at the Queen, though they knew that her face was composed, and that her needle moved steadily.

August 31
In the last of the twilight a man came and knocked at the door of the parsonage at Marrick. Gib was in, sitting at his

supper of bread and cheese, beans, and a salad of cresses and radishes.

The stranger said, "Friend, are you the parson of Marrick?"

Gib stowed half a radish in his cheek, and said that he was.

"Sir Gilbert Dawe?" the stranger persisted, and again Gib said "Aye—that's me."

The other man came in then. He was very dusty and hot, and brown as a nut; so brown that his hair and sandy beard were paler than his face. He shut the door, in spite of the warmth of the evening, and said, "Ned Tanner of York told me of you. He said you were of us, a 'known man.' "

Gib kissed him and sat him down to supper. When it was dark, and the old mother had gone to bed, they barred the door and the shutters, and lit a rushlight, and so together read a chapter from the Apocalypse in an English translation of the Scriptures that the stranger brought out from a pocket very cunningly hidden in the back of his pouch. It was a different translation from the one that Gib kept under the floor. The stranger made a twit of that one, saying that it was old and rude, and the one he had, much better. So they read in his.

And the sun was as black as sackcloth made of hair, and the moon waxed red as blood, and the stars of heaven fell into the earth, even as a fig tree casteth her figs when she is shaken of a mighty wind. And all mountains and isles moved out of their places. And the Kings of the earth, and the great men, and the rich men, and the chief captains, and every bondman and every free man hid themselves in dens and rocks of the little hills.

The stranger stopped here to explain that King Henry was not such a King, for he was a noble Prince, and executor of the wrath of the Lamb upon wicked men and fools, such as those who believed that the Bishop of Rome had any primacy among other Bishops.

September 1

Next morning Gib saw him take the track across the fells towards Washfold while it was still barely light. Then he went back to the bed where they had slept together, but his thoughts followed Master Trudgeover; that was what the stranger had called himself, and though Gib did not believe that it was his real name, one name was as good as another. Gib thought with envy of him tramping through England empty almost as an animal of the care of worldly things, and full of the marvellous riches of the spirit; less a man than a trumpet to sound to judgement and to destruction of God's enemies. Here lay he, Gib Dawe, as eloquent, as fervent, as truly grounded in the truth, but shut up in the narrow Dale to preach to clods, who thought small beer of him because he was a Marrick man born, and no stranger like Trudgeover. And besides being shut up in the narrow Dale, he was shut up too in the parsonage, with an old woman and a dumb brat.

September 4

The Princess Mary sat at dinner in the royal house of Beaulieu in Essex. Only the Countess of Salisbury dined at the same table as the Princess; the other ladies, and those gentlemen who were not on duty carving or waiting, sat at a table nearer the door. They were cheerful enough, though subduing their voices out of respect for their betters, but the Princess sat silent, and the Countess did not try to rally her. She herself knew what lay like a shadow across the girl's mind, for it darkened her own too as they waited for the news that might come any day now. But besides that, Master Hugh Pennington was serving at table, "and although he's a good youth," thought the Countess, "and of gentle conditions, yet he has the most careless and chancy hand at waiting of them all." She fixed her eyes upon the plate he was setting down before the Princess: he had carved the pork well, cutting it finely without disturbing the almonds that were stuck all over the crackling. But the gravy, rich and full of raisins and spices, all but swam over the roped edge of the silver plate as he set it down. The Countess breathed deeply in relief, and then because she saw the Princess's hands suddenly clutch upon the table, she looked up and forgot Hugh Pennington.

Mary was staring down the room to the door which was just closing. Now she turned to the Countess.

"Madame, I saw Charles. I know I did. Send for him to come in. No I'll not wait. At once."

The Countess frowned, though not because it was unnatural in a girl of seventeen to be impatient for her mother's message. It was natural, and it would have been right, if things had not been so wholly and shamefully wrong. But as

[253]

they were so wrong this royal child would have need of a fortitude greater than natural, and it had been the Countess's aim, in the last unhappy years, to train her charge to such a self-command that nothing should shake her. The Countess, herself, of the old blood-royal, and of a masculine courage, had wished, during wakeful nights, that she could somehow give to the girl of her own strength; that could not be done, and now she doubted if there would be time for the Princess to acquire it from practice or precept, for she believed that the hour drew near.

She raised her hand, and told one of the servants to bring in the man Charles.

He came in, and knelt before the table opposite the Princess, When she asked him how the Queen did, he said, "Well," and no more. When she asked him, had he a letter, he said, "No. No letter."

"Then," said the Princess, "what message?"

He glanced over his shoulder, and the Countess too looked down the room. At her glance the ladies and gentlemen at the lower table turned quickly to their food again; David Lloyd, making music with two others, had just shaken out his recorder and now held it to his mouth again, his lips pursed to blow, but instead of blowing he only stared and listened. When he caught her eye he put the instrument so hastily to his mouth that it let out a faint, involuntary toot.

"The Queen's Grace," said Charles, in a voice too low for any but the Princess and the Countess to hear, now that the music was playing again—"The Queen's Grace sent me to tell Your Grace that the Marchioness of Pembroke hath been brought to bed of a child."

"Man or woman?" It was the Countess who asked the question.

"A girl."

"Ah!" Mary sighed, and they guessed how much she had dreaded to hear the other. But Charles said, "The heralds proclaimed the bastard 'Princess of Wales' at the Cross in Cheap."

There was a silence in which only the gay warbling of the recorder and flutes made a fountain of bubbling sound. Then the Princess said, neither to the Countess nor to her mother's servant, but to the food on her plate, "It may die." And then, "I have heard, and am persuaded, that it is not my father's child at all."

The Countess said, "Hush!" though Charles was discreet as death, and no one else but herself could hear.

Mary looked at her with a little elderly, poisoned smile, which even the Countess, good hater as she was, found shocking on so young a face.

September 6

Queen Anne lay propped up with pillows in the carved, painted and gilded bed that had been brought from the King's Great Wardrobe for the occasion of the birth of the heir. The rings of the curtains, drawn wide apart now, were of silver gilt and ran along silver gilt rods. The hangings of the bed were of white and green brocaded velvet, and the counterpane which they had thrown over the bed for the King's visit was of cloth of gold. It lay very heavy upon the Queen, making her think of the leaden shrouds in which the dead are wound—the great dead, who lie in proud tombs—but as cold as any beggar. Her cheeks and eyes were still bright with fever, and fancies such as these, each of them tainted with horror, filled her mind with moving shadows. Beside her, upon a cushion of cloth of gold, lay the small tight shape of the one-day-old child, swaddled to the neck, and wearing a little tight cap exquisitely worked in silk. Between the swaddling bands and the cap, the puckered, querulous, aged face was of a dusky red.

There was a stir at the door, and one of the gentlemen announced the King. He came down the length of the chamber, tall and immensely broad in his puffed and slashed doublet of sanguine velvet, which to her fancy suddenly took on the likeness of raw, bloodied flesh, while the white satin that showed at the slashes was white bone. He came alone, having, by a motion of his hand, stayed those that were following him. The Queen's people, seeing this, also drew away. They stood in two groups, not mingling, hers by the hearth, his just inside the door.

But she was looking only at the King. He came on, his head a little bent, his shoulders swinging, till he stood beside the bed. He asked, courteously and formally, after her health. She said she did well. He said that he rejoiced therefor. She thanked him for his gracious visit. He said that she should command him in anything she wished. She replied that there was nothing she desired but only his gracious favour. That, he told her, she had, and promised that not only in the

[255]

Royal Chapel, but in all churches and chantries, her welfare should be petitioned for. Then he went away.

Her ladies came back. They removed the heavy coverlet and laid over her instead one of velvet brocaded in a pattern of true lovers' knots and roses. One of them asked her, "Shall we leave with you this noble lady?" rocking in her arms the child who had wakened with a shrill, piping cry.

"No," said the Queen, "I shall sleep."

She shut her eyes so that they should think she slept. He had not touched, he had not once looked at the miserable little creature that had caused her all that wasted pain. She could, for the present at least, feel nothing but loathing for the girl who should have been a boy.

September 11

Dame Anne Ladyman had been to Grinton. As she climbed the stair to the Prioress's chamber she wiped her hot face with a lappet of her veil, for the weather was like high summer, and anticipated with pleasure the long, cool drink of ale, which, she confided, would soon be slipping down her throat as they two sat together, she resting her tired feet and retailing all her news—and to-day one piece of such laughable news.

But when she opened the door she knew that all her anticipation had been vain. Opposite Dame Christabel sat the Prioress of St. Bernard's Ladies from down the river, as erect and as iron as the fire-dogs on the hearth.

The Dale grudgingly credited Dame Euphemia with a kind of sanctity; for how could any woman so completely ignore every comfort of life unless she had at least some tincture of holiness? But if she were holy, she was not beloved. Those who might kept clear; those who must be about her endured with what philosophy they could muster. She marched through life, rigid, cheerless, dispensing gloom, and not even taking pleasure in that. The whole world lay under her condemnation; her Nuns were soft indulgent creatures, yearning for worldly delights; laymen were close-fisted wretches, careless of the hardships of St. Bernard's poor Ladies; her own House she grudged at for its poverty, Marrick Priory for its plumper endowments; her kin she condemned for proud men who believed that ancient and noble blood would save a man at the last tremendous Day (which Day was perhaps the one occasion to which she looked forward with any enthusiasm); those of lower degree than herself and her family she despised. She was of the few people who could, by means of sheer

[256]

blind, bludgeoning, remorseless pride, set down Christabel Cowper, Prioress of Marrick.

So now, when Dame Anne Ladyman came in, she found St. Bernard's Lady with her usual look of one who has tasted verjuice; the Prioress of Marrick was flushed, but maintained an expression of smooth, controlled politeness.

Dame Anne found herself affected, as everyone else, by the visitor's temper. Some were struck silent by it; but she took refuge in loud and rapid garrulity. So, while Dame Euphemia's deep and burning eyes looked down her important nose, Dame Anne rattled through the heads of the less startling items of news which she had gathered when in Grinton: how that the harvest was the greatest that any could remember; that the wheelwright's wife had twins; that one of the hinds who had sliced his leg reaping was now doing well; that parson's rheumatism was better. Then, breaking off, she tittered, and struck her hands together.

"And now, I'll tell you greater news than all these. I wager you knew not, Madame, that we have a holy woman among us—one that sees visions of heavenly things."

When St. Bernard's Lady had arrived Dame Christabel had been reading "The Death of the Duchess" in an old, beautifully written copy of Geoffrey Chaucer's poems that had belonged to her mother. She had seen how Dame Euphemia's eyes fastened on it, yearning to know by the title what book it was that occupied the Marrick Prioress's leisure, but unable to read it upside down. Now, because she guessed what satisfaction Dame Anne's loudness gave the other woman, she determined to flaunt her own frivolity, ramming down the visitor's throat, as it were, the worldliness of St. Benedict's Nuns. So she laid the book on the rushes at her feet, carefully disposed so that the title was easy to read, and even, with a provocative smile, pushed it nearer to Dame Euphemia with her foot.

"No," she answered Dame Anne, "I know none such. A woman who sees visions?"

"And what will you say when I tell you that this same is our serving woman Malle?"

"By St. Eustace!" the Prioress began, but then Dame Anne burst out laughing, her high trilling laugh which the Prioress so hated. Nor would she stop, except to interrupt herself with such exclamations as, "The Holy Malle. . . . Her

Feast will be All Fools' Day. . . . If she have a halo it will smoke like the kitchen fire. . . ."

"And what," asked Dame Euphemia, so suddenly and harshly that Dame Anne fairly jumped about to face her, "what hath this wench of yours seen—or says she hath seen?"

It was those last words, spoken in a tone which stripped the Ladies of St. Benedict of any right to hope for heavenly favours, which gave the Prioress of Marrick her cue. When Dame Anne's eyes came back to her she nodded. "Tell us," she said.

Dame Anne took a moment to recover, and then began, stumbling a little.

"I'd been to the mill, to ask if the young goslings we're to have are ready. They are ready and I told her—but that was after. Well, I'd come nigh to the bridge and there I saw Malle, among a crowd of idlers and children, staring into the Blackburne's yard.

"There's a wedding there this day," she added, with a sidelong smile.

The Prioress knew that smile well. "So I heard." She was curt.

But it took more than a tone of voice to shoulder Dame Anne off from the subject of a wedding.

"A bonny, bouncing lass, that one of Chris Blackburne's, but I'll warrant that when she goes to bed with a man this eve it won't be for the first time."

The Prioress did no more than raise her eyebrows at that, and Dame Anne went on, with story and supposition, things seen by this or that one of the servants on summer nights or at winter ales. The Prioress of St. Bernard sat with her eyes cast down in a dangerous stillness, which Dame Anne missed but the Prioress did not.

"Well, there was that fool peeking and peering in." Dame Anne stood half crouching, her hands on her bent knees, and swung her head from side to side with goggling eyes and mouth open. "Like that," said she, and laughed.

"So I called to her, to have her away—wasting her time, the idle slut! She came to me, but then she caught my sleeve in her dirty hands, crying out, 'He's there within.' 'And who?' says I, very short with her, and, 'Get you back to Marrick at once,' says I.

"But she had me by the arm dragging me towards the gate and I could not but go. 'Look,' quod she, 'here they come again to the well to draw water for the wine.' 'Fie,' quod

I, 'Goodman Blackburne won't have wine at the wedding, even with water in it. Wine's for gentles.'

"But she says, not listening to me but staring in at the window, and speaking very quiet, 'I can't hear His voice for all that din they make. They are so merry to have among them the King of Heaven. But when He comes out we shall see Him.'

"'The King of Heaven,' quod I, and I boxed her ears soundly and bade her not be a fool, and she cried and whimpered a deal, but I said, 'Off with you to the mill, and bring those goslings back to the Priory' (for the miller's wife had told me they were ready for the fetching). 'And if you linger,' says I, 'you'll be beaten.'"

"Madame," said Dame Euphemia to the Prioress of Marrick, ignoring Dame Anne as completely as she ignored a bluebottle which swung about the room, "Madame, will you suffer such idle talk? It were strange that such a one as a serving-woman—" she paused, and added, "of your House" (meaning clearly "of any House but mine") "should see such holy things."

The Prioress of Marrick did not even look in her direction.

"Tell me," she said to Dame Anne, "did she see a light, hear heavenly music, fall into a trance?"

Dame Anne stared. "Lord," she cried, "it cannot be that you believe—? Why, she's mad as a goose. I asked her why she should think to see Our Blessed Lord at Grinton, and in Chris Blackburne's house. Quod she, 'He went to a wedding. And I saw the light shine.'"

The Prioress bent her head, crossed herself, and said, "*Benedicite*."

That brought Dame Euphemia to her feet.

"What! Should Our Saviour come to the house of a plain yeoman, nor no good sober man neither, but a lousy, upstart, swilling fellow—"

"We read that He went about," said the Prioress with smooth satisfaction, "among common folk."

Dame Euphemia gulped. It was true. Yet she was sure that if those had been common folk they had been so in a different way from the people of the Dale. That impropriety, however, was not the worst of it. She could have borne that a vision should have been seen in the Blackburnes' house if only it had not been a Marrick serving-wench that had seen it. For a moment the outrage held her dumb, and into the silence Dame Anne let forth another of her high trilling laughs.

" 'Light?' quod I. 'What light? Why,' quod I, 'what you saw was the sun dazzle on a pewter plate on a shelf within.' "

The Prioress of Marrick rose.

"It may be so," she said, very stately and judicial. "I shall look into this. I shall question this woman. If God in His Grace hath favoured our poor House with a very holy thing, the world shall know that it is no feigned vision, no trumped-relic that we claim to have received."

Dame Euphemia stood up; her white cheeks were patched with red. That matter of the horse harness, or the belt of St. Maura, whichever it might have been, lay years behind; it should have been by this time forgotten. Now she knew it would never be forgotten.

She moved to the door. The Prioress opened it for her. The two religious Ladies kissed, cheek laid not very near to cheek, and lips sucked in to make a noise like young chickens cheeping.

"God," said Dame Euphemia over her shoulder, "God grant this holy vision may be for your comfort. Yet remember, if you mell in such matters, that the Nun of Kent is sent for to be questioned of treason."

St. Bernard's Lady went out; she was defeated, but a scorpion's sting is in its tail. The Prioress of Marrick might give no sign. She might not even know that she had been touched. But soon she would know.

For a while after the visitor and Dame Anne had left her, Dame Christabel leaned at the window, her hands on the warmed stone of the sill, and looked out, not up the drowsy, blue-misted Dale, but at things closer at hand. That patch of new slate in the stable roof; it had cost what she could ill spare. A man led in two horses from the field and brought them to the trough in the Court below; he leaned against the rough quarter of one of them as they drank with long breathings and gurgling noises. She herself had bought that near horse at a great price; he was from Jervaulx where the Monks breed the best horses of the North; but good beasts are costly.

If only the House might become a place where men came to pay honour to God, for the sake of its particular holiness, then, she thought—but her thought was no more than the clear sight, in her mind, of the last page in the Priory accounts.

Her eye was caught by someone moving slowly through the fields from the direction of Grinton. It was Malle, driving the young geese before her with a long lissom willow switch.

"Now," said Christabel Cowper to herself, "I must have her in, and question her."

But even as she thought that, she shut the window and turned away, knowing that she would not question the woman, for least said about this matter of visions, soonest mended. She sat in her chair by the hearth, and bit her fingers. It seemed to her most unjust that when this hope of prosperity and honour was offered to the House, for caution's sake it must be allowed to go by. Better safe than sorry, but the necessity galled her soul; the more so because she felt, though illogically, that it was Dame Euphemia who stood between Marrick and the pleasant prospect of gainful holiness.

October 10

At breakfast Sir John Bulmer swore at the mutton pie for being mutton pie again, and then sat eating it savagely, leaning his head on his hand so that he should not see his wife's face, because her mouth, with the black moustache along the upper lip, was shaking, and now and again jerked down at the corners before she could steady it. That Dame Anne looked ridiculous in her grief, as fifteen stone and forty-five years old must look ridiculous, made Sir John yet more angry.

He had a right to be angry, he thought, stabbing a bit of the pie with his knife so fiercely that the point grated on the pewter plate. For while the eldest son had been at home Sir John had not ridden to Pinchinthorpe for more than a couple of nights at a time—or only when the boy was away at Settrington, hunting with his mother's nephews, the Bigods. But now that the lad had gone to London to keep his first term at Gray's Inn, why should not his father stay a while at his own Manor of Pinchinthorpe? Must not a man see to his lands and farms? And what right had a man's wife to suppose that he was tiring of his bawd, just because he was too nicely considerate of his eldest son to linger with her when the lad was at home? And again what right had she, when after so long he went once more to his bawd, to snivel over her buttered eggs at breakfast-time?

To show that he was at ease in his conscience he told young Rafe Bigod, his wife's younger nephew, who was staying with them, a very merry story that had been going around the taverns of London last spring. He himself laughed at it loudly, and Rafe laughed feebly, crimson to his ears, and never raising his eyes from his plate. "Tchah!" thought Sir John. "Mincing young fool!" and included Rafe in his anger. "If he dared," he thought, "he'd chide me for his aunt's sake, but he daren't, and so he chafes and frets."

He finished his ale and a dish of fried eggs, and then stood up in the midst of a company grown suddenly silent.

"Tell them to bring the horses. I'll ride the Blackbird to-day," he said to the servants.

He made himself look at his wife. She had both hands laid flat on the table, and bent forward with her head lowered like someone who is preparing to speak. But she was silent.

"I'm riding to Whitby," he said, more loudly than he meant. "D'you want aught?"

She jerked up her head. "No. Yes. Oh, Sir! the herrings," and began to cry openly.

"God rot the herrings!" He stamped out.

Young Rafe Bigod leaned at the door of the Hall when Sir John had ridden away, and the household was busy about its ordinary tasks. The autumn sunshine fell pleasantly on his face, but Rafe's look was black. He wriggled his shoulders in his over-fine green hunting coat, and knew that he was a gawky lad, with a fair skin that flushed as easily as a girl's. He knew too that he did not dare rebuke Sir John for his own aunt's sake, and that he had not dared even rebuke him for a bawdy story, by silence, and a stern, unsmiling face.

He turned to find Dame Anne beside him. She did not look at him as she spoke, but her voice and her lips were quite steady.

"Rafe," said she, "I go to Pinchinthorpe. Will you go with me?"

He gaped at her. "Pinchinthorpe? For why?"

"I must," she said, "look on her." She added quickly, before he could speak, "And I need a—a kinsman with me."

That made him feel a man. "I'll come," he said grandly; and awkwardly, but with honest feeling, he caught and kissed her hand.

Pinchinthorpe was a very different place from the empty and deserted house to which Sir John had brought Margaret in the autumn. The little green Court was shorn and neat; the brambles had been grubbed up, and by the Hall door Meg's hawk sat on a perch in the sun. Inside there was change too. There were painted hangings all round the wall, and in the parlour two new chairs with cushions. The little elm cupboard now held a salt of silver, two silver cups, a couple of bowls and three silver spoons. On top of it sat Meg's regals, and underneath it her lute.

It was all very trim, and on a morning like this with the sun shining in, a pleasant place, but the house in which Margaret Cheyne lived was like a house without doors and windows, through which a high wind blew. The wind could be warm, or shrewdly biting, but it was never still.

This morning the wind blew fair. Meg had ridden out before breakfast, and come back glowing; after breakfast she played in the yard with a litter of pups, was in and out of the kitchens and dairy pretending to be a good housewife, pulled out all her gowns from the presses saying she would make ready against the time when Sir John would take her to York and she would want to go gay. She had soon tired of that, and now July, in the old orchard, could hear her singing about the house.

The old orchard was still waiting to be tidied up, and remained a pleasant wilderness, and a refuge for July, who withdrew here when she wanted to be quiet and to feel safe. It lay tucked under the wall of the house, so close that she could hear if she was called and hurry in, but so well screened by trailing clumps of bramble and the crowded old apple-trees, that she was out of sight, and, with luck, might thus be out of mind.

To-day the late apples, high up and already warmed in the sun, smelt sweet, and the brambles were colouring, scarlet, yellow, and purple red; they and the grass alike were soaked in a foggy dew, for the sun had not yet reached them, so that the grass looked as grey as if hoar frost had touched it.

July picked up a windfall apple and went down the little twisting path that led to the gate; there had been a moat all around the house at one time, but this side was dry, and planks had been laid across so that people coming from Pinchinthorpe village might take this short cut instead of going round by the road.

July stood on the second bar of the gate, clutched the top with her elbows, and began to eat her apple. From here she could see one of the big fields of the village, pale where the stubble yet stood, but with brown ridges of ploughed land spreading over it. Four of the eight ox teams were working there now; one was so near that she could hear the creak of the yokes as the oxen plodded by. Gulls, swinging in the sunshine and dropping lower, settled on the new furrows, followed by crowds of smaller birds; above, the blue sky was stately with white clouds sailing.

Then from beyond the sandy bank below the pines, round

which the road ran, two riders came—a man and a woman. That was all that July could tell at first, but as they drew nearer she could see that the woman was huge; a vast bulk in a flowing plum-coloured cloak; the man was not so much a man as a boy, thin and angular, with straight fair hair and a cheek of as pretty a colour almost as Meg's own. July stared, wondering who they were, and where were their servants, for they were not the kind of people who should have been riding unattended.

She was so lost in the security of her solitude, that she was still hanging over the gate when they drew abreast. Only, for shyness, she dropped her eyes, and bit deep into the apple. Then she looked up because they had halted.

"That's no Pinchinthorpe lass," said the lady.

"But she's no more than a child," said the boy.

The lady pushed her big brown horse close to the gate. July, looking up at her, thought that she had never seen anyone so bulky; she wished she had run away before they had come near.

"Are you," the lady asked, in a voice astonishingly high and harsh for one of her comfortable looks—"Are you Sir John's strumpet?"

July felt her face grow cold. She knew now who the lady was. "No," she mumbled.

"Then who are you?"

It had come to pass, that which July had dreaded. Here was Dame Anne Bulmer, who had for distant kinsman Robert Aske. And here, at Pinchinthorpe, were Meg, Sir John's strumpet, and July, Meg's sister.

She said, "I am her sister," and felt the blood flow up into her cold cheeks until she burned visibly with her shame.

There was a long silence which seemed to her worse than anything, and then Dame Anne said, "Poor child, you should not be in such a house. You—I have a mind to carry you—" She stopped. July was staring at her. She hesitated and then said again, but as if she had intended other words, "No, indeed you should not be here." And then hastily to the young man, "Come, Rafe."

She rode on, but he lingered.

"Is—she—within?" he asked July, in a low voice, and July believed that he would have been glad to hear that Meg was not.

It came to her suddenly that they must not go in to Meg. "No," she cried. "No. She rode out. Do not go in."

The young man shook his head; clearly he wanted to believe her but could not. "We'll do her no harm," he said loftily, and went on after the lady.

July clung to the gate watching them out of sight. "Harm?" Those two gentle, good people—she knew that they were gentle and good, it was written all over them—those two, so kind and so defenceless, were going to see Meg. And Meg, impossible to bind as a fish or a flame, cold as the one and cruel as the other, Meg who could stab with words, would be as cruel to them as she knew how.

The nearest of the plough teams passed and re-passed twice before July moved from the gate. Something new had come into her mind, so new that time was needed to consider and accept it. Meg and she were separable. All her life till now July had counted them inseparable, but Dame Anne had separated them easily, with a few words. It was a great thought that made July feel free, as though she had passed over a threshold, and come out from a close room into open day.

She went back at last up the little slope of the orchard, into the old postern, and along the passage that led to the yard. But she stopped before she came out into the sunshine. The young man and Dame Anne had not yet gone. He was just now heaving up the great bulk of the lady into the saddle. At the well-head some of the Pinchinthorpe servants stood and tittered, and July heard Meg's laughter, musical and wild; she must be watching from the door of the Hall.

For the first time in her life July was aware that she hated Meg.

November 3

Most of the ladies of Princess Mary's Household were gathered about the big fire when she came in; they drew back, leaving place for her, but she only bowed her head in her shy, awkward way, and hurried through the room. But Mistress Mary Brown, who had followed her, told them that, "My Lady's Grace has a letter from the Queen," which silenced their talking and laughing for a few minutes, and made more than one of them stare at the door which the Princess had shut behind her.

It was dusk when the Countess of Salisbury came into the Princess's chamber, for she had been out riding. She saw Mary stand, a dark shape at the narrow, deep-set window, for this was not the pleasant house at Beaulieu, but the Castle of Hertford; the King had given Beaulieu to Queen Anne's brother, and had sent his daughter here.

Mary turned, saw the Countess with a candle in her hand, and turned back to the window. But she spoke, jerking the words out as though she could manage only a few at a time.

"A letter—from my mother—and a message for you. Read it." She stuck out a hand behind her, and the Countess took the letter from it and read.

DAUGHTER,

I hear such tidings to-day that I do perceive, if it be true, the time is come that Almighty God will prove you, and I am very glad of it.

She read on, the delicate proud stillness of her face untroubled, though many would have wept at the courage and nobility and tenderness of the letter. She came near to the end before she found any message for herself.

And now you shall begin, and by likelihood I shall follow. I set not a rush by it; for when they have done the uttermost they can, then I am sure of amendment. I pray you recommend me unto my good lady of Salisbury, and pray her have a good heart, for we never come to the Kingdom of Heaven but by trouble. Daughter, wheresoever you be come, take no pains to send to me, for if I may I will send to you. By your loving Mother, Katherine the Queen.

"What," asked the Countess, "does it mean?" She guessed that some message must have come with the letter.

"That my father will send me to the household of the bastard."

The Countess was silent.

"I am," said Mary, "to be one of her waiting women." Her voice was steady, but, as she spoke out of the shadows, it had no more body than if a shadow had been speaking.

"His Grace," she went on, "is persuaded that you—that my people—encourage me to resist his will, calling myself Princess of Wales."

"By God's Death! so we do, and so we shall."

Mary went on to the end of what she must say. "Therefore I am to go alone."

[266]

This time the Countess did not use any oath. She stood silent, and without movement, except that she turned the letter over and over in her fingers. She was a woman very strong in silence; therefore till she had resolved what to say she would not speak. The thing might not be true; but she could not say that, lest it should be true. She could not say, "Poor child," because this child had been born too high for pity. She decided upon something that must be said, and, taking the Princess hard by the wrist, she spoke at last.

"You must fear nothing, and you must yield nothing."

Now that she touched Mary she knew that the girl was shaking, but she only tightened her hold.

"In Her Grace's letter one thing is most true and most grave—"

"That I should obey my father?"

"That, of course." But it was not of that the Countess wished to speak, nor of those little tender trifles of advice, such as that the girl should keep her own keys if there were need, or recreate herself on her lute and virginals, if they allowed her to have any. "No," said the Countess, "but it is 'that you should keep your heart with a chaste mind, not thinking or desiring any husband.'"

"Yes," said Mary, "yes," but the Countess knew that she turned her head away.

"What?" she thought. "Not yet! She cannot favour any yet!"

She ran over in her mind all the men, young or not so young, here or at Beaulieu. Of preference towards any of them the girl had given no sign, and yet the Countess guessed rather than knew that she was one who would need greatly to love.

She said, because she must somehow find out what the averted face meant, "It is of course fitting that Your Grace should be married before long. But you cannot regret any of those betrothed to you by this treaty or that. The Emperor—you only saw him once, the Dauphin—never."

"No."

"Then," said the Countess, and let the girl's wrist drop. Mary turned away and leaned her hands on the stone sill, staring out into the garden which she could not now see.

"It is not any man. But I have thought of children—of a child—a little boy best," she said in a whisper.

The Countess went away across the room till she stood beside the bed. She laid her hand on one of the curtains, and stared at it as though she learnt the pattern by heart.

"Your Grace," she said at last, "Your Grace must put away such thoughts."

When Mary was silent she added, "For the love that you do owe to God."

"To God—" said Mary.

"And to your Mother, the Queen."

"To my . . ." the girl began, and then hurriedly—"Go. Leave me. Yes. I will be alone."

1534

January 1

Dame Anne Bulmer sat for a long time in front of her mirror, though not because she took thought for what she saw in it. She sat there because she needed time to be quiet, and once the mistress of the house launches herself upon the day she has little hope of quiet, especially during the Twelve Days of Christmas, when the house is full of company, and every meal is a feast. So when her woman had pinned in place the red velvet, looped-up hood, with its gable-shaped frame of gold wire and little pearls to lift it from the face; and had put round Dame Anne's neck a chain with a ruby hanging from it, and a shorter chain that carried a little gold case in which was a hair of St. John of Beverley; and had clasped the gilt and enamel girdle with its swinging pomander ball, Dame Anne told her to go, and sat still in the cold room. The bed, in which she had slept alone, was disordered; a thin mist crept through the window shutters, so that the candles burnt in a haze. The huge, heavy woman, with her square, swarthy face, sat still, leaning her elbows on the arms of the chair and staring straight in front of her; you would have said that she thought of the bread, beef, or beer needed in the kitchen, or of subtleties for the master's table; but it was not so. She had put all thoughts of these out of her mind and now she meditated upon Calvary.

When her nephew Rafe knocked and came in she turned her face slowly towards him, and smiled. Rafe being, as she was, a Bigod, neither missed nor misunderstood the beauty of the smile, but it made him angrier, and more determined to say all that he had come to say.

She let him go through with it, listening patiently, not looking at him, but now and again moving the powder box on the hutch in front of her, or the comb or the nightcap, in her slow heavy way. And when he had finished she took her time before she answered him.

"I bear it because it is that which Our Saviour has laid upon me to bear, and—"

"But it dishonours us—it dishonours you and Frank and me —that he should have brought his bawd into this house."

She shook her head, rebuking him for the interruption, and finished, "and so I follow Him, though a long way off, and halting."

"God's Death!" cried Rafe, in a hot rage, but when she hushed him he was ashamed, for he understood her, since he shared with her, and with his elder brother, that same quality which made some call them the mad Bigods—as if a lute string had been tuned to a note too high for ordinary ears.

Dame Anne lumbered up, like a cow rising in the meadow; she laid her hand for an instant along his cheek, meaning that the touch should speak for her, and it did. Rafe caught her hand to kiss it, and muttered, "Then we can suffer it too," while the blood ran up, bright as a girl's, to his hair.

"And now, nephew," Dame Anne said, going away from him to a chest at the foot of the bed, "you shall do an errand for me, if you will."

He said he would, and willingly, but when she told him what it was he was astonished and reluctant.

"Yea, yea," he cried impatiently, "I can see that it is not the child's fault that her sister is a bawd, but that you should send her a New Year's gift—it seems—it seems—"

Dame Anne came back and laid on his knee a little gay bunch of ribbon points.

"Give them to her and bid her Merry Christmas. I chose them of bright colours such as children love." She went away from him, her heavy crimson gown hissing over the rushes. "Rafe," she said, not turning to him, but fingering the dribbled wax that had run down the side of a candle, "Rafe, she is not like a child, that poor little maid. I have watched her since—they came. None of the servants will speak with her, not one. And the lads tease her. One of them threw a dead cat at her. She didn't cry out, or run, like a child. But she went past me, white as a ghost, and her eyes cast back like a hare's when the dogs are close. A child should not look so."

"Oh!" said Rafe. "Well, I'll give it to her," and he went out.

July was hovering at the kitchen door, looking and smelling. Inside the cooks ran about very hurried and hot, yet today never out of temper, and always with time enough to change jokes with any of the guests' servants who sat along a bench, each man dandling a cup of ale. On the long spits at the fire there were rows of small birds, as well as capons and partridges, which whirled slowly this way, then that way as the scullion boy turned the wheel. Below them on a bigger spit were rounds of beef, and a young pig, cut off at its middle and joined to the body of a fat goose. All these things hissed and spat, and smelt most toothsome. There were piles of mince pies on the table, and veal collops waiting for their sauce, and eggs, saffron, raisins of the sun, half a sugar loaf, and a lot of little bottles of spices waiting to flavour the sauces: from the Pastry came the sweet scent of pies and tarts baking. July's mouth watered, and then someone came up behind her and touched her arm, and she jumped round and away in the same movement.

"Mistress," said Rafe, "I am to bid you Merry Christmas and to pray you have this gift from my Lady Anne."

July looked at the little bunch of bright ribbons, and Rafe looked at her and saw what Dame Anne had seen, a child too young to have the right to that look of fear with which she had sprung from him. He was not only a Bigod, but also very young, and his mood changed in less than a breath from condemnation and disgust, to pity and rage for her sake. In the perturbation and enthusiasm of his feelings he cast the distance of the five years that were between them, and spoke like a boy of her own age.

"Mistress July," he said, "have you seen that room where they found the bones of the man long dead, with gold pieces between his fingers?"

"Oh!" she whispered. "No!"

"Shall I show it to you?"

"Oh!—Yes!"

The little room he led her to was in the oldest part of the house, and Rafe pointed out the arched doorway which had been walled up and forgotten for many years. The room beyond was small, and even by day almost dark, because there was nothing to light it but a slot window, set high up in one wall. Rafe had to make a light and set it to a candle that stood on the heavy table. Besides the table there was only a trussing bed, a small iron-bound coffer, a few old swords in one corner, and a mousetrap in another.

But here, at the table, Rafe said, they had once found a dead man, or at least his bones. The bones had been dressed in a gown of red silk such as came from Cathay, with patterns on it like feathers; a heavy belt had hung sagging about the thigh bones, made of square gilt bosses of goldsmith's work and a precious stone in each square. On the table the dry white finger-bones had clutched gold pieces of more than a hundred years ago.

July shuddered with a not unpleasant horror. She was indeed so warm with happiness that even the terror of a dead man could not chill her. Dame Anne had forgiven her for being Meg's sister.

She sat down beside Master Rafe Bigod upon the bed. She was shy of him now, and would look nowhere but at the pretty ribbons as she turned them about her fingers. He, though she could not have supposed it of one so old and important, was shy too; his long sensitive face was bright with embarrassed colour. There were, he was discovering, so few things that he could say to her, seeing that she was Meg Cheyne's sister. He wished, with passion, that he had not brought her here, then remembered his motive, and thereby found a topic which was not forbidden.

"Mistress July," he broke out abruptly on the silence, "you should thank God that has given you license to live in this time, for the Gospel of Christ was never so truly preached as it is now."

She looked up at him, startled and quite uncomprehending, and in the blankness of her surprise he read her need of instruction. He lost his shyness, and began to talk eagerly, looking at her, or beyond her, but always with a strange lit look, as though the things he spoke of were bright as a coloured sunset. July did not miss that look, but could not guess what caused it; he was telling her that the Mass was nothing, priest nothing, the Pope nothing, Our Lady nothing. Such a sweeping elimination left her disturbed and a little shocked, but not otherwise moved, for these matters were not such as she was used to give much thought to.

Yet when he told her to come to the little room again tomorrow she promised him that she would.

"I'll read to you in a book I have. It is a godly book called *The Prick of Conscience*."

July did not find the title promising, but Rafe was Dame

Anne's nephew, and he and his aunt were the only people in the world—that she could remember—who treated her as herself, and not as Meg's sister.

January 5

July came back to Meg's room in the dusk. There was a little table near the fire set for two—that meant Sir John Bulmer would be coming to sup with Meg. Two boys with viols, and a flute player, whom Sir John had sent up, were tuning and trying their instruments, and even now the little fat lad, whom Sir John had given Meg for a page, was on his knee before her with a bowl of water, and the towel for her hands laid ready over his shoulder.

July had hoped to slip in unnoticed, but Meg saw her directly, and called, "Sister! Sister!"

July went near, till she stood behind the kneeling page, who turned his round apple-blossom face and blue eyes to stare at her; the women stared too, and July's heart sank as she curtseyed.

"And where," asked Meg, with her wild laughing glance that took in all the room, "where have you come from, creeping in so quiet as a nun?"

July looked at her with her dark, unchildish look, but was silent.

"Marry!" Meg lifted her finger-tips from the water, and, laughing, splashed a few drops in July's face. "Marry! Mistress Sly, but I know, and I'll tell you—where, and who, and what. And when too—and when is to-day and every day of this New Year."

She told them also, truly enough, where and who, but when she began to tell what, July, whose face had changed from burning to white, stopped her.

"We did not—he did not—I sat beside him on the bed, but—"

The women so screeched with laughter that she stopped. Meg laughed too. "What then did he—and thou—and the pair of you if you did not that?"

"He talked to me—of—of—he said the Mass was but a May game."

They cried "Fie! Fie!" but they laughed again, perhaps believing her, for all knew the two young Bigods for the maddest heretics, yet teasing her. At last, hearing Sir John on the stairs, Meg hushed them. "Not a word more. But," she whispered before the door opened, "next time perhaps there'll be a different tale to tell, for even godly young men may wax wanton at Christmas-time."

That night July lay long awake. Meg's two women lay in the same room; one snored steadily; the other muttered now and again in her sleep. Outside the wind had risen; it moved like a great beast in the valley; sometimes by the sound it seemed to turn over and over and thrash about with its tail; sometimes it passed roaring by.

July, cold and very unhappy, listened, trying to resolve what she must do. If she went not to the little room to-morrow Master Rafe would think her ungrateful. If she went—Meg had so soiled her with the words she used that July believed he would see it in her face. Besides, it seemed that Meg had soiled him too.

The wind flung drumming showers against the window; after that there was a steady hush of rain as the wind ebbed; at last came the empty silence which wind and rain had left behind them, and in which snow began to fall. July slept. She had made up her mind that she could not bear to go.

January 6

It was nearly supper time and already dark. July had sat all afternoon and evening industriously sewing, or obligingly singing, according as Meg desired silence or music. Now she began to believe that the day would pass safely, and perhaps to-morrow would take Master Rafe hunting, and the day after that—but she would go no further than to-day.

Then the hue and cry began after Pourquoi, Meg's little dog, who had a French name because he had been brought from Calais, and who was very dear to his mistress. They sought everywhere, under beds, on beds, in the attics, and at last Meg said that July and the women should go round and about the castle and even through the yards and outbuildings, carrying lights and whistling and calling for Pourquoi.

So July went, but would in no wise part from the elder of the two women, though Gill had bidded her several times, "Go seek you in that direction and I'll go in this." "No! No!" July would say. "Let us go together."

They were crossing a little yard between the old spicery and the carpenter's shop, when two gentlemen with a lanthorn came out of one of the buildings. At the sight of July and Gill standing in the midst calling, "Pourquoi! Pourquoi!" the shorter and stouter of these raised a laugh and a shout.

"Mass!" he cried, coming swaggering over to them. "What's here? Bring the light, Rafe." Gill, giggling delightedly, would have boxed his ears; he caught her by the wrists, laughing, then swearing, then silent, because she was a strong wench and bold. They struggled together, in a violent, unseemly fashion that grew more and more ugly, until his foot slipped in the trodden snow of the yard, and then he stumbled and loosed her. She fled, but when he had recovered he was after her. The other two heard her scream, heard him laugh, and then there was silence, and they stood alone in the little yard, Rafe Bulmer still stupidly holding aloft the lanthorn that the other had bidden him bring near.

By its light July could see that he was dressed very fine in brocade the colour of ripening corn; she saw too that his face was flushed and loosened with wine.

He looked down at her. After what they had just seen her shrinking was a provocation. He remembered also that her sister was John Bulmer's bawd.

"I—I seek my sister's little dog," she said breathlessly, hoping to fend off with words that which Meg loved to angle for.

"Why did you not come to the little chamber this forenoon?" he asked. When she only shook her head, "Nay. You shall tell me," he persisted.

Her eyes, avoiding his, were caught by the gleam of the jewels in his cap. She tried, faintly, and clumsily, to fence with him.

"What is that pretty thing?"

"What thing?"

"In your cap."

He pulled off his cap and looked at the little gold and jewelled brooch.

"Leda and her swan," he told her, and met her eyes and saw them flinch. "No, by the Mass," he thought, "she's no innocent."

He was sure of it when she persisted, with a smile he took for brazen, "Who—who was she?"

"I'll tell you the story. Come up with me to the little room."

She went, dumb and helpless. She was helpless because he was Dame Anne's nephew—one of the good people, quite different from Meg. She knew that he was so, therefore if she said she would not go, she could not tell him why. Indeed there was no reason, for surely there could be nothing to fear. Yet she shook with fear.

There was a little stair leading up from the old spicery into the ancient part of the castle. They climbed up it, by the light of Rafe's lanthorn, July going first, he coming after with his hand on her all the time.

Dame Anne had gone down to speak to the Clerk of the Kitchen because when Sir John had called for figs to eat at the fireside in the Great Chamber, where he and his guests sat together talking and telling stories, and singing now and again, the Clerk of the Kitchen had sent back word that there were no figs.

So Dame Anne went down, found the Clerk and took him with her to look; she moved about in the dark corners of the store-room, while he carried a torch after her.

"I know there was a coppet of figs," she muttered. "I know it was not opened. What is that?"

"A coppet of great raisins, Madame."

"I know," she repeated, dogged and distressed, "that there is a coppet of figs." Then she turned, to tell him to bring the torch nearer, and saw that he had backed a little away, and was staring out along the little passage, staring and smiling. She did not like the smile.

"What is it?" she demanded.

"Madame, nothing." He was grave at once, and came near again with the torch.

She went to the door and looked out.

"There is no one there." Her mind returned to the figs. Sir John was displeased that they were lacking, displeased too that she had come to look for them. He would be more displeased still if she were away long. She turned again into the stillroom, and as she turned remembered the little dim room along the passage. She guessed what sort of thing it was that the Clerk had seen, and was angry.

"Did you," she asked him, "see someone go into the chamber there?"

He hesitated, and she stamped her foot.

"You did? Who? Who?"

He mumbled something about Christmas.

"And you think the men and wenches have license to be wanton because it is a holy feast. But I'll not have it. Not in my—" she stopped short because it came back into her mind with a new shame and desolation that her own husband thought he had license to be wanton, in her house. But though she flushed a hot, ugly red before the man's face she did not turn away.

"Go and knock on the door," she told him. "Bid them come out."

"Madame," he said, hastily and confusedly, "let alone. It is nothing. They have come here each day," he added, as if that made it better.

She went out of the stillroom, and he came behind her, half sorry, half relishing the humour of it. When she had thumped on the door and flung it open he was at her shoulder, peering in.

But Dame Anne did not let him stay, and when she had driven him off she sent Rafe also away. He, who had never before seen his aunt angry, was frightened by her. He tried to hold his ground, tried to assure her lightly that a few kisses were all; all he intended, all he'd got, and that they were nothing. "There was no more." He turned to July for her to confirm that, but she had her hands still over her face, and they could see her whole body shake.

He shouted at her, suddenly angry.

"As if you knew naught of such things. As if you had never seen, nor heard—you with a sister who—"

He went then because Dame Anne said, "Go," and he dared not linger. She shut the door behind him, and then she turned and spoke to July. She had suffered her husband to bring his bawd to the house where she lived. She would not suffer that another of that corrupt blood should befoul Rafe—Rafe who was almost more her own than her own boys, being Bigod as she herself was Bigod. She proceeded, slowly and implacably, to maul July with words. If she could have killed with words, she would have killed.

January 8

Lord Darcy had with him his steward, Thomas Strangways, who had just reached London. They had turned their backs on the table, littered with papers, pens and ink, rolls of accounts, and the sheepskin pouches that held wax, seals, laces, scissors, and all the things needed for letters or chirographs. Now they sat side by side on the settle before the fire, with a dish of winter apples between them, exchanging news of the North for news of London where doings were greater and graver.

Strangways listened while Darcy talked, rasping his forefinger down the bristles of his hard weather-beaten cheek.

He was a man of a few years younger than Darcy, with a look open, choleric and bold. They had been good friends ever since the days when Darcy had been Captain of Berwick Castle and Strangways gentleman porter of the city.

"And so," said my Lord, "this Parliament is set to do fine things, at the King's bidding. For the King will make Bishops now, and is Head of the Church, and not the Pope."

"That," said Strangways, "he cannot be. How can a secular man be Head of the Church? Will he be Head of all Christendom?" His face was flushed up to his hair by the heat of the fire or by indignation.

"Not of all Christendom, but of the Church in England only."

"But there's no more than one Church Catholic." When Darcy let that go in silence Strangways muttered, "Will this thing be suffered?" and a little later, "If man will not, then shall we surely see God Himself take a hand."

"There was—" Darcy spoke at last, "this Nun in Kent with her visions that the King should not live, but he has lived, and she and those that trusted her are like to die instead. Soon there will be a Bill brought in to attaint them."

He looked sideways at Strangways as if uncertain whether to say more or hold his tongue. Then he said:

"I did myself, with many others, think that God might speak by that poor soul. If it had been so—" He broke off. "When I was a younger man than I am now, I took upon me a Crusade." Again he glanced at Strangways, sharply, as if with suspicion. "But in this matter I know not—I know not—" he muttered.

Strangways shook his head heavily. He said that there was a woman that they talked of in Swaledale at a Priory there, that had seen a vision of late. Or so it was said in those parts.

Darcy swung round at him. Who was she, this woman? Nun or no? Who had told Strangways of her? Was she known for a person of holy life? Last of all he asked, "What was it then that she saw?"

Strangways said that it was a showing of shepherds and angels on Christmas Eve.

"How? Tell me as you heard it."

Strangways crossed his legs, and picking up an apple from the dish dandled it in his palm as he talked. The woman had seen—no, had heard, and partly by starlight seen—said she had heard and seen the blessed shepherds go by as she looked out at a little low window; they were going to find the Holy Child. And she said also that she had heard the angels sing that same night, though the words they sang she could not rehearse, "being a simple creature, as I was told."

"Go on," said my Lord.

"The fellow told me that the woman said, 'It was deep, deep dark, smelling of frost, with stars by the thousand. I heard them laugh and shout, and their dogs bark.' And she says, 'The shepherds sang "Ut hoy," and "Tirly Tirlow." ' "

"And the singing of the angels?"

"That was after."

"She saw them?"

"They say, no. She said, 'I saw them not, for I suppose they had put out all the lights of heaven and set open the windows that they might see him in the stable low down in the Dale.' She spoke much of peace also, so they say." Strangways pulled down the corners of his mouth and shook his head, but sadly.

"It will serve," said Lord Darcy, and he laughed softly.

Strangways turned and stared. The old Lord had his chin on his fist, gazing into the fire. As he sat there with his fine features, proud head, and hair warmed again to gold by the light of the fire, he looked almost a young man.

"You cannot," said Strangways, "give the tale credit! Why! Shall she not have heard some fellows go singing by to the ale-house? And as to the angels, what of the Ladies at their Matins and Lauds?"

"Many will credit it," said Darcy. "Shall I tell you for why? Listen then. This Nun of Kent saw, or said she saw, devils whispering Queen Anne Boleyn in the ear; and when the Cardinal died, a disputation of devils. Such things move discontents. Such things may be feigned of men, using a fool, in order to move discontents.

"But this talk of angels and of shepherds—it is so simple it smells all of truth indeed."

Strangways fidgeted on the bench. "Yet," he said, "there is in it nothing to our purpose."

"She can be taught to utter some words of solemnity, and so we can use her and her visions."

Strangways scowled and muttered something about, ". . . like this poor fool of Kent." Darcy looked at him quickly.

"You would not have me use her?"

"They spoke her as a very simple poor creature."

"Ah! Tom," said Darcy, "none would think, to look at

[278]

that leathern face of yours, that it hid so pitiful a mind. You'd not have me bring another poor fool into peril of her life?"

"If the North rise for a right cause," Strangways grumbled, "what need to use her?"

Lord Darcy did not answer. A strange doubt had touched him. For if these things were indeed of God, "It is my own soul I bring in peril," he thought.

After a moment he laid his arm across Strangways' shoulders, and said, "God forgive us worldly men, and bless the poor humble folk, for Christ was born in a manger."

January 9

Meg stopped July at the door of the winter parlour. She caught July's shoulder and pressed it so hard that her rings bit on July's bone.

"Now mark and remember!" she whispered. "Whether or no there was more than kisses I shall say there was, for so shall I wring out advantage for you. And do you say the same."

July wriggled in silence; Meg loosed her shoulder, opened the door, and marched in, braving them all with her heavy body, great with a seven-months' child, and her face quick as bright flame.

Sir John stood with one foot on the hearth; Dame Anne sat opposite him, her fingers straining at her beads; Rafe straddled a bench under the window, and glowered down a little toy of a dagger he wore. His brother, Sir Francis Bigod, older, thinner, and with a kind of noble ferocity of look, sat on a settle, and kept his eyes, blue and hard, upon his brother. Beside Sir Francis on the settle was Sir John Bulmer's brother, Sir Rafe Bulmer of Marrick, and beyond him Sir Rafe's wife Nan followed with her finger down to the page of a book on her knee, reading how best to shoe jennets.

There was no place for Meg, except Sir John's own great chair, and Dame Anne, sitting broad as a crouching frog, dared Meg with her eyes to take it. But then Sir Francis sprang up, and Meg, going by him with a very sweet, kind look, sat down in his seat. He met that look with one of such disgust that even Meg's cheeks tingled at it, and on the settle Sir Rafe slid himself away from her, crowding up on his wife. No one marked July, stiff as wood by the door.

Meg looked round at them all and laughed her high wild laugh, and plunged at once into battle.

The clamour of tongues died after a while. Meg sat panting,

her hand to her side, biting her lip at Sir John who had just bid her be silent for a fool; she was mad to think that Rafe should marry the little bastard—no matter whether the lad had—

Dame Anne broke in there in her harsh deep voice, speaking only to her husband.

"And no matter whether, either she or I shall go from Wilton."

"Fie!" cried Meg, "turn from the door a gentlewoman so wronged!"

"A wanton and a bastard."

"God's Death! Peace!" cried Sir John, for this was to begin all over again, and then he repeated for the third or fourth time that there'd be no harm done, and no blame if they married the little wench to a good, sober yeoman.

"Disparagement!" Meg cried once more, and shot a flaming proud glance at them all. "Bastard she may be, but of a House that overmatches any blood here."

Sir Rafe Bulmer of Marrick had said nothing all the time, but now he broke in with a laugh, liking Meg for her beauty and her spirit.

"Make the lass a nun," said he.

"No!" said Sir Francis Bigod.

They all turned to look at him. He came and stood in the midst, and again said, "No." There was on his face that shining look July had seen in Rafe.

"Will you," he asked, "so choose them that are to serve God? If my brother have deflowered the maid he shall marry her."

"Frank!" cried Dame Anne, "I'll not endure it."

"Aunt," he rebuked her, "you and I and he alike must endure it. It is the punishment of his sin."

"But," Nan Bulmer's cool light voice came gently upon a shocked silence, "if the little wench should choose to be a nun?"

"She? She will not!" Dame Anne looked at July and the look said, plain as words, "A whore, and a whore's sister."

"But ask her."

"Do you then," Rafe Bulmer told his wife.

"Would you," said Nan, "be married, Mistress, or be a nun?"

July, seeing all their faces turned on her, grew white and choked. She had not followed all that was said, but now this was clear.

She cried suddenly, shrill as a whistle—

"I will not be married to him. I will be a nun."

When all the rest had gone out, July the last of them and least noticed, Rafe Bulmer drew his wife to the window.

"How will this fadge?" said he. "Bastards should not be nuns."

"Dame Christabel will not care for that, so as the wench brings her dower."

He whistled. "Dame Christabel! You mean—fetch her to Marrick? 'A God's name, why?"

"I do not like her sister," Nan told him; and when he laughed at her and said that was because Meg was so fair and beautiful a creature, she said no, it was not for that reason. "You know I like well that women should be fair. But I like not her."

He pondered over that a moment and then came back to the matter in hand.

"The other Ladies may not be willing to have the girl."

She smiled. "Dame Christabel will not care for that neither." After a moment she gave a small laugh. "Those mad Bigods! There goes Frank braying out that young Rafe must suffer for wronging the wench, and the wench was never wronged."

"How dost thou know?"

Nan looked at him with her faint grave smile.

"I asked her, since none else thought to. She said, 'No.' "

"Then why—? But she may have lied."

Nan said no, she was sure July had not lied, "And she is virtuous."

"What! With that sister? Though she's but little more than a child."

"Child or woman, so she is," Nan told him positively. "And that is why she hates her sister."

January 20

Those two of Queen Katherine's ladies whose duty it was to-day to fetch food for the Queen's breakfast met again near the door of the Pastry. Both had pink noses and blue fingers, for the air was sharp, and the perpetual winter chill of the waterlogged country all round made it colder still in the late dawn. One of the two had been waiting for the milking; watching from the door of the dark shippen, where the lanterns cast huge shadows, and caught here the cross beams of the roof, there the wide shining eye of a cow, and there the thin steam of its breath, puffing, spreading and fainting from sight. Now she brought again the pitchers full of the warm, frothed milk, and found the other waiting, stamping her feet, with a white loaf and some eggs in a basket, and on top of the eggs a fish.

Neither of these ladies was young, and therefore there was nothing amusing, either in having to fetch the food, or in having to cook it over the fire in the Queen's Chamber. They did what they had to do in silence for the most part, and with set lips; they beat the eggs for the posset with anger and impatience, and having set the fish to broil, fastidiously wiped their fingers. From the further side of the room, a yet older lady came and looked down at the fish, already hissing and steaming in the heat.

"Is that—safe?"

The lady who brought it nodded. "Quite safe. I took it from among those for the Chamberlain's own table. I tumbled off all that were on top. No one could have known that this was the one I would take. And I did the same with the loaves."

"Well," said the elder lady doubtfully, "I suppose there can be nothing unhonest therein." Not for worlds would any of them have used the word "poison."

"Jesu! You'd have Her Grace live wholly upon eggs, I think," the other replied sharply, having been a little proud of her foraging. But then they were silent, because the door opened and Queen Katherine came in from Mass. She smiled at them all, a smile which was sweet as it had always been, but which left her face dead when it faded. She sat down at the table and leaned her head upon her hand; even when they served her she still seemed to need that help to bear it up, and so toyed with the food listlessly, with one hand.

While she was eating there came to the door the new servants appointed by the King to her Household, with dishes for her breakfast. They were told that my Lady's Grace was already served, and went away without surprise or demur; it was well known to them by now that the Princess Dowager would now eat nothing but what was fetched and cooked by her own people.

February 1

The setting sun was flooding the top of the fells with gold as Sir Rafe Bulmer and his people came back towards Marrick. Near Langshaw Cross they caught up with the shepherd bringing back the Manor sheep. The servant behind whom July rode stopped to talk to Shepherd; the sheep strayed about him; when you looked at them against the golden light they seemed all to be steeped in violent purple.

By the time the servant had finished his talk with Shepherd, and gone on after the others to the Manor, and was ready to bring July down to the Priory, the sun had set, though the sky was still bright and warm over towards the west. But as they dropped down the hill twilight met them; soon all the air was washed through with a kind of clear darkness. The earth was turning back from day towards its nightly privacy, and man, who had during the light been master, now moved as a stranger, ignored rather than unwelcome, upon whom, departing, doors were softly closed. July, riding pillion behind the silent servant, lifted her eyes and saw the first star prick out among the bare sharp branches of an ash tree, in a sky as green as it was blue. Another light, nearer and warmer, caught her eye, and when she turned she could see the lit windows of the Priory. Candles burned in the upper rooms with a clear, twinkling flame, but the painted windows of the Church were lit with a coloured steady glow.

She looked back down the Dale, and would have been glad to stay hidden there, unnoticed in the deep tranquillity, and covered by the rising dark. But the servant rode on to the gate-house.

He sat awhile with Jankin the Nuns' porter, while July went in to wait on the Prioress in the Parlour. He told Jankin a great deal about July's sister; Jankin would not believe that she was so beautiful as he said, but did not doubt that she was as bad. As to July, the Bulmers' man admitted that one said this and another that; but Jankin was always happy to believe the worst.

February 18

Robert Aske shifted some crumbs on the table one way and another with the curve of his hand; he made them into a neat pile, and scattered them again with his finger. The Hall of Gray's Inn was full of barristers and benchers at table, of the good smell from their supper, of the sound of their talking, and of the trembling flames of many candles.

For once Aske himself was not talking but listening, his heavy brows drawn together, his big mouth pouted forward and very tight at the corners. His neighbours were disputing as to how that clause had come into Magna Charta by which

Ecclesia Anglicana libera sit, and what was meant by it. Those round about him spoke of the words as words written in ink upon parchment, which, like pieces in a game of chess, would be set against other words; to move words thus against each other made a very good game. It was a game too that Aske liked well to play, but not to-night, not with these words, because these meant something too real to play with. If Parliament should give, as Parliament was busy giving, all power over the Church in England into the hands of the King, how should the Church in England be free?

Aske covered the crumbled bread with his hand, and stared unseeing at the thin grey beard on a Bencher's chin that wagged between him and a candle flame as the old man talked. These new laws that were being made overshadowed his mind with something of the unease and oppression that goes before a thunder-storm. And away down below that and almost out of hearing there was a voice that asked a question—"If these things were done, what should a man do?" But that meant, "What shall *I* do?"

When supper was over and all stood up he shook his shoulders as if he shrugged off a cloak, and went away to his own chamber. Will Wall was there, turning some clothes out of a chest. He had in his hands an old velvet coat of his master's, and as he looked up, his long, dark, melancholy face was so full of trouble that Aske cried out to know what was wrong.

"Perdy!" said Will, "the pile of this velvet is so rubbed as a rye-field beat down with rain. I don't like to see you go so poorly, Master Robin, as to wear such a thing."

Aske laughed, and, on his way to the bench by the fire, flicked Will's shoulder lightly with his hand, feeling a sudden warmth of relief and assurance in the old and close tie that bound the two of them. Parliament nor the King could not change Will, nor change all the settled faithfulness between man and man—so settled that you forgot about it till you found yourself stand in the midst of change.

He said, as he got down his book from the shelf, "Then take it for yourself, Will. It'll trim your grey camlet gown."

Will's face lit, but he hesitated. "It'd trim that red doublet of yours, Master."

"Lord!" Aske said, "I'm beautiful enough without any such adorning," and grinned at him, and began to read. Will went away with the velvet coat over his arm, to get his supper.

After a while Aske laid the book on his knee and reached for a bundle of parchments, the evidences of the Kentish squire who had briefed him lately—charters and chirographs all tied together by a hawk's creance, and kept in a soiled bag of white leather. He had forgotten the troubles of the times and now was whistling through his teeth, for he saw the way he could plead, to establish his own case and undermine the other; argument and counter-argument came so trippingly to his mind that suddenly he drove his fist down upon the end of the bench, swearing, "By God's Passion, I'll have them there!" and felt power, like a shiver, go right down his spine.

April 16

The Benchers and Barristers of the Inns were called to Lambeth this day, to take the oath. There was a great crowd in the Hall of the Archbishop's Palace, mostly of men of law, but also of other gentlemen; those of them who stood near the fire steamed like a wet washing day, for the rain had beat on them as they crossed the river, and now it rattled upon the windows of the Hall, and hissed in the swirling flames of the fire.

At the upper end of the room the Archbishop, the Chancellor, and the Dukes of Norfolk and Suffolk sat behind the table. They took no part in what was going on, except that at times one or another of them would lift his hand to his cap in answer to a greeting from some Bencher or Sergeant-at-Law among the crowd. For the most part the Lords talked softly, together; the Archbishop did not talk but seemed to watch each man's face as he came up to take the oath; there was a pewter pot in front of him with daffodils and sprigs of rosemary in it, and now and then his fingers fidgeted with the flowers. In front of the table two clerks stood; each had a book in one hand and a copy of the oath in the other; not that they needed any copy by now, so well they had the words by heart after having repeated them to so many.

Hal Hatfield and Wat Clifton found themselves at the head of the slowly moving line. The clerks bent their heads, listening, then made a motion with their hands, and the two barristers passed on towards the door. Aske had come in with them, but the three had got separated in the crowd. He had just now come to stand before one of the clerks; Hatfield and Clifton muttered, "Stay a moment," each without hearing what the other said; their eyes were on Aske.

[285]

The clerk repeated the oath, phrase by phrase, as he had done for each man; Aske said it after him; they could hear his voice over the shuffling of feet and the subdued sound of talking. He joined them at the door and together they went out.

The shower was taking off as they came slowly from under the gate-house. Hal drew in a great breath of rain-sweetened air.

"There are," he said, "many good reasons—many good reasons in law why no man should scruple to swear."

"Aye," said Clifton. "Many."

Hal ran through a few of them; they were at his tongue's end, for at Gray's Inn the matter had been fully debated ever since Parliament had, more than a fortnight ago, ordered that every man and woman in the kingdom should take the oath to uphold the King's second daughter for his lawful heir, born of a lawful marriage. That meant that his first marriage was no marriage at all, and that, again, the Pope's dispensation for the marriage was nothing. Matters such as these, of great moment and of as great complexity, had provided ample material for argument.

"I," said Clifton, glancing at Aske who was silent, "I took the oath adding 'so far as the law of Christ allows.' "

"They did not stickle at it?" Clifton shook his head. Hal turned to Aske. "Did you the same, Robin?"

"No," said Aske, and they looked away from him.

But next moment he had put his arms so roughly about their necks that he bobbed their heads together.

"Come," he said loudly, "let's drink! This taking of oaths makes me thirsty."

They sat in front of their pint pots till it was past noon, with not another thing said of the business that had brought them to Lambeth. When they went down to the river to take a boat they were arguing about fishing, each was extolling that fly, or bait, which above all others, so he said, was beloved of trout and grayling. They came down to the Hard which, as the tide was low, stretched a long way out through the washed, smooth sands. The wind had dropped, the rain was over, and against the grey, quiet sky the gulls showed coldly white. Aske brought the dispute to a sudden and tame conclusion.

"Oh! well, maybe you will take them as well with one fly as with another. Though," he muttered, "in our fenny waters—" He broke off there, shrugged and let it alone.

He was silent for a minute and then said, as if he were in a hurry to have it spoken before they stepped into the wherry, "Sir Thomas More and the Bishop of Rochester lie this day in the Tower. Yet is their conscience clean."

April 20

When Chapter was over and everyone back in the Cloister the two other novices, good little girls who had not received correction in Chapter, drew themselves away from July. They had known that she told lies, and mimicked the Ladies behind their backs, but now that everybody knew it and July had been birched before all the House they did not wish to be seen associating with her.

So July stood alone, smiling, because that was the way to hide anything that hurt. But it is difficult to maintain a smile for a long time, especially when it is only for the sake of defence; the smile became a grin, then a grimace. She was very glad when the bell rang for Terce and they must all go into Church.

When they came out from Chapter Mass lessons began again. July, crouching within herself, did not for some time observe that her companions seemed to have forgotten that she had on her something which she had supposed to be indelible as the mark of Cain. But when the Novice Mistress dropped her book, and almost overset her chair as she bent to recover it, the other two novices, confining their giggles by hands pressed over their mouths, turned their eyes, shining with laughter, upon her, to share the fun. And a little later the Novice Mistress, who had laid on the birch, commended July's reading.

At first July was incredulous. Yet it was true. These people here were as kind as happy. And that evening old Dame Eleanor Maxwell, deaf as a post, slow as a cow, and sweet as new-made bread, gave July a little carved box. Dame Eleanor had been one of those whom July had mimicked, and when the old lady put her box into her hands she almost dropped it, and blushed up to her veil for shame. But Dame Eleanor, muttering, "To keep your bobbins in. To keep your bobbins tidy," patted July's hand and closed her fingers round the box. July went away, still with a very hot face, glad that Dame Eleanor had missed the part of the accusations in Chapter, and dreading lest someone should now tell her.

She went away to the room where she slept and took out from the trussing coffer her bobbins and her thimble and laid them in Dame Eleanor's box. The twilight was coming in very quietly, and here and there in the woods birds were singing which had felt the first motion of the spring this sweet still day. July lingered. There was a doubt in her mind; it was vaguer than a question, but yet it was there. Was there any need to tell lies and to mock in this quiet place? The doubt, even though she did not try to resolve it, brought a kind of ease like that which the quiet evening had brought to the Dale; outside the windows, as dusk gathered, fields and trees turned to sleep too softly even for the release of a sigh.

May 14

The ostler of the White Horse at Cambridge tossed up the saddle of the bay mare onto the peg and looped the irons over it. Then he came back to take off the bridle, but his mind was not on that but on the argument that had risen between him and Mr. Patchett's servant, who now leaned against the door prodding at the cobbles with a faggot-stick he had picked up in the yard, and declaring that the Pope should put all right, and make King Harry take his own wife again.

"There is no Pope," cried the ostler, and jagged at a buckle so sharply that the bay threw up her head and laid back her ears. He left her and went to the doorway. "There is no Pope," he repeated, "but only a Bishop of Rome." A few loiterers outside, hearing the note of controversy, came nearer to listen.

Mr. Patchett's servant ground the end of the faggot-stick into the crack between two cobbles. "There is a Pope," said he, "and they that hold the contrary are strong heretics."

"Hah!" cried the ostler. "If I am a heretic yet I have the King's Grace who holds of my part."

"Then are both you a heretic and the King another. And this business never would have been if the King had not married that strumpet Nan Boleyn."

"Fie!" cried the ostler, who was a little man but stringy and tough, whereas Mr. Patchett's servant was a large, soft man.

The loiterers outside closed in; a dog came and skulked about round the outside of the group. In the midst the two were arguing ever more hotly. "Knave!" the ostler called his opponent and then Mr. Patchett's servant raised the faggot-stick and broke the ostler's head.

At that moment a company of grave gentlemen were coming out of the door of the White Horse; most of them were

Doctors of the University, but among them was the Mayor. He stopped, and then crossed the yard.

"What's this?"

The ostler with his hands to his head clamoured, "Master Mayor! Master Mayor!" When the Mayor had heard his story he looked very grim. "For it smelleth to me of treason what you, fellow, have said," and he frowned on Mr. Patchett's servant.

"Mass!" said he, being a man of temper and courage for all his fat look. "Mass! then is half the realm in treason with me; for as I say, they think."

June 2

"Now," said the Novice Mistress, "we shall read again in *The Revelation of Divine Love* of Dame Julian of Norwich. The First Revelation—the Fourth Chapter. Take you the book." She gave the book to the eldest novice, who began to read:

And in this, suddenly I saw the red blood running down from under the garland, hot and freshly, plenteously and lively, right as it was in the time that the garland of thorns was pressed on his blessed head, right so both God and man the same that suffered for me.

July leaned her elbows on her knees and slid her hands up inside her veil so that she could press her fingers into her ears to keep out the words. She succeeded so well that she nearly got herself into trouble, because when it came to her turn to read, Bridget had to jog her arm, and, even when she took the book, she had no idea of the place, for instead of following over Bridget's shoulder she had shut her eyes tight too.

"Where?" she whispered urgently, and Bridget's finger came down on the page—

Notwithstanding, the bleeding continued till many things were seen—and understood,

she began breathlessly, but Bridget jogged her again, and pointed.

The plenteousness is like to the drops of water that fall off the eavesing of an house after a great shower of rain, that fall so thick that no man may number them with

[289]

any bodily wit. And for the roundness, they were like to the scale of herring in the spreading of the forehead.

These three things came to my mind in the time: pellets, for the roundness in the coming out of the blood; the scale of herring, for the roundness in the spreading: the drops of the eavesing of an house, for the plenteousness unnumerable.

This showing was quick and lively, and hideous and dreadful, and sweet and lovely.

July gabbed on as fast as she could, trying not to understand what she read. To her the showing was hideous and dreadful indeed, but it was nothing else.

When the Novice Mistress said, "Enough," July shut the book with alacrity. "Now it is time," said the Novice Mistress, "that ye should turn to your broidering. But in your minds ponder that ye have read."

They sat thereafter in a demure silence. The Cloister was empty of the Ladies, who, this fine warm day, were gone out to the dale-side to sit among the young bracken and in the shade of the thorn bushes, spinning and sewing. Only the Sacrist's big striped cat lay at ease in the sunshine on the paving of the North Cloister walk. From the Great Court came voices of servants, men and women, and sometimes the soft gabbling of ducks. There was also a steady hum of bees in the flowers of the Cloister garth.

July, glancing up sharply from her work, tried to read the Novice Mistress's face. It was absorbed and serene as she stooped over a little purse of scarlet silk. July did not understand how it could be serene after the horror of pain that the book had laid bare. She grew angry with the Novice Mistress—did she not understand what she was doing, to make them read such things? The little Priory between the dale-side and the quick-running Swale had become for Julian a lodge of leafy branches built on a summer day, so pleasant, so flimsy as that. She did not want the woven branches torn open to let in the sight of God suffering. She wanted not to know—or rather to un-know—that there was suffering everywhere.

July 12

Early in the morning the hay-makers set out from the Priory to carry in from the last and farthest of the Priory closes. The Cellaress went a little later, and with her the three novices, and the mother of the youngest of them. It was only because she had asked it of the Prioress that the three were allowed the treat of spending the day in the hay-field. Jane's mother knew what little girls liked; she was young herself and pretty, and plump; not heavily plump, but with something of the soft, airy roundness of a dandelion clock.

So with bread and meat, cheese and beer, and a pannier of cherries, they set off from the Priory gate across the open field to the gate at the foot of Marrick Steps. Here and there in the grass at their feet there shone a soft blink of wet gold, where the sun caught a dewy cobweb. But in the woods the shade was thick, and the air damp and green. Jane, who lived in her own private world of marvels, heroisms, and holinesses, walked behind the others with her finger on her lips and treading softly because someone, she was sure, had said "Hush!" to the trees, and there was somewhere under a great stone a monstrous fairy toad, with a gold crown on his head. If the trees kept quiet long enough he might look out from under the stone. Her mother and the Cellaress talked pleasantly of grown-up matters. July and the eldest novice forged ahead to reach the hay-making quickly.

After a long morning in the open, burning field, and dinner eaten in the shade of an ash tree with all the hay-makers, the girls were content for a while to lie idle, watching the women move along the swathes with their rakes, the men gathering the small pikes into kyles, then tossing up the kyles onto the wains. Their voices came pleasantly in the heat, and pleasantly too the thin hiss of the hone on a scythe blade from a nearby Close, where one of the Marrick yeomen was cutting his hay.

The two elder novices dozed, slept, wakened, and dozed again. Jane had curled herself up against her mother's thigh; whenever the other two wakened they heard her talking.

She said, "Madame, there were many knights that had their pavilions set at the ford below the Priory . . . where the stepping-stones are . . . I saw a dipper there yesterday; he told me he had three eggs in his nest . . . He said he would show them to me one day when he had leisure. . . . There was a red pavilion, a gold pavilion, and one all stripes of blue and green. Every day the knights ride into the Dale to find Paynim knights to joust with, and damsels to deliver." She paused to stretch and yawn like a puppy, then laid her cheek down on her mother's knee. After a while, "Madame," said she in a drowsy voice, "wot you that there is a mermaid at the Priory?"

Her mother, never surprised, never incredulous, remarked placidly, "Nay. In truth?"

Jane sat up to explain that "she was a mermaid but the Lady said she could not be so she was not." She hesitated, then said, "Some say she is a fool, and some that she is a holy creature though foolish. But we must not speak abroad of what she has seen, because the Lady will be angry."

She wriggled herself nearer. "I asked her, Madame, how it was to live beneath the sea, and of the caves and palaces there. She would not tell. But she told me what she saw last Twelfth Night. Can I tell you?"

Her mother snipped off a length of green silk, puckering up her eyes against the light. "Tell me, but not others," she said.

"Malle," said Jane, "—her name is Malle—Malle went up to the Manor that night to fetch a feather bed; there were so many guests at the Priory that there were not beds enough, and then Dame Anne Ladyman's sister came." She giggled. "July and I had to sleep in the same bed, and we talked till the Ladies woke for Matins." She turned to smile at July, but July's eyes were shut.

"It was the time of the great snow, and the moon shone, Malle said. And as she came back by the woodside there ran two boys after her down the hill, and about the snowy field, the one chasing the other. He who was chased was laughing full sweetly, Malle said. She said that when she heard Him laugh she knew it was God's little Son. She said none other but He could laugh so happily as that, since none but only He knew joy so nigh. And, Madame, Malle said—"

"Did Malle say that?" Jane's mother asked.

Jane stopped, considering. "I think she did."

The eldest novice, who had wakened, interrupted here, with brutal frankness.

"Jane is making it up. Malle doesn't talk like that. She is only a fool, and stutters when she talks. She would not say such things."

Jane flushed. She shrugged the eldest novice off with her shoulder, and spoke only to her mother.

"That is what she meant to tell me. That is what she saw."

"And," said the eldest novice, "you know, Jane, that we are forbidden to tell her foolish sayings."

Jane's mother turned the conversation easily and pleasantly by reaching out a dangling handful of cherries from the little pannier, and bobbing them against Jane's lips. The others sat up too, and all ate cherries, and soon after tied on their straw hats, and went out again to help with the hay.

As the two elder girls went raking one after the other along a swathe, the eldest novice spoke gravely of Jane's disobedience in talking of Malle's crazy sayings.

"Humph!" said July, and would not, though the other tried to persuade her, say any more for a time, only, "Let her alone. There's no harm in that."

"Dost thou then," the eldest novice asked, "believe in this foolishness?"

July thought, "If it is true! If God knows joy! If we coming toward Him come nearer to joy, and that without fear!"

To the other novice she said, "Nay."

"For," said that young lady, who had reached her priggish age, "if any were to see such a vision, it would not be a wench like Malle, but the Prioress, or one of the Ladies, or even . . ." She stopped there, without mentioning novices.

July thought, "Jesu! Mary! St. Andrew! Let it be true!" Then she thought, "I shall find Malle and make her tell me that it is true." But very soon she knew that she would not dare do that, for fear she should find out that it was a lie.

August 20

The King came in to sup with the Queen in her apartments. In the antechamber one of her ladies was playing on the virginals, others were reading, or whispering together; two of the youngest were playing with a kitten. Everything seemed as usual, but when the King had looked sharply round, not one of them, as they rose to curtsey, would meet his eye. He indicated with a wave of his hand that no one should follow him into the Privy Chamber beyond, and went by quickly.

The Queen sat there, alone, between the yellow candles and a lowering red sunset. She got up from her chair and curtseyed very low; her eyes were on the ground but at the look of her the King knew that he had guessed right, and that though in the antechamber all seemed pleasant pastime and cheerfulness, a storm had raged here lately. Besides, it had by no means escaped his notice that one of the Queen's Maids who should have been in attendance was not.

"Madame," he said, lowering his head, and going straight at the point, "where is—"

The Queen did not even give him time to speak the girl's name.

"She is not here. She is not here," she burst out; and now she raised her eyes and braved him. "I will not have her here. Oh! I know. Jesu! But I can see. And I'll have no rutting here among my maids. She shall go home." She gave a sudden sharp cackle of laughter. "Christ! Now you will say that it means nothing that you must sit by her, and lean over her and paw her—Ah!"

She stopped because he had moved so abruptly.

"No, Madame," he said, not speaking loudly at all, but— she could not help herself. She started back as if he had raised his fist to her, and could only hope he did not see how fast her breath went.

"No, Madame, I shall not say that. But I shall remind you of what I have done in raising you, and what you were before I raised you. And I shall counsel you to be content with what I have done, the more because if it were to do again, I would not do it."

He smiled at her unpleasantly, and she covered her face with her hands, and sank into the chair again. She looked beaten, but as she sobbed, partly from the trembling of her nerves, and partly for design, she had indeed snatched her courage to her again.

"It is my great love—my great love for Your Grace," she murmured.

He began to fidget about the room, and she let her sobs cease, but she fetched a trembling sigh.

He said, "Well, well. Come to supper."

She caught his hand and kissed it, and then covered her mouth with her fingers, because he had pulled away from her so sharply that the claw setting of a great ruby on his finger had torn her lip.

August 28

Robert Aske was coming back from Aughton Landing. One of the barges which brought goods up into the country from Hull had arrived there after dinner-time, and Aske had hoped that among the stuff for Aughton would be a ream of paper that he had sent for. But the master of the barge knew nought of it, though he had set ashore barrels of fish, several casks of wine, the lock of the parlour door which had gone to be mended, and two sugar loaves. Aske left the servants to bring these up, and started for home alone.

The evening had fallen quiet after a windy day, and white

clouds, plump and pillowy, wallowed lazily across the sky. In that huge open countryside it was like being below the water of the sea, and looking up at the hulls of a fleet of ships sailing by above. Beside him his shadow, stretched and lean, slid smoothly, or flickered over unevennesses in the grass of the ings. Just before he left the river bank he startled a swan which had been standing there; it tottered clumsily towards the water, leaning forward with its wings spread; in a second more it was in the air, beating with great slow wailing flaps down the course of the river; only when it had gone far along did it rise, and then for minutes he could see it still, sailing towards Bubwith, white against the white clouds that lay low on the horizon there.

As he came near to Aughton the church bell began to ring; it must mean that the harvest was over, and that the great open field from which the corn had been carried was now broken, so that the cattle could be driven in to pasture upon the stubbles. But as well as the clanging of the bell he could hear, as he came up beside the old grassy mound where the de la Hayes had had their castle, that there was an unusual stir in the house. Dogs were barking and men shouting; he walked more quickly; it would surely be Jack, come home after a fortnight's visit to Marrick—both to Marrick Manor and to the Priory, since Dame Nan Bulmer at the one and old Dame Eleanor Maxwell at the other were both kinswomen, the one on the Aske side, the other on the Clifford.

Jack it was, and very pleased to be home. At supper all the talk was of what had happened at Aughton since he went away—to the children, the harvest, the beasts, the dogs. After supper he and Robert went out in a late clear afterglow, so that Jack might have a look round; he was not content to wait till morning, so eager was he to be truly Aske of Aughton again.

Yet as they leaned on the stackyard gate looking out on the lane Jack did not talk at all, for a while at least, of Aughton, but of their people at Marrick. As Robert listened, hearing news of Dame Nan's hawks, and Dame Eleanor's rheumatism, he wondered if Jack knew that it was better not to talk before his wife of Aske kin; he wondered too how anyone could be so jealous, and with so little cause, as Nell.

But then—his mind wandered—Nell's tempers were small things, sharp and sudden, like flaws of wind on the water, but like those only shaking the surface of life, which, here in

Aughton, was all unstirred below. Here, but for such shallow troubles, was a great familiar peace. He looked down the lane; the elms were gathering twilight in their dusky leaves; tags and streamers of the harvest hung from their lower branches to show where the wains had passed; now a herd of cows came lazing along, driven by a young fellow in a green hood, who gave out now and again hollow, owl-like cries, which in no wise hastened the slow beasts. With the boy was an old man, who carried aloft on his shoulder a dumpling-faced infant. Both young man and old must have sworn that oath that every grown person in England had sworn, except so very few. Jack too had taken it, and Robert dared not ask him what he made of it all. Yet here perhaps it might seem to Jack and the others that there was no force at all in the oath; what King Harry did in London came to Aughton as no more than hearsay, and would not change a thing. "At least," Robert Aske thought to himself, "nothing has changed here. At least here for a while I need not to think that it has changed. At least I can forget London where I know that all has changed."

The cows were passing. Jack, forgetting for the moment Marrick matters, told Robert the age, the parentage, the quality of each beast as they went by, swinging their heads, switching tails, and casting a wild look sidelong on the men at the gate. When they had gone the whole air was sweet with the smell of milk.

Jack turned so that he leaned his shoulders against the gate. "Tell me, Robin," he said in a doubtful, hesitating way, "what think you of visions?"

"Visions? What visions?"

Jack laughed, as it were apologetically. "You'll call me a fool for thinking on it. But there was that in the poor creature—though they say she's crazed—yet there was that made me—"

When Robert interrupted, demanding to know what in God's name he was talking of, he said, "Of that poor fool the Nuns call Malle." He twisted his head to look down the lane, and added, "I'd not use the Nuns' cows to play a patch on ours."

"What visions?" Robert Aske rapped out, so sharply that Jack turned towards him. But he, lest Jack should see his face, had hitched himself up to sit on the top bar of the gate. "What visions?" he asked for the third time.

So Jack went on. "This Malle, who—well, I'll tell you it, Robin, as it happened. I was up at Marrick, coming back to the Manor at dusk, in a great rain that drove so hard that I had my head down and saw nothing till the horse turned aside. *She* was in the way; she'd a great bundle of faggots on her shoulder, and she stood in the rain, as soaked as a washing-day clout, but she never moved, only stood staring.

"Staring at what?"

"Into the window—but it was shuttered—of the last toft of the village, for I had come just to the town end.

"She said, without looking at me. 'He is within. He blesses the children.' "

"Wait a moment," said Robert. "You said the last toft. That's where that wench Cis—"

Jack held up his hand. "I know what you'll say, Robin, but let me end. Quod she, 'I looked in. The shutters weren't close. Cis was stirring the pot for supper, and the pigs and hens were driven in for the night. I could see the sow lie in the corner, and the hens roosting.' Then she said—but, of course—however—she said—'I saw Him, a young man by the fire, tired from way-faring. He had his boots off to ease his feet. One of the little wenches leaned against his thigh and the babe was on his knee, and two of the little knaves played in the ashes at his feet. I saw him,' quod she, 'lay his hand on the little wench's head.' "

When Robert said nothing at all Jack said:

"I know you'll tell me it were no strange thing to see a young man, or men not so young, in that toft at night. Her husband's dead now—not that it made much odds when she had a husband. The Bulmers say not more than half that string of brats were his begetting."

"Did you," said Robert, "see in? Was there—was there— one with her?"

"No. The shutters were close when I came." Jack turned now, and looked up at his brother. Robin sat humped on the top bar of the gate, watching, with his one eye puckered up, the bats that swung busily in the darkening air.

"I knew," said Jack, "that you would laugh. And indeed the common talk is that the woman is crazed."

"I? Laugh?"

"Robin! You believe that indeed she saw—"

Robert Aske had jumped down from the gate, and now moved away towards the house. As he went he said:

"I warrant that when He went about in Jewry He did not deny to bless bawds' children, being so merciful as He was."

"But," Jack persisted, "you believe it a true vision?"

"If ever," said Robert, marching on ahead and speaking in a voice that sounded angry, "if ever there were a day in which Christian men needed a sign to ensure them of God's forgiveness, and if ever there were a place, that day's to-day, and that place England. And if any man needs it in special—"

"But such a simple creature, so ignorant."

"I shall go to Marrick, and find out for myself."

"When will you go?"

"Sometime," Robert Aske answered, roughly, because as soon as he said he would go he knew that he would not go. He would not act the lawyer with God's word, to doubt it, to haggle, and probe. "No," said he to himself, "I'll take it, thanking God for his mercy."

September 30

M. Eustache Chapuys looked up from the letter he was writing, stared, with eyes that did not see, at a cupboard with a jug of wine and a silver pot on it, and stroked his lips with the end of the quill he was using. These long despatches of the Imperial Ambassador to his master took up both time and thought. He bent again to his writing, and for a while the pen chirruped almost as steadily as a cricket by a warm hearth.

At last M. Chapuys cast down the pen, yawned, stretched elaborately, and picking up a glass of late carnations sniffed deeply at the spicy scent. Then he threw one leg over the arm of the chair and began to hum softly. Now and again he glanced over his shoulder at the letter; it was a good letter, he thought. He was of the opinion that the Emperor Charles was lucky to have such a man as himself in England in these difficult times. An ambassador here today, he thought, needs to be fearless, subtle, ingenious, perspicuous; he must be such an one as is able to keep on good terms with the King and Thomas Cromwell, now Master Secretary; for otherwise he could do nothing to help Queen Katherine and the Princess. All these qualities M. Chapuys conceived himself to have. And, being no fool, but a good judge of men even when it was himself he judged, he was right. Not exactly young, he had a young man's nicety in dress, as well as other qualities which a man usually leaves behind him before he reaches middle age. He was still sanguine, flippant, and eager; he was also wary, or he would not have served the Emperor

Charles, but it was as though he played a game in which caution was necessary, and amused himself thereby.

After a little while he swung to his feet and went across to the window. It was a large window, of five casements in a row, with wooden mullions between. If he had opened one and looked out and up he would have seen, as well as a row of empty swallows' nests, a tangle of rich and various carvings —vine leaves, grape bunches, twists of ribbon, peacocks, unicorns, and wild men whose hair became vine tendrils, and whose bodies tailed off into fishes. Opposite, on the far side of the Cheap, the houses were adorned with similar, though even more opulent, carving; for on that side as on this the goldsmiths lived, and their houses, not so very long builded, were the pride of Londoners and the admiration of strangers.

Below M. Chapuys' chambers were the workshops, as well as the kitchens, hall, and shop of his host. When his door was open he could hear the gasp and roar of the furnace as the bellows governed it; but the stammering tap of the goldsmiths' hammers came to him all day long, whether the door were shut or open. So now for the noise they made he did not hear the footsteps of one coming up the stairs outside. At a knock on the door he turned quickly.

"Ah!" he said to himself, and more loudly, "Enter!" and the man he was waiting for came into the room, and straight across to the table. Chapuys met him there.

"Did you see him?"

"Yes, M. l'Ambassadeur."

Chapuys said, "A moment," and opening the door shouted for Gilles. There was a muffled answer. Chapuys said in a low but clear voice, "Gilles, I wish to be private." When he came back into the room he was smiling.

"From the sound of Gilles' voice," he observed, "I judge that he had his face in a pint pot. Being a Fleming he takes kindly to this barbarity they call beer."

He sat down at the table, resting his elbows on the letter which lay there, and became at once serious and intent.

"You can speak freely now."

The man, who was tall, pale and bald, shifted his feet among the rushes, and paused a moment before he said: "I saw him."

"Lord Darcy himself?"

"Yes, Monsieur."

"Secretly?"

"Very secretly."

"Where?"

"In a privy chamber. His steward brought me there. Only my Lord and he go in."

"Did he know you, this steward?"

"Yes, Monsieur. But he is safe."

"And my Lord? Is that true which Lord Hussey said of him? He'll do more than talk?"

"He said he would."

Chapuys said "Tchk!" under his breath. To get news out of this Burgundian was like pressing a cheese. Screw, a dribble. Screw. Another dribble. Screw. A little flow of whey. Yet if he had not been so discreet he would not have been so useful.

"Tell me all he said to you."

"First he made me swear to be secret, or it might be death to him. He said not even his sons must know."

"God forbid they should. One stands so well with Cromwell that he hath lately made him captain of one of those islands . . ."

"Jersey," said the Burgundian, who always had his facts clear.

Chapuys stretched out his hand suddenly, and jabbed the table under the other's nose with his finger.

"Tell me. Have you heard any say that it was my Lord himself who asked this favour, the Captaincy of this isle Jersey, from Cromwell?"

"I have. It is true."

"But—" cried Chapuys. "Then is Darcy then playing with us?"

The Burgundian shook his head.

"Monsieur," he said, "I was once at Etaples in France and there I heard the Bishop of Meaux read in French from the Bible. It was not fobidden then."

Chapuys nodded. "I know."

"He read a story of how the people of Israel came out of Egypt. That day they left they took from the people of Egypt jewels—rings, brooches, collars."

Chapuys waited. After a while he said persuasively, "Yes?"

"My Lord Darcy wishes very much, Monsieur, to go back to Yorkshire."

Chapuys chuckled. "Out of Egypt."

"And before he goes he would spoil the Egyptians." The Burgundian allowed himself a faint smile. He took his finger-tips from the table, and spreading his hands under his eyes, seemed interested in the trimming of his nails. "I think—" he began.

Chapuys did not move.

"I think, Monsieur, that my Lord remembers the time of the wars, when there were two kings in England."

"He's past seventy. Yes, he must remember."

"I think he remembers it well."

"But what of that?" Chapuys asked.

"Kings were cheaper then. He thinks of kings not as men think now, but as a man of those past days."

"I see." Chapuys tapped with the tips of his fingers on his teeth.

"Yes. I see," he repeated.

"And there is yet another thing, Monsieur. It may be the greatest thing."

Chapuys did not interrupt by a question. He only lifted his eyebrows.

"My Lord said that in this quarrel he would raise the banner of the Crucifix beside the Emperor's banner. He said those very words."

Chapuys' face lit with excitement and then became appropriately solemn.

"It's true. This King is nothing but a heretic." He added quickly, "Did he say what force he could raise?"

"Sixteen hundred Northern men. He said, Monsieur, that I should tell you this—that he is more loyal to his Prince than most men, in matters that go not against his conscience and honour, but seeing that things are done here contrary to reason and hateful to God, he cannot be consenting thereto, neither as an honest man nor a good Christian."

Chapuys bowed his head. "I count it myself," he said, and crossed himself, "even as a Crusade." He struck the table with his fist and laughed. "And what a stroke at the throat of France if we could pull down this King and set up the Princess Mary."

When the Burgundian had gone Chapuys turned again to his letter, writing out first in rough and then fairly what the man had said. When it was done he sent Gilles for a taper, sealed the letter, and shoved it inside the breast of his doublet. The rough copy he held to the flame of the taper till it blazed, then threw it on the hearth, and watched while the paper writhed, and blackened, and lay still, making the tiniest sharp ticking sounds. When he had broken the frail thing down to finest black ash his caution was satisfied.

At Chapter the Prioress told the Ladies that the King's Commissioner would be at Marrick this morning to take the oath of each one of them to the Act of Succession.

"And of the servants, too?" Dame Anne Ladyman asked.

"Of the servants, too."

"Mass! How should their oaths matter?"

The Prioress was shrugging her shoulders over that when Dame Margery Conyers stood up, and said that she for one would not take the oath.

They all stared at her and someone, in a loud whisper, mentioned the Tower.

But the Prioress said, "Nonsense. Why should you not swear? All but a very few have sworn, throughout the whole realm. Will you be more careful of right than they?"

Dame Margery had grown very red, and shut her lips tight; she shook her head in silence, because, as usual when she was excited, tears were gathering in her eyes.

The Prioress looked at her, and then at the faces of the others. Dame Elizabeth Close was leaning forward; her hands were gripped tight together; in a moment she would be on her feet. The Prioress saw that Dame Margery's refusal might be an infection to spread.

She said, speaking calmly, but in a matter of grave moment: "Yet before you refuse consider what will fall, not only upon you, but upon the House. For to refuse is treason, and if you and others should refuse, that will happen at Marrick which has happened to the Franciscan Observants. The Priory will be suppressed."

In the dank chill of the November morning cold shivers ran up the backs of several of the Nuns. In the minds of all what the Prioress had said was a blast of bleak wind, not to be endured.

Dame Margery sat down, then stood up again.

"Madame," she said rather grandly, "then I discharge my conscience and I charge yours."

The Prioress bowed her head. Her conscience was ready to bear the charge.

That afternoon in the old Frater, they took the oath tendered them by the Commissioner, a portly, cheerful man, who before the business began had talked over wine and wafers of his little girls at home, and the first boy, the heir, still in swaddling bands. Such humanity and kindliness had greatly eased the Ladies' minds; they could not but feel that an oath proffered by such an individual must be innocuous.

When they had taken it the servants came in, and after them the men from the fields. Dinner was late, but when the Ladies sat down to it, hungry but cheerful, they looked back at the day's work with equanimity.

1535

January 1

None but his own servants gave New Year gifts to the Emperor's Ambassador on the first morning of the New Year, for his friends and his kin were not here, and the English Lords knew better than to make presents to one whose master was so ill a friend of their master.

But soon after dark had fallen a little grey-haired Priest came to the door below, asking for Gilles the Fleming. He spoke English like a stranger himself, being in fact a Hainaulter, so there was nothing out of the way in his coming. Gilles, however, when he had brought him in, led him upstairs and into the Ambassador's room, where M. Chapuys sat throwing dice, one hand against the other. After that Gilles sat down on the stairs outside the door.

The Priest from Hainault wished the Emperor's Ambassador "A happy Christmas from my Lord," and laid in his hands a long slim parcel lapped in leather. When Chapuys undid the wrappings he found a fine sword in a sheath of crimson leather.

"It's a choice gift," said Chapuys, "and I send many thanks for it to my Lord." His eyes were on the Priest's face, as though he waited for something more.

"What will be in this New Year—" the Priest began, and then spread his hands and let them fall.

"No man can tell," Chapuys ended for him. "But I think my Lord sends me this gift because he'd have me know that the time is near when we shall play with steel."

The Hainault Priest shook his head heavily, and said that the times were very ill.

Chapuys slid the sword out of the scabbard, laid it to his cheek and looked along the blade. As he lowered it the firelight shone red upon the clear steel.

"God help us to mend the times," said he, and the Priest said, "Amen."

February 2

Lord Abergavenny murmured, "Bring me your ear closer," and the Earl of Huntingdon stooped over the brazier where they warmed their hands, so that their faces were near together.

"In my hearing," said Abergavenny, "My Lord of Northumberland called her 'the great whore.' "

Huntingdon raised his eyebrows and pulled down the corners of his mouth but made no answer.

"So many," Abergavenny went on softly, "hate her, and what she has brought on this realm. If the King tire of her—"

He stopped because Huntingdon had whispered "Sh!" at the King's name, and they both turned from the glowing red of the charcoal to look between the crowd to where, at the far end of the Great Gallery, the King and the French Envoy, M. Palmèdes Gontier, Treasurer of Brittany, moved to and fro in front of the great hearth. A monkey with a jewelled collar slunk and gambolled inconsequently after the King at the end of a gilt chain; it chattered with rage when the chain pulled it up at every turn and it must follow whether it would or no.

The King was all in white satin, stitched with gold thread and sewn over with emeralds, in honour of the feast, and the Envoy beside him in his black velvet and grey satin looked like a long thin evening shadow. It was pretty clear to anyone who knew the King that he was growing testy; now and again he leaned upon the Frenchman's furred shoulder, but for the most part his hands were behind his back—not clasped, but with the back of one laid flat on the other palm, and he kept clapping them together in a fidgety, impatient way.

"The business," Huntingdon murmured, "goeth not well."

Abergavenny took a discreet look over his shoulder at the King and the Frenchman, turning just now at the window.

Huntingdon went on, as though he spoke to the thin blue smoke of the charcoal. "I have heard that the French will have none of the Princess Elizabeth, but require the old treaty to be kept, and the Lady Mary to be given to the Dauphin. That will not please His Grace."

Abergavenny turned slowly back.

"His Grace seems to me," he whispered, "to go halt upon his left leg."

"Sh!" said Huntingdon sharply, but when Abergavenny muttered "An ulcer?" he nodded, and said, "The physician told one of my gentlemen so. There are two things I would know——" He broke off there, and said in a different tone—— "Ah! my Lord Duke!" as the Duke of Norfolk, huddled to his long nose in fur, joined them beside the brazier.

"And what be those two, my Lord?" said he, with the frank smile that he could use when he chose.

"One is—whence they have that fine gravel for the tilt yard," said Huntingdon promptly.

"That I can tell you," said the Duke, and the three began chatting lightly of such matters, now warming their hands over the brazier, now tucking them under their arms, and most of the time stepping gently with their feet among the rushes to keep the blood coursing, for the day was very cold.

That same afternoon Mr. Thomas Cromwell brought the French Envoy to Queen Anne. She was in one of the smaller rooms leading off the Presence Chamber, yet the room was large enough to have two fireplaces, one at each end, and for thirty or forty people to be able to divide themselves into two quite separate groups. The larger group by far was that about the King, who stood with his back to one of the fires, pulling tight his white satin trunks across his broad backside, and now and again bending slightly forward, the more exquisitely to toast his rear.

The Queen sat beside the fire at the farther end of the room with a lute on her knee, and some of her ladies and a few young gentlemen about her. The fire sent out puffs and gushes of sweetness for they had not long since scattered spices on the logs.

One of the young gentlemen near the Queen had the King's monkey by its chain and he and a gentlewoman were feeding it with sweetmeats while most of the rest looked on and laughed. As M. Palamèdes came near he noticed that the Queen was watching the monkey too, but with loathing, and so intently that she did not see the two gentlemen approach.

As they paused the strange creature sidled over to the Queen till it stood crouching before her. She shrank back. "Mother of God! I hate monkeys" It laid one of its long, wrinkled, dark grey hands on the strings of the lute. and with the other grabbed at a sweetmeat in the Queen's fingers.

Then it was away, with its paw at its mouth. The discordant twang of the strings under the tiny clutching fingers was echoed by a cry from the Queen, who brought her own hand up to her mouth in a gesture strangely like that of the animal.

"Oh! He scratches!" she said, just as M. Palamèdes bowed and went down on one knee.

Neither he nor Cromwell missed the start that the Queen gave. Cromwell glanced round at those standing near; he did no more but it was enough. The group about the fire broke up and drew away, leaving the three of them alone.

As the Queen's hand lay upon Gontier's and he stooped to kiss it he knew it was trembling. He lifted his head, and his eyes, caught by the shifting sparkle of jewels, rested for a second on her bosom. Her blood-red velvet gown, brocaded with gold, had an edging of pearls and small sapphires along which the firelight ran with a broken flash, quickly gone, and then running again from point to point in time with the Queen's quick breathing. The woman, M. Palmèdes realized, was panting—no less—yet when he looked in her face, she smiled, and as she spoke in French of how she had loved France, and how ill she now used his lovely French tongue, she laughed, shrilly, a laugh with as little meaning as the strained smile, while her eyes darted past his head to watch what was going on at the farther end of the room.

Then, with desperate urgency, but always with that same smile on her face and with laughter that tinkled emptily, she began to press him "to use dispatch in this business of the marriage of my daughter the Princess Elizabeth's Grace." Dispatch! Dispatch! That was the word, over and over. "For if you do not I shall be in worse danger than before I was married. Worse danger!" She laughed with fear looking through the mask of her face. Her head jerked and she craned her neck to see beyond him. Gontier felt his flesh creep, and yet he knew that nothing had happened of more moment than that the musicians in the room beyond were tuning their instruments and that the King had moved away from the other hearth.

The Queen held out her hand; the Frenchman bent and kissed it again and felt her nails nip into his flesh.

"I dare not speak longer," she said breathlessly. "I cannot tell you more. The King is watching us. Someone said I should not anger him. But if I did not he would think I am afraid." She seemed to choke, then said, "As (dear Mother of God!) I am afraid."

She did not seem to know that she was still clutching his

hand, but he freed it gently and asked if he might wait on Her Grace another day.

"No. No. I can't see you again—or write—or stay longer. He has gone. They are dancing already."

She sprang up, laughing again. The room was nearly empty. Only a few of her ladies were there to follow her as she moved towards the door through which came the sound of fiddles and recorders.

February 12

When the physician had gone out Queen Katherine sat for a long time pricking with her needle at a leaf on the corporax case she was embroidering, but making no stitches. From time to time she sighed. It was hard enough to be separated from a daughter; it was worse if the child were ill; and she had been ill for months. The child—the Queen realized that the girl of fifteen whom she had last seen, would be nineteen in four days' time.

She thought, "If I could go to her! If only he would go!" meaning her physician. But he had seemed not eager to go. He had said he could not leave Her Grace, and indeed, thought the Queen, "I had done ill without him while I was so sick. But now—why will he not go?"

As an answer to that came into her mind she grew very still. For a minute she sat stiff in her chair, staring straight before her while her face whitened, and her mouth formed a silent "Oh!" which she did not utter. Then she snatched up the little bell on the table and rang it, and went on ringing it till the door opened and two or three ladies, with scared faces, looked into the room.

"Quick," said the Queen. "Bring me pen and ink. Quick. And one of you find Charles. He must ride to London at once."

They had thought her ill. Now they almost thought her mad.

"Go! Go!" she stormed at them. "Don't stand staring. Pen—ink—paper." She began to walk up and down the room and to bite her nails. But before any of them came back she had drawn out a crucifix from her breast, and sitting herself down at the table, bowed over it. When the eldest of her ladies came in, shutting the door softly, the Queen looked up at her with a grey face, but calmly.

"I think," she said, "that he does not dare to go to my daughter because he fears there is poison given her, and that if she—if she die, they will lay it at his door."

The elderly lady cried out at that, but the Queen hushed her with a word, and began to write to M. Chapuys, Ambassador of the Emperor's Majesty.

For a while there was no sound in the room but the complaint of the driven pen. When that stopped for a minute the lady-in-waiting looked round, and caught a glimpse of the Queen's face. It was less like a living face than a carving in stone, chiselled to represent, changelessly and for years on years, the uttermost of woe. She did not look again.

So [wrote the Queen], because it appears to me that what I ask is just, and for the service of God, I beg you will speak to His Highness, and desire him on my behalf to do such charity as to send his daughter and mine where I am; because treating her with my own hands, and by the advice of other physicians and of my own, if God please to take her from this world my heart will rest satisfied; otherwise in great pain.

You shall also say to His Highness that there is no need of any other person but myself to nurse her; that I will put her in my own bed where I sleep, and will watch her when is needful.

I have recourse to you, knowing that there is no one in this kingdom who dare say to the King my Lord that which I desire you to say; and I pray God reward you for the diligence that you will make.

She signed it then, "Katherine the Queen," and dated it, "Kimbolton, the first Friday in Lent."

May 4

The King sat in his study at York Place in Westminster with a small harp on his knee and music on a desk before him. His hands, white, fat, yet at once both nimble and powerful upon the strings, plucked out from the instrument its voices of trembling sweetness. He played first a love-song, then a *Nunc Dimittis*—very gentle and slow; he swayed his head to the plaintive measure and his face was calm and purged.

Someone knocked at the door, and without pausing in his playing he bade, "Enter." But when he saw Mr. Norris come in he set down the harp so roughly that the strings tingled in one soft discord.

"It is done?"

Mr. Norris shut the door. "It is done," he said. Then he tittered. "There are four fewer Carthusian brethren in the realm to confuse Your Grace's Supremacy and hold by the Pope. Four fewer alive, that is, but if every piece of every monk of these four were to count a whole monk than hath Your Grace increased the sum to—" he reckoned on his fingers, "four quarters each, and their arms torn off, and every man his bowels and his heart—" He began to laugh noisily.

The King pressed the lips of his small mouth close and his eyes roamed about with the lowering hot glance of a boar. He said, "And they lived yet when they were cut down?"

"One of them lived even till both arms were off. But all while they were opened and drawn."

The King bowed his head. He seemed to consider with attention a diamond on his finger.

"The executioner did his work with a will?" he asked.

"With a will. He rubbed their very hearts, hot and steaming, over their mouths."

"Ah!" said the King, and after a while stood up. "Shall we make a match at the butts?" He went to the window and opened it. The day was more like April than May, with a racing wind, blue sky and light flying clouds. Just now one covered the sun, and it was as though he had shut an eye. The King said, "The wind's strong, but steady. I'll use that new great bow." Yet he stood still staring out of the window.

"Did they cry for mercy?" he asked suddenly.

Norris said that they did. It was a lie, but the King nodded as if pleased, and that was what Norris cared for.

This evening Robert Aske came late into the room where Clifton and Hatfield sat over a flagon of wine. When they asked him where had he been he said only, "Riding." He would not drink with them, but sat down on a bench and took a book on his knee, but after a little Hal nudged Wat and motioned with his head towards Aske, and Wat saw that the book lay upside-down.

Presently Wat said:

"If you have ridden out into the country you may not know that the Brothers of the Charterhouse were executed this morning."

Aske moved so sharply that the book fell between his knees. "I do know," said he. And then with a jerk, "I was there."

"Mass! You were there!"

Aske's face twisted into a sort of grin. "I was not the only one. Many of the Court were there to see the brave sight."

"Tell us the truth then," said Wat. "Were they hanged in monks' frocks—not degraded from their clergy?"

"They—" Aske began, but instead of answering the question he said, huddling the words together, "Let them tell you who were not there. I cannot say it."

He put down his hand to take up the book again and then stopped and they saw him stare down at his wrist where the sleeve had drawn back as he stretched his arm; there was a dark brown stain on it. He looked up at them with a sick face.

"I did not know I was spattered with it. But I stood so near as that." He got up hastily. "I must wash it off."

At the door he stopped and they saw him draw the fingers of one hand across his eye and shake them as if he would shake off something which clung like a cobweb. "I can wash it from my wrist," he muttered, and then went away.

May 7

Gib went up the stair from the houseplace to the chamber that was above. There he prised up a board in one corner and took out a book. This was his latest hiding-place for his latest purchase—a small old manuscript of Wycliffe's Testament; it had painted initial letters of red and blue, but the back was shabby, and besides that scorched right through the leather to the board beneath in one place.

Gib did not intend to read indoors; both discretion and the fair morning urged him out. When he came downstairs again he laid the Testament in a basket, put a handful of hay over it, and called to his mother that he was away to Kexwith to fetch the sitting of eggs that one of the Burleymen up there had promised him.

It was a morning of brisk wind, warm sun, and bright sailing cloud that might darken and gather later. Just now the sun was pleasant, and more than one of the old women of Marrick stood at the doors, each with the distaff tucked under one arm, and the spindle swinging and whirling at the end of the lengthening thread. Gib gave them good-day sternly, and was glad to be through the village. These ignorant old souls were, he knew well, irrevocably sunken in superstition; he could do nothing with them.

Beyond the last fields he reached the crest of the rise and suddenly all the fells were opened before him, blue and green like the sea, with grape-purple shadows of the clouds lying here and there; for miles on every side but one there was nothing but wave after wave, with Mozedel rising higher yet in the far distance; only near by, ahead and to the left, the ground fell away to the trees and the profound sheltered peace of the Dale.

The Nuns' bailiff and his man came into sight near Langshaw Cross on the road from Owlands. Gib knew the bailiff even from this distance by his white horse and the big brown dog that ran alongside. He did not wish to meet him or anyone else, so he left the road for the turf, taking the green track that joined the way up from Grinton. When he was out of sight beyond the swell of the ground he sat down, and took his book from the basket, secure in the austere emptiness of the fells, and in a great quiet, for here the wind passed in silence and of all the birds only the larks had confidence to fly strongly and sing aloud; the rest made short flights close to the ground and spoke with small stony twitterings and chinkings. Nor were there any flowers up here, other than the tiniest sort among the grasses, except where the golden wild pansies were spilt upon a sunny bank.

Gib opened the book and began to read.

He entered into a synagogue and a man was there and his right hand was dry. And the Pharisees espied him if he should heal him in the Sabbath, that they should find cause to accuse him. Soothly he wist the hearts of them.

"Black hearts," Gib thought, who saw the Pharisees as a row of Abbots, sitting in their carved stalls, each man different in face, yet each with the same air of command and confidence.

He saith to the man that had a dry hand, Rise up into the middle and stand.

Gib smiled at the thought of the discomfiture of that rank of grave and scornful prelates; his imagination increased their number now by two or three Bishops.

Soothly Jesus saith to them, I ask of you if it is lawful for to do well in the Sabbath or to do evil, for to make a soul safe, or for to loose? And all men looked about—

At that Gib gave a small sharp laugh; he could see their proud yet shifty eyes glancing from the rushes on the floor to the brass eagle that carried the Gospel Book on its wings, and then up to the painted vault of the roof, not one of them daring to catch His eyes, not one with a word to answer.

He said to the man, Hold forth thy hand, and he held forth, and his hand is restored to health.

"Hah!" said Gib half aloud, and then jerked his head up, because a shadow slid across the grass beyond his feet. Malle, the Priory servant, had come near and now stood, red-faced and puffing; she had a very young calf in her arms; its ears flapped, and the long, heavily jointed legs dangled helplessly.

"This one," said Malle, and dumped the creature on the grass, "this one ran away. He came out of the ox-house only to-day, and the world frightened him. So when he found a hole in the wattles he broke through, and ran, and never left running till he had no breath left. But at last I caught him."

The calf, after trembling and quaking for a moment, flopped down, its forelegs doubled under it; it looked softly at them with its large, shining eyes, and swept a thick tongue over its nose; it lowered its head and they heard the gentle sound of its breathing as it nuzzled at the turf.

Gib frowned at the little beast, and frowned at Malle's bare feet; he had his hand over the page, yet knew it was not hidden, and was angry to know that he feared lest it should be seen; he looked up at her face, and saw that her eyes were on the book.

"Sir," she cried, and came close. "Is yon the book in which you find news of Him?"

He shut it then, shuffling it between his knees before he remembered that Greek, Latin, Hebrew, or English, it was all one to her, who could read no letters. He said, the more harshly because of his fear, and the shame it left behind, "The book is not for such as you to read in." He said that, and suffered at once from a sharper twinge. It was of the very breath of the New Learning that it should be open to all; yet, he told himself, not to this woman, who was utterly a fool.

She laid her hand across the two tight knobbed curls on the calf's brow which would be horns later, and he could not be sure if it were she who sighed or the creature who breathed a deeper breath in the turf. Then she smiled.

"Perhaps He will come again," she said, and then, "Up, little one!" and gathered up the calf into her arms, and lumbered on.

Gib opened the book again.

"And it is done afterwards," he read, "that Jesus made journey by cities and castles—" but he could not keep his mind to the words. He looked after Malle, trudging along with her head-kerchief flapping in the wind; he even drew his breath to shout after her and bid her come back, but then he saw beyond her, and quite a long way off, the Marrick flock of sheep and lambs, like the white edge of a wave lapping towards him over the green turf; the shepherd walked before them; his dog, restless and quiet as the shadow of a moving leaf, slid beside them, now on this flank, now on that. Gib picked up his basket, and huddled the book under the hay; when the shepherd came alongside, five minutes later, Gib was beating with a stone at a nail in his shoe. He waved his hand, put on the shoe again, and stood up. They walked along together then, the sheep following them, the dog circling on noiseless feet, but the whole air full of the plaintive bleating of the flock as that above sea cliffs is of the gulls' yelping.

Gib said he was going to Kexwith for a sitting of eggs. He said that a nail in the sole of his shoe had galled his toe. The shepherd, walking alongside, with his pipe to his mouth and fingers moving but playing only a soundless tune, bowed his head and made no answer. He was a very silent man and so used to thinking his own thoughts that often he forgot to listen to what others said; sometimes too, when he did speak, he seemed not to know if others listened.

"How many lambs this year?" Gib asked, and got no answer.

" 'Most white. That's right,' " said Gib, "but black ones enough for black hosen too."

Shepherd nodded. Then he said:

"She said she saw Him. Yet it's strange—here—in these days."

When Gib asked who "he" was, and who had seen "him," the shepherd did not answer, but stopped, and turned to look back the way he had come. Malle was by now out of sight, but as they looked the bailiff rode over the crest of the rise, and disappeared, going down into the village.

Then, leaning on his long hooked staff, with his wind-puckered eyes looking into the light of the sun which had even yet not risen very high, Shepherd said:

"I was over to Harkerside Moor t'other day, and coming back I saw yon wench hoving by the roadside. I thought 'twas far forth of her way, so I stopped and asked what she did there."

After that he let so long a space of silence pass that Gib felt himself forced to ask, "Well, what did she?"

Shepherd's eyes came to him, and then seemed to look through him.

"Quod she, '*He* hath gone by below,' and she pointed at the corpse-road going towards Keld. 'A young man,' quod she, 'with twelve other young men, all talking merrily and walking fast this shining afternoon. But *He* went ahead of them all; I heard the iron shoe of his staff clack on the stones of the road. And the birds,' quod she, 'sang Osanna fit to brast their throats.' "

Gib said something, hardly a word indeed, but it brought back Shepherd's eyes to his face. "And then?" cried Gib.

"Nought else. Except she said: 'They know not yet with whom they walk, but only have great joy to be with Him.' I thought," said Shepherd after a moment, "that a Priest'd know if such a thing could be. But there—" He met Gib's stern look and sighed.

Gib turned away. He would not let Shepherd see how mightily this thing had moved him. But surely here was a sign from God, spoken and shown to his very soul. Those young men, following that other young man up the Dale, they were going forth into the world to preach. Well—and if he could not go after them, could he not write? And did not books, coming fast now from printing presses, speak to more—aye, and more surely—than the words of a preacher? His heart went up like thistledown floating in autumn, and he heard in his mind, as if someone had spoken—"There is much ripe corn, and few workmen; therefore pray ye the Lord of the ripe corn that he send workmen into his ripe corn."

He said, in his harshest voice, "I will call the woman, and inquire further of this matter. The truth shall be proven."

They walked on together a little way, but then Gib said he must make haste so as to be back at noon. So he left Shepherd moving slowly, his shadow and the shadows of the sheep slipping smoothly over the short turf in front of them. As all good shepherds do, he would lead the flock westward till the noon sun stood high; in the afternoon, when it had a little declined, he would turn and bring them home again, so that always the sun shone from behind them, never in their faces.

Gib swung on again at a great pace; he was a fast, impatient walker, and besides that, the way was far. Yet he walked faster even than usual, so buoyed up was he with that which Shepherd had told him.

Sweating, with his face harshly red, he came to Nungate Top, and began to go down towards Dales Beck. A couple of small children stumped along just ahead, carrying a bag of flour on a pole between them. They were not ill-looking children like Wat, but fair and sturdy; he noted himself taking pleasure in watching them, and that confirmed his confidence. "Jesu! Mary!" he thought to himself. "If I may be free to proclaim His word, I shall love all His creatures, every one." But something trembled in his mind when he thought—"Even Wat."

Yet he went to Kexwith and back in very good cheer, in a settled mood of confidence, too exalted for any grip of fear. Only in one matter did his mind change. When he came to think it over he decided he would speak no word of this vision to the woman Malle. What Shepherd had told him was enough. "If I speak with her," he thought, "it may puff her up to believe that this seeing comes to her by cause of holiness. Thus shall she lose her humble meekness which, manifestly, is that in her which is pleasing to God." So he told himself, but he knew that he could not endure to ask her of her seeing—as if she, the poor fool, stood closer to God than he who was Priest, and God's chosen messenger.

May 10

Summer had not yet come to Yorkshire. To-day was cold, with cloud, strong wind, and occasional flaws of sunshine. When the sun shone the river winked with light, and far up the Dale you could see a bright white flicker come and go upon the water. Gib met the Nuns' Priest near the East Close. He was walking with his head bent against the wind, and pinching his hood tight under his chin with one hand to keep it on and to keep his ears warm; so he did not see Gib. But Gib, who was bringing his two cows back to the milling, held out his arms across the track, and the Nuns' Priest jerked up his head with a start when he felt someone in front of him, and came to a stand. The cows slewed to the right and left and maundered on towards home with their swinging, dilatory gait.

"Sir," Gib said, leaning on the hedge-stake he carried, "Sir, last Sunday I heard you pray for the Bishop of Rome."

"You heard me—?"

"I was in the Parish Church. I heard you well through the grille. You said quite clear, *'Oremus et pro beatissimo Papa nostro.'*"

The Nuns' Priest ruffled up and became very dignified.

"I shall so pray," said he, "till I have further command to the contrary."

Gib heard footsteps behind him above the tumult of the wind. He turned and saw that the smith was coming up and was indeed quite near. In a moment he ranged up alongside Gib and stood looking down at the Nuns' Priest.

"It is forbidden that any priest should pray for the Bishop of Rome," Gib said in his grating voice, and hearing that the smith cried, "Ho! Marry! Say you so. Doth he pray yet for the Bishop of Rome?"

The Nuns' Priest had grown red and a little flustered, but he held his ground, saying again that he would so pray till commanded to the contrary.

"Yea! Cock's Bones!" shouted the smith who had been drinking at Grinton. "Will you pray for Dr. Pupsie though it's forbidden?" and he began to slap his thighs and to laugh uproariously at his joke, repeating, "Dr. Pupsie! Dr. Pupsie!"

The little Priest grew nearly purple and he spluttered.

"Mass!" he cried, "and if it be forbidden by these new laws! Yea, nowadays we have many new laws. And if we take no heed I trow we shall have a new God shortly," and he put his head down and moved forward with such decision that both Gib and the smith made way, and the Nuns' Priest went on towards the Priory.

Gib and the smith continued along the road in the other direction. The smith was very noisy, laughing and hooting and shouting, "Dr. Pupsie." Gib stalked on in silence, angry almost as much with him as with the Nuns' Priest and all other idolaters.

May 15

"What does it mean?" said the old Treasurer of Paul's who had kept one of the three keys of the Cathedral Treasure for the last thirty years. He turned over the letter of Master Cromwell, the King's Chief Secretary, and peered at it upside-down.

"Surely," one of the Canons told him, "it means that the King has been informed of this precious little crucifix of ours and hath taken a high affection and pleasure of the sight of the same, even as the letter saith."

"And," said another Canon, a big, gaunt man, with a sour face, "it means that seeings will be keepings."

"Fie!" the first rebuked him, while the old Treasurer looked from one to another. "It means that we shall tender the same to His Grace as a free gift, trusting in his charitable goodness towards our Church of St. Paul."

"And as little daring to refuse," said the tall Canon, "as any wayfaring traveller dare refuse a robber his desire."

"Fie!" the first Canon cried again, and others too. "To liken the King's Grace to a robber!"

The tall Canon denied that he had done so. "It is the Chief Secretary that writ the letter," he argued.

But all of them felt that the less said the better, and that, whether they liked it or not, they had no choice but to make the gift. So the first Canon was set to write a letter to Master Cromwell, and the old Treasurer together with the Dean and the Sacrist went with their three keys to open the Treasure House, where the precious little crucifix lay.

And when he had taken it out the old Treasurer dandled it in his hands, trying, with his bleared old eyes, to see it by the light of the torch they had brought. It was very precious and beautiful, for it was of pure gold, with a rich ruby in the side, besides four great diamonds, four great emeralds, four large balases, and twelve great orient pearls. The old man began to cry over it, because indeed he could not think that it was right that the King should have it, seeing that it belonged to God and to St. Paul.

May 20

Of a sudden it was summer. The sun shone and cuckoo shouted day long. Among the thorn bushes below Gawnless Wood the grass was clouded blue with blue-bells. The Nuns' Priest climbing the stairs to the Prioress's Chamber felt the delicate stir of the gracious season, which was warmth and a vibration, and a note of singing just too high for human hearing; but he sighed as he raised his hand to knock.

The Prioress was feeding the small brown bitch which had whelped lately, so she heard him first with only half her attention. But when his meaning became clear she put down the platter for the animal to feed or not as it would. He was asking her whether she would have him disobey the King's command, and continue to pray for the Pope.

"Disobey?" she cried, at once seeing danger to the House. "No, you shall not."

"I have till now disobeyed," he said.

She had not noticed it, but then one did not attend to every word that was said in Church.

She repeated, "You shall not disobey. It might imperil the House."

He fidgeted with his feet and ran the thong of his belt backwards and forwards through the buckle so that the leather made little sharp slaps as he drew it tight.

"I thought——" he began, "I fear——Madame, I cannot think it well, that which is now done. There is the whole Church Catholic which prays for His Holiness; how can we alone forbear?"

The Prioress sat down in her chair and looked him over with more attention than she had given him for many a long day. She could not have expected, she thought, to find such a strain of scrupulosity in a man so round, so pampered, so easy. His gown was of very fine cloth of a dark crimson, and the sleeves were lined with silk; his fair hair, thin now, was as carefully laid in waves as ever; but his little mouth was troubled. She was honestly sorry for him, but he must not be allowed to damage the House. She tried subtlety.

"Sir," said she, "I think you are in the right. But these things which are new——I do not look for them long to endure. Soon we shall see them laid by, and all return as it was."

"You think so?" he cried. He was ready to think so himself. He had said, miserably, what conscience had goaded him to say, but he had no lust for the martyr's part. He had been a sorely frightened man when he came in to the Prioress, and here was balm.

She told him she did think so indeed, and truly!

"Then what shall I do?"

She was going to say "Conform!" but something obstinate about his look made her alter that into, "Go away from here for a little time. Let me say you are sick. Go and stay with the good yeoman your brother. There you can sing your Masses to the sheep and none wiser if you pray for the Pope or no."

He demurred a little, but not much. Only, what would the Ladies do for a Priest? The Prioress said, "Sir Gilbert can sing our Masses for us."

The Priest frowned at that and muttered that he thought sometimes Sir Gilbert was half a heretic.

"Then," cried the Prioress gaily, "when you return you

[318]

shall convert and lead us back into Holy Church. And we'll all bear faggots on our necks and wear white shifts."

She would not take the matter seriously any more, and soon the Priest cheered up, and drank some wine before he left.

He stood for a moment outside the Prioress's door and felt again the touch of the sweet day on his face. When he had paused here before, the chill of fear had impaired the sweetness. Now, as well as a blessed relief, there was only a very slight twinge of dissatisfaction in his mind; but that, he was sure, would pass.

July 1

The flecks of blue and ruby and thin grass green which the sun cast on the pavement through the coloured windows of Westminster Hall had slid only an imperceptible distance when the jury came back, so short a time had it taken them to decide on their verdict.

Sir Thomas More saw them file in and lifted his head to meet what was to come.

When they were silent Lord Chancellor Audley asked them, "Guilty, or not guilty?"

"Guilty," they said, and the Chancellor stood up and pronounced the sentence of death.

More, who had sat so still, shifted now in his chair. He unclasped his hands from the little ivory crucifix on his knee, laid them instead upon the arms of the chair, and leaned forward. They all watched him and silence fell as the crowd in the Hall hushed itself to listen.

"My Lords," he said, "since I am condemned—and God knows how—I wish to speak freely of your statute, for the discharge of my conscience." Audley opened his mouth and shut it again. "For the seven years that I have studied the matter, I have not read in any approved doctor of the Church that a temporal Lord could or ought to be head of the Spiritualty."

"What, More!" cried the Chancellor now, and laughed derisively. "You wish to be considered wiser and of better conscience than all the Bishops and Nobles of the realm?" and he picked up the posy of sweet-smelling flowers and herbs before him, and smelt at it, and laughed again, glancing at the other Lords for their approval. Sir Thomas waited till a few of them had laughed, and then began speaking again.

"My Lord Chancellor, for one Bishop of your opinion I have a hundred Saints of mine; and for one Parliament of yours, and God knows of what kind, I have all the General Councils for a thousand years. And for one kingdom, I have France and all the kingdoms of Christendom."

"Now," Norfolk broke in, and beat his fist on the table before him, "now is your malice clear!"

"My Lord," said More, "what I say is necessary for the discharge of my conscience and satisfaction of my soul, and to this I call God to witness, the sole searcher of human hearts.

"I say further that your Statute is ill made, because you have sworn never to do anything against the Church, which through all Christendom is one and undivided, and you have no authority, without the common consent of all Christians, to make a law, or Act of Parliament, or Council, against the unity of Christendom."

He paused and seemed to have finished, but as Audley half stood up he raised his hand, and the Lord Chancellor sat down again, and then fidgetted upon his chair as though the seat were red hot; but much as he might have liked to interrupt, he did not.

"I know well," said Sir Thomas More, "that the reason why you have condemned me is because I have never been willing to consent to the King's second marriage."

He looked along the row of his judges, his eyes dwelling longest on Audley and Norfolk, and there came into his face the flicker of a smile only a little merry, but very gentle.

"I hope, my Lords, in the divine goodness and mercy, that as St. Paul, and St. Stephen whom he persecuted, are now friends in Paradise, so we, though differing in this world, shall be united in perfect charity in the other. And I pray God to protect the King, and give him good counsel."

They all knew that he had finished there, but you could have counted ten before the Lord Chancellor stood up.

"Take the prisoner away," he said.

July 3

Gib came back with the other men from the harvest; it was dusk now and they had been out since daybreak, yet still the fields were only half cut, and if this short spell of fine weather broke in thunder, as it was threatening, there was little hope of saving a quarter of the hay, after all the weeks of rain. It was of this that the men talked, looking up at the heavy sky, as they tramped homewards, weary as dogs that have hunted day long. One by one they turned off to their houses; by the time Gib came in sight of the smithy he was alone.

One of the smith's little girls stood inside the wide door; he could see in the dark the glimmer of her shift, which was all she wore. As he came nearer she skipped back into the shop, and when Gib came abreast of the doorway the smith was there. "Hi! Sir Gilbert," said he. "Come in."

"Not now," Gib was saying, but he saw the smith make a sign with his hand; it was a sign Gib understood, so he turned in at once. The little girl had been lurking in the shadows of the smithy, but she slipped away into the yard behind as Gib came in.

"When did he come?" asked Gib, as the smith laid his hand on the latch of the house door.

"Not half an hour ago."

He opened the door and Gib saw Master Trudgeover sitting by the hearth, with the smith's two youngest, one on each of his knees, his big rough bristly face bent over them while they looked up at him with eyes as round as birds' eyes, and chirped to him in their small voices which were almost the voices of birds.

The smith wanted Gib to sit down to supper with them all, but Gib would not, and would have Master Trudgeover come along at once to the parsonage, "for he'll be safest there," said he; but what he wanted more was to have Master Trudgeover's attention drawn from these piping youngsters and turned instead upon heavenly things. Gib wished to discourse with him upon the blessedness of the new knowledge of God, and with that upon the rewards prepared for those that accepted it, and the vengeance for those who refused.

So, though Trudgeover seemed a little unwilling, Gib insisted. "Bring the others with you when it grows dark," said he to the smith. "If they came here there's no knowing who might not chance in." That was true enough, while on the other hand few knocked at the door of the parsonage, except the smith and these same known men, who would come there to read together in their books.

Trudgeover put down the two children and laid his large hands on their heads; Gib heard him bless them. They went out into the twilight. Once Trudgeover stopped and looked back; the smith's children were strung out right across the road waving to him, but in silence, because even the smallest knew that he was a secret; he waved back, and kissed his hand.

A minute after Gib heard him sigh and say, "I've five childer at home in Norfolk."

Gib had never known that Trudgeover was a married man, and it meant little to him now. He thought of him only as the tramping preacher, whom sometimes he despised for his lack of learning and clumsy schoolboy jokes, and sometimes admired to the pitch of reverence for his way of kindling the simple, heavy countrymen till they glowed like the iron on the smith's anvil, and laughed or shed tears, as Trudgeover chose.

"I've heard no word of them for this four month," the preacher told him; but Gib said nothing to that, and in a few minutes asked what the news was where he had come from, and Trudgeover began to tell him how Master Cromwell, now the King's Vicar General over the whole Church of England, was with the King in his hunting this summer, and, as the King hunted, Master Cromwell visited the monasteries, making record of their treasures, turning away those monks and nuns that had taken the vow too young, giving licence to depart to any who chose, and threatening the rest with such an enforced strictness in keeping the Rule that none would be able to abide it. Trudgeover was very merry at the expense of the monks, and Gib endured it with a bitter smile, because it was good news to him, but nothing to the purpose for making jokes.

At the parsonage they found supper behindhand because Wat had gone off on some business of his own without drawing water. "And I," said Gib's mother, "must needs wait an hour or more till Goodman Tod came by and I could ask him to bring me a pailful." The old woman could not now do all that she had used to do, being often ailing, and sometimes in great pain.

Master Trudgeover said that for his part he was well content to wait for supper, but Gib was very angry. He went out into the garden, and they heard him calling for Wat, each time more fiercely. After a while he gave up calling, and soon came back with his hands full of salad stuff from the garden. "We'll begin with cheese and these," said he, "while the bacon's seething." He lingered at the door for a minute and said, "The rain won't be long." Then he barred the door.

The rain began while they were still eating bread and

cheese and the cool, dripping salad stuff. It was very heavy. Soon after it began they all heard the latch rattle.

The old woman tittered. "There's my fine varlet." Trudgeover looked at Gib, but Gib helped himself to more cheese and said nothing. Trudgeover fidgetted, kept looking towards the door and losing the thread of his talk. At last he broke off.

"Brother, let the little lad in to his supper."

Gib crunched a radish between his teeth. "There's no supper for him." "Then let him in to bed." "He can bed with the pigs. He's an ill-conditioned knave."

Trudgeover laid down his knife.

"I shall let him in."

Gib stood up too. He met Trudgeover's eye, and then, to his extreme anger, found that he could not meet it. He unbarred the door, and Wat came slinking in; he had his cap in his hands, full of wild raspberries.

Gib caught him by the collar of his jacket, and, when he had driven the door to with his foot, shook him. The lad was so thin and ragged, and now so drenched, that he looked like an old clout hung on the line and shaken by the wind. Then Gib hauled him over to the little closet under the stairs and throwing him in shot the bolt on him.

They finished their supper in silence, and even when the smith and the other "known men" had come in Master Trudgeover seemed different—less eloquent than usual, speaking of mildness and mercy rather than of God's glory of God's judgements. And when the rest of the company had gone, in the last of the dwindling rain, he and Gib did not sit up together reading and talking by the rushlight. Trudgeover said he would to bed betimes against the morning, and certainly he was yawning, so that all his big yellow teeth showed. Gib said he was weary with the reaping, and they went up together in silence, and in silence undressed.

Trudgeover soon fell asleep, but Gib could not. At first he said to himself that it was the heat, or his bedfellow's snoring, which was indeed prodigious. But at last he admitted to himself that it was neither of these which kept him awake. How could any man suffer patiently a dumb fool like Wat, an ill-conditioned, idle, malicious imp? Lads must learn by beating. He himself had been beaten often enough. But for him Wat would have been a miners' lad, and what was that better than a slave? Yet always, as he disputed with his own thoughts, he knew clearly at last a thing he had long blindly known: in Wat he had brought the old sin to dog his steps close as his own shadow; he hated Wat, and that was a new sin. With horror the thought came to him that he had, as it were, begotten sin upon sin.

July 5

Gib heard the women from the Priory pass by before it was light. First, even before they came near, he heard their voices, then the jangle of the chains by which the wooden pails swung from the yokes they carried, last of all their footsteps, for they all went barefoot, so that they made less noise upon the road than as many sheep. They were going up to the Priory flock which the shepherd kept just now above Gawnless Wood, to milk the ewes for summer cheeses.

When they had gone by he got up, and lighting a candle sat down by the window to write. He had in his head many and piercing arguments against the usurped power of the Bishop of Rome; when he woke they would begin to move in his head so that he could not sleep again. So it was better to leave his bed and write.

As he wrote the dawn came without his noticing it. Only when he heard the women coming back he raised his eyes from the page, and saw that the candle flame looked sickly in the daylight, while outside the window the shadows lay long and pointed across the fields, and the sky was delicately blue and full of brightness.

He thought—"I could do well with a draught of milk"— but to ask a gift of anyone grated on him, and it would be worse to ask from one of that cackling crowd. He heard them laugh and call to each other, and then shriek louder to the men out in the fields.

Gib got up and began to put on his coat, meaning to shake Wat from his bed and send him out to milk the cow. But he heard Wat stirring and opening the door below, so he sat down again.

"Ho! Priest's bastard!" cried one of the women, and "Fie on the ugly brat!" another; then there was a squawk and a shout. "Drop that stone! Let me get at thee!" and Gib saw Wat go across the road, running doubled almost like an animal. He was behind the big elm tree; a second stone flew and there was another squawk.

Then the women began to go on again; he heard their angry voices; they spoke now not only of bastards but of heretics. He took up his pen but laid it down again when he

[324]

saw that one of them was still below. She stood in the road, holding out a hand towards the tree, from which Wat danced out for long enough to fling another stone.

It caught the woman Malle on the arm, and she gave a little cry and began to rub the place, then she held out her hand again.

"Nay! Nay!" she said, and had to dodge a clod of earth. After that she gave it up. Gib saw her shake her head, and go trudging off after the other women with the milk lipping at the edge of the swinging pails, and now and again slopping out to make blue-water patches in the dusty road.

July 6

Just before dinner time an elderly serving man in a greasy torn coat and leather hosen turned into the gate arch of the house at Mortlake which Lord Darcy had rented. He asked for my Lord and was told "Within," but when he came into the house they said, "Without in the garden." So he went straight on, though more than one tried to detain to ask, "What news? Is it done?" But he would not stay to talk, being a discreet man, nor even to shift the old coat for Darcy's bright popinjay green livery with the Buck's Head badge; he knew that my Lord waited for his news.

He found his master walking in the little walled rose-garden where the fountain, forlorn and cheerless, wept softly under the grey sky into the grey water of the basin, or was flung spattering by a gusty wind that made the roses shiver and flutter. A couple of women knelt together, weeding; when they saw the servant come in under the arch they sat back on their heels to stare.

Darcy, looking the man hard in the face, raised his eyebrows. The fellow nodded with a very grim mouth.

"We'll go beyond." Darcy led the way down the yew alley to the river bank. Yet when they had come there they stood in silence. Darcy's mind was searching back into the past, thinking of this King Harry, and of his father, and of the King whose naked hacked body had been brought into Market Bosworth tied on the back of a rough-coated farmer's pony. "But now," he thought, "is no man to set up his will against this King; no, not one."

The old serving man at his shoulder was seeing a crowd and a scaffold. His chest tightened again at the silence that had fallen when the headsman swung up the axe above the neck of Sir Thomas More; and again he heard the blade chop down with just that sound, only louder and greater, that housewives hear unmoved as they stand by the butchers' stalls talking of the weather and of the children's ailments; but this time there were few, men or women, whose breath did not catch at the sound. And then, with a bump and a rustle, the head, which had been one of the wisest and wittiest in Christendom, had tumbled forward into the straw.

"Did they suffer him to speak to the people?"

"Aye."

'What did he say?"

"Not much."

"God's Passion!" Darcy shouted at him. "What?"

The elderly serving man screwed up his face and braced his shoulders as if for a heavy bit of work.

"He says, leaning on the rail, and speaking slow, 'Good people pray for me, and I shall pray for you whither I go. And you shall also pray God send the King good counsel. As for me, I die a loyal servant of His Grace, but God's first.' "

Darcy pondered on that, recollected himself to make the sign of the cross and murmur a prayer, then pondered again.

"Well, it was enough. And yet—maybe they had commanded that he should use few words." He was, indeed, a little disappointed. This man who had died for conscience's sake might have left behind him words that could be passed from mouth to mouth to hearten other men, if the chance offered, for a different, armed resistance. Then he thought, "There's no chance—yet—or the chance is past," but if past he did not know when, nor how it could have been seized. He turned away along the river bank, saying over his shoulder, "Go and get off those rags," and then halted to ask, "Did you know any that were there?"

The man named the Lieutenant of the Tower, and the King's Great Chamberlain. Darcy interrupted.

"Not them. Any that were friend to Sir Thomas?"

"A serving man of my Lord Marquess, and of Lord Montague. And a man of the Emperor's Ambassador."

"In their liveries?"

"Nay," said the fellow, and with a sour smile plucked at his own ragged doublet. "Only the Ambassador's."

Darcy gave an angry laugh. "The rest of us don't dare show even our servants' noses." He struck his staff into the ground; the sodden earth clucked and hissed as he pulled it out again. He waved his hand, to dismiss the man, and then, as the horns blew in the house for dinner, turned and followed him in.

At table no one spoke of what had been done that morning on Tower Hill; no one spoke much at all. Darcy, observing the faces of his gentlemen, could see in them a look as of men unsure of their way; he knew how they felt. Under his own feet what had been the solid, known earth seemed now to crack and splinter like ice breaking. He could just remember times when there had been in England men marching or skulking in the lanes, charging across the quiet, familiar fields, dying on the banks of the brooks where as children they had used to fish for minnows. But this was a different thing, for there was peace, and in peace Cromwell—whose pale face, placid but for the quick eyes, was very present in Darcy's mind—Cromwell pulled down, one by one, those who resisted the King's will.

After dinner, in the privacy of his bedchamber, my Lord gave instructions to the Hainault Priest for Masses to be sung, secretly, for the soul of Sir Thomas More, and John Fisher, Bishop of Rochester.

"A very noble death—a martyr's death," said the Priest, whose face showed that he had been crying. "God give us grace to follow such an example."

Darcy crossed himself. "God rest his soul. *Miserere Domine!*"

But he thought, although he did not say, "How would that serve? It is not martyrs that will bring down Cromwell. If every good man died a martyr, who would profit but heretics and harlots? How would God be served?"

When the Priest had gone he sat long on the side of the bed, considering in his mind the power and the clogging burdens of the Emperor, the strength of French friendship for King Harry, the chance of an attack from Scotland. The longer he thought, the more sure he became that, without the Emperor would move, the only thing to do was to bide the time.

August 20

The Nuns' Church at Marrick was, of course, small, but since Dame Christabel had been Prioress it was very neatly kept. There were hangings of green say with a trellis pattern of flowers all round the Chancel now, and the big silver cross that had used quite often to be brown and discoloured had always in these days a high polish.

Just now the Nuns were not in Church, as it was the time

for Parlement, that is, for good and religious conversation in the Cloister for the ordinary Nuns, and for the officers of the House the ordering of their particular charges. Both the doors from the Cloister into the Church—the Prioress's door at the east end of the north Cloister wall, and the Nuns' door at the west end—stood open, but so still was the day that no breath of wind came into the Church, only the sunshine, stained and enriched by the painted glass where it fell upon the floor, but in the air nothing more than ghostly slants of something paler than the general brown dimness of the Church.

Julian Savage knelt at the Chancel steps, telling her beads. She had already said 29 of the 50 Paternosters which were her penance for bringing Dame Margaret Lovechild's rabbit into the Cloister, and she was keeping up a very good pace, being anxious to be done, and then perhaps the Novice Mistress would let her go out with the others into the field where the first reaping was to begin to-day among the oats.

Then she heard the clack of the latch on the door of the Parish Church beyond the screen, and the unmistakable wheeze of the door opening, and a man's voice said:

"Sir, take an offering and sing me a Mass for the soul of the Founder of this Church and the House of the Nuns. For I'm a man of that same family, though of the younger branch."

After the first two words July knew the voice, and a shock of delight and, somehow, of delightful dread, ran through her, so that she heard the voice only and not the words, until Master Aske said, in a different tone, "Why! I have seen you before."

"Since I was born in Marrick," Gib growled, "that's not strange," and July, listening now with all her ears, heard the Priest go away to the vestry. As she could not hear any other footsteps she did not know what Master Aske was doing, but she guessed him to be down on his knees, as she was, and somewhere quite near.

For a while that was enough, but then she thought, "I must see him."

She did not know how she could do it, but one thing was certain: she must be out of the Church as quickly as she could. She got up and tiptoed down to the Nuns' door. There was no one in the west walk of the Cloister. She peeped along the north walk. Dame Bess and Dame Margaret sat with their heads close together presumably in good and religious conversation. Beyond them there was a knot of Ladies near the

Prioress's door. They were also engaged in conversation but the tone of their voices was high and sharp.

July clutched her beads to her so that not a click should betray her, drew a long breath as though she were going to dive into deep water, and stole out into the Cloister. She knew that she must not look round, but the skin of her back prickled as if she felt the Ladies' eyes through her habit. Then she was in the little low passage between the Cellaress's Office and the Church tower—almost safe—then out in the Great Court, and shutting the door of the passage behind her —for the moment quite safe. But what was she to do next? She had never thought of that, but must think of it now, and the shelter of the stable opposite seemed a better place for thinking than the open Court; but while she still hesitated she heard a knocking, and his voice cried at the gate, "Ho! Porter!"

She forgot all about shelter then, and came out in the middle of the Court. He stood in the shadow of the gate talking to Jankin and leaning one hand on the wattled wall. She could hear the sound of his voice, though no words, and she could look at him. Instead of the crimson and black, watchet blue and murrey which she remembered in London, he was dressed to-day in an old patched coat of the dull colours that men wore for hawking, and a hawk sat on his left hand. July learnt him all over again as she watched; yet really he was just the same, and in herself she was aware of no difference.

After a moment Jankin left him, lifting a finger to the edge of his hood, and went across the Court to the Cloister door. Master Aske came out into the sunshine and sat down on the horse-block in the sun. For a moment there was no one else in the Great Court—only the hens picking and scratching, and on the roof of the gate-house a few pigeons which sidled, dipping their necks, or rooted with their bills under their wings, or lifted a coral-coloured foot to scratch; on the horse-block there was Master Aske, and by the stable door July, all under the warm still blue sky.

She went quickly across the Court till she stood in front of him.

"Master Aske!" she said, and then, "Oh! you've forgotten me."

"Mistress—" he began, puckering up his one eye against the brightness behind her head. Ought he to remember her? He did not. Then he did, and, so quick is thought, he remembered the last time he had seen her, holding a mirror for Meg, who laughed at him with her eyes over the mirror and over the girl's head; and he remembered the last time he had seen Meg, with her hair spread all over the pillow. That recollection made his mind sick.

July stood in front of him watching his face. If she could have gone away she would. If she could have cried she would have wailed aloud. But she could do neither, and so she simply stood and looked at him, dumb as a stone.

A more stupid man than Robert Aske would have seen that he had hurt her, and a less kindly man would have been sorry. He struck himself a sharp slap on the brow with his open palm.

"By the Rood!" he cried, so loud that the hawk jerked and flapped on his fist. "It's my other little July! I didn't know you, grown so great a girl. But I did not know you were here neither."

July came to life again. "I knew you were here. I heard you in the Church. I was doing penance for bringing Dame Margaret's rabbit into the Cloister. I live here. The Ladies let me feed their rabbits." She heard Jankin coming up behind her, and the Prioress's door opening.

"Where have you come from?" she scrambled out quickly, determined to know. "Do you stay here? When did you come? For why are you here?"

He laughed at her with the bright teasing eye she remembered.

"Mistress, one at a time and that the last. I'm come to see my kinswoman, Dame Eleanor."

That struck July dumb. To think that she had never known. To think that she had once made a laughing stock of his kinswoman.

The Prioress's voice called her by name and bade her begone to the Cloister. She went, not looking back, but she had the look of him with her, laughing, browner than she had known him, in his old stained, grey-green hood. She thought that if she had to do more penance the look of him would last her through many Paternosters.

August 29

July walked to Grinton with Dame Eleanor and Dame Bess; two men-servants came behind to carry for them. The day was very fair, after many days of rain, warm but with a pleasant breathing air to temper the sun's heat. The two Ladies were pleased to have an errand to take them out on

[330]

such a fair day, but July, who was in herself one of the motives for the expedition, found the sunshine as cheerless as black night, since she was going to Grinton to have a tooth pulled out.

To step into the cottage where the deed was to be done was like stepping into prison. The Monk from Bridlington, who had the knack of drawing teeth, got up from beside the fire where the wife was busy with white puddings seething in the pot. He put his hand (he meant it kindly) on July's shoulder, and led her to a bench under the window. The two Ladies abandoned her, as one past human help. As her knees doubled under her and she sank on the stool she could hear their voices, loud because of Dame Eleanor's deafness, talking by the fire, but the sense of their words could not penetrate the terror, which, like a wall of glass, enclosed her, narrowing always.

The Father took hold of her chin; the wall of glass came so close as to suffocate her; she opened her mouth, gasping. Then he thrust into her mouth a great pair of pincers which rattled against her teeth. She struggled a little, but he had her tight. Pain shattered the wall of glass. She screamed, and the tooth was before her eyes, small, bloody, and now quite strange after years of closest companionship. When Father Richard loosened his grip on her jaw, as if he had given her face back to her, she covered it tenderly and tremblingly with her hands and sobbed.

"That fellow," said the good Father cheerfully, "that fellow won't trouble you any more, no, not till Doomsday."

At the words relief began to creep into her mind, but it was soon a flood of pure joy. When they came out of the cottage she saw the sunshine for the fairest that ever shone. Even Dame Eleanor's disjointed comments upon everything they bought could not fret her this morning: there was time for them on this sweet day; there was time for anything, for time stretched ahead with nothing in it which was not pleasant to do, with no fear such as that which had stood in the way as they came to Grinton. She was so happy that she could even spurn from her the thought that though to-day was free from fear there would come another day, when another tooth must be outed. She swung the basket recklessly.

She and Dame Eleanor were to meet Dame Bess on the bridge, but when they reached it there was no Dame Bess, and now Dame Eleanor clapped her hands together in distress. "There!" she cried. "The linen for the Lady's stockings.

Gregory was fetching it from Richmond. And I've forgotten it." And now what was to be done?

No, July could not go because the Prioress had been particular that Dame Eleanor must see that it was the right, fine, Flanders weave. And Dame Eleanor could not leave July on the bridge, because that would not be seemly. And they could not go both together, because Dame Bess would come and would not know where to find them. The problem seemed insoluble. "And there will be no time if we wait, for now there's but time to be back for dinner." Dame Eleanor looked towards Fremington Edge and wrung her hands together; no help was visible in that direction; she looked back over the bridge towards Grinton and her face brightened. She pushed July gently aside, and moving a few paces held out her arms wide as if to stop a runaway horse.

Master Aske, who was strolling across the bridge idly twirling in his fingers a young foxglove spike, stopped, pulled off his cap and wished her, "Good-day, cousin. What's your will?"

She explained the dilemma to him, holding him firmly by the wrist, and talking a great deal and fast, with soft mumbling motions of her lips rather like a rabbit. He listened gravely but once or twice his eye caught July's and she could have sworn that there was a laugh in it.

"So cousin," the old lady concluded, "if you should stay here with this young gentlewoman till I return, all will be well."

He said he would, and nodded so that she should get his meaning.

"You will not leave her?"

He said he would not, and shook his head.

"You will stay here till I come back? You understand?"

He said he understood, and she went off, in a great hurry, but turned and came again to say that he need not stay if Dame Bess returned. "But not to leave the young gentlewoman alone."

When she had gone right away he turned his eye on July, and the laughter in it was plain to see.

"If I mistake, correct me. But I think I am to stay with you," said he.

There were quite a number of people passing one way and another over the bridge, and now a train of pack-horses came along, their bells jangling. Master Aske led July to one of the angels over the buttresses of the bridge. He leaned his elbows on the parapet and looked down at the river. She looked at him.

He talked, lightly, of this and that. He was staying up at Marrick Manor. He had lost a hawk the other day in the woods. Fenland such as he knew at home he liked better for hawking than these thick woods. By and by he plucked one little glove finger from the foxglove spike and stuck it onto his forefinger.

"That," he said, poking it up to show her, "was what we did when we were little brats."

He was surprised when her hand came down and snatched it off.

"There is poison in it," she cried. "It will do you a mischief." He saw that her eyes were very round and serious, and he laughed.

"That's fiddlesticks. I've done it a thousand times."

She faltered, "There is poison in it. Anyone will tell you," and she slipped it on her own finger.

"Silly little wench," he said, but kindly. "You see, you don't believe it yourself."

Yet she did at least half believe it, and was afraid in a kind of misty way, but much more glad to be sharing the danger with him.

He was silent for a little while, and again July watched him. Now that he was neither laughing nor talking his mouth was shut very tight and hard, and his heavy brows were drawn into a straight frown. She cried suddenly, feeling as if the shadow of a cloud had fallen on her face, chilling it, "Oh Sir! What's amiss?"

He started round, frowning now at her—a thin girl at her most awkward raw stage, and looking younger than her fifteen years.

She said, with her eyes on his, "I would do anything for you, Master Aske."

He flushed at that, though she did not. "What a child!" he thought, and felt suddenly warm towards her, forgetting for a moment that she was Margaret Cheyne's sister.

"That's a large offer," he said lightly, but yet he was moved, though he did not come near to guessing how amply true her words were.

She repeated, "What is amiss?" and the frown returned to his face as he looked up the Dale to where the great hump of Calva drowsed in the heat.

She thought that he was not going to answer, and she had

no other words to move him, but suddenly he began to speak. It was about Statutes, Laws, Parliament, Thomas Cromwell, the Bishops, the King. In all this she did not follow him well, but when he spoke of headings and hangings, and, driving the words through his teeth, of butchering deeds that he had himself seen done, then she understood only too well and felt her face and her very heart grow cold from fear, even when he broke off short and muttered, "No need for you to know these things." But it was as if she had always known them.

After a while he turned to her again with a sharp, bitter look.

"This is treason now, by these new laws, only to speak as I have done to you."

"You will not speak so to others," she urged him, and he shook his head and turned away. To Will Wall he had spoken, because Will would betray him as soon as his own hand, and now he was speaking to this child and it did not occur to him to wonder why.

"So," he said bitterly, and shrugged, "we have now taken that oath."

She said, eagerly, "Why! Yes!" being thankful to find him disposed to talk of such a harmless, unbloodied topic as an oath. "We took it in the Chapter House, each one of us. The Prioress said we should, or the House would suffer."

"That was how we all took it. Priests and Monks so that the Church should not suffer, and I—"

"Oh!" she cried. "Oh! your hand!"

He looked down at it. His knuckles were bleeding where he had struck his fist against the coping of the bridge. He put it to his mouth and then lowered it to tell her, "It's nothing," and whipped it behind his back as he saw Dame Eleanor and Dame Bess bearing down on them, and the two Priory servants carrying baskets and bundles.

That afternoon when the Novice Mistress set the girls their task of reading, July asked that she might read in the book called *The Revelation of Divine Love*, and when told she might, fetched it, and settled herself in very studious solitude apart from the others.

She had feared that the pages for her reading might be prescribed, but no, she was free to choose, and it did not take her long to find the place that she wanted, and to slip into it, unnoticed of any, the foxglove cup which she had taken from Master Aske's finger.

When she had done that she let out a soft breath of relief. This doing of hers was a spell or an invocation—she didn't know which. But as the poisonous foxglove had no power to harm him "so," she thought, "if I lay it on that page, among those very words, and it stays safe there, he shall be safe." Not even to herself would she own what it was against which she wished to assure him, but seeing that he was dearest, she must fear for him always the worst.

To comfort and give herself confidence she read over many times that afternoon the words in which the charm consisted, turning back again and again to where the foxglove cup, limp now and flat, lay pressed between two pages.

"See I am God," the book said—

See I am in all things. See I do all things. See I never left my hands of my works ne never shall without end: see I lead all things to the end that I ordained it to, fro without beginning, by the same might, wisdom, and love, that I made it with. How should anything be amiss?

October 1

"Get me out the King's letter. There is the key."

The Archbishop dropped the key of the painted coffer on the table and went away to the window. There was little there to be seen but rain driving before the wind, the tossing branches of the trees and leaves that streamed away among the rain.

The little wainscoted room, with its books, and viol on one table and recorder on the livery cupboard, and the brightly burning fire, was much pleasanter, but it was unwillingly that Dr. Cranmer moved back to the table where his secretary had laid out the King's letter. It was dated just a fortnight ago, and this was not the first time that the Archbishop's secretary had taken it out of the coffer, and afterwards laid it there again, with its command not yet fulfilled.

The Archbishop stooped over it, as though he must read it through in order to master it; his secretary picked up a quill and tried the nib on his nail. He kept as much of his attention on that as was necessary not to seem to watch his master, but enough of it was free to make him raise his head as the Archbishop lifted his eyes from the letter.

"If," said the Archbishop, "I should put it to His Grace once more how the Scripture may be so interpreted, and indeed I think truly so interpreted, indeed I do—" He lost himself and began again. "If I put it to him and show him in Scripture how the Bishop's jurisdiction is by the law of God—"

He waited, but the secretary seemed now to be completely absorbed in testing the quill.

"You think I should not?" The secretary almost imperceptibly shook his head.

"There are," the Archbishop admitted, "other ways of interpreting the same Scripture." He sighed. "And if our jurisdiction come neither from Scripture, nor from the Bishop of Rome, as none holds now, then is Master Cromwell true to his logic when he argueth that it must come from the King, and so, by the King may be intermitted."

He drew a quick breath as though he had reached a decision, and said, "Write—'To the Bishop of Winchester.'"

But after that he got no further. He stood up and began to roam round the room.

"It is strange," he said, speaking to the secretary, but looking into the fire. "It is strange and new that the Bishop's visitation of their own dioceses should be inhibited, and Master Cromwell visit here and there throughout my province. It is very strange—I did not think . . ." He coughed.

"What other letters are there?" he asked.

The secretary said letters from Lord Lisle and others about the weirs in Hampshire.

"A troublesome business," says the Archbishop. "Read me the letters."

When the letters about the weirs had been answered it was time for the Archbishop to go to dinner. The secretary locked up the King's letter in the painted coffer and gave the key to his master.

"To-morrow," said the Archbishop, "I shall write to the Bishops what is the King's command."

October 5

The Nuns' Priest had been back at the Priory for a week. He had told the Prioress, in private, that his conscience was quieted, and he rattled past the omitted words in the Office so confidently that it was plain he had well rehearsed the new Office. Rarely, before he went away, had he had anything to do with Gib Dawe, but to-day, meeting him by the churchyard gate, he brought Gib up to his snug room, where a fire burnt pleasantly, and there was a jug of French wine in the cupboard.

The Nuns' Priest told him to sit down, and poured out some of the wine for each, and then began to talk about the woman Malle and her visions. He said that he wanted to know Sir Gilbert's opinion, and in the caressing way he had he patted Gib's bony forearm with his plump, smooth hand; but it seemed rather that he wished to tell Gib that he himself thought visions to be awkward, chancy things to deal with. "Marry," said he, "though she be no Nun of Kent, seeing visions of Kings and Queens to bring her to the gallows, still less would I be as those unhappy priests who were hanged together with the Nun," and his hand went down to his silver-plated belt and caressed the roundness under it, as if he reassured his belly against the executioner's knife and scrabbling hand. Indeed it seemed that his thoughts had gone that way, for he shuddered, and for a minute his face became quite pinched and pale.

"So," said he, "I would have nought to do with these things, but I think to warn the Lady that there is much talk of them, which, I believe, she doth not hear."

"And also," said the Nun's Priest, reaching out for his wine, "what has this poor soul seen and heard but common folk and common things—neither saints nor angels, nor Our Lady and Her Son throned in bliss, but a young poor man, and simple shepherds? And not in Church neither, but openly in the Dale. Mass! It's not seemly."

He tipped up his can and drank, and Gib watched his throat working as the wine ran down; it was a thick throat and above it a plump, close-shaven jowl. Gib got up abruptly.

"Seemly?" said he, very harsh. "And what were those holy shepherds but plain, poor, homespun men such as our shepherds to-day? And what was the Lord Himself but a carpenter's son that swinked and sweated over a bench?" He stopped, and even in his anger must laugh at the way the other's jaw had dropped at his fierceness.

"So you believe," said the little fat Priest, "that these be true visions?"

Gib began to say that he did, but that was purely out of contrariness; it was long since he had put any faith in Malle's visions, and honesty pulled him up short, so that he had nothing better to say than "Tsha!" He left the Nuns' Priest by the fire with the wine at his elbow, and a dish of filberts, and a book of tales beside him on the bench, and went out into the wind, and into a cold driving rain that had begun to fall.

At the parsonage house the chimney was smoking and the pottage was burnt. It was a very scurvy dinner. Then Wat managed to trip and spill some of his pottage over Gib's shoe. Gib got up and beat him, and throwing him into the shed beyond the dairy, shot the bolt on him. But when he came back to the house place he could still hear Wat's whimpering, and after a bit he took his own bowl and tipped what was in it on to the fire, making a worse foul stink than ever.

After that he sat with his arms tight about his knees, staring before him at the bunches of herbs hanging from the rafters, a long string of onions, and the ox harness for the plough.

He wished he could have denounced the Nuns' Priest for unbelief, but himself he could not believe the visions, though not for the same reason. That talk of the young men going up to Keld, which had seemed to mean freedom, he had long put away from him. And surely, if God showed visions to any these days, it would be of threatenings of wrath and judgement. An angel with a burning sword, devils dragging rich men to hell—these he could have readily believed. But Malle, so far as he could hear, had talked only of bliss and of peace. Wat's whimpering went on and Gib shifted his shoulders as if something galled him. To be rid of it he went and fetched the book of the Scriptures and, opening at the Book of the Revelation, read of the casting down of Babylon. As a background to the mighty winds and trumpets of that book his mother breathed hard at the pain that gnawed her belly, and sometimes groaned; occasionally Wat cried out, but at last he seemed to fall asleep.

October 8

The two Ambassadors of his most Christian Majesty, Francis I of France, to the King of England, sat together at a table on which their wine stood among a litter of paper, pens and ink. Monseigneur Antoine de Castelnau, Bishop of Tarbes, had been writing with his own hand instructions for his fellow, the Bailly of Troyes, who to-morrow would return to France to report to their master. The instructions lay now spread out before them, sprinkled over with fine powder of cuttle-fish shell, ground small, to dry the ink. As they waited, the Bishop stretched out a hand for his wine; it was in a goblet of Venice glass, and it was wine of his own country; he held it towards the candle flames till the edges grew translucent, with a glorious colour. Then he lifted it to his mouth, breathed in the faint, vinous aroma, and at last drank.

"Hah!" said he pensively, "I know the vineyard where those grapes grew," and his mind saw it, and the bleached rocks of the higher hills above, while his eyes rested on the lined and bearded face of the Bailly. "And you will be home in time for the vintage." He sighed, and began to talk about a new vineyard he had planted, and a garden at a small house in the hills which was very dear to him. Outside a wild wind caught the notes of the chimes from a nearby church, swinging them close and away as if they had been a shaken banner of sound. After the chimes ceased there came the sharp rattle of heavy rain upon the window, and smoke swirled out from the hearth.

The Bishop recalled himself from his thoughts of France, and none too soon, for the Bailly, an impatient man, was drumming his fingers on the table edge. The Bishop tipped the powder back from the paper into the box, blew the last grains from the page, and gathered the other sheets together.

"As I see it," he said, "our master can do what he will with this King, so great is King Harry's need of a friend, and so many his enemies."

The Bailly nodded shortly. All this was in the written instructions, but he knew the Bishop too well to think that he would get off without a repetition of it, unless he avoided that by taking his leave; but the Bishop's wine was good and plenty, and while this storm of rain lasted he would remain; better the Bishop's prosings than to be abroad, exposed to this sacred climate of England.

"If any Prince, the Emperor or another—"

"What other?" the Bailly cried scornfully.

"If there were any other. If any Prince were to take up the quarrel of the Queen Katherine and her daughter, the people love them so well they would rise."

"Hm!" said the Bailly.

"Such is the opinion of noblemen, and commons; yea, and I have heard it spoken even by the King his servants. You yourself—"

"They talk," said the Bailly.

"There's too much talk to take lightly. See how openly the poor folk cry out against this Queen Anne, calling her—" He hesitated, and the Bailly with his curt laugh supplied a string of names which the poor folk, and others not so poor, called Queen Anne.

The Bishop held up his hand. "There is also the subversion of religion. Also this terrible weather, whereby the harvest's half destroyed."

"*Mordieu!*" said the Bailly. "You do not need to tell me about the weather."

"And they fear also an interruption of trade with the Emperor's countries. That, with the scarcity of bread, would be a shrewd blow, especially if our master were to refuse corn. And if the Emperor were to move war—"

"He will not," said the Bailly.

The Archbishop was nettled. "How do you know?" he inquired tartly. "If he does, they will rise for the old Queen, and the Princess, but especially for the Princess. Be very sure you make our master understand how they still, notwithstanding all the laws made in their Parliament, count her as Princess. And especially tell him of those citizens' wives that came about her when she was brought last from that palace down the river, weeping and crying out that she was still Princess, whatever laws the men might make."

The Bailly, during the pause in which the Bishop took another sip of wine, turned his head to listen. There was now no sound of rain on the windows. He stood up.

"Tell him also," said the Bishop, "how all, even gentlemen at Court, at first believed that we came to pronounce excommunication against the King, and that they prayed for us."

The Bailly had taken up the written instructions, folded them, and slipped them into the breast-pocket of his doublet. Now as he buttoned himself again he said, "It is written here," and he tapped his breast.

Yet the Bishop followed him to the door, and held him there with a hand on his shoulder, still telling him how all England, and the Princess Mary herself, thought of nothing but that marriage of the Princess to the Dauphin should at last be made, and so save the Princess her rights.

When the Bailly had twitched his shoulder free and gone, the Bishop came back to the table. He burnt all the half written sheets that lay there, and then settled himself comfortably with a book and his wine. But now and again his mind would go back to the small house and its garden, and the vineyards round about, and above the vineyards little woods of pines, where, when the singing of the vintagers ceased, you heard the warm, dry note of the cicadas.

M. Chapuys' servant was shaving him, when his discreet Burgundian secretary knocked and came in. He remained near the door, but Chapuys could see who it was in the wall mirror, and said, "Another ten minutes, Philippe," and gave his face again to the razor.

But the secretary did not go away, and the Ambassador, waving the servant off, turned to look at him. Then he saw that the sober and correct M. Philippe had his cap in his hands, and the cap was full of brown eggs.

"And have you been robbing a farm-yard?" asked M. Chapuys pleasantly, but the secretary told him "No," and came nearer so that he stood between his master and the man who was shaving him. "A country woman is below, who brought these eggs," he said; but unseen by the servant his finger pointed at a little posy of late flowers that lay among the eggs. There were a few marigolds, tied up with some pansy leaves.

"Ah!" said the Ambassador, "I'll buy them. Go and bring her in." And to the servant, "Make haste."

"She is within," Philippe said, and went and sat down by the door with the cap full of eggs, and the posy in which were marigolds for Mary and pansies for Pole, between his respectable black knees.

The servant found his master hurried and fidgety that morning. "That'll do. That'll do," he said, and caught up the towel to wipe off the last of the lather from his face. "Come, truss up these points. Now, the sanguine gown. No, I'll not stay for a doublet."

Then the Ambassador and his secretary passed out into the big room that looked over Cheapside, M. Chapuys in shirt and hosen and loose gown, though he was used to dress early and always with the most exact care.

"Is she from the Marchioness?" he asked as soon as the door was shut behind them. A fortnight ago the Marchioness of Exeter had sent her Chaplain to tell the Ambassador that the King threatened to have done at last with Queen Katherine and Princess Mary.

"She does not speak."

"Dumb?"

The secretary allowed himself the slightest smile and shake of the head.

"You said a country-woman?"

"She has a basket, and garments convenable."

"But—?"

"Her hands are not such as brew, bake, and milk kine."

"Bring her here."

When she came in, following the secretary, Chapuys saw a small plump woman with a big white veil flapping on each side of her face, a grey homespun petticoat, a brown kirtle hitched up on one side over a stout leather belt, and strong shoes. The shoes were too big for her, and when he looked at her hands he saw that Philippe was right. She carried a basket, but even as he looked at her she held it out to him, and, from that instinctive gesture of one used to be served, he knew who she was.

"My Lady!" he said, and led her to a chair, and poured out wine, and served her himself. The Burgundian secretary had gone out softly, and Chapuys knew that now he would be keeping the door.

The Marchioness drank, and set the cup down, and he noted that her hand shook.

"My Lord Marquess would have come," she said, "but I said he must not, for he might be known."

Chapuys nodded. The Marquess with his great height and long sad face was hard to disguise.

"Therefore I came myself—so that I may make you believe the danger—the danger—the danger I sent word of a fortnight ago."

"Madame, I do believe it. I promise you on God's Passion."

"I thought that perhaps when I sent that message you did not believe." She looked hard at him. "But you must make the Emperor believe."

He said, "Tell me, Madame, what I shall tell him from you and my Lord Marquess."

She gripped her hands together at her breast and told him. The King was determined, when Parliament met again (and but for the Sickness it would have been sitting now), that the Queen Katherine and her daughter should follow where Fisher and More had gone; and on the same charge, for neither had they sworn the oath.

"And he will do it. I heard him swear by God's Majesty that he'd do it, if he lost his crown in the doing. Sir," the Marchioness looked up into Chapuys' attentive, serious face, "sometimes I think he is mad—or all the world is mad—or I myself."

Chapuys shook his head.

"The Queen—" he began, meaning Queen Katherine, but

the Marchioness mistook him, since at Court "the Queen" had for so long meant Queen Anne.

"Jesu! yes!" she said. "It is Anne Boleyn that has done all this. And now works against the Princess. She hates her the more because she fears her."

"Fears her?"

"She has heard a prophecy of which she told us all, openly. There were her maids, and other ladies, not a few gentlemen, and that pretty singing fellow Smeton sitting at her feet. I did not hear how they came to talk of it, but I heard her say, 'No, by the Mass, I do not love my step-daughter Mary. And,' says she, 'I know well that she is my death and I am hers; for so it is by the stars.' Then she laid her hand on Mark Smeton's head, toying and tugging at his curls. 'Therefore,' quod she, 'I will take good care that she shall not laugh at *me* when I am dead.' And she began to laugh."

The Marchioness shivered. "She would laugh indeed if the Princess died."

"Madame," Chapuys tried to comfort himself and her, "God will preserve from harm those two good ladies."

"God," the Marchioness said with bitterness, "is very patient. He did not preserve neither the Bishop of Rochester nor Sir Thomas More, nor yet the brethren of the Charterhouse. It is the Emperor who must—"

"I will write," he told her eagerly, yet when she had gone he wondered whether the Emperor's patience might not exceed even that of God. The doubt did not however prevent him writing a letter which was most urgent and energetic in asking help for Queen Katherine and the Princess.

1536

January 7

At Kimbolton Castle the Groom of the Chamber and the Candlemaker heard the clock strike eleven as they finished the worst part of their work, and washed their hands, letting the water run over their forearms, till the basin looked as if it was full of raspberry juice. Then, having tidied up the mess, and set aside the earthern jar in which were enclosed the heart and entrails, they kicked the bloody clothes out of the way of their feet, and set to work to cere the body, wrapping it in fold after fold of waxed linen cloth, with handfuls of spices laid on, till the sickly smell of blood was over-laid by the sharp scents of cinnamon and myrrh. By the time they were done it was close on midnight, and all at Kimbolton asleep except those who waited to watch beside the bier till day. The Groom of the Chamber unlocked the door, and he and the other went out, leaving alone the body of Katherine who had been Queen. It lay now stiff as wood, and bulked out to unnatural rotundity by the folds of the cerecloth; only the face showed, wax white and sharp in the light of the candle flames which shivered when the wind whined through the shutters.

Outside on the dark stair the Groom of the Chamber let out a great sigh, and said that By Cock! he had a sore thirst. As the Chandler had the same they went off together to shake up one of the buttery lads. When he had found ale and bread for them, they blew up the cinders of the fire in the almoner's room, and sat down to warm their feet and drink their ale. A big tabby cat, dislodged from the cushion of the settle, stretched and yawned, showing teeth curved and sharp as thorns, but milk white; then it leapt, light as a leaf, on the lap of the Chandler and at once fell asleep again.

Not till their cans were half empty did either of the two men speak, and even then the Groom of the Chamber was sparing of words. But the Chandler became garrulous. He said it was a pity to see the good Queen lie dead, and no harm now to call her Queen for that Queen she had been and now was no more, nor was anything any more, God have mercy on her soul. "And," said he, "all her ladies saying that since the Emperor's Ambassador came to see her on New Year's Day, that she fared the better for it, and would recover. Aye and surely it must have given the poor soul comfort to speak to one of the Emperor's people once more."

The Groom of the Chamber grunted. He was a lean, sharp, worried man, never talkative, and now he would not raise his eyes from the fire. The Chandler went on:

"That fat man of the Imperial Ambassador, the one that spoke English, told me the poor lady took heart so from his master coming, that he heard her, when they were talking, laugh, and more than once."

"Did she laugh?" the Groom muttered, but it was less a question than a sort of sour comment.

"Aye that she did. And asked for the fat man—you know what a merry talker he was—to make her sport that evening."

After a silence the Chandler shifted a little on the seat to look at the Groom of the Chamber.

"Even last night the women were saying that she was so much better that she called for a comb and dressed and tied her hair for herself."

The Groom of the Chamber twitched his thin nose, frowned, squinted into the can that he held on his knee, and said nothing.

"And to-night," said the Chandler, fondling the cat with one hand, but keeping his eyes on the Groom, "to-night—there she lies, dead." As he lifted his chin towards the painted beams of the ceiling they both thought of the little close room above, of the reek of the blood, and of the dismal work they had accomplished on the shrunken body of the grey-haired woman that had come to England nearly thirty years before, a young girl, plump and merry, afraid a little, yet hoping more than fearing, because of the ignorance and potency of youth.

"Why," the Chandler leaned along the settle and spoke softly, "why did you cut through the heart when it was forth of the body?"

The Groom's eyes came quickly to his in a sharp look. But all he said was, "Because so it should be done."

"Perdy, *I* never saw it so done before."

The Groom of the Chamber got up. He said he was for bed, and went away. But before he went to bed he found the dead woman's Chaplain, the Bishop of Llandaff, who, with others, was watching about the body, and told him, very secretly, a dreadful thing—how that the heart of Dame Katherine, Princess Dowager, was black and hideous all through, and to the surface of it clung a small black globule. The Groom of the Chamber knew just so much of surgery as to be very positive. He told the Bishop, who was a Spaniard, that from the state of the heart he knew that the Princess Dowager had been poisoned. The Bishop wrote a letter that night to Master Chapuys, telling him what the Groom had said. "And if it is poison," he wrote, "surely none other but the Concubine hath devised it."

January 8

Not only the Queen Anne but the King himself joined in the dancing this night, and both showed very good cheer. Many remarked it, and thought, if they did not whisper, of the messenger who had come that morning from Kimbolton, announcing the Princess Dowager's death. At last, quite late, the King clapped his hands to quiet the musicians and bring the galliard to an end. Then he called for wine and candles, and for his gentlemen to put him to bed. The Queen and her ladies, having curtseyed to the King, withdrew to her apartments.

In the King's bed-chamber the gentlemen on duty took off the King's rings, and chain, the dagger in a crimson velvet sheath the hilt of which was frosty with small diamonds. One of them laid by his yellow satin cap with a white feather, and a sapphire brooch to hold the feather. Two others helped him to take off the yellow satin doublet. The King whistled softly a tune that they had danced to just now; he yawned, whistled again, and smiled privately to himself.

They had put on him by now his night-shirt, and the gold embroidered night-cap; when he had slipped his arms into a green and white velvet nightgown he spread them out in a great luxurious stretch, yawning again, wide as a cat, so that all his fine teeth showed, and his pink tongue.

He kept Norris behind when the others had gone, talking with him of the buck hounds, and of a new goldsmith out of Germany, a very skilful craftsman; but at last he got into bed and lay there with his eyes shut, and his face, with the fine sharp beaked nose, turned up to the ceilour of the bed, while Norris drew the curtains softly, and thought, with a sort of start in his mind, how the King would one day—one day—lie just so, with face composed and eyes shut; but on that day the eyes would not open again.

They opened now and met Norris's, and Norris felt his heart quicken, as though the King could read his thought.

"How," the King asked, "goes this business of your marriage?"

"But lamely," said Norris, and asked himself, "Can one have told him that I wait to stand in his shoes?"

"You should make haste," said the King, closing his eyes again, yet smiling with his mouth. "And how think you," he asked, "should a man choose a wife? For wit, or for beauty, or for what other quality in her?"

Norris, because he had been for a moment afraid, now became pert. He said that himself he favoured a plump dower.

But the King, frowning a little, went on, as if he had not spoken. "Of all things," said he, "let her be meek," adding hastily, "given virtue, of course, given virtue."

Norris agreed, "Of course." And then, since Katherine, Queen or Princess Dowager, was to-night, though un-named, in the minds of all, he began to say that though Her Highness had been virtuous, meek she had not been. But he stopped short, having remembered the awkward fact that it was not for him to consider her as the King's wife at all.

Yet the King only smiled at Norris's stumbling. "No matter—no matter. She is dead." He crossed his breast under the sheet and murmured, "*Deus misereatur . . .*"

"God be praised," he said aloud. "Now am I free from any threat of war with the Emperor. Now I shall have peace."

After Norris had left him the King humped himself more comfortably into the warmth of the bed, drowsily watching where a dimly luminous glow in the curtains showed that the great candle burned outside. "Peace with the Emperor," he thought, "peace at home."

"My little fair sweetheart," he murmured, and thought— "Meek as a dove, and as a lamb innocent."

January 18

It was Dame Margery Conyers who was the first to see the King's Visitors. She was up in the Vine Chamber in the dorter which she shared with Dame Joan Barningham and Dame Eleanor Maxwell; it was called the Vine Chamber because a long time ago the beams of the ceiling had been painted with a pattern of vine leaves and grape bunches; the paint was faded now and dark, but on a sunshiny morning you could now and then catch a gleam of gold among the leaves.

The gleam was there to-day, because of the brightness outside, where a white frost lay on the ground and on the roofs, and the sun shone over all, yellow and clear. The servants had lit the fire and redded up the room while the Ladies had been in Church, and now the flames were climbing merrily up the chimney; beside the hearth, between the settle and a stool, a table was laid for Mixtum with a white fresh cloth.

The day was so fair that for mere pleasure of the sunlight Dame Margery went over to the window, which fronted the sun across the Dale. The little panes were all patterned by the frost with pictures of marvellous things. Crusted upon the glass there were woods, sharp hills, lakes still and frozen, fountaining shapes of unknown leaves, all frost-white, yet lit through by the yellow sun with a warm glow of rose.

Dame Margery opened the window, and met the sunshine that came swimming into the room on a faint lit mist and with the clean smell of rime. Across the frozen grass the trees laid lavender blue shadows. Just as she drew a deep breath of the sparkling morning she caught sight of the dozen or so riders who were crossing the ford; they were almost in the sun's eye for her, but she could see one, tall and thin, who wore a big red felt riding hat; another bulky man rode a little askew in his saddle, and as she looked he raised a hand and pointed as if he had seen her at the window.

And as if he had seen her she slammed the casement to. She knew who these were. The Nuns' miller had heard from one of the Stainton hinds, who had it from a lead miner, who was told by the Leyburn shepherd, that the King's Visitors were come to Coverham Abbey; the shepherd had heard the Monks' carter say so at the ale-house in Leyburn.

Dame Margery made haste to go down, but it was as if the stone stairs had turned soft as feather pillows under her feet, and the flags of the Cloister like quaking marsh land. These Visitors, sent about to every Monastery in the country, were here to pry, to pick on faults, to question. And at the end of it their meaning was to turn out the Ladies from Marrick. She was sure of it. Houses in the South Country had been served so; now it would be their turn.

The Prioress was busy counting tallies in the little office halfway along the passage between the Cloister and the Great Court when Dame Margery found her. "Well?" she asked, without looking round, and the light slivers of wood clicked as she counted, "Four boon days; five; six," and then again, "Well?"

"Madame," cried Dame Margery, and tears of excitement rushed to her eyes. "They are coming—from Coverham. They are at the ford." She listened, for by now they must be past the ford. Her right hand, clenched among the folds of her gown, was lacking, though she herself did not know it, the hilt of the sword that her father, and his fathers before him, had carried. "Can we bar the gate and keep them out?" she asked breathlessly.

"By the Rood! that we cannot," the Prioress said. She laid down the tallies on the Convent chest. For a moment she considered; then she told the Chambress what to do, precisely and in detail; cut her short with, "Silence! On your obedience!" and turned again to her counting.

Dame Margery, crimson and smudging tears hastily from her face, went back into the Cloister, and found that the news had come there already. All the Ladies stood close, gabbling together like so many ducks, but much shriller. They cried out to her, and she to them, and the noise grew; most of them were sure as she was of the worst; a few were doubtful; only old Dame Joan Barningham was confident that our Blessed Lady would protect Her daughters.

Dame Margery pushed through them, answering questions as she went. "Have you seen them?" "Yea." "Where are you going?" "To the kitchen." "What for? Does the Lady know? What does she say?" There was a silence when that was asked.

Dame Margery had her hand on the door of the buttery passage. She gave them the answer loudly.

"She says, 'Make ready a breakfast for them.' She says, 'Have herbs strewn in the guest-house. Have the maids light a fire, and see they well blow it up before they leave it. Get out the silver spoons.' She says, 'Set before them the wild boar pasty.' "

She had opened the kitchen door, and now slammed it behind her. The Ladies were left to make what they could of the Prioress's orders. They found many interpretations of them; Dame Bess Dalton even suggested tentatively that the Prioress intended to put poison in the pasty. Dame Anne Ladyman came nearest to the truth when she said, rolling her great black eyes, that, Mother of God! all men were alike. Feed them well and they'd be kind.

That would not have ended the debate, but the sound of voices, and of knocking at the gate, cut it short. The Ladies, hushing each other loudly and urgently, made with one accord for the Buttery which had a window on the Great Court.

July and Dame Eleanor Maxwell were left alone in the Cloister. Dame Eleanor sat still on her bench; she had at first hoped to learn what it was that had so excited the other Ladies. She had plucked at a sleeve here, a gown there, but if any had tried by shouting in her ear to make her understand, the hubbub had been too great for their words to penetrate her deafness.

So the old woman had given up her attempts, slipping back into the prison of her body, which had windows, but in which no sound, except the most muffled and indistinct, was ever heard. She sighed and trembled a little, frightened by a turmoil which had for her no meaning except that it must mean ill. Uncomprehending almost as a baby, but far more patient, she sat very still, her hands crossed upon her big belly, her lips moving in prayers that were just audible.

Behind her, and keeping out of her sight, July stood stiff as a clothes peg, looking down at the grass in the Cloister Garth, where frost had laid such jewellery upon every blade, dead leaf, and common stone, as none of the King's goldsmiths could by any means have equalled. Her eyes saw, but her mind did not perceive, that exquisite transient craftsmanship, being filled with a dismay too deep yet for any feeling. They would all be put forth from Marrick; she was far more sure of that than the most despairing of the Ladies, because she had known always that disaster was the order of the world.

As the Ladies sat down to their Mixtum, very late, and most of them with the doors set a little ajar, they could hear now and then men's voices, and footsteps heavy and strange. Listening, they knew by the sounds just how the King's Visitors were going about their business; the door that clapped to so noisily was the door of the Frater; a board in the floor of the warming-house creaked; the loose handle on the parlour door rattled, and they thought of their embroidery turned over, perhaps trampled upon by these terrible persons. When the Chapter Bell rang they came down circumspectly, as if wolves waited below, and sure enough in the Chapter House there were two men, one standing by the lectern, the other sitting in the Prioress's chair. This one was heavy and bulky, with a broad face that had purple veins like tiny worms upon his cheeks. The other, who flipped over the pages of the Rule as if he disdained it, was much longer and thinner; he was younger too, and dressed in fine red cloth and crimson velvet; he had a haughty look, and his jaw thrust out dangerously like the jaw of a pike.

When the bulky man, who was Dr. Layton, had read the Commission of the Visitation, the Prioress knelt and kissed the seal that dangled from it. It was only a little seal, being Master Cromwell's and not the Great Seal of England; for it was not the King but the Chief Secretary who had sent out these men. Then Dr. Layton told them that the King had heard of the corruptions and wickednesses which had defiled the small Houses of Religion. They looked at each other and were silent; last year the Bishop had visited them, but, though severe, he had not seemed to think their faults very black, so perhaps all might yet be well.

"Therefore," Dr. Layton concluded, "we shall speak with each of you severally, to learn in what state this House stands. We shall begin, as is the custom, with the youngest of you."

That was July, because the youngest Novice had gone home for a christening. So they left her, standing in her place looking down at her clenched hands. She did not see Dr. Layton crook his finger to her, but when he ordered her to "Come—come near," she gave a start, and went and stood behind him, but would look no higher than his boots, which were of light brown leather, rubbed dark and shiny where the stirrup irons had worn them.

The other man, who was Dr. Legh, came near, and the two of them spoke together, but not to her. "Too young to know much . . ."

"But *ex ore parvulorum* . . ." "Well, well, ask her. Little pitchers have long ears."

In the end it was Dr. Legh who began by asking her whether the divine service was fully and meetly kept.

"Oh yes," said July, and they both laughed, Dr. Legh with a thin high whinnying laugh that she much disliked.

"Too fully and meetly," he tittered. "You're not very devout, Mistress. And now as to fasting . . . ?"

Dr. Layton interrupted after a little. He said it was no use "putting such questions as you put to this child. She cannot know how the officers of the House lay out the revenues."

Dr. Legh asked, "Why not? Put them all through it. Truth comes out by little and little, like whey from the press."

But Dr. Layton overrode him, and July thought for a moment that he was the more bearable of the two, while he asked her how old she was, and when she was to be professed.

She told him fifteen first, then sixteen. Then she said, "Yea, sixteen, and I shall take the vows at Easter."

"God's Blood! sixteen!" cried Dr. Layton. "That's how scandals grow. My young gentlewoman, in another ten years we'll have you kicking against the vows, and maybe committing fornication with some pretty wanton priest."

He laughed, low and richly, and July thought him worse than Dr. Legh.

"Or if not with Master Priest," he ran on, "then with some fine gentleman who comes and goes, in and out of the house. For I hear from certain of the servants—" he spoke over his shoulder to Legh—"you heard it too—that your Prioress will let men speak with the Nuns in the Cloister and the Parlour. Now can you say who entertained these men, and whether any sent or received love-letters or tokens, pretty trifles such as ribbon knots, or rings with posies? Or did any man haunt the Church alone after dusk? Jesu! things can be done in the Church after dusk that you wouldn't think for." He laughed again, and asked Dr. Legh didn't they know it by now, both of Monks and Nuns? Legh smiled, but sourly and as it were with disdain.

"Now," Layton said, and laid his warm fingers on July's hands, clasped in front of her. "Now can you remember of any gentlemen who came into the Cloister—yea, even though you saw nothing amiss done?"

July unclasped her hands and put them behind her back.

"No," she said, "None."

"None? You're sure?"

"None," she told him again, and he caught her look and in it read hate. He could not know what she hated him for, nor that when he spoke of men it meant for her nothing but one man, and when he spoke of wantonness it was as if his soft pawing hands were feeling towards the name of Master Aske, to soil it with their touch.

They asked her more questions after that, but she shut her lips and only shook her head or nodded for answer, so they rated her for an obstinate forward stubborn wench, and after a little, since they got no more out of her, sent her away to bring them the eldest of the Novices.

January 19

Next morning, early, because they would leave Marrick at once after breakfast, the two Visitors sat in the guest-house chamber, drawing up their report on the Priory. There was a fire, but, in spite of much work with the bellows, a gusty wind was puffing smoke and more smoke down the chimney and into the room. Dr. Legh flapped it from his face with a long, impatient hand. "The devil's in the fire," he said and coughed, and bade the clerk open the window, "for it's better to freeze than stifle."

The clerk, who sat much nearer the window than he, thought otherwise, but did what he was bid in silence.

"Are you ready?" Layton asked. He sat the other side of the hearth from Legh; the Prioress's red buckram bag lay on his knee, and from it he was pulling out bundles of old charters with cracked or crumbling seals dangling—seals of red wax, or heather-honey brown, or oily green.

The clerk, having sat down again and tucked his left hand under his thigh to warm it, said that yea, he was ready. Layton began to dictate; this was all of the revenues of the Priory from meadows and closes, sheep walks and messuages that had been given in old time to the House—at Marske, and Downholm, Richmond and Newton-le-Willows. He stopped once to flourish a small, very old charter.

"Here's a pretty thing! 'Henry le Scrope 14th year of King Edward son of King Edward'—that'll be Edward II—'holds ten acres of Margaret, Prioress of Marrick, at a rent of a red rose in the time of roses for all services.' Was she then his minion? Were Nuns, think you, as loose then as now?"

Legh said scornfully that such a rent was nothing uncommon, but Layton would not be deprived of his ancient scandal. "For look you," said he, "that same payment was after commuted to sixpence."

When all the spiritual ties and temporalities of the House were written down, they came to the Nuns themselves, beginning with Christabel Cowper, Prioress and Treasurer.

Dr. Legh said at once that there was little against her, except that it was said of her—that fat Nun Elizabeth Dalton said it—that she wore petticoats of brocade and gilt pins on her veil. "But I make little of that," said he, waving his hand against the smoke, and then holding it before him to look at a gold ring on his finger with one sapphire stone in it. He thought that Dr. Layton did not know that the Prioress had given him the ring.

"What," asked Layton, "of those mistakes in the Account Roll?"

Legh chuckled. "Jesus!" said he. "No mistakes. They're all on her side, and I think I know where the money went that was so subtly hidden in them. You've seen the Prioress's chamber? Yea. Very fair. Very neat. Good wainscot work and made to last many a year. Indeed," he looked very superciliously at the clerk, and a little less so at Layton, "indeed, for my part, I think it a pity that this House should not continue, so I gave the Lady the best counsel that I might." He half closed his eyes to look again at the sapphire on his finger, and added, "Of course, she said the House was too poor to offer so great sum to the Chief Secretary for its continuance." He smiled to himself, making the same mistake with regard to Dr. Layton that the Prioress had made.

But he had far less excuse than she, for by this time he should have known that Layton, for all that he was a man of one idea, was no fool.

For a moment Layton said nothing, but scratched his thigh and savoured his keen dislike of his fellow Visitor. Then—

"What of that that was said of her as to being found with a boy in her bed one night?"

"Tcha! And how many years ago? Even that black-eyed scandal-monger that told it could not say but that it was a matter of two children. And such as she—" he looked at Layton with a look that said, "and such as you,"—"would find matter to traduce a saint."

"Well, well," Layton let it go.

"Who next?"

"Dame Margery Conyers."

"That bag of bones!"

"Confederate with the Prioress, I think," Layton put in, but Legh disregarded this, which might have been a warning to him. So they went on through the Nuns. Nothing much could be objected against the House except that the Nuns were accustomed to go out from the Cloister to funerals and christenings, staying away an unconscionable time, and that it had been known for gentlemen to be entertained in the Cloister and the Parlour. One Nun, professed two years ago, at the age of twenty-three, must go forth; they both agreed to that, though their Commission only gave them power to send away any under twenty-two years of age who had taken the vows.

"As for that novice," said Legh, meaning July, "she shall not take the vows this Easter."

"And it would be well," Layton added sourly, "if she took them not at all."

At last Legh stood up and stretched himself till his joints cracked. He said, well, that was an end, and now for the mulled ale the Prioress had ordered for them, and to saddle.

The Clerk began to shuffle his papers together, and then Layton spoke.

"Have you forgot," said he, "this matter of the wench who sees visions?"

"Visions?" Legh was taken between wind and water.

"Or have you not heard?" Layton purred, knowing well Legh had heard. "I thought it," he said, "a grave matter."

Legh sat down again. In his mind he abandoned the cause of the Prioress, and with less compunction because the ring, though pretty, was of no great value, and he suspected that it was not her best. "Tell me," he said, as if this talk of visions was news to him.

So Layton told him of the serving woman, Malle, who, certain of the servants averred, saw visions of Our Saviour, of Our Lady, of saints and angels and devils too.

"And doth she prophecy treasonably?" Legh inquired with the due amount of apprehension that a loyal subject should show.

But Layton was satisfied; he had given the young man a lesson. He said that there were no prophecies that he could hear of, nor naught treasonable in the visions, but that it seemed the wench was but a poor, crazed, harmless creature. "Nevertheless," he concluded, "it were well that I should admonish the Prioress that such things are dangerous. Write it down so," he bade the clerk.

Legh understood precisely why he said that "I" and not "*we*" should admonish the Prioress. Nor when they rode from Marrick, warmed by the mulled ale, did he need to inquire how Dr. Layton had come by a handsome brooch that he wore; it was a thing of a good deal more value than the sapphire ring on his own finger.

January 29

Sunshine was blown across the empty countryside like straw before the wind; in the great Church of the Abbey of Peterborough the coloured windows glowed and gloomed as the light filled them and was wiped away. As well as the changeable brightness of the day the strong tide of air found its way into the Church in little trickles and eddies and swayed the flames of many torches and tapers lit for the burial of Katherine, once Queen of England. Sometimes a stronger breath moved the drooping banners, upon which candlelight and sunlight chased each other, showing the arms of England, of the Emperor, of Spain, Aragon, and Sicily; there were also little pennons bearing devices such as the bundle of arrows, the pomegranate, the lion and the greyhound, which commemorated old alliances as far back as John of Gaunt, who had married a Spanish Princess. Besides all these banners there were four great golden standards on which were painted the Trinity, Our Lady, St. Katherine, and

St. George, while round about the walls hung clothes painted with the dead woman's chosen motto, "Humble et loyale," in tall gold letters. All that was left in England of Katherine, Queen or Princess Dowager, lay in the midst of the lights and the banners in its leaden coffin, under a cloth of gold frieze with a great cross of crimson velvet.

The mourners, of whom the King had chosen for chief his niece, Eleanor, daughter of the Dowager French Queen and the Duke of Suffolk, sat in black rows upon the benches, while Bishop Hilsey of Rochester preached to them against the power of the Pope, and against the incestuous marriage of Katherine, widow of Prince Arthur, to Henry, then Prince of Wales. Lady Eleanor sat, hearing, yet not hearing, with every appearance of decorous attention; her mind was running upon the delinquencies and impertinences of one of her waiting women, and on the piercing phrases of her next rebuke. But the ladies and gentlemen who had been of the dead woman's Household heard and attended well enough to what he was saying. Many of the gentlemen scowled; those of the ladies who were not crying shuffled their feet upon the hassocks of rushes. The Imperial Ambassador, M. Eustace Chapuys, who was placed among the great mourners, neither scowled nor shuffled, but sat very stiff with a face empty of expression. Only when the Bishop, warming to his work, declared that the Princess in the hour of death had confessed that she had never rightly and lawfully been Queen of England, the Ambassador's sanguine complexion deepened to crimson; he lifted his head and stared at the Bishop, in a look giving him the lie. But the Bishop would not catch his glance, keeping his eyes all the time on the words of his dissertation.

When the solemn Mass was over they buried her before the lowest step of the high altar, laying over the stone a simple black cloth.

That same day at Westminster, as rain began to slash at the palace windows in an early twilight, a man in a sober black gown came to the door in the palace, knocked, and with a backward glance to see that none watched him, slipped in.

A young man, with a long, pale, disdainful face, was writing at a table. He let his eyebrows run up towards his fair hair at the intrusion. But the other said, "My master is one of the doctors to the Queen's Grace."

"Ah." Sir Edward Seymour stood up. Under his dignity he was eager. "Well?" he asked.

"She hath miscarried."

"Of a boy or girl?"

"Of a male child."

"Not that that matters," Sir Edward corrected himself coldly, and the doctor's servant let the corners of his lips drop in a sour smile. It mattered much for the Queen's Grace.

"Tell me—" Seymour was easing a pearl ring from his fore-finger, and the other, keeping his eyes away from it, began to talk, doctor's stuff at first, which were mere words to the uninstructed, but afterwards things more understandable.

"As soon as she could speak," said he, "she asked her woman, 'Knave or girl?' and when they said, 'Knave,' she let out a cry, and on that same moment swore that the fault was her uncle's the Duke of Norfolk, because he had told her that the King had fallen in the tilt-yard. 'And he looked so white and wizen,' says she, 'I thought his Grace was dead, the which pierced my heart like a dagger, and I shrieked, and the pains came.' "

"His Grace hath been told?"

The doctor's servant nodded as he took the ring from Sey-mour's fingers, and now he let his eyes take a look at it, be-fore he put it by in his pouch, and tightened and knotted the strings. It was a ring of price, and according to his lights he was a man who liked to be honest, and give value for money. He came close and whispered.

"I spoke with him who brought the news to His Grace. He heard the King say that now he was sure that black sorcery had been the means by which he was brought to this present unhappy marriage."

Sir Edward put by the fellow's hand from his arm, and said stiffly that news, so it were true, should always find its reward. When the doctor's servant had gone off, circumspectly, he also came out from the room, and went up through the Pal-ace towards the chambers of the Queen's Maids, to find his sister, Mistress Jane Seymour. He thought it well she should be told all that he had just heard.

February 4

Dinner at Marrick Manor began with veal chawetts, and for a while the Prioress and Dame Nan talked of how these should be cooked. The Priory made its chawetts with wine, a little verjuice, and dates, raisins, currants and mace. These chawetts of the Bulmers had green cheese in them, and no wine nor dried fruits. The Prioress professed herself eager for the receipt, and Dame Nan said over her shoulder, "See to it, John," and one of the men waiting answered her, "Aye, Mistress."

But after that more and more the Prioress directed her conversation towards Sir Rafe, so that by the time the cloths were drawn, the servants gone away, and the three of them private (which was what the Prioress had asked for), Dame Nan's face was set hard as a stone, and she sat beside the Prioress on the settle, remote and pale, looking down at her hands idle in her lap, while the Prioress leaned towards Sir Rafe in his chair, and told him of all that the Visitors had done and said, of Dr. Layton's warnings, and Dr. Legh's counsel, and thus came to the point of her errand, and the dire need of the House.

"Well," said Sir Rafe at the end of it all, "if you will sell me those closes up at Owlands—"

"No. But I will lease you the west side of Owlands Bargh."

"Sell it, and you shall have that which will content Cromwell."

They haggled about that for some time, while Dame Nan sat mute, only her chin lifted a little higher.

When they had agreed at last, the Prioress got up to go, so they all stood, but Dame Nan moved a pace aside to separate herself from them, and looked out of the window at the garden deep in snow and shining in the sun. The Prioress was telling Sir Rafe how his brother Sir John would not pay the dower of Julian Savage this Easter, seeing that the Visitors had forbidden that she should be professed. "So how," the Prioress asked, throwing her hands wide, "how can I keep a growing young wench without dower till she be twenty-four, and the House squeezing out money to buy our continuance, if it may be? Nay, marry, I cannot do it. I cannot. She must away again to Sir John."

Sir Rafe began to hum! and ha! He made it clear without exactly saying so, that he thought his brother in the right, since to pay a dower when the Priory might not stand, was only to put money out of his own into the King's pocket. If the money were July's own, left by her uncle, that made no difference.

It was then that Dame Nan spoke, surprising both of the others.

"I will have the young gentlewoman here at Marrick, if Sir John and—" she paused, "and his Lady allow."

"Why Nan—" Sir Rafe cried.

"I need another gentlewoman," she said, never turning her face from the window.

"Well, well," the Prioress murmured. She was indifferent what became of Julian Savage, so long as she did not eat up so much as a groat of the Priory revenue. She asked Sir Rafe when she might have the money in her hand for the lease-hold, and they went out together, leaving Dame Nan just rising from a needlessly deep and stately curtsey.

After a few minutes Sir Rafe came in again, and sat down. He looked at his wife's back, regretted, as he often did, that things were come to be so often at cross-purposes between them, and, not being wise enough to let ill alone, said, "I cannot see for why you should need another gentlewoman, nor, if you do, why you should take that young wench who's a bastard."

"And sister to your brother's wife," Nan caught him up. "At last his wife," she added smoothly, and saw him scowl. He was not glad to be reminded that since Dame Anne Bulmer had died last autumn Meg Cheyne had become Meg Bulmer. And when Dame Nan added that she thought it not well that a young wench, who was to have been a nun, should go to such a sister as Meg, he was too much in agreement with her to find any retort.

"And I hope," Nan concluded, with jagged ice in her tone, "I hope I may at least choose my own gentlewomen."

He cried then, "Death of God! It's that, is it, that you grudge at? That I deal for you in a matter of land and leases, though before your face, mark you? Shall not a husband do so?"

"You have tried to buy that which my ancestors gave to the Nuns."

Sir Rafe threw his hands wide, caught his knuckle smartly on the settle, and swore again.

"There was a time you wanted the closes at Owlands," he told her, and she, remembering that time, and all those times when they had been one in mind and in heart, was pierced by the pain of remembering.

"My ancestor, Roger Aske," she began stubbornly, but Sir Rafe cried a murrain on all Askes, and inquired whether she would not have the Priory to continue.

"I would," she said in the voice which she kept for their worst quarrels.

"But you would not have me help the Prioress to one hundred marks?"

"One hundred marks to bribe Cromwell with."

"Well—would you that, or that the House were suppressed?"

"I would not the King left his business in the hands of a rogue."

"Fie on such words!"

"Fie on him for a rogue! Yea, fie on the King too! My fathers gave lands that God should be served down at Marrick. Will the King do well if he take those lands that were never his?"

Sir Rafe rebuked her. Then, because in this also they did not really differ, only that he thought it unseemly for a woman to speak so bluntly against the King, he said, to turn the subject, that it was well the Priory had that manner woman for its Prioress these days.

"Is it?"

"God's Bread!" he cried, "is it not? You know how well she has cherished the House."

"I know how she cherishes that which is her own. I know what manner woman she is, and what it is she loves. Not God, nor poverty, nor charity. No. But her will, and her way, and her goods."

"Tcha!" was all he could say to that.

"And she says that if that poor soul Malle speak more of heavenly things she's to have a sore whipping: You heard her say it. That is how Christ is served at Marrick."

"Mercy of God!" he asked her, did she think that the woman Malle was anything other than a poor crazed fool?

"Fool or saint," she said, "it would be all one to my Lady Prioress."

"Oh!" he cried, and got up. "Here is but spite and ill-will and a woman's shrewishness," and he left her there. She stood for a long time by the window looking out. The sun had gone down now, and the snow was bright no longer, but only a shroud over the frozen earth. She laid her face against the bubbled quarrels of the casement, and kept it so till it ached with the cold, smelling the thin, chill smell of the glass, and feeling her heart like the flesh of her cheek, both aching and cold.

A servant had been sent down from Marrick Manor with a mule, and a Priory servant was to go up with Mistress Julian Savage to fetch back the baggage pony that carried her little trussing coffer and bed, which was all she had brought to Marrick. Two of the Ladies, Dame Margaret Lovechild and Dame Bet Singleton, came to the gate-house with her, and saw her lifted up on the mule, and cried to her to come and see them often, and that she was not far away, and must not forget them. They waved their hands to her, and then turned back into the Great Court, because they ought not to have been there at all, but in the Cloister, and the bell in the tower was ringing for None. As they picked their way through the trampled snow, which the great frost kept crisp yet, Dame Margaret was wiping her eyes.

"Poor child," said she, "poor little wench."

"But when I asked her yesterday was she sad to be gone from us, she said, 'It matters not. It is all one.' And to-day she did not shed a tear."

"Ah! But she was sad for all that. And perhaps she meant that it was all one, if the House did not continue."

Dame Bet cried out, "Fie! we shall continue," for the Ladies were getting their courage again, and could not conceive that Marrick should be suppressed, and the Priory void, and they all sent away to those homes that they had seen only now and again for many years.

Meanwhile July and the two servants went up by the longer way to Marrick Manor through the bright day, July riding a little in front of the men. She did not once look back, but neither did she look forward, only down at the mule's shoulders where the muscles slid under the mouse-grey hide.

Just about the time that July sat down to her dinner at Marrick Manor the Nuns' bailiff came back to the Priory; he had been on the road from London for the last three days, but he was brought at once to the Prioress, delivered his message and handed her a letter.

She looked down at it in her hand, and asked again, though she had heard him well enough, "You say the Chief Secretary promised to be good lord to us, and bade us not to fear?"

"He said to me those very words."

She broke the seal then, and opened the letter. The same was written by one of Master Secretary's clerks, and signed with Thomas Cromwell's own hand; the Ladies of Marrick should not fear if in their House God's service was well kept, "for it is not the King's intent to suppress any but Abbeys in which manifest sin, vicious, carnal and abominable living is daily used." So Master Cromwell accepted the gelding, and promised to accept one hundred marks next year.

Within the hour the news became known in the parlour where the Ladies sat, and then all pretence of silence and meditation ceased.

Never, they told each other, had they believed that Marrick should fall, and that was true, but for the last few weeks they had not been easy, so that now, as their confidence returned, they grew very cheerful. Yet it did not take them long to grow accustomed to this security which was so natural to their thoughts. Before suppertime Dame Anne Ladyman was heard to lament that, it being a Friday, they would have to eat "those everlasting beans once more." And Dame Bess Dalton, who was darning a tenter-hook rent in the skirt of her habit, remarked that she supposed there'd be no new gowns for them now for many a year, aye, and long after the Lady had redeemed Owlands Bargh. "Surely," said Dame Bess, "this same pretext will serve her bravely whenever she will stint us of this or that."

March 6

The Prioress looking from her window saw the bailiff talking to one of the hinds who was ploughing. So she put on her pattens, and a big cloak, for the evening was setting in fine and frosty, under a clear sky, and hurried out to catch Master Bailiff before he went off to the ale-house at Grinton.

She caught him, and kept him standing first on one leg, then on the other, at the edge of the field, while the hind trudged up and down the furrows. There was much to be spoken of, for barley sowing was on hand, and harrowing would follow. Then grafting must be finished in the orchard before the moon began to wane. And this year white peason should be sown in more plenty, for the Prioress thought she should have enough for the pot, and to sell also.

At last she let him go, and herself came back towards the Priory. Along the hedge the blackthorn blossom tufted on the dark boughs was like pearls, like stars; away on the edges of the wood it was like spilt foam. She turned into the orchard gate, and for a while walked among the trees, pausing specially long to look at the new graftings; on the big old Bittersweet apple tree she had had the bailiff set three grafts, of Pomewater, Ricardon, and Blandrelle. So in five years' time, or seven, that tree would bear his four manner apples; a great sublety it would be and much admired.

Before she left the orchard she took a look also at the three young walnut trees, clean, slim, and silver grey. They would be slower; perhaps in twenty years the Nuns would have of them plenty of nuts. She looked at them kindly; she did not wish to hustle them. She doubted if even in twenty years' time their neighbours, the Ladies of St. Bernard, would have thought of planting walnut trees—that is if, in twenty years' time there were any Ladies in the little House a mile down the river. And then she reflected with some satisfaction on the elimination of the Ladies of St. Bernard, who had not Thomas Cromwell to their friend.

So, as she latched the orchard gate carefully behind her, her mood was contented, and in tune with the quiet evening. And she smiled to see that big lad, Piers Conyers, bumping along from Grinton on a chestnut cob. He smiled too, and pulled up to walk the pony alongside her, his blue cap in his hand.

"Well," said she, "and what mischief have you had in hand?"

He grinned, then laughed. There was down on his chin, but his cheeks were yet soft and round as a child's cheeks; and so was the nape of his neck, where the brown hair fell in a soft curve. He said, demurely, "Madame, no mischief, but an errand for my lady."

"Faith!" she told him, "I thought you had helped yourself to Mistress Doll's little cob."

"And so I did."

They both laughed, and she said, "I'll not tell. Get on. Get on with you. But rub him down well and water him, for I can see you've been riding races."

So he went, shouting, and beating the little beast to a canter with his heels, and she came on slowly, smiling at him, and smiling in her mind at another boy, younger than he, and a long time ago. John was in her thoughts as he had not been for many a day, he and Piers together. She felt their kindness for her, and it was as if John and she were still as young and silly as they had been. Then she laughed outright, as she remembered Dame Anne coming in with the candle in her hand, and all her solemn horror, so palpably enjoyed. She had never laughed at that before, only, if she thought of it, had been able to smile bitterly. But now she thought, "Mother of God! How silly we all were!" and she laughed comfortably in her mind at all of them. Then she thought, "It is because I grow old that I can laugh." It did not grieve her to think of growing old, but gave her a feeling of greater security and quietness.

As she turned under the gate-house she heard Jankin's fire crackling merrily, and saw the light of the flames sliding and shaking upon the opposite wall. It was a pleasant sound, and when she came into the Great Court it was pleasant and a great surprise to see the Lent Pedlar and his tall white donkey. Jankin was unloading the donkey, but the Pedlar stood near, and Dame Margery Conyers, and Dame Anne Ladyman were with him. They saw her and they all stood stiff, as if they had been caught at some shocking deed. Jankin stood with one of the packs held against his stomach, Dame Margery's hand went up to her mouth, Dame Anne and the Pedlar stood still staring.

Then the two Ladies cried, as if with one voice—"Madame! Madame! Have you heard?"

They told her, the Pedlar, Jankin and the two Ladies chiming together like dogs, that Parliament had given into the King's hands all the Abbeys. "No," said the Pedlar louder than all, "only the little Abbeys, such as this one," to be suppressed and altogether brought to an end.

When they had finished telling her there was a silence so complete that she could hear again the crackle of the sticks in Jankin's fire in the gatehouse. She said at last, to Jankin, and pointing to the Pedlar, "Give him to eat, and his beast," and then went up into her Chamber. She had not told the Ladies to follow her, but she was not surprised to find them in the room with her.

She sat down in her chair, and they side by side upon the bench. Dame Anne twiddled her fingers together, Dame Margery had her hands tight locked; the Prioress saw them sit like that and then turned her eyes to the window. Calva lay there sharp-edged and dark against the last of the dying light.

Margery Conyers suddenly wrenched one hand from the other and beat it on the bench beside her.

"Shall they do it? Will not men rise to forbid them? Oh! Shame! Then let's bar the gate. Let them take us like a besieged city if they dare."

She burst into tears then, and the Prioress told her that such a thing could not be, to hold the House against the King's will. But she did not speak sharply, and patted Dame Margery on the shoulder, bidding her take heart. Margery was a fool, but she loved the Priory, and Dame Christabel felt kindly towards her.

"Jesu!" Dame Anne said, "if there are to be any of such doings let me forth first," and she laughed. She had given up twisting her fingers together, and now she pinched her veil on this side and on that, and drew a little farther from under it a curl of dark hair which showed upon her forehead, where it should not, by the Rule, have showed at all.

"Well!" said she, giving herself a little shake like a bird that has just preened its feathers, "if they choose to put us forth what can we do but seek husbands. Fie on such a need! God's Mother! I shall die of shame to feel a man's hand on me."

The Prioress turned and looked at her, and under the look Dame Anne grew red and giggled. Then the Prioress turned her eyes away. It seemed to her now that there had never been a time when she had not detested Dame Anne. "At her age!" she thought. "Her head's like a brothel!" And she was filled with a fury of scorn and disgust.

But when the two had left her, and the warming fury had died, then the Prioress knew the blank of final defeat. All the Abbeys must go—all the little Abbeys that is—and she had got out of Jake the Pedlar that proof which should try and depart great from little. She bit at her knuckles, and at her nails. It was useless to unlock the chest and to go through the Priory accounts. Never she knew could she make Marrick even appear to possess revenue of £200 a year. Yet she could not but try. Soon she sat at her desk with rolls and books spread out, reckoning up, and reckoning up again. It was as hopeless as she had known it would be. At last she allowed the rolls to slip away and rattle to the floor at her feet. She set her elbows on the desk, and her forehead fell into her hands.

March 28

They were winnowing in the big garner—the last of the wheat, which the Prioress looked to sell at a good price at Grinton. Because of the dust it was very thirsty work, and long before noon the bailiff winked his eye to one of the men, and walked away towards the kitchen. The rest of them followed soon, keeping close to the wall and out of sight of the windows, in case the Prioress was looking out. Malle trailed after them, last of all.

Cook already had his face behind a can of ale, and a man

they did not know sat with him, black, shaggy-haired, in patched leather hosen; a man of not much more than thirty by his look, but with lines bitten into his face by hunger, or sorrow, or by some stress beyond the common lot. Yet when those who came in from the winnowing grew merry over their ale, he was laughing with them, and more than once it was a shrewd saying of his, or a homely salty story that had set them laughing. Certainly, for all the raggedness and wretchedness of his look, he was one of those that have a way with them; even the bailiff listened when he spoke, and Cook, a man of uneasy temper, treated him with unusual sweetness, so that the drinking time in the kitchen lasted longer than anyone had thought for. But at last they must go back to their work, so by ones and twos they drifted away.

Malle had not come into the kitchen. She had stood all the time at the door, gaping in. Now they had to shoulder past her, so stupid she was, and so taken up with staring goggle-eyed at the stranger. Only when all had gone except Cook and him, and he got up, and came towards the door, she skipped back out of the way, standing aside in the shadowed passage till he had bidden "God be with you!" to the Cook, and gone out. Then she followed him.

There was no one in the Great Court to bid mad Malle back to work, but the Prioress herself saw her, for she stood at her window with Dame Anne Ladyman. First they saw the stranger come out. "There goes an ugly vagabond knave!" said the Prioress. "Whence is he?" Dame Anne agreed that surely he was a rough one to look at. She supposed he might be Sir Rafe's new shepherd's man from over towards Lunesdale, where folk are very poor and wild.

When Malle went by following after him it was Dame Anne who said with a titter, "See the fool running after him!" The Prioress "Tushed," impatient of Dame Anne's meaning, and for that reason would not open the window to send the woman back to the winnowing. Also her thought was more taken up by the man.

"Fie!" said she. "If Sir Rafe hath brought that one into the Dale he hath brought a very stout rogue. See how he goes." He passed just then under the lintel of the gate-house, and something in the way he carried himself made it seem, though it was amply high, too low and mean for him to pass beneath.

"Fie!" she said again, feeling herself strangely and strongly moved against the fellow. "I warrant this is one of those whose humour it is to grudge at rich men, and would pull down all to be as wretched as they."

When the Man came out from the Priory gate there was Wat, Gib Dawe's brat, sitting by the Nuns' duck pond, hugging his knees. He got up at once, and came slinking down to the lane-way, as the Man went past the church-yard towards the Nuns' Steps; he came alongside Malle, and gave her a quick glinting look, a strange look, but neither frightened, nor wary, nor wicked; his face was slobbered with tears, but that did not matter, for she was crying too. They smiled at each other, and when she held out her hand he took it. So they went both together after the Man.

By now He had come nearly to the gate in the wall that divided the Priory land just here from the Bulmers'. He went slowly, with His head bent, as though He marked the young grass growing, for it was a very fair bright day, and for the first time the grass smelt of spring. After Him, but some way behind, came Malle and Wat. The brown ducks that had been preening and scratching and shaking themselves with much fuss and flutter on the edge of the pond went now in line, following Him towards the gate, and a few of the Priory sheep, which the shepherd had brought down from Owlands, moved that way too, slowly, with little pauses and starts.

When the Man had gone through the gate, letting the weight swing it to after Him, He turned for a moment and looked at them all. They stood still, nor did any of those creatures move again until He went on, more quickly now, up the Nuns' Steps and into the wood.

Only then they came to the gate, and Malle and Wat stood looking over it and watching Him as He went. The ducks gathered about their feet, and the sheep too in a little crowd, and looked between the pales. The sun, not yet very high, struck right in among the bare trees, finding out the bright watery green of the trunks, and unlocking all the distances. The wind, moving strongly through the wood, filled it with sliding shadows, as if the air bore light upon its back as a running river bears ripples. So He went up and out of sight, under the great branches that bowed and swung, while the little twigs seemed to clap themselves together for joy.

A cloud covered the sun. He had gone, and Malle and Wat came back to the bare hillside among the boulders, where now the wind brought only chill. But for Malle it was golden harvest weather; the ears of corn were full, wrought four-square, firm as a rope, exact as goldsmiths' work; like rope ends they struck her thighs as she moved through them, loaded with goodness.

She plumped down on the ground, and caught Wat by his knees so that he tumbled against her. Then they sat together, rocking to and fro, and Malle kept on babbling, "We shall brast, Wat, we shall brast," while Wat made shocking faces and groaned in his throat; it hurt them so, the joy that was far too big for them, and the dread. For God, that was too great to be holden even of everywhere and forever, had bound Himself into the narrow room of here and now. He that was in all things had, for pity, prisoned Himself in flesh and in simple bread. He that thought winds, waters and stars, had made of Himself a dying man.

But at last, as if it were a great head of water that had poured itself with noise, and splashing, and white foam leaping into a pool, and now, rising higher, covered its own inflow, and so ran silent, though no less strong—now they were lifted up and borne lightly as a fisherman's floats, and as stilly.

They crouched on the hillside, looking towards God, feeling God under their spread palms on the grass, and through the soles of their feet. Beyond, beyond, beyond, and beyond again, yet always that which went still beyond—God. And here with only a low wooden gate between, that thing which man could never of himself have thought, and would never come to the depth of for all his thinking, here that thing impossible was true as daylight, here was God in man, here All in a point.

April 3

Robert Aske went shopping that morning, before the Courts were open. It was chilly in the streets, though the sky was bright above, so he and Will walked smartly along Distaff Lane stopping only to buy a new lute string at the sign of the Cock and Hen, and at the Mermaid a sugar loaf, and a pot of treacle, because in the last letter from home Jack had one of his great colds, and there was no treacle to be had in York. Nell, Jack's wife, wrote also to know the cost of all sorts of spices, because she thought the York shopman cheated her. Robert stopped at the corner of Friday Street, in the swimming warm sunlight, to read again—"Pepper, cloves, mace, ginger, almonds, rice, saffron—!" He groaned— "Mass! We must ask the price of all those, and yet buy none." When they came to the sign—"'Do you go in!" he said to Will. But Will made way. "After you, Master." They came out not only with the prices all neatly written, but also with some oranges and a jar of green ginger, "Because we are two great cowards," said Aske. "It's only women can so brave shopmen," said Will.

After that they went back up Friday street and into the Cheap, to buy stuff for a new coat for Aske. The street was wide here, so that they came suddenly out into sunshine. All the gilding and painting along the front of Goldsmiths' Row caught the light, and already the busy chinking of the craftsmen's hammers could be heard from within, as well as the voices and laughter of the prentice boys and maids standing about the conduit with their pitchers and pails, waiting to draw water.

"There, Master," Will said, plucking Aske's sleeve and pointing across the road to a shop where the wife, in a red gown and fine white kerchief, was setting out bales of cloth, with a brave scarlet on top.

"Not scarlet, Will."

"No. But the murrey."

They crossed the road. The woman smiled at them; she had grey hair and only two teeth in front, but her look was kind and her eyes merry. Aske leaned against the front of the booth, pushed his cap back on his head and prepared for pleasantry.

"Fie, Sir!" the woman cried, after they had talked of the fair day, and the Dame's good cloth, and Aske's need—so he said —of a new coat to go wooing in—"Fie on the smooth tongue you have! It's God's mercy I'm not a young maid, or you'd have the heart out of me following at your heels."

"Will," says Aske, "take me home, or I'll be plighted to this fair gentlewoman before I know it."

At that she pretended to fetch him a box on the ear, and vowed she'd call her husband.

"Don't vex the good man. Let's speak of the murrey cloth. What's it an ell?"

They settled to a brisk haggle; the price went down from eight shillings to five, and then stuck.

"Four and a kiss," Aske offered.

"God bless the man! Is he always so saucy?" she asked Will, but he glowered at her, and turned his back. He did not like his master to be so familiar with the common people.

In the end Aske paid five shillings an ell for fifteen ells.

"And it's good width, two ells and a half," said she, as she rolled it out with soft heavy bumps, while the cloth billowed like the waves of the sea. "You can call the meter to measure it. Will you so, or trust me?"

Aske did not call the meter, but when the cloth was cut and folded gave it to Will to carry back with the rest of the stuff, while he himself made for Westminster.

At the corner of the street he turned to wave his hand and kiss his fingers to the cloth merchant's wife; she threw up both hands and laughed at him, and went inside to give her husband the money and to tell him about the merry gentleman—"a lawyer by his filed tongue and inked fingers" —and what he had said to her and she to him.

"And I said—'Call the meter if you will.' And he says, 'Not I!' says he, 'I know who'll cheat me, and who I can trust,' says he. And I says, 'Well, you can trust me,' I says, and he says, 'I can well see that,' and he laughs at me out of his one bright eye. Our Lady! It was bright too, and gamesome. And he says, 'I know who I can trust,' says he."

Her husband ran his finger down the pages of his ledger. "If he thinks he knows that he's a fool," he murmured.

"Fie!" she told him, "Fie! And he's no fool."

He did not argue the matter.

April 7

It was early, the sun not yet up over the opposite side of the Dale, but already Gib sat reading, close to the window, and tilting his book to get all the light. It was safer to read thus early the book that he was reading, when no one was likely to come in and ask questions. Only the old mother was about, muttering as she moved to and fro in the house, and out to the cow-shed to the milking. She was telling herself, and Gib, if he cared to listen, what a hiding she would give that useless idle brat, that had slipped out the devil knew where, when there was fire to light, and beasts to tend, and water to fetch.

Gib was reading, with great satisfaction and a cordial anger, "The Epistle of Paul to the Colossians."

> Beware lest any man come and spoil you thorowe philosophy and disceitful vanitie, thorowe the traditions of men and ordinations after the world and not after Christ. For in him dwelleth all the fulness of the godhead.

He turned the page and by accident dropped the book, and as he stooped for it heard his mother screeching outside once more for "Wat! Wat!" She passed the window next moment, her mouth working with anger, the yoke across her shoulders and the empty buckets swinging.

Gib opened the book again at random and his eye, running down the page, caught here and there a phrase—

And he came to Nazareth where he was nursed . . .

and then—

To preach the gospel to the poor he hath sent me. And to heal them which are troubled in their hearts. To preach deliverance to the captive. And sight to the blind. And freely to set at liberty them that are bruised. And to preach the acceptable year of the lord.

After that he did not turn on to find Colossians again, but instead sat thinking, with the book on his knee and triumph mounting in his brain, because this very year surely was the acceptable year of the lord. The power of the Pope was minished in England; soon it might be done quite away and the pure truth of the gospel preached. The King was as valiant for truth as King David (a good similitude, for Gib felt a qualm when he thought of the King's love. But even so had David lusted after a fair woman, and yet David was God's servant).

Gib got up. There were wheels that went turning in his head like the interlocking wheels of a mill, but instead of soft, white, silent flour, they ground out arguments. He had begun to write them down two days ago; now the mood was hot in him again. First he would put away the English Gospels, but because of his impatience the old hiding place must serve. So he went to the corner where was the loose flag-stone, and knelt to prise it up with his knife and lay the book again in its hiding place.

It was then that Wat came in, most untimely for both. Gib beat him, both for coming in at that moment, and for not coming earlier; only after Wat had run out again whimpering did Gib remember that the knave could not speak, and therefore could hardly betray.

But one beating more or less did not much signify. Spare

the rod, spoil the child. He put the book away and swept the dust and scanty rushes over the stone again with his hand, got his ink and pen from the shelf and the last sheet of his paper, and sat down to write till it was time to go to the Church.

The wheels in his brain worked, spinning this way and that. Some would have said that what came out of it was confusion, but Gib knew better. There was something higher and more terrible than ordinary reason, and the cold logic of the schools. His pen spluttered and squeaked as he drove it fast along the page. He dealt with the Pope and turned his attention to the Bishops.

> And that a subject can hold no land by no righteousness of God under the sun, but it be measured and meted by the King's standard right of God's law above the sun. The King knoweth not his own right of his head office; he hath given his head right to his subjects, which by his own laws hath robbed his kingly image by his sufferance to their wills; hath given it away from him to the Spiritualty, holden contrary to God's laws.

He stopped there, looked out of the window to see how the light had grown, and realized that time had run on while he wrote, so that now he must go at once to Church. Besides, he was at the bottom of his last page. He scrawled hastily, "Here I made an end for lack of paper," bundled the sheets together and hid them away.

Though he had made an end of writing his thoughts did not break off, but, as he went he was full of excitement and triumph. "To preach the gospel to the poor he hath sent me . . . the acceptable year of the lord." He was an instrument in a mighty hand. He walked so fast that his breath came short, and he took great gulps of the clean morning air. Had the prophet Elisha, he asked the trees of the wood, spared the forty and two ribald children who mocked him? And—No—he muttered in defiance.

As he came to the corner of the church-yard wall something that stirred and rustled made him glance aside, and he saw Malle's face bob up. It was as easy to see from her look that she spied out for someone, as that Gib was not that one she spied for. At once she ducked down again, and when he came close tried to hide behind the big holly bush that grew in the corner.

"What are you at? Come out!" he told her, and when she

came, rueful and dumb, "What are you at?" he asked again.

She mumbled that she wanted—she thought—she hoped—
"Lest He should come again this way," she said.

He frowned his harshest at her. She had not even youth as
excuse for wantonness, yet she was woman enough, with
her large, sagging breasts, and broad haunches, to throw him
into a fury of disgust.

"Off you go!" he cried. "Off to your work, or the Lady
shall know, and you shall be soundly beat."

He watched her as she went, ungainly and slow, and with
many backward glances towards the wood, till she turned in
under the Priory gate-house.

April 8

To-morrow was Palm Sunday, but the weather had turned
back to bitter cold. Every one of the Ladies at Marrick Priory
had a cough, and not one would take any remedy more effi-
cient and less agreeable than honey. Some indeed talked of
lemon juice mixed with honey as being very sovereign, but
since there were no lemons nearer, at the best, than York,
their eagerness to undergo such a cure was of little im-
mediate use. The Prioress therefore, having endured the
combined, indeed, she fancied, the competitive, coughing of
the House for three days in Church and in chapter, descended
this morning to the still-room, carrying with her a rushlight, because the shelf where the simples were kept was in a
dark corner.

And there, as so often happened, she found that where her
eye had not been, old chaos reigned. For one thing none of
the jars was labelled; for another, when she laboriously began to take off the bladders that covered the jars, she found
things that ought never to have been on this shelf at all—that
is to say, distilled water of primroses, and the dried violets
which would be made into sugar comfits at Christmas.

So, revolving in her mind just what she would say to Dame
Margery, she set to work to look through jar after jar. First
came the dried lime flowers; then the coltsfoot, grey-green
and soft, which rustled as she stirred it with her fingers;
next two jars full of the light brown chips of the bark of
wild cherry. And here—she lifted first one and then another
down and set them by the rushlight on the table—here were
the wrinkled black stems of comfrey, and here the faded
pins of juniper. These, efficacious if unpalatable, should be
the lot of every Lady who was heard even to clear her throat.

It was just then that she heard the clack of pattens and recognized Dame Margery's quick, scuttering walk.

The Prioress had been minded to call her by name, to receive the prepared rebuke, but there was no need. The door opened and in burst the Chambress, and came hastily over to the table where the rushlight, shaken by the sudden draught, streamed aside with a lazy tail of fume. She had come in as though on some urgent errand, yet now she stood still, staring at the Prioress; the flame of the rush, steadying, swam brightly in her eyes, and shining from below threw strange, distorted shadows upon her face.

"Madame," she began, and again, "Madame."

"What is it?" In the old days the Prioress would have been proof against the infection of her excitement, but the times were too precarious now for her to remain unshaken. She blenched, but managed to preserve her calm.

"Madame, the Mermaid—she hath seen a vision."

So it was not that the King had sent to drive them all from Marrick out of hand. The Prioress found herself extremely angry, the more so because her hand shook on the jar of comfrey it held. Worse than that, she felt her mouth also shake.

"I thought," she cried furiously, "I thought—" and she turned away, but not quite in time.

"Madame!" Dame Margery was quite at a loss.

"It is," said the Prioress, away in the darkest corner, and rummaging among the jars so that they clashed together, "it is," she said on a high, unnatural note, "my many fears for the House."

Dame Margery knew those fears too. All the Ladies knew them. But she and some others differed from the Prioress as to the means that should be taken to save Marrick. Up till now they had only muttered together in corners of "the arm of flesh which shall not help us," or of "God and His Saints to our warranty," lacking courage both to brave the Lady by protest, and, should she yield to their protest, to shoulder responsibility for the consequences.

But now, crimson and tearful, and caught in a strong flow of emotion, Dame Margery cried—

"But if, Madame, if this be a sign that God is on our side— if this be a showing of God—"

The Prioress stood, turned away, silent and wooden. Dame Margery's eloquence died.

"*Peccavi! Peccavi!*" said the Prioress, and knocked on her chest with her fist.

But she meant, "I have been a fool! A fool!" That first vision—O that she had trusted her instinct and put her eggs into that basket! Instead she had taken Cromwell for her saviour, and he had failed her. Now it was too late to turn back. No, not too late, for of course God was merciful. And perhaps it would work; at least it was worth trying. "*Miserere mei Domine,*" she cried, meaning, "God! God! Do *Thou* what the King's Vicar General will not. Save the House of Marrick!" She turned back to Dame Margery.

"What—what was the showing?"

The Chambress told her, tumbling it out as if spilling dried peas from a jar.

"The pear tree on the cloister wall, that storm two nights ago—there's a big branch broke loose. She—Malle—went to Grinton to buy nails; Cook sent her, for he says there'll be no pears if that branch goes on thrashing at the wall like it has—"

"Tchk!" said the Prioress.

"And there was the Pedlar's donkey, she saw it, tied to the door of the wool store by Master Blackburn's house." Dame Margery gulped. "Just as it says in the Office book, where two roads meet. And they came and fetched it away, and Malle went after them and she saw Him ride—"

"Well?"

Dame Margery whispered the rest.

"And she saw Him ride on it across Grinton Bridge."

The Prioress kept her eyes upon the candle flame for so long that when she looked up she could see nothing for the floating light that still dazzled them.

"Where is the woman?"

Dame Margery began to explain how Malle had been along the river bank gathering pussy-willow for the Palm Cross to-morrow, but the Prioress cut her short.

"Where is she now?"

"Up the Daleside after primroses." Dame Margery pointed towards the hill behind the Priory, and found herself alone in the still-room.

The Prioress came out of the gate-house, and looked upwards. At the top of the open steep slope, under the edge of the woods, a woman in a brown gown moved and stooped; a little lad was with her. That was Malle, and the lad was the Priest's bastard.

Only when she began to climb the hill did the Prioress remember that she had not asked why Dame Margery was so sure that it was a vision sent from heaven. "But that," she thought, "I'll find out better for myself."

When she had gone some way up she stopped for breath. As soon as she had it she called Malle by name. The two above turned and looked down; then the lad slipped away into the woods. The Prioress beckoned with her hand and waited for Malle to come down to her. She did not watch her as she came, but instead looked down to where the whole Priory lay spread out below her, the Great Court, the Nuns' Court, the orchard, all the farm buildings, and the Church—like the picture of a priory. The servants were busy in the Great Court; a woman came out with buckets swinging on a yoke, and went into the Nuns' Court where the well was. Behind the stables a man in a red hood was carting dung.

She knew that Malle stood beside her, and turned. She looked, stared, then lowered her eyes from the creature's face. Never had she supposed that such a look could be. It was not a smile. It was not a light.

"What . . . ?" the prioress began, and must stop to clear her throat. It came to her with a shock that now she feared to be told what the woman had seen. She would have been glad to go away without another word said. But she drove off the fear; what else but good should God, Our Lady and Saint Andrew intend to their servants? Yet she knew that of that good she was as much afraid as if God were her enemy.

"Come," she said, and heard her own voice harsh, weak and strange. "What is this thing I hear? What have you seen?"

With a wrench, as it were, she took her eyes from Malle's face. When she did that, and looked down again at the Priory, her mind steadied.

"Mad as a goose," she thought. "That look is of her folly. I shall say to her, 'Fie! fool, hold your tongue of these things!' "

But when she looked at Malle she could not say it.

Malle said:

"There was a great wind of light blowing, and sore pain."

The Prioress shivered. A tide of air, snow-cold, steady and strong, rushed by them. The morning's blue was now threatened by a cloud that rose and darkened across half the sky. With her eyes on Malle's face the Prioress began, fumbling her words in a way that the Convent did not know—

"If it is— If you saw— If it was shown— I pray you," she got it out at last, "what in your mind is God's meaning to us in this showing?"

While she waited the wind shifted and rustled among the grass at their feet. Against the deepening darkness of the whelming cloud the frail green mist on the elm trees was visible as it had not been against the bright sky, and far away along the fringes of the wood the bare ash branches showed white like clean bone. Suddenly the cloud broke in a snowy shower, so that looking up the Prioress saw a thousand thousand flakes spinning down, sharp white against the looming grey above, and so hard frozen that they rattled among the oak leaves in the grass.

"Marrick?" the Prioress cried, coming to the heart of the matter. "Was it shown to you of our House? Shall it fall? Not our House, and the Church that's hallowed to God and His Mother and Saint Andrew? Not Grinton Church?" she pleaded, though she cared not a button for Grinton Church.

But Malle did not answer and at last the Prioress turned away and went slowly down the hill.

By the time she came back to the Great Court the sky was clear again, and the clouds sailing in it light and bright as suds. The tower of the Nuns' Church took the sun bravely. It was of stone, and built upon stone, but as the Prioress looked at it, it seemed to totter, and her heart failed. "Jesu!" she cried under her breath. Then she realized that only the fast-driven cloud behind it moved; the tower stood firm.

"And shall stand," she muttered, and ground her teeth together, while her fists clenched at her sides in the folds of her gown.

April 12

The roof of Master Cromwell's new house beside the Church of the Augustines in Broad Street was not yet tiled, though the rafters were all in place, and threw down sharp bars of shade upon the sawdust and butt ends of wood, upon the carpenter's benches and tools that were below.

Master Cromwell stood with his backside hitched on to the edge of one of these benches as he talked to my Lord Darcy in the empty, bright skeleton of his house. The carpenters were at work laying battens for the roof tiles; they whistled, sang or shouted to one another up against the blue, where fat white clouds sailed. Now and again someone would drop the end of a plank with a clanging noise and a hollow bursting echo.

"The horse" said my Lord Darcy, "is a good horse. He hath a fair pace and easy, and the harness will be worth a hundred marks."

He did not know if Cromwell was attending to him, or to the workmen; for the Chief Secretary's eyes went sharply about, watching what the men did on the springing ladders, or flat on their stomachs upon the roof timbers.

"But," my Lord said, "if I may have leave of the King to go home I shall have no need of the horse, and would beg you take him for the sake of friendship and in token of kindness. And," he added, "in Yorkshire I could be of service to the King's Grace upon the Commission of Peace that is appointed."

"So you could," said Cromwell, not as though it were a new idea, but merely confirming Darcy's words. Then he said it again, fingering a palmful of sawdust as though there might be something hidden in it. After a pause he said, "And I thank you for the gift, my Lord, and your good will to me."

Darcy said that the gift was naught compared to the love he bore to Master Cromwell. "And shall I have the King's leave in writing?"

"You shall." Cromwell reached up and clapped him on the shoulder, and kept his hand there as he led him about the house, showing him where the kitchens would be, and where the great hearth, and how choice a prospect there would be of a little privy garden from the window of a closet behind the Hall.

In that closet they stood a while at the empty window-frame looking into the garden. Near by there were piles of slates and nails dropped about in the grass so that there was nothing but disorder, but beyond, a pear-tree, loaded with its snow, stood remote in beauty as a ship far off at sea. Perhaps because the door had swung to behind them the two gentlemen, leaning at the window in the sunshine, began to talk of matters of greater moment, and calling for greater privacy than the plans of the new house.

They spoke of the Queen's late miscarriage, and the sorrow of His Grace at the loss of this hope of male issue.

Then Cromwell said, with his eyes on the heap of tiles under the window, "His Grace takes comfort from going down to Greenwich."

"It's a fair palace," Darcy's face was decorously grave, but Cromwell hid a small glinting smile by again lowering his eyelids, and covering his mouth with his hand.

"And a fair flower grows there of late," said Master Secretary.

"You mean Mistress Jane Seymour."

Cromwell laughed out and called Darcy a right North Countryman with his free tongue.

Then he said, rubbing his back up and down upon the window-frame—"A fair flower, but discreet too as any greybeard. Did you hear how His Grace sent her a crimson velvet purse full of sovereigns, with a letter begging her to spend them for her disport, and calling her—well no matter."

"I've heard the like before," Darcy said.

Cromwell caught him by the shoulder again, laughing and as if much pleased.

"Yet this is not Mistress Anne," said he. "I told you this lady was discreet. Down she goes on her knees, kisses the letter, and then gives that and the pretty, plump purse back into the hands of the messenger, begging him to pray the King consider that she was a gentlewoman of good and honourable parents, who had no greater treasure in the world than her honour, and that if he would give her such a costly gift it might not be till her parents had made for her some honourable match."

Darcy shrugged, and muttered something about women knowing how to hold a man off so as to keep him on?

"You think it's her own wit devised the answer?" Cromwell asked quickly, and Darcy met that quick stabbing glance, and began to have an inkling of what Master Secretary was angling for. So he only shrugged, and let the other go on.

"So," said Cromwell, "the King's love waxes at the sight of so delicate a virtue, wherefore that she should know he loved her honourably, he sent to her a promise that he would never try to speak with her except in the presence of one or other of her kin. And," he laughed ruefully, "to that end was I bundled out of my chambers at Greenwich, and Sir Edward Seymour there planted in my stead, because there's a privy way thither from the King's apartments."

He moved from the window and taking Darcy by the arm led him to the door, but stayed before he opened it.

"You think it's but a maid's modesty? Yet it would not be strange if she were instructed by her friends, so as to bring His Grace hookwise crookwise to marriage. As indeed I think she hath been instructed by some, perhaps not so much her friends, to persuade the King against his present marriage, because these same friends, or sinister back friends let's call 'em, want to bring back the old ways, and the power of the Bishop of Rome."

He had his hand on the door and turned so that the two looked at each other. Now Darcy was sure of what he was after, and according to his custom he replied with a something that was as much true as it was beside the point. He said that in his fantasy the King would not, for any woman, easily give up that power which he had taken into his hand.

"I think as you. I think as you," Cromwell said, but still held Darcy a second longer, trying to read his face before he opened the door and led my Lord out, and to his litter, parting with him with the greatest pleasantness and courtesy.

In the litter Darcy let himself smile. He did not think that the Chief Secretary was any the wiser for that talk of theirs in the little closet looking on the garden. Cromwell might guess that my Lord knew from M. Eustache Chapuys how carefully and earnestly certain persons had advised Mistress Jane Seymour to speak to the King. He might guess that my Lord was one of those who liked the new ways little. But of neither of these suppositions was he any more sure than he had been before.

As my Lord smiled—a sharp smile with his handsome old head high—he was dusting his shoulder and his arm where Cromwell's hand had rested. "The place is full of sawdust," he said, catching the eye of one of his gentlemen who went alongside; but there had been no sawdust to be seen upon his coat.

April 20

My Lord Darcy's company came from under the arch of St. Mary's Gate and on over the five-arched bridge. When the way no longer rang hollow under the hoofs they had left Doncaster behind, had crossed the Don and were, at last, in their own country.

Darcy dragged the leather curtains of the litter aside and leaned out. "Hi! lads! Halt at the first ale-house. There's one a mile or so beyond. We'll drink there to the North Country and home-coming."

The gawky pages yelled, the gentlemen smiled, and the serving-men's brown faces split with grins from ear to ear. Darcy smiled too, leaning back in the litter. It was good to be coming home, whatever was lost and whatever time had swallowed up.

Darcy remembered the little ale-house from the first time

that he had come riding with his father to London, when he was ten years old. Since that day he had never stopped at it, for it was a poor place. But to-day, because they came home after so long a time, and because that once he had halted there—to-day they should stop and drink.

The servants riding ahead turned off the road; the rest followed along the bank of a little brook where half a dozen children, naked as fishes, were wading and wallowing; these stood to stare at the riders, then turned their attention again to the minnows and the rat-holes.

In front of the ale-house there were three horse-chestnut trees, and a little green. Darcy sat down on the ale-bench, stretched his long legs, and looked up into the young leaves, through which the sun thrust swimming shafts of white light. The serving men had gone away to the kitchen door; the pages had flung themselves down on the grass like puppies, and now like puppies began to fight and scramble together; the gentlemen stood about, their riding hats pushed off and dangling down their backs by the laces; several of them had peeled off hoods too, so warm the morning was for April.

The inn-keeper came out with his wife and a man carrying horn cups, and one pewter pot, "for my Lord Darcy," says he.

"You know me." Darcy was pleased.

"I've known the Buck's head since I've known aught," and the fellow began to talk about what his father had told him of my Lord's father.

"Draw for yourself," said Darcy, when he had come to an end, and, "Thank ye," said the man, curt and rough in good North Country fashion, and went off. Darcy smiled up into the deep, lit green of the big tree; such as this man would not be easily bent to new ways. "By God's Passion," he said to himself, "the King doth not know the Northern parts nor the men that here bide. Yet one day, maybe, he'll learn that heart and stomach they are of."

When my Lord was in his litter and on the road again Tom Strangways the steward came up alongside. He had all the news of the North from the ale-house keeper, and he retailed it as they went along, including that story of a deal that the Abbot of Jervaulx had carried through with the Earl of Northumberland over some horses; they both chuckled over it, then Strangways grew grave, and seemed to Darcy to be casting at him looks that were curious and probing. "Well, Tom," said he, "out with it," and laughed to see Strangways start.

"It is," he said after a slight hesitation, "more of that same tale I told you a while ago. There's talk again of the serving woman of Marrick in Swaledale."

"Serving woman? At Marrick?" Darcy could remember nothing about it.

"Of whom they say that she hath seen visions."

"Oh that!" said Darcy, as something of it came back to him, and he remarked that doubtless the Priory had made a pretty profit of such a woman.

"Not in these days," Strangways reminded him, with anger in his voice. "It's said the Prioress will not suffer the woman to speak of what she sees, lest it embroil the Priory in greater troubles than those that are laid upon all by this late Act."

"Hah!" said Darcy, softly and slowly. "Is it so?" After a moment he said, still speaking low, though the trampling hoofs and creak of harness drowned their voices, "Then in these visions the King's proceedings are in some manner condemned?"

"Jesu!" Strangways snorted, "and it would be strange if they were not, unless it be that Heaven is deaf."

"But what do they say of her visions?"

"That she saw Our Saviour bodily as when He rode into Jerusalem on Palm Sunday."

Laus Deo!" Darcy muttered, crossing himself. As he leaned back in the litter, easing himself into the best position to endure the joggle of it, he was thinking that one day, if the times did not mend, this woman and her visions might be of value. Things were not at such a pass that he and others must even use whatever lay to their hands. No hope now to be too finicking. But not yet, he thought, not yet. It might be that this new love of the King's would bring him back to the old ways, though Darcy himself had little hope of it. And anyway, just now there was no help to be looked for from the Emperor, who, by all seeming, would have a war with France upon his hands before autumn, and who, besides, was not readily to mell himself in English matters now, with Queen Katherine dead, when he had so long refrained while she was alive.

So my Lord reflected, but in silence, because Strangways, he knew, was impatient of policy, and loved things to be plain yea or nay, right or wrong. When he put his head out of the litter it was to say, "It might be well to seek the wench and question her."

This time Strangways said that he thought it would be well.

May 2

The Groom Porter went first down the stair in the White Tower, with the keys he carried lightly chiming one against the other. Then came Mr. Lieutenant of the Tower, Sir William Kingston, and after him Queen Anne, with her ladies, scared and white, following close. But at the low round arch of the stair, that burrowed both up and down through the huge walls, the Queen seemed to stumble, and stayed, laying her hand upon the rough cold skin of the stone, while her ladies bunched together behind her.

"Down?" she cried.

Sir William, already going down, said over his shoulder, "If you please, Madame."

But the Queen still stood, clutching at the wall, and looking down into the twilight of the stair.

"Shall I go into a dungeon?"

Sir William's voice came hollowly from below them. "No, Madame. You shall go into the lodging you lay in at your coronation."

At that she let out a cry.

"It is too good for me," she said, and began to go down, but weeping now, and trembling, and crying, "Jesu have mercy on me."

In the great chamber where she had lain before her coronation there were ashes of a dead fire on the hearth, and candles that had guttered low before they had been blown out. For a moment she thought, as she stood in the doorway, "They have not touched it since that night," and that the candles were those that had then made a glancing golden haze, and the cold ashes the ashes of the fire that had hissed and spurted out sweetness to the room from the spices that were cast on it. She moved on a few paces into the room and then could hold herself up no longer, but went down on her knees, crying again and again, "Jesu have mercy on me!"

Sir William drove her women towards her. They took her hands and after dealing with her a little, quieted her. He, at the door, was for turning his back and going away, since this was now no chamber of audience; but the Queen cried to him, begging him to move the King's Highness to let her have the sacrament in the chamber with her. "That I may pray for mercy," said she, still shaking so that he could see her flesh tremble. "For I am clear from the company of man, as for sin, as I am clear from you, and am the King's true wedded wife."

Then she put aside the women, and came close to him, catching his wrist and peering into his face. "Mr. Kingston, do you know why I am here?"

"No," said he, lying.

She began to ask him of the King, of her father and of her brother, and Kingston did what he could to keep to the letter of truth and yet hide from her, what he knew well, that her brother, Lord Rochford, was already in the Tower. And, lest she should ask more, he tried to loosen her hand from his arm and begone, but she would not let him go.

"For," said she, "I hear say I shall be accused with three men. And I can say no more but nay. Without I shall open my body," and at that she tore at the breast of her gown, and, as she met his eyes, huddled it together again, turning her head aside and crying, "Oh! Norris, hast thou accused me? Thou art in the Tower with me, and thou and I shall die together," and then, all in a jumble, spoke of Mark Smeton the spinet player, and my Lady of Worcester, and of the child that had never seen the light.

"Mr. Kingston," she cried at last, "shall I have justice?"

"The poorest subject the King hath," he told her, "hath justice."

At that she threw up her arms and began to laugh, so that he thought it best to leave her, with however little courtesy. When he had shut the door behind him he could not hear the voices of her women, trying to compose her, but her laughter only.

May 16

Robert Aske knocked at the door of Master Snow's room at Gray's Inn. His finger was on the latch when he heard Snow's voice cry sharply from inside, "Who's that?" and then, in a different tone, "Come in! Come in!" So he went in, and found not only Snow but Clifton and Hatfield and another gentleman whom he knew by sight for a man of Lincoln's Inn.

"Come in," said Snow again to Aske, with great cordiality, and to the other gentleman, "You may speak before him."

Aske shook his head at the stool that Snow shoved towards

him with his foot. "I come but a-borrowing," and named a Year Book he needed.

"You shall have it. But sit down now."

"Not craving company. I'll come again for the book."

He was going out when Clifton called to him, "Robin! Robin! come back."

Aske came back. "Well?"

Snow said, "Shut the door," and Aske, after a sharp, hard look at him, shut it, frowning.

"Master Stonor," said Clifton then, waving a hand towards the stranger, "is telling us of this trial of the Queen," and again Snow pushed forward the stool. Aske did not take it; instead he set his shoulders against the door, and shoved his hands through his belt, and so listened, while Master Stonor told all he knew, and that was much and on good testimony, for he had it of a Sergeant-at-Law of Clifford's Inn, who had been present at the trial of the Queen and her brother in the Tower.

When he had finished not one of them spoke or moved till Hal got up from the bed with a sort of laugh.

"And meanwhile," he said, going over to the door, "they say that the King goes junketing on the river all these sweet fair evenings, with minstrels playing, as if he rejoiced to be a cuckold. And you should rejoice too at her fall," he said, looking down into Aske's face which was grim. "You have been always set against this Queen." And then, "Let me out, Robin," he said, because Aske had not budged.

"You said," Aske spoke to Stonor as though he had not heard Hal, "you said there were no witnesses called?"

"Never a one."

"And that though the Queen and the Lord Rochford both denied the charges?"

Stonor bowed his head.

"It is done so in the King's Courts?" Aske looked around at them all, and Clifton grumbled, "By the Rood! No!" but Hal cried out, "Let be! Let be!" putting his hand on Aske's shoulder again, to let him pass out.

This time Aske opened the door for him, and when it was shut again said, as if there had been no interruption, "And of all these accusations, save that great one of co-habitation with those three men, there is naught but what would make men laugh in a Twelfth-tide play. God's Death! She and Rochford made mock of the King and his clothes! She showed openly she loved His Grace no longer. They two laughed at the King's ballads. Well then, bundle up all those charges together with that which you cannot prove, hand a man a written accusation, forbidding him to read it aloud, frown heavily on the jury—and then, by God's Passion, law and justice being fairly kept, pass sentence of death."

Clifton growled, "You've said it," and Stonor tightened his mouth and nodded his head, but Snow got up and began to fidget about the room, protesting that it was unmeet to say such things.

"For why?" said Aske.

"For that—"

Aske caught him up. "For that they are not true?" and Snow began to say, "No, but—"

"I'll tell you for why," Aske interrupted. "For that it's come to this, that not one of us dares lay his hand on the latch to lift it and cry aloud, for only man to hear, that in this trial neither law nor justice is done, but only the King's will, and Cromwell's."

He looked round at them again, and they were silent.

"Each of us," he said, "knows that it is so. But none knows to what pass we shall be brought before the end."

He opened the door then and went away, with Wat Clifton following close behind.

May 18

The Ladies had sung Lauds and gone back to bed some time before, and all the House had fallen silent again for the short hours till dawn. But my Lord Darcy was waking in the Guest Chamber that was above the gate-house; he lay on his side with his face towards the westward window, through which looked in an orange moon with two large stars beside it, standing clear in the ashen sky of this hour before dawn.

The first cock crew, but sleepily; and faintly out of the distance another answered it.

"Tom," said my Lord, "Tom!" and Thomas Strangways sat up on his pallet rubbing sleep from his eyes. "The servants will be stirring soon," said my Lord, and Strangways, groaning and yawning, got out of bed, dressed himself, and then helped his master to dress.

By the time that was done there were footsteps and voices below; a latch lifted, a door banged, the dogs barked, and there came the jingle of harness and stamping of horses led out to plough.

Strangways said, "I'll find and bring her to you," and went out.

My Lord sat down on his bed, with his back to the old, round-headed window that looked eastward down the Dale. This Guest Room, which was the oldest part of the Priory, ran right across the upper floor of the gate-house, with a window at each end and an open hearth in the midst with a louvre above. It was still dark in the room, because of the smallness of the windows, so Strangways had lit two rushlights and set them on the bench. But outside the sky was paling slowly, as all but the greater stars withdrew before the coming day.

Darcy sat absently fingering his beard and considering this venture on which he had set out. He could not be sure that the Prioress, that woman with the keen eyes and deep voice, believed that he and Strangways were, as they said, merchants going over into Wensleydale to buy horses. Yet even if she doubted, it was no matter, so long as she did not know, and did not discover, who indeed he was. And if she did know or discover—God's Passion! he did not greatly care, now that he was once again in the North Country. Yet, he thought, in coming here he might prove to have been a fool for his pains. It was not probable that a serving wench of a small, poor House like Marrick should have anything to tell that would serve in so great a matter as that would be if it came to raising the realm against Cromwell and the King.

Strangways came up the ladder into the room, saying over his shoulder to someone below, "Come up! Come up! None'll hurt you. And you shall have a groat for your trouble for lighting of the fire. But my—my friend is of a humour that cannot suffer these cold mornings."

Then Malle came up into the room with her apron full of sticks and dried bracken for kindling, and having bobbed to my Lord upon the bed went down on her knees and began to blow upon the pale ashes of last night's fire, and paused a moment sitting back on her heels to say that for all it was May it was shivering weather; then she crouched again, puffing noisily.

While she was at it Darcy looked at her, and looked at Strangways. He lifted an eyebrow and shook his head, and Strangways shook his too. The woman had a patient, cheerful face, but she looked to have as much wit as the handle of my Lord's walking staff.

"Well," said Darcy, when she had done, and the flame

licked up and the smoke swayed and crawled and curled a-long the hearth, "here's for your labour," and he held out a groat.

Malle came near and he put it into her hand, but she held it so slackly that it fell between them.

"Are you she," he asked—because having come here he would at least put the question—"Are you she of whom they say that you have seen in a vision or dream holy things?"

He looked down quickly at the groat which she had dropped, and again at her face; then he got up quickly from the bed; the two rushlights were behind her; no gleam of their flames shone on her face, nor was it, when he looked again, any light at all that he saw there, only something which might be to light as man's thought to his spoken word.

"I pray you," Darcy urged, when she was silent, "to tell me what it is that you have seen."

Malle said: "There was a great wind of light blowing, and sore pain."

He waited for her to say more, not looking at her now, but turned towards the window beyond which the eastern sky showed pale, cold and strange, not coloured yet, but flecked with small dark cloud. He had to make an effort to recall what it was he had hoped to get from this woman; something that could be passed from mouth to mouth among common men and gentle too; something that showed it was God's will they should resist the King's proceedings in religion; something that promised the downfall of Master Cromwell, Chief Secretary.

"But," he said, having fished all this up from the bottom of his mind, as if these were things long forgotten and now become unfamiliar and unreal, "was it told you that God is angry with them that have counselled the King against Holy Church? And that He will have them brought low?" When she said nothing he persisted "In these days there are deeds done—there are wicked men—" He glanced at Strangways for help, but Strangway's eyes were fixed on the woman.

"In times past," Darcy urged, "when His birth-place and His sepulchre were in the hands of the heathen, He spoke by the mouths of Popes and Saints to call on men to take arms and guard His honour. Is it not so now? Is not this the meaning of what you saw?"

He tried to see her face again, but she had turned aside, and the torn and crumpled kerchief she wore hid all but the tip of her blunt nose. He lifted his hand and beat with one clenched fist on the palm of the other.

"He would not resist His enemies. That I know. But for us it is different. Shall we stand by and see—and not—"

But, though he waited, Malle made no answer.

He moved at last and went from her down the length of the room to the window that looked up the Dale. For a moment he stayed there, looking out to where, above the humped back of Calva, the moon hung in the sky, pale and round as a white cheese. When he came back Malle was gone and Strangways stood at the top of the ladder, staring down after her. Darcy went by him restlessly to the other window, as if there he might learn something that he needed to know; as if what was not to be found in the dim west might be written upon the brightening east. And upon this side the dawn had come. Harsh thin flame had lit all the small clouds, and, even as he looked out, the light changed, grew warmer and softer, till the cold fire had turned to rose colour against a heavenly blue.

"Tom!" cried Darcy. "If all honest men were to hold their hands would not knaves rule all?" He knew he had said that before, and then knew that he had said it to his wife, and the remembrance cut him, and joined with this woman's silence to condemn him. But he cried, "Surely God would not have us stand by while His enemies work their will?"

"Surely not," Strangways said confidently; but then the weight of the decision did not fall upon his shoulders.

And Darcy said never a word more of using the woman's vision to hearten men to resist the King's doings.

June 15

The sun was shining into the upstairs room in which Master William Ibgrave, the old embroiderer, sat with his three workmen. It was from the hands of these cunning craftsmen that those sumptuous garments came that the King and his Queens—one or another—wore at high feasts of the Church or on other solemn occasions. Round about the walls hung doublets and kirtles, mantles and petticoats, and among them, hardly more glorious, was stuff for the King's Chapel—copes, orfreys, chasubles and frontals.

Master William had, laid across his knees, a doublet of white and green satin of Bruges, with the pattern faintly traced upon it, which was to be embroidered for the King; and now one of the men brought to him a little locked coffer from the carved chest by the window. Master William took the key from his pouch, unlocked the coffer and lifted from it two packages of soft leather. He unrolled them upon the bench beside him; in one there were eighteen emeralds set in gold; in the other twenty-nine little things like brooches, but without the pin, of pearls set in gold in the shape of the letter I, for the initial of the new Queen Jane's name. Master William and his men were to stitch them upon the green and white satin doublet, the pearl letters on the green, the emeralds upon the white, and all in an intricate mesh of embroidery in silks and gold thread.

Of the three other men who sat in the sunny room one was stitching small pearls upon a pair of crimson sleeves; another was busy with gold thread upon a black damask girdle; and the third, who had brought the coffer to his master, and who was to help with the green and white doublet, sat with his hands on his knees and his eyes cast down; he was a mournful man of Lutheran belief, tormented by fears of damnation, but he was the best workman that Master William had.

He who was sewing at the crimson sleeves paused to let his needle hang twirling at the end of the thread till the twisted silk ran sweetly again. But then, instead of stooping once more to his work, he lifted his head.

"Surely it is that they come," he said, and nodded towards the window. There had been a good deal of noise in the street all morning, of voices, footsteps, and the tread of horses. But now a sound of shouting was growing in the distance, and flowing nearer.

"Tcha!" said the Lutheran, as his two fellows got up and hurried to the window, to hang out, straining to see farthest. Master William, however, only shook his head gently. Though he disapproved of such interruptions, being himself tirelessly industrious, he did not rebuke his men, for he was of a very patient and pacific humour, and willing to suffer the infirmity of more frivolous minds. So he went on, delicately tacking the emeralds and the pearl and gold letters upon the doublet while the road below filled with a moving flood of velvet and satin, jewels, steel and feathers, as noblemen, bishops, ladies, knights and gentlemen, and the King and Queen went by to the Corpus Christi Day Mass at Westminster.

When all had passed the two men came back to their work, and were perhaps the brisker at it for the interlude. Now, as they sat stitching, they told Master Ibgrave how very fairly the embroidery of the Queen's kirtle had showed; they all knew that kirtle by heart, for between them they had embroidered the grey satin with gold, and among the gold had set on no less than 1562 pearls which, in to-day's sunshine, had given the whole a sort of milky radiance. They commented too, upon the new Queen's fair face and gentle demeanour, comparing her favourably with her predecessor. The Lutheran, on the other hand, defended Queen Anne, declaring her to have been a great favourer of the Gospel, and, in his mind, to have been done to death, innocent, by those who were enemies of the true light. Master William through it all sat contently stitching with his knotted deft fingers, and on the eaves of the roof above the windows the swallows, with the sun on their breasts, kept up a tuneless, ecstatic twittering.

Much later on this same day, so late indeed that all in the house at Hunsdon were asleep except herself, the Princess Mary sat leaning her elbow on the table and her head on her hand. Her head ached with a great knocking throb, because she had cried for so long. The room was close and airless, which made the ache worse, but if the shutters were set open on the warm summer air the moths would come in and blunder into the candles, so that she must stop writing till they had staggered out again, maimed and helpless, to spin themselves to death upon the table.

Yet she was not writing; and now because her fingers were clammy with heat she laid down the pen and wiped them on her gown, and afterwards sat looking at the pen, and not looking at the piece of paper beside which it lay. All she had to do—but she had sat here for hours, and it was yet undone—was to sign her name three times upon that piece of paper. If she did that she would declare the King her father to be the Head of Christ's Church, his laws good and just, and herself to be born of a marriage "by God's law and man's incestuous and unlawful."

"Oh!" she whispered, "I shall be sick. I shall be sick," and then crammed her knuckles against her mouth to stifle the word that had come to her lips. She could not cry "Mother!" because she knew that she was going to sign the paper.

And she must do it quickly, before the heavy hammers began to beat again in her head, hammering out arguments, for and against, as they had hammered them out for days. It was wrong. The Emperor's Ambassador said it was right.

They would kill her. Then she would be a martyr. It was right to obey a father. It was horribly wrong to deny the truth.

She snatched up the pen and set her name to each of the three Articles, then folded and sealed the paper, but clumsily and spilling the wax because of the trembling of her fingers.

When it was done and the thing lay there, signed and sealed, she sat looking at it. It was done, and for a few moments her mind was quite empty except for a dull and heavy sense of relief. She did not remember the dwindling hope of the last week, the growing fears, the letters she had written, submitting, praying for pardon always more abjectly, yet always stopping short of that which now she had done. She did not remember how a couple of days ago she had sat in this chair while two of the King's Privy Council, the Duke of Norfolk and the Earl of Sussex, had stood over her shouting that if she had been the daughter of either of them her head should have been beaten against the wall till it was soft as a rotten apple. She remembered and thought of nothing now except that now the thing was done.

She stood up clinging to the chair for a minute to keep herself steady, and then went crookedly towards the door. Behind her, upon the table between the two candles, lay the sealed paper. She did not turn her head to see it, but it filled her mind, because that small square of white with the clumsy botched seal on it, was that by which she had cut herself off from her mother, from the Church Catholic, from God. Even now she might have gone back to the table and set the paper to one of the candle flames; but she did not.

When she came to the door her fingers fumbled for the latch. She was muttering to herself.

"So it's done. I can sleep now. I must sleep."

June 29

The rain caught them again as they were approaching the Priory, so Dame Nan Bulmer sent the two men servants on to the Manor, and herself, with little Doll and her younger waiting gentlewoman, who was Julian Savage, and the servant behind whom July rode, turned into the Priory gate. Dame Nan and Mistress Doll were brought up to the Prioress's Chamber, and at once there was calling for wine and wafers, strawberries, and a dish of cherries. The servant went off to the kitchen where he greatly enlivened a dull and disagreeable morning for the Cook, his boy, and as many of the wenches who could find excuse to pretend business in that direction. July slipped away to the Cloister, and, finding that empty, to the Parlour.

There the Ladies were, all but Dame Anne Ladyman who was with the Prioress, and Dame Joan Barningham who was now so old that for the most part she kept her bed.

"Lord!" they cried, "it's July!" and shook Dame Eleanor Maxwell by the shoulder to rouse her, shouting in her ear that it was July, and pointing to where the girl stood by the door in a grey gown with a red petticoat. It was a moment before the old lady recognized her in this guise, but then she lumbered up, very slowly, while all the rest were crowding round July, crying out that she's grown and was now quite a woman, asking her why she had never yet been to see them till this day, bidding her tell them if she'd rather be at the Manor or here, and then never listening to a word she said, but pouring out all that had happened at the Priory since she left. Dame Margaret's little dog was dead, and Dame Bet's brother promised her one of those talking popinjay birds but it never came, and Dame Joan had had all her teeth out, and had a very great cough even though it was summer.

Then they made way for Dame Eleanor, who, leaning heavily on her stick, leaned also on July's shoulder as she bent and kissed her, saying in her flat toneless voice that it was good to see her. July, who did not like to be kissed or touched, stood stiff, and then, looking into Dame Eleanor's face, forgot everything but the change she saw there; in these weeks Dame Eleanor's firm, freshly coloured fat had sagged and paled; her eyes, which had been cheerful, now seemed to be bleared with tears, and her big mouth trembled.

So, all the time July sat with the Ladies and they talked and showed her their new embroidery works and plied her with cherries and strawberries ("but we can't give you wine for the Lady hath the keys"), she kept stealing a look at Dame Eleanor. When Dame Bet Singleton would have her come upstairs to look at a murrey cloth gown that had been left to her in a sister's will, and they were alone together, July began to say, "Dame Eleanor—" and then did not know how to go on.

But Dame Bet understood.

"Alas! You saw? Even we who are with her can see how she's changed."

Dame Bet laid her hand on the lid of the coffer, where the

murrey gown lay, but did not open it. Instead she sighed, "I do think that when—that if—they turn us out from Marrick, that day will be her death."

July could make no sound in answer, and Dame Bet said in a different tone, "Ah well! You are gone forth into the world. It cannot be the same to you as to us." Then she opened the coffer, and in displaying the gown became more cheerful.

But when they sat together on the top of the coffer with the gown across their knees, Dame Bet seemed to remember that all this time she had learnt nothing of how July was getting on at the Manor, and began to question her. Was it merry among all those folk? Wasn't Mistress Doll a sweet little maid? Was Dame Nan kind? July said, "Yes," to all, because that was safest, but she spoke with so little spirit that perhaps Dame Bet guessed how often the truth would have been, "No," for she heaved a sigh and said inconsequently, "Alas! now we may prove in ourselves the mutability of things temporal," and from that went on to tell July that the Prioress, being of so stout a heart as she was, maintained that all would yet be well with the Priory, though Monks and Nuns in the South were even now turned out. "But the rest of us are sore afraid. Only one—" she obviously had difficulty in swallowing back the name—"*one* would not be unwilling to be put forth, I do think. She has a gown of carnation colour in her coffer and she embroiders a pair of grey sleeves as if she were a maid preparing for a bridal." Dame Bet looked down on the murrey-coloured cloth that she was stroking with one hand and added as if it needed some explanation, "This is of a sad colour, and, besides, will be only for a petticoat, and the gown over it open but a little way."

July, whose eyes had wandered to the window, got up hastily.

"The rain has stopped. I shall be chidden. I must go."

They were indeed calling for her below, and she got sharp words from Dame Nan when she came. What made it worse was that the rain began again before they had gone far, and Doll began to cry, and Sir Rafe, hearing her grizzling as they came into the Manor, rebuked his wife for not having more care of the child. All this, July knew, would like curses come home to roost with her. And then she thought of Dame Eleanor Maxwell, shrinking and dwindling to a helpless, wretched old woman, and all the Ladies except the Prioress and Dame Anne Ladyman, dreading the day when they would be put out of the Priory, leaving behind them the kind, quiet life, to live as July had come to live, in some crowded house in which they had no place.

She was at table now, and listening to all the chatter and shouting, laughter and bickering, she thought of the Priory as a place of peace. Those tiffs which from time to time divided the Ladies were no more than ripples on the placid surface of their life. Here—July looked along the table—here this lad was quarrelsome because a wench would not look at him, and there that wench was cock-a-hoop and giggling because the lad she liked had handled her in a dark corner. From behind the shut doors of the summer parlour came the sound of Sir Rafe's voice raised and harsh. You would never hear Dame Nan speak loud in anger, but July knew just how she would be answering, cold and bitter and cruel as she could be in the fewest words; July did not love Dame Nan, but she knew, without having thought about it all, that here was another who was unhappy, and whose security had been taken from her as it had been taken from July, and would be taken from the Ladies of Marrick Priory.

Just before supper July was sent to the still-room to turn the green walnuts in their pickle. On her way back instead of coming at once to the parlour, she slipped across the little yard and out into the dripping garden, for the rain had at last taken off after a drenching day, and now the clouds were parting and showing in the west a hint of the sun. She heard footsteps, and looking down at the road below the little stone terrace she saw Malle coming along carrying a bolt of homespun linen that one of the Marrick women had woven for the Priory.

July let her pass, and then, in a great hurry, ran down the steps to the little gate; the key was in the lock; she pulled open the door. "Malle! Malle!" she called.

Malle stopped, turned, and came back. July wished that she had not called her. "No matter," she began to say, and then remembered how much it did matter. If only the Ladies might have peace. If only for them there might be still that quiet island in the troubles of the world. Even though July herself must be buffeted on the high seas it would be comfort to know that there were some safe in a sheltered haven.

"Malle," she said, "tell me. They say that the Saints show you what shall come to pass. Malle, what of the Ladies? Shall they be turned out?"

Malle said nothing.

"Oh, Malle, tell me, I'll give you my brooch. They say that Our Saviour appeared to you, riding over Grinton bridge. Tell me what it meant." She was busy unfastening it, but it caught in a thread of her gown, and looking up she saw Malle's face, and after that forgot about the brooch, and was pierced through by a sudden sharpness of hope.

"Malle," she cried. "Is it well? Is it? Oh! what did you see that you look so—so—"

Malle said:

"There was a great wind of light blowing, and sore pain."

July flinched. She still had her hand on the latch of the gate, and her fingers grew cold on the cold iron, though she could feel warmth on her cheek from the sun which now shone through the scattering clouds, edging them with flame. She stood waiting, then glanced again at Malle's face, and saw that there lingered on it still that shining that was not from the brightening west.

"You say 'pain' and you smile. What do you mean?" July cried out, though Malle's look was no smile either. Malle did not answer. She went slowly away along the wall of the garden, and July watched her till something moving on the road below the big gate of the Manor caught her eye. It was one of the hinds toiling up with an oak beam on his shoulder for mending the Hall roof; he was coming up from the saw-pit. Beyond him lay the depth of the Dale, now so brimmed with sunshine that it seemed to be full at once of drenched green air and fiery gold; it was as though July looked down into the deep sea, and saw there a great fire lit and burning below the green water, with flames at once glorious and fatal.

"They hanged Him on the Cross," she thought, and in the furthest corner of her mind cringed away from sight and sound of the big round-headed iron nails biting through flesh as the hammer drove them. Malle's look of light meant nothing. There was always, round about the whole world, an ocean of pain. It crept towards the Ladies of Marrick; it lapped to the feet of the one she could least bear to have suffer. "But he's well, and in no danger," she assured herself. Then—

"Oh!" she cried, wringing her hands together. "You are a fool!" she cried after Malle's broad lumpish shoulders and bent head, "A fool!"

She went back into the garden, slamming the gate so that a branch of sweet briar above it, smelling like paradise after the rain, shook down on her cold drops that struck as sudden as little knives.

July 24

There was a posy of clove-scented pinks, white and fringed and each with a deep crimson eye, on the sill of the open window by which the King leaned. The Lady Mary, his daughter, standing before him with her hands clasped upon the velvet brocade petticoat of her gown, looked no higher than the stems of the flowers which showed, lean and jointed, through the Venice glass; little shining bubbles clung to the stems.

"Therefore," the King said, "I charge you tell me if from your heart, and truly, you have submitted yourself." He paused, but not long enough for an answer. "I tell you," said he, "I hate nothing more than a dissembler. My Lord of Norfolk, or Master Cromwell—Lord Privy Seal—" he corrected himself, for such was Cromwell now and Baron too, "either of those, and other of my Council, would often have me dissemble with Ambassadors of foreign Princes. But I'll never do so. Now, good daughter, will you in this show yourself my daughter indeed?"

He laid his hand, warm and heavy, on her shoulder, and she knew she must meet his eyes.

She did it, curtseying to the ground, and taking his hand to kiss it. She said that most truly, most humbly, as his bounden subject and penitent, unworthy child, she submitted herself with unfeigned heart to his will, "such as has been and shall be declared unto me for my obedience to—to—" She stumbled and the sentence trailed away, because his eyes were still on her. "Oh truly, truly, Sir," she cried.

He nodded then, and smiled before he turned away. But he said over his shoulder that she would want to write to her kinsman the Emperor, and to the Bishop of Rome, how freely and of a good conscience she renounced her mother's marriage as incestuous, and took her father as Supreme Head of the Church in England.

She stood there for a long time after he had gone, looking again at the posy of pinks, and wondering whether, with practice, lying came more easily.

She gave a great jump as someone came up behind her. It was one of the King's gentlemen.

He held out a little green silk purse. The King's Grace had sent it to her for a token of his love and favour. There was a ring with a fine diamond inside the purse. She thought, "So I'm to be paid for lying." That made it worse.

August 23

July was glad not to find Jankin at the gate when she and little Ned, the Bulmers' new page, came into the Priory. Neither she nor Ned had any good reason for coming here, and July had been trying all the way down the hill to think of a good excuse, but the wind and the rain seemed to make it impossible to think, so another moment or two was welcome. Once inside the gate she edged Ned quickly to the right, and when he asked, "Where are we going? What's in here? Why do we go in here?" she told him truly, "To look at the horses."

But as they came to the door of the stable kept for the horses of guests, they found Malle, sitting on the ground with a great wet pile of rushes beside her, that ran water to meet the water that was blowing in from outside. The reeds had all been cut in summer, as time served, and had since then lain in the river, tied up into bundles, and each bundle moored to a big stone. Now Malle was peeling them for rushlights; all about her feet the curled peel lay green and sopping, and on one side there was a pile of thin lengths of white pith, each with its rib of green; these were the lights.

"See," said July, "there are the horses."

There was a sorrel horse, and beyond it a bay.

"Is that all?" Ned objected. "My father has far more. My father has ten horses, twenty horses. My father has forty horses."

"Has he?" July laughed at the child's brag because she was so happy. It was true, what they had said at the Manor last night. Master Aske had come to the Priory. The sorrel horse must be his, and the bay his servant's. But still she had not thought what she would say to explain why she and Ned had come here. She could not say, "I had to know." Still less, "I thought I might see him."

"Come on," said Ned, and tried to drag her to the door. But when they had reached it it was he who hung back to make a dive for one of the fine curls of green peel from the rushes. July let herself be checked, and stood in the doorway of the stable looking out into the rain that rushed down out of a lowering, sombre sky, filling the empty Great Court with noises of gurgling, splashing, dripping, all overlaid by the great steady swish of its fall.

As she stood there Master Aske came through the gate-house. He carried a straw basket, and a fishing-rod over his shoulder; as he tilted it up again, clear of the gateway arch, the thin end danced high above him. He came straight to the stable door, his head down against the rain. July slipped back, and he pulled up abruptly with an apology that he left unfinished.

"Why," said he, peering into the dark stable, "it's—it's little Mistress July, grown big!"

He came in, laid down his basket, and set the rod against the wall.

"I suppose," he said, "the fishes I left behind me in the Swale aren't wetter than I," and he bent his head down to peel off his soaked hood, and wrung out his hair, and laughed at July, his face wet with rain and his eye very bright and gay.

"Sir," Ned asked, not waiting for an introduction, "have you caught any?"

"Would you see?" Aske picked up the basket and opened it, and Ned and he stopped together, their heads close, but July drew back; she had no wish to look at the gasping, wretched things flapping about in the hay there.

"Marry!" Ned piped in his clear voice. "It's a great catch—three big fellows and two, three small ones."

"That's no mastery," said Master Aske, "on such a day as this," but July could see he was pleased, and he took Ned and tossed him up on the back of the sorrel horse. When they came again to July, still standing beside the door, Ned had Master Aske by the hand and was wanting to know all about what Malle was doing.

"Why does she peel them all wet?"

"Because they won't peel else."

"And what will she do next?"

"Lay them out in the dew a few nights, then dry them in the sun."

"Then the Ladies will burn them to read their books by?"

"They will—when cook has dipped them in the scum from the bacon pot."

"Oh," said Ned, and stood with his feet wide, staring at Malle, and putting away in his head all this information.

But Master Aske came over to July. He smiled at her, swinging his wet hood, and then she saw his thick straight brows knot together in a frown.

"Mistress," he began, and then with a hesitation unusual

for him, "I thought—you wore a novice's habit when I was here last year."

July nodded.

"And now?"

"I'm waiting gentlewoman to Dame Anne," and July nodded towards Marrick up the hill.

"Did you choose so?"

She shook her head and he continued to look at her, very hard and intent. He had not seen till now that pinched, defensive, eastwind look, which others knew so well; but now he saw it.

She said, in a flat matter-of-fact voice, "Sir John would not pay my dower till I was professed, and that cannot be now, the Visitors said, till I should be twenty-two. So the Lady would not keep me."

He turned away from her, biting his lips and frowning. This—an unhappy, frightened little wench—was one tiny fragment of the destruction that the King and Cromwell were making.

He said, continuing his thought aloud, "And there's my kinswoman, Dame Eleanor." Those two, July and the old lady, were present and painful in his mind, and beyond them all the others, known or unknown, now turned out. "Some," he went on, arguing it out, "some will go to the greater Abbeys, but old folk—such as Dame Eleanor—that's not for them. But you—" He hesitated.

"By the time I am old enough there'll be no Abbeys."

"God's Cross!" He turned to her. "Who told you? It's not possible. Our King cannot change all that has been for a thousand years, and in all Christendom. Who said it to you?"

She said, "No one," and he rebuked her for putting about such a word, and went on to show her at length how impossible it was that such a thing should be. "I cannot think how you should suppose it," he said; and she, dumb because he was angry, could not tell him the reason, which was indeed no reason at all—but a conviction that just because the fragile peace of the little House at Marrick was the only peace she had known, therefore it would surely be destroyed.

"If it should come to that—" he said, "if it should come to that—" She heard him grind his teeth together, and she clutched at his sleeve.

"Oh! do not—do not— What would you do?"

He put his hand on hers and lifted it from his arm, but

gently, and for a second he held it in his. Yet she knew that if he was not angry with her neither was he thinking of her at all.

"There's nothing a man may do now," he muttered. "Not rightly do."

Then he left her and went across the Court to the outer stairway up to the Guest House. She took Ned with her into the Parlour, for he had become clamourous to know why they had come to the Priory. She counted, and rightly, that so young and plump a small boy, with his comical parade of manhood, would wile sufficient sweetmeats out of the good Ladies to satisfy him as to why.

But she would not let him stay long, and the Ladies found her fidgety, inattentive and abrupt. They did not realize how she was looking at them with eyes which were almost, if not quite, hostile. But it was so, because now the King's dealings with the Abbeys meant to her nothing more nor less than danger to Master Aske. If the quick, utter and unresisted suppression of every Abbey in the country could have been procured by July nodding her head she would have nodded, lest otherwise Master Aske should somehow be dragged into the quarrel. "There's nothing a man could do," she told herself, repeating his words for comfort. Since, however, he was different from every other man in the world, the words, though so obviously true, did not comfort her much.

August 27

Will came unsteadily into the room, tripped over a stool and dropped the saddle-bag he had brought upstairs; this morning his master and he had come up from the Priory to the Manor, because Aske was to spend a few days there, being kinsman to Dame Nan, though distant.

"Mass!" Aske cried. "Already! Could you not wait even an hour before you must drink yourself sodden?"

Will stooped to grope for what he had dropped, but the floor was tipped too dangerously for him. He stood up again and laughed.

"By Cock! but a temperate man'd be tempted, so many pretty trulls there are below stairs. There's one called Cis, and another—called—called— Well I can't mind her name now, but there's *thy* old trull here, Master; Mistress Meg no-better-than-should-be Bulmer."

Aske got up then and struck Will a blow which knocked him flat, and the fellow turned tearful and penitent and would kiss Aske's hand. He swore he'd never take such a word on his tongue again, nor never drink no more than he could carry. "And God knows I know you are as clean from sin for her as it's sure I'm a sinful man and an evil-tongued, graceless servant."

Aske left him, disgusted with himself, angry with Will, and put out too at the knowledge that Meg Bulmer was here. He'd not have come if he'd known, and now that he knew he thought of staying but one night, and then making an excuse to go. But he had met that little July in the gateway as they came in, and he had seen her face kindle as purely as the wick of a candle taking light. He had thought of her more than once, since they had talked in the stable, with compunction and great gentleness, wishing that there was something that he could do to amend what it seemed could not be amended. Now he thought, "Why! it is that she lacks friends in this strange place, and she takes me for an old friend. Poor little wench!" he said to himself, "I'll be as true friend to her as I may." So he could not have found it in his heart to go away at once, guessing just how the light in her face would be quenched if he were to tell her, "I'm for Aughton to-morrow."

August 28

Sir John Bulmer came into the room while Margaret's woman Bet was lacing her mistress into the leather corset, busked with wood, and with side pads at the waist to hold out the over-petticoat and the gown. Sir John had been out hawking early with some of the other guests, but rain had come on heavily when they were far up the valley, and had blown in their teeth all the way home. He was very wet and out of temper, and began at once casting off hood and coat and doublet, and pulling down his hosen. Margaret said he'd make Bet blush, and Bet pretended to hide her eyes, but peeped at him from behind her hand, laughing. He said if she was going to be married she'd best get used to the sight of a man. "O fie, Sir!" cried Bet, but she went by him with a look that was anything but coy.

When she came back she had Margaret's bodice and petticoats on her arm. She slipped on the bodice and tied the points, then the petticoats, and asked which gown and sleeves. Margaret said, "The blue, and the damask sleeves."

Sir John was sitting on the bed, rubbing his wet legs with a towel. He told Bet to fetch him a pair of hosen and a

gown from the trussing coffer. Margaret nodded, so Bet left
her mistress to get the things and tie his points for him.
Then she came back to Margaret, and he lolled on the bed,
warm and comfortable again, watching Margaret turn or
stand still, raise her arms or thrust them into the wide
sleeves that Bet laced up to the bodice. Whatever she did
was lovely, and once he came from the bed, pushed Bet
away, and lifting Meg's hair kissed her neck.

Bet was fastening the last petticoat which was of crane-
coloured damask like the sleeves. Then Meg dived her head
into the gown, and came out with her bright hair tumbled.

"How much longer?" he cried.

"Not long," she told him, "not long. Bet has to do my hair.
Are you hungry?"

"You'd be hungry if you'd ridden as I have through the
rain."

Margaret had sat down in front of the mirror and Bet
began fastening up her hair; neither of them had any intention of being hurried, but Meg leaned forward so that she
could keep an eye upon his face in the glass, in case he grew
too impatient.

"Who went with you?" she said to him; and to Bet, "Draw
out that pin again. There's a hair pulls. That's better."

He was naming the other guests; Aske's name came last,
and Sir John chuckled, but sourly. "He's lost his hawk. I told
him he would. She's not yet fully reclaimed, though she's a
handsome enough eyas. He cast her off after a couple of
mallard and she flew wild, and got into the trees at the top of
Gill Beck. He's riding a young mare too, that's but half managed. I told him so, but he's a man that thinks he knows better than any, though he was very sorry to lose his hawk, and
acknowledged I had been right."

Margaret had met her own eyes in the mirror at the mention of Aske's name. Now she smiled and murmured, half
aloud, "Poor Robin!" and because she was smiling at herself
did not see Sir John lift his head. She took a long look at her
own lovely face thinking, "Jesu! no! It was because he loved
me too much that he never came again. And that is why he
remains a bachelor." Then she glanced at the reflection of Sir
John. He was drumming with his fingers on his knee. He
looked up suddenly and said to Bet, "You can go. Yes, go. No
—leave that alone." Bet went hastily, but for a full minute
he said nothing, and Margaret sat, with her hands in her

[403]

lap and eyes lowered, in her pose as still and easy as a fish in a quiet pool, and as ready to flash into life.

"I marvel," said Sir John, still frowning at his knuckles, "that Robin Aske has never married."

That chimed so exactly with her thoughts that Meg turned about on the stool, to look at him with a new respect. Could it be that the slow ox had hid such perception behind his dull face all these years? At the thought that there might be some smoulder of anger under his sluggish devotion she brightened visibly like a flame.

"I have marvelled too," she said sweetly.

"You have?" He looked up and was aware of the brilliance of her beauty. He stared at her, and she saw anger, pain and a hungry worship trouble the dullness of his inexpressive face. She said, on a sudden inspiration, "Shall we marry him to July?" and watched him, all wifely submission outwardly, and with her spirit dancing and daring him within. Laughter bubbled up in her too as she saw him trying to work out how this might relate to that which he suspected.

He dropped his eyes and muttered that July was well enough here with Dame Nan.

"This," she told him, "was but for a time. I'm her sister. I must see the child provided for. We cannot keep her dower for ever. Robin Aske—or another—but as she hath small looks, it were well soon rather than late."

She stood up and moved to the door. Let him puzzle his head as to whether or no she cared whom Robin Aske married. He got up heavily and followed her. "I must think on it," he said.

August 29

Robert Aske was very pleased with himself when he marked his lost hawk rather high up in one of the trees near the top of Grinton Beck. "It's well," he thought, "that I came." Sir John Bulmer had been positive he'd never find her.

He got down from the saddle and slipped the bridle over a low bough; the young mare was a joy to ride, footed like a fairy, and would soon lose her whimsies. "There, there, my sweeting!" he said, smoothing his hand down her neck, before he started to climb the tree.

About two minutes later, with a great crack of a breaking bough, he came down, rushing through the leaves with a prodigious and startling commotion. When he had picked himself up he sat down again hastily, and began to assess the damage. He had torn his doublet; something was very wrong with one ankle; the mare, taking fright at his sudden and noisy descent, had dragged the bridle from the bough and was away; he could hear her go clattering down the beck, slipping and stumbling and churning through the water in one of the pools—he could only hope she would not break a leg.

It is tempting, but it is unwise, for a man whose ankle is swelling inside his boot to try a short cut. Before long Aske knew that it was so, but because he was obstinate he would not turn back. When he came to the road running from Grinton up the Dale below Harkerside he was going very halt. He had thought to find someone on horseback who would take him up behind, but, as luck would have it, only those on foot were going his way, and these were children and women; those on horseback going towards Keld he would not ask to turn for him.

So he went slowly, and in pain, and had made up his mind to go in to the Manor, though the bailiff and a few servants would be the only people there, when Gib Dawe, coming briskly up from behind, drew level, stopped and asked what was to do.

Aske told him what had happened, and Gib, in a stiff, harsh way, offered his help. Aske hesitated, then accepted; it had long been in his mind to speak a word to the Marrick Priest, and perhaps this was as good an opportunity as another; he did not reckon that the pain he was in would make it difficult to keep his temper. They went on together then, but with some embarrassment, and, for Aske, a good deal of discomfort, since Gib was by so much the taller that to lean on his shoulder was difficult, and besides that Gib did little to moderate his pace in order to make it easy for a limping man.

So it was abruptly that Aske opened his matter.

"Sir Gilbert, from all I can hear you are one of those who teach heresy to the simple poor folk."

"Sir," said Gib, very harsh, "that you call heresy I call the true word of God."

"That I call heresy General Councils of the Church have called heresy."

"As what?"

Aske bit his lip as his foot turned on a stone. "I'll not dispute it with you," he said shortly. "You know well enough what things are contrary to that which the Church has always taught."

"Ha!" cried Gib, triumphantly. "But now it is all to be reformed. The King and the Vicar General—"

Aske cried, "Out on Thomas Cromwell! Was he to make and unmake what men should believe?"

"Yea. He and the King. Because that is the work to which God hath sent them. You have seen what is done already—superstitious practices forbidden, the Pope's authority broken; carnal ill-living Monks and Nuns driven like conies out from their buries—"

Aske stopped and took his arm from Gib's shoulder and faced him on the road.

"I'll hear no more of this—" he began, but Gib did not wait for him to finish.

"Aye, but you shall hear more of it. The work's only now begun. But the field shall be reaped clean, and it is the King that has laid his hand to the sickle."

He gave a sort of laugh, but cut it short at the sound of Aske's voice when he spoke.

"Sir Priest," said he, "the King will do what he will. But here in the North the time for these things is not yet, and I swear to you I shall some way let you from this preaching. I'll be loath to bring a man into trouble, but you shall not so deceive the simple commons. I shall see to it."

"Against the King's will?" Gib said, and was angrier almost with himself than with the other, because his own voice lacked that ring of sureness that Mr. Aske's had.

"I've told you. I shall see to it."

They measured each other, eye to eye, then Gib's dropped; he shrugged his shoulders and turned away. But when he had gone a step or two he came back.

"Lean on my shoulder," he said.

"I shall make shift well enough without."

So when Gib went on again alone each of them was much out of temper—Gib because he had not been able to out-face Master Aske, but Aske for a deeper and more grievous reason. What Gib had said of the King and of the work yet to be done was only too true. And though he himself should be able to have one preacher silenced what would that avail? As he limped on downhill towards the mill and the yew trees in the churchyard he contemplated a prospect of such total ruin that he could hardly yet believe it possible. Then he remembered a story that was going about, of a simple fellow who had come to the churchyard of a village, near-by a Monastery to which the King's Commissioners were come to suppress it. This fellow had a spade and mattock on his shoulder and when he was asked why, "Marry," quod he, "because I am here to bury Jesus Christ." "Fie," quod they, "on such a word!" "Marry!" quod he, "but it is sure he must be dead. Whoever heard of a man's goods being appraised while he was still alive."

The Church clock struck, leisurely and sweet, the hour of seven. Aske, abreast of the gate, stopped, hesitated, and turned in. "Indeed," he thought, "I can't go further." There was a bench under the south wall where folks sat who came to Mass on Sundays from far up the Dale, bringing their bread and cheese, pork and beer, to eat and drink in the churchyard. He got that far and plumped down on it, and then, taking out his knife, began to slit away the boot from his leg. It took long, for the pain increased as he jagged at the leather, so that he must go gingerly. A small child came and stood close to watch, but Aske had no attention for him; his hands were shaking now and there was a darkness in his eye, and roaring, as if the Swale were in flood, in his ears. He heard someone say, "You've dropped the knife," and he muttered crossly, "I know that," not connecting the voice with the child, because it seemed to come from so far away; but though he groped for the knife he could not lay his hand on it.

Then he knew that someone was lifting his foot from the ground. There was a wrench that spun blackness and noise together into one, and then relief; the roaring died to no more than a rustling, and the blackness to flying spots that cleared and let in the brightness of the day. He saw that Malle, the Priory serving wench, had his knife in her hand; she had got his boot off and was slitting away the lacing of the gusset of his hosen at the ankle. He wiped his forehead clumsily with the back of his hand, and said "That's better. Thank you," smiling at her, and she smiled back with her dull, indeterminate smile.

He did not speak to her again till she had bound up his ankle with a strip of linen borrowed from the Miller's wife, who would have come to attend the gentleman, she told Malle, who told Aske, but that she was baking, and her husband should have the cob saddled for him so that he might ride at his ease back to the Manor. Malle had soaked the rag in well-water, deliciously chill, and Aske sat, enjoying with a vacant mind mere physical sensations, the warmth of the sun on his hand, and face, ease after pain, and the simple but primary pleasure of light.

While Malle stooped over his foot he looked about the churchyard where the long, low hummocks of the graves made soft shadows in the grass. There were three yew trees along the wall, two to one side of the gate, one to the other. The rumble and splash of the millwheel filled the air with comfortable sound, and now and again came voices, speaking or singing, from the village beyond the wall. Up the Dale there was the great heather-red flank of Harkerside; looking down, past the roofs of Grinton, he could see the steep woods behind Marrick Priory. It was always a strange thing for him, a fenland man, to find himself so deep among the hills, which, like great silent beasts, lay to this side and that of the quick-flowing river. Sometimes he felt stifled by the depth of the Dale, but to-day the fells, steeped in sunshine, stood up as if to shelter this quiet place.

"Montes in circuitu ejus, et Dominus in circuitu populi sui; ex hoc nunc usque in saeculum."

The well known words slipped into his mind so aptly that it was as if someone had heard and answered the thought in his mind, and answering had led him out into a great peace.

As the hills about Jerusalem, and as the hills about the Dale, even so God stood round about His people.

Malle sat back on her heels. "There, Master," said she, "I'll help you stand and bring you to the gate."

"No. No. Wait a minute."

He had never, except that first time when Jack had spoken of them, taken much account of what he had heard of her dreams, or visions, or whatever they were, having heard at the same time that she was but a crazy creature, and knowing how poor folk will make a marvel out of nothing. It was, he thought, a gold chain to a duck's egg that whatever she had seen was but part of her madness. But now, having talked with her, he knew that though she might be simple she was certainly not crazed; and if simple might not God have spoken to her simplicity?

Suddenly, with relief, he felt his own littleness, as he had felt a few moments ago the greatness of that which stood round about to shelter.

He said aloud—but it was to himself that he spoke—"It is sure that God must prevail." And he leaned forward, laying a hand on her shoulder.

"Tell me," he said, "has there been word given to you, or a sign shown, that God will come to our help?"

Malle said:

"There was a great wind of light blowing, and sore pain."

She lifted her head, so that now he could see her face.

He got up hurriedly from the bench; she got up too and stood; it was he who went down on his knees and knelt in front of her on the grass.

After a moment he uncovered his eyes, and drawing a deep breath let it out with, *"Deo gratias!* Then it's true. You saw Him. Tell me."

When she said nothing he instead began to tell her, but as if she knew all about it already, how he needed—"How we all need, we that fear—that think—" He broke off. "I have needed the comfort of that blessed sight which was shown you."

But when she still was silent he cried, as if in anger, "Him that the Jews crucified, you saw ride in triumph. It was in triumph?" He caught at her gown and shook it.

But Malle made no answer. He joined his two hands together and bit at his knuckles, and in a minute got to his feet and without looking at her went heavily towards the gate of the churchyard. She had tried to help him, but he put her by, though gently, so she stood and watched him limp away. He checked once and half turned, for he had remembered that he had given her nothing for her service to him, but he knew that now he could not give her money, so he went on, and found a boy in a red coat and ragged hosen standing looking in at the gate, the bridle of the miller's white pony over his arm, and his eyes like two round O's. When Aske had got into the saddle and was riding off he looked back, and saw the boy speak to a man passing by with a sack of meal on his shoulder. The man dumped the meal, and together they stood staring into the churchyard. When Aske turned again there was a little crowd there, all looking towards the place where he had knelt before the Priory wench, Malle.

August 31

Gib Dawe was wakened just before daylight by a knocking on the door. When he opened he found Perkin a' Court standing outside with a lantern; Perkin was an old man who lived in a hut up Cogden Beck in a very lonely place. He said that his wife was dying and asked Gib to come.

So Gib dressed, and came down again. As he went out of the door the old goodwife, his mother, called sharply, "Gib! Gib!" and he answered her that he was going out. He heard her call again as he shut the door.

The sun was up, but hidden from the Dale in a white, weeping mist when he came back. He took a short cut along the side of one of the hay closes where the aftermath stood pretty tall, and crossed the Swale below the stepping-stones, then up past the Nuns' fishponds with his wet gown slapping uncomfortably against the calves of his legs. He intended to go straight home, break his fast, and only later to return the oil and the Pyx to Church. Let any that saw him disapprove if they chose. Such things to him were superstition, and often his conscience pricked him that for the sake of quiet, and lest the Prioress should deprive him of his benefice, he ever performed such rites.

When he came to the door of the parsonage it was open. He shouted for Wat, but there was no answer. He called to his mother, but got no answer from her either.

When he went in he found her body, wizened, twisted, shrunk, sprawled half out of bed, but she was not in her body any longer. Wat did not come back till suppertime, having an animal's dislike of death.

September 2

Sir John Bulmer and Robert Aske were playing chess in the window of the summer parlour. It was evening and the sharp fierce gold of sunset, pouring through the trees, turned all the leaves to a burning green, while the flies shone gold as they jigged in the light. Through the open casement came the voices of Dame Nan and others of the Ladies who sat together under the apple trees: further off some of the village children were playing a singing game that went to a sweet plaintive tune. Aske sat astride of the bench, very still; when it was not his turn to play he kept his hands on his knees; when he should make a move he bent his head a little lower, and sometimes, if the game went badly, sucked in his cheeks; then he lifted one hand from his knee, made his move, and sat still again. Sir John, on the other hand, was both indecisive and fidgety; he would keep his fingers on a piece, push it this way, set it back, and begin all over again with another; when it was not his turn to play he drummed tunes on the edge of the board. Yet for all that he was a wily opponent, and it was long before Aske murmured softly,

"Ah!" and, having moved a rook, "Check." Ten minutes later he said, "Mate," and raised his arms to stretch them over his head; it was like seeing a bent bow slacked to see the intent look pass from his face.

"You are too good for me," said Sir John.

Aske smiled, "Nay—nay," but then he turned his head to the window; just outside, Sir Rafe and one of the older guests walked up and down along the terrace. They spoke of great matters, and, Aske thought, rashly, making no bones but that they were much discontented with the King's doings. But then, Aske remembered, it was not in the North Country as it was in London, that a man must guard his tongue every minute. He turned back to the room, for Sir John was speaking.

"Anon?" said he.

"Have you ever thought of marrying?"

"Marrying?" Aske was vague.

"They say," and Sir John stared at him as if to read it written upon him, "they say you have a Manor in the South for which you pay your brother eight pounds a year."

"So I have."

"For life?"

Aske said yes, for life.

"And land in Yorkshire—worth twenty pounds a year they say."

"They say too much. But why all this?"

"If you thought to marry— Do you think?"

"I might."

"What would you say to a dower of two hundred marks?"

Aske picked up one of the pieces from the board, and began to rub his finger over it. He had not thought of marriage lately, but the idea was not unpleasant. It had a good settled sound in these unsettled times. "Maid or widow?" he asked.

"Maid," Sir John said.

"And the dower in money or land?"

"Money."

"Who is she?"

"Meg's sister."

"Little July? Surely she's not of an age to be married?"

Sir John said she was fifteen or sixteen at the least. "It's only that she's so lean and small," he said.

Aske looked down at the chess piece in his hand. Such a thing he had never thought of, yet after all why not? He'd promised himself to be good friend to her, and in this manner he would be. He began to smile, partly with amusement, because still the notion seemed comical, but partly also for gentleness.

Sir Rafe and the old man he walked with had come back and were standing just outside the window. The older man was speaking.

"Throgmorton himself told me so. They had spoken in the King's presence how his Grace was troubled in his conscience for his marriage to his brother's wife. And Throgmorton said he feared that if his Grace married Queen Anne his conscience would be more troubled at the length, 'for that it is thought,' said he, speaking to the King's Grace himself, 'that ye have meddled with both the mother and the sister of her.' To the which His Grace replied, 'Never with the mother.' From which it is manifest that His Grace had first the one sister and then the other."

Sir Rafe gave a snort.

"And that if the first marriage was incest, so was the second."

"First the one sister, and then the other . . ." Aske felt his face reddening. He set down the chess piece upon the board and said to Sir John, "No." But then, realizing that he could not let the blank flat negative stand alone, he added, "She is too young for me."

Sir John got up. He stooped over Aske, thrusting his face close. He was a slow man, but he had been on the watch, and he had missed nothing.

"Is that all your reason?" he said, and Aske knew that he was dangerous, and why. As they faced each other eye to eye Aske had time to marvel that suspicion should have lain working in Sir John's mind for so long. But he must think of an answer that would put an end to the business, and yet not be the truth.

He said, with a hard look, "No. If you will have it, I'll not marry with a bastard," and he thought, "How long will it take to work through his thick skull that that is what he has done? And will he then strike me?" He saw in his mind the two of them scrapping together on the floor like a couple of pages. Or would Sir John take his dagger out?

None of that happened. Relief, rather than anger, and some perplexity, perturbed the other's face.

He said vaguely, "Well. Well. If you will not . . ." and went away, leaving Aske to sit alone with the disordered chess board, and to feel reviving within him a deep disgust and anger against himself. It was not that he wished with any vehemence to marry poor little Julian Savage, even now when he knew it impossible, but it went clean against all the grain of his pride that he should be let from marrying her for such a reason.

July was stooping and gathering among the raspberry canes in the dusk. She and several of the servants had been at it all evening since supper, because to-morrow, guests or no guests, Dame Nan was determined to preserve the fruit. July was alone now, the servants having gone in; she intended to fill her basket and then follow them. It was while she was working down the last of the rows that Meg Bulmer came by with Bet. July saw them, but took care that they did not see her. She bent lower and kept very still as they passed by, and as they passed she heard Meg tell Bet that Sir John was speaking to Master Aske of marriage with "that ill-favoured sister of mine," and then Meg laughed and said something else that July did not catch.

After that it took July long to fill her basket, because at first, when Meg had gone, she stood still in a sort of maze, and even when she went to work again she kept forgetting what it was that she was doing, and would come to herself and realize that she was letting the raspberries drop on the ground instead of into the basket.

At first she could hardly take it in. Then she could not imagine that for her such a thing should ever be. Then just because it would be a thing so absolute, so like the perfection and certitude of a completed circle, so contrary to anything which she had ever thought of, like a voice speaking from heaven, she began to contemplate it as a thing which, by its very incredibility, might come true.

She was glad when it was time to go to bed, where she could be private, and lie awake, playing delicately with little imaginings of how it would be if she were Master Aske's wife. She would have a puppy dog. She would make for Master Aske rishaws such as they used to make at the Priory. He and she would take a boat out on the Thames in summer evenings, with green and flowering branches to deck it, and a fiddler and a singing boy to make music. She would walk beside him through London, while he talked and looked down upon her with his bright, laughing eye.

It was late when she went to sleep, and then she dreamed

that she and some others, Meg and Dame Nan and Sir Rafe Bulmer among them, sat together in the Prioress's Chamber down in the Dale, looking out at Calva. One of them asked, where was Gray's Inn? And then Robert Aske was standing close behind her. He laid his arm on her shoulder and pointed out through the window saying, "That way it lies."

That was all. She woke, and lay in a sureness and peace far more profound and potent than any bliss, because among that company she and he had belonged one to the other, and the circle was indeed closed, complete, and of a perfection infinite.

September 7

Rain had washed the sky as clean as if it were made new, and the sun was warm on the wall where the flies basked. Master Aske stood on the terrace below the window of the summer parlour, dressed for riding, with a hood on his head and a cap over that, and the stirrup cup in his hand, for he was leaving this morning. Now as he waited for Will Wall to bring out the horses he talked to Dame Nan and Sir Rafe inside the room.

Dame Nan was teasing him. She was very cheerful with him always, and far more easy than with most others, as if his cheerfulness and ease gave her confidence. It had even, for the moment at least, given her back confidence towards Sir Rafe, and she looked at her husband laughing, as she called Aske "good-for-nothing knave," and then she stretched out her hand and flipped Aske's ear with her finger.

He was just raising the pot of ale to his mouth, and, in trying to dodge, he jogged his elbow on the wall and the ale slopped out. He clapped the pot down on the sill and began to shake the drops from his cuff.

"Now I shall smell like an ale-house. And what a waste of good ale too," he said.

She told him it served him right, and went away laughing, but Sir Rafe said there was no lack of ale at least, and called to July, who was going round among the other guests filling their cups from a pitcher. But the pitcher was just now empty, so, "Go and draw some more for Master Aske," he told her.

She had drawn the ale and was crossing the passage on the way back to the parlour when she saw, through the open door at the end, that Master Aske had left the terrace and was standing under one of the apple trees. Doll was with him and he was reaching down an apple for her, for those on that tree were the earliest of all to ripen. July went out of the door and across the grass to him. He glanced towards her and smiled, but with some constraint, and he affected to be watching Doll who had run off with her apple, so that he was half turned from July as she filled his can again, and only murmured thanks when it was done, without again looking at her.

July stepped back, and then stood still. He was going away. Certainly he must have refused Sir John's offer of her marriage, of which indeed no one had spoken to her from first to last. She did not hope anything now, yet to let him go away without a word was to drown and not cry out for a line to be thrown.

She jerked out, "Sir," and as he turned, stretched a hand towards him, because she wanted so much to have it taken and held, and besides she was unable now to think of anything that she could say.

He looked at her, but did not, or would not, see her hand. Only he smiled again and said, "Good-bye, little July—and thanks for the ale."

She knew that he was trying to put her off, and had never seen him so ill at ease. It gave her courage. "Sir," she said, though in a very small voice, "Sir, they—they—offered you me —to marry?"

He nodded.

"But you will not?"

He said, "No, July," and grew red and went on hurriedly, "I have no thought just now to marry. These are evil times."

That was so far from the reason which she had guessed that she began almost to hope. "Sir," she urged, coming closer, "could you not? I would cost you very little. There's not as much stuff in my gowns by two ells as Alice needs" (that was Dame Nan's elder gentlewoman). "And I can sew and spin; Dame Anne says I spin well when I try. I would try."

To that he could only shake his head.

"I—I can make rishaws. I would make them for you."

At such a child's plea he almost smiled, but, to her, rishaws had brought back the brief hours of that happy night when her castle in Spain had been a house in London with a kitchen in which she herself would make rishaws for him.

She cried, "Oh, why will you not? If you would tell me why not. Is it me—me myself?" If he had looked at her—but he would not look—he would have seen on her face more than a child's misery.

"No," he said. "No." And his voice was so angry and troubled that she whispered, "It does not matter, never mind."

He took no notice of the words, if indeed he heard them. "See here, July," he said. "Let's have a token between us that we are friends and shall be always." He clapped his hand on his pouch as if to find a token there, then looked round, and with a sort of laugh reached up and plucked an apple. "And you shall eat one half and I the other," he said, taking out his knife and splitting the apple. "And we'll plant two seeds, and when next I come to Marrick you shall show me where our two little apple trees grow." He thought he was talking to a child, and smiled down at her, and was glad when she smiled.

They ate the apple standing there under the tree, and when only the core was left he asked, "Where'll we plant the seeds?" She said, "By the bee-hives," and took him there, and knelt to plant them, because she said he must not soil his hands.

So he stood looking down at her while she dug with her fingers into the wet, warm earth, planted the seeds, and patted the place smooth again. When she had done that she still knelt, her hand cupped above where they were buried, while her eyes were on his feet as he stood by her; he had on riding boots of brownish red leather, and there was a patch on one of them; she knew, as she looked, that she loved all of him, from his head to his feet; not that Meg would have recognized it for love, though Will Wall might have. And he was going away; the apple wasn't a token of anything more than that, and the seeds that she had buried in a grave would never live; that was only a foolishness. She crouched there in the sunshine, with a light soft wind touching her face, and with the pleasant murmur of the hives in her ears, but it was on the edges of the world that she knelt, looking over into the naked, lifeless, sunless places.

"July," said Aske suddenly, "there's nothing amiss here, is there? Nan—my kinswoman—your mistress—she's kind?"

She had never before armoured herself against him, but now, in her extremity, she looked up at him with a little smile that cost a huge effort.

"Nothing much amiss. My lady's often out of temper, but what's that? At least she is easy to take in."

"What?"

"She believes whatever we tell her."

July found that what had seemed as bad as it could be was now worse, much worse. A moment ago she had not cared that she should displease him, but now she did care, yet it could not be undone.

He said, "July, you must not tell lies. Never. To no one. Promise me!"

She cried out, "You don't know what you are talking about." Then they heard Dame Nan calling "Robin!" and Sir Rafe also, "Robin! Robin!" and he went away from her quickly, with no more than a muttered word that might have been farewell or anything.

September 8

It was just dark when Aske and Will Wall got home to Aughton. Supper was long over, and the tables taken down in the Hall, but Will went off to the kitchen for his supper, and Mistress Nell had the servants bring cold beef and salad, beer and a dish of apples to the summer parlour for his master.

So Robert Aske sat eating by candlelight, while Dame Nell sewed, Hob, Jack's eldest boy, read and yawned over a book of law, and Julian, his youngest girl, between spurts of sewing, watched her uncle; Julian, fourteen years old now, so unlike her father or mother, being stocky and solid, with a square, dark-browed face, might easily have passed as her uncle's daughter.

Jack Aske sat at the table facing Robert, and told him of all that had happened at Aughton—small beer it would have been for anyone but an Aske, but not for Jack, and not for Robert, though his life had taken him out from Aughton; when he came home again he felt that he and Aughton were no stranger to each other than buckle is to thong. So he munched lettuce and listened, and nodded, putting in a word here and there, or stopped eating and gave his advice at length, whether asked for or not, or teased Jack with the old crusted jokes that went back through many years, and were always the better for keeping. He was very happy to be at home.

But when Julian had been sent off to bed with Mistress Nell's gentlewoman, Jack fell silent, and began to fidget. It was clear that his attention was not on what Robert was saying, though it was in answer to a question he had asked about Rafe Bulmer's sheep.

Then he turned his face to his wife.

"I shall show him the letter," he said.

"I do not see need," said she.

"I am not of your mind in the matter," said Jack, and got up. While he went to the little old coffer in the corner and unlocked it Nell bent her head over her sewing, tightening her lips, and Robert fiddled with the core of an apple on his plate, spinning it about by the stalk, and wishing that Jack would either keep his wife out of his affairs, or not try to bring his brothers in.

Jack came back to the table, and threw down a letter in front of his brother. He leaned over him as he read, a hand on his shoulder.

When he had finished reading Robert laid the letter down on the table, and then flipped it from him with one finger. "Well?" said he.

"Uncle," Hob broke in suddenly, and Robert turned to him. Hob had been christened Robert after old Sir Robert and himself, though, to distinguish, he was never called by his proper name. He was eighteen now and in October the two of them would go up to London together, as the young man was to read law.

"Uncle!" said the lad again, and then, red and stammering a little, "Oh! isn't it shameful this fellow Cromwell should be able to write to whom he will to let him have this or the other for his servants."

"Well," said Robert Aske pleasantly, "he may write—"

"You think I should refuse?" Jack cried, and Mistress Nell in the same breath, "No! No! I told you he would say so. But do not listen."

Jack bade her hush, and repeated, "You think I should refuse, Robin?"

"I did not say so."

"No, but you mean it," cried Hob triumphantly, and his father bade him also be silent.

"Come, Robin," he said, "what's your counsel?"

"You will have it?"

Jack said, "Yea." and Dame Nell got up suddenly and went out. Jack picked up the sewing she had dropped, and flung it on her chair. He looked troubled and sorry, but he said: "Well now—"

So Robert gave his counsel, at length, and with many good reasons, and when he had finished they were all silent. This request of my lord Privy Seal—that a servant of his should have the farm of the 300 acres of the Askes' saltmarsh, near Pevensey—was a small thing, but as a straw which is a small thing, it showed which way the wind blew.

"I said it was a shame," Hob muttered, with his eyes moving between his father and his uncle.

"I shall say nay." Jack stood up. He went close to Robert again, and again laid a hand on his shoulder. "You're right, and Hob's right, saying it's a shame this man should rule over us, changing and breaking, and doing as he will. And," said he, "I see now clearly for the first time, since you have showed us, how greatly and grievously our freedoms have been minished by all these Acts lately passed. Whoever heard before that a man's word should be counted treason?" He looked about the candle-lit room frowning, as though something was in it to disturb and threaten its quiet. Then he said; "Who knows but that the time may come when we must take dreadful measures to amend what has been done amiss."

"God forbid!" Robert Aske muttered.

Hob asked him what he meant, but he only shook his head, and Jack Aske took no notice of what he had said, but repeated, "I shall say him nay."

He got out pen and paper and wrote and sealed it while they sat watching him. Then he put it in his pouch. "Now to bed," said he, "and that's a thing well done."

September 9

Marrick Manor was almost empty of guests now, but not quite. Two remained—if you did not count as guests Sir John Bulmer and his lady—the elderly man who had walked with Rafe on the terrace when Aske and John Bulmer were playing chess, and his wife. Old Sir Christopher might have stayed for ever without putting anyone out, but his lady was a different matter; she talked. All Yorkshire knew how she talked, and Dame Nan, teasing Aske one day, had proposed the question whether Cousin Robin or the lady had the longest tongue. "By the Rood!" said Aske at that, "if there's a doubt I see I must tie knots in mine."

Now, with all the other guests gone, she was more difficult to avoid, while the penalty for being caught was more prolonged, since it was likely that only the horn blown for the next mealtime would bring release. It was for this reason that Sir Rafe had dodged into the shed where the gardener kept his tools and baskets and twine, to lurk there in the brown twilight that smelt of dust and potting soil and dung, and it was for this same reason that Dame Nan, lifting the latch with caution, slid quietly in and as quietly shut the door. They saw each other then, and they laughed.

"What are you doing here?" he asked. "And what are you?" said she. They laughed again, and standing close listened for footsteps. Sir Rafe put his hand to his wife's waist, and she laid hers on it, moving slightly so that she almost leaned on him, though not quite. She turned her head and they smiled at each other.

"Hark!" he whispered.

"What'll we say if—" she murmured, and then came closer yet. In that moment, with all of it unsaid, she was able to renounce the unanswerable, unforgivable words that had burned and swelled in her for months about the woman that he kept at Richmond; nor would she think on the creature again, but things should be as they had once been. And Sir Rafe, also without a word spoken, swore to himself that he'd go no more to that trull. He had, in fact, been tired of her for some time, but it was pleasant to be able to make a virtue of it. He and his wife stood close as boy and girl shyly approaching love, like them wishing to dare more, yet exquisitely content.

When it was safe for them to come out of hiding they went together to look at the new cow-shippon that Sir Rafe was building. Dame Nan had not seen it before, but they must ignore that, because now everything was to be as it used to be. At first she praised all, then was silent, remembering that she had been used to no such insincerities, and at last, forgetting that anything had ever been different, said roundly that this or the other seemed to her to be wrong. And once more, as he had used to listen, Sir Rafe listened to her advice.

So they were at a very sweet accord when they came again into the sunshine, and lingered, willing to prolong their companionship. It was then that she said, "Rafe, I shall tell your brother's—I shall tell Dame Meg to take her sister from here."

"Well," said he, "I never liked her much."

Dame Nan seemed to think more explanation was needed. She was sorry for the girl, she said, a bastard, and with such a sister, and she glanced a little apprehensively at Sir Rafe, whose brother had married that sister.

"Speak not to me of her," said he, in a tone that told his wife she could say what she liked.

"It is my fault. I should not have brought the girl here. She cannot help herself that she is come of such blood. Yet though she is young I doubt she is not as a young maid should be."

"Oh!" Sir Rafe narrowly avoided the mistake of reminding his wife how positively she had proclaimed July's virtue.

"I saw her go up to Robin just before he left. She would not leave him. She stood by him and stretched out a hand to him."

Sir Rafe would have liked to inquire if Aske had taken it, but had sense to see that the question would be untimely. He tried to look shocked, but, disabled by a sudden recollection of his dealings with the trull at Richmond, succeeded only in looking sheepish.

"The way she stood," Dame Nan said disgustedly. "It was pure invitation. Thus—" She showed him how July had stood. Sir Rafe shook his head. It was no use reminding Nan that the girl was too plain to be likely to attract a man, unless one with a very strange taste.

"Is that," he asked, "why you spoke privily to Robin just before he got to saddle?"

She flushed a little.

"He first spoke to me of her. He meant nothing but kindness. He thinks of her still as a child."

"And did you—"

"I said nothing of what I'd seen. But I told him the girl's a liar in grain, and that's a thing he hates worse than any other. 'And,' said I, 'after all, she's Meg Cheyne's sister.' He said, 'I know that.' He was angry but perhaps he'll think of it."

"Well—" Sir Rafe had been going to say, "it's none of our business," but changed it hastily to, "Well, let Meg Bulmer take her sister away."

"When will they go?"

"God knows!" said Sir Rafe.

That evening Meg's woman Bet had the colic, so Dame Nan sent July to help her sister to bed. Meg did not talk about anything in particular while July undressed her and brushed out her hair, except to make fun of Dame Nan, and a little also of Sir Rafe, though she admitted he was a fine figure of a man. "Not so like a well-stuffed sausage as my blossom," she said, and made a face at the curtains of the bed as if Sir John lay there already.

When she was between the sheets she began to talk about Sir John, saying things that would have sent Bet into squeals of delight. July heard them alright, but said nothing, and moved about the room, doing what was necessary, with her black scowling look. At last, as she passed the bed, Meg flung out an arm and caught the skirt of her gown, and then sat up, dragging her nearer, and shaking her a little, angry, but still laughing.

"And you need not behave like a nun now, mistress," she cried. "For if I can I'll have you married before the month's out, and you'll learn such things for yourself, though I doubt your husband will not be so hungry for you as mine is for me."

She felt July stiffen in her hand, and smiled into her face, a malicious, pointed smile.

"Why shouldn't I stay here?" said July.

"Because Dame Nan is sick of you, and will have me take you away. And it is by good fortune that I hear of a bridegroom for you in London, so you shall ride there with Sir John when he goes thither two days hence, on his affairs." When July said nothing Meg asked did she not want to know her bridegroom's name.

"It does not matter," said July.

"Fie!" cried Meg, "and that and a scowl is all the thanks I get for trouble enough. Here am I, doing a sister's part, with Sir John grudging all the time to lift his hand from your dowry." Then she laughed and said, "It's as well you don't care to know his name, for by the Mass! I've forgotten it. But he's a man of substance—a widower. It is his dead wife's brother that has writ to me so timely, asking could I help his brother-in-law to a good sober wife. He says he remembers me well, but I can call neither of them to mind, though he says he is one of William Cheyne's friends."

"Oh!" cried July.

"Well, you must be content. I'd have done better for you if I could. Aye, and you know not what, nor how well I would have done. Far above your deservings I'd have set you, with one I myself might have matched with had he not been a younger son with little gold in the kist. If it does not matter who it shall be, will you know who it should have been, only that he would not take you?"

July did not speak, but Meg told her, "Robin Aske! There! And now will you thank me for that, though, for no fault of mine, he would not." When July stood silent Meg flung her away with a push. "There's gratitude for you," she said.

"I know," said July, "why he would not."

Meg gave her a sharp look and then began to laugh very much.

"God's Mother, that you do not."

"By God!" July said, and for once the proud Stafford spoke in her, "I do. It is because I am your sister."

Meg was silent, staring at her.

"Who told you then? Did he? No, for he said he never had nor would tell any. Mother Judde? Did she tell you he came to me one night when Sir John was away?"

"I'll not believe it."

At the shrinking horror in July's face Meg stared again.

"How then? You did not know. Then what did you mean when you said he would not because you're my sister?"

She saw how July shook, and began to nod her head and to laugh. "Lord! You thought that it was because your sister's a wicked wanton he'd have none of you. But, you see, you're wrong, for I was good enough for him. Good enough? I was his bliss and his heaven."

She grabbed July again, and peered at her closely. "Jealous, sister?" she whispered.

July was not jealous, because what Meg had had from Robert Aske she nor knew nor thought anything of. But she saw the candle flames reflected bright and trembling, in Meg's eyes; she could smell her bare, warm flesh, and the perfume of orris that she used, and she shut her own eyes because she felt sick.

Meg smiled at her blind face and shook her gently to and fro.

"Nay," said she, "but I think I know indeed why he would not have you. He said to me it was because it would be incest, after he had had me. But I think the truth is that he would not because he wants me still, and fears he could not command himself were he too often near me. Poor Robin! Poor fool!" she purred, and smiled and sighed.

July opened her eyes.

"He hates you," she said. Watching him as she did, and

having by heart every expression of his face and tone of his voice, she knew that.

"Hate lies close to love, they say," said Meg lightly.

July said, "*I* know it doth not."

Then Meg began to shake her, crying, "Take your eyes from me, little black-faced witch that you are."

Outside the door July lingered a few moments on the dark stair before she went to serve Dame Nan, for her knees were shaking.

It was no wonder, she thought, that he hated Meg. But he did not need to hate so perfectly, with such a deadly killing hate as July. If Meg had not caught him in that way that July had seen her catch other men—and yet she, July, did not know how—"If Meg had not caught him," she thought, "he might have taken me. He might."

It was a while later that she remembered she was to marry one of Master Cheyne's friends.

September 10

When Gib drew near the churchyard he paused. In the woods the highest branches of the trees swung in the wind, but below they hung still and heavy, burdened with rain; and there was quiet, except for the sound of fat drops falling. But from ahead there came the noise of shouting and hallooing, with barking of dogs; it might have been that the last of the corn was being cut, and the boys and dogs setting on after rabbits, had the day been one of harvest weather.

Yet when he reached the stile to the churchyard and looked in he saw that it was indeed some of the reapers who shouted and laughed—strangers these were who came from over the hills to work for hire, and who were keeping about the Priory now, waiting for the weather to clear so that they could finish the barley.

They and their dogs were after game too, though the game was not rabbits but the woman Malle, who stood in the angle of a buttress, threshing about her with a rake to keep the curs off, while the men threw sticks and small stones at her shouting, "Hue! Hue! Run, wench, run!"

A few of the Marrick hinds had been watching it all from the shelter of the wall. They came out as Gib climbed the stile, looking at once surly and sheepish. The Lady, they said, had bid the bailiff turn off Malle, and when she would not go the bailiff had set the strangers and their dogs on her.

As they spoke Gib's eye was drawn, by a slight movement there, to the window of the Prioress's chamber which looked out this way. Dame Anne Ladyman, scared and truly shocked, had peeped out and as quickly withdrawn. But Gib thought that the Lady was looking out upon her handi-work—though furtively—and the obliquity and tyranny of women, running together in his mind, were not to be endured.

"God's Passion! The Lady!" he cried. Here was rule. Here was power. Here was one of the worldly rulers of the darkness of this world. Then her he would defy. Against her he would wrestle manfully.

He ran forward shouting. One man he caught with a buffet on the ear; the other he tripped up, more by chance than design, as the fellow backed away. No more than that was needed. Gib was left alone with Malle; behind him the Marrick hinds saw the reapers off; they were glad to have the poor wench ridded, though they had not liked to risk the Lady's anger by doing it themselves.

"Now," said Gib, well pleased with himself, "you may go safe."

But she did not move.

"Go," he said again, and waved his hands towards the gate.

"Whither?" she asked him, as if he could tell her.

Half Gib's mind remembered the shifts and discomforts that there had been at the parsonage since the old woman, his mother, had died; the other half chewed triumphant upon the rich iniquity of Prioresses, who drove out poor wretches to starve.

"If you will," said he, "you shall come home with me. I need a servant to tend the house." He looked up towards the Lady's window and shook his fist that way, then wished that he had used a gesture more suitable to an ecclesiastic. He nodded to Malle with a stern look and went into the Church. Let her wait for him or go otherwhere as she chose.

While he said his Office he heard a sound at the door which was not one of the sounds of the rising wind outside. He turned to look over his shoulder, and frowned, seeing Malle come in and peer about. She came no nearer though. A little after this it struck him that he did not know why the Prior-ess had turned her away. If it was for thieving—well—he'd find that out from her; he would shelter no thieves, no, nor a loose woman, if that had been the trouble. So he went on with the office, while the wind snored in the tower and whistled shrilly through a broken pane in the vestry; when

[425]

he paused for a moment he could hear the turmoil of the beaten woods outside.

He found Malle sitting by the door. She stood up and bobbed to him.

"Now," he said, speaking sternly, "tell me this. Why are you turned out?"

"For that which I saw."

"For that which you saw? What did you see?" he asked her, though he knew well all the talk of her seeing Our Lord Himself riding the pedlar's donkey over Grinton Bridge. He had sworn to himself that he would never speak to her of it, telling himself that if he heard her speak the words, presumptuous, blasphemous, he would come near to striking her down for her wicked folly. But the fact was he dared not take the risk of finding that so poor an ignorant creature as she, had in truth seen this wonder. Now, suddenly, because of the pride of the Prioress, and because he had routed the fellows she had set on, he dared take the risk. And if the thing were true he would make it ring in all men's ears; they should not silence him. They—

"Come!" he said.

She was silent, standing with her hands hanging and head bent.

"Come!" he said more sharply, and brought his face close to hers, for it had grown very dark in the church.

He drew back, blinking. It was not that there was any brightness in her face, seen dimly in the dusk. Rather it was as if, peering at her, he had looked into some shadowed secret place in the woods, and there found the scent of violets, or heard water running sweetly.

Malle said:

"There was a great wind of light blowing, and sore pain."

Gib found himself bumping against the sharp corner of the Founder's tomb, and only then knew how he had turned from her and moved blindly away. He gripped the edge of the chiselled stone while his thoughts ran this way and that in confusion. He was hugely angry, and glad. He was angry because she had seen this thing; he was glad of the thing which she had seen. He was far more angry with the rich and great whom Christ in His righteousness had come to judge. "Now," he thought, "we shall see the day of wrath for those who turn their faces from the Gospel. Now the Lord comes once more, wearing a poor man's coat, and poor men will follow Him."

He came back to Malle.

"This means that the hour is come. In this vision God speaks through you to me. It is time I lay my hand to the plow. It is time I go out from the Dale to proclaim the day of the Lord. This was the meaning of that other showing."

He saw himself, gaunt and fierce as one of the ancient prophets, preaching and exhorting endlong and overthwart all England. "I shall be greater than Trudgeover," he thought. "I shall be a new Fore-runner. I shall tell them of the crowd of poor men that went along the road, jostling and thrutching, tearing down of branches, throwing down of coats, crying 'Osanna.'"

"That is the meaning of what you saw," he said to Malle again, and more urgently.

"The day of the Lord. Osanna," he almost shouted at her. But Malle made no answer.

He caught his hand to his breast like a man who has run on steel. "Osanna!" he said again, but in a faint and shaken voice, and laying his finger on the door-latch lifted it.

At that the wind burst into the church, snatching the door from his hand and sending it clattering back against the wall. The flames of the lamps on the screen of the Founder's Chapel rocked and streamed aside; even the light on the Rood-loft of the Nuns' Church leapt up, so that the dimness was filled with the noise of wind and the pulsations of living light.

Gib stepped out, his head down against the wind. "Osanna," he had cried at Malle, and had remembered that that was the word by which the children greeted the Son of David in the Temple of God. All those children crying "Osanna" in Jerusalem, and one child here, the dumb half savage brat who was Gib's son. Not for Gib to guide the plow or sow the seed for Christ's harvest. It was not Gib's voice which should sound through the King's realm, nor his name that should be feared by the wicked and the great. He must stay in Marrick, shackled, like any grazing beast on the sykes, to the clog that kept it from straying. Wat was the clog, the child that Gib might not leave, and could not come anywhere near to loving.

He looked over his shoulder. Malle followed slowly after him, unquestioning as any dog; the wind beat at her skirts and flapped her kerchief across her face.

"She saw nothing!" he told himself. "Nothing! Nothing!"

But as his feet squelched on through the deep mire of the

road it was to the tune of other words that repeated themselves in his mind against his will—

"Depart from me! Depart from me! If any should offend against the least of these little ones—"

September 14

Kit Aske had come home to-day from the Earl of Cumberland's Household, and directly after dinner he must go out and see how the new church tower was getting on. The tower was his tower; it had been his idea to rebuild it, and stone, timber, and work were being paid for by him. He was passionate for it, as if it were a living creature and his child.

So he was all in a fidget to be off and see how it had grown, and wanted Jack to go with him. But Jack had a great cold, and Dame Nell would not let him out, so instead Robin must come. They went off together through the orchard and across the bridge over the moat. Kit, though he went nowadays a little bent and limping, was ahead all the way and kept on saying, "Come, Robin! Come on!"

At the churchyard wall they stood back to get a good view, and to be clear of all the masons' and carpenters' stuff that lay about. It was a fine stalwart tower, not high but strong; broad based, with splayed buttresses at the corners. It looked as though it had strode out of the very verge of the marsh, and there stood, defying the waters.

"Your tower'll last, Kit," said Robert Aske. "We shall not see him come tumbling down in a gale." That had been the end, three years ago now, of the old tower.

Kit was pleased.

"And look," he pointed up, "my name in stone to tell who was the builder." High up on the wall there were shields of arms carved, and the words, *"Christopher second fils Robert Aske Chevalier. Oublier ne doy. Anno Domini 1536."*

They went nearer, through the piled sand and lime and the stacks of clean planks, meaning to go about the church to look at the new work from the other side. But just under the tower they met the master mason, with a bit of oily rag in one hand and a chisel in the other. So they stayed talking to him with the wind whipping the skirts of their coats while the sun went behind heavier cloud, and a few driven spatters of rain flew by them.

The master mason, who was a sad-looking little man with a rare smile that gave him, while it lasted, the look of an old and wise child, was very deferential to Kit, promising that the work should be finished in a few weeks now, and taking Kit's chiding for the slowness of it with a chastened air. But just as the brothers were going on he looked to Robert and smiled.

"And have you found your aske, Master, that you bade me carve you on a stone?"

"I?" said Robert. "Did I so?"

"That you did. For you said if there was the name of one Aske carved up there, so should there be an aske out of the fen carved for to remember you by. So there I carved him for you," and he pointed behind them, where low down on the west wall of the tower an aske, as the fen-men called a newt, wriggled his tail across a stone.

"Why," Robert cried, "so I did. I remember it now," and he began to laugh, and then, seeing Kit's face, checked himself.

Kit was very angry. "God's Death! To deface my tower with such foolishness!" His passion startled the master mason, who stepped back before him. Kit even had his fist raised, but Robert stepped in between, hastily, so that his shoulder jogged Kit's chest.

"Easy, Kit," said he.

"Easy!" cried Kit in a high, furious voice.

Robert heard the mason clicking his tongue soothingly in the background.

"If there's blame it's mine," he said. "But indeed—" he shrugged because really it was so small a thing, and one he had never intended, his words to the mason having been of the idlest.

" 'Indeed?' Yea indeed. Indeed it is you, always, all the time, spoiling my works, making mock of me behind my back."

"Dear, dear, dear!" the master mason lamented softly and distressfully as Kit went limping away from them. "Would I had not done it, but I thought—"

"Think no more of it. It is nothing," Robert said in a loud and cheerful voice, so that Kit should hear.

For he was angry too, and that which he called "nothing" was to him, as to Kit, all the past rolled into a ball—all their bickerings, emulations, angers, grudgings—present with them again; for these, like wood-lice under a stone, needed only a touch to wake and set them squirming and busy.

After he had talked a while, to hearten and console the master mason, he went off, not to the house, being too sorely out of temper for that, but round about to the workshops. He was thinking that all the sins that Kit must be hoarding against him, and he could remember quite a string of them, going back and forth through the years—a broken bow, a page torn in a book, a gold button borrowed and lost—all these, he thought to himself, don't amount to the price of a man's eye.

He found Will Wall at work in the carpenter's shop sharpening a knife on the grindstone. He nodded to him, then went over to a corner where there was an iron pot containing an ill-looking black mixture; he croodled down on his heels by it, to see the better, and picking up a chip of wood from the floor, lifted the lock of hair, taken from Jack Aske's white horse's tail, out of the mixture of strong ale and soot in which it was steeping. It had lain in soak for a day and a night but yet it was not dark enough to twist into a line fit for fishing in the black cloudy waters of the marsh land.

He was staring at it moodily, when the slithering, petulant hiss of the grindstone ceased, and Will spoke.

"Master," said he, "I was over to Thicket yesterday."

Aske did not turn his head nor answer.

"They've been stripping the lead off the Nuns' Church, and the rain's come through something cruel."

"There's puddles all about the altar," he said.

Aske got up and went over to the bench. He began to root about in the litter there.

"Where's that whoreson quarrel needle?" he muttered, and having found it began to work the bellows of the little fire till the soft ash flew about.

"God's Body!" he cried suddenly, and let the bellows die on a long breath. "What of it then? So I suppose will it be in many a church these days."

Will came over to him, and taking the horn-tipped handle of the bellows began to blow gently and persuasively, till the tiny heart of red in the fire had spread through the whole. Aske gave him a quick glance, and then set the quarrel needle between the tongs and thrust it into the fire. They watched in silence while the little black thing changed and brightened till it was indistinguishable from the glowing charcoal. Aske drew it out and began to work on it with a knife. "I want a small fishhook," he said gruffly to Will, and left him, to quench the quarrel in a pail of water.

It was not till it was again glowing and sparkling, and Aske was bending it to a hook, that he spoke again.

"Why do you say this to me?"

[430]

"Because—is it— Master, in your conscience, do you think it is right?"

Aske stopped his work with the hammer. He took a long while to answer. Then he said, "In my conscience, I think it is not right."

"Then—"

This time Aske did not give Will time to finish.

"It is the great lords temporal that must bear the blame. It was for them to take such order that this should not have come to pass. It's for them to amend it."

"But, Master, will they amend it?"

Aske laughed shortly. "God knows what they will do."

"And if they do not?" Will watched him with an underlook, then said, "They're saying that if none else dare, then the gentlemen and the poor commons must amend it."

Aske tossed down the hammer on the bench and stood staring out of the window, but knowing nothing of what he saw.

"That," said he at last, "would be rebellion against the King."

"But," Will mumbled, "there's the King's King, Master, to think on."

Aske turned to him with a look that seemed startled, and went away out of the workshop as if he had not heard.

But it was this chiefly, of all that Will had said, which was in his mind that evening when Jack, Kit and he were standing about with Nell and Master Thomas Rudston and his wife, who were staying at Aughton. They had their wine cups in their hands, and the candles stood lit and ready on the sideboard to carry up to bed. But there they stood disputing, as they had disputed for the past hour, and like dogs in a fight, not one of them would break away for long enough to let the dispute stop.

What they were arguing was all the same that Will had meant, and yet was totally different. For on the one side, they spoke of the poverty of the North, and how the King's taxes were too heavy and might not be paid, and how much of the relief of the poor commons was in the Abbeys, who would suffer sorely by their suppression—such was the line which Jack, Master Rudston and Robert Aske took. But Kit spoke of how the King's will must be done or the realm fall into confusion, and that there was much to be reformed among the spiritual men, and that heretics would before long be put down, and nothing but the lordship of the

Pope broken in England, and that perhaps only for a time. Of the two ladies Mistress Rudston said nothing, but Nell Aske cried Kit on, and now and again gave Robert glances of fury.

"Furthermore," said Mr. Rudston, "there is this Statute by which the King may bequeath the Crown to whom he will. That's no good thing," and he turned to Aske as to another lawyer, for they were both men of Gray's Inn. Aske shook his head.

"And on the other hand," Mr. Rudston continued, "there's a Statute to forbid us willing our lands to any but our heirs, which is injustice manifest."

"Aye," said Robert Aske, seduced once more into the argument by the fascinating complexities of the law—"Aye, but, as I think, as there are now more ways than there were before this Statute to defeat the King of his right—" and he plunged into a subtle and ingenious exposition to which even Nell Aske listened with respect, and all the others, saving Kit, with approbation. But Kit broke into it.

"Lord!" he cried. "Hark to Mr. Justice Aske declaring the law," and he slammed his wine cup down on the sideboard and snatched up his candle and went away upstairs.

In a few minutes the rest came after, Nell first with her chin high and a stiff, flushed look on her face, the Rudstons next, and Jack and Robert last. Robert, stealing a glance at his eldest brother, could smile, though sourly, to think that the Rudstons alone would find peace in their bed, for Jack must go to Nell, and he and Kit were sharing a room together.

Kit was already in shirt and hosen when Robert came into the room. He said he'd sent away Mat, his servant, "And that's a pity," thought Robert, setting his candle down.

"I always think," Kit said behind him, in a soft, unpleasant voice, "that with you, Robin, it matters little what's right or wrong, what's good or ill, so that you can play on it to show your wit."

Robert swung round.

"Oh! That's what you think?"

"So you will egg on Jack and others to talk treason enough to hang us all."

"God's Blood!" Robert threw back at him, with equal unpleasantness. "And if any hang it will be that you have informed against them. For, but yourself, there was none that thought other than as I said."

And then they were standing in the middle of the room

[432]

shouting at each other, while their shadows crawled up the walls and shrank down as the flames of the candles were flung by their furious gestures.

At last Robert tried to get a hold on himself—

"Mass!" he said. "Kit, let's leave it at that."

"Aye," Kit sneered, "because you can't deny but it is treason against the King you have been saying."

Robert threw his hands wide, as if to ask an invisible witness to bear him out that he had tried to disengage from the quarrel.

"But I can deny it. And if it were true there's a worse thing than treason. Hark you, Kit, it was a poor man of the commons said to me but to-day, 'There's the King's King, Master, to think on.'"

"A poor man of the commons?" cried Kit. "You give such fellows leave to come and grudge and mutter to you? Why? Shall they rise, and choose you to be their leader forsooth?"

Robert had his fist clenched. He was glad indeed to find that Will had come into the room and was standing behind them. How much Will had heard he did not know, and anyway it did not matter. The great thing was that the interruption had come in time to prevent him striking Kit.

"Be off with you, Will," said he, and, turning from Kit, sat down on the bed and began to take off his shoes and unlace the gussets of his hosen. Kit went on talking, but Robert kept his face like wood, and after a while Kit gave it up and they got to bed in silence.

September 17

Four men, Will Wall, the Miller from Ellerton, an Aughton yeoman and a stranger, a man out of Lincolnshire, were hanging with their elbows over the gate of Goose Green Close where a dozen of the Askes' horses were grazing; these had been brought up out of the ings earlier in the day, because all three Aske brothers, and Master Hob too, were leaving tomorrow, early, for Ellerker, to get a fortnight's cub hunting with the cousins there before Robert Aske, and his nephews, Hob Aske and young Jack Ellerker, started for London to keep the law term.

As the four leaned on the gate it was the Lincolnshire man who was talking. He was a thin fellow, red as a fox, with quick eyes, and quick wits in his narrow head. He had come, he said, from Louth (they'd heard of Louth?) and he came to Yorkshire, said he, because brothers and neighbours should help each other. "For now there be things devised against the commons too grievous to be borne, as that every man shall be sworn what goods he hath, and if he have more than so much all his goods shall be taken away. Likewise there is a Statute made that none shall eat white bread, goose nor capon, but if he pay pennies to the King. Likewise another that none shall be christened, wedded nor buried but at the price of a noble. For these days there is a sort of Lollards and traitors that rule about the King, and have brought him to such a covetous mind that if the Thames flowed with gold and silver it would not quench his thirst."

The Miller and the Aughton yeoman could only murmur approval, but Will Wall, as one who knew London, and moved in learned circles there, was more forward. He had, he said, heard his master declare that the Statute of the King's Supremacy was an evil Statute because by it came division from the Church Catholic, and that no king before this king had had the cure of souls. "And I have heard other gentlemen too—"

The Lincolnshire man interrupted impatiently, "Fie on your gentlemen! For what will they do but talk? I'd have none of them. There are in Lincolnshire who say 'We must have gentlemen to lead us.' But I say 'Nay.' For if they would lead us it should be for no longer than serves their own purses and purposes, and then they will fall away, betraying us so that they can save their necks while ours stretch in a halter."

Will cried, "That's not my master!" and the Miller and the yeoman backed him up, and they began to tell the Lincolnshire man stories about Master Robin, all trifling, but to them these trifles had significance. He listened, fidgeting, and waiting to take up the word again. But it was Will who interrupted by jerking the Miller in the ribs and muttering, "Here he comes."

They all turned at that. Robert Aske was coming towards them over the sharp, springing stubbles that showed yellow and shining in the new deep green of the reaped fields; he had a capful of corn in his hand. He nodded to them as they made way for him, cast a sharp glance on the Lincolnshire man, and opened the gate. They watched him in silence, and as though he were a strange sight, and because he gave them no second look, and no word at all, they felt that somehow, though he could not have heard what they said, he must know the subject of the Lincolnshire man's discourse. They let him go halfway across the field towards the horses and then slunk away along the hedge.

It was not that, however, which had made Aske keep his mouth shut, and pass them with only a nod. It was because he saw that the Lincolnshire man was a stranger and of no stranger did he want to ask, "What news?" since in these days all was bad news. So he went on to where the young mare moved slowly, switching her tail against flies as she cropped, and keeping a soft, wild eye on him as he drew near. When he reached her she lifted and shook her pretty head, whinnying, and then nuzzled in his cap for the corn. He stood for quite a long time, smoothing his hand down her neck till his fingers were dusty and sticky from the warm, dusty hide. When he looked back to the gate there was no one there. He was relieved; then he thought, with a sharp misgiving, "Had that fellow news?" and then, "Mass! I shall put it all by for this fortnight at the least."

When the Aughton men and the stranger left the gate of Goose Green Close one of them suggested that they should drink together before they set the man from Lincolnshire on his way. But as they went they began to jangle, so that they parted before the door of the ale-house was reached. The cause of their disagreement was that Will had begun again on the subject of Master Robin.

"And if you had him to your leader," said he, "in the stead of this one you call the Cobbler—"

"Pooh!" the stranger interrupted. "Him! A little man like that with but one eye, and too proud withal to speak to common men!"

The Miller put him right on the last point. "It's not his way to pass without a word. Most times he'd have come and set his shoulder to the bar of the gate and stood among us to talk. But if he'd wind of your business—"

"Fie then—" the Lincolnshire man began, but thought best to leave the rest unsaid. "Well," said he, "by your leave I may say he's a man of no great station nor worship, and of a name unknown."

They told him, angrily, that if Master Aske were not known in *his* country, "yet there's many in Yorkshire knows him; all this countryside, and by Wressel to Beverley and south to Humber. And in Swaledale too."

"Aye," says Will grandly, "and further north yet, to the Border itself, and wherever the Percy's name runs. For in his young years my Master was of the Earl's Council, and for all he was young the old Earl leant much on him."

"So," the Miller summed it all up, "though he's a little man, and one-eyed, a lawyer and no knight, we'd sooner go out behind his back than any other's, and we'd know that he'd die with us if it came to the pass."

"How'd ye know that?" the Louth man sneered.

They could not say how they knew, only that they did know.

"And," said one of them, "it's my belief you could hack Master Robin into gobbets, and every one of them'd tell the same tale, and that'd be the truth. And you couldn't make them gobbets hold their tongues neither."

September 24

There was a sharp knocking on the door of the Prioress's Chamber and one that she did not know, though she knew the manner in which every one of the Ladies, or of the servants would knock. When she cried out to come in, in came Piers, Sir Rafe's elder page. He pulled his cap off, shut the door behind him and stood against it, his eyes and cheeks very bright; it was plain that he had been running.

"I could not steal the pony. So—I ran," he said with gasps, and she stood up, crying out, "What is it? Is it news?"

He nodded.

"I heard Sir Rafe say it to my lady when he had read the letter. He'll send a message to you but I came out to tell you quick."

"What was it you overheard?" Now she would know whether Marrick should stand or fall.

"I was waiting upon them. I did not overhear it. They knew I was there," he corrected her.

She did not care for that, although he did. "What?" she cried.

"Sir Rafe said, 'Here's from my brother. He hath done the Lady's business for her. The King hath given licence that Marrick shall continue. There's his seal.'"

"Ah," cried the Prioress on a deep breath, and then, "The King's Seal? You're sure?"

"Sure!" said the lad, and he grinned at her, friendly and impudent, and the bearer of these tidings. For a second she thought to kiss him, and he knew it. She saw how he stiffened and flushed, and instead she held out her hand. "No. Not to kiss, but to take you by the hand for a good true friend," she said, as he ducked his head with an awkward bob to kiss it. So they shook hands together smiling at each other, and she smiled inwardly with amusement and with pleasure.

"I am glad," he said, out of his young simplicity. "I'm all for the monasteries to stand, and I think it shame that the King should be in the hands of such a rascal as Cromwell. They say, and indeed I think it's full likely, that there'll be rebellion soon if he should continue about the King. The great lords, they say, will take up arms to compel the King to put him away. That would be a thing to see," and he looked at her, gaily as a robin.

"Aye," said the Prioress. She did not want rebellion, since Marrick was to continue, but she was not going to damp the boy's anticipations. She let him talk, in a very grown-up strain, and with his eyes dancing, of how this Lord and that was said to have harnessed men ready in his lands. She said, very gravely from time to time, "Truly?" and, "You think even so?"

At last he remembered how time was passing, and gave a whistle, and said he'd get a box on the ear if he didn't get back quick. She kept him while she got out from the coffer a bag of money, and putting two angels into her own little silk purse gave it to him—"For bringing me good news."

He kissed her hand this time, and went out. She heard him go whooping down the outer stair in two bounds.

After a little while she followed him. The evening was coming in still and overcast, with the fells showing damson-blue through the rainy air. Summer had gone by. There was over all a sense of returning, of withdrawing, of coming home, so that even the poached mud of the Great Court seemed to speak of quiet. Winter was to come, but the world was ready; like a dormouse it was curling itself up. And the little world of the Priory would light its fires, bar its shutters and snuggle down safe at home. Even though gales tore through the gaping doors and empty rooms of other less fortunate Houses of Religious, Marrick would snuggle down, safe and permanent.

She went towards the gate-house, meaning to look out and along the Dale—much as the dormouse may look out, to taste more sweetly the comfort of his security. One of the women was feeding the hens. She tossed the good corn out in handfuls, then emptied out the last of it from the wooden measure; it rattled on the stiff wing feathers of the nearer birds. They were all dipping and dabbing at it on the ground; fussing, quarreling, clucking, gobbling as quick as they might. Among the hens a few pigeons sidled, swinging their tails.

The Prioress came to the gate-house arch and saw, striding along outside on his way back from Grinton, with a full poke slung from a stick on his shoulder, Sir Gilbert Dawe.

Because, if she spoke to him, it must be to rebuke him for letting the altar linen get dirty and also spotted with damp; and because tonight all should be peace, she turned hastily back as if she had not seen him and went in and up to her chamber.

But Gib knew she had seen him, and snorted aloud with indignant laughter. Had she let him come up with her he would have denounced her: her tyranny, her love of money, her easy living, her cruelty to the poor creature Malle. But she feared him. She had fled from him.

The triumph of that thought warmed him. He refused to consider what the presence of Malle in his house did indeed mean. It meant that there was a woman to do the woman's work, but it meant a woman's tongue too. It had never entered his head—even if he had stayed to think it never would have entered his head—that the woman could speak except to answer him when he chose to speak to her.

But she talked to Wat, cheerfully, foolishly, endlessly.

September 26

On the evening before his wedding Master Laurence Machyn dressed himself in his best doublet of yellow cloth faced with grey sarcenet, and taking with him the brother of his late wife, he went to greet his bride, who had been brought to London by Sir John Bulmer, and left in the charge of Sir John Uvedale and his lady.

It was Laurence's brother-in-law who shouted to the servants at the Cardinal's Hat to find Sir John Uvedale; and his brother-in-law who so took the lead in conversation with Sir John's lady, that she thought for several minutes that he was the groom. Even when she learnt that he was not she tended to address to him all the complexity of her explanations—how her husband and Sir Rafe Bulmer were acquainted because both had been in the Household of the poor little Duke of Richmond, that sweet child, alas too early taken—and so Sir John Bulmer had entrusted the young gentlewoman to her, but, alas! to-day is the poor young maid sick—

"Sick!" Laurence's brother-in-law boomed, so that both Laurence and the lady jumped; and she explained hastily that it was no contagious sickness, but merely a disordered stomach, "but she retches so sore I would not bid her come down to greet ye."

"No. No," said Laurence hastily, speaking almost for the first time.

"Jesu!" the lady ran on, "it is but the weariness of the journey and her fears maybe, and time will mend all. Yet perhaps it was enough to scare the child, to be brought so suddenly to her marriage. But Sir John could not wait, and there was but two days for her to prepare, and so here she is with no more than six good shifts of her own, and a bundle of her sister's gowns that's far too big for her, but that was all there was time to provide, and they can be cut down. Not that the shifts aren't good and fine, and I told her a husband loved better that his wife should bring to her marriage good shifts that he alone should see, rather than great plenty of outward gear that other men should admire, and nothing but patches and rents beneath. So I said to comfort her, but—"

She had to stop there because Laurence's brother so slapped his thigh and roared out a laugh crying, "Marry! but that's good counsel for a bride. Marry! but that's good."

They did not stay long after that, and Master Laurence's brother-in-law was still laughing as they took their leave; his laughter and his big voice filled the courtyard of the Cardinal's Hat, so that men and maids turned from their work to look at him. Sir John Uvedale's lady's gentlewoman looked too, peeping out from the window of the room upstairs where July lay limp and abject.

"Hark, there he goes, your groom," she cried, and opened the casement to watch the better. "Such a big man," she told July, "with black hair that bristles on his head. And that's his voice—great as a bull's. Do you hear it?"

July said faintly, yes, she heard it.

"But who is it goes with him? Is he a widower? Hath he a son?"

July murmured that she had been told that he was a widower, but of a son she knew nothing.

"Well," said the woman, shutting the window, "you must rest you now, and sleep well while you may, for such a man will give you no rest to-morrow's night."

July shut her eyes. She felt ill enough to die, but had no

hope to be so lucky. It was a few moments later that she drove herself to ask, "What manner of man is he?"

"Big. Black—as I told you."

"But of countenance and favour?"

The gentlewoman had not seen more than his back so could not say. July was left to picture an ogre, huge as a bull, and black-bristled, yet with the gleaming, thin malevolence of a friend of William Cheyne.

September 28

Master Laurence Machyn lived in Knightrider Street, almost next door to the Church of St. Andrew in the Wardrobe. The house from the front looked very small, because Laurence's grandfather, who had built it, had squeezed it in between a fishmonger's house on one side and on the other a much older house of stone, which had belonged to the Black Prince, but which now had a shoemaker's sign—the Cow & Garland—hung over its stately but half ruinous gate.

Inside, the Machyns' house was larger than it looked. You came, by the door from the street, to the passage beside the screens, with the great chamber opening off on the right. There had been no room to build the kitchen and offices opposite the screens in the usual way, so these—a kitchen, a little buttery and a pantry—lay at the back of the house through a door opposite the street door. Upstairs there was quite a big solar over the great chamber, and leading off that the bedroom in which Laurence Machyn had been born, and in which last night he and his bride had been bedded. Above there were smaller rooms where two of Laurence's men and three serving women slept, and one little empty attic where an old chest and a couple of trussing coffers were stored.

Behind the house, opposite the kitchen, stood the long workshop where the men made the coffins, for Laurence, who belonged to the Guild of the Merchant Taylors, furnished forth burials. A woodstore opened out of it, and above was a dark loft, where the candles, big and little, were stacked, some as stout as flails, some no thicker than ash twigs. In presses there, kept under lock and key, there were palls of rich stuff which Laurence hired out; being for rich dead men they were very fine, woven with gold among the colours; lesser folk would hire a pall from their parish church, but those, of course, were not so splendid. Sometimes the loft was gay with the painted buckram shields that Laurence had

had painted to be carried after the dead, and always, hanging on pegs, there were black gowns worn by poor men who followed the dead, carrying the lighted candles and banners.

Pinched in between the buttery and the workshop, and enclosing a little yard where there were flowers, mixed up with parsley, thyme, sage, pennyroyal and other kitchen stuff, there was a brew-house, and if you went past that by a covered passage you came to a little garden. Most of it was taken up by an old mulberry-tree, but along one wall there was an alley built with poles and planted with honeysuckle and with a vine that bore tiny grapes like green beads.

July wakened in the big bed in the room off the solar. The curtains were drawn close but she could see that there was daylight beyond them. She started up, then, because of a sick faintness, lay down again, and buried her face in the pillow and cried.

Yet that she could cry at all meant that the worst had not come upon her. If it had been as she had feared she must have hardened herself to stone or to cold iron. As it was she could cry. For when they had brought her to church and she had made as if to give her hand to the big, black-bristled man, it had been taken by another, not indeed very attractive to look at, since he was lean and light, with pale brown sparse hair, and a thin face with a ridiculously large mouth. When he smiled his smile was more gentle than merry, and he showed very black and bad teeth, which made his breath unpleasant to her when he kissed her. But at least he was not alarming like the other, and nothing at all like William Cheyne.

Yet even so, and though during the feasting and the dancing she caught him sometimes looking at her with a kind look, the day had been a nightmare of fears and sickness, and then came the night. Now she lay with her face hidden. She did not realize how great his forbearance had been, but, as she thought of that night, she believed she had not slept at all till the light came, for even when he slept she had lain awake hearing the bells from the Black Friars' Church ring so loud that they might have been in the room.

Now they rang again, and other bells, more distant, on this side and that, with a sweet, wandering music. But since the hour was so late she must get up quickly. Why had he not roused her? He—they all—would be angry. Where were her clothes? And what must she do when she had them on? Call the women? Go to look for him?

Trembling and clumsy she began to dress. But she could not put on the gown she had worn yesterday; that was for feasts only. She had to tumble out all Meg's gay stuff upon the floor to find one of her own, and at last was ready to go down, in her old brown gown and grey petticoat.

It was absurd, and also acutely embarrassing, to be creeping about the house like this, an intruder, and yet one who might not go away. And she began to know that she was terribly, achingly hungry. She thought that if she found the kitchen one of the women might give her bread and perhaps a drink of ale. She came down into the great chamber. It was yet in disarray after yesterday's company: dishes and cans on the table, and a cat crunching delicately at a chop bone under a bench. It occurred to her that she too might find something to eat fallen among the rushes, and so stay her stomach. But if they caught her so employed, or asked her after how she had breakfasted—? She could not risk it.

Yet where were the kitchens? Confused, she opened a door, and found herself looking out upon the street. She came to the other door, opposite, and had her hand on the latch to open it when it swung in suddenly, so that she had to spring back as her husband came in hastily.

He stepped back too, and they stared at each other, in an equal embarrassment. "Where are you going?" he asked, not being able to think of anything to say, and at that she began to stammer excuses in so palpable a fright that it helped him to recover himself.

He looked down at her, small, thin, and dressed as meekly as any night-flying moth in grey and brown. And she feared him. For a moment he thought to take her hand and say, "Sweetheart, I left you to sleep." But no. He must be sure of his foothold before he encouraged her to take liberties. He looked grave.

"No matter, wife," he said; and then, "Shall I—I shall call Marget to show you the house."

"If you will, Sir."

She looked utterly miserable. "But you've not break-fasted," he cried, and, forgetting that he must at all costs make himself master in these early days, he left her hurriedly to call on the women in the kitchen to be quick—"Be quick and bring your mistress breakfast."

When one came in with it he came back too, and pushed aside the cups and platters from the end of the table in the great chamber by which July had sat herself down forlornly. While she ate he sat opposite her, not saying much and keeping, when he remembered, a solemn and even a frowning countenance, and when he did not remember, looking at her with gentleness, pity, curiosity, and lessening apprehension.

On the whole he felt greatly reassured by her appearance and behaviour. He thought that it was impossible she should prove to be such another wife as his first. The late Mistress Machyn had been five years older than he, and a widow when he took her. She was, besides, a great hearty creature, with a complexion like a farmer's wife, and a voice like an usher in the courts. You would have thought that she would have outlasted half-a-dozen such as Laurence Machyn, and when she died of the sweating sickness he had been so amazed that he had quite forgotten to fear that he might die of it himself.

So he watched July, noting with approval that she ate most daintily. But, he thought, if she's too dainty how shall I ensure that she well orders the house? And he began to foresee troubles other than those which he had already suffered.

But when, having finished eating, she looked up at him with a little colour in her cheeks and life in her eyes, he smiled at her and began to fumble in his pouch.

"See, Sweeting," he said, "there's four angels for you to spend as you will," and then he coughed, and told her sternly that the women must be set to clear out the chamber before dinner-time—"And that's not long," said he, "for it must be near ten of the clock, and look at all this!" He swept his hand about to direct her attention to the confusion on the tables, as though it was all her fault. "I shall send you old Marget," he said, and left her.

September 30

Will Wall said, as he held Aske's stirrup this morning, "You did ought to have let me take the mare to be shod. That off fore is working loose," And then, as though it were all part of the same reproach, "They're turning forth the Canons from North Ferriby this morning."

"It'll last me to-day," Aske said cheerfully, as if he had heard only Will's warning about the loose shoe.

But when the mare dropped it, and Aske lost the rest of the hunt, instead of going back to the smith at Swanland he began to walk her downhill towards where the tower of North Ferriby stood up amongst the trees of the village.

The smith told him that all the Canons had gone away early this morning—"except Dom Philip Cawood," said he, "and you'll find him, I doubt not, at the ale-house." But Aske was only too glad to hear that he need not see any of those who were turned out; and if one of them were to seek solace in drinking himself silly Aske did not blame him. He left his horse at the smithy, and walked along the empty street of the village towards the Priory: only the ducks and the hens were about, but already he could hear the sound of voices which told him where were all the absent villagers.

In front of the Priory Gate-House a row of carts were drawn up; three men were already loading up a big iron-bound coffer, and as Aske went past them another came out with a bundle of woven hangings on his back. Inside the first court a group of women stood close, peering in through the doorway that led into the Canons' offices. They fell back when they saw Aske, and let him go by in silence; he looked over his shoulder, and they had come a few paces after him and then stood again, silent and staring.

But in the Church itself there was no silence but a great noise of voices, and the shouts of children skylarking up and down the Canons' night stairs. There was a sound of hammering too, and wrenching of wood, as wainscoting was stripped from the walls of a vestry beyond. Now and again there came a louder outcry when one of the villagers was caught pilfering from among all that which was now the King's, and which the Receiver's men were collecting in great piles in the Church and Cloister. Aske stuck his hands through his belt and stood watching it for a long time; until, in fact, the fellow in charge turned all out of the Church and locked the door behind him. He gave Aske good day politely, and then looked curiously at him, before he went to his dinner. Aske took his horse again at the smith's and started off in the direction of Ellerker, but at the lane that led to the Manor he did not turn; instead he rode on along the old Roman Road northward.

It was dark when he came again to Ellerker, and so late that as he approached the house he could see no light at all. Yet he had hardly knocked when the gate was opened by Will.

Aske rode in and dismounted stiffly. The mare had had

enough too. Will swept his lantern over her and then lifted it so that he could see his master's face.

"Have you—Sir," he cried, "have you been over the water?"

"Over Humber? Why should you think I went over Humber?"

Will did not say, and Aske did not care enough to press him. Of all fruitless journeys and foolish, surely his had been the most fruitless, most foolish. "But at least," he thought, "I have seen with mine own eyes, what it is that is done." He had seen, as at Ferriby, so at Pocklington, and at York, the emptied shells of what had been Houses of Religious. He had even been so near home as Thicket, and in the last glimmer of dusk had felt his way into the little Church where, Will had said, the rain was coming in upon the altar. It was too dark for him to see, but certainly the place smelt of damp, and already of decay.

Will brought him some supper now from the kitchen and put it down at the end of a table in the Hall where Aske already sat, with a rushlight making only a small and faint island of light in the darkness.

"Master," said Will, "they do not guess where you have been."

Aske looked at him dully. How could they guess?

"I said you had sent word by a pedlar that came. I said you had met one of the gentlemen from Gray's Inn that was going to Hull and that you had gone thither to dine with him."

Aske said, "Will, go to bed. What are you talking about?" but he did not in the least want to know, and Will went off without answering.

Aske sat on a long time in the Hall, very weary, stupidly eating and staring at the rushlight, and as stupidly forgetting to eat. At last he pushed his plate away, took up the rushlight and started to go upstairs.

Outside the door of the room which he was sharing with Kit and young Hob he blew out the light and stood in the blank dark, hearing the night noises of the old house—a faint sigh, a creak, a tiny but sharp crack. It had not seemed to him that he was thinking while he sat alone below. But now two things were clear, which till now, had been clouded; or perhaps it was that they were isolated by the general dullness of his mind, and so seemed clear as the little flame of the rushlight had seemed bright in the dark and empty Hall. The first he could put into words.

"If I move," he said in his mind, "I do wrong. If I move not wrong is done."

The other, which was a dumb thing, was fear—the fear lest he should stand alone, a man disowned by kin and friends; there in the dark he knew in a foretaste the weight and desolation of that loneliness. His hand, groping, found the latch of the door; as it opened he heard Kit cry sleepily, "Who's there?"

He answered, "Robin."

October 1

Lord Darcy sat in the garden at Templehurst. In this sheltered place, under the lee of the house and the chapel, it was warm as summer, and the dogs lay flat on the stones twitching when the flies teased them. Below, in a little strip of orchard, a gardener and his boy were gathering apples.

In front of Lord Darcy a fat man with a broad brown face sat on a small stool; he wore my Lord's green coat, and the Buck's Head on his breast and back.

Darcy said, "This man who told you was truly what he said—a servant of the King's Commissioners?"

The fat man could only say that he'd never doubted him. Darcy nodded; it was enough; the fat man, for all his pudding face, was no fool.

"He was riding in haste. He did but bait at York. He'd slept at Howden maybe, or even Lincoln."

"And he told that the Austin Canons of Hexham have resisted the Commissioners?"

"Aye. He said that when his masters came to Hexham there was a pretty crowd in the streets, with bows, bills and leather jackets he said. And the town rang the common bell, and they in the Priory rang the great bell there; it was tang-tang-bom-bom-bom, he said, like as it might be a day when the Scots are into England, he said. And when the Commissioners came nigh the Priory there were the gates shut against them, and one of the Canons came up on the leads, harnessed he was too with a steel cap on his head. He hollers down to the Commissioners saying that there were twenty brothers with him in the House would die or they should have it. So he showed them a writing, with the King's broad seal dangling, saying it was writing for writing and seal for seal against that which the Commissioners had. And then he says, shouting between his two hands that all the town should hear, 'We think it not to the King's honour to give

[446]

forth one seal contrary to another. And afore any of our lands, goods, or house be taken from us we shall all die, and there is our full answer!' "

"Hah!" said Darcy, and nothing else for some time, till he asked, "Did this man tell you of any stirring in the North, other than these Canons of Hexham?"

"No."

"Did you ask him?"

The fat man looked down for a moment, the comic parody of a coy girl. "I said to him, 'Though Northumberland's ever unruly, yet I'll think it strange if there be no more troubles here in the North with this suppressing of Abbeys?' And he said, 'Well, there's none stirring yet.' "

Darcy nodded and sent him away to draw his livery of bread, beer, and mutton at the buttery and pantry. But my Lord sat long after the servant had gone, letting his mind range back through dangerous old times, and forward through times that might be as dangerous; but then he did not think danger a very evil thing. While his narrowed eyes glanced about the sunny bit of garden, or followed the cruising bees, he was calculating chances. What would this man do if—and that man if instead— Would Exeter make up his slow mind, or the Poles swallow their scruples? And if they should once move, would the Emperor— He did not think so —not now—whatever it might have been three years ago. And then—

He broke it all off. There was nothing stirring in the North parts but only these Canons of Hexham.

He took up again that book of Lydgate's that he had been reading when the fat man came lightly along the path to him. But once he sighed.

October 4

Robert Aske drank the last of his ale, wiped his knife on a piece of bread and slipped it into its case.

All those at breakfast in the parlour at Ellerker looked at him as he stood up.

"Come on, Hob. Come, John," he said to his nephews, "or we'll miss the tide and the ferry."

The boys got up. Will Ellerker, John's father, half rose, then sat down again. One of the servants brought water and a towel, and Aske dipped and wiped his fingers and tossed the towel to Hob.

"You're set to go?" said Jack Aske.

"Since Rafe can't hunt, but must be about taking this cursed subsidy."

"Fie!" cried Kit. "That's no word for the King's will."

"By the Rood!" Robert answered in the cheerfully impudent tone that always enraged his brother, "I use no worse than that Rafe used."

Rafe Ellerker, Will's eldest brother, should have been with them these last few days for the hunting, but because he had been appointed one of the gentlemen to collect the subsidy he could not come. So yesterday Robert Aske had declared that next morning, and not the day after, he would set out for London, and that the two boys, John and Hob, who were both to begin their studies at law, must be ready to ride with him. "Because," he had said, "we shall ride the more easily with another day to spare before term begins."

But now Jack Aske said, "You'll not wait to know if it was true what that Summoner out of Lincolnshire said? 'The commons all up about Louth,' he said."

"I don't go by Louth," Robert said obstinately.

"Mass, let him go. For he will go," cried Kit.

"I shall go," Robert answered him with a hard, hostile look, and then was sorry. It was not good to part from a brother in ill will. "The boys need not go," he said.

But John and Hob were not to be stopped. "What's a rabble of poor tradesmen and husbandmen?" cried John confidently. "Should we not have heard, Sir—" Hob began to ask his uncle more soberly, but Robert Aske was already at the door and went out without looking back.

They were nearly halfway to North Ferriby when he said to the boys, "There's a word I must say to your Uncle Kit." He turned his horse about. "I'll be with you in time for the ferry," and he went back, riding hard.

He came again, only just in time. The servants and horses were all on board, and the boatmen waiting with the sweeps ready. Hob and John, however, stood on the staithes; they caught Robert's bridle as he swung out of the saddle.

"Sir," said Hob, and laid his hand on his uncle's arm as he was for stepping into the boat.

"Tide's turning, Master!" the boatman cried. "I can't wait no longer."

Robert Aske said, "Come on," and went into the boat.

So they got his horse in, and pulled the gangway after them. When that was done, and the boatmen poling the big barge offshore, Aske left the boys and went forward. There was a coil of rope in the bows; he sat down on it as the boat swung slowly into the river. The men settled down to their oars and now they met the wind from off the sea, which, running against the first turn of the tide, cast up little waves that slapped and gurgled against the bows, and ran alongside hissing.

Aske sat with his chin on his fist and a dark look on his face. The nephews, watching him, could guess well enough that whatever word it was that he had ridden back to speak to Uncle Kit he wished now that it had been left unspoken. "But," said Hob, and squared his shoulders, "I shall tell him what they say. He might think we should turn back."

He came and stood near his uncle.

"Well?" said Aske shortly, without looking up.

"Sir, the boatmen say that all Lincolnshire is in a floughter, and ringing their bells awkward. As well as Louth, Caister is up, and Horncastle, they think. The commons are taking any gentlemen they can and swearing them to an oath. And they've killed the Bishop's Chancellor—dragged him from his horse and beat him to death with staves, and killed others too, they say."

When his uncle neither answered nor looked up, Hob touched him on the shoulder.

"Do you hear, Sir?"

"Yes. There's no ferry back till to-morrow morning."

"Would you go back?"

"No."

"The ferrymen would not go about."

"No."

"Unless you should persuade them."

"You can try if you will."

Completely puzzled Hob went off. He spoke a while with John Ellerker, then with the master boatman. At last he came back to the bows.

"No. They will not."

"I thought not," said his uncle, and no more. When Hob had gone away he sat still, his eye upon the widening rift of palest blue above the dove-coloured water, which showed where, far down the broadening river, the sea lay. Now he could not turn back.

They rode up from the ferry staithes towards Barton village, keeping pretty close; the boys and the servants were spying about them all the time, as though the dykes might be full of ambushed men. In the village itself, just as a touch of sun flooded over the flat land, they came on the first sign of trouble. Two men stepped out from the door of one of the tofts; they saw the riders, and went in again; one of them had a bow slung at his back and a long woodman's knife at his belt. The other carried a pike.

At the duck-pond where, from the straight road to Lincoln, a little narrow lane branched off between a barn and an orchard, Robert Aske wheeled to the right. "We'll make for Sawcliffe," he told them over his shoulder. The others had been expecting that, since the ferrymen had told them that they'd never make Lincoln by the high road. At Sawcliffe lived Sir Thomas Portington, who had married Robert Aske's eldest sister Julian, and never married again since she died.

Aske had been riding always a little ahead; now the distance increased; when they came to Barton Windmill, whose sails were turning briskly with a whirring noise while the shadows of the sails raced upon the road with an endless quick flickering, they could see him a hundred yards ahead. But when they were quite clear of the village, and riding in the open with the wide river on their right, flashing now in sunshine, he was so far that even in that flat land they kept losing sight of him, as they had altogether lost sight of Will Wall and the Ellerker servant behind.

It was quite suddenly that they came up with their uncle again in the street of South Ferriby. He was in the midst of a small crowd of men, one, with a black coat and grey beard, on horseback; the others, close on a score of them, on foot, but armed. As Hob and John Ellerker came round the corner into the village they saw one of these shorten his pike and move in till the point of it was close to Aske's breastbone.

"Mass!" cried Hob, and spurred, then pulled in, his horse. Their uncle's voice came clearly to them.

"Friend," said he, "that spit of yours is too long for a small fowl like me," and he put the blade aside with his arm, and, taking one foot from the stirrup, gave the fellow a gentle shove in the chest, so that he went backwards. The boys heard some of the men laugh, and one of them cried that here was a little cock but it crowed gamely.

"But," said the grey-bearded man, "you shall take the oath or not pass undamaged."

"The oath, or you shall die," they began to shout, and

then someone said, "What of these others?" and pointed back along the road.

Aske turned and saw the boys. He lifted his hand and they thought he meant to wave them back, but he must have changed his mind, for he called them to come on.

"Well," said he, as if now they were all friends together, "and what is your oath?"

"To be true to God, the King, and the Commonwealth."

"There is no treason in that," said Aske, "but it stands well with that oath I took before."

"The easier then," said they, "for you to take it. Nor shall you pass otherwise."

So he took it, laying his hand upon the book they had. But when they would have had the lads take it he would not, but began to argue with them, till Hob pulled him by the sleeve.

"Sir, I'll take it so that we may pass."

"You shall not," he told him angrily. "You are minors at law. Come on. No, no! They shall not."

He put his horse forward at the group of men, and they must use force to keep him, or let him go through them. They let him go, and the boys followed after him a little way behind, until they heard him say, but without looking round, "Range up on either side of me."

When they had done that he said, "Lean down, Hob, as if you looked at your gelding's feet, and tell me do they follow us."

"No," said Hob; only a woman with a pitcher of water and a child at her skirts was watching them.

"Well," Aske said, "that's well." He laughed suddenly. "There it is. And it is done."

After that he did not ride forward alone, but went with them and talked a lot, merrily and learnedly, and sometimes listened to what they said.

When they came to Sawcliffe the big gates were shut. From within the Court they could hear oxen lowing and the bleating of sheep, as if market were being held there.

"Hammer on the gate, someone," said Aske, and Will, who had caught up with them by now, got down and beat on the doors with the handle of his knife. After a little while the shuttered window above the gate-house was opened, and Hal Portington and his younger brother Tom looked out. "Oh! It's you!" they cried, and seemed very glad of it. "The commons are up all about," they said.

"We know that," Aske told them.

"And they've taken my father," said Hal. "The girls fear lest—"

"Well," said Aske, "let us in."

They were indeed very glad to have him in. Hal and Tom put such a face on it as if they could have done well enough without him, but Sir John Portington's sister wept on his shoulder, and little Meg flung her arms about his knees and wept into the skirts of his coat. When he had comforted them with a grave face, and a twinkle in his eye to the lads over the lady's head, he went away to the kitchen. They heard his voice rating the servants, they heard the sound of someone getting a drubbing, and then they heard his voice again, not angry now, but laughing. After a while he came back with a big dish of eggs and told them that he thought a wooden spoon was as good as a stick for beating a lad's backside, "and better perhaps, for it covers more ground, and also the noise it makes is more ghastful."

Then the servants came in with the rest of a hastily prepared dinner, and when they sat down to it, they all felt more cheerful. "And," he told them, "there's no need to fear harm to your father, who hath in nothing offended the commons. They'll but have taken him, as they took me, and made him swear the oath. And if they keep him it is because he has land in Lincolnshire, and they need his counsel."

So the rest of the day was cheerful, if strange and disorganized, and they sang in the evening to Hob's lute. When bedtime came Hal Portington took John Ellerker to sleep with him and Tom; Hob went off to Sir Thomas's own bed with his uncle; it did not take him long to get to sleep, and if Robert Aske watched Hob did not know it.

He did not know either what time it was when Aske wakened him. When the boy sat up, mazed with sleep, he saw that his uncle was dressed and ready to ride. He sat down on the bed by Hob, saying, "Wake up, sluggard. Now listen." Then he said that he was going to try to cross over from Wintringham back into Yorkshire.

"Back?" Hob was confounded both by such a sudden change of purpose and by an uncertainty and haste in his uncle's manner that was altogether strange.

"God's Death!" cried Aske in a sudden flame of anger. Then he began to argue. For if, he said, the oath he had taken stood well with his first oath to the King, then so, semblable, did that oath stand with this, and in keeping of the first he could not but observe the second. "Therefore," he summed it all up at length, "I'll get back if I may." He got up and stood biting his knuckles, then said, "Nor is this my country that I should take hand in this matter," and turned away to the door.

Hob flung out of bed. "I'll come with you." "No." "Then I'll call Will." Aske turned on him, causelessly angry again. "But you shall help me saddle and lock the door on me," he said, and put his hand a moment on the boy's shoulder.

When he had gone Hob got back into bed and thought that, for listening to sounds, he would never sleep. And the next thing he knew was that a handful of pebbles was rattling against the shutters. He looked out and saw his uncle below.

"Well," said Aske, when he was back again in the room, "here I am and here I'll bide, as the cat said when she fell into the milk-pail." His cheek was raw, and the knuckles of one hand, and his thumb was swelling prettily. He said that they had caught him even at the river-side, for their watch was good. "One of them," said he, "will have to bite apples with the side of his face, for his front teeth aren't there where God planted them. But they got me down and sat on my head as though I were a horse. Then the fools let me get into the saddle again."

He stood listening, but there was no sound but that of the wind in the chimney, and the ticking of the cool embers on the hearth.

"It must be close on midnight. Let's sleep while we may," he said.

October 5

It was still dark when the family at Sawcliffe, half-dressed, cold and miserable, came together around the embers of the Hall fire. Robert Aske was not with them, nor Will Wall, because half an hour ago a big band of the commons had come knocking at the gate and calling for "Master Aske of Aughton. And you shall not deny him to us, for we know he's here." He had spoken to them out of the gate-house window, and in the end had ridden away with them into the dark.

Between the time when the great knocking on the gate had set all the dogs barking and the cattle in the Court lowing and the women screaming in the house, and the time when the men servants barred the gate behind him, there had been leisure for almost no words between the three young men and their uncle. Only, he had told Hob and

John Ellerker to get them back over Humber early next morning. "For it seems," said he, "that the commons will be drawing to the southward. And if so be you find the way clear and safe, send back a servant to Hal here. Then shall you, Hal, follow after with the women and the little ones."

That had been while he was dressing, and Will Wall trussing up a suit of harness for him, borrowed from among those of Sir John Portington. And a few moments after he had gone, with no word more, but only a gesture of his hand and a hard glance that seemed to pass them by as if he had already forgotten them.

Now, when the women and children had gone again to bed, the three had time to talk it over, and at first they could make nothing of it—how their uncle had taken the oath that afternoon, and tried to make his way back over Humber last night, and this morning had gone off with the commons. Hal argued that it was not strange the commons should say they knew him, and that therefore he must go with them, because Kit Aske's lands lay close over Trent in Marshland. But Hob doubted that there was something in it that needed to be bolted out, and, growing sharper in argument, cried out at last, "My mother says she will never trust him, but that he will bring himself and others into trouble by his tongue. There is one thing mine uncle has never learnt to do —you know the song—" and he quoted it sententiously—

> Whatsoever be in thy thought
> Hear and see and say right nought:
> Then shall men say thou art well taught,
> To bare a horn and blow it not.

"But now," he said, "I do fear he is confederate with the commons."

"Fie!" cried Hal and John Ellerker together, and John said, "No gentleman could be. Surely, it cannot be so." Then he frowned and said, "But it appeared that they let themselves be ruled by him in that they consented that we should return to Yorkshire." Before they concluded the discussion Hob and John thought very gravely of their uncle's behaviour, and if Hal argued for him it seemed to be more for cussedness than from conviction.

Meanwhile Robert Aske rode southward knowing in the darkness only that there was a great company both before and behind upon the road, and that most of them were on foot, though he could hear some horses. Only when the darkness thinned could he see their numbers, and their arms, which to a Yorkshireman, used to the harnessed men who would turn out to fight off the Scots, seemed wretched indeed, for their harness was mostly no more than a leather coat, and their arms very often only quarterstaves and clubs.

Daylight came, but a murk daylight deadened by heavy mist, just as they reached Appleby. They were still in Appleby when, several hours later, the fog was shredding into a light, shining mist. Aske sat on his horse in a yeoman's stackyard. All through the little town and out into the fields the commons were crowded, shaggy-haired, dirty fellows many of them, and with a pale sick look, for Lincolnshire was a poor country and agueish.

Round about him they were mostly of the better sort—that is to say, the horsemen, and such as had bows or bills, or here and there a broadsword. He had come in here half an hour ago to chivvy off two or three ragged fellows who were set to rob the yeoman's hen houses, and these others had followed him, much as dogs follow a man, from a habit grown so strong that it has become a need. So far as he could see there was no other gentleman in all that host, though he guessed there must be pretty near two thousand of the commons.

All about him he could hear them talking of what had been done—"Aye, Cock's bones! and it was well done," at Louth and Caistor and Horncastle. They talked also of what should be done next, and, as they talked they would break off and look to him, and wait an instant, as if that he might speak. But Aske had not spoken.

And still they did not move. The fog had quite cleared: it was not now even a mist, but only gave a delicate bloom and sparkle to the sunshine. The yellow straw of the stacks was a shining silky gold against the blue air; a red cock and his hens picked about between the feet of the horses; the cock jerked the fringed feathers of his neck petulantly, and the light wind blew the arched, cascading feathers of his tail about him, like a woman's veil; he sloped his head and stared up at Aske with a fierce round stare as he stepped under the horse's belly.

It was only when the cock, clucking fiercely, hustled out on the other side and made off with a furious pounding stride, that Aske knew he had shifted his heel and put his horse forward.

As he moved all the talking round about him ceased, all heads turned in his direction. The men on the green beyond the stackyard turned too, and came nearer. When he spoke he lifted his voice, meaning that they also should hear.

"Masters," said he, "what will you do? The day's passing. There's no gain in staying here for ever. Where next?"

After a pause someone said that Aske had already heard many times that morning, that Lord Brough had sent to raise the men of Kirton in Lindsay and all the Soke. "But they'll not move against us," another cried. "We'll call them up to join us instead."

"Well," said Aske, "let us set about it then. Let some go to Kirton, and some about the Soke, calling on all to join the commons."

They said that would be a good thing to do, a very good thing, and then began asking each other who would go where. They stopped at last because Aske spoke.

"Let the Sokemen go to Kirton. I will raise the Soke."

The Sokemen came from out of the rest like the salt beads of water out of butter. Then Aske stood up in his stirrups, put his hands to his mouth and shouted—

"Twoscore men to ride with me along Humberside to raise the commons there!"

He had them very soon, and was riding out of Appleby towards the Humber, saying to himself, "This is treason."

It was between one and two in the afternoon that he and his twoscore came to Kirton in Lindsay to rejoin the Sokemen. He had seen enough that morning of the poverty and simplicity and indiscipline of these poor commons of Lincolnshire to give his face a very grim look. Now, as he rode into the township, he glanced around at the scattered mob of footmen who, having eaten, lounged about in groups or lay asleep; a few of them shouted to him as he rode by. "And that's about all they're good for," he muttered to Will beside him. Will pretended not to hear.

The Sokemen were sitting about in the churchyard round the foot of the cross. But that they were all awake he could not see that they were doing more than the poor footmen outside. He pushed between them till he came to the step of the cross, set his foot on it, and looked down on them. They looked up at him, waiting.

"God help us," he thought. "Sheep. Very sheep." He said— "And what now?"

They told him that they planned to go towards Caistor, to meet the host of Caistor, which was mustering.

"So Jake said," one of them put in.

"He saw many riding thither," said another.

"But when Will came by Briggs no one knew if Caistor were up or no."

"God's Bones! Of course they're up!"

"If they're not up—" someone began, in a voice that sounded scared.

Aske did not let him finish.

"Is there any man who can tell me surely whether there's a host of Caistor or no?"

They stopped arguing it and looked one to the other for the answer. At last an old man with watery eyes said, "No, but they thought it was so, for so the talk went in the country. But they knew it not for truth."

Aske turned from them. He laid one hand flat on the stone shaft of the cross. The stone was warm, but his heart was cold and very heavy. He said:

"Who will go and see whether it is true or not?"

He kept his eye on his hand for what seemed an age. No one spoke out loud, though he could hear them whispering together. He took his hand from the cross and looked at them again.

"Well then, if none will go, I will go."

He went out of the churchyard to where Will waited in the saddle, as he had been bidden, holding Aske's horse. "To Caistor, Will," he said. As he picked up the reins some of the Sokemen called to him to stay till he had dined. He laughed at them, too angry to answer. Three of those that had ridden with him that morning came running after him, stuffing hunks of bread and bacon into their faces. He did not wait, but they scrambled into the saddle and beat their horses till they drew level with him beyond the village.

"What about your dinner?" he threw at them.

They grinned, shamefaced.

"Those fellows," said one of them, "would make a pig sick."

But Aske's heart was lightened.

Late in the afternoon the host was still at Kirton. They had lit fires about the green and were cooking supper now. The Sokemen were all together in a farm, at table still, having well eaten.

Aske came in to them with Will and the three men who had

gone after him. He stood at the end of the board, setting his hands on it because he was so stiff with riding that he did not well know where his legs were.

"Caistor host," he said, "will be at Downham Meadow to-morrow, and there you shall meet them."

"And you, Master," cried one of them, "you're going to Caistor with us."

"No. I'm for Sawcliffe and then Yorkshire."

"No, by God, you're not," someone shouted.

Aske looked at him. "Why not?"

"By cause we know you gentlemen. You'd all skulk and hang back while we commons bear the brunt."

Aske looked over his shoulder to the Lincoln men who had ridden with him about Kirton Soke, to Kirton, to Caistor, and back to Kirton. They laughed aloud angrily.

"Where hast thou been to-day, Tom?" cried one of them.

"Ah," said another, "Tom's the nose that must smell out alehouses for the host. He's a great man at that, he is. He can't be spared to ride about on errands."

There was some laughter from the other Sokemen, but Aske said—

"I can make Sawcliffe to-night before dark. I'll cross into Marshland to-morrow where my brother has Manors, and men know me; then to Howden, where also I am known, being a Yorkshireman. For it's not one county that will bring so great a matter as ours to a good end, but all the North must rise, yea, poor commons, gentlemen, and noblemen too, if they know their duty to God. So I will make a beginning of raising those parts, and return. And now, shove along, shove along. We're hungry."

"How do we know that you'll return?" someone jeered.

Aske gave him no answer: but one of the men who had ridden with him did, bidding him in a fierce whisper to shut hit face for a fool. "He's said he'll return, and, by God's Nails! so he will."

October 6

The Burton Staithes ferry boat ran silently aground on the soft mud by the landing, and Aske and Will Wall led their horses out of it. The hoofs made a great noise on the hollow timbers of the Staithes, and then suddenly none at all on the wet meadow grass. They rode off, past the shuttered inn, for it was so early that the light was barely come; but before they had gone a hundred yards they turned at a noise behind them; the ferryman was beating upon the door of the inn. Aske consigned him to the devil. The Marshland men knew paths that a horseman could not take which cut miles out of a journey. "By the time we come anywhere," he said, "all but the rabbits and the waterfowl will know as much as we do."

He was right. It was daylight when they came to Reedness, but there were no men in the fields, and yet the village street was full. The steward, with his oxhorn slung at his back, was making no attempt to call them to the ploughing; it was he who caught Aske's bridle, crying, "Master, shall we ring our bells and muster?"

Aske did not answer for a minute. Then he said,—

"Wait till you hear the bells of Howdenshire ring over the water."

He told the same to every village along the river, where, as at Reedness, the commons thronged the street, and so they came to the ferry across to Howden town itself. The place was like market day for crowds, only to-day the shops were shut because the journeymen were all out in the streets, and would not go in for anything that their masters would do. Aske pushed his horse as fast as he could through the throng, answering questions over his shoulder, but never staying. When they cried out to know if they should ring their bells awkward, and muster, he said, "Wait till you hear them ring in Marshland."

When they were clear of the town he turned, frowning, to Will's puzzled face.

"But, Master, I thought——" said Will.

"What did you think?"

"Why did you bid Marshland men wait for Howden bells, and here in Howdenshire you say they shall wait for Marshland? Will you have none rise?"

Aske looked at him as if he were an enemy.

"Do you think I'm in this for my pleasure?" he asked bitterly. "I'd give my right hand to be clear of it. Lincolnshire has sent articles to the King. If he should give a gracious answer shall Yorkshiremen rise? And shall I put a halter round my own neck? If," he muttered, "I have not already."

"Master!" cried Will, but Aske said, "Now, ride!" and spurred so fiercely that it was a little while before Will could come up with him to ask whither.

"Home. Aughton. Fool!"

But when they had ridden at that furious pace for some while Aske slackened, and turned again to Will, who had come up beside him.

"My brother Kit," he said—and his eye seemed to search Will's face—"My brother Kit and I do not agree over these things. Perhaps I cannot even now make him see—but the Master" (he meant Jack) "he and I think semblable in this. He said that himself when we spoke of how he should make answer to a letter of Cromwell's.

"So," he concluded, watching Will all the time, "so I do not doubt, though he may at the first think it strange I should so mell in insurrection, being a man of peace as I am . . ."

When he left that unfinished, Will said, fervently, "You will be able to show him why it is right, Master Robin."

"Yes, that is what I think," said Aske.

They came between the thin, wind-torn woods to Aughton crossroads, and turned away westward. The track dipped down to an arm of the Fen, grew heavy and boggy, and crossed a sluggish course of dark water lined with browning reeds by a little wooden bridge. When they came up again to the level they could see, beyond the village, Kit's new church tower. Aske said, "Come on. We'll not stop to answer any," and so they went through the village with the wind whistling past their ears, hearing the shouts of those who ran out and ran after them drop quickly behind.

The gate of the house was open. They rode into the court, and Aske was out of the saddle and up the steps to the Hall door while the servants were running out from the offices and from the stackyard beyond.

The Hall, though now it was getting on for dinner-time, was still littered with the men's pallets, and the tables with last night's supper; as he came in two of the young dogs leapt down from among the plates and slunk away.

He went on to the Parlour, though indeed he knew now that he would find no one there. He opened the door and stood for a while, staring stupidly at a pot of dead flowers on the window sill; the hearth was cold, the sideboard was empty of the silver cups, salts, and flagons that should stand there, and there was dust everywhere. Beside what had been old Sir Robert's chair a book lay upon the floor, with a straw to mark the reader's place, who had laid it down beside him. On the table, at the very place where Jack had sat to write his letter to Master Cromwell almost exactly a month ago, lay a quill pen, as though that letter had been written yesterday, or as though time had run back through all the days between. Aske looked about at it all, then went away.

The key of the church door hung in its place upon the nail in the screens passage just beyond the pantry. He took it, and let himself out of the house by the little old door into the orchard.

When he came out of the church Will Wall jumped up from the bench in the porch, and, taking the key from Aske's hand, made a great business of locking the door.

"Master, they have all gone away," he said, as though that were news. "Master Kit went first. He had money of my Lord of Cumberland's. He swore he'd get through, and that a rabble of lousy commons should not stop him."

"He'll get through," Aske said, wishing he could have told Kit (only he never could) how well he knew the measure of his brother's intrepid and impetuous spirit. "And—Jack?" he asked.

"Master Jack sent Mistress Nell and the children to Master Monkton's."

Aske took that for an answer. It made no difference whither Jack had gone, since he was gone.

"The court's full of folk, Master," said Will. "They wait for you to tell them what to do."

As they went together into the house Aske said that he would name Shipworth Moor as the place where, if the bells rang, they should muster; it was a place just over the river Derwent from Aughton. "For thence," he said, "they can pass over the river at Bubwith to go eastward, if the commons are rising on that hand, or northward towards York, or to Selby, or south to Howden."

"Yes, Master," said Will. While Aske spoke to the men in the court, telling them to be ready, to see to the buckles of their harness, their swords, bills, and bows, to have their good wives boil bacon for them to carry in their pokes, Will watched him with the eyes of a dog.

The rest of that day was most busy. Aske wore out the quill pen that he had seen lying on the table in the Parlour, and another after it, and Aughton servants and men from the villages round about were riding off this way and that way all the time with the letters he wrote. Then there were the arrows and bows to count in the Church tower, and harness both for master and men to find, and clean, and pack.

When at last he and Will left Aughton it was evening. A strong, clean wind blew out of the west, and as they took the road through the village, the clouds behind them drew up in a great pomp of purple and gold about the golden sunset.

Sir George Darcy and his score of riders did not get back to Templehurst till about an hour before midnight, but the porter who let them in had word for him from my lord to go up at once. As he spoke the porter's eyes were wandering beyond Sir George to watch the rest of the riders come in under the gate lantern, for all in Templehurst knew what business it was that had taken Sir George off just after dark, with a coil of rope hanging at the saddle of one of the horses. But when the horsemen were in it was clear that the rope had been useless, for there was no prisoner trussed up behind any of the riders.

My Lord's voice, clear as ever for all his age, cried, "Come in," as Sir George knocked. When he went in the same young voice, and this time with a sort of laugh in it, asked, "Well, and have you him safe by the heels?"

Sir George came round the high-backed settle and found, sitting side by side upon it, his father and Sir Robert Constable, each in his velvet and fur-lined nightgown, and each toasting his bare, hairy shins before the fire. There was a dice-board between them, and even now my Lord threw and cried out in triumph at a double-six. George, who was already ill-tempered from failure, took such levity much to heart.

He paused just long enough for his silence to be significant, then said: "I have him not, for he was warned, and fled."

"God's Bones!" said Darcy, "and that's a pity."

"How could I help——" cried George, and began to tell how coming near to Howden he had sent scouts this way and that, to hold the roads——"Aye, and to the ferry to keep that. There was no way but I had it stopped. But when we came to that house where it was told us he lay—he was gone, though the bed was warm."

"By the gardens no doubt, to lie snug in some other toft till you were away."

Again—"How could I help?" Sir George protested angrily, and much more till my Lord told him sternly, "not to speak so to me." "And it's likely that if you'd used less guile, and ridden straight ways, you'd have caught our man. Na! Na!" he added sharply, and held up his hand. "If you will be so het, son George, then leave us. But if you can command your-self, sit beside Sir Robert, and let's take counsel what next."

After a pause Sir George plumped down on the settle, though he could not bring himself to speak for a few moments, but listened to his father and Sir Robert discussing what were best to do next.

"Where will he lie to-night?" Darcy asked his son, and George answered gruffly that it was said he was going to Lincoln, "because it is bruited that the King has sent answer to the rebels' articles."

"If that be a fair answer—" Sir Robert began, but Darcy laughed.

"That answer will be such as may set the whole North on flame, if I know the King's Grace, and if the commons can find them leaders."

"That was why," Constable said, "I came in such haste as soon as I heard at Holmes that Robert Aske was in it. I heard yesterday that there was in Lincolnshire one gentleman was very active for the commons. And then to-day, when I knew how Aske was at Aughton, and how the people flowed to him—"

"Why do they so?" Darcy was interested. "You know what manner of man he is. Tell us."

Constable tweaked at the hairs of his shin, frowning into the fire. "I'd not have thought him, mind you, of such ill condition as to meddle in treason. But once in he's a man of such obstinacy and audacity as to be very dangerous. And he hath a very pregnant wit too."

"A very pestilent traitor!" cried Sir George, and getting up announced that he was for bed. "A vile villain," he said. "Even the commons speak of him as they could of no gentleman. When he left Howden they were singing in the streets a song— 'Then came a worm, an Aske with one eye!'" He pulled open the door with a jerk, grinding his teeth as he remembered how, as well as singing, there had been laughter in Howden streets as they came away, and though Sir George was spared hearing his own name in a song, yet people had called from the upper windows words that showed no due respect to their Sheriff.

When he had gone Lord Darcy sat in silence for a little, stroking his nightgown over his knee.

"Robert," said he at last with a little laugh, "by what you say of this man Aske you show me such a bold, ready man, as, were he not a traitor, I could love."

"God's Cross!" cried Sir Robert, "I do not love him. In the Percy's Council we were always at odds. For a more positive, opinionated, obstinate fellow does not live than he."

"And if," thought Darcy, with an inward smile, "he excels in those qualities the man beside me, then indeed——" but he knew better than to hint at such a thought. And besides, there were matters of urgency to speak of. He said, "We must lay for him again, to take him whenever he shall come again into Yorkshire. For with one or two such taken and hanged incontinent, it's not like the commons will stir."

Sir Robert nodded, but with a glum look. He stretched out his fist, clenching it so that the muscles of his forearm stood up. "We must needs take him," he said, and then, with a jerk, "I do not say that he is not a man of very open and honest manner of dealing."

"He should ha' kept out of treason," said Darcy cheerfully.

October 7

July was in the kitchen, and her fingers were all bloody from gutting the smelts that Arnold the journeyman had brought in. Laurence came through, wanting hot water for a glue pot, just as she was laying them in the pan. He put the glue pot down and laid hands on her to kiss her. She turned her face from him, and pushed him away, leaving red stains on his green doublet, so he let her go and she went to the table to fetch the board on which were set out the sliced lemon, the little piles of nutmeg, ginger, mace, and chopped bay leaves.

She knew he was watching her but she kept her eyes down. She was always expecting him to be angry with her, though as yet he had been patient. "I have no wine vinegar," she said.

"Then send out."

"But, Sir, I know there are some dregs of red wine souring in a pot, ready to use."

"Well," he began, and then remembered that he kept the keys. The late Mistress Machyn had been a most abundant housekeeper when it came to feasting friends, and, to make up, the diet of days in between had often been lean. Laurence had a little grudged at that, but far more at the noise and jollity which seemed almost perpetual in the house. So, he had thought, this new wife should be curbed from the start.

That had seemed easy enough, and July had made no objection, no comment even, but usually asked him for the keys whenever she needed them. But now, because she would not let him kiss her, and because she had not asked, he was smitten through with a pang of fear. He had offended her. She was shutting him away because she knew he distrusted her (though God knows he'd never thought whether he trusted her or no, nor thought indeed at all, only had floundered deeper and deeper in love, till he feared his feet would soon lose the bottom).

He pulled the keys out of his pouch. They still were attached to the fine broad lace of blue and yellow that he remembered well swinging against the first Mistress Machyn's gown. That gave him warning. He must pull himself up. He must not be a weak fool—or must not let his wife see that he was a weak fool. He said shortly, "Here they are."

July came to take them. She saw where she had smudged his coat with blood, and raised her eyes no higher than that, but held out her hand for the keys. She thought he would surely be angry when he saw the stains.

He said suddenly, "Sweetheart, would it please you to keep the keys? Do not be displeased with me that I did not at first— it was because she—I feared—I did not know—"

July took the keys and he gave up trying to find a suitable explanation.

"Give me a kiss, Sweeting," he said, and when she allowed it kissed her very gently, and went away, not sure if she were pleased or displeased, willing or unwilling, but sure that to deal with her, withdrawn, fugitive, almost hostile, and yet so dear, was as delicate a business as to walk on egg shells.

When the smelts were in their bath of pickle, July tied on a hat over her hood, and, taking one of the women with her, went out shopping. The keys swung from her waist, and she found the occasional jingle they made quite pleasant. She was still only playing at being Mistress Machyn, but it was a pleasant enough game for all its drawbacks. Laurence she could make little of, and their relationship was a puzzle to her, though one on which she had not spent much thought. When the serving-woman said with a little laugh, "Anyone can see you are able to twist the Master about your finger," she cried, "How can you be so foolish?" Such a thing was to her too new and too foreign to all her experience to be easily believed.

They were going along towards the Stocks Market to buy meat when July's heart jumped suddenly up into her throat. Further along, going in their direction, she saw in the crowd a man with dark hair, a dull red coat and black hosen. "He's back to London," she thought, and then saw that it was not Master Aske, nor even very like him. She went on feeling light and shaken, like a cloth drying on a line on a breezy day. After that it was not of the meat for tomorrow's dinner, nor of the chink of the keys at her girdle, nor of playing at being Mrs. Machyn, nor of her husband that she thought. All those had become unimportant to her as thistledown drifting.

October 10

The ferryman at Burton Stather was weary of Mr. Aske's demands to be put across into Marshland again. Surly and unwilling he came down once more to the swollen river and swung his lantern over the dark edge of the water. It still swirled by above drowned grass, but between their feet and the lip of the water there was a couple of feet of meadow, sodden, muddied, and strewn with sticks and water weeds.

"See how the river has fallen since dusk," said Aske.

"See how it has risen since last week," said the ferryman, and pointed to the mooring post of the barge, feet away from them across the hurrying water.

"It has not rained since noon. I have listened." At Sawcliffe Aske had indeed listened and watched, all afternoon, ever since sunset, and ever since in the first dark, he and Will had come to the ferryman's door, urging him to put them over—but he would not.

Nor would he this time. At last Aske gave it up, and went slowly over to where Will held the horses. They got to saddle and rode up the steep, brief hill, which rises above Trent here, facing west across the marshy flats opposite, and in daytime even commanding parts of the northern shore of Ouse and Humber.

Aske was cursing the ferryman under his breath. Will, to comfort him, said there was no harm done, and he was sure that none knew where they were hiding.

"God's Passion!" cried Aske. "We left Lincoln yesterday morning. To-morrow is Tuesday. Another night, and another day, lying listening and waiting, and not knowing what —not knowing—"

They came at the top of the hill to Burton Stather village, and turned at the church to take the lane to Thealby. The night was very still, with a smell of sodden ground after the great rain that had fallen since Saturday, filling all the rivers and turning every road to deep mire. But overhead the clouds were beginning to break; here and there stars showed. In the sky to the northeast there was a red-golden star that grew huge in the hollow gulf of night; it spread to a smudgy flame. Further to the west another red star sprang and trembled.

Aske pulled up his horse. They both sat staring. "They've lit the beacons," said Will. "That's Yorkswold over that way." But Aske had swung his horse round, and was floundering back through the quaggy lane, so Will followed him.

The ferryman, just warm in bed, stuck his head out of the window and swore at them. Aske's face, a blur of white in the darkness, was all he could see, a little way below him.

"I'll not put ye over. And so I told you before, and a murrain on you!"

Aske said, "They've lit the beacons along Yorkswold. If you'll not put us over, by God! I'll break your door down and take you out and throw you in the river."

Afterwards the ferryman remembered that Master Aske, though so fierce, was but a little man, his servant a mere weed, and the bar of the door amply strong to have withstood anything that they might have done. Now, however, grumbling and cursing, he turned out and led them down to the ferry; the big sweeps over his shoulder, and the lantern swinging from his hand.

"I'll take one," said Aske, and sat down on the thwart beside the ferryman. Will had the horses in and shoved off. "Ye'll have to pull hard," said the ferryman.

But in a minute he said, "Steady! Ye'll jerk the guts out of you if you tug at the oar like that, besides swinging her across the river." Aske only grunted, but pulled less violently; above the whine of the row-locks and the swash and hiss of angry unseen water his ears were straining to catch the sound of bells. But beyond the river noises there was only a great silence, and silence when they landed in Marshland.

They went through Aldingfleet and Ousefleet without a check, but this side Whitgift Aske eased his horse to a walk.

He said suddenly, "There's a poor man, a fowler, that lives aside from the road by a clump of alders. You turn by a long pool."

They went on a few yards. A faint looming in the darkness at the side of the road hinted at water. Aske pulled up his horse.

"This is the place," he said, and then sat still.

"But, Master—"

Aske cried out suddenly, "I said I would go back, and I went. And they tried to kill me in Lincoln; whether it were gentlemen or commons matters not. You know how they would have taken me in my bed if the host of the Angel had not warned me. They would have killed me because I went back to Yorkshire to do what I might there. When I had returned, keeping my promise to them, they would have killed me."

When he had said that he was silent again, and Will dared not speak.

"And," his master went on after a minute, not violently now but earnestly, as if appealing to a judge, "And you know how I bid Marshland wait on Howden, and Howden on Marshland. Now, when Lincolnshire is breaking to flinders like a faggot of dead wood, they light their beacons. They'll ring their bells next. But in it I've no part, no word."

"Why do you say nothing?" he cried, and then thrust his horse across Will's, and took the little sludgy track beside the long pool, towards a darker patch in the darkness which was a clump of alders, and a cottage beside it.

He said, as Will came up behind. "You shall take off the harness and hide it in the house. The man will show you a place to turn out the horses, that they be not seen. We can lie here till—till—"

"Master," Will cried, when that seemed to be all that Aske would say, "but, Master, will you not— Will you not—"

He got no answer till they stood at the door of the little, lonely, tumbledown toft. Then Aske for an instant interrupted his gentle, insistent knocking to say—

"I must sleep. Four nights I have not slept. I must sleep."

But between his teeth, and to the door, he said, "I must have time."

The poor man, the fowler, let them in. He showed Will where to lead the horses into the fen so that they could graze unnoticed. When they came back Aske was not where they had left him, sitting beside the hearth with his head between his hands, but they heard his voice from the loft above telling them he would lie there, and none should disturb him. "And see to it that you tell no man where I am. D'ye hear?"

"Yes, Master Robin," said the fowler, who remembered Aske as a lad at Wressel, for he was a man of the Percy's.

"And you, Will?" Aske cried sharply.

Will said, "Aye, Master."

But for Will it was a long day, and glum. The fowler went out with his net and did not come back. At what he guessed to be about noon Will went off softly up the ladder with a bowl of pottage, a spoon and a piece of black bread. He could just see Aske lie, with his hands behind his head, on a pile of bracken.

"Put it down," said he, and Will put it down and went back to the fireside, to listen for the sound of his master going across the boards to take up the bowl. There was, however, no sound at all, so perhaps he slept.

It was late afternoon, and the light waning, when Will got up at last, stood listening, and then, with infinite caution, let himself out of the toft. He would, he thought, go towards the fen to look for the fowler, but instead he turned along the track that led to the road. It could do no harm, he thought, to walk that way, if he did not go so far as the road.

But in the end he came to Whitgift village, and found it very busy, and the smith busiest of all, for besides those men the rivets of whose harness the smith was fettling, or whose horses the smith's man was shoeing, there was a crowd of others, hanging about the side doorway and talking to the tune of the gulping bellows and the dan-dan-dan-trinkety-dan of the hammers. Will, a small man, and not of any noticeable or distinguishing appearance, slipped quietly in among them to listen.

But when he had had enough, and was for dodging back out of the press, someone cried out, "Hi! I know you," and laid his hand on his shoulder, crying loudly, "Here's Master Aske's man."

Then they all crowded round, clamouring, "Where is he? Is he here? Has he sent you to us?"

"No," said Will, lying stoutly. "But he went to Lincoln, and left me at Sawcliffe."

"By Cock! Let him be," cried a big yeoman. "We'll not need such as Master Aske if we follow the Buck's Head and the popinjay green coats," and he jerked his head towards the road beyond the crowded smithy.

"What's that?" Will, being so small a man, could not see what he saw.

"Aye," said the yeoman, "Lord Darcy's own servant here, in his master's livery, bringing the Articles out of Lincolnshire to us of Marshland." And he cried, laughing a little, "A

Darcy!" The press in the smithy broke a little just then, and Will could see, going by, two gentleman's servants, one in a tawny coat, the other in green like young leaves in spring. This man waved his hand. "Na! Na!" he said, but he laughed.

The thoughts were running round in Will's brain like a mouse in a cage. If my Lord Darcy were in it other lords would be in it too, and the King would have to be gracious; no one would be hanged. Master Robin forsake the commons? Never! Not he! He had only turned in to the fowler's toft so that he might sleep.

He grabbed at the yeoman's great arm.

"Hark ye!" The yeoman leaned down his ear that sprouted bristled red hair. "My Lord Darcy sent to take my master at Howden." The yeoman nodded. He had heard that before. "Now you say my Lord's servant brings the commons' Articles. It's no treachery?"

The yeoman said, "He saith my Lord was never pleased that the Abbeys should fall. He saith he knows, though my Lord may not declare himself yet, that he's for us."

"Then," said Will, "if there's no treachery I'll bring you to my master. And bring you my Lord Darcy's men, with the Articles of Lincolnshire."

"Ho!" cried the yeoman, clapping his big hand on Will's back. "That's a better song to sing." He shouted, in a bull's bellow, "Here is Master Aske come. His man will bring us to him."

While Will was still coughing the smithy emptied and he was on the road with them, going back towards the fowler's toft. When they had gone a little way someone cried, "We should ring our bells. It means that we should ring, now that he is come again." By that time Will was very frightened at what he had done. When the cracked jangle of Whitgift bell began behind them his heart gave a great throb in his chest. Master Robin had said Lincolnshire was a faggot of dead wood breaking. He'd told Marshland and Howden to ring no bells till he bade them. And if he would lie hid—safe —and have Yorkshire also to keep quiet, that was not to forsake the commons. Will would have liked to turn back, but, "Where does he lie?" they asked him, and when he told them —"Why did he not show himself?"

"Because he's foredone for lack of sleep," said Will, and tried to hang back, but they said, "He'll have slept enough by now."

Aske had not, however, slept. Not sleep but time to think was what he must have, though all the hasty ride from Lincoln and all the two days and a night and half a night at Sawcliffe, waiting for the water of Trent to fall, he had been thinking, and thinking.

He thought now how crookedly, how almost, as it were, backwards, he had come into the rising; so that now, it seemed to him, he was less resolved than he had been that night at Ellerker to do whatever should be laid upon him.

He thought—"Even yet I do not know what I shall do," not understanding that the drift of a man's will can persist under many eddies of hesitation, to carry him at the last either with his conscience or against it, as he had once chosen. For indeed, though he thought the choice not made, he had chosen long before. Yet now he muttered to himself, "I must have even a little time longer to be sure what I will do."

For he was sure now that the Lincolnshire men were as he had said to Will, no better than a rotten faggot, so easy it was to see how gentlemen hated commons, and commons mistrusted gentlemen. Therefore, if the Yorkshiremen rose, they were like to stand alone. And if one county stood against the King that meant failure, and failure meant— He clenched his teeth, and lay stiff in the darkness of the loft. It would be no worse for him than for any man to suffer the shocking outrage of a traitor's death. "Yet," he thought, "as not all will be hanged, so not a leader will be spared," and one of his hands went down to draw upon his own body that line which he had seen the executioner mark on the bodies of the Carthusians, before he began his bloody work. He snatched his hand back and thrust it under his head; if he could by no means rid himself of that fear at least he could trample on it.

But he thought of Aughton then. He had come home, and found himself alone, like a leper from whom his brothers fled. At that it seemed that indeed the weight of this thing that they would lay upon him was too great for him to endure, and he must even now resolve to lay it down.

"I have laid it down," he thought. "They sought to kill me. So I have laid it down."

And then, as if he had not yet laid it down, a sharp and trembling qualm ran through his mind. If to rebel were truly against the will of God, as it was against the law of man—

[471]

He sat up, and groaned aloud, *"Miserere mei Domine!"* he muttered, and then was silent, but with his soul at a stretch to reach help.

When he got up from the bracken he was stiff, and very cold, so that he stumbled as he made for the ladder. But there was a quiet in his mind, and, so it seemed to him, enlightenment. A year ago, against his conscience, he had sworn an oath; now he must take on his conscience, another sin to set right the first. The chain of his own sin bound him, and he must suffer the bond. "And do Thou," he said, just aloud, "forgive me in the one as in the other, for now I can no other than this."

He groped his way down the ladder. The house-place was quite dark because the fire had died down to ash. When he opened the door the grey soft light of late afternoon surprised and almost dazzled him; he stood, leaning against the site-post of the door. The fowler's tethered goat gave him an intolerant, pallid glare from one protruding eye, and bent again to its grazing; nothing else in the wide, empty country was alive, except the flop-winged plovers; a few of them went by overhead, but towards the north the whole sky was full of their wide wheeling drifts. He stayed there for a long time, mind as well as body lapped in a great quiet.

The sound came to him, sweetened by distance, of church bells ringing. Almost before he knew that he heard them his hand tightened on the doorpost. Each note was sweet, but, like a rising scream, the ascending instead of the descending peal meant alarm. He listened, his ears straining, his back growing cold under his shirt. From further away to the west he heard other bells, but again in that undue order, and from the southward, more. They were ringing awkward to arm and muster. Then while he still tried to doubt, he heard, dull and distant, the note, which he could not mistake, of Howden great bell.

October 12

It was just after noon on a bright day, with a light, whisking wind, when the mounted men of Howdenshire and the East Riding came to Market Weighton. Among the first of them rode a big, elderly yeoman from near Wressel, and in the stirrup beside his foot was set the foot of the great cross from Howden Church; as his horse moved the brightness of the sun flowed in waves down the gilt shaft, like light ripples upon water, and shot out coloured sparkles and un-coloured blazes from the jewels set in the gold; all about and behind the cross the sunshine blinked and flickered more coldly on the pikes and spears of the horsemen that filled the road.

The host was very orderly. Men went into Market Weighton asking for leave to sleep in barns and garners, or in the kitchens and outhouses. But when, in the afternoon, the foot-men came up, there was more trouble, for these were the poorer folk, and some of them already hungry, and not knowing whether to be angry or scared. As well as these foot-men, to add to the crowding and confusion, there came in also the men from Beverley and Holderness; so now it was not all neighbours together, but there were strangers about a man whom he had never seen before.

As it was in the host, so it was among the captains, who sat around on the tossed piles of yellow straw in a rick-yard, eating bread and cheese and drinking ale. There were the Howdenshire people who knew each other, whether gentle-men like Sir Thomas Metham, and Master Saltmarsh, or men of the commons like the miller of Snaith with his flour-whitened hair, and flour in the wrinkles of his big, fleshy face. But besides these there were townsmen and yeomen from Beverley and Yorkswold, strangers to the others; as yet the two groups did not mingle, but eyed each other across their ale cans.

Then, as they sat in comfort of sun and ease of the yield-ing straw, a Weighton man came running to say that cer-tain footmen—of what party he knew not—were driving away Weighton cattle to kill for supper.

There was silence among the Captains for a minute, ex-cept that Sir Thomas Metham murmured, "Let the com-mons' own fellows call them off," and he looked towards the miller of Snaith. But Aske lodged his can carefully in a pocket of straw, and got up.

"We must stop all spoil," he said, and went towards the horses; then he paused, and looked about at the Beverley men, searching their faces for a moment. Among them was a big fellow with a broad, brown face, eyes of a windy blue, and hair that curled lightly over his head. "Come you with me," said Aske, and the big yeoman stood up. The miller had got up too, and the three of them took their horses and rode away.

It was not very long before they came back; those in the

rick-yard saw them ride among the paling, and get down at the gate where Will Wall was waiting to take the horses. The big yeoman and the miller came in after Aske. When he stopped they stopped too, standing on each side of him but a little behind.

"I have given order," Aske spoke so that all in the rick-yard should hear, "I have given order that there shall be no spoiling of cattle, no rifling of farm-yards. The man who makes spoil shall hang."

No one spoke as he sat down and took up his can again. The miller and the yeoman went back to their places too, and those about the yeoman plucked him by the sleeve and rowned him in the ear, and he and they muttered together, looking across at Aske, and at the other Howdenshire gentlemen.

It was this yeoman who, when they had finished eating, stood up in the midst and said: "Masters, when the host is gathered, what do we next?"

He caught Aske's eye, then looked from one to another, then again to Aske, who, when no one else spoke, said that in his mind the host should divide, part to move on Hull, the other part on York.

But then Sir Thomas Metham cried out that this was folly. "York has walls, and Hull too, and we have no engines for assault."

"What then," said Aske, "would you have us do?"

Mr. Saltmarsh, who sat beside Sir Thomas, said that they should wait till the host was greater, for that men were coming in every hour.

"That's my counsel too," said Sir Thomas.

"And then?"

"Why, then——" Sir Thomas waved a hand, "then we can see."

A sort of growl came from the big yeoman, and Aske spoke hastily. He had seen this thing before in Lincolnshire (and God, He alone knew to what end it would bring them there): gentlemen against commons and commons against gentlemen, each fearing and distrusting the other. "We cannot wait to see. My lord of Shrewsbury is already at Nottingham, and the Duke of Norfolk gathers men and is named the King's Lieutenant against us." He looked round at them, and those who felt dismay at those names and at the thought of the King's power behind the names, did what they could, at his look, to keep dismay out of their faces.

"Besides," he said, "if we wait, doing nothing, for one man who comes in to us, three will go home."

"Aye, aye," came from several of the yeomen there who thought of their fields lying unploughed.

"But," cried Mr. Saltmarsh in a sharp voice, "it's treason to march in arms against the King's Lieutenant."

Aske did not answer that. He said again that his counsel was they should first make sure of York and Hull. "Then when the King's host draws nigh we can go to meet with them, and, by the King's Lieutenant, send unto the King's Grace our petition for the remedy of our grievances. But York and Hull we must have first."

Sir Thomas Metham and Mr. Saltmarsh began to protest. "It's treason." "We have no siege train." "York will shut its gates." Others joined with them.

The big yeoman with blue eyes broke in. He spoke for all to hear, but to Aske alone.

"I'll answer for the commons, Master. They'll go to York or to Hull with you. Which first?"

Aske said, "There's nine thousand of us, and all lies in speed. Give me half, and to-morrow I'll go towards York; the rest to Hull."

Sir Thomas Metham jumped up, and swore by God's Nails he would know why a man who was no knight should set himself over them all in that matter.

"I'll tell you," said the big yeoman. "It's because the commons will follow Master Aske. That's why."

It was after dark that the commons who had taken Will Monkton and Hob Aske in Monkton's house brought them to Market Weighton, and to the farm where the Captains were.

Monkton, always a silent man, had ridden in silence, but Hob had fallen back to join those of the commons who came behind; he found them very ready to talk; one and all they wanted to tell him of what Master Aske had been doing; they also wanted to tell them about his uncle. That Hob found to be difficult, since the conclusion that he and Jack Ellerker had reached on that night at Sawcliffe was clearly not to be mentioned here. If he had told the truth Hob must have said that until a week ago he had never really considered his uncle at all, but taken him for granted, as he took his bed and his breakfast for granted, and the house and fields at Aughton—all things necessary to sustain or to form a background for Master Hob Aske. So he could only think to tell them that Uncle Robert liked much mustard with his meat, and that he wrote in a book whatever tombs of noblemen and gentlemen were to be found in any church he saw.

But this was not the kind of thing that they wanted to know, so they fell back on talking among themselves about Captain Aske while Hob listened. It might have been a stranger that they spoke of, so much they saw in Uncle Robin which Hob had never noticed; he began to feel himself not a little important to be his nephew.

They got down from the saddle in a farm-yard, by the faint light of a clouded moon, and as they came to the door of the farm it opened and a man stepped out with the light behind him. Hob went back so smartly that he trod on Will Monkton's toe. The man coming out stopped too.

"Ah!" he said. "You are come. Are you come willingly?"

They knew him then by his voice, and Hob cried, "Uncle! By the Cross, right willingly!" He felt that needed something to back it up and added, "You know I would have taken the oath that day at Ferriby, if you'd have suffered me."

Aske said, "Yea," and thought, "Would it had been Jack—or Kit—instead!" But he turned the thought from his mind, and kissed the young man heartily. Will, from behind Hob, said: "Nan would have had me come to you when you were at Aughton, but I would not. For one thing I had Nell and the children on my hands. But now I am glad to be here."

"And, oh Will!" Aske cried, and kissed him too. "I'm glad to have you." Then he said sharply, "Listen!"

As they stood listening they heard a sound, no greater than the click of knitting needles, but they knew it for the sound of a horse's hoofs, ridden hard, far off, but coming nearer.

"Go in," said Aske, and they went in, but he shut the door on them and did not follow.

It was not very long before he came into the room, walking lightly with his chin high. Monkton and Hob were at the fire talking, rather uneasily, with others there, some gentlemen, some men of the commons, under the big hams hanging from the beams, and the bunches of dried herbs.

Aske said, "There is a messenger come from Lincolnshire. He brings news."

"Good news then!" cried Hob, watching his uncle's face.

"No. Not good," said he, answering Hob's question, but he spoke to Will Monkton. Then he told them what the news was—that the Lincolnshire men would surrender themselves, without terms made, to the King's mercy.

Sir Thomas Metham started up from the seat in the chimney corner. "Then—" he cried, "then what shall we do?"

"Go forward," said Aske.

The big yeoman, who was called John Hallom of the Wold, got up too. He eased his sword-belt round, so that the hilt was more ready to his hand.

"I never did think much," said he, "of them as lives across Humber. It's better as it is. Now we shall know where we are."

His blue eyes met Aske's eye with a reckless dancing look, and Aske looked back at him steadily. Each had the same thought in his mind, "This is a man to have at a man's back."

October 13

Even in the Great Chamber at Pomfret, where Lord Darcy sat at dinner, there was an air of disarray; a pile of cloaks and a riding whip cast down on the carpet in a window, and paper, ink, and pens pushed aside but not taken away from the board when the table was laid. My Lord sat on an elm seat with carved ends, with his back to the fire; on his left side was Sir Robert Constable, on his right an empty place. There was another table in the room, but not near enough for those who sat there to hear what my Lord and Sir Robert might say if they spoke low.

"Well," my Lord said, taking up his spoon, "you have seen what provision is here against a siege. Not one gun ready to shoot, arrows and bows few and bad, money and gunners none, and of powder—" He pointed to a dish of nuts before them—"enough to fill a walnut shell. And this" (he leaned his head closer), "this is the King's strong castle of Pomfret, even the most simply furnished that ever, I think, was any man to defend."

"Tchk!" said Sir Robert sympathetically, and then saw a sort of spark leap in Darcy's eye as the door opened and an old man came into the chamber, leaning on the arm of a young priest. The old man wore a long violet gown with silver buttons down the front of it; from under the violet velvet cap that covered his head his silver hair waved delicately back from a face that was handsome, dignified and petulant.

"I fear," said the Archbishop of York, "that I am late." He dipped his fingers in the water that a page brought and wiped them on the napkin from the lad's shoulder. "I had forgot time in my devotions." He sighed. "And in sad thoughts of these sad times."

"It is no matter unless you will grudge at your pottage being cold," said Darcy, just on the hither side of discourtesy.

"Pottage?" says the Archbishop, and sniffed at the plate. "Leek pottage again?"

"The leeks grow in the garden," said Darcy. "When they are at an end maybe we'll sup pottage without even leeks to flavour it. For if it comes to a siege there'll be little to eat."

The Archbishop turned in his chair. "Do you not take victuals into the castle?" he asked.

"And did your grandmother not know how to suck eggs? I would take in victuals if I could get them. But what the townsmen will bring in is nought, and these rebels are taking up all about."

"Have you then," the Archbishop asked, with a slight shake in his voice, "written to the King's Grace to send help?"

"Once, and had no answer. And again to-day," said Darcy, and helped himself to a handful of nuts and began to crack them between his teeth. He glanced again at Constable, and again the spark of anger and angry laughter was in his eyes.

"But," said Sir Robert, whose sense of propriety was a little troubled by my Lord's baiting of so reverend a spiritual personage, "but it is not to be thought that a rout of poor commons and husbandmen will assault such a castle as Pomfret."

"No," said the Archbishop.

"No?" said Darcy. "If I thought that I should sleep the easier. But I think they will, and shall I tell you for why?"

The Archbishop took out the spoon from his pottage and laid it on his tranch of bread. He waved his hand to show that they should take away the pottage, and his gesture conveyed by its delicate languor that worn though he might be by the cares of his high station, and in need of sustenance, yet to set leek pottage before him was not so much a stupidity as an irreverence.

"Shall I, my Lord Archbishop," said Darcy again, "tell you for why?" and leaned towards him and said, nailing his words, as it were, to the wood of the table with a stiff forefinger, "Because you, my Lord, are come into the castle, therefore the commons will not pass it by."

"I?" said the Archbishop haughtily. "What have I done against them?" He looked at the plate of cold rabbit pie set before him with a pained disgust. "I have done nothing against them," he muttered, with a trace of anxiety in his voice.

"It is not what you have done against them, but what you shall do for them," said Darcy.

"For them? I'll do nothing for them."

Sir Robert asked what should my Lord do for them, and Darcy turned to him to say, "Why, write the Articles of their grievances that they shall send to the King."

"No," cried the Archbishop from his other hand. "Never! Never! I will die first before I should give aid or counsel to traitors."

"But see, my Lord," Darcy turned to him, "see what they do for you—perilling their necks to save the privilege of the spiritual men, and defend the faith of the Church! Meetly —as it seems to me—might they ask of your counsel, and think to have you go along with them." He turned again to Sir Robert. "You'll have heard how they call this their 'pilgrimage,' so it is seen that in their eyes it is all for the sake of the Church, and of the spiritual men."

"They are mistook. The Faith is in no peril. The King hath so provided by his late book. It is rebellion. I would see them all hanged, every one. You hear me say it."

"Then let us pray," said Darcy, "that it cometh not to that pass that I must surrender the castle to them."

The Archbishop's mouth opened as though to breathe, "Surrender?" but he shut it again. Then he said hastily and softly, "I am not well," and got up from the board and went out.

Darcy gave a sharp laugh and stood up. "Come on, Robert," he said, "let's take view of the well, and the offices. And I told the carpenters to look to the timbers of the bridge and tell me how they stand."

They had seen to all these things, and found all in bad state, and were on their way back to the Great Chamber; my Lord said he would write a letter to the Earl of Shrewsbury, who lay at Nottingham, gathering men. "But they come in slowly," said Sir Robert, who had this very morning come from there. They opened the door of the brew-house yard, and came on a little space of garden beside an old pear tree on a wall, where great tits, handsome and bold, swung and sported. There were leeks growing here, proudly fountaining their dagger-pointed leaves, which from the plait-pattern in the centre sprang up and out, to drop with a sudden stately fall.

"Pottage for the Archbishop," said Darcy grimly, and laughed.

"What," asked Sir Robert, "was the news that fellow brought you just now?" A man in a homespun coat and clouted shoes, but with a sharper face than a poor country hind was like to have, had whispered with my Lord in the wood-yard.

"He? Oh! he saith that the Howdenshire men and those beyond Derwent were yesterday at Weighton. That means Howdenshire has joined itself with Beverley and Holderness."

Sir Robert looked grave at that, and stood frowning along the ranks of leeks. At last he said: "And yet it sticks, like a crumb in my throat, that what we hold for the King we hold to keep that hound Cromwell in place, and others as great heretics as he." He glanced at Darcy and then added, "Yet we can do no other."

Darcy looked down at him, and the corners of his mouth twitched. Constable, when he would be indirect, was so transparent.

"Ask me outright, Robert, 'Will you surrender Pomfret?' But first answer me this. Do you conceive me a man lightly to surrender such a castle to such an enemy?"

"No," Sir Robert muttered, a little red, "that I do not."

"But," cried Darcy, "our most reverend father in God, the Archbishop, by God's Passion I am sick to hear him!" and he laughed a little. "I like to make him quake, now for fear of the King, and now of the commons."

October 15

Julian was in bed already, and Laurence was just pulling his shirt off over his head. She let her eyes slide away from his thin shanks, and looked beyond him to the press, which had the story of Deborah, Jael and Sisera carved on it; July did not know it, but Deborah, a stalwart lady in a wide starched veil, always reminded Laurence of the first Mistress Machyn.

"They say," said Laurence, through his shirt, "that this rebellion in Lincolnshire is worse than was thought."

"I supposed," July murmured, "that it had been put down." After a great scare, when she had first heard of "trouble in the North," she had ceased to take any interest in the business. Lincolnshire was not Yorkshire.

Laurence folded his shirt neatly and padded across the rushes to the bed where his night-shirt lay. "The Lincolnshire

[480]

traitors are put down. But now they rise in Yorkshire, under one Aske. What he is, I know not—some low fellow."

July sat up in bed. Laurence, slipping the night-shirt over his head, did not see her wide, frightened eyes, nor the hand which covered her open mouth. He turned and blew out the candle. When he groped his way into bed he put his hands out to draw her to him.

But she pushed him stiffly away, and he knew she was shaking all over.

"What is it, sweet?" he asked hastily, thinking her to be ill.

For a minute she could only hold him off, saying nothing. Then she muttered, "Who? Where?"

At first he did not know what she was asking. But she said, "Who—leads this—this new insurrection?" and he told her again, "It is one Aske, so they say. But you do not know him?"

"No," she said. "No."

Laurence heard her teeth chatter together as she spoke. He thought, "She is as scared as a bird," and his heart melted, as if it laughed and cried over her at once.

He said, "Peace, peace, my sweeting. They shall not come here." He might have been soothing a child wakened out of a nightmare.

Not because of his words, but because his hands ceased to constrain her, she suddenly flung herself towards him in the bed, clutching him by the wrists.

"It's not that. It—it is—it is—" She stopped, and then made herself speak. "It is what is done to traitors."

He did his best to soothe her then, using all the gentleness he knew, and, at last, when he thought she slept, he lay long awake, pondering upon her, upon her terrors, and upon the frightened child, the frightened lass, whose life, fugitive as any wild, hunted thing, these terrors seemed to betray.

"But," he thought, "if God would give us a child— Then it would be well with her. For," he said to himself, "she should see it grow and thrive, God of His grace permitting, like a flower. And nor it, nor would I, do anything that might frighten her. And so she would forget to be afraid."

October 16

Robert Aske rode, the first of all the host, through Walmgate Bar into York. Under the ringing hollow of the arch the sound of his own horse's hoofs swelled so that it overmastered even the tramp of all the horsemen behind him. Then he came out into the street beyond, and was met by the shouting of a great crowd. And while the people still shouted the bells began to peal, from all the church towers in York, and among them the bells of the Minster, dancing up and down unseen stairways of sound, till the air was wild with their flying feet, running after each other, overtaking, clanging together.

The long procession of horsemen came out from Petergate into the great space before the West door of the Cathedral. There had been rain that day, and a high wind which had only dropped towards sunset, leaving the air very clear, and the sky swept and blue. There were pools in the paving, and great leaves blown from the chestnut trees lay scattered there. The chestnut leaves were bright gold, and the pools reflected all the colours of the riders' cloaks, in flashes and gleams of scarlet, green, sanguine, murrey and blue.

When they had got down from their horses the Minster bells stopped ringing, leaving a great silence troubled only by little and near noises, and by the dancing of more distant bells. Then those who stood close to the West doors heard the great bolts run back; the doors groaned as they swung inward, and at that same moment the choir began to sing just inside, boys and men, sweet and deep, high and low, while beyond the organ pealed and rumbled. So they went in, the choir leading, then the priests, vested in cloth of gold and silver, in satin and velvet, spangled with jewels and stiff with gold embroideries, a Paradise garden of colour, towards the High Altar. The Captains followed the priests, Aske first, and after him the other Captains, and after them the host, till the great church was crammed.

Through all the solemnity of Vespers Aske knelt, stood, knelt again, and knew no meaning in what he did. Trifles possessed his mind; the miller of Snaith's cloak had a long darn on one shoulder; there was a priest in a blue velvet vestment who was very like old Dom Henry at Ellerton, but with a wart on his nose. And a foolish anxiety beset him—lest he should miss the signal which would call him from his stall to make his offering upon the High Altar. He did not miss the signal, and in a few moments he was back again, and a blue velvet purse fringed with silver lay on the altar; now his thoughts strayed to the farm at Bubwith which he had pledged to raise the money in the purse; there was the rick-yard stuffed for winter, the oxen were coming slowly home from ploughing in the last light, and hens were scratching round the kitchen door.

They knelt again. The priest at the altar raised his hand for the blessing, and in a moment the voices of the choir flowered again in the silence. Aske, in the darkness that his hands made before his face, tried to collect his thoughts. But he could not do it; the most he could reach was a confusion of words as empty of meaning as chaff is of the winnowed grain. "*Deo gratias! Miserere mei Domine!*" he muttered, and did not know whether he gave thanks or prayed for mercy.

Close on midnight Will Wall knocked at the door of the chamber in Sir George Lawson's house where his master was to sleep. But he was not sleeping yet. His voice called out to come in, and, when Will went in, there he sat at the table, with Master Monkton on one hand and Master Rudston on the other, and the three of them busy writing. Gervase Cawood, a man from Howden and a Captain in the host, was on the settle by the fire notching tallies with his knife as they called out numbers to him.

Will shut the door before he said that there was one come in secret.

"He says he is my Lord Darcy's steward."

"Ha!" cried Master Rudston, and clapped his hand down open on the table. "So my Lord would be with us!"

Aske said, "Bring him in. And keep the door, Will."

So Will brought him in—a big, gaunt, grey-haired man with a red face.

Will kept the door for perhaps half an hour, and then out came Rudston, Monkton, Gervase Cawood, and my Lord Darcy's steward. So after they had been gone downstairs a little while Will went in to his master, and found him sitting at the table with pen in his hand and paper before him, but staring at the page as if he did not see it.

Will went softly about the room for a while, glancing at Aske from time to time, but he did not move.

At last Will said, "Master, will you not sleep?" And then, "Oh, Master Robin, this is a blessed day. Listen yonder!" From the streets, which should have been quiet hours ago, came a distant sound of pipes, tabrets and fiddles. Just below the window a boy went by singing very sweetly, "Salve Regina." "The commons," said Will, "are putting in the Monks that have been turned out. They will do it, late as it is, and this night God shall be worshipped again," and he ran to Aske and knelt and would have kissed his hand.

"Will! Will!" said Aske, touched, but more displeased. If only this strange, unaccountable creature that was his serving-man would cease to swing between moods of devotion and beastly drunkenness, "then," thought Aske, "it would be the better for both of us."

"No, Master," Will cried, mistaking Aske's tone, "I've not drunk. Not to-night. I would not touch the ale to-night," and he fell to crying wildly.

"Tchk!" said Aske under his breath, and patted Will on the shoulder, and, to quiet him, began to talk about Lord Darcy's steward. My Lord, it seems, had sent him to bring away a copy of the commons' Oath, and of their Articles, "And he asked to know whether we would agree to a head Captain, if the Articles should please my Lord."

"God's Passion!" cried Will hotly. "You're our chief Captain."

"I told him," Aske said, as if Will had not spoken, "that a nobleman of the King's Council was more like to send a spy than a true messenger to know the purpose of the commons. This man, Strangways, promised us we should have Pomfret if we came there. Would God that we might. But my Lord would never yield up the King's strong castle."

"Would he not? Why not?"

"No man would," said Aske, but he meant, "I would not," and then, he got rid of Will by sending him, late as it was, with the copy of the Oath of Lincolnshire. "And bid Master Strangways be forth out of York before daybreak, for I'll not have my Lord Darcy's man see the muster," said he, "when it is held."

After Will had gone he sat awhile, thinking of my Lord —of all that he knew of him in the past, and of what Darcy's steward had said of his master—and there was little of it that pleased him, for he said to himself, "He's a man of deep counsels, wily, full of statecraft. That which we have entered on is not for such as him."

And suddenly he knew clearly what it was that they were entered on. He took a fresh quill, and a fresh sheet, and wrote—

The Oath of the Honourable men,

and under that—

Ye shall not enter into this our Pilgrimage of Grace for the Commonwealth, but only for the love that ye do bear unto Almighty God, his Faith, and to Holy Church militant and the maintenance thereof, to the preservation of the King's person and issue, to the purifying of the nobility, and to expulse all villein blood and evil Councillors against the Commonwealth from his Grace and his Privy Council of the same. And that ye shall not enter into our said Pilgrimage for no particular profit to yourself, nor to do displeasure to any private person, but by counsel of the Commonwealth, nor slay nor murder for no envy, but in your hearts put away all fear and dread, and take afore you the Cross of Christ, and in your hearts his faith.

Will came in. Aske said, "I have nearly done." After a moment more he laid down his pen.

"Here is the Oath that we shall swear to-morrow," he said, and read it aloud.

October 17

Thomas Strangways found Sir Robert Constable in the Great Chamber at Pomfret; it was crowded, but Sir Robert sat in a corner bent over a chessboard upon which he had set out a random number of pieces; he was plotting subtle moves and dark serpentine approaches against an imaginary opponent, and his face when he looked up wore an expression of pure, blissful absorption. But as he saw Strangways it changed.

"Ah!" he cried. "You! You are to go in. My Lord's in his bath, but he will not care for that."

So they went in together to the smaller Privy Chamber beyond where my Lord simmered, pink and sweating, in his tub, with one soaping his back. The room smelt damp and sweet from the steam and the sweet herbs strewed on the water.

"You!" said my Lord, as Sir Robert had done, and told the servant to put a towel round his shoulders and then go away. "Well," said he, when they were alone, "and what treason have you been pledging me to, you old whoreson?" and he laughed.

But Strangways was solemn.

"I've the copy of their oath, and the articles that you bade me bring," said he, and my Lord beckoned and bade him hold it for him to read, "For my hands are wet," he said.

So they were silent while my Lord read the two papers, making little dabbling noises in the water under the towel as he read, and sometimes swearing and sometimes laughing below his breath.

Then he said, waving Strangways away: "What are the numbers of their muster?"

Strangways said he could not tell, for he had come to York long after dark, "And their Captains said I must forth before day-break that I might not see them. But York seemed stuffed with men, as for an expedition against the Scots."

"Tcha!" cried Darcy. "A rabble of poor commons."

"And I saw Lord Lumley's banner hang out," said Strangways with a stubborn look, "and Lord Latimer's. And the rest that are not gentlemen are yeomen of Yorkshire, harnessed and horsed every man. The poor commons that go on foot lie outside the city. And order is kept as good as in the King's palace at Westminster."

"You hear?" Darcy turned to Constable. "The fellow's as full of treason as an egg of meat. And did you say," he asked lightly, as if the matter was nothing but a jest, "that I would lead them if they would go the way I will?"

"I said as you bade me," Strangways answered, and shut his mouth like a trap.

"And no further?" Darcy teased him.

"I spoke for myself what was the truth."

"And was rank treason, I'll be bound. Well, and what did they answer?"

"One of the Captains said it was more like you would send a spy among them than a true messenger."

"Which of them was that?" Darcy rapped out.

"Master Aske—I knew him by his one eye."

"Well," said Darcy, and laughed softly, "he may have but one eye, but it seems he can see as far through a wall as another man."

After that he questioned Strangways sharply about many things, and at last bade him and Sir Robert go and let him get dressed.

Strangways, once they were out of the Privy Chamber, would have gone away to find breakfast, but Constable laid hold on his arm.

"What does he mean?" He tipped his head towards the room they had just left. Strangways shook his head.

"But what will he do?" cried Sir Robert.

"I'll tell you one thing he will not do. He'll not hold Pomfret."

Constable cried out at that, "God's Wounds! But he will!"

"If the commons come this way to knock on the gate no man in Pomfret, save the gentlemen only, will fight."

"God's Wounds!" said Sir Robert again between his teeth, thinking it to be only too true.

Then he said: "But will he yield with a good heart? Does he approve their purposes? I—" he hesitated, "I like it ill that we who stand against the commons stand between them and that rascal Cromwell and those that he has set on to spoil the Church."

Strangways looked at him searchingly. "So that is your conscience in the matter?" He took his arm from under Sir Robert's hand, and lifted the latch of the further door. But before he opened it he said: "What my Lord means now, nor I nor any man can know. He has a deep, working brain, and more wit and wisdom than all of us. But I know this, that since the commons' cause is the right cause, and the cause of all true men, my Lord will be with them one day. For there's no man truer nor he."

Then he went out, and left Sir Robert not much less puzzled than before.

A tramping tinker told the news to the yeoman at Oxcue, who told it to a Marrick hind, who brought it to the smithy at Marrick, quite early on a fine morning. The smith was busy over a plough, which two improvident fellows had brought in to have the coulter re-set; they said it was leaving a rest-balk between the ridges which would breed thistles next year, and so it might, but any good husbandman would have seen to it long ago, not left it till the very ploughing season itself.

So those two lounged and leaned at one side of the smithy doors, and the Nuns' shepherd stood at the other; the bag of his pipes was under his arm, and now and again he would set his lips to the mouthpiece and blow a low and thoughtful note, which was, for the most part, his only contribution to the conversation. His life made him a very silent man, and set him, as it were, always at a distance: even when the Marrick hind told the news of how the commons had taken York the shepherd did not watch the face of the speaker, but seemed to measure with his eyes the long shadows which the bright morning laid across the fields.

The owners of the plough were jubilant at the news, their nature being to take pleasure in trouble. The smith, stooping over the coulter, said little, but by his silence managed to convey doubt of the truth of the hind's story; he did not want to believe it, since, being all for the new ways, he had been very cock-a-hoop about the pulling down of the Abbeys. The hind, however, was positive. "Sure it was truth," he protested, and the two others rammed it home by every means they could, calling upon Shepherd to agree with them how good news it was. All he would say was, however, "Marry, that such things should be! What a coil in the country! What'll come of it?"

Then—"Here's Priest!" cried the hind, and as Gib Dawe came by, bent under a load of bracken for winter bedding, the two Marrick men hailed him, telling him the news, which, they guessed rightly, would please him as little as it pleased the smith.

Gib halted, holding his pikel with one hand, and with the other wiping the sweat from his face.

"So," cried one of the two, "Master Cromwell and his heretic Bishops shall down," and he began to sing a song that was going about in those days—

> Much ill cometh of a small mote
> As a Crumwell set in a man's throat,
> That shall put many other to pain, God wot!
> But when Crumwell is brought alow—

"Yea, yea," said the other, cocking a snook, neither exactly in the direction of Gib, nor yet far off. "Our valiant North countrymen that have gone forth for the sake of Christ Crucified shall knock on the King his doors—"

"Aye!" cried Gib, "and you're valiant men too. And yet I would have you wait a while till you have seen the King his doors; namely, the great gates of his Tower of London, and the guns therein, very many; aye, and that which may sooner cool you—the gates of London Bridge, where the flies buzz about the meat of traitors thicker than round the butchers' stalls. And what will a lousy pack of countrymen do against the King's high nobility with their men-at-arms and the King's—tcha!" he broke off, "I'll answer you no further," and he tramped on, leaving them, for the moment, silenced.

But he himself was ill-satisfied with what he had said, having, as it were, conjured up the great and the rich to set down poor men. Yet those poor men, fools and blind, were such as spurned the pure new light of the Gospel; and among them as leaders were proud, overweening men such as Master Robert Aske.

" 'Christ Crucified!' " He spat out the words. "They'll cry on Christ Crucified when the hangman's hand is on them!" Yet it was all awry, to have poor men rise for such a cause, and also to prosper in it. He was angry, but his anger could find no sure aim. He came, panting because of his wrathful hurried pace, to the gate of the parsonage, and pushed through it, his wide burden of dry bracken hissing against the posts of the gate.

Dame Nan Bulmer brought the news to the Ladies at the Priory, coming hastily into the Prioress's Chamber, handsome more than ordinary in her untidy, hungry-looking way.

She interrupted Dame Christabel at Mixtum, would not shut the door, would not sit down, would not eat, yet, as she stood talking took up from the table and broke and munched the fresh manchet bread, and then reached for the Prioress's plate of quails, and ate from this small choice morsels casually yet delicately.

None of these things pleased the Prioress, who had a sore cold, and for whom, alone of the Ladies, there were quails, a present from her sister. Nor did the news please her.

"And so," Dame Nan concluded, "before them all my kinsman went into the Minster, and before them all laid his gift upon the altar. They say," she declared, "that there are forty thousand men to follow him, gentlemen and commons. And in the South Country will be many more to rise with our people. So you need not fear," said she, "that this House shall be brought to an end."

She was holding out her fingers vaguely, as if she expected the Prioress to hand her the water to dip them in. Dame Christabel did not move, so she wiped them on the cloth. Dame Christabel looked at the greasy marks and said, "I did not fear it. We have my Lord Privy Seal's promise for our continuance, and the King's." '

"Mass!" Dame Nan laughed. "You trust to your bribes to bind such a rascal as that fellow Cromwell?"

"Fie! To speak so of the King's servants!"

"Fie on such a servant of the King!" And Dame Nun turned away. "I must on to tell the Ladies of St. Bernard this good, great news," said she, and went, leaving the door open with the fresh morning wind flapping the table-cloth, and scattering light wood ash from the hearth over plates and dishes. Dame Christabel did not, even for courtesy's sake, follow her across the Great Court to see her away. Instead she shut the door with an angry, quiet care, and, going back to the fire, stood looking at the bright sparks running along a blackened log, and one hand jagging at the beads at her girdle.

"Ill," she said, half aloud, "will come of it. Ill will come of it." She did not know how; she did not fear any ill in particular, but because Master Aske and these others had blundered in where they were not needed, she would be ready to blame them if ill should come. And then she remembered Dame Nan's last words—she would away to tell the Ladies of St. Bernard the news. The Prioress heard the beads, the string of which a sharper unconscious jerk of her hand had snapped, begin to patter on the hearth, and into the rushes. It had been indeed these last words that pricked her most nearly. Should the rebels succeed in their purpose not only Marrick, but all Abbeys should stand. For long now, hardly recognized but dearly cherished, there had lain at the bottom of her mind the thought of Marrick continuing secure, thrifty, prosperous in barn and byre; while in the House of St. Bernard's Nuns, down the river, the wind would blow through the unshuttered, empty rooms, where no more were there any Ladies in the white gowns of the Cistercians.

"But," she said to herself, as she stooped to search for the beads, which were of pretty carved box-wood, "rebellion doth not prosper, because God hateth it."

She had to endure much that day from the Ladies, to whom Dame Nan had managed to scatter the news on her way across the Great Court, as though it were corn, and they a company of clucking hens.

And clucking hens the Prioress found them, assembled as they were, a noisy excited company in the warmest corner of the Cloister. Dame Margery Conyers, her face crimson and eyes streaming, had her hands clasped, and was crying: "*Deo gratias! Deo gratias!* Our House is saved! Our House is saved!" (As if Christabel Cowper, Prioress, had not already saved it.) And there was Dame Anne Ladyman, shaking her head, and casting her eyes this way and that in the very manner of a brainless hen, and declaiming upon "that sweet noble gentleman Master Aske. Jesu! he hath all our hearts at his feet."

The Prioress came near them and the tumult a little hushed, but then Dame Margery cried out, demanding that they should send money to the commons to help the cause. "And if not money," said she, with surprising common sense, "then we have cattle that can be driven thither for their meat, and none of us will grudge to go a little hungry this winter for those men that are our defenders."

The Prioress only looked at her, but she spoke to Dame Anne Ladyman.

"How old are you? How old?" They all knew as well as Dame Anne herself, which was not precisely, but dismally near enough. "And you talk of your heart, and of sweet noble gentlemen! Oh!" she cried, "if you had committed fornication I could better forgive it than such very foolishness. Yet that you never did, but only and always cackle of it, cackle, cackle!"

There was, however, one who, in the Prioress's opinion, spoke with propriety of this unlawful scurry of the commons. In Chapter that morning Dame Margery's suggestion was debated by the Ladies, but, by the force of the Prioress's resistance, defeated. In the charged silence that followed, Dame Eleanor Maxwell slowly rose. They all turned to her, staring. Not one could remember when it was that she had last spoken in Chapter, but they thought they could be sure enough of what she would say concerning this great news of her kinsman, which someone had shouted into her ear.

And then she began, in her faint, light, toneless voice, to tell them that though she could not herself well recall the evil times when men fought for the two Roses, yet she had very often heard her father speak of them. "And evil times they were, though you think not of them, nor does that rash boy. Nor can he nor any other serve God by moving war against his Prince when the realm is in peace." And she sat down again, her face trembling, and her hand shaking on her stick.

One of the Manor ploughmen told the news to Malle. He was an old Aske servant, and so he took great pride in what Master Robin had done, since Aske was Aske to him, whether of the older or younger branch.

Malle had come out with her spindle to drive Gib's cow to pasture on the grass along the verges of the road. The sun was still not yet high, and the shadows were long. In a neighbour's croft a man was digging; as he drew the spade out the earth-scoured iron flashed white; the new-turned earth of the plough furrows glittered too, sticky wet, and the polished quarters of the two horses shone dark, yet bright.

"Hi! mad Malle!" cried the ploughman. "Have ye heard this good news?"

Malle stopped, letting the spindle run down and hang still at her knee. But when he told her she did not seem to make much of it, only mumbling, "What will they be at?" Then she moved on, after the slowly moving cow. The ploughman shrugged, slapped the rope rein against the horses' flanks to start them again, and tramped away with a good heart, looking forward to the drinking and talking there would be at the alehouse, when dusk brought all home from the fields.

That night, when the door and shutters were barred, Malle was cutting bread for Wat's supper and hers; bread and lard was their supper; Gib had had his, and gone up to bed with the rushlight to read there, so they groped by the last light of the fire and must speak only in whispers. But it was pleasant here and friendly; Wat had his bare feet in the ashes that had a touch soft as silk, and warm. Before Gib went he had told them, sharply and angrily, the news from York. Wat was rubbing his belly over it now, as if he had eaten something very good. He was always pleased at things which displeased his father. But Malle mumbled to herself over the loaf.

"So there *is* news," said she suddenly, in as loud a whisper as she dared. "A marvel is the news. God is here comen to us. That is the news!" She flapped her left hand in the air as though Gib's news was a fly which she drove away.

"How can He put on," she said, "such a homespun coat, and not burn all up with the touch of Him? If he shouldered down the sun, and quenched light with His coming, it would be no marvel."

Wat scrambled up, and catching a handful of her gown shook it impatiently, being hungry. Malle shoved into his hands two thick slabs of bread with lard between, and he went back to the hearth. But she lingered at the table. "Instead," she murmured, "He came stilly as rain, and even now cometh into the darkness of our bellies—God in a bit of bread, to bring morning to our souls. *There* is news."

Gib called angrily from the room above. Wat looked up with

a glare, but shrank away from the fire and into the safer shadows. Malle cried that they two would not be long. She laid her finger on her lips, and laughed silently at Wat, to wipe away his scared look.

October 18

All the Captains except Robert Aske stood in a wide, deep window in the house of Master Collins, the Treasurer, in York. The window was open, and the late afternoon sunshine and mild air came pleasantly in. The Captains had put on what they had with them of best clothes to sup with Master Collins; some had bought a new cloak or doublet or a finer sword since they came to York, so that they made a cheerful show. They talked cheerfully too, for Master Collins was known to keep a good table, and the smells that they had met on coming in had promised well.

They heard someone come pounding up the stairs, and then Aske burst into the room. He had a quill pen stuck behind his ear, inky fingers, and a smudge of ink on his cheek.

"Master Collins," he said, "I pray thee have me excused, but here's no time to sup to-day." He turned to the others. "The Vicar of Brayton has come to me. He says that Strangways, my Lord Darcy's steward—you know him, Cawood, Rudston—" He looked to them and they nodded. "The parson says Strangways has shown him a way to enter into the Castle. What Castle? Marry, Pomfret. But whether that word of Strangways be truth or trick the parson says this is sure— that the servants and even my Lord's men will not stand up against us. Which of you will come with me? How soon can we muster to ride?"

"Wait a moment." Mr. Saltmarsh pushed his way forward. "Where is this Vicar of Brayton? Let's have him in to question him?"

"He's gone. I sent him back forthwith. He'll have ways to—"

Sir Thomas Metham's sharp voice came from the midst of the group.

"God's Death! You sent him? And now you'd send us?" and he laughed in a silence.

"Aye, Mr. Aske," Saltmarsh said, with more courtesy, but no less malice in his voice. "It seems to me also that the messenger should have come to all the captains, and if he came to one, that one should have brought him to the rest."

"Mass!" Aske began, and had been about to say the truth,

that indeed he had never thought of it, and now was sorry. But Sir Thomas snickered again, and—"Mass!" said Aske instead, "what does it matter? There's the news. Now—"

"Yet," Mr. Saltmarsh objected in his smooth voice, "yet tarry."

"I'll not tarry. Pomfret we must have. I tell you—"

"You tell us too much, Master Aske." Mr. Saltmarsh looked round about for approval. "Are you head Captain over us?"

"Aye," cried Sir Thomas, "are you?"

"I tell you—" Aske said again, his voice easily overmastering their voices, and thereafter for a few minutes the servants below, and passersby outside, could hear the clamour and sometimes the words of a very pretty quarrel.

At last—"We cannot," Aske cried, "wait on further news from Lincolnshire. We hear news enough."

"Yet no sure news."

"Enough. And so ill news that I am sick to hear it."

"Then the better to wait."

Aske caught at his temper.

"If," he said slowly, "if they have yielded already in Lincolnshire there is nothing we should wait for. If they have not yielded, and we hold Pomfret, they may take courage from it."

"Then," Mr. Saltmarsh dropped the words one by one, provocatively, "then, if Pomfret must be taken, a' God's Name go and take it."

"A' God's Name I'll go if I go alone," Aske cried, in such a voice and with such a blaze of anger in his eye that till he slammed the door on them not one of those left behind spoke or moved.

But then Lord Latimer drew towards Lord Scrope, and they put their heads close. Master Collins came up beside Lord Lumley; he, pleasant good man, was distressed to think of the good dinner so interrupted and left spoiling, for already two or three of the Howdenshire Captains had gone hurrying after Captain Aske.

Metham and Saltmarsh had come together at the open window. Metham leaned out; he laughed, then pointed his finger:

"There he goes. And in what a fume!"

Saltmarsh leaned out too, and together they watched Aske, a little man, very angry, and in a great hurry; they saw him snatch the quill from behind his ear, stare at it as if it were strange to him, and throw it down.

"Let him go," Saltmarsh said; he was still much huffed, and red about the ears. "He is," said he, "of too rude and tyrannical a humour to be borne."

Aske came to his lodging still angry, and still very much in a hurry. As he ran up the stairs he was calling for the men to turn out, and for "Ned! Ned!" to come and arm him; and he was thinking it was well Ned should do it, because he was a quick handy lad, and always cheerful; but if Will Wall had been on his feet, instead of ill in bed, Ned would have been driven off for Will to fumble and bungle, and, besides that, to start a bickering with his master. "For he's a difficult fellow these days," thought Aske, "or else I am," as he flung open the door of his chamber.

Will stood up from the bed. His face was like paper, and he looked about as sturdy as a rag in the wind.

"What! Are you here?" Aske cried, and added hastily, "I'm glad of it. You're better?" But already he had seen Will's face fall and his mouth shake. Then he saw beside Will's feet, neatly laid out in order, all the pieces of Sir Robert Aske's armour, which he had brought from Aughton. They were ready for him to put on, and Will, stooping slowly, was lifting the padded coat that went on first. Aske ripped open the buttons of his doublet, and threw it and his coat together on the bed. He must even suffer Will; he could do no other. When Ned put his bright, smiling face round the door Aske bade him to see to the horses.

So while Will armed him he stood very still, helping when he might, as unobtrusively as possible. But often Will would push his hands away, and then fiddle over a catch or a buckle that might have been righted in an instant. One thing there was to the good; he did not talk; but that, Aske supposed, was because he needed all his strength; sometimes when Will's hands came down on his shoulders he thought it was only thus that the man managed to keep himself upright.

When at last it was done, and Will stooped over the buckle of the sword belt, Aske struck him lightly on the shoulder in place of farewell, and thanks, and all that was not to be said.

"And now off you pack to bed again, and lie snug till I come back from Pomfret," he told him cheerfully.

But Will, straightening himself, showed a face tragical and quivering.

"And," said he, "if I was not the sot that I am, I'd be beside you, to die there. For here you go to the assault of a strong castle, and there over the water of Humber—they have—they have—"

Aske turned his eye away from Will's face. He could hear the horses stamp on the cobbles of the yard; it must be much longer than the half hour he had given the others to be ready at Micklegate Bar.

"Have they surrendered then, in Lincolnshire?"

"You know it?" Will cried. "They told you as you came in."

"It was easy to guess." Aske gave a little laugh, and then was silent for a moment. "Well, I must not fail of Pomfret, let Lord Darcy shut his gates or no."

He touched Will on the shoulder again, but absently, as if already his mind was on the road, and went out. Will blundered back to the bed, flopped down there, and cried shamelessly for a while. But in the end he took comfort, seeing, in his mind, Master Robin stand, and hearing him laugh. Will remembered the hero called Samson, who had plucked up posts, gates, bars and all from some Jewish city, and carried them away on his shoulders. Master Robin looked, Will thought, like as if he could carry away the world on his shoulders, if he should resolve to carry it.

There were about three hundred men waiting at the Bar, Howdenshire men mostly, with some from Beverley. It was few enough; but Aske hid his chagrin; and anyway, speed was more than force in this, he told himself. Besides, though few, they were of the best sort of yeomen, and there were Aughton fellows grinning at him in the front ranks, and Will Monkton with them.

They made such good speed that in order not to reach Pomfret in daylight, and so betray their little strength, they must lie up somewhere for a while. So for an hour of twilight they waited in the cold whispering shadows of a little wood just across the Aire.

Aske and Monkton tramped up and down together to keep warm, while the wind flapped the hem of their cloaks against their steel back and breast pieces with a hollow sound. Monkton glanced aside more than once at Aske, but he plodded in silence, and with a grim face. At last Monkton spoke:

"Robin!"

"Anon?"

"You did not well to rate Metham and Saltmarsh with so rough a tongue."

"Did I not? Oh? I did not well?"

"Now, Robin," Monkton began, but Aske bore him down.

"No, I'll not hold my tongue, neither for you nor no man. Why would you all have me whisper, cog, speak smooth?"

Certainly he was not whispering. The men stared at them, and Monkton wished with fervour that Robin's voice were less powerful, or his patience longer. "Robin," he thought, "used to be a good-humoured fellow," but not seldom in these days he had felt that he did not know this brother-in-law of his, whom, for so many years, he would have said he knew.

He declared, with more than his usual doggedness, that such language as Aske held towards the others might estrange them from the commons' cause.

That brought Aske's anger to blow against himself. What! did he think there were any such in the host? "No, by God's Passion! for I think there are none with us but are willing to go forward in their hearts," and Monkton could see, even in the dusk, how his face had turned darkly red. "There are none," said he again, as if by vehemence he could make it be so.

Yet after he seemed to wait, as if he knew that that was not all.

"And listen," said Monkton, "to what I heard. For those two were at the window when you were gone, but I stood below in the doorway. Saltmarsh said you should break your teeth against the walls of Pomfret. And Metham said—let you go and have your will, so as, if our pilgrimage miscarried you should be clearly seen to be ringleader, and so come under the King's vengeance in especial."

Aske flung away, laughing loudly. "Shall I listen or care to hear such talk as this?"

He stood apart, biting at his knuckles. The long, impatient sighing of the wind went through the wood, and there were incessant small noises like water trickling, but it was dry leaves that fell spindling past branches, and past other dry leaves not yet fallen.

He came back to Monkton. "It'll be full dark by we make Pomfret now," said he, and shouted to the men to make ready. He became suddenly cheerful, and Monkton could not see that his words had been at all heeded. Yet what he had said was there in Aske's mind, unregarded as a thorn in a man's thumb, which he will feel only when there is pressure put on it.

October 19

Aske, having waited at the gate of Pomfret Castle in a heavy cold rain till the hostage for him (it was George Darcy's eldest son) was brought out, now had to wait again in the Great Hall, while the gentleman went up to announce him to Lord Darcy and the great men above. There were a few young gentlemen, none of whom he knew, standing at the hearth; they looked over their shoulders, drew themselves closer together, and went on with their guarded talking. The servants who were clearing away the tables after dinner had, he could see, one eye on the gentlemen and one eye on him. But he would not look at them; he guessed that if he gave them half a chance they would be all about him, and shouting for the commons. Even as it was, when the gentleman who brought him in came back to bid him in to my Lord, one of the women at the screens cried out shrilly, "God save you, Sir, in your pilgrimage!" Aske turned and raised his hand, but he neither smiled nor spoke, and went on upstairs.

In the Great Chamber there were many lights, which, after the dark afternoon outside, dazzled his eye. For a minute he could see only lights—firelight, candlelight, torchlight—and among these the forms and faces of many men, but none of them clearly. Then, as his vision steadied, he could see my Lord Darcy on a high-backed settle beside the hearth, and beside him, haughty and beautiful in his violet velvet, the Archbishop. Sir Robert Constable sat on my Lord's other hand upon a stool; his sword trailed out behind him like a long, black, silver-tipped tail. On the hither side of the Archbishop was another priest with a clever, ugly, inscrutable frog's face. Beyond, and behind these, there were faces he half knew or did not know at all. He bowed to them and some of them did the same to him, but all watched him, in silence, waiting to see what he would do.

He went, his wet cloak dripping, to the hearth, set his foot on the edge of it and stretched out his hands to the warmth, not looking at any but keeping his eye on the flames, because he was thinking of what he should say, when he must speak. It mattered very much, he considered, what he should say.

Lord Darcy bade someone, "Take his cloak," and a gentleman came near, to whom he slung off the heavy wet fustian, and who then went away out of the room with it.

"What is that you carry?" Darcy asked.

"What? This?" Aske touched the white rod which he had tucked under his arm, then told them, what my Lord already knew, that it was the rod of his Captainship of the commons.

"And you carry it here—within the King's castle?"

"It was given me," Aske said, his eye still on the fire, and his thoughts on the words he should speak, "so I carry it."

Constable muttered under his breath that this was the same Robin Aske as ever! He glanced at Darcy, but could make nothing of his face, except that he was watching Aske closely. The Archbishop ceaselessly twirled a ring upon his finger without raising his eyes.

In a moment Aske said:

"My Lord, shall I speak?"

Darcy bowed his head in a very stately fashion.

"Speak freely!"

"Freely?" said Aske, but half to himself, as if he were still within his thoughts. "Surely I shall speak freely." But still for a little longer he was silent, and to more than one of them as they sat watching him it seemed that he gathered up some strength that was in him, before he lifted his head and spoke.

When he had done he looked round about at them, and then only at my Lord. "And now," said he, "it is for you to answer me."

Lord Darcy said that he must take counsel, so Aske was led away into the Privy Chamber beyond. When he had gone each man waited for his neighbour to speak.

"Well," said my Lord to the Archbishop, who had flushed to his silver hair. "It was to you he spoke first. Let us have your counsel then."

"Fie!" cried the Archbishop, "that such a man should so rebuke the Lords Spiritual who have the cure of souls of all lay persons, saying we have failed of our duty in that we have not been plain with the King's Highness—" He stopped there, because Lord Darcy laughed shortly, remarking that, well, surely this man Aske had been plain.

"Plain!" the Archbishop repeated, heightening the word by his tone of outrage. "But for us—for me—I vow before God I would have stood against the King's Grace's will in —er—certain things—to the death, if I could have prevailed. But it would have served nothing. To have resisted would have been death, and," he added hastily, "death profitless," and then went on to say that perhaps on the other hand this man Aske spoke not much amiss with regard to the temporal Lords, who should have warned the King.

"Enough!" Darcy interrupted him, and turned to Sir Robert Constable because he felt him fidgeting alongside.

"And you?" he asked sharply.

Sir Robert gave up fretting with his feet among the rushes; he planted them squarely, and tugged his sword round so that it was near to his hand.

"I think," he said, "that he speaks as an honest man."

George Darcy sprang up with such amazement, incredulity and disgust written upon his face that his father laughed aloud. But my Lord said, before George could speak, "Come now, here's little to the purpose. You all heard him say that he and his would assault to-night. How shall we answer him?"

"But," cried the Archbishop, "he cannot so soon. And my Lord of Shrewsbury will be here—"

He looked round, much less confident than his words, and caught Constable's eye, who growled that to his knowledge Master Aske was a man who acted with speed.

"By the Rood!" Sir George Darcy said with bitter disdain. "Let the commons assault! What then? Here's the King's strong castle to be held."

"Mother of God!" cried Darcy, "to be held by whom, son George, and held by what? Here are we few, two of us spiritual men, and there are a parcel of gentlemen of ours that will fight. And what of the rest?" He looked all about and no one answered. They had heard enough of the muttering that went on in corners, and seen the unwilling service that was done by servants and soldiers alike. "And," my Lord concluded, "with what shall we hold Pomfret? Marry, with quarter-staves and fleshing knives, for of munitions of war there be none."

"Yet," the Archbishop protested, obstinately, but with a quaver in his voice, "so great a castle—do we but shut the gates—"

"Mother of God!" Darcy broke in. "Can you no better counsel than that?" and there was a silence broken by Constable, who asked, "Shall you then surrender the castle, and, as he saith, take their oath?"

Darcy gave him an angry look and answered that if the castle had been well furnished "nor he nor any should have had neither the one nor the other but to his pain." Then he said: "Well, here's my counsel. Call him in and say we must have till Saturday eve. If he will tarry till Saturday may be he'll tarry till Monday, and by Monday, who knows?"

So Aske was fetched in again, and my Lord said, speaking haughtily and roughly:

"Well, here's your answer. I neither can nor will give up the King's castle."

"Nor join us," said Aske slowly, "in our Pilgrimage?"

"That's a fine new name for an unlawful scurry against the King's Grace and the peace of the realm."

It came to Aske then, like a great blow, that he had failed. He had spoken as well as he knew, plainly and truly, and they looked at him still with unbending, wooden hostility.

It was more difficult now to meet their eyes, knowing that he had failed, but he made himself do it lest there should be one among them who would be of the commons' fellowship; he found himself looking first, and also last, at Sir Robert Constable, but he would not raise his head, and Aske thought — "Why should I think it? Always he would be set against me."

He said: "Then we shall assault you, by every means whenever we will. You cannot hold the castle. Not one of your servants, nor of the soldiers neither, but is on our side." Then he struck his hands together, being much moved by failure and a sort of bewilderment it had brought him into, that they should not understand, or should not believe what was so plain to him.

"Yet," he said, "I had looked for more than to have Pomfret in our hand. I thought to have had you with me in our high cause; some of you at least. You, my Lord," he looked at the Archbishop, "you in especial."

The Archbishop caught the changed tone of his voice and grew haughty.

"And what would you have had of me?"

When Aske said, "To have your counsel, and that you should be mediator for us with the King," the Archbishop took him up.

"Then it were not well I should be joined with you, for a mediator should be neither of the one party nor of t'other."

Aske looked at him, saying nothing, and he went on, with an offer to come on a safe conduct and declare his mind to the commons, as to the righteousness of their cause.

Still Aske was silent, and the Archbishop, growing bolder, said, with the judicial air of one teaching logic in the schools, that, as for giving counsel, first it must be considered whether their enterprise were lawful, "for," said he, with a noble and lofty look, "you may have my body by constraint, yet never not my heart in the cause unless—"

"No, my Lord," Aske interrupted him, speaking softly, "I shall not give you safe conduct to come out to speak to the commons." Then he cried, in a voice that startled them all, "Oh! you Churchmen, Archbishops and bishops, and all the sort of you, will you never deal plainly with a man? Did you stay to speak with the commons when they came to you at Cawood? By God's Wounds! I have heard how you fled away. And you did well, for there are men among them would be without mercy, should you fall into their hands. Safe conduct? God's Bones! That you may so snarl up a plain thread that none can disentangle it. For you Archbishops and bishops are able to find wherewith to justify yourselves that ye let not out the squeak of a mouse against the King's doings. But we that have taken arms can see—" He stamped his foot, and then, ashamed to have let himself be so mastered by anger, turned back to my Lord. "So there's no more to be said."

But Darcy, looking proud and disdainful, bade him wait a while. "Give us," said he (this being Thursday), "till Saturday before you assault."

"Till to-morrow morning," said Aske; and when my Lord pressed him, "Till to-morrow morning at eight of the clock. For I know what is in your thought and it is in mine too—that my Lord of Shrewsbury may come; but I, as I deal plainly, I do not fear to speak of that I fear."

He swung round and went to the door. Lord Darcy waved his hand to Mr. Bapthorpe, who got up quickly and followed him. But Aske turned back. For a moment he stood looking at the ground and even now he thought, "No use to say more. No use." Then he lifted his head and spoke.

"Whether that I have said be true I put to your conscience. But if you fight against us, and win, you put both us, and you, and your heirs, and ours, in bondage for ever; for if you will not come with us, be sure we will fight against you, and against all that stop us. And we trust, by the Grace of God, that ye shall have small speed."

He put by Master Bapthorpe's hand, stretched out to unlatch the door, and opened it himself.

After he had gone there was a deal of talking, but few could find much that was new to say, the facts were so baldly plain. Lord Darcy lamented to the Archbishop how little hope there was that my Lord Steward (that was the Earl of Shrewsbury) should come in time. He beat his fist on his knee and cried that had he but munitions he would hold the castle till all the food was gone—"and that would give us eight days, or ten, or more if we should endure awhile the extremity of hunger," and he looked searchingly into the face of the Archbishop, who replied, but faintly, that indeed they would all be ready to suffer to the death, in their service to the King's Grace.

"Aye," said Darcy solemnly, "so would each man of us," and turned to lay his hand on Constable's shoulder who stood beside them. "Come, Robert, since these lousels are all about us, and may make assault any time—"

"But he granted us truce," cried Constable.

"Tush! Will you trust them? We'll make sure. Safe bind, safe find," he said, and pushed Constable towards the door.

They went out and about the castle, each noticing, but in silence, how indifferently watch was kept, and how surly were the looks of those whom they passed. At last, in the still, uncoloured air that the rain had left very keen and clear, they stood on the top of the keep, looking towards Micklegate and the town above. The commons were busy there, and, it seemed, cheerful about their work. The two on the tower saw the quick cold flash of axes above the heads of a little knot of men; the choked ringing note of the steel came to them just after each white flicker.

"What are they at?" Darcy muttered, and then answered himself. "Hah! a ram to bring down our gates." He looked down at Constable, and then said: "And what's amiss with you, Robert?"

Constable continued to scowl at the stones of the breast-work, which he was kicking with his foot. He said: "Will you send a message to Shrewsbury?"

"No, I will not. For he cannot reach us now. Nor can we get a message through to him."

"Then why—why this truce? A' God's Name if we must yield, let's yield."

Darcy looked at him, but he would not look up.

"And take their Oath? And join us with the commons?"

Constable was silent. Then he blurted out, angrily and in a hurry, that for himself he would be ready to take their Oath — "By cause that what he spoke was truth," said he, and met Darcy's eyes.

That my Lord was smiling a little made him angrier and he cried out that surely such was his opinion, and he'd not hide it. "But what yours is, Tom, in all these windings and turnings that you make—God alone knoweth it."

Darcy laughed at him again, and began to explain, very calmly and reasonably, that he had spoken as he had spoken, and done as he had done, so that men should report him to the King not as one who flung away a great castle lightly, and lightly joined with rebels.

"And who shall report you?" Constable grumbled.

"My Lord Archbishop." Darcy laughed again at Constable's expression. "Or any other." But on that he ceased to laugh, for like a flaw in crackled ice the thought struck through both their minds of George Darcy, with his look of pregnant disapproval. "By God's Cross, Robert," said Darcy, throwing off that thought, "you too may be glad if things go ill, that by these same windings and turnings of mine it is made clear that we are forced to their Oath and to their company."

"Oh!" Sir Robert groaned. "Here's policy! But—"

Darcy clapped him on the shoulder. "And why not policy? But—what?"

"But—Mass! But did you not in your conscience think that he spoke the truth to us?"

"So you and Strangways are of a sort in this!" Darcy pulled a face, then, catching Sir Robert's glowering look, said that none could deny but Aske had spoken boldly.

"And—truly?"

Darcy looked away into the town, where the smoke trails from evening fires were going up, straight in the stillness, with only the slightest pulsation from the living heat below to trouble them. "I wish," he muttered, "I knew how many he brought with him from York." Then he said, "Nor I'll not deny that to me he seemed, in the main, to speak the truth. More especially with regard to the spiritual men."

"Then," cried Sir Robert, "shall we that are gentlemen dread to take a good cause in hand, when the poor commons dread not?"

"And be hanged with them for traitors?" Darcy mocked.

"This Pilgrimage of theirs," Sir Robert went on doggedly, "I'll undertake it with a good will."

"Well," said Darcy, "it seems we'll all undertake it, will we nill we. But," he added, unexpectedly, "what plagues me is I cannot for the life of me remember where I saw the man before. "Twas in a great sunlight. But where?"

October 21

Lancaster Herald waved his hand to the commons, whom he had been haranguing, and rode on towards Pomfret more briskly than they could go, tied as they were to the pace of the wain that was loaded up with certain carcasses of salt beef, three sides of bacon, five sacks of flour and two barrels of beer.

He rode cheerfully as well as briskly, for it was a cheerful day, with sunshine and a fine galloping wind that swept down from the west over the wide, mounting fells that lay that way. Besides, after his persuasions, those fellows, who had sweated much to bring the wain safely over a small but swollen stream, had told him that indeed they were weary of the life they were in, since this business began, and would gladly go to their houses. So that it seemed to him that he had done very well already in his errand, for these last had been a great band, and he had spoken in the same vein, showing them how little reason they had to rise against their gracious Prince, to many others on the way. Therefore he jogged along merrily, with two servants in green and white behind him, and the golden leopards and lilies of the King's arms on his breast glowing bravely in the sun. It was well, however, for his good cheer, that he did not overhear the disputing with which those same commons, coming slowly after, wiled away the time beside the slow-trudging oxen. For at first telling each other how true it was, that that the Herald had said, and indeed never in words contradicting it, they had, by about the third milestone after he left them, returned contentedly to their conviction that this business of the Pilgrimage was a main good thing, and that the commonalty should set all right again in the realm, as the Great Captain said, and should be thanked of all men, even of the King's Grace, for what they were doing. That Lord Darcy had so soon surrendered Pomfret Castle, and that he and all the gentlemen with him had taken the Pilgrims' Oath, these were stronger arguments than any words Herald Lancaster could use.

The streets of Pomfret Lancaster found to be crowded with men and horses. In place of last summer's pea-sticks, bundles of pikes and halberds were stacked up against walls, and the smiths were far busier with steel caps and rivets on steel breast and back plates, than ever they were with shoeing horses, even on Fair days.

When the people saw Lancaster they ran along to see him better, some shouting that the King had sent to answer their griefs, and some just shouting, so that very soon he moved in a great crowd, and slowly, till he came to the Market Cross. There he stopped, and bade that one of his servants who was not incommoded by his master's trussed-up gear, to blow his trumpet, and cry "Oyez! Oyez! Oyez!" But while the last of the proud mounting notes of the trumpet was dying among the chimney stacks of the houses and the servant was drawing his breath to shout, and Lancaster was unlacing the thongs of his purse to get at his proclamation, the faces of his audience, so unanimous in their attention, began to turn this way and that, as a murmur went through the crowd. Men craned their necks, not to see Lancaster in his bravery of blue, scarlet and gold, beside the Cross, but to learn what it was that caused a stir in the crowd beyond. "It's the Grand Captain. No—it's Captain Monkton," someone cried, and Lancaster found that a big man in leather hosen, and a padded privy coat of fence, had a hand on the bridle of his horse, and was inviting him to come to the Castle.

"Gladly, when I have read the proclamation that I am charged withal," said Lancaster, and snatched at his reins, for Monkton was already leading him away.

"The Grand Captain said you should read no proclamation," said Monkton, "at the least, not yet," and went on. The half dozen pikemen who had come with him formed up alongside, and Lancaster saw no possibility but to sit in the saddle and go where he was led. Once he said, "So you have Lord Darcy now to your Grand Captain. I trust I shall persuade him and others—" He stopped then. "Why should you laugh?" he rebuked one of the pikemen.

"By cause Lord Darcy is not our Grand Captain."

"Then who?"

"Captain Aske."

"Chosen," said the pikeman, stepping closer, with an ugly upward look at Lancaster, "chosen by all the nobles, gentles, *and* the Commonalty of the Pilgrims. And why should *you* laugh?"

"Sim!" Will Monkton threw over his shoulder, and Sim fell into line again.

Lancaster had preserved his temper and his dignity through this episode. He was able to glance sharply about as he was led through the three wards of the castle, noting, for report, the many harnessed men, and the porters, one for each ward gate, and each with a white staff of office, as had been proper if this had been the palace of a great Prince. In the Hall they left him awhile, with only two pikemen to keep a space about him in a great crowd of what seemed to him mainly the better sort of yeomen and lesser gentlemen. Here, he thought, was his opportunity, and with a vague word to his guards he pushed his way towards the upper end of the Hall and stepped up beside the high table. The pikemen followed him, but did no more. For lack of a servant he cried his own, "Oyez," and began to speak. But he had hardly opened to them the cause of his coming when a hand was laid on his arm, and the big man Monkton stood by him, saying that the Grand Captain had sent for him. That did upset Lancaster. "Had it been Lord Darcy—" he thought, "But this fellow Aske—" He tried to wrench his arm from Monkton's hand, then desisted and went along, but wrathfully. "God's Bones!" he said to himself, "I shall show him. He shall have from me so much courtesy as a vile traitor should."

The Great Chamber was pleasant with both firelight and sunlight. Lord Darcy sat in his chair by the fire, his knees wrapped in a gown of velvet and marten skins. The Archbishop and the Archdeacon were side by side on the settle; these two Lancaster knew, but he looked quickly about among the half dozen or so gentlemen who stood or sat nearby, to find the traitor Aske, without being able to pitch on any that should certainly be the Grand Captain. Since he was determined, when he did see this Aske, to pay him no respect, he would spare only that hasty glance, and then with great, indeed with exaggerated, courtesy, singled out the Archbishop and Lord Darcy for his salutation. To them he took off his cap, made a leg, and began to declare his business—how he came from the Right Honourable Lord, the Earl of Shrewsbury, Lord Steward of the King's most honourable Household, and Lieutenant General from the Trent northward, and the Right Honourable Earls of Rutland and Huntingdon, of the King's most honourable Council, bearing a proclamation to be read amongst the traitorous and rebellious persons assembled at Pomfret, contrary to the King's laws.

He had got so far when someone behind him said, "Herald Lancaster!" and partly because everyone was now looking beyond, to the man who had spoken, but more because the voice was such that he could not ignore it, he turned half about, also to look.

Along the whole of that side of the room ran the dais of two degrees, on which the high table stood, still littered with plates and cups from breakfast, and besides these with pens and sheets of paper. At the far end, beyond the table, there was a window, through the glass of which great shafts of coloured light struck down, in which the motes danced. A gentleman leaned there, as if he had been sunning himself, a short, black-haired man in a scarlet coat and doublet. He came from the window now, yawning and stretching: when the bright sunshine was no longer behind him Lancaster could see that he had only one eye. He came and stood before the table, his feet set wide apart, his hands thrust into his belt, and from there he looked down into Lancaster Herald's face. He had heavy brows that drew into a straight black line, and a big mouth that shut very firmly. Lancaster took an instant and vehement dislike to him—"Keeping thus," he thought, "his port and countenance as though he had been a great prince!"

"Since," said this gentleman, "I am chosen Great Captain of these same traitorous and rebellious persons, it is to me, Master Herald, that you shall do your errand."

It only needed that Lancaster should meet his eye with a casual, scornful glance, and then turn his back, and continue to address my Lord and the Archbishop. Nothing could have been simpler; nothing, the Herald would have thought, easier, but now he found it to be impossible. Instead, hot with anger, and the hotter as he felt himself growing flustered, he turned his back, not on the Great Captain, but upon my Lord Darcy, and began his recital again, from the beginning, gabbling it a little.

When Aske stopped him, saying shortly, "Show me the proclamation you say you carry," Lancaster fumbled his purse open, and gave him the folded paper.

"Well," said Aske, "now I will read it." And he read it steadily through, loud enough for all to hear, and gave it back to Lancaster, who took it with a snatch.

"In this," said Aske, "is no cure at all for our griefs, nor even pardon offered, so it shall not need to call no counsel for the answer of it, but I will of my own wit give you the answer." Then he said:

"Herald, as a messenger you are welcome to me and all my company, who intend as I do. But as for this proclamation, sent from the Lords from whence you come, it shall not be read at the Market Cross nor in any place among my people, which be all under my guiding: it doth not enter into our hearts to fear loss of life, lands nor goods, nor the power that is against us, but we are all of one accord, with the points of our Articles, clearly intending to see a reformation or die in these causes."

"And what," Lancaster asked, "are these Articles?"

"I shall tell you," said the Great Captain, and he rehearsed those words of the Pilgrims' Oath which he had written down that night at York. At the end he said: "And you may trust to this, for it shall be done, or I will die for it," and shut his mouth so hard that the Herald could see the muscles tighten over the jaw-bone.

When he thought over his mission afterwards Lancaster knew it was at this moment that he had begun to feel sure that however boldly the Grand Captain spoke of "my company" and "my people," and however true it might be that the ignorant commons would follow him, yet he had no certainty that those others—my Lord, the Archbishop, and the knights and gentlemen whom he had taken yesterday in Pomfret, and who now listened in silence—were, in their hearts, anything but pressed men on whom no certain dependence could be put. And with that there came into the Herald's mind a way to reward this proud and traitorous Captain's insensate pride.

"Sir," said he, in a tone at once more courteous and more easy than he had yet used, "I would ye should give me these Articles in writing, for my capacity will not serve to bear away the whole tenour of them."

"With a good will," said the Grand Captain, and, "Who has a copy of the Oath? For," he explained to Lancaster, "the Articles are comprehended therein," and he turned to the table behind and began hunting among the papers there. As his back was turned Lancaster could smile; it was a pretty thing to see the fellow walking into a trap that a wiser and a humbler man would have shunned. But he was properly grave when he took the paper from the Grand Captain's hand, and asked:

"Will you, Sir, set your hand to this bill?"

For an instant then he doubted whether indeed the man was not aware of the trap, so sharp and scornful was his look. Lancaster tried, but could not continue, to meet his eye, as the Great Captain, stooping, twitched the paper from his hands and turned away to shove aside some of the clutter on the table, take up a pen and bend over the writing; in the silence they could hear how hard he drove the quill.

"And," said he when he had done, in a great voice that rang in the vaulting of the room, "this is mine act, whoever shall say to the contrary."

Lancaster made himself glance up; but the Grand Captain's eye was not on him. Once more he was looking beyond the Herald, with a dark, hard stare, and a set mouth, to where my Lord Darcy and the others sat.

When the Grand Captain had gone out of the room, himself leading Lancaster Herald by the arm to see him safely out of the gate, the others melted away too, leaving alone the Archbishop, Lord Darcy and Sir Robert Constable. It was the Archbishop who spoke first, crying out that it was not well that Master Aske—"The Grand Captain," Darcy put in, and no one could tell against whom the irony of his voice was directed— "The Grand Captain, as he calls himself," said the Archbishop. "He doth not well to speak rebellion so openly, saying that he will see a reformation or die in these causes. And saying that the commons shall to London to the King's Grace. It's treason against the King's person."

"He said," Constable broke in, "that we meant no harm to the King's person, but to see reformation."

"So say all rebels," the Archbishop answered him fretfully.

"And so say I," Constable affirmed stoutly.

"Well," said Darcy, "since we were willing to take him for Captain, we must e'en abide by it." He gave a little laugh. "We cannot say we knew not what manner of man he was."

The Archbishop thought that he was a man of an ungentle and rude port, and said so. He also said that in his mind it was great pity that when Master Aske would have laid down the white rod and the Head Captainship my Lord would not take it up.

Darcy interrupted. "You heard what I said. There are other Lords in this business now. They would grudge were one of their own fellows set over them. Besides," he smiled into the Archbishop's face, "how if I, no more than you, most Reverend Father, wish not to appear to the King's Grace to be the foremost in this Pilgrimage."

The Archbishop got up rather hurriedly, and went out, saying something to the effect that he was the King's most loyal subject and so it should appear.

"And sworn to this Pilgrimage," my Lord threw after him;

but the Archbishop shut the door on that and did not answer.

Darcy looked at Constable smiling, with dancing lights in his eyes that gave him the look of a lad in mischief. But Constable was jagging at the tongue of his belt and scowling into the fire.

"Tom," said he with a jerk, "is that the true reason why you refused to be Great Captain?"

"Must I tell the truth to the Archbishop? It were a waste of good coin."

"Then it wasn't the truth?" Constable met Darcy's smile with an angry, obstinate look.

"Well, would you have me, like Master Aske, to dash my name on to the paper at the foot of a list of treasons?"

Constable muttered, "He should not ha' done it. Why did he do it?"

"Because he's a man that drives his furrow as straight as a stone falls."

Constable looked up sharply. "You think that of him?" He considered it a moment and then said, "Mass, it was even so. But yet," he said, "I had supposed you should find him too proud and unreverent."

Darcy reached out his staff, and lifted back to the fire a log that had rolled off.

"The salmon, Robert," he said, "is a great fish, strong and courageous, so that it pleases a man well to take him."

"What's this talk of salmon?" asked Constable crossly, and added, not without malice, that if one of those two, my Lord or the Great Captain, were a salmon, it was not the Great Captain that was taken with a hook in his jaw.

Darcy laughed at him. But then he said, not laughing, "The salmon is Master Aske. My thought was that a man might be as glad to have him for a friend as to take the biggest salmon of them all."

That same afternoon those in the castle heard the sound of cheering run like a March dust storm through the streets of Pomfret. When some ran up to the top of the keep to look, they saw the Percy crimson and black filling the streets among the cold broken gleams of pikes and halberds. They could see now the silver crescent of the Percys' on the banner, and the man who rode beside, in half-armour, with a red cap and red feathers, a long leggy man on a tall bay gelding.

"That's Sir Thomas Percy," they cried on the top of the

keep, and cheered him so that he looked up and waved his hand. For all Sir Thomas and Sir Ingram Percy had been disinherited by their brother, poor sick Earl Henry, no one in the North but took them for the true Percy heirs, for what the Earl had done was, they were confident, only by the contrivance of that minion Reynold Carnaby with Thomas Cromwell himself.

Thomas Percy came late into the Great Chamber, so that it was already full of men standing about while the boys and servants went round with water and towels for washing of hands. Percy stood for a moment with his back to the door, and craned his neck to see over the heads of the rest, which he was able to do because of his length. Then he elbowed his way through the crowd till he was close behind Sir Robert Constable and Master Robert Aske, who stood in front of the fire; they had been all afternoon on St. Thomas's Hill together, outside the town, taking musters of the commons who came in every hour, more and more. Now they talked together as they warmed themselves.

Percy put his elbow on the Great Captain's shoulder and leaned heavily on it. "Ha! my little Robin," he said, "you've not grown any taller for all your greatness."

Aske turned about. He and Sir Thomas had gone fowling together in the days when Aske was a lad in Earl Henry the Magnificent's Household; they had learnt their Latin and the lute-playing together, and known the sting of the same birch.

"No," said Aske, "but you've sprouted feathers," and he put up a hand and flipped the end of the crimson feathers in Sir Thomas's cap, at which Sir Thomas laughed his wild shouting laugh, showing all his fine teeth.

"Behold me," he turned himself about, "and admire, for it has not cost me a penny, coat, doublet, feathers and all. But Master Collins the Treasurer has gone surety for it."

"Mind you pay him then."

"Or will you hang me?" Percy asked, lightly but dangerously.

"I'll have no spoil taken."

Percy eyed the Grand Captain for a moment, then laughed again, and thrust his arm through his, swinging him round towards the high table.

"Get me and Ingram our rights again," he said, "and we're with you to the death."

Gib chose the way down alongside the river, though it was a little longer, because he did not wish to go up through the village, where it might be remarked on that he was carrying a bundle tied on his staff. "Whither goest thou, priest?" He could hear them so calling to him, and himself lying, along with the truth—"To Richmond. To Richmond only, with some of the wench's homespun to sell."

Last night had been one of stormy wind and rain; indeed, it was while he lay awake hearing the pelting rattle of the driven showers that he had at last resolved, after the thing had lain long working in his mind like yeast, to do what this morning he was setting forth upon.

The woods, as he went through them, seemed strange to his eyes, and being so intent upon his own resolve he thought they were so because he was leaving them for ever, since a man sees a place, as it were, newly when he knows he will never see it again; yet the truth was simpler than that; rain and wind had brought down most of the leaves during the night, stripping the boughs bare; brightness had fallen from the air, and now lay in drifts of copper, gold, or golden green to be trodden underfoot.

Now the sky had cleared to blue; at the foot of the hillside the river ran, shallow and quick, winking back the sunshine into Gib's eyes with every flicker of its ripples. He walked fast, feeling, as the distance lengthened between him and Marrick, a growing sense of freedom and relief. He saw only one man as he went and that was the Marrick swineherd, but him Gib could not avoid, for he stood under a tree watching the swine that thronged all the road, trampling and shoving, squealing and rootling in the mud for the acorns which the wind had brought down. Gib must wait till the swineherd saw him and cleared a way, with much shouting and many blows that sounded dully on the tough, dusty quarters of the swine. Then the fellow would walk along a piece with Gib, chewing a beechnut and spitting it out, and talking, with an intolerable slow pertinacity, of a diseased pig, of its long, mysterious illness, of its death.

At last Gib shook him off and settled down to his own brisk pace again. Almost he had been driven, as he had walked beside the swineherd, to grit his teeth together to contain this impatience. Yet now, alone again, the very sharpness of his relief promised so well for the future that he was glad he had not passed the man by with a word. "Lord!" he thought, and drew a deep breath, "in London I shall not suffer from such fellows, but there wits be keen."

In the street at Marske the Conyers' Priest hailed him, and would have had him in to breakfast. Gib refused, but since it was the last time he should have to suffer this fool also (for he conceived the Marske priest to be a garrulous, and also an idolatrous fool) he consented to drink a cup of ale at the garden fence.

So, in the pleasant sunshine, they drank a can of ale together, while the women and pretty young girls went by to the well, the pails swinging on the yokes, and now and again a long plaintive chirrup sounding from the creaking well-wheel. Now that the sun was warm a white steam went up from the thatch, and smoke went up too, trembling, hyacinth blue against the hillside, but a stain upon the brighter blue of the air.

When the ale was finished Gib went on. As he had expected, the Marske priest had talked a great deal, and, whether it were of old Perkin or of young Hodge's little brat, or of how the King should take heed to his Kingdom—"but give him an apple and a pretty wench to play withal and he'll not stir from the fireside, but leave it all to these rogues of heretics'—whether it were of this or that it was all foolishness.

"Surely," he found himself saying again as he climbed the hill out of Marske, "such shall I not need to suffer in London," and he kicked out fiercely at the stones of the road. Here was he—a man of learning, though that learning might, from his sojourn among want-wits, be a little rusted over— here was he, a man (as he knew) whose thought moved quicker and stronger and more vehement than other men's slow, turbid thoughts, as Swale ran brighter than a marsh-land stream—here was he, lit and burning with eagerness to render to God his due service—"No! No!" he cried aloud suddenly, quite scaring two horses that hung their heads over the gate of a little close. "No! No!" he said to himself. It could not be that God meant him to bide in Marrick, only to drone the idolatrous Mass to a few ignorant blocks, and to harbour in his house a simpleton and a lad that was less human, he thought, than a monkey that he had once watched in the window of a great house in London, scratching and picking at itself.

He switched his thoughts quickly from Marrick parsonage, where perhaps even now Malle was halloing to him to come in to breakfast. Instead he would chew upon one of those grudges and resentments that lay so thickly scattered on the floor of his mind. If there had been any in these barbarously ignorant Northern parts that could have recognized of what quality the man was behind the harsh and hungry looks of the Marrick parson, then, thought Gib, I might have endured to stay. But there was none that had the penetration to see it. Sir Rafe? An ignorant, careless, proud gentleman. His dame? More ignorant, and prouder than he. Trudgeover? A coarse, unlettered fellow, though eloquent, and if he were coarse and unlettered what might be said of the "known men" that were in Marrick, of whom the smith was the best instructed? So, there was none. Yea, but there was one who came and went, one who knew London and London wits, one who might have recognized what manner of man was Sir Gilbert Dawe, Priest. For the rest of the way to Richmond his thoughts circled, angrily yet with a bitter satisfaction, about the oblivious, confident, victorious Master Aske. Never once would Gib let them slink back to the parsonage at Marrick.

Richmond was full, for it was market day. He saw Sir Rafe Bulmer's bailiff, and turned hastily down Friars' Wynd to avoid him. Well, this way lay his road, so why linger where the wall of the Grey Friars began? He said to himself: "Because I'll go the better if I break my fast here, and keep that I have in my poke for dinner. Besides, if I wait awhile there may be those going from the fair with a spare nag that I can ride. So shall I make much better speed."

With such good reasons he turned back into the big market place, and bought a piece of hot mutton pie, and ate it sitting on a doorstep. From here he could see, about five houses along, the round jutting window with which Will Cowper had improved the small, frowning face of old Andrew Cowper's house. The stonework of this window was new and white; one of the glass casements stood open, so that Gib could see right through to the upper light of the window on the far side, which was filled with golden-coloured glass upon which was a white lily, the whole very pretty and bright in the sunshine. A plump woman came to the open window and looked out for a moment; her sleeve that hung over the sill was turned back with sapphire velvet. Gib dropped his eyes and bit into his mutton pie. He greatly and bitterly disliked all Cowpers, and with them all those who had so much money that they could spend it upon new round windows, upon golden-coloured glass, and sapphire velvet.

But it was not this which now blackened away the sunshine, and kept his eyes upon the cobbles, where bits of straw and cabbage stalk and all manner of household rubbish lay scattered. The sight of Will Cowper's house had brought him up with a round turn and he must perforce remember first the Prioress, and then the parsonage at Marrick. It seemed now that his mind (or else it was his conscience) had never forgotten it.

Someone stopped in front of him; he saw a pair of boots, grey hosen, a brown coat. The Bulmers' bailiff cried his name; he was already a little drunk or he would not have bidden Gib to an ale-house. "And you shall ride back after behind one of the men. If you've done your business." Gib said he had done his business, and went, and drank, silently and savagely. As the drink worked on him, and his thoughts grew nimbler, and more lightsome, he was chasing one question, yet could not resolve it. Was it God who drove him back, or the devil who wiled him? Had he determined to go back because (God have mercy!) Malle's angel and Wat's angel beheld always the face of the Father in Heaven? Or had he determined to go back so that the Prioress should stand condemned, because she had thrust out the poor creature Malle, whom he had saved? He could not tell, for the two thoughts were twined in his mind like strands of a rope, and his head by now was ringing.

It was black dark when the horses stopped and the servant said: "Here y'are, parson," and with his hand rather spilt than helped Gib down from behind him. They rode on, cackling, and then their laughter and slurred words died in the deep silence. He found the gate, and his thought was only, "Well, here I can lie down and sleep. Here's home."

His hand, groping, touched the door, which yielded; it was neither barred nor latched. He pushed it open, and saw the little house-place by the dullest red glow of a dying fire, but after the total dark it was bright enough to his eyes.

Wat lay sprawling just clear of the ashes, his shirt was wide open over his thin, ridged ribs. He was wriggling, wildly throwing arms and legs about, his mouth wide open, and the gurgles that with him passed for laughter came thickly from his dumb throat. Malle knelt beside him; she was laughing too, and tickling his bare skin with a peacock's feather.

She looked up first and saw Gib.

[516]

"Jesu Mercy!" she cried.

Wat sprang up with one quick move, and slipped away so that he stood with his back to the wall. Neither laughed now.

Gib said: "Bar the door," and went past them without more words, and up to bed. He pulled off his clothes in the dark, and pitched into the corner the bundle which he had carried all day. It fell with a thud, for there was in it, besides Gib's best gown and hosen, and two shirts, his copy of the Gospels Englished.

Well, here he was home again, shackled by conscience; he was where duty sent him, but that tender loving kindness which was all God's service—he could as well render it, as with his fingers make one of the light flashes on the ripples of the Swale.

October 25

July propped herself against the edge of the table in Mistress Holland's kitchen, and nibbled at an almond wafer. She did not want the wafer, having little appetite these days. She did not want to be in the kitchen either, though it was a pleasant room into which this morning the sun came. It smelt pleasantly too of Mistress Holland's baking, of the herbs that hung in neat bunches from the beams, and of several little birds now turning on the spit against dinner time. It was a far pleasanter kitchen than July's own, for which she took no care, and which therefore showed accordingly.

Mistress Holland talked with one of her maid servants, earnestly, as two speak who are concerned with grave matters; their communication was of mincemeat. A big woman, twenty years and more older than July, with a plain face and contented, shrewd eyes, Mistress Holland found young Mistress Machyn rather a trying guest—"shy" she tried to think, though "proud" she feared shot nearer to the mark; but whether the one or the other it would do no harm to leave her for a few minutes to herself. So July sat, and nibbled the sweet crisp wafer, and felt sick, and felt the panic of waiting for disaster to rise again into her throat. Since she had always known that what she waited for must happen, why must it be waited for so long? Then—"Jesu Mercy!" she cried inside her mind, since she had caught herself wishing to hasten the cruelty that dogged Master Aske's footsteps.

Mistress Holland came and sat upon the edge of the table by her. She also began to eat a wafer, but with a hearty appetite and critical appreciation.

"It was the Ladies of St. Helen's told me how to make these," she said, more because she felt it to be courteous to talk to a guest than because she hoped to interest July. "St. Helen's for almond wafers, St. John Baptist of Holywell for crispey. Every House of Religious, I dare say, has its own choice dish."

"It was rishaws at the House at Marrick," said July.

"Marrick? Is that where you had your schooling?" Mistress Holland took with both hands this first voluntary remark of her guest.

"I was a novice. I should have been a nun," July said, looking straight in front of her at Mistress Holland's scrubbed board, and at the cupboard where the slipware cooking bowls and crocks stood with light winking on their brown sides through the latticed doors. But she saw the Great Court at Marrick, under a hot afternoon sky, and Master Aske leaning his hand against the gate-house arch, and talking to Jankin the porter.

"Then why—"

July gave her a glance, dark and sullen seeming.

"Because my sister would not let me bide."

Mistress Holland remembered Margaret Cheyne, since the good Master Holland was merchant of that same worshipful Company of Vintners as William Cheyne; her remembrance of Margaret had indeed weighted heavy in the scale against July, although Mistress Holland was too honest a creature not to own to herself that there seemed to be nothing in this sister of the other, except it were her pride—which might be shyness.

So now, knowing by July's tone that there was one subject on which they agreed, she put her arm quickly about the girl's waist, hugging her, and at once letting her go. The less the young wench liked her sister, the better would Mistress Holland like her.

"Yet," she said, answering July's words and speaking as became a good wife, and a happy one, "now you are wedded you would not be a nun there."

"I would. I would I were there. I would I might have bided there always."

Mistress Holland was startled by her vehemence. She could

not know that Marrick, in July's mind, was a place enclosed, protected, inviolate. There, forever, Master Aske went about, carrying his fishing rod through the rain, loitering at ease across Grinton Bridge. Mistress Holland, not knowing this, must suppose that Laurence Machyn's wife had either a cruel, unfeeling husband, or a great devotion to the holy state of chastity. Mistress Holland knew Laurence too well to think the first. Therefore it must be the second. She looked at July, still gazing straight before her with a pinched mouth, and was filled with a sudden almost awed compassion. This was enough to account for the girl's distance, silence, strangeness. Mistress Holland, who was very devout, put July at once into the category of those holy and religious women who long for no earthly bridegroom.

So she shook her head, and was silent. Beside her July brooded, passing and repassing, light as air and quick as thought, through the fields, ways and chambers of Marrick. The woman with whom Mistress Holland had conferred went off to fetch onions from the larder; the other opened the door on the street and stepped outside to look for the men who, every morning, came selling water from the conduit. Mistress Holland and July were alone.

"And to think," said Mistress Holland, "that the King, following the counsel of that man Cromwell—no, I'll not call him Lord nor nothing but his unchancy name—that the King would have pulled down and destroyed all such Houses of Religious, had not these brave commons of the North letted him."

"But," July turned on her with a look so startled as to be almost wild, "but I hear them say that the Northern men are surrendered, and that now there will be—be an end." She could not say the words she had heard spoken, "That now there will be hanging of the wretches that led them, and there an end."

Mistress Holland tossed up her chin.

"*Benedicite!*" she said, "let them wait till they have sure news before they say so much. For my husband saith" (she brought her mouth near to July's headkerchief, and murmured softly), "he saith there is other news; that the King must send the Duke of Norfolk to treat with them, so great an host as they are, being all the North parts, gentlemen, lords and commons, in arms for the sake of the Church."

July, staring at her, could only whisper, "Is it so?"

"And besides that and better," said Mistress Holland, "I

say that God will be their surety, who venture their lives in His service. He will be found at the last to be beside them in need."

July looked at her again, with caution this time; almost with suspicion. But Mistress Holland did not speak defensively, hardily, but almost, as it were, comfortably. It was not as if she clung with toes and fingers on the face of the naked scar at Fremington Edge, desperate and trembling like the boy who fell from there when he was taking an eagle's nest. July had dreamed, waking, of that boy many and many a time, feeling as he felt when his hand slipped, and the air rushed up past him, and he knew he was falling. No—when Mistress Holland spoke it was as if she sat on the warm turf of the sunny fell side, leaning, at ease, upon the safe kind bosom of the wide earth. Suddenly, unbelievably, July's heart, for a time at least, laid down its load.

"Where is this place Marrick?" Mistress Holland asked idly.

"In Yorkshire."

"Nay then, have you acquaintance with any of these noble gentlemen?"

"No," said July. "No."

Mistress Holland glanced at her and saw a smile shining, gentle, rapt.

October 26

Malle and Wat were burning garden rubbish; the heap was crackling merrily; below the busy flames were sliding their quick fingers above the dry wizened stalks, feeling along, licking up; above smoke, reeking of rottenness, poured out, leaned sideways, swirled wide and swept over half the garden. Malle and Wat, casting down fork and rake, fled out of it to the clear air to breathe, and leaned together upon the wall.

"Wat," said Malle, "have you thought that He has stained Himself, soiled Himself, being not only with men, but Himself a man. What's that, to be man? Look at me. Look at you."

They looked at each other, and one saw a dusty wretched dumb lad, and the other saw a heavy slatternly woman.

Malle said: "It's to be that which shoots down the birds out of the free air, and slaughters dumb beasts, and kills his own kind in wars."

She looked away up the Dale towards Calva, rust-red with dead bracken, smouldering under the cold sky.

"And it wasn't that He put on man like a jacket to take off

at night, or to bathe or to play. But man He was, as man is man, the Maker made himself the made; God was un-Godded by His own hand."

She put her hands to her face, and was silent, till Wat pulled them away.

"He was God," she said, "from before the beginning, and now never to be clean God again. Never again. Alas!" she said, and then, "Osanna!"

October 27

The whole host of the commons lay on the north bank of the Don, the King's on the other side of the river, and Doncaster between them. Early this morning thirty of the King's lords and thirty of the commons' leaders had come together upon the bridge on the north side of the town, the commons to speak their grievances, the Lords to answer them, that, in the end, some appointment might be made between them.

It was growing dusk now, and still the conference on the bridge went on. Earlier it had been possible for the commons to see, from where their ranks were drawn up, the crowd on the bridge, thirty lords and gentlemen from their party, and thirty from the King's host. But now, though lights were pricking out in the town beyond, the bridge was drowned from them in the twilight.

Robert Aske had half turned his horse, to ride again across the front line of the commons' host. This was what he and other Captains had been doing at intervals since late afternoon, and he knew only too well how necessary it was, and how increasingly the commons were breaking line to clog into companies that muttered with their heads together, and only fell apart when one of the Captains drew near. By now it was almost a good sign if any man of them would call angrily to know, "When will they on the bridge be done with talking?"

He heard a horseman coming up fast behind him; so he did not turn, but waited. Will Monkton ranged alongside.

"The Bishopric men are saying 'Treason.' They say, 'Let's run upon them that are betraying us to the King's lords, and kill them.' "

Aske swung his horse about. "No—slowly, Will," he said, so they rode slowly across the face of the host, till they came to the midst where the banner of St. Cuthbert stood, the crimson dulled to shadow in the dusk, the white velvet and the gold of the embroidery still faintly bright. But the banner was now the centre of a jam of men who shouted at each other, waving their arms. Aske said: "One is better than two here. Stay, unless I raise my hand." Then he rode into the crowd.

It was longer than Monkton liked that he had to wait, but after a while the voices dropped; there were times, and more times, when only Aske was speaking; at last he came back and together the two continued to ride along the line.

"Phew!" said Monkton, and then, "We'll not hold them much longer."

"But if we must, we shall."

Monkton shook his head. Then he said, leaning over to speak low:

"Robin, would they betray the commons?"

He could only see Aske's face dimly as he turned, but he knew all the same that he was angry.

"Would I? Would you? If it had been our part to go to the parley?"

The clock struck six from the Friars' Church, and at last the appointment between my Lords of Norfolk and Shrewsbury on the one side, and the leaders of the commons on the other, was concluded. Now the servants brought torches, and the men began to move about, stamping their cold feet.

Lord Darcy found himself for a moment alone in the diminishing crowd by the side of the bridge; then someone pressed his arm and he turned.

"Ha! Talbot!" he cried, and the two stood in a momentary silence till Shrewsbury said he was sorry to see my Lord Darcy on that side which he had chosen.

Darcy turned to lean on the bridge. Shrewsbury leaned beside him; in the torchlight Darcy could see his face, thin, long, infinitely wrinkled, and set on a neck as lank as that of a plucked chicken. Beyond Shrewsbury's head he saw also two of the gentlemen who had spoken for the Pilgrims. So he chose his words carefully.

"All the world knows (if there is justice) why I am of that party." He bent his head as if to peer over the bridge to where the current made a slight lisping sound against the piers: further off flames of the torches showed on the dark water in smooth oily undulations, becoming there wavering peacocks' feathers of gold, each with a dimpled eye of darkness.

"I must needs join with them to save my life," he said softly; Shrewsbury, he knew, was not one to be easy with words of double meaning.

As it was the Earl frowned for a moment before he said doubtfully, "Yet you will not now join yourself with us."

"Talbot," Darcy with his forefinger tapped the back of the Earl's hand as it lay on the stonework of the bridge—"Talbot, hold up thy long claw and promise me that I shall have the King's favour, and my case be indifferently heard, and I will come back with you to Doncaster this night."

Shrewsbury pulled at his ear for a minute; at last he shook his head: "Well then, my Lord Darcy, you shall not come."

Darcy laughed softly and scornfully.

"And so I thought. He that will lay his head on the block may have it soon stricken off." He held out his hand, and Shrewsbury took it; they had known each other many years and had always been good friends.

October 30

Robert Aske was sitting on a stool beside the great bed of the Earl of Northumberland at Wressel Castle. He looked not at the Earl, but at the embroidered curtains of the bed, rich old embroidery in silks and silver thread, but the silver was tarnished and the silks fraying. His clenched hands were thrust between his knees; he looked down at them now, and, as he unclasped them, learnt by the stiffness of his fingers what a pressure he had put on them. He drew a deep breath, meaning to let it out in a sigh, but Earl Henry mistook the significance of the sound.

"No," he cried, "it's no use to say more. You shall not move me. My brothers shall have nothing of me. And I care not to die. I can die but once. Strike off my head, and you will but rid me of much pain."

He was crying by now, and Aske jumped up. "Sir!" he said, "Sir! I pray you—have done. I'll speak no more of it." He went over to the window and stood there, trying not to hear the Earl's whimpering, and wishing he might be able to recall some of the words he had flung at the wretched man in the bed—words that should have stormed him, or scourged or mocked him into consent. Yet for all the force and bitterness, aye—and cruelty, he had put into it, Earl Henry had not consented, but had answered over and over, wretchedly and obstinately, that his word was given unto the

King; so Aske, who had begun long before to be ashamed, was now very much ashamed indeed.

He heard a noise from the bed that was not a whimper. There was a silence, and then Earl Henry groaned again. Aske went quickly back and stood close to him; the Earl turned his head, but very stiffly and cautiously, and as if all his mind was waiting, watching, listening for something which should arrive. Aske saw his face change and could not take his eye away from it, though he wished to look away; yet he knew that the Earl did not care whether he looked or no, being now quite cut off from him in the privacy of extreme pain.

It lasted but a few minutes. When it was over Aske sat down again till he saw the Earl lift his face a little from the pillow, looking for him. Then he asked, speaking almost in a whisper—

"Is it like this?"

"Sometimes bad, as now, and longer. Sometimes not so bad."

Aske said, "I should not have spoken. Yet—" He checked himself abruptly, and said, "Forgive me."

Earl Henry gave him a little smile. "You are very earnest in this business, Robin."

It was a long time before Aske spoke. Then he said—

"Sir, I have thought of myself sometimes in this as a horse set to lug timber in the woods in deep mire of winter. There's the weight to move, that's one thing, and for another the wheels will not turn. So the horses must haul as to break their hearts, if they will shift the tree. But," he said, "I shall shift it."

The Earl said softly, "It'd be a great load, Robin, that you did not shift."

"Surely," said Aske, "I shall see reformation done, or I shall die for it. But," he muttered too low and hastily for the Earl to be certain of his words, "but I'll not be taken and judged as a traitor. I'll die on the field."

Then he began to tell of the course of the negotiations, and how at Doncaster it had been appointed that Robert Bowes and Rafe Ellerker should go with the Duke of Norfolk to Windsor, to carry to the King's Grace the grievances of the North, while both hosts should disperse until the King's answer came. "But surely," his face and voice kindled, "surely I think that if we would have chosen battle rather than to send our petition we should have had the better of them. For those gentlemen and commons that went with them went unwilling; but in our host I saw neither gentleman nor commons willing to depart, but to proceed in the quarrel, yea, and that to the death," and he drove his clenched hand down on his knee. And then, speaking in a hurry, "I would with all my heart, Sir, that you were with us, for before God I do know our cause is just. How can a secular Prince—"

He broke off because the Earl had moved sharply, and certainly this was to begin all over again. So they were silent until the Earl began to talk about that stuff of his which the commons had seized, and Aske had saved from spoil. "You shall have it," said he, "and I would it were of more worth," and then he said, "And—yea, you shall have my great spice plate that lies in the keeping of the brethren at Watton."

So, as the spice plate was worth £40, and money was needed by the commons, Aske kissed the Earl's hand and thanked him. Then he made up the fire, pressed and strained the juice of some oranges that were in the livery cupboard, and sprinkled rose-water about the room to sweeten the staleness of the air. It pleased them both that he should do this old accustomed, long-discontinued service.

After the close, scented room the air in the dark court tasted strangely clean. Aske stood for a few minutes letting the wind stir his hair, and looking round about at the lights in the windows. From the tower where the kitchens were came not only light but noise, for the servants were washing dishes after supper. He could hear them shouting to one another. "Yet they always shout," he thought, "even when they stand side by side at the same kneading trough." A woman in wooden shoes went clattering down the flagged passage to the dairy; he knew the way she went, and how the great bowls of cream would stand all along the stone benches; many a time he had stolen in to ladle out cream for himself, and come skulking out wiping his mouth with the back of his hand.

Through an arched passage just beside him lay the herb garden of the castle; if it had been light he could have seen from where he now stood the trim beds of herbs edged with clipped box; but it did not need daylight for him to see it all quite clearly in his mind. And as he saw it, so he remembered how angry the old Earl had been when he found out that the cooks had been buying herbs at Howden and Hemmingburgh. He had started off into the garden to see for himself if there were not herbs enough, with the sulky chief cook on one side of him, and on the other a gardener to show him where every herb grew that a cook might need. When they found the herb the cook got a rating, and when they found it not, the gardener, so neither could crow over the other. When he had seen all the Earl came back and had it written down in the Great Book of the Household:

"That from henceforth that there be no herbs bought seeing that the Cooks may have herb enow in my Lord's Gardens."

Aske smiled as he remembered it, and he remembered it well, for he himself had written it, being just then in the office of the clerk of the kitchen in the Earl's Household.

He went across the Court, loitering, as his mind was loitering through past times. Then he turned into the Spicery, and calling a servant asked for a pricket of wax; he had a mind to go up to the Chamber that was called Paradise because in that pleasant, peaceful, sunny room the old Earl kept his books; there they stood about in their presses, and in the midst of the room for convenience in reading, there were the hinged, latticed desks, which he had been so proud of. "For a little while," Aske thought, "I'll read there." But the truth was that he did not want to meet Sir Thomas Percy just yet, to tell him that the Earl had utterly refused, and to hear what he would say about his brother.

But when he had shut the door of Paradise behind him he found that there was a light already in the room, and the very man he had hoped to avoid was flipping over the pages of a book with an impatient hand.

"Well?" cried Thomas Percy.

"He will not."

Then Thomas began, and Aske, having tried to soothe him, was caught into an argument. Both were angry, and Aske was angry with himself too, because there was much in what Thomas Percy said that he himself had said to Earl Henry, and as Thomas now stormed at him, so had he stormed at the Earl, as he lay tossing miserably in bed. So it was manifestly unfair that he should take the contrary part now; and yet he must, for Thomas wanted to break into the Earl's chamber, "and then see will he still refuse. And I can do it," he cried, "with my folk and those you have with you, maugre any men of his here that will withstand us." But Aske would not have it so.

As they grew hotter the argument ranged wider. Thomas

said Aske cared nothing for his old friends but only for the new. Aske told him not to talk so like a shrewish chiding woman. Thomas cried, "Friends? Sinister back friends I'll call them that'll do you a shrewd turn one day," and began to rail on Lord Darcy, raking back over the old Lord's past years, into what was hearsay for both of them—how it had been said that he had tricked old Lord Monteagle, and wasted the heir's wealth when the lad was his ward and Hussey's. "And here is this same man, but older, and you take him in Pomfret like a bird in a gin, and he swears an oath perforce, and you think that he will stand to it, and not escape away to the King if he might."

"Fie!" Aske shouted then. "God's Blood! Say that to his face, for I'll not hear it of him!" And he went out slamming the door, and only remembered when he stood in the black dark of the stairway that he had left behind him his candle standing on the desk.

So he began to feel his way down, and, as if by the touch of the cold stone against his fingers, his anger began to cool. He had not gone halfway when he stopped to argue with himself whether he should go up again. Just then he heard the latch of the room above lift with a click, and saw the stair and the newel and the curve of the wall swing unsteadily in the light of the candle which Thomas Percy carried.

"Tom," he cried, speaking on an impulse, "to-morrow I'll speak again with the Earl. Perhaps I may move him."

Sir Thomas answered only by a grunt. But in a moment he said: "Here, take your candle that you left behind you." So Aske waited for him on the stair, and they went down together, in silence but with dwindling enmity.

November 2

The Duke of Norfolk, Sir Rafe Ellerker and Master Robert Bowes waited together in a window at Windsor. Close to them gentlemen and yeomen of the King's Guard stood at the door of the King's Privy Chamber. This end of the long room was almost empty except for the Guard, the three gentlemen, and a few grave pacing couples, who looked soberly with frowning faces and spoke quietly to each other. Further away the crowd talked more cheerfully and louder; among the men's voices could be heard women's too, and their light sweet laughter above the deeper hum of talk.

The Duke was discoursing well and wittily. The two younger men listened, or seemed to listen, and tried to think collectedly of what they must say to the King when they had their audience. Sir Rafe kept his long, pale, placid face bent; yet it was neither so placid as usual, nor so pale, but a little flushed and frowning. Robert Bowes' heavy features and half-shut, guarded eyes did not easily betray either his feelings or the keen brain behind them, but even he was restless, shifting his shoulders inside his dark blue doublet that looked far less fine here, in spite of all its gold buttons, than it did at home in the North. Only Norfolk was, it seemed, at ease, chatting on about horses.

Somewhere beyond the room a little bell jangled softly. The Duke, leaving a favourite and much vaunted black gelding in the midst of one of its most remarkable jumps, stopped speaking, and turned his head over his shoulder to listen.

A quiet-stepping, round man in grey velvet came out of the King's Chamber; he was carrying a great many papers in a red leather pouch. He went away down the room, with pursed lips, and absent, calculating eyes; yet to Bowes it seemed that he had taken in the three of them in one sliding glance.

"Who is that?" he asked, and Norfolk told him, "Privy Seal."

Bowes nodded. He had never seen Cromwell before, yet he had hardly needed to ask the question. One of the gentlemen was coming towards them.

"If you show yourself humble and penitent I make no doubt His Grace will use you with mercy and his customary benignity," Norfolk said, speaking hastily. "But if you stand stiffly—"

He moved to meet the Gentleman Usher who drew near.

"His Grace hath sent for me?" His voice was cheerful, and he went briskly towards the door of the King's Chamber. The two Yorkshire gentlemen envied his confidence; they had been too preoccupied with their own apprehensions to notice how, at the pretty silver note of the bell, the Duke's chin had jerked, and his voice died.

Inside the Privy Chamber the King stood before the fire; he wore velvet the colour of flame, his feet were set wide apart, his head was bent and his chin sank into roll upon roll of bristled fat above the gold-stitched collar. His bulk, blocking out the firelight on that darkly overcast forenoon, seemed enormous; Norfolk could hear something—perhaps it was the King's belt—which lightly creaked every time he breathed. Himself a man of a very spare habit of body, he felt a qualm both of disgust and dread at the physical grossness of the King. He knelt; he kissed the King's hand, and, as the King did not raise him, he continued to kneel.

"Well?"

This, and no better, was the sort of welcome that Norfolk was prepared for. To meet it he had already resolved to use a cheerful, soldierly frankness.

"By the Mass," said he, "here am I a true loyal man imploring pardon for that which was no fault of mine, since neither for ease nor danger have I spared this little poor carcass that you see. Yet with a good will I would be prisoner in Turkey rather than to have had the matter at the point it is now. Fie! Fie! upon the Lord Darcy, the most arrant traitor living."

The King did not speak, but he moved sharply, and that shook Norfolk from his cheerful vein.

"Woe! woe worth the time!" he cried, "that my Lord of Shrewsbury went so far forth. An he had not done, you should have had other news."

"Cousin," said the King, and from his quiet voice the Duke knew that this was going to be an audience of the worst sort; for the King was at his cruellest when he spoke like that— "Cousin, we have called to our remembrance the whole discourse and progress of this matter, with your advertisements made in the time of the same; which we find so repugnant and contrarious, the one and the other, that we cannot forbear frankly to make a recapitulation of the same; to the only intent, that you shall perceive that you have not therein observed that gravity and circumspection that in your person towards Us was requisite."

"Sir," cried the Duke, but the King held up his hand. He went away from Norfolk and sat down on a big velvet goldfringed chair beside the hearth and from there continued his rebuke. So the Duke was left kneeling before the fire, ridiculous, humiliated; what with anger, fear, and the heat of the flames, now no longer masked from him by the King's person, the veins of his temples began to throb as if they would burst.

"Alas," he cried, in his agitation interrupting the King. "Alas! for I have served Your Highness many times without reproach, and now, having been enforced to appoint with the rebels, my heart is near broken!" And he felt that indeed it was, and wrung his hands together.

"Suffer me," said the King, with a yet more deadly gentleness, "to speak my whole mind," and he continued to speak it.

"And now," he said at last, and paused to shift one leg over the other, "now We have uttered unto you, as to him that We love and trust, Our whole stomach, which if you do, in your person, weigh towards Us, as We do utter Our love in the declaration thereof to you, We doubt not but you will both humbly thank Us for the same, and with your deeds give Us cause to thank you accordingly."

Norfolk could not raise his eyes; for one thing he dared not; for another, if he did, the King would see in them that anguish of rage that shook him in time with his heart beats; so that again he dared not. Looking only upon the King's broad black velvet shoe, he mumbled that surely he was thankful, and if the King's Gracious Highness of His benignity—

He looked up, saw that the King was raking his face with a slant, secret look, and found that words died on his tongue.

"There is," said the King, "another matter which must be touched on."

Norfolk waited.

"You said that in Our service you would esteem no promise you made to the rebels. Was that truth?"

"Very truth."

"Saying also that you would not think your honour touched in the breach and violation of any such promise. Are ye yet in that same mind?"

Norfolk cried that surely, and God help him, he was in that very mind, "and most humbly I pray You, Sir, to take it in good part that I think and repute none oath nor promise can distain me, so that it be made for policy, and to serve You, mine only master and sovereign. For," he plucked at the breast of his doublet, cleared his throat, and declared, "I shall be torn into a million of pieces, rather than to show one point of cowardice or untruth to Your Majesty."

"Well!" said the King. "That is well," and he smiled. Norfolk, glancing up, caught the end of the smile, and it was the bitterest and most searching torment of all to see that look on the King's face, a look satisfied, contemptuous.

"And now," said the King, "as to that villain Aske. Have you used any means with Lord Latimer or other of those lords to induce them to contain the wretch?"

Norfolk protested that at Doncaster was no time; that the rebels stood so stiffly to their demands; that all policy was needed to persuade them to disperse. "And besides," said he, "this Aske was manifestly leader over them all, lords and commons alike."

It seemed to Norfolk that rage puffed the King out to a larger bulk than ever.

"So," he said, speaking with the utmost gentleness, "so you think it no marvel that the nobility of the North suffer such a vile villain to be ruler over them? What was he in Our Courts but a common pedlar of the law? Is it aught but his filed tongue hath brought him in such estimation?"

Norfolk muttered that indeed the North parts were mad in these days.

"Yet," said the King, "you have done nothing against this wretch, though We and all Our Nobles that are here with Us think Our honour greatly touched in that he abideth free."

In the silence Norfolk heard the first gouts of a windy shower strike against the window panes. He cried, his hands straining upon the brim of his cap, that to know his gracious Prince so used by ungracious naughty subjects was death to him.

"If I have done nothing," he protested, "yet I have thought —if great policy should be used—if one of the lords might be brought to deliver him up by promise of favour—"

At that he saw the King lean forward.

"A way," said Norfolk, "might be found. If I wrote to—"

The King's hand checked him. "How, shall be your concern." And then—"Where are those two of the rebels that have come to ask Our pardon?"

Norfolk said that they were without, that he had brought them with him, that he had so wrought with them that they were, he conceived, most truly penitent.

"Go and fetch them."

The Duke got up, in haste to do the office of an usher.

November 10

Lord Darcy was sitting in the little garden at Templehurst, which lay between the house, the jutting chapel wall, and the moat. Always a very sheltered place, except when the south wind blew, to-day—a day of St. Martin's little summer— it was so warm that even a bee or two worked among the last carnations. As well as Lord Darcy's gentlemen, strolling to and fro along the paved walk, and my Lord, who, wrapped in a fur-lined cloak, sat at a table dictating to a clerk, there were half-a-dozen or so of yeomen or squires from round about Templehurst. They had heard that a messenger had reached Doncaster and had sent asking for a safe conduct. They meant to know what letters and what news that messenger brought, so they hung about in the lower part of the garden where it dipped to the moat, eating my Lord's apples from his trees, and throwing the cores into the water, where the silly fish rose at them. Sometimes a few would come unobtrusively nearer, but if they hoped to catch any words of moment from my Lord's lips they were disappointed, for all they heard was, "charcoal for the Great Chamber fire, because the smoke of sea-coal will hurt my Arras," or again, "Great wood for fires too, because coals will not burn without wood."

But at last the door at the top of the stairs leading down to the garden was opened, and servants in green coats came out, bringing with them a small grey man, who looked stupid, but who was only very weary with hard riding.

"Ha!" cried Darcy, and got up. "Welcome, Perce Creswell."

Creswell, who had been Lord Hussey's servant, and now was Norfolk's, came down the steps stiffly as though his legs were made of wood and not well jointed. He said, speaking hoarsely because his throat was dry, that he had a letter. He put one into Darcy's hand.

Darcy turned it over, looking at the seal. "The ermine and the bows," he said. "It is from Sir Robert Bowes?"

"And Sir Rafe Ellerker."

"And you bring news? And good news, I hope."

"Good enough, my Lord, for I trust all will be well." Creswell added then so that only Darcy could hear, "I have a privy letter."

Darcy turned. He knew that his gentlemen had stopped their pacing and were listening; he knew that the commons were edging nearer, listening too.

"You hear that, my masters," he said loudly. "That all will be well." And then, "Who will bring the news to the Great Captain, and bring him here again?"

"I'll go." "And I." "And I." Three of the commons began to move away, then stopped and hung uncertain, when Darcy asked, "Where will you find him?"

Someone said, "Wressel." Someone else said, "Hull." "Or any other town or castle in all Yorkshire." They all laughed at that; it was well known that the Great Captain was apt not to be long in one place, and that he covered the ground quickly.

"Come, Perce," said Darcy, when they had gone, and put his hand on Creswell's shoulder, and led him into the house. All the rest followed, the clerk coming first, bearing the cushions my Lord had used, the papers, rolls of accounts, bundle of pens and a pot of ink. In the way between the Chaundry and the Boiling House, just before they came out upon the passage beside the screens, Lord Darcy half turned, and slipping the big fur-lined cloak from his shoulders, tossed it to the clerk, but so maladroitly that the skirt of it flapped paper, ink and pens, cushion and all, out of the man's hands.

"Tchk!" said Darcy, and went on with Creswell beside him, leaving the clerk and the others who came after to pick up what had been scattered. They could not know, when they came up again with my Lord and the messenger going through the Hall to the Great Chamber, that a letter sealed with the Duke of Norfolk's seal lay snug in the long hanging sleeve of Darcy's green damask velvet gown.

Alone in his own Privy Chamber Darcy lingered for a minute before he shut the door. He had left Perce Creswell outside in the Great Chamber, with the others, to ease his stiffness by the fire, and to drink a cup of wine. Now Darcy could hear them begin to question him of Thomas Cromwell, Lord Privy Seal, and now to say what they themselves thought of him; that, Darcy conceived, would keep them busy long enough; he shut the door, latched it, and went away to the deep window on the far side of the room. There were cushions there on the stone seat, and the sweet smell of the herbs strawed on the floor came to him as he stirred them with his feet. Outside the window the country stretched away, still and golden green, with blue above, and mist of a deeper blue lurking in the further trees. He opened the letter and read what Norfolk had written.

Not till he came near to the end could he guess why for the delivery of this letter such secretness had been needed. Then he understood.

He read the whole through not once, but three times, then laid it on his knee, upside down; yet he could not take his eyes off the Duke's clerk's neat, pretty penmanship. At last, after a very long time, he picked it up, and looked it all over, most narrowly, examining the writing, seal and all. Then he folded it, put it back into his sleeve, and opened the door into the Great Chamber.

Perce Creswell was sitting by the fire, dandling an empty winecup in his hand. He looked a much nimbler man than when he had come in, and he swung round quickly as he heard the door open.

His quickness was a mistake. The commons jumped up, as when one dog wakes, all wake. They boggled that Darcy should speak with Creswell alone; they thought they should hear it too. Yet when Darcy told them he would but speak a while with an old friend, reminding them too how Lord Hussey, whose servant Perce had been, was now a prisoner for the Lincolnshire rising, they consented. "And you shall hear all anon," said Darcy, as Perce followed him in.

Darcy sat down again in the window-seat. Perce Creswell took a stool.

"Now," Darcy asked him, "what is your credence for this?" and he swung the end of his long sleeve between them.

"The same," said Creswell, "as is the effect of the letters. That my Lord of Norfolk, my master, bids you account him your true friend to follow his advice in this, that in order to declare yourself ye shall by your policy find the means to take, alive or dead, but specially alive if ye can, that most arrant traitor Aske. Which," said Creswell, "my Lord my master doubts not by your wise policy ye shall well find the means to do."

Robert Aske was in the parlour of the Buck's Head at Selby. Will Wall, still as thin as a straw, but now not quite transparent, was writing to his dictation at the table by the window; Aske would not sit, but went up and down between the hearth and the table. He had come from Wressel this morning and would return before dinner. At Wressel was Kit, and they had quarrelled before he left. And here at Selby a letter had reached him which said that the brethren of Watton would not hand over the Earl of Northumberland's spice plate; the letter said much more than that—such things that Aske had first crumpled it in his hands, then torn it into pieces and thrown them into the fire.

He swung about at the hearth. "Have you writ that?" Will, his pen still scurrying, nodded.

"Then write this," Aske said, tramping off in the other direction: " 'For I will assure you that I will have nothing of

no man, but that it may be lawful and reasonable done.' "
He stopped, biting at his knuckles, said—" 'Wherefore' "—
Then, "No, it's enough. Conclude—'And therefore fare you
well from Selby, the tenth day of November.' "

But though he had said it was enough, when he had read
through what was written he twitched the pen out of Will's
fingers, and, with one knee on the bench, began to write a
postscriptum. "If you have the spice plate, send it me with
haste." The pen flew over the paper. "It is pity apart from
God's sake to do anything for that House that so unkindly
doth order me." Will looked up to Aske's face with its black
frown; these days, Will thought, his master was angry where
he had been positive, bitter where he had been stubborn, and
very seldom merry.

Then he saw that Master Robin had stopped writing to
listen. "Open the window, Will," he said, but before it was
open Will had heard the sound of a horse ridden very hard.
Aske ran out into the street.

Yet, when he had stopped the messenger and almost
hauled him out of the saddle, he came back in silence into
the parlour with the fellow behind him, and sat down on the
bench.

"Well," he said then, "what's your errand?"

"My Lord Darcy says, 'Come back to Templehurst. There's
a letter from Sir Robert Bowes and Sir—' "

"Did he say no more?"

"He told us all in the garden, 'This messenger says all will
be well.' "

Aske got slowly from the bench. He turned his back on
them and went down on his knees with his head between his
fists against the edge of the table. Will knelt too, and the
messenger, after fidgeting with his belt a moment, did the
same.

No more than two minutes after that, Aske set off for
Templehurst, on the horse which the messenger had ridden.
He would not have Will come; he must go back to Wressel.
But he laid his arm for a minute across Will's shoulder and
said, softly and quickly in his ear, "Oh! Will, I had forgotten that God might have mercy on us, and lay to His hand on
our party."

Then he looked down at his knees. "See, I have knelt in a
puddle of ale." He laughed, and Will heard him laughing as
he went out and swung up into the saddle.

Lord Darcy and his people were at dinner when Aske reached Templehurst. He came up the length of the Great Chamber just behind a big ham and an apple pie; he laid his hands on the shoulders of two who sat opposite my Lord. "Come, make room, make room," he bade them, and vaulted over the bench to the place between them.

Lord Darcy said: "Where did they find you?"

"At Selby."

"And the messenger? And your servants?"

"Oh! Somewhere behind." Aske waved his hand vaguely. But when he had eaten a little he looked up and around from one to another, and laid down his knife.

"Your messenger said, 'All will be well.' Is it well? What does Bowes write?"

"Well, there it is." Darcy threw the letter to him over the table.

When Aske had read it he slammed it down on the table and then gave it a great blow with his fist so that the dishes jumped.

"It's a lie that I moved war newly since we were at Doncaster. You all know that I have not. I have stayed the people wherever I could. And after Pomfret, God knows, I could stay them hardly."

"Good Master Aske," Darcy interrupted him, "we shall answer these letters, but after dinner."

"I shall answer them article by article," said Aske, and after that sat eating without lifting his head. After such hope as he had had this was too sore a trouble for him to take it lightly.

When dinner was over my Lord said it would be well to send out messengers to fetch some of the other Captains, because, besides Aske's answer, this letter should receive an answer from them all. So those of the commons who had come to Templehurst to hear the news went off, as well as certain servants of my Lord. Darcy himself went into his Privy Chamber; Aske took pen and paper to the little Chequer Chamber where he could be undisturbed.

He had barely finished his answer when a lad came saying that my Lord would speak with him, and so led him through the house. It was a great house, and crowded with servants, all in the green livery, besides gentlemen sitting talking, singing or dicing round the fires, for evening was closing in, and within doors it was almost dusk. Every here and there, in little closets or at the wider parts of passages, there were barrels of arrows, or stacks of bow staves or of pikes. Aske thought to himself as he went after the lad, that my Lord Darcy was master of a big meiny, and well furnished; he remembered how he had, like every lawyer, condemned the bad old days when the lords had each an army of men in his own livery, to fight for one or other of the two Roses; but now it heartened him a little to see Lord Darcy's strength.

"And I need heartening," he thought, with an uncheerful smile, as he came to the Privy Chamber. Kit's words at Wressel, the letter he had answered at Selby, now this lying accusation which Bowes and Rafe Ellerker had believed—all these things together had borne him down.

He sat down by my Lord upon the settle. Darcy put a letter into his hands, and then got up, and began to move about the room behind him. Aske leaned forward, holding the letter aslant to catch the light of the fire, and so read it to the end.

He did not stir when he had read it, and he knew that his face did not alter, whatever was the alteration in his mind. When he first took the meaning of what the Duke bade Darcy do, he thought: "He would not do it," and then hearing how Darcy prowled restlessly behind him, and between him and the door, down went his confidence like a shot bird. He thought, "It was always what I feared," and he read again—

"In your life I think ye never did such service that both to His Majesty shall be more acceptable taken, nor that shall more redound to your honour and profit. My Lord, the bearer, your old acquaintance, can show you how like a friend I have used me to you all this time."

"Like a friend." And the letter was signed—"Your loving friend, T. Norfolk."

So the Duke of Norfolk, who was Darcy's friend, expected him to do it.

Darcy had stopped moving about and now stood still. "Well," thought Aske, "I must say something." But he was thinking that there were five gentlemen and several of Darcy's servants in the room outside, and himself one man alone.

He said, in a flat voice without looking up: "They want me 'alive or dead, but better alive.' " He had been about to say, "I'll see it's not alive," when Darcy cried—

"Alive, or your head in a sack. He said that to me. God's Bones! but that he was mine old acquaintance, and besides came on a safe conduct—" He broke off, and coming to the settle leaned over, and snatched the letter from Aske's hand.

"What I have answered to Thomas Howard," he said, "is between me and him. But there was need I should show you that letter. God's Bones!" he cried again, and Aske heard him rap out with his staff at the frame of the bed as he went by it. Then he stooped for a long time over a fine little coffer bound with steel and with five locks of steel, till he had put away the letter and locked it safely in.

Aske stayed where he was, his face burning, and not with the heat of the fire. He felt himself, for his suspicion, no better than a cur.

He said the same to Sir Robert Constable that night. They were sharing a bed; Sir Robert lay already between the sheets; Aske had sent away the servant, and now he sat down on the edge of the bed in his shirt and hosen.

"Did you conceive," cried Sir Robert, when Aske told him, "that Tom Darcy would act so?"

Aske hung his head without answering.

"It's well you did not say it. He could not have forgiven you, I think."

Aske muttered that he thought shame ever to have—but—

Constable, watching him, felt a spark of their old enmity kindle. But it was the last spark. He had never seen Aske utterly abashed before, never, in all his experience. To see it now tickled his vanity; the cause of it wakened his generosity; so the spark dwindled and was quenched.

"Never," he said, "would Tom betray a man. Though I grant you I myself find him over fond of policy and subtlety sometimes. But then he hath a very busy working head. But this is a different matter."

"I did not know," said Aske, "what to think of him." He twitched his shirt out, and as he plucked it over his head he said: "I knew, and did not know, I think."

"Well, you know now."

"By God!" Aske turned his face. "Now I do know."

There was something so warm, and so moved, in his look that Constable was moved too. They faced each other for a short instant. Then Constable, drawing up his knees, drove with his feet at Aske's backside, hoisting him off the bed.

"A murrain on you!" Aske cried, rubbing himself. He was laughing, but each of them knew that a line had been passed.

November 14

It was a perfect hunting morning, blue above, lightly crusted with hoar frost underfoot; the shadows of the bare

trees, delicately pencilled and perfect in every branch, lay
stretched across the clean ridged plough lands, as the King
and his Court went by with noise of trampling hoofs, jingling
of bells and the tantara of horns; above them the gulls, in
from the sea, turned with a flash, then flowered into golden
white, sailing.

The King was in a good humour. The Duke of Norfolk, who
rode beside him on the one hand, and my Lord Privy Seal,
who rode on the other, got each a teasing that the King
pitched loud enough to be heard by those that came behind;
so when the King laughed, these laughed too; their laughter,
which Lord Privy Seal bore with apparent complacency, was
to Norfolk a hair shirt on his shoulders.

So when, within the forest, they waited for the huntsman's
horn to tell them of the game afoot, Norfolk let himself
be edged to the outside of the crowd, in the midst of which
the King's green velvet cap and white feather could be seen
above the rest, mounted as he was upon a tall black gelding.
Norfolk did not look that way, but downwards and side-long;
winning for the moment, in spite of the crowd, a fragile,
narrow privacy.

There had been murder done just here, sometime this
bright morning; a scatter of feathers filled a little grassy hollow; a spot of royal sanguine, on which the dogs pored and
sniffed, lay upon the dark, soft earth. The feathers were
grey, and black and grey like mussel shells; Norfolk's eyes
being on them he saw instead, in his mind, the long low
shore opposite Orford, and the heaps of mussels there. It
was lonely on Orford ness, lonely and quiet unless tides and
winds were angry. At Orford and thereabouts, and at Framlingham, and in all those places where Howards were lords of
the soil, Thomas Howard was a man different from the Duke
of Norfolk who had ridden by the King's side, his ears burning, cackling with a sick and raging heart at the King's
baiting. He wished now that he was there and not at Court; he
almost truly wished it.

One of the huntsmen came trotting by, circling the crowd,
with the dogs after him; the hoofs of his horse trampled the
spilt feathers, not with the brittle cracklings of mussel
shells, but in the silence of a trodden cloud. Then a dog
bayed, the horns blew, and the hunt crashed away down the
glade, with the slipping, flickering shadows of the bare boughs

racing over them. Norfolk rode light, and rode boldly, so he was soon able to choose his place. He came to the King's bridle hand, and clung there, not to be dislodged by any other, for the rest of the hunt.

When he came again into the chamber he had been given at Windsor, there was Perce Creswell waiting for him beside the fire. So Norfolk sent everyone away, and then Perce drew out of his doublet the letter which Lord Darcy had written three days ago at Templehurst. The Duke took it, but before he opened it he asked:

"Will he do according to my counsel?"

Perce shook his head. "By no means could I prevail on him."

So Norfolk read the letter through, hurrying on to the part he least liked to read, and reading with a shrinking mind.

"Alas, my good lord," it was written in Darcy's bold, round, tumbling hand,—

> Alas that ever ye, being a man of so much honour, and great experience, should advise or choose me to be a man of any such sort of fashion, to betray or deceive any living man, French, Scot, yea or Turk. Of my faith! to get and win to me and my heirs four of the best duke's lands in France, or to be King there, I would not do it, to no living person.

About an hour later Perce Creswell stood before my Lord Privy Seal, looking down at the table which was heaped with papers; among them was a very dainty silver-studded leash for a hound; there was a little wrought coffer, too, of steel work overlaying some light-coloured horn; the coffer stood open, and from it trailed a pair of beads of ivory and cornelian; the room was warm and smelt heavily, though sweetly, of musk.

"What my Lord Darcy wrote to my master," Perce said, "I do not know."

"No?" Cromwell did not raise his eyes from his two plump hands, spread starfish wise, on the table before him. "But if there were words that you can remember—"

Perce said: "My Lord Darcy showed himself much displeased at my master's letter. He went about the room, halting on his staff, saying, 'I cannot do it. I cannot do it, in no wise, for I have made promise to the contrary.'"

"Ah!" Cromwell snatched at a word. "A promise?"

"So he said. And he said further—'It shall never be said that old Tom shall have one traitor's tooth in his head. Not the King nor none other alive shall make me do an unlawful act.' "

"Fie!" said Cromwell, but softly, "is it an unlawful act to take or kill a rebel?"

"I say what I heard," Perce mumbled, and Cromwell nodded for him to proceed. "Then he, leaning at a window and fretting at the catch thereof, said: 'My coat armour was never stained with any such blot.' And he said: 'My Lord's Grace, your master, knows well enough what a nobleman's promise is.' And again: 'For he that promiseth to be true to one and deceiveth him may be called a traitor, which shall never be said of me.' "

"Why," said Cromwell, "here's a great talk of promise, and promise again." He looked up, so that Perce saw his bland, quiet face, with the sharp pig's eyes. "And did my Lord Darcy seem to bear your master an ill will for his counsel?"

Perce looked down at his cap. "He believed not that it came of my Lord's device."

"Then of whom did he conceive that it came?"

Perce shook his head. He wished he did not so clearly remember what my Lord had said as to that man of whose device he conceived this thing had come.

Cromwell picked up the pair of beads, and began to run the pretty things through his fingers, but he was not praying. He smiled, thinking, "Surely my ears should have burned—" Then he stopped smiling. "Surely, God willing," he thought, "those words shall return home to roost."

"And was that all?" he asked.

Perce, greatly relieved, said: "That was all, bating sundry great oaths."

November 18

From the windows of Wressel Castle you could not see twenty yards across the flat deserted meadows, the mist lay so thick. It crept also into the house, filling the rooms with a clinging chill, for it was a fog that followed on frost. Kit Aske, waiting while the servant went up to enquire whether the Grand Captain would receive him, felt the ache of his back which came with such weather, and chewed the bitterness of having to wait on Robin's convenience, and of hearing Robin called "the Grand Captain."

When they brought him upstairs to the Earl's bed-chamber
—"No less," thought Kit, "will content his pride"—Robin was
standing in doublet and hosen while Will Wall helped him
into the velvet and steel brigandine.

He put Will by and crossed the room to Kit, shrugging
himself into the coat as he came, and laying his hands on
Kit's shoulders, kissed him lightly and went back to the fire.
Kit was nothing softened by the greeting, nor by Robin's
casual, "Well, Kit, you're welcome. Now about those fellows
of Skipton—" Not even if Robin were in a hurry to be gone
did that excuse his positive dictatorial brevity, the manner
in which he interrupted, or contradicted, Kit; Kit did not
even try to conceal his resentment; soon they were at it
ding-dong, disputing whether or no, had the Grand Captain
chosen to attack, he could have taken Skipton Castle.

Yet the quarrel, which might have eased Kit's mind, was
constantly interrupted; a gentleman would knock and look in
to ask a question; the clerk steadily writing at the corner of
the room in a welter of papers would come forward with a
pen for the Grand Captain to put his name to a letter; Robin
must, for this, that or t'other reason, take his attention
from the argument, so that he only seemed to sustain his
part in it for a pastime; and that was bitter to Kit.

So, at last, he himself broke it off, saying, "But whether it
were Skipton or the King's Tower at London you would say
you should take it. Yet it was not to speak of this that I came.
Shall I speak with you alone?"

Aske looked at him. "You shall. But I may not stay long."

They were silent till Will, the clerk, and a boy who was
trussing up such of Aske's harness as he was not to wear,
went out of the room.

"Well," said Aske, "now what will you say?"

If ever there had been any motive of brotherly kindness
which had brought Kit here, by now he had forgotten it;
certainly he found a sour pleasure in the news he brought.

"There is," said he, "a general pardon offered, but ten are
exempted therefrom, of whom, you, brother, are the first."

Robin had gone away across the room. On a stool between
the windows there was a trussing coffer bound with iron. He
tried the lid, and when he found it locked nodded to himself. Then, but as if Kit had only half his attention, he said:

"That I knew," and went to the bed and began to rum-
mage among the stuff cast down there, muttering something
about a key. Yet he did hear what Kit said, for when Kit had

finished urging him—"for the sake of all us Askes that be loyal"—to sue for his pardon at the next meeting with the Duke of Norfolk at Doncaster, he answered sharply that he would do it only in so far as all the commons did, "And as the King shall grant our just demands. And now," said he, "if that be all you want with me, I can stay no longer," and, giving Kit barely time to reply, went out of the chamber.

Kit stood still where he was for one long minute. He had come, he told himself, to give a brother warning. Well, he would stay for another purpose, and it was Robin's own fault that he did so. But in order to accomplish that purpose Kit must appear to be good friends with the Great Captain. He went off, as quickly as he might, after his brother.

Robin was standing in the Great Court with the reins in his hand. Kit went near, and spoke in his ear.

"You'd best take care."

"How?"

"Not so loud." Kit tipped his head back towards the Hall. "They are using ugly talk in there, grudging at you because you would make them ride in haste without their dinner. They say that a man is worth his meat, or else his service is but ill. And one said that you use them no better than slaves."

"Well?"

Kit said: "It is not well," but the talk of the commons had been balm to his sore mind. "The end," he said, "will be that either they'll kill you, or deliver you over as a traitor, like Jacques Dartnell, or William Wallace the Scot."

Robert Aske cried out suddenly, very loud, "Jesus! Will they?" and laughed in Kit's face. He left Kit standing by the horses and went running up the steps to the door of the Hall. Kit lost sight of him then, but he could hear his voice, as he rated the men with a kind of cheerful ferocity and in very damaging terms; sow-bellied swill-bowls was the prettiest name he had for them.

Kit clenched his hands. "Now! Now! Will ye endure it?" He did not speak the words but something in him was crying after that fashion to the men in the Hall.

"Come on you!" He heard Robin's voice again with a laugh in it. "Out you go first, since you are the smallest"; and the Great Captain came to the door again holding by the ear and one wrist a big, bearded fellow who yelled and swung his other arm like a flail, but aimlessly. At the top of the steps Aske loosed him with a shove that sent him sprawling down into the yard. There was a crowd of commons in the doorway now; one of them laughed, and then they all laughed with a great gust.

When the Great Captain had gone, and the men, for whom he would not wait, were scurrying to get horses saddled and away, Kit went back to the Earl's Chamber upstairs. Will Wall had been busy here. His master's coat and doublet were folded and laid on top of a chest at the bed foot. The litter of stuff on the bed was tidied away too; not a paper was to be seen anywhere; the clerk had gone, taking with him his little desk and all his writing gear. But the trussing coffer was still there.

The great house was very quiet now that all the men had gone clattering out after Aske. The fire was dying down; Will Wall, nor no one, Kit thought, cared for the comfort of the Great Captain's brother. He listened. He went, stepping softly on the rushes, to the door, to see that the latch had fallen home. Then he came to the great bed, and, still listening, began to shift the curtains along the tester rod; the old silk and velvet smelt sharply of dust as he moved them.

Something fell with a little thud. He stooped and picked up a dark green leather pouch; it had silver-gilt aglets on the ends of the thongs that drew up the throat of it.

Kit, with his eyes on the door, undid the thongs, and felt inside, and found the key that he had hoped for.

When he had at last put away again all the papers in the little trussing coffer, and locked it, his hands were very cold, but sweat was running down his back. He sat down by the fire, and as he stirred the logs to get a blaze he ran over in his mind the heads of all the matters that he had learnt, especially the plan for marching south in three hosts which should unite again after Trent was passed.

Then he thought of Robin riding post to Lord Darcy at Templehurst, and the men hammering along the road after him. "But he hasn't my hands on a horse's mouth," he thought. He warmed himself also with thinking how clever he had been to find both the key, and that one writing among all the others that was of such moment. "And it's not every man," he thought, "could have got it all pat so soon. Robin couldn't—at least no sooner." And Robin had done all he might to ruin the whole Aske family, so it was but just if one of them did what he could to save the house by discovering to the King the detestable, traitorous plans of the rebels.

Lord Darcy sat by the fire in the Privy Chamber at Temple-hurst. He said: "Thomas Cromwell was with the King before you came to him?"

Bowes nodded; he was sparing of words. Rafe Ellerker said that they'd seen him come out as they waited. "But," he added, "I think he's painted blacker than need be. After, when he spoke to us, he said he wishes well to the North Country and we should know it."

"He does, does he?"

Aske, speaking from beyond the group beside the fire, said it was time they came to the tenour of the messengers' charge, and Lord Darcy agreed. So they sat down much as they stood, my Lord, Sir Robert Constable, Sir Rafe, Bowes, and Master Challoner at the fire—Aske astride of a bench beside the table; he drew a pile of clean paper to him and tried a pen on his nail. There would be letters to write after this news.

Sir Rafe and Master Bowes, one prompting the other, gave their account of their mission to the King. None of the others said a word while they spoke; Lord Darcy listened, resting his elbow on the arm of the chair and his head on his hand; Constable stared at his feet; Master Challoner teased at the Pilgrim's Badge on his breast, pulling and twirling at a loose thread between his fingers; Aske after a little threw his leg across the bench and sat with his back to them all, jabbing with the pen at the table.

When the messengers had finished there was a little silence, and then Aske said, without turning about:

"Why did you not tell the truth to the King?"

"The truth?" Rafe Ellerker cried sharply.

"You say you told him that the gentlemen were taken by the commons and forced to swear the oath."

"And we were. You were too. You told us so yourself."

Aske turned and looked at him. "Would you go down into the Hall now, Rafe, and tell my fellows what you told the King? Well? Will you not answer?"

Bowes answered instead of Ellerker. "The King's Grace," he said, "was very angry. I think we only spoke what we dared. I know I dared not have spoken bolder."

"But," said Aske, "if none dare tell the King the truth how can he know it? It was your charge, to tell him, and you did not dare."

"Of course," put in Ellerker in a cold, unpleasant tone, "Robin would have dared."

Darcy lifted his hand.

"The Captain is right. Let the King and Cromwell think that there is the thickness of a thumb nail between the gentlemen and the commons, and they'll go about to drive in a wedge will split a mill post."

Bowes stood up, and then Rafe Ellerker; it was Rafe who spoke.

"We have made our report to you. If there's no more ye would know, give us leave—" They moved towards the door, and none of the others bade them stay. But at the door Bowes hung back.

"Among other words of reproach His Grace said these, or near as I can remember—'Now the intent of your pilgrimage with the devotion of the pilgrims may appear, for who can reckon that foundation good which is contrary to God's commandment, or the executors to be good men, which contrary to their allegiance, presume to order their Prince, whom God,' said he, 'commanded them to obey, whatever he be, yea though he should not direct them justly.' The which hearing, no subject but must be troubled in his conscience, being in arms against his Prince."

"Ho!" cried Darcy, "and is your conscience even so?"

Bowes replied that yea, so it was, and went away with unshaken dignity.

When he had gone there was a silence, and then Darcy spoke:

"Well, Master Aske, and what do you think of this answer of the King's?"

"I think," said Aske, "that it is no answer at all."

November 19

When most people in the great house at Templehurst were asleep Aske still sat writing in Lord Darcy's chamber. The old Lord was in bed, but awake, sitting propped up against pillows, in a fine embroidered linen night-shirt and cap, with a black velvet nightgown about his shoulders.

Aske got up, sighed, stretched, yawned and went over to the fire. He threw on a couple of logs and dusted his hand on his hosen.

"Are you done?" my Lord asked.

"Near done." He clapped his hands upon his backside and gave a little laugh. "You know, my Lord, they say that a lawyer needs three things—an iron hand, a brazen face, and a leaden breach. But I have fallen out of the way of much sitting these last months."

He went back to the table and took up his pen again. "I've near done," he said again, and now he was not laughing. "I wish we were as near the end of our great affair."

Darcy said, by the Mass, he wished so too, and just then a servant knocked and let in Sir Robert Constable. He sat down on the settle, and let his gown fall away from his knees so that the fire should warm his bare shins.

"Have you opened it to him?" he asked of my Lord, tipping his head towards Aske.

"No."

"Opened what? I've done now," Aske said, without looking round. He tipped the sand back off the last letter, folded it, and tossed it on to the pile of those that were ready for sealing. Then he came over to the fire. "Well?" he prompted Sir Robert.

But it was Darcy who said: "We all think alike of the King's answer. If I mistake not, we all think now that the matter shall come to battle."

He waited, and Aske, looking down into the fire, muttered that the North was ready. "And where erst we took up one man to go on our Pilgrimage, if we go forward now, we shall take up seven."

Darcy said: "One trained man-at-arms is better than seven of your armed husbandmen. The Emperor has the best men-at-arms in Christendom."

Aske began to say, with some heat, that Yorkshire yeomen were as good as any—then he stopped short. "What do you mean?" he asked sharply.

"Look outside the door!" Darcy bade him. Aske raised his eyebrows, but did as he was told.

"Rawlyns is there?" Darcy asked when he came back.
Aske said: "At the stair foot."

"Good. You ask what I mean. Then this, in a word. We must send and ask help of the Emperor."

"No," said Aske quickly, but Darcy went on—"Two years ago Master Chapuys, the Emperor's Ambassador, promised help. There were those then who thought that the King's proceedings would not be endured. Now, if we ask, and if the Emperor will send men, we have Hull for a port for their landing—"

"And we have the friar," Sir Robert broke in, leaning forward to look up into Aske's face, "for a messenger."

"What friar?"

"An old man, and honest. Waldby. You know him. He will go."

Aske went away to the table and stood quite a long time fiddling with the pens there. They watched him all the time. At last he came back.

"My Lord," said he, "Sir Robert—this Pilgrimage that we have set forth upon—it's God's business, though"—he dropped his voice and spoke so low and hurriedly that they hardly heard the words—"though it is done our way not His. But," he looked from one to the other of them, "let's finish it with His help, and without more treason than we need."

Sir Robert said in his plain way, "We knew you would not like it."

But Darcy began to argue. Just because it was God's business, they must bring it to a good end. "If we fail, the Church and all our liberties will be quite overset. Cromwell, his servants, and these new Bishops will pull all down. Would you have that?"

"No. No."

"And you would fight that it should not be?"

"Oh!" cried Aske. "But this is another matter."

"And it is yet another to suffer God's Church in England to be rooted out, heretics to bear rule, and teach what they will. Why, in fifty years, if they have their way, there will be none, barring a few old men, who have heard anything but that which the King hath been pleased they shall learn."

Aske said, "I must think." He began to walk about the room, and they let him alone. At last he came back and stood looking down at Sir Robert.

"Are you for it?"

"I'm with Tom," Constable said. "Here's Cromwell making Bowes—even Bowes—believe he loves our commons well, and the same day he writes that letter we took, saying he'll make a fearful example of them, and of us, to all subjects while the world shall last. What will they else but trick us if they may?"

Aske gave a sort of groan. "So we shall trick them first. I think I know now what it means—'*Quicunque enim acceperint gladium, gladio peribunt.*' It's not only that man shall be killed by the sword. But all he fights for perishes, while he fights, and it perishes by his own sword. Well—" He threw out his hands. "Since I am in I must wade on till I'm over.

But God knows whether once there I'll find I have left Him behind me on the hither side."

"Then—you consent—" said Darcy.

Aske nodded. So Constable went to the door and bade Rawlyns to fetch the friar.

November 24

This was the last day of the Council of the Commons at York, and the stormiest. They disputed till the candles were lit, and the painted glass in the windows of the great Chapter House showed only looming gloomy colours in which the flames were dully reflected. This day they spoke of their grievances, and men, growing angry, hammered with their fists on the arms of the monks' stalls, and the commons used the same oaths that they used for swearing at their sheep dogs and plough beasts.

It was against Cromwell that they spoke most freely, but they grew very bold also against the King, Sir Francis Bigod recalling how Rehoboam, by young foolish counsel, had so used the commons of Israel that they would no longer suffer him to reign over them. Then another of the gentlemen said it did not need Israel for a lesson, "For in this noble realm who reads the Chronicles of Edward II shall learn what jeopardy he was in by reason of Piers de Gaveston, and other such counsellors."

"Aye," cried one of the commons from near the Border, "and a Prince should rule by justice mixed with mercy and pity, and not by rigour to put men to death; for though it is said that our bodies be the King's, when he has killed a man he cannot make him live again."

Another asked, "What of the King's vices, which men may say truly have most need to be spoken on, to be reformed of all things, for if the head be sick, how can the body be whole?"

And then they came round to Cromwell again, calling him "the Loller and false flatterer." "He says," said Sir Richard Tempest, "that he will make the King the richest Prince in Christendom," and at that one of the rough fellows from the dales broke in—"But he can have no more of us than we have, and that he hath already, nor is not satisfied—as a man can have no more of a cat than to have its skin." They must have their laugh at that, before Sir Richard could go on. "Yet I think this Cromwell," said he, "goes about to make the King the poorest Prince in Christendom, for when by such pillage he has lost the hearts of his baronage and poor commons, the riches of the realm are spent."

Then a big man with a beard jumped up, a yeoman from beyond Beverley.

"If that traitor live," he cried, "none of us who are head yeomen or gentlemen can trust to any pardon. Some other device will be found whereby we shall lose our life, goods and lands. It is better to try battle than to submit."

"Aye, and good to take time when time is fair," said another.

When they saw Sir Robert Constable on his feet they were all silent, for they knew that he was one of the chief leaders. He said his counsel was that as they had already broken one point with the King (he meant by taking and keeping a ship that had come into Hull), he for his part would break another. "Let's have no meeting with my Lord of Norfolk at Doncaster yet, but make all the country sure from Trent northwards, and then I doubt not but all Lancashire, Cheshire, Derbyshire and the parts thereabouts will join with us. Then" (and he laughed), "then I would condescend to a meeting."

But at that Aske got up slowly, leaning with his hands on the arms of his chair. He said surely the commons must go to Doncaster. "It's all our whole duty to declare our griefs to the King. If he refuses, then our cause is just. But first we shall ask for a free pardon and a free Parliament."

There was a great outcry then, one advising battle, and another to treat. When the noise died a little one of the Captains, called Walker, a man with a voice like a bull's, cried to the Great Captain, "Look you well upon that matter, to have a free Parliament, for it is your charge. For if you do not you shall repent it."

Aske, who had sat down again, gave no more answer than to bow his head. It was Sir Robert and the other gentlemen who at last quieted the commons. After some more debate the meeting broke up, and all went away, excepting the Great Captain. He, when Constable asked was he coming, only shook his head; he had a paper in his hand, one of the many petitions of grievances, and seemed to be studying it. Sir Robert, who had thought just now that Aske had spoken too roundly in differing from a friend, was nettled by his silence, so, shrugging his shoulders, went off, leaving him there, with all the candles burning around him, in the empty Chapter House. When once Aske was alone, and no one there to see, he leaned forward, letting his head hang down, as he hugged the great pain that wrung him.

Will Wall, who waited at the Silver Crescent with the other servants, took quite a long time to cover the short distance between the tavern and the Chapter House, being, by the time the meeting broke up, pretty sodden with drink. When he reached the Chapter House only the porter stood there, swinging his keys. Will leaned against the door jamb and looked into the high, vaulted place. He rumpled up his hair all over his head and said, in a blurred, reflective tone, "They've gone away. Where've they gone to?"

"The Grand Captain's there."

"By Cock! He is, is he?" said Will. "And what's he doing there? Cock's Bones! I'll go see."

Aske heard him coming and raised his head. He knew from the sound of Will's footsteps, before ever he saw him, what the fellow had been up to. And now Will was leaning over him, swaying and bleary. Aske gave him a push.

"Take your ugly face away. You stink of ale. I shall be sick." He got up heavily and began to go towards the door.

"Lord!" cried Will, with a cackle of laughter, when he saw Aske stumble, "if I'm drunk, you're drunk too."

Aske said through his teeth, the pain being very severe, "I'm not. It's the colic." But Will would have it that his master was drunken too, and linking arms rambled on beside him out of the Chapter House and into the moonlit streets singing loudly. In spite of the pain Aske could not help an inward wry smile, so like to a pair of homing roysterers they must appear; the height of the dismal joke came when they two with one consent diverged in order to be vilely sick. "God's Mother!" said Aske to himself, wiping his forehead with a shaking hand and laughing feebly. "Like man, like master!"

They got back somehow, and after some time, and Aske called to Chris Clark to come and undress him. But Chris came up the stairs saying there was "a gentleman from the South," and he looked at Aske with a look that meant more than the words. So Aske sat down on the bed and the gentleman came in, and delivered his news, which was of moment, and urgent, and very secret; and then Aske must write a letter to my Lord Darcy, and Chris Clark must mount and take it. By this time Will was snoring, and all the others in the house off to bed, so Aske lay down, dressed as he was, to sweat and shiver, to fall dizzily to sleep, and to waken hearing a voice cry in his ear, "Look you well upon that matter, for it is your charge. For if you do not you shall repent it." In his dream it had been his charge to prop up with his two hands the tower of the Church at Aughton, which was toppling over, and he had known that his hands could not avail.

November 30

Malle and Wat stood on the edge of the Swale just below the steppingstones. Malle had the Nuns' big mule, Black Thomas, by the bridle; the steward had lent him to Gib to take a sack of wheat and a sack of rye to the mill to be ground for maslin. Thomas stooped his grey velvet muzzle, soft as a night-moth, down to the water, and began to draw in deep gurgling draughts.

Malle let him finish and then nudged him with her elbow and he began to go over. The water was biting cold so that Malle and Wat went trampling and splashing to be quick across, but Thomas trod as daintily as though he could walk upon eggs without cracking them, tossing his ears and switching his long tail.

When they were over Malle stopped to wring out the skirts of her gown, and Wat began to dance about to warm his feet again. Black Thomas tripped the bridle out of Malle's hand and went on along the track by himself.

Malle said, in a muffled voice, for her head was between her knees as she tried to reach the hem of her skirt behind—

"All's smitten through with Him. Love, frail as smoke, piercing as a needle—near—here. He that's light has come into the clod."

She stood up and for a minute seemed to listen to the unceasing voice of the Swale.

"So," she said, "yon brown cows, and the grass, and us, all things that's flesh, for that He is flesh, are brothers now to God."

Then, "Look." she cried, "look. There's Thomas rubbing off the rye sack against the tree. Run! Run!"

So they ran, while Malle cried out "Shoo! Tom. Shoo! Tom, wicked old whoreson!"

December 9

Robert Aske came home to Aughton in the dusk. The windows of the Hall were lit, and he could see, as he crossed the Court and the dogs met him, the arms of Aske, de la Haye,

Clifford, and Bigod shining coloured upon the colourless twilight. Inside the Hall door there was a warm steamy smell, such as would always hang about the house once a month while the ale was brewing. A couple of servants were just coming out of the kitchens; they were carrying dishes of eels in broth; when they saw him they cried, "God's Mother!" and "It's Master Robin!" and "Hast 'a come home, Master?" and one of them tipped his dish so that the broth ran over, as he turned to shout over his shoulder that Master Robin was come home. So Aske must stay a while in the Hall while the servants crowded in, to tell them what had been concluded at Doncaster yesterday. When he stopped speaking there was a deal of shouting, and as he went down the passage to the Parlour, a great burst of talking and laughter, and someone singing a song of the Pilgrims that others took up.

He went into the Parlour and shut the door behind him, and the noise outside was cut off. "Give you good evening," he said, but for a moment they all sat in silence round the table, staring at him, and saying not a word.

Then Jack cried, "Robin!" and started a fit of coughing that bent him double. Dame Nell turned her eyes from Jack to his brother, with a look as fiercely accusing as if Robin had been to blame for Jack's cough as well as for everything else. Beside Nell was a young girl, very pretty, whom Aske had never seen before. She half got up, and then sat down again. Jack's two younger boys, together on a bench, lifted their eyes from their trenchers and stared as they ate. But Julian, Jack's youngest daughter, came rushing across the room, oversetting a cup of ale on the table; she threw her arms about Aske's neck and kissed him.

"Julian!" said her mother, and the girl went back to her place, but with a smouldering, obstinate look.

Jack got up then and kissed his brother and asked, very husky, "Well, Robin, what news?" but Dame Nell cried, "No, I'll have no talk of these treasonous doings."

So Robert sat down, and since no one else spoke, asked, "Where's Hob?"

It was Nell answered him. "Hob's in London—safe."

"Good!" said he, in that same cheerful tone that always enraged Kit, and now had the same effect on Nell, who cried, "And no thanks to you for that."

But Jack said hastily, "This is Hob's wife," and Robin

[553]

looked at the pretty girl, who smiled again at him, though dubiously, and with a sidelong glance at her mother-in-law.

As they ate their supper, talking disjointedly, and in a thorny, uneasy way, Robert wondered if Will Monkton were having such a cold homecoming as this. He thought also of my Lord Darcy, of Constable, of many other men both gentle and simple with whom he had been in company so lately. His heart felt hollow as a bucket and heavy as lead.

It was early yet when he stood up, and said now he'd take his candle and go to bed.

"Julian and the little ones," said Dame Nell, looking down at her sewing, "have the room you and Kit had. But there's a bed in the room over the buttery, and Will Wall can carry up a pallet from the Hall."

The room over the buttery was an upper servant's room but Robert did not care for that. He said, "I'll tell Will," and then Julian jumped up.

"I'll see to it," she said, and went out in front of him with such a look over her shoulder at her mother as made Robert think, "Here's one that needs marrying, or there'll be bickering in this house." Jack certainly ought to have beaten her before things came to such a pitch that a maid could behave so to her mother.

But as they went side by side through the Hall she tripped up his thoughts about her by suddenly coming very close, and taking his hand in hers. She gave it a hard, quick squeeze, with a sort of shake, and dropped it again, saying, "You shall sleep in your own room. No, you shall. Dickon and Jack will never wake at moving." So, as they went up after Will and a maid servant, Robert Aske was thinking not of her ill behaviour to her mother, but of the way she had caught his hand, and how she alone of them all had welcomed him.

Upstairs, when the two little boys had been carried off sleeping, and the room put to rights, and Will had been sent off by Julian to fetch candle for his master, Aske took his niece by her two hands meaning to kiss her good night. But instead of letting herself be kissed she shoved him masterfully back towards the bed, sat down herself, and dragged him down beside her.

"Now," said she, "tell me what you stayed to tell the folk in the Hall tonight. For I heard your voice before you came in."

He looked at her sitting beside him on the bed. She was at that stage of growth when a girl can change in a few months, and she had changed since he saw her last September.

Then she had been a coltish creature, with abrupt, almost harsh, features, dark straight brows and a square face. Now she was ungainly no longer, though she was big, broad, and strongly built, being far more like in that to the Cliffords than she was either to Askes or to her mother's Rither kin. In face she had a likeness to old Sir Robert—and, Aske supposed, to himself—being a maid far from maidenly prettiness, with a dark line of hair upon her upper lip; yet she had a fine mantling flush at times, that gave her a sudden comeliness, and she wore it now.

"Tell me—everything," she urged.

"Do they know nothing at Aughton?" he asked, half teasing.

"Who would tell *me*?" she cried, rudely and scornfully. "You heard my mother to-night. And my father dare not—" His look checked her but she added obstinately, "The servants think that I am as my mother and my father."

Aske thought, "Surely she should be well beaten. Or should have been a lad."

"But," she said, as if she knew his thought, "if I'd been Hob, Uncle Robin, I'd not have left you."

"I sent Hob back," he told her sternly.

"You couldn't have stopped me from coming on."

He turned his face and looked at her. It was all wrong that she should speak so. She was a wilful, saucy, unbroken wench, but to be with her was like warming his hands at a fire. He half smiled. "Truly, and I think I could not, neither. Well. What shall I tell you?"

"There was a great council at York. I know that but no more."

"Then we came to Pomfret—" He locked his hands about one knee and began to talk. As he talked he forgot the familiar room in which he knew by heart each knot and shake in the beams, every twist of the painted leafy trellis pattern on the walls; he forgot the single candle burning on the stool by them, and casting their shadows huge and distorted, across the floor and halfway up the door; he forgot his niece in her old rayed gown of blue and red, and white country kerchief. Instead of these he saw the crowded Hall at Pomfret where my Lord Darcy, Constable, and all the rest, gentlemen and commons, sat on benches, like the King's Parliament at Westminster, a great, solemn and an earnest company of men.

"The best blood of the North," he told her, "was there, and

that's not all noble blood, July, but also the yeomen and the poor commons of Yorkshire." He stopped and she saw his eye had kindled, but when he went on it was more lightly.

"We talked and talked. And when we did not talk, I wrote. We drew up Articles that the Duke should be given to carry to the King. We took three days over it, and the spiritual men over their Articles took two more."

"And then?"

"Then ten of us went to Doncaster. No. Not I. But those ten carried the Articles, and asked for safe conducts. Next day three hundred from our part rode into Doncaster. We lay at the Grey Friars and my Lord of Norfolk at the White Friars. Then we chose twenty, and those twenty of us went to him. And there, being chosen to speak for all, I argued the Articles."

"You!" she cried with a bright flush, and a ring of pride in her voice that he could not miss. He put his arm round her, and felt her body, young, solid, yet supple, close against his.

"The Duke read out to us the King's free pardon for us all, and declared His Grace's promise of a free Parliament, and pledged his own word that the Abbeys should stand till that Parliament be met.

"When I got back to Pomfret that night it was too late to declare the same to the commons, but next morning early I sent the bellman round, and had them all to the Cross and told them. After, I went again to Doncaster, but then comes one riding in haste from Lord Lumley, saying that the commons would not be content but if they saw the King's Pardon and the Great Seal. They were crying again to fire the beacons, and that we gentlemen had betrayed them."

"Shame on them!" she cried.

He shook his head. "The commons," he told her, "are like dogs that have been scared when they were whelps. They'll trust a man, and then at a word or a look they'll remember what men once did to them, and, when they remember, they'll either run, or bite. And after they'll trust again.

"So back I went to Pomfret, by consent of all, and the rest of that day I talked. Mass! I marvel my tongue was not quite worn out talking to the commons there. Good men they are, niece, but obstinate, and some of them have skulls as thick as a clog sole, and it's as difficult to draw a notion out of their heads as to drive it in. But by evening I had contented them, and sent to Doncaster to have Herald Lancaster with the Pardon; who came, after dark."

He looked at Julian, and gave a little laugh. "There were, among those gentlemen with me, I'll not say who, that would have had me turn all out once more that night to hear the Herald's message, fearing, they said, that the commons should murder us in our beds. But I said, 'Well, if tonight I be murdered, in my bed it shall be, for nothing shall keep me out of it longer!'

"So next morning, on St. Thomas's Hill, where Constable and I had used to take the musters, the King's Pardon was declared to the commons, and received of them, and then—"

He stopped abruptly, and looked at Julian as though he saw her again after being away at a great distance. "Then—they all went way—I watched them most of that morning, from the top of the keep. When they'd all gone, and the town was empty, except for us few gentlemen—I—could have wept."

She asked, after a little silence, "Was that this morning?"

"No. Yesterday," But to him it seemed half a year ago already. He said, more to himself than to her, "And I should be on my knees to God for His grace to us, instead of talking so like a thankless fool."

"What then?"

He went on, after a moment, "Then we that were left rode back again to Doncaster, and there, in the White Friars' Frater we all, kneeling on our knees, tore off our badges—look, you can see the mark." She looked, and saw where his finger touched the breast of his doublet, a line of stitching and a patch where the colour seemed deeper than round about. "I prayed, and they granted me, that they would never call me Captain any more. The white rod I carried I tried to break across my knee, but I could not."

"What did you do with it then?"

"Kicked it under the table. The poor Friars will have a fine sweeping up to do with our badges and all."

He was smiling, but she stretched out her arms with the hands clenched, and letting out a deep breath cried, "So you did that which you set out to do."

"If God speed us. The Duke will go to the King now, and the King must ratify the terms."

She started round, and stared at him.

"So it's not finished yet?"

"Our part is finished. And—yes—it is as good as finished."

[557]

She sat brooding with her chin on her fists, and after a while he answered her silence, almost as though she had been a man, not a chit of a girl.

"The Duke," he said, "spoke in the King's name, knowing the King's mind. With a free pardon, and a free Parliament, we need fear nothing. The rest will be done by that free Parliament, held here in York."

"And the Duke?" She turned to him with her obstinate, truculent look. "You will trust him? And the King?"

He rebuked her sternly, almost fiercely for that, saying that he marvelled to hear her speak so. "For if," he said, confusedly but with vehemence, "if I may not trust—if such men—if—surely I would rather die." Then he was silent, for in the bottom of his mind there was a thought which he could not find words for, nor even plainly know its meaning. But like a dread in a dream it lay there nameless—if there could be such treachery as that she glanced at, he had rather not have been born, for God Himself could not prevail against it.

But he shook it off, and came back to the ordinary world. Julian sat beside him, crimson and scowling after his rebuke. He put his hand on her shoulder.

"I thought once," he said, "much as you do about my Lord of Norfolk, because of a thing that was told me. He would have had one to—well, to betray me."

"But that one would not?"

"He would not. And now I see that the Duke so dealt because of his loyalty to the King. So I count he shall be loyal also to us. He spoke long with me, Julian, most graciously and frankly too, standing in a window at the Grey Friars."

"I see. So it is well." She jumped up from the bed, then put her clenched fists against either of his cheeks, chafing them roughly.

"You great hoyden!" he said, laughing and catching her wrists.

"It is because I am so glad."

He got up and kissed her, bidding her "Good night, sweetheart."

December 18

Julian Aske slipped into the dairy, sure that no one had seen her. She dipped a canful of cream, and stood with it in her hand behind the door, spying through the crack between the hinges till Uncle Robin should come through the gate. From the window upstairs she had seen him walking across the Ings, so there would not be long to wait. When he came she would walk out, with the can of cream in her hand, meet him in the Court as if by chance, and give him warning. Then he had only to turn and go out of the gate again, and to Aughton Landing where already Will Wall and Uncle Will Monkton must be waiting with the horses.

It was a beautiful plan, all her own in conception and execution, but it failed. She had not been in the dairy two minutes when she heard her mother calling, "Julian! Julian!" She stood still, making no answer. But one of the servants cried, "Mistress July's in the dairy." "Send her to me," Mistress Nell answered. Julian whisked out into the Court. If she was quick enough it might be possible to do her mother's bidding and be back in time. But it was not possible. She had only lifted down from its peg the big fat hank of woollen yarn for which her mother sent her, when she heard her father's voice hailing, "Hey! Robin, what have you been at?"

"I've been at missing every duck I aimed for between here and Bubwith. All but this one, and he, I swear, ran on my bolt for pure charity. And, for pure amazement to see him fall, I fell into the bog."

Julian looking down from the little low window of the weaving loft could see them below—her father, who must this moment have returned from Selby, on horseback; her uncle, mired to the waist, and drenched with rain beside, for there had been sharp sleety showers driven on a northerly wind since sunrise. He had a crossbow on his shoulder, and the charitable duck dangled from his hand. Now he waved its corpse in farewell, and went on to the Hall.

Julian knew that in the Hall waited Master Peter Mewtas, Gentleman of the King's Bedchamber, with the King's letter summoning Master Aske to London.

Too late to give him warning, but as soon as she might, she went after her uncle. He and Mr. Mewtas stood facing each other in the great tower window of the Hall where the bow racks stood. Mr. Mewtas was a big well-looking man of about thirty, both fine and neat from his curling fair hair and short beard to his broad-toed velvet shoes, for he had had time to shift from his wet clothes into a suit of fine black cloth with carnation-coloured sleeves; there were jewels in his ears that gave a winking flash in the fire-light when he moved his head.

Robert Aske, dribbling bog-water from his boots, coat and hosen, stood with his head bent over a letter. His hood was off, and he held it dangling beside his knee; Julian, watching him from the shadow of the screens, could see that his jaw was very set, and that the hand that held the hood shook, though ever so little. She thought, with a sort of pang, "He's frightened," and was both shocked and horribly daunted. Then she called herself a fool. Of course it was the chill of his drenched clothes. She moved forward, and he turned quickly and saw her.

She knew, by the way he turned and by his look, that he had needed someone. She was glad to be that one who had come. But she dropped her eyes as she curtseyed, lest Mr. Mewtas should divine from a glance that there was any confederacy between them.

"Niece," Aske said, "will you be pleased to send us some wine. And let someone set me dry stuff ready in my chamber."

"I will see to it, Sir," she said, and went.

She wanted to bring the wine again herself, but did not because he had said, "Send us wine," and she would exactly obey. But as she waited a long time upon the stairs, hearing below the voices of her father and mother, as well as those of Mr. Mewtas and Uncle Robin, her teeth were chattering, partly for excitement, partly for dread that she had not rightly understood him.

When he came up, and she saw how he spied about and how his face lit when he saw her, she knew that she had not mistaken.

"I have set everything ready," she told him.

He laughed silently, and whispered as he came up after her, "I said I must put off my wet clothes. I stood close to the fire till the bog mud stank, and Mr. Mewtas could not speak for holding his nose."

But when they were together in his room and the door shut he did not laugh.

"Julian," said he, "will you help me?"

She scowled at him because he needed to ask, and he understood and gave her a smile. "Find me Will, or Chris Clark," he said, "and send him for me to your Uncle Monkton at Ellerton."

She laughed out at that. "I have already sent Chris. I sent him as soon as that perfumed popinjay bird below came in."

"Tut! niece," he murmured, "the King's messenger. But—"

"Listen," she cried impatiently, and reached up her hands to untie his doublet at the neck. She did it with a sharp tug, and began to undo the buttons, telling him as she did so that, "that fellow's servants watch the stables, I think, but if you should go out by the orchard and so to the Ings, it's like they shall not see you. I told Chris to tell Uncle Monkton to wait by the thicket of thorns. There are four horses down on the Ings still. Arrowsmith's the best, and then Pippin. I told Chris to saddle those two."

He caught her by the wrists. "But for what?"

"To ride. To get away." She stamped her foot at him.

"Where should I ride? Into the sea? To the Scots?"

She understood then that all her plan was foolishness, and hung her head sullenly. "You will think I am a great goose."

"No." He did not smile, and there was no gentleness in his look, but she knew that this was how he searched a man's face, to judge his worth and his truth. "I think," he said, "that you are bold, ready, and faithful."

At that she flushed her finest crimson. "But," she said, "will you ride to the King?"

"This very day. Mr. Mewtas will have it so. He says it is the King's command, and indeed so the letter says, to use all despatch. He says it must be to-day because there was snow near Lincoln yesterday. With this wind there is like to be more to-morrow. That is true—" Yet he was frowning as he turned to cast his doublet down on a bench.

It was then Julian remembered that he had said: "Find me Chris Clark," So, "What will you have Chris do?" she asked.

"This," he told her. "The King writes that I shall make no man privy to his letter. But my Lord Darcy I must tell of it, and send him a copy. Can you have it copied and sent, so that none knows but you and I, Chris Clark, who shall copy it, and your Uncle Monkton, who shall fetch it to my Lord?"

"I shall do it," she said, and took the letter, and left him.

When she came back, and tapped on the door, she found that he was dressed, ready to ride. The suddenness of it struck her then with a great clap of fear, and she caught him by both elbows.

"Uncle, why must you go to-day?"

"To-day or to-morrow is all one."

"But—must you go?"

He looked at her very soberly for a minute, before he said: "I must go. Some man must tell His Grace the truth of these matters. No one has told him yet how wholly all this part of his realm, lords, gentlemen, commons, are set against his proceedings. And besides these there are also many of our way of thinking in the South. If no one will tell him, then I will tell him." He smiled at her. "So it is good that the King should send for me."

"If it is good," she muttered, "why do you write secretly to my Lord Darcy?"

"You're a lawyer, are you?" he teased her, but she would not smile. "Because, though I think it is good, yet, if it should prove the contrary my Lord should know on what credence and safe conduct I went."

"Uncle!" she cried, "don't—"

He shook his head at her, and she was silent.

"Now," he said, smiling at her, "down we go to meet again this—what name did you call him by?—this perfumed pop-injay bird. And like two true plotters let us look strangely on each other. And I shall chide my niece, and my niece will be forward with her uncle, which, I do fear, she is most apt to be."

She would not answer his smile, but gave him over her shoulder a fierce, glowering look, as though she dared him to make light of himself, or of her, or of the affair in which together they were concerned. Yet the truth was she was near to tears, which she would not for the world have let him see.

Will Monkton came to Templehurst a little before sunset. It was snowing, though not heavily, and in the house it was so dark that the candles were lit already. They were just going to table when Monkton came in, so my Lord bade them set for another at his own table, and Monkton sat down opposite my Lord and Sir George Darcy.

It was Sir George who said, "You bring news from Master Aske?"

"Time enough after supper," said my Lord, and, "You've no wine in your cup, George." But Sir George was not to be put off. "If it is a privy matter and urgent will you not, Sir, speak at once apart with Master Monkton?" and he looked from one to the other. He was no wiser for what he saw in my Lord's face, but it was plain that the big, slow man opposite sat, as it were, on thorns.

"Have you," my Lord asked, "a letter?"

Will Monkton answered, after a pause, that he brought the copy of a letter.

"And a message?" Sir George suggested, but my Lord was holding out his hand, and Monkton put the copy of the King's letter into it in silence.

When my Lord had read it he laid it down beside his plate, on the side farther from his son, and began to talk about indifferent matters. But while he discoursed to Master Monkton of the price of lime and of the weight of fat porkers killed and salted last month Sir George was looking across him to the copy of the King's letter, spread open on the board. Suddenly Lord Darcy took it up and laid it before him—"For else," said he, "I can see that your eyes will take a lasting cast, from glancing so long aside."

Sir George flushed very hot at that, but he read the letter and then said to his father—yet looking also at Master Monkton:

"Will Master Aske, think you, do well to go?"

"I think," said my Lord, "that he will do well, having the King's word for his safe conduct."

After that Sir George was silent, and when supper was over one of his servants came in, saying that the horses were ready and the snow falling heavy.

"So," said my Lord, "you must haste away, or you shall not make Gateforth before dark."

Sir George went, having kissed his father's hand, and given Will Monkton a sour good night.

Then my Lord led Monkton to a window. It was cold here away from the fire, for the wind was clotting the flakes thickly against the glass, and chill air came filtering through the lead of the window frames. But it was private, and that was what they needed.

"When," my Lord asked, "will he go?"

"By now he is already some hours gone."

"Gone?"

"My niece sent this word: 'Tell my Lord—he would go.'"

"Tchk!" Darcy said, and then, "By the Rood! yes. That he would." He dabbled absently with his finger tips in some of the melted snow that dribbled through the casement, and shook the drops off.

"How many did he take with him?"

"Six, and a horse-boy."

"Good men? Trusty?"

"All born at Aughton."

"And that means the same." Darcy gave a little laugh. Then—"Can you catch him up if you should ride now?"

"I could try. I ride heavy."

"You shall have a good horse. Come up with him if you can, and tell him he shall leave a man and a horse at divers places along the road—Which now?" He screwed up his eyes, peering through the muffled and darkening window, but seeing the long road that led to London, and the towns strung out along it. "At Lincoln," he said, "and at Stamford, Huntingdon, Royston, and at Ware. Then if this letter and safe conduct be a trap to take him, that servant who comes with him to London can warn his fellow at Ware, and so each the next, and in a day or but little more I shall know of it. And then—" my Lord drove his staff down upon the stone floor of the window—"By God's Death, I'll fetch him out of the Tower if it should cost twenty thousand men's lives."

Monkton said: "Where is the horse?"

But very late that night he knocked again at the gate of Templehurst. When they brought him in they had to lift him down from the saddle, so stiff he was with cold. He had lost himself hours ago, and ridden, he supposed, in a circle. At last, because there was nothing else for it, he had laid the reins on the horse's neck, and let it find its own way home.

December 21

Lord Privy Seal was in the great closet, overlooking the tilt-yard. Before him on the table lay lists of the King's debts, under three heads—"Merchants that be contented to forbear unto a longer day," "Small sums to be paid forthwith," and "Greater sums to be paid forthwith." Privy Seal was working down the second list, checking from another paper those names against which a clerk had written, "Sol": to show that the bill was paid.

"Henry Annottes, fish monger.

"Humphrey Barrows, ire monger.

"John Sturgeon, haberdasher.

"John Horn, tallow chandler."

There was a knock at the door, and a gentleman put his head inside the room.

"My Lord," said he, "His Grace comes even now through the Great Gallery."

Cromwell looked up, nodded, and went on with his work. Yet his ears were pricking. When the King came in he was halfway to the door, and his cap in his hand.

The King let himself down into the chair that stood beyond the table, and near to the fire. It was a fine chair, very wide and ample, and its red Spanish leather was stamped with roses and lions, and fringed with gilt and crimson. He bit his lip and eased one leg to a better position, then shot a glance at Cromwell as if he warned him not to know that the King's ulcer pained him; Cromwell stood like any clerk, pen in one hand, cap in the other, and eyes cast down demurely; yet he missed nothing.

The King said, "You sent me word he was come."

"Last night, Your Grace, late."

"Well, what manner of man?"

"A man with one eye. A little man with a big voice." Cromwell, not forgetting that the King's voice was small and high-pitched for his great bulk, added, "Over big."

The King snapped, "As to his eye, we have been told that already. As to his bigness and voice we can see for ourselves. Of what manner is he in the inward man?"

If Privy Seal had been less quick he would have accepted the rebuke. But instead he turned it neatly. "Surely," said he, "Your Grace's wit will pierce more sharply into the inward man of him than could mine. But so far as I was able to perceive he is very confident."

"Of our clemency?"

"Of that, and, as I think, also of himself."

There was a silence in which Privy Seal turned away to lay the pen in his fingers beside the others on the table.

"He came," the King asked in his voice of dangerous gentleness, "he came then willingly and without delay?"

"Doubtless," said Cromwell, "in his heart he feared, remembering his late horrid treasons. But for all Master Mewtas could see, he came willingly and cheerfully. He talked much, Master Mewtas said, by the way."

"Talked?" The King leapt on the word. "Of what?"

"Of light matters, such as shooting with the long bow."

Master Mewtas had reported, not without malice, that Master Aske had spoken very freely of the hatred which the whole North Country bore to Lord Privy Seal, being so angry with him that they would, Master Aske said, in a manner eat him.

That had not prepared Cromwell to like Aske, nor had their interview last night bettered matters, since Cromwell had found him not at all respectful.

For my Lord Privy Seal had begun graciously, promising that Master Aske should find him good Lord to him.

Aske thanked him gravely for that.

"And you, for your part," said Cromwell, "shall be plain with me, opening freely to me your whole mind and stomach."

"My Lord," Aske said, "I am, I think, plain with all men. But my whole mind and stomach I shall open to the King alone."

"I am His Grace's servant."

"Yes," said Aske, and left a very definite silence.

So now Cromwell said, watching the King, yet not seeming to watch him, "Of light matters, such as shooting with the long bow." He saw the King's hand clench on the handle of the little dagger that hung by a gold lace about his shoulders, and added hastily, since for him policy came before private malice—"I think, with my Lord of Norfolk, that if Your Grace uses him with fair words he will tell much, both of himself and the other traitors."

The King uncrooked his fingers from about the handle of the dagger. "You shall see how I shall use him. Have him in."

When Aske came in he saw Privy Seal first and made a gesture with his hand to his cap. Then he saw the King. He pulled his cap off and went down on his knees.

"Well, Master Aske," the King leaned forward, staring into his face, "you have come. For what have you come?"

"To hear your most merciful pardon from Your Grace's own mouth, that I have already under your Great Seal. And to answer plainly and frankly as your Grace commands, whatever it shall please you to ask me."

The King heaved himself up from his chair. He went to the window, and came back, tramping heavily, forgetting altogether to disguise the lameness of his diseased leg. He stood over Aske; Aske raised his head and they looked each other between the eyes.

"I shall," said Aske, "if Your Grace gives me good leave, tell you the truth of the causes of our Pilgrimage."

There was a silence. Then the King said to Privy Seal:

"Go. Leave us alone. See that we are not interrupted."

Cromwell went out very thoughtful. It might be—he hoped it was—that His Grace could not endure that any should see him so braved. It might be—he hoped it was not—that His Grace had taken a liking to Master Aske. For the King could like, at times, a bold man, and certainly this man was extreme bold.

December 22

Master Laurence Machyn and his wife sat late at breakfast. The servants had finished theirs and gone away on their several occasions; every now and then one or other of them would go past the screens to the street door with a bundle of mourning robes over his arm, or a sheaf of long candles, or a load of painted buckram escutcheons upon staves, for there was a great burial to-day at St. Laurence Pountney. But Laurence and his wife sat on; they had argued all breakfast time, and the argument was not yet concluded.

July said: "Well, Sir, if you will not go, I cannot."

"Oh, Sweet! It's not that I will not go. I cannot. I must be at this great burial."

July flung down upon the board that one of Laurence's big gilt spoons of the Apostles with the figure of St. Peter on it, as if it had been no better than a spoon of tin.

"Why should they bury him to-day, when the King goes to Greenwich?"

"He has been dead four days."

"There's a quarter of mutton in the larder," she declared callously, "that's been dead longer than that. In this great frost—"

But he stopped her there with a fair show of sternness, which, however, he knew he should not be able to keep up for long. And true enough, when he saw July sit there, drooping glumly over the table, all light gone from her face, he had to think of a way of setting things right.

"I'll tell you, wife, what I shall do." He stood up, and, standing so, felt that he could speak as a husband should, who, if he chose to be indulgent, was firm withal.

"I'll send the boy to fetch Mistress Holland. She loves a show. You shall go together." July was picking with her finger nail at the blue stripe that was woven across the board cloth. She did not look up. "And Mat shall go with you, so you shall have a man to attend you in the crowd." Mat was Laurence's eldest journeyman; to send him away on a busy day meant much, and July knew it; but still she sulked.

"There, Sweet," Laurence cast from him the last rag of simulated firmness, and pleaded openly. "There, Sweet, be merry. Give me a kiss, and you shall have a gold noble to spend."

When he had taken his kiss, and paid his gold noble, he went away to see to all that he had promised July before he set to work on the business of the burial. He told himself that he had a dutiful wife—she was dutiful, he repeated to himself, in the main. Also she was hardly more than a child; whenever he chose to make a stand, then she must yield.

Yet the truth was not so, and he knew it. Already she took her way as freely as ever the first Mistress Machyn, and in return he got less comfort, for she would not be troubled to see after the maids. And lately, since he had given her a fine green nightgown lined with budge, she had shown herself a sad slug-a-bed, even trailing down to breakfast in it. He prepared a rebuke, yet when he saw her lay her cheek on the soft fur of the collar, and snuggle the green folds about her, his disapproval was quite swamped by pleasure in her pleasure, and pity for her pride in the gown, for, in her first delight, she had cried, "Oh! I never had none such before! My sister had no finer."

Laurence had spoken to Mat, who looked down and side-long, disapproving. He stood for a moment at the door watching the boy go off on his errand to Mistress Holland. The briskness of frost and sunshine had got into the lad's toes, and at the street door he must take off in a great leap, so as to brush the lintel with his hand; then he was away with a bound and a hoot, as though he had escaped from a cage.

Laurence smiled and shut the door. In the darkness of the passage he stood a moment, as his thoughts went back and hung over July. He did not know how often in a day he would stand like this, apparently vacant, but in reality searching, wondering, learning.

Now he shook his head. He did not care if she was by no means as meek as she had been. "One of her birth," he thought, "must find it ill to be wife to such as I." With her growth—and she had shot up tall since last autumn—she had put on a look as of fugitive, proscribed nobility. Sometimes she was imperious, though defiantly rather than with any confidence; sometimes, when among company, there was a sort of dark sparkle about her. "And if," thought Laurence "she be so set on this show, it's but as it should be." It came to him with a pang of tenderness that when she was first his wife she was so frightened a thing as to have no heart for pleasure. He could not guess that she would have had no heart for it to-day, only that she had heard his friends talk last night of the Yorkshire rebels, saying that the King had pardoned them every one. That was why she was so set on holiday-making.

The boy came back jigging on his toes and snapping his fingers behind Mistress Holland, who moved at a slow pace which his feet could not well endure. Mistress Holland, having kissed both July and Laurence, explained that she had been ready to go out to watch the show with Mistress Pacey, but just before Laurence's lad came she had heard that Mistress Pacey could not go, she having fallen down the cellar steps, nine steps, and broken her leg. "I told her," said Mistress Holland, "I told her she would be sorry when she had the picture of the blessed St. Christopher in the parlour whitewashed over, and a motto—something about Fortune—painted over it. 'It may be new fashion,' I said to her, 'but you'll be sorry therefor.'" Then she kissed July again, and pushed into her hands a little box of comfits.

So July, far from losing her dignity, was able to feel that she was doing Mistress Holland a kindness on going with her to watch the King riding to Greenwich, not as usual by water, but, because the Thames was quite frozen over, through London and over London Bridge.

They came through crowded streets, where the stones rang with frost, and the heaps of scattered garbage were hard almost as the stones, and laced over with patterns of white rime, to London Bridge, and following the crowd passed under the arches of the gate-house there and a little way along the bridge till from a space between two of the houses they could look down upon the river, like a great dark green highway, with people walking about on it in the sunshine, and boys sliding, and some few people gliding at great speed upon bones tied under their feet; one of these, less skilful than the rest, was most popular with the crowd because of his frequent and comical tumbles.

But while Mistress Holland and Mat looked down July turned her back and looked up towards the sun, because its light was so blessed as it moved, in greater splendour than King Harry's across the sky which in these last days was empty of clouds from dawn to the red setting, and now of as clear a blue as any summer morning. She forgot everything in that pure light, and the delicate warmth on her cheeks, and, half-smiling, turned her eyes this way and that, enjoying everything without thought. There were many banners set out in their brackets over the gate to-day; they stirred a little, sleepily, unfolding their colours and their gold against the sun, then, drooping, hung close again. July looked below them, to the ledge just above the arch, and she startled Mistress Holland by catching her arm and letting out a shrill cackle of laughter.

"Oh!" she cried. "See him grin with never a tooth in his top jaw. And his hair—red hair—it moves in the wind."

Mistress Holland looked where July pointed, and pulled her hand down.

"Sh!" she said, low but very urgent. "That is one of the Monks of the Charterhouse. They were holy men. Martyrs. You should not laugh."

July stopped laughing with a gulp. When she spoke, what with the way her voice shook and her teeth chattered, Mistress Holland could make little of it, and it seemed no explanation at all for July to say—if that was what she did say—"I laughed because they will not do so to the Yorkshiremen now."

Mistress Holland could see, however, that the girl was near now to tears. "Tut! Tut!" she said, comfortingly, tucked July's arm under hers and talked cheerfully of easy, everyday things. She also took some pains to shake off Mat so that she could ask July a few close questions; but July gave her none of the answers she hoped for, and certainly the girl was thin as a rake handle with no signs yet that she was breeding.

Soon the King and Queen went by, and small, pale Lady Mary, the King's elder daughter, who had once been Princess of Wales, close after them. The Queen smiled, and drew her hand out of her mantle of Russian furs to wave to the people as they shouted, and the King looked about too, with a gracious expression, and put up his hand to his cap now and then. But the Lady Mary went by them with a look like a sleep-walker.

After that Mistress Holland and July went down by Old Swan Stairs onto the ice, stepping on it very gingerly at first, then with more confidence. It was deep green, it showed feet thick, and had bubbles in it. July, staring down, thought it beautiful, and thought of the river flowing beneath the ice, all alone in its own silence, seen and yet unseen, for though the ice was clearish, like thick green glass, you could not see the water through it; or else you did not know which was water and which was the ice through which you saw the water. She thought that the river must feel now very safe, moving thus solitary below its frozen skin.

When they had had enough of walking about July and Mistress Holland began to look for Mat, but could not find him. "Well, we'll stand and wait," said Mistress Holland, and they stood back to back, the Vintner's wife scanning the crowds on the ice, July looking up at the wharf above, till her eyes were dazzled by the bright sky beyond the people's heads.

Behind her she heard, among many scraps of meaningless talk, this, spoken in a man's voice:

". . . A great brush and a pail of ink, and he inked every sign from Paul's to Old Bailey."

Whoever spoke had gone by now. Another voice answered him from farther away with a great laugh, and, "Ha! you lie!"

July whipped round.

Master Aske and a taller man had passed, and were swinging on up towards the Vintry at a good pace. July seized Mistress Holland by the hand. "There he is," she cried, and dragged her along. Mistress Holland, in her anxiety to recover Mat, was willing to show what nimbleness she could. Only when she found that July was plucking by the sleeve a strange gentleman did she pull her back, assuring her hastily that, "This is not Mat, Mistress Machyn."

Master Aske had stopped and turned. He looked first blank, then astonished, and then pleased.

"Mass!" he said. "Mistress July here!"

July stood dumb, only looking at him. If there were any thought in her mind it was that it would be enough for her could she look at him always and listen when he spoke. The perfection and quiescence of her sudden joy so warmed and lit her face as to make her, for those few moments, almost beautiful.

But Mistress Holland was insisting that she should know who was this gentleman.

July told her, "Master Aske."

"Not—not the Captain of the Yorkshire men?"

July, without taking her eyes for a moment from his face, said yes, this was he. She did not remember, and would not have cared had she remembered, that she had lied to Mistress Holland, saying that she knew none of the Yorkshire gentlemen.

Mistress Holland herself did not precisely remember it yet, though it lurked in her mind, creating a slight confusion there. But of one thing she was sure, since little Mistress Machyn was acquainted with Master Aske, she herself should shake him by the hand, and having shaken him by the hand would bid him home to supper, and his friend too.

His friend it seemed was promised forth. Master Aske, after an instant's hesitation, remembered that the chimney at the "Cardinal's Hat" smoked, and said he'd come, and gladly.

At the Vintner's house they supped and drank well, and afterwards in the last coloured light went to an upper parlour that looked upon the river. A servant poured more wine, and set down wafers, sugar comfits, and a dish of oranges. When he had shut the door and gone away Master Holland stood up.

"Sir," said he, "we and all England may well thank you, under God, for you and your fellows have saved religion," and he drank to Master Aske, standing.

Aske flushed and his eye shone. He was as ready to tell them about the Pilgrimage as they were to hear. "And," said he at last, "now there is nothing to fear. The King is a very gracious Prince. He only needed to know the truth, which was kept from him."

Mistress Holland cried out that she'd said so all along. "It's that Cromwell," she said.

The Vintner asked quickly, "Was Lord Privy Seal there while you spoke with the King?"

"At first, but the King drove him out."

"Is it possible?" said Master Holland. He looked shrewdly at Aske. "The King heard you patiently?"

"He heard me." Aske leaned forward looking from one to another, half smiling. "I'll tell you now what I've told no man. I rode here in great fear of my life. But the King's no dissembler. If he'd been smooth with me I'd have doubted him. But he was not so. I knelt there for half an hour, I think, while he rated me. But then, at the last, he said I should write down all that I had been telling him of the grievances of the North, and he would take counsel on them."

"Ho!" said the Vintner, "you spoke of grievances to him?"

"When he let me speak." Aske gave a little laugh. "I thought he'd have knocked his dagger about my ears before I'd done. Yet in the end he gave me his hand to kiss."

He sat for a moment in silence, staring down at his wine, which, in the silver cup, showed no colour, but only a surface that was dark, and darkly shining. He could see again the King's hand laid on his own, a plump, wide, white hand, with finely tapering fingers and many rings. He said, thinking aloud, "It's strange how when you have stood against any true man you love him all the better for it. There's Sir Robert Constable. We had each other always in displeasure in the old days. But now I know him, and he me. So too with my Lord Darcy. And so with the King's Grace; I never would have done him hurt, but now I'd die for him."

He looked up, and this time was aware of how July was watching him. He smiled at her. "He gave me a crimson satin jacket of his own," he said, "so you'll see me going very fine."

She dropped her eyes from his face to his breast for a second. "Is that it?" she asked, in a bemused sort of way, though the jacket he wore was of cloth, pretty well worn and not at all fine.

"Goose!" he said, and laughed. "Not this one. And that jacket will have to be mightily cut down or I wear it, so much bigger a man is the King than I. I told His Grace it'd be as in the fable of the ass and the lion's skin." He turned to the others and said, to explain his familiarity with July, "This maid I have known for many years since she was so high," and showed them with his hand.

But Mistress Holland cried out, "Maid? She's a married wife this three months."

"*Benedicite!*" said Master Aske, and looked again at July, more narrowly and more kindly. He thought to himself that he had never before seen her eyes so shining; he was glad to think that this must mean she'd got a good man, and was at last, as it were, warm, sheltered, and out of the wind.

1537

January 2

After the dullness of grey ice the pool in the old knot garden at Wilton gleamed dark with the reflection of the wall and the yew trees, bright with the pale sky. It was pleasant to see the water quiver as a breath of wind touched it, after so long immobility, just as it was pleasant to walk in the air, and feel it soft and clean on the cheek, after the biting chills or heat of great fires in perfumed, shuttered rooms, which all had endured for the last weeks. So Sir John Bulmer and Sir Francis Bigod paced together in the garden, followed by Meg with a nurse carrying her latest born, a boy now a month old.

Here, in Dame Anne's time it had not been thought amiss to dry linen yarn or new bleached cloths along the flat, clipped tops of box that edged the convoluted beds. But now that it was Dame Meg instead of Dame Anne such things were not done in the old knot garden: indeed already part of it had been grubbed up to make Dame Meg one of those newer gardens, such as the King had, and some great nobles, where the owner's coat armour was most cunningly picked out in colours, with, for gold, yellow sand or crumbled and pounded Flanders tile, chalk or well-burnt plaster for the herald's argent, sifted coaldust for sable, bricks broken to dust for red, and so on. This display of coat armour, where Bulmer impaled Stafford (and Stafford with no sinister bend), had been Meg's first flourish in her altered state, when from mistress she became a lawful wedded wife. She had set the gardeners about it in the first fine days of last spring, before even she began to root through all those coffers and chests which contained Dame Anne's stuff—old-fashioned, enormously ample gowns, hosen of gigantic proportions, shoes easy, large, and slovenly trodden over. Of all these things Meg had made great mock to her women, though not when Sir John was there, for he exacted more respect for a dead wife than he had done for one alive and going heavily about her duties at Wilton with an invincible silent patience.

For a while Meg carried in her arms the stiff little bundle that was young John Bulmer of Pinchinthorpe, rocking him, making sweet silly noises to him, bidding him watch the birds as they flew, and bending her lovely face above him, lovelier than ever after the stress of child-birth. Partly she did it for sheer pleasure, because she was proud to be the mother of a true-born son, but also she was aware how Sir Francis Bigod marked her, as he and Sir John turned; his eyes lingered as if he saw her in a new guise, and with new kindness; that being so, and she what she was, she could not keep her claws from him, though she might hide them in the most demure gentleness of approach.

So, when John of Pinchinthorpe set up a high thin wail, Meg pushed the child into the nurse's arms. "In! In with him!" she said. "For I can see he's cold—oh, such cold cheeks!" She let her lips travel with a bee's light cruising kiss over the child's face, then caught Sir John's arm and leaned upon him, looking across him to Sir Francis with a faint smile.

For a little the three of them moved in silence. They came

so to the small round pool, and stood, looking down. Then Sir John said:

"Frank will not believe the word that Rafe sent me from Marrick, sweetheart."

"No," said Bigod, "I will not think Master Aske a man to accuse his fellows to the King in London. Rather I fear that it's true what they are saying at Fountains—that when he came to London the King had him headed."

"Jesu Mercy!" cried Meg, but Sir John, giving over for a moment biting his nails, muttered that whether it were so, or t'other way about, yet Rafe's counsel was good—"that for no fair letters nor fair words we should not stir forth of the North Country."

Sir Francis looked from one to other of them with that lit, wild look of the Bigods.

"I tell you, Jack, that's not enough—to stay still nor stir not. For my part I am sworn to go forward again with the commons."

"No!" Sir John said, "No!" with his fingers at his mouth. "When my Lord of Norfolk comes—"

"When he comes I doubt he will rather bring us into captivity with them of Lincolnshire, than fulfil our petitions."

"But," Sir John persisted, "the commons'll not follow you, Frank. See how near they came to killing you at Pomfret for your traffic with Cromwell and your known learning in these English Scriptures."

"Yea," Sir Francis cried, "but now it is not so. They know me and acknowledge my truth," and he began to explain, not for the first time, how he had come to take arms with the commons, saying that it was manifestly against God's will for a secular man, a King, to be supreme head over the Church; and he went on from there, subtly dividing what authority might belong to the Pope, what to a Bishop, and what to a King.

At the end of it all Sir John put up his hands to his head and tugged at his hair. "So it may be. So it may be. But to rise again! And if Aske hath betrayed us—or is taken—what can we do?"

"Shame!" cried Meg so suddenly, and with such a sharp and ringing note in her voice, that they who had taken no account of her at all in their argument were astonished into silence. And then she began, urging as Francis Bigod had urged, but with more vehemence, that to stay still was to lose all, that these ships which Rafe Bulmer wrote of from

Swaledale were sent north by the King so that they might set on the North Country; that it was now, or else never, and that the commons were ready if only they should find leaders; and she caught a hand of each and looked into their eyes, eagerness quickening her beauty as wind draws up a flame, so that for a moment they could only stare at her.

Sir Francis cried, "God be my Judge, all this is true," but Sir John tore his hand away and went off, crying that he'd hear no more—not one word.

Yet he did hear more, and that which came nearer the truth, when he lay beside Meg that night in the darkness. For when he tried to fondle her she struck his hands away and would have none of him.

"You," she cried, "you, of a great house, yet who will take no part, but to follow other men, littler men such as Robin Aske! And now he is high in the King's favour, and you—"

"Or he is dead—headed or hanged, as Frank says."

"He?" she cried. "Never! He's not one to let himself be tricked, but to climb upon other men's heads to a high place. Did you not see it in the old days? But I did. I knew it in him. As the devil he is ambitious."

"Well!" He was sullen. "What then can I do?"

"Do? Nothing. You'll do nothing. No, but if the commons need a leader it shall be little Robin Aske, or that madman Bigod, but never Sir John Bulmer."

They wrangled for a time, but at last he pleaded, half promised, then wholly promised that he would be forward to lead, if there were those who would follow. Only then would she yield. When he slept she lay awake awhile in the dark, remembering how this morning, when both Sir John and Frank Bigod left her, she had stood alone by the coldly shining, lightly shivering pool. She had leaned forward, to see her own face in the water; it showed there, wan and deathly, but she knew it well enough in her glass to know what beauty it was that that proud fellow, whom she had once loved, had despised. For that was the truth, which she had known all along; though she had made a pretence to herself that he loved her only too well; the truth was that he had despised her. And this was he, forsooth, who, if he were dead, all the courage of the North Country must die too.

But, truly, she could not think him dead. Then, if alive, he was at Court, high in the King's favour, richly rewarded. "Yet," she told herself, "the last word's not spoken. If one, then another can prosper by that same means. And shall, if I can goad him to it."

There were several young gentlemen sitting at cards outside the door of the King's Privy Chamber at Greenwich. "He must," said one of them as another dealt from the pack, "he must have been with His Grace the best part of an hour."

"They say the King favours him greatly."

"Were I the King," cried one of them, "I'd have sent him home with never a tongue, the scurvy little traitor with his one eye."

"Did you hear how he spoke to the King's Grace?"

"What did he say?"

"It wasn't the words. I heard them not. It was how he spoke."

They fell to play again, but at the end of that game one of them, who had lost more than he could well afford, got up saying he had played enough, and began to ramble about the room, picking up a book and ruffling the leaves, twanging with his fingers the strings of a lute which lay on a bench. His aimless wanderings brought him near to the door of the King's Chamber. He stood still a moment, then beckoned to the others. "Listen!" he said.

They cried fie on him! and told him he'd be losing his ears in the pillory.

"I cannot hear their words. It is, as you said, *how* he speaks."

The others did not leave their play, but he stayed a few moments listening. Inside the King's Privy Chamber a man's voice, confident, resonant, positive, went on and on. It was not the King's voice.

Master Aske came out at last. He looked hard at the young men with his one eye, but saw them not at all. He saw instead a work accomplished, and it was a work that he had never fully believed could be brought to a good end. It seemed to him now a small thing that this morning a man had come to the Cardinal's Hat—a man he did not know—bringing news of fresh trouble in the North. This fellow said he had it from a friend at Buntingford, who knew a man at Royston, whose cousin . . . Aske could guess that if you went back over the slot you would trace it stage by stage, from mouth to mouth, all the way between London and Yorkshire.

The news was that the North was all of a floughter. Some

were saying that the Grand Captain had been bought by the King; some that he was dead, or in the Tower. And the man who had a friend at Buntingford put into Aske's hand a soiled strip of parchment which must have been torn from an old book of church-wardens' accounts, for there were on the one side of it entries of money spent on candles for the rood-loft, wine for the altar, and beer for the ringers. But on the other was written in a staggering, scrawling hand—

"Commons keep well your harness. Trust you no gentlemen. Rise all at once. God shall be your governor and I shall be your Captain."

It was signed at the bottom by the word "Poverty," and at each of the four corners the parchment was rent, because it had been snatched from the church door to which it had been nailed. So now Aske thought, "I must make haste home, to stay the people with the good news." But he thought that would be an easy thing to do.

A few minutes after he had left the King's bell jangled. That young gentleman who answered it came back and went away towards the gallery. The others questioned him in silence with lifted eyebrows, and he answered them in a whisper—"Privy Seal."

When Cromwell came to the Privy Chamber the King sat at the table bent over some papers. He gave no sign that he knew of Cromwell's presence, but, after Privy Seal had been on his knees a second or two, the King's hand made a motion for him to stand. So he stood, and let his eyes flicker lightly over the King, from his hair, once red-gold but grizzling and paling now; by the round roll of fat above the gold-stitched collar, the wide purple brocade shoulders, and so to the hands; as the King stooped over a bundle of papers his fingers drummed upon the table. It was certain that the King was angry; Cromwell would have given much to know against whom his anger was directed.

"This," said the King in his sharpest voice, "is the declaration of Aske. I have dismissed him to go North again." He looked up and suddenly cast the papers across the table. "Read it," he said, and sat back in the chair, his chin sunk on his chest.

Cromwell sat down, and began to read—"The manner of the taking of Robert Aske in Lincolnshire, and the use of the same Robert unto his passage to York." It took a long time, but the King now sat in silence, and quite still, except that the fingers of one hand twined and untwined about themselves the gold chain that hung round his neck, so that the jewel which swung from it tinkled on the emerald buttons of his doublet.

Cromwell read it through carefully, but as quickly as he might; only towards the end he read more slowly.

> And the said Aske saith that in all parts of the realm men's hearts grudge, with the suppression of the abbeys and first fruits, by reason the same would be the destruction of the whole religion of England. And their especial grudge is against the Lord Cromwell, being reputed the destroyer of the Commonwealth, as well amongst the most part of the lords as all other worshipful men and commons, for as far as the said Aske can perceive there is none earthly man so evil beloved as the Lord Cromwell is with the commons, albeit the said Aske saith that the Lord Cromwell never gave him occasion to report of him, but he only doth declare the hearts of your Grace's people.

There was not much more after that, but when he had finished Cromwell sat feigning still to read, while he weighed two different means of penetrating the King's intentions. Should he sigh and say, "Alas! I am content to be misjudged in your Grace's service," or should he, speaking in a frank open manner, say, "Here's a very honest man"?

He chose the latter, as being more provocative, but since he did not dare to meet the King's eye he shaded his own with his hand,

The King looked across at him, then down at the table. A sluggish winter fly crept there. His Grace put his thumb down slowly and firmly upon the creature; when he lifted it again he looked for a long instant at what had been a fly, before he scraped off the mess on the board's edge.

"Honest?" he said in a voice that told Cromwell nothing. "Yea, I think he is honest."

The Duke of Norfolk, loitering alone in a small oriel that looked from the southern side of the Great Gallery towards the river, congratulated himself that it was Cromwell and not he who had been sent for by the King, and had been with him for so long a time. The Duke, and almost everyone else in the palace, knew that the King was in a rage; who had incensed His Grace mattered little; those that came near him would suffer.

There was a small desk in the oriel, and a stool. On the desk lay a Book of Hours bound in stamped leather. Norfolk set his knee on the bench, and began to turn the pages. It was a sumptuous work, not new, for it had belonged to the King's father before him, but none the less beautiful in the Duke's eyes for that. He let the silky, strong parchment leaves slip crackling by under his fingers, catching glimpses of opulent gold, scarlet, lapis-blue: there were initial letters that held all of a scripture story, or only a grotesque animal: pictured pages where the golden haloes of saints beamed among English farms and fields: margins all a spray of flowers and leaves, and among the twined tendrils a monkey beating a drum, an archer aiming at a black and white magpie, half as big as himself, or a chaffinch painted to the life in his proper tinctures.

"What's the new printing," the Duke said to himself, "to this?" and he thought scorn of all those worthy folk who must buy printed books because they could not pay the price of such craftsmanship. Yet there was uneasiness mingled in his scorn; Howard needed not to buy cheap; he might still commission as costly a book as this—yet it would not be so fair. In his mind he felt the breath of change, chilling as the east wind in blackthorn winter. Nothing new was quite the same, and God only knew how far mutation would reach.

Someone tapped him on the shoulder and he whipped round to find the King standing beside him. Cromwell was just beyond, pale, and placidly twinkling as ever. If the King had trounced him, none could guess it from his look; not even the tips of ears were burning, but already Norfolk felt the colour climbing towards his own eyes.

"A fair work," he said hastily, waving towards the book the cap he had snatched off.

"Humph." The King put out his hand, and slapped the pages over angrily and hastily, searching for something.

Cromwell said he had seen in Italy a book printed for one of the Strozzis more perfect than a man could imagine, so exact yet flowing the letters of it, and the miniatures painted so graciously. "I remember," he said, "a grove of laurel painted there. A man might have walked into it to shade himself from the sun, and laid himself down under those trees, so masterly was the painter's hand."

"Humph!" said the King again, belittling the Strozzi's book.

Then he said, "Ha! See here, Thomas Howard, you that are papist at heart and a friend of naughty monks."

They looked down then, and saw that his finger pointed to where there was a blank in one of the prayers, where some words had been scratched and scrubbed out, leaving the parchment's smooth surface blurred; neither of them needed to be told whose name had stood there before the King decreed that in Rome there was but a Bishop, and he no greater in honour than any other.

"Before God!" cried Norfolk. "Your Grace is misinformed. I am no papist, nor no favourer of naughty religious persons. Nay! by Christ's Passion! but when I was in the North parts, and lay of necessity at one of the abbeys, several of my gentlemen warned me to take heed, for fear of prison, of what I drank there, so roundly I had spoken against them."

Cromwell put in eagerly, as if to help a friend, that such words had been reported to him. "My Lord speaks the truth," said he.

The Duke blinked at that, as if a glove had been flipped across his mouth. But the King said harshly that words were easy things. "And what lieth in a man's heart and stomach appeareth not so much by his words as by his deeds." When Norfolk began to protest that by words and deeds his true heart should appear, the King stopped him.

"Do you then," he asked, and let his small, keen eyes bore into the Duke's, "do you in your conscience approve and heartily embrace the laws that we have made in all these causes of religion?"

Norfolk pressed his two hands together. "Your Majesty, I do know you to be a Prince of such virtue and knowledge, that whatsoever laws you have in times past made, or hereafter shall make, I shall to the extremity of my power stick unto them."

"Well," said the King, "if that were true, it were enough."

January 7

Master Purefoy, a Master Scrivener and a very distant cousin of Laurence Machyn, sat for a while upstairs in the parlour of the Machyn house, waiting for Laurence to come home. He sat all the time with his head between his fists, never lifting it. Sometimes he muttered to himself, between his teeth. "He might 'a lived. He might 'a lived." And once, at a thought of one of the boy's merry sayings, he wrung his hands together and groaned aloud. But for the most part he

[581]

was too smitten to feel anything other than the great weight of loss for the son who had died yesterday; the one son, and the one child.

At the end of half an hour he could endure his thoughts no longer. He must be moving, though he knew that far or fast as he might go sorrow would come after, close as his shadow, not to be shaken off. So he went down into the Hall below, and, finding none there, let himself out into the street, and turned in the direction of Paul's. He had not gone far when Laurence Machyn stopped him by putting a hand on his shoulder, for he had heard the news and could not let Master Purefoy go by, solitary in his grief. Yet now that he had held him up Laurence could think of nothing to say, but stood, with averted face, gripping the Scrivener's shoulder.

His meaning was clear though, for kind intent can speak in a silence, and after a moment Master Purefoy turned, and went along beside him, telling of the little lad, and letting the tears run as they would. Laurence walked him up and down Knightrider Street for a long time, and heard, all in a jumble, of the boy's death, of his pretty ways, of how he had fallen sick, and what a solemn burial it should be. Laurence must see to that, "and stint nothing—stint nothing. For it was all for him, and now I care not to save, since now he—" "Ah, peace! peace!" said Laurence. "He is at peace."

When it was growing dusk they parted. Master Purefoy would not go back to the house with Laurence, and had not said, because in his grief he had quite forgotten, that ever he had gone in and waited, and come away again without a word.

So when the young shock-headed prentice lad Dickon, who opened the door to Laurence, told his master that he'd let in a gentleman and set him in the parlour upstairs, and yet he wasn't there now, and no one had seen him go, and no one knew what he had come for, Laurence could make nothing of it. "Who was the gentleman?" But Dickon, who had only been a week in the Machyn house, knew him not. Of what like then? Dickon had not noticed, but to get himself out of the scrape he muttered that the mistress would know, because she had been within in the bed-chamber.

Just then July came out of the kitchen carrying a lighted candle. Laurence cuffed the boy, but not hard, and told him he must be more heedful. "By not asking his name," said he, "you might have lost a customer."

He caught July just as she came to the foot of the stairs, put his arm about her and kissed her.

She pushed him away crying, "Keep off! Your breath smells most ill-favouredly."

"It is my teeth," he said meekly, and let her go.

"Then you should have 'em pulled out."

She began to go up, but he said, "Wife!" and she paused. "Who was this gentleman who came and who went again?"

"Gentleman? I know of no gentleman."

"Dickon let one in."

"Then ask Dickon."

"He knew him not."

"Well," said July, "and I saw him not," and she went on upstairs, leaving Laurence to come up after her.

Yet July had seen Master Purefoy very well, both coming and going, from the garret window, for she had spent all this afternoon in turning out an old chest up there. There were gowns in the chest, stuffy-smelling, stained, and some of them moth-eaten. There were swaddling bands for children, and little white embroidered caps, yellowish through being laid by. There was an old, a very old, headdress of tattered grass green silk and gilded wire; it was crumpled, but she straightened out the frame, pulled off her own white linen cap and veil, and put on the other. When she looked in an old steel mirror which she found wrapped in a bit of kidskin she could not but laugh at the strange fashion.

Time had passed pleasantly up there, for the sun came warmly through the window, and as she toyed with the stuff in the chest she could think her own thoughts. But she did not wish Laurence to know that she had idled away the afternoon, instead of seeing that the maids set the house to rights after the disorder of the Days of Christmas. And now she remembered that she had left the stuff all about the floor of the garret, having come down hastily because one of the maids had called her.

So she went straight on up the stairs, saying nothing more to Laurence, but with her ears, as it were, cast back like a dog's, to hear what he would do.

She heard him stop outside the parlour door, and then turn in. So she was alone again, except for the living candle flame that swayed in the draught like a dancer, like a spirit in cloth of gold. She stood on the stair to let the light steady, and stared at it till her eyes were dazzled; it was a pale saffron crocus, growing within a golden yellow crocus; it was a joyful thing to see. It was joyful because to-day Master Aske (he had said so) would be riding home, free and safe. As she moved on, groping with her hand, yet with her eyes still fixed on the candle-flame, July began to sing.

Laurence heard her and stood still.

"Who?" he said to himself, and "Jesu! I never heard her sing before," and he began to smile. Then something pierced painfully into his mind, like a needle into the quick under a finger nail, as he remembered how this afternoon Holland, the Vintner, had spoken of "your good wife's friend, that same Master Aske that was Captain of the Northern men." And Mistress Holland had said, "To think that your little July should have known him since she was a child," yet July had said of Aske that she knew him not; and now Laurence remembered with a sort of horror how she had lain shaking in bed beside him, the night he told her that Aske was Captain of the Northern men. And this afternoon a man had come to the house and gone again, without leaving any word. Yet July had said that she saw him not. And now she began to sing, sudden and sweet as a wren in the hedge, for the first time since she came to this house.

Laurence went to the settle and plumped down on it. He began to gnaw his knuckles; then he wiped his forehead with his hand.

"It was because she has been frightened that she will lie," he told himself; but that which had comforted him often was nothing to the point now. After a moment he sprang up as if the settle was red-hot, because a thought which he would not entertain had shown him the two of them sitting there together. "It will prove to be some other. It will prove to be nothing," he assured himself. "I shall find out." But he knew that he could not dare to ask anyone who might be able to give him the true answer.

January 8

Malle opened the door of the bread-oven beside the hearth and peered in. This time the loaves were well risen; she thanked God for that, and when they were all set out on the table, fresh, sweet-smelling, pale brown mounds, each with a bloom of flour upon it, she hung over them sniffing up the sweet savour and smiling.

While the loaves were still warm, but after she had redded up the houseplace and set bowls and spoons out for supper, she cut some thick spongy slices off one of the loaves and spread them thick with the herb-scented lard which the Priory cook had given to Gib. Then she tied the bread into a corner of her apron and went out looking for Wat.

She found him where she expected, gathering sticks for kindling along the edge of the wood. It was growing dusk, with a small moon in an empty sky; there would be a hoar-frost before morning; already the grass felt crisp under foot.

She stooped to gather with him, and then straightened herself to wipe the back of her hand across her nose. "Wat, there's naught any more to fear. For already, already God has done it. Whatsoever ill news cometh, that good news cometh after. Already, already it is done."

They saw Gib go by beneath them along the road; he did not look their way, but they kept very still till he was out of sight.

"Already! Already!" Malle said, as though that word was key to a marvel. She ruffled Wat's hair with her hand. " 'What's done?' says you? Why, that you know well, having seen Him. It's His work, it's God's great work that is done. Afore time was He thought it, and as He built the world He built His own hurt into the walls of it, for mortar to hold the walls to stand for ever."

She said—"See here, what I have brought you for your supper," and untied the corner of her apron, so that Wat grabbed at the bread and began to eat. "So," said Malle, "you needn't be seen by your father this night."

"Wuf!" said Wat, and "Gur!" for that pleased him as much as the fine fresh bread, oozy with half-melted lard.

"So it is," said Malle, "that already, little as they may know it, He hath all men taken in His net. And when He will, He may hale in, to bring us all home. How else? Shall that strong One fail of His purpose? Or that Wise, Who made all, be mistook?"

January 10

Archbishop Lee said, in a whisper, though the door was safe shut, and no one in the little warm room, with its painted and gilded wainscot, but himself and Gib Dawe, "You have the letter safe?"

"In my shoe's sole."

"They will give you a horse at the stables. I have put money in your purse. If you are questioned show the other letter, the one to the Bishop of London."

[585]

Gib bowed his head and said nothing. There was no need for the Archbishop to tell him all this again, since he was, he conceived, no fool. He looked down at the Archbishop's delicate hands, poised over his silver plate; one held a knife with a silver-gilt handle, the other a little two-pronged thing, also of silver-gilt, with which he now spitted the body of a wild duck, in an action that seemed to Gib intolerably and fantastically dainty.

"You understand? You will show the other letter to none, till you come to my Lord Privy Seal. Then give it to him, and such news as he will have of you of the new rebellious stirrings here." Having thus delivered his final instructions the Archbishop popped into his mouth a neat sliver of the wild duck. "Go now, go now," he said, and was raising the cup of wine to his lips as Gib laid his hand on the latch. The Archbishop's blessing, an afterthought, and hasty, followed Gib into the passage, and then he shut the door of this Prince of the Church, snug as a hare in her form, and as timid—thought Gib—eating his meat off silver (like a fine court lady) too dainty to touch it with his fingers; duck for him, and beans and bacon for such as us. . . . So, as if jolted by each step of the stairs, the little spurts of malice jetted up in his mind. "And a poor wretched nag it will be that they'll give me," he thought, forgetting to be glad that he would have a nag at all for his journey to London.

The horse was, indeed, nothing much to look at, but it proved itself a serviceable beast, so that he went through Doncaster as the sun drew near to setting. Beyond Doncaster, where the road ran up a hill beside a wood, with a village a little way below upon the right, he stopped, and for a moment looked back, and around him. The quiet sunny afternoon was closing in peace; the village, with the veiled orange glow of the sunset behind it, and the big stacks standing up smiling security, as much at ease as a man sitting down on his settle by the fire in the twilight, slipping off his shoes, warming his fingers and toes, thinking of his meat.

Gib, having cast one last glance back over his shoulder towards the North, where all was grey, and night coming up in a creeping mist, turned down the lane to the village. He too was at ease in his mind, wonderfully at ease.

Clearly, he thought to himself, as he jogged down towards the gathering of small houses and big stacks among the elm trees—clearly it was a man's duty to his Prince to carry news of treasonable words, discontented mutterings, threatenings of insurrection. Yet this, which had been his pretext when he came yesterday to the Archbishop at Cawood, and found him, surely by the dispensation of Providence, in need of a secret messenger, was not the chief cause of Gib's inner content.

That which had begun in pure, simple, almost physical relief, just to be clear of the Dale, of Richmond, and of any country he knew, had grown deeper as he rode, had become, he was sure of it—most sure, God be thanked—a refreshment of the spirit such as he could not have dreamed of, nor hoped.

For he had confessed to God, not, as the Papist idolators, to man, not in a church made with man's hands, but under no less a vault than the floor of Heaven itself built before the world—his thoughts swinging in widening arcs, like a hawk mounting, lost touch with words. He only again remembered the melting as of frost, as of grief into tears, that came when he had cried in his heart, "Lord, I have failed. Lord, I am not able to do it." And then, out of a great self-loathing and despair, "Master, if Thou wilt, Thou canst make me clean." At that moment came the melting, and the tears, and a great welling-up of comfort and humble confidence. He told himself now, "I am a sinner and can do no good thing. But I am forgiven." And once in London he would strive, not only against God's enemies, but against himself, God's worthless servant.

He came to where, as it reached the village, the road narrowed sharply, hemmed in between a steep bank with the church-yard wall on top, and the stone flank of a barn on the other side; beyond these it swung left-handed, so that the corner was blind as well as narrow. And there Gib knew that had the Angel stood in his way, and had the Archbishop's nag turned aside crushing his foot against the wall, as the ass crushed Balaam's foot, then he would have beaten the nag till he had forced it on, or he would have gone by on foot, or he would have gone about. But not for God's own angel would he have turned and ridden back again to Marrick. He knew this, but he shut the door upon the knowledge, locked the door, and drowned the key.

No angel stood in his way. He rounded the corner, saw the geese on the green and cows driven home, and heard the bell begin to jow in the church. Everything was sweet, kindly, and at peace.

When it was supper-time Dame Eleanor Maxwell came into the Prioress's Chamber and settled herself at table, with noisy sighs and breathings of which she herself heard nothing. The Prioress did not yet move from her chair beside the fire. A servant was laying for supper, a pewter plate and a wooden plate, the Prioress's great cup, and the little horn cup that was used by whichever of the Ladies sat with her at table. She set on cheese and bread, a dish of lemons and a jug of ale. Now she went off to fetch the salt herrings, and the eels, for to-day was Friday.

Dame Eleanor sighed yet more loudly and said, "Now that the Priest's gone—and God knows where—the woman and that child will starve."

The Prioress said nothing. It was useless to say anything to Dame Eleanor; only a shout in her ear could penetrate her deafness. But she nodded to show that she knew what the old lady was talking about.

"If," said Dame Eleanor, "Malle should come back here —the henwife's rheumatism is worse each year." A few minutes later she said, "Why should she not come back?" and she looked at the Prioress and waited.

"Now," thought Christabel, "neither to nod nor shake my head will answer her that." Nor did she truly know how to answer. Now that Marrick Priory had the King's letter for its continuance, and, on top of that, now that this late rebellion had braved the King for the sake of the Abbeys, she need not fear. Surely it would take more than a fool's babbling to endanger the House.

She nodded her head.

"Ah!" cried Dame Eleanor, and pressed her hands together. "Then she may come back and bring the child with her?"

The Prioress nodded again, and so it was settled. After that they sat in silence, except that the Prioress who had a lute upon her knee let her fingers toy with the strings, plucking no more than a tingling silver thrill from the minikin strings, and from the solemn bass a humming reverberation.

She bent her head; she would not look again at Dame Eleanor, because beyond her was the little secret recess which the Master Carpenter had made when he wainscoted the Chamber. Not half an hour ago, with the door barred, the Prioress had drawn from her breast the key, warm with the warmth of her flesh, and set it in the cunningly hidden lock. She had opened the door panel and looked in; even in that dark corner the firelight found the jewels in the little golden pyx inside the recess; the gold was in a buckskin bag lined with scarlet damask silk—rose nobles and angels—in value still a good sum, and always the same in the beauty of its sultry sullen gleam, as she poured it out upon her palm, and, covering it with the other, clenched both hands upon it.

Now, with Dame Eleanor in the room she would not look that way, but she thought of the pyx, and of the gold. Not for all their talking should the Ladies have the pyx back again in the Church. Let them guess, and guess again, whether or how the King's Visitors had laid hands on it and taken it away. It should not go back into the Church, to be seen and coveted by other new Visitors that might be sent by the King; next time, there was no telling, these Visitors might come to take away the holy vessels, such as were of value. And then the Ladies would be sorry. But the little pyx was safe where it lay; and moreover while it was in the hidden recess it was as good as her own.

"No," said Christabel Cowper in her mind, as if Dame Eleanor had spoken an accusation, instead of only venting one of her wordless grunts. "It is not that I am avaricious. The Pyx I keep for the sake of the House"—almost she was able to think "for the sake of God,"—but let that pass; she'd be honest and set her claim too low rather than too high. "And the gold," she thought, "it is not that I love the gold itself." She bent lower over the strings of her lute. Gold was a soft cushion to sit on. Gold was a rod to rule with. Gold bought things of good craftsmanship, things that were beautiful, things that made the heart rejoice. Without gold man in this world went very nakedly and wretchedly; with gold, strong and hearty, he might the better praise God. "Gold," she thought, "it's gold that bought this fair lute," and suddenly struck a full chord in which the voice of the strings mingled tingling sweetness and a sombre compassionate solemnity. She listened while the notes pulsated, dwindled and died.

Without raising her head she looked up at the old woman who sat mumbling with her lips like a rabbit.

"Surely," said the Prioress, in a low but defiant tone, "surely gold is good."

Dame Eleanor sighed deeply.

It was a bright open day, cold, with a strong wind that went through the three beech trees on top of the moot hill at Settrington like a tide of hurrying water, but with little noise because of their winter bareness. Now and again the wind sent up a cloud of dead leaves from the fallen drifts under the trees, lifting and spinning them against the blue sky; even when almost all had dropped again a few would loiter high in the sunshine, like butterflies.

Thirty or so husbandmen stood on the moot hill looking down towards Settrington, and talking together, but neither loudly nor freely, for none knew why they were here, except that Settrington beacon had been fired last night, and that could only mean tidings of discomfort.

At last one said, "There's horsemen coming through the Coppins!" and all could see the winking flicker of sunshine on the steel caps of horsemen down there. So after that they waited in silence while Sir Francis Bigod and close on forty gentlemen and yeomen came up the hill.

Sir Francis was armed, except for a helmet. When he had wheeled his horse amongst the beech trees he pulled off his cap, waved it to them all, and began to tell them why the beacon had been fired.

It was indeed ill news. At the first he made them catch their breath by telling them that if they did not look well upon many causes, all they should shortly be destroyed.

"For," said he, "the gentlemen of the country have deceived the commons."

He let that sink in, and then, looking about and smiling, promised them that the Bishopric and Cleveland were up under Sir John Bulmer, to ensure that the commons be not tricked, "trusting," said he, "that you will not leave them in the dust, seeing that they took your part before, and that it is in the defence of all your weals."

He waited then for a shout, but, though there was a murmur, most looked on their neighbours silently and with glum faces. So he went on, leaning forward in the saddle, his voice rising higher and the wild Bigod look more apparent in his glance.

"For my Lord of Norfolk comes with twenty thousand men to take Hull and Scarborough, and other haven towns, which shall be our destruction unless we prevent him therein, and take them before; and so I and my fellow Hallom purpose to do."

They shouted then for the first time, for Hallom was one of themselves, and if he were in this——! They pressed closer, and Sir Francis, seeing it, took fire, and from this time on he had them hanging on him, so that they groaned when he said that they were deceived by the colour of a pardon, which though it were called a pardon was none, but a proclamation; and one cried out to curse Privy Seal. Then they were silent again as death, while he read over to them the words of that same so-called pardon.

"But that," he told them, when he had done, "is no more but as I would say unto you, 'The King's Grace will give you a pardon,' and bade you go to the Chancery to fetch it. Also herein you are called rebels, by the which ye shall acknowledge yourselves to have done against the King, which is contrary to your Oath."

They all began to cry out then, one saying, "The King hath sent us the fawcet but keepeth the spigot. Which is to say we shall none of us taste of the ale." And another shouted that as for the pardon "it makes no matter whether we have any or not, for we never offended the King nor his laws." "Nay," said another, "therefore we need no pardon."

"Well then," Sir Francis stopped there, and again they looked, all of them, to him. "Hear you further. A Parliament is appointed, as they say, but neither the place nor the time is appointed. And also here," and he tapped on the pardon with his fingers, "here is written that the King should have care both of your body and soul, which is plain false, for it is against the Gospel of Christ, and that I will justify, even to my death."

He looked about at them with his eyes burning in his head, and then cast up his right hand clenched.

"And therefore," he cried, "if ye will take my part in this and defend it, I will not fail you so long as I live, to the uttermost of my power; and who will do so, assure me by your hands and hold them up."

Upon which up went all their hands, and they shouted so that a ploughman tramping down the furrow a mile away heard the cry and stopped the horses to listen and wonder what might be afoot.

Then Sir Francis told them what must be done—he to go to Hull, which by now Hallam should have command of, others to make sure of Scarborough, and a letter to be sent to bring out Sir Thomas Percy on their side—and so he and his horsemen rode away down the hill. The others watched them go;

the morning was cheerful and their spirits warmed by enthusiasm and indignation at once.

"Blessed is the day," one told another, "that Sir Francis Bigod and Jack Hallom met together; for an if they had not set their heads together, this matter had not been bolted out."

Then, after a little talk and some argument, they broke up, to fetch their horses, and meet again at the White Cross, and so march against Scarborough.

January 19

Julian Aske came, abruptly as usual, into the winter parlour, having just put Dickon to bed. Her father and mother sat side by side, yet apart, on the settle; Tony and Chris were on the bench under the window, making an appearance of learning their Latin; a little apart her mother's waiting gentlewoman was busy cutting down one of Tony's old coats for Dickon.

When Julian opened the door they were all, except the gentlewoman, talking at once. But when she shut it after her they were silent. Then her mother cried, as if for the last of many times—

"Then you will do nothing! Nothing!"

"I can't," said her father, "turn away mine own brother from his house."

Julian went over to the fire. She set her foot on the raised brick hearth and rested one hand on the chimney. She did not think that just so her uncle would stand, nor how like him she was now, with her eyes bright and her mouth set hard.

"Then," her mother said, in the same sharp voice, "then must we flee away from it ourselves, all of us, as we did in the first insurrection."

Jack fidgeted with the pages of a book he had open on his knee. He said that this time it was different. No man could have done more than Robin to stay the people.

"Why!" Nell laughed. "So he does, with the one hand, and with the other he is trying to shield these traitors. You heard him say how he and Constable wrote that Frank Bigod's messengers should be set free, because, forsooth, 'It's none honest,' says he, 'to keep messengers.' "

"They're poor ignorant fellows—"Jack put in, but half-heartedly.

"Oh! He's taught you. But I'm not so tender of poor ignorant fellows. Let him be tender of his brother and of his father's house. *We* shall suffer for his tenderness."

Tony said, in his new man's voice, and with the air of importance he had grown into since Hob left home—"I think my mother is right. Why should he not go to my Uncle Will Monkton's. Or to one of these great men with whom he sorted in the insurrection. Let them have him. We do not hold with him in his treasons."

"Speak for your own self!" July said so suddenly and so fiercely that they all started and stared. "I do. I hold with him. But it's no treason, but lawful petition of grievances made by all the commonalty and gentry of the North."

"Hold your tongue!" her mother cried; and Tony, "Parrot! Parrot! Who taught you words to speak so pat?" "Quiet! Quiet!" Jack bade all of them.

When he had got silence he began to explain to July, with far more patience than any of the others liked, just why all that her uncle had done before the pardon was treason and needed pardon.

"He says," Julian muttered obstinately, "that he could not in his conscience have let such things happen, as the destruction of the Abbeys, and preaching of heretics."

"Well then," said her father, still reasonable and patient, "what will be the end, if every man, because his conscience grudges at what the King does, shall count himself free to move war. Will it not be as in the days of the two Roses? Will it not be so? Come. Answer me."

Julian's face was burning, and she hung her head.

"I can't answer. But he could."

"Ho!" cried Tony, and he and Chris laughed loudly and insultingly at her.

Julian lifted her head, and looked at her mother. "But," she said, "if he goes from this house, I go too."

"God's Passion!" Nell sprang up. "Nay, but you shall go. I'll send you waiting woman to my sister, till you be married to a man that shall teach you reverence and quietness, and that soon."

When Julian had said that she would go from the house she had meant it, but as soon as it was said she thought, with a great jolt, "Where shall I go?" Something came into her mind, giving her answer. She lifted her chin, and scowled back at her mother over her shoulder as she went to the door. She had her finger on the latch, then turned.

"You shall send me where you will. But you shall not marry me. For I will be a nun."

In the darkness outside, when she had shut herself out from them, she was conscious at first only of the impressiveness of the moment she had created, at random as it were, almost it seemed now, out of nothing. But once more she realized the practical difficulty with which she was faced. What should she do now? It would be altogether tame if she returned to the parlour. It was too early to go to bed. The Hall would be cluttered with servants getting ready for supper. She could not well lurk on the stairway till it was bedtime. Then she knew where she could go, and her heart lifted again to the height of her defiance, yet this time not angrily but in solemnity. She could go to church.

Outside was a night of full moon, heavily clouded: it was too dark to see, but she could hear a great noise of wind in the orchard trees and in the elms of the churchyard, where the branches strained and ground together, as the gale poured itself through them from the flat countryside. She reached the church porch and only then remembered she had not brought the key, which hung always at the end of the passage by the screens. But just as she realized this, her fingers, groping over the door, touched the cold iron of the key standing in the lock. "Huh!" she thought, as she pushed the door open, "the old man's forgotten again," for the priest from Ellerton, who came here to sing Vespers, was a careless, forgetful old thing.

She shut herself into the church, and into a different world. Here it was black dark, wholly quiet, except for a thin, wailing noise the wind made in the tower; and that seemed to come from a long way off. The air here, though it was still, and smelt of damp, stale rushes, of incense and candle reek, was colder than the living air outside.

She stood for a moment, because it was so dark, and suddenly so quiet, then moved forward. She could see nothing, but knew that the way was clear, if she avoided the bench which stood against the wall just beyond the door.

Then she tripped over something, cried, "Oh!" almost fell, and saved herself by clutching the man's arm who sat there with his feet sprawling out in front of him.

"Who? It's you, Julian!"

The voice was sufficiently like her uncle's voice for her to know him by it. It was so very unlike as to give her a new fright.

"Oh!" she cried again, "what is it? What are you doing here?" and her hands began to feel over him, but he put them away, and said:

"Doing? Nothing."

She had forgotten herself and the reason that brought her here. She sat down by him and laid her hands on his arm.

"Uncle Robin, what is wrong?"

He took a long time to answer and then spoke with a sort of harsh lightness.

"God's Passion! I think everything is wrong."

"Tell me. You must tell me, Sir."

"Why? You know it," he cried, as if he could not endure her importunity. Then he muttered, "They took Hallom of the Wold in an attempt on Hull. They've taken Bigod now."

She felt his arm harden under her hands and knew that he clenched his fist.

"And that Bigod's taken, I thank God. For it was he that set Hallom on after I had stayed him and the rest from rising at Beverley. Let Bigod suffer!" Close to her ear in the darkness she heard his teeth grind together, and the sound appalled her by its force and fury. Yet when he spoke it was not anger that altered his voice.

"Hallom's this manner man, July. They say that when none would rise in Hull to take his part, he came safe out of the gate, and as far as the windmill, whence he might without pain have come clear away. But one cried out on him, 'Fie! Will ye go your ways and leave your men behind you?' So he turned back and came to the gate. And so they took him."

"And so," he said after there had been a long silence, "I sit here doing—nothing. I can do nothing. But that I can I will. I have written that they should not try Hallom yet, saying that the North's all dry tinder that a spark will set afire—and that's the truth. And I've sent your Uncle Monkton to bid them—Whom? Oh! Rafe Ellerker and the rest—to bid them a God's name let go on bail all those poor souls taken with Hallom and with Bigod, except only the leaders. So, by the Duke comes, they may be forgotten and escape judgement. But I think," he ended bitterly, "I think Rafe Ellerker, like many another, remembers too near how he was with us to dare show mercy."

She hunted in her mind for comfort, but there seemed none to give him. Then she thought of one who could help. "The King," she began uncertainly—

"I have written to the King," he took her up. "Constable said I wrote too plain, and that he may be displeased. Yet how can I write but the truth? And truth *is* plain."

"He has promised," Julian began. This time he had not spoken, but something rigid in his silence stopped her short.

He said, speaking in a hurry after a long time, "He has promised—I told them so at Beverley. I told them he was gracious lord to us all. So he is. There must be hangings after this late rising, for it's treason, though the people were misled. But he'll keep his promise that he made. I don't doubt it."

"No," she said.

"No. With his own mouth he—"

He started up, and went a few steps away from her.

"I say—'no,' " he said out of the darkness. "But now they may say that we have broken the appointment, so the King need not keep his promise to us."

She knew then what had brought him to lurk here in the church, and for a moment it struck her dumb.

Then she remembered, and was startled to think that she had forgotten why she herself had come there. So she told him.

He did not for a moment take it in. "A nun?" he repeated —"You, a nun? Why, niece?"

"Because I will undertake Christ's cause, and in that stand beside you as I may. And—and—He will prevail." She had begun grandly, but the grandeur trailed off as she thought, "It doesn't sound like the truth. Yet it is the truth."

He knew it for that, but he made no answer, except to say under his breath, "Jesu! Saviour!" and then after a long pause—"There was a poor wench at Marrick, a servant. They said she had seen Him go over Grinton Bridge on a pedlar's donkey. She would have it He was here, in the realm, now."

Julian could not understand why he told her this, unless it were because she had said, "Christ will prevail," and this was a sign to confirm that saying. Yet it seemed to her that he spoke not at all in triumph, but as if he was reluctant to recall what the woman had seen.

So they sat together, following their own thoughts. She saw herself declared, committed, sealed to the cause of Christ which he had chosen. Once more his mind looked, shrinking, down a road the end of which he dreaded to see. To-night, as if distress had cleared his sight, he saw further along it than ever before. Were Christ, he asked himself, were Christ in the realm now, and came to London, a poor man, speaking humbleness, poverty, truth, and the compassion of God, should He prevail, or should He be judged as a malefactor, and so, again, die?

February 3

Very early this morning, when the town of Pomfret was just beginning to stir, and the castle gate had not long been opened, Lord Darcy's litter, with a pretty good number of gentlemen and men-at-arms riding behind it, came to the gate of the Barbican. My Lord's litter came through into the ward beyond the gate, but then the guard, who were George Darcy's men, stopped the rest before they could pass in. So Lord Darcy pulled open the leather curtains of the litter, and asked, "Why do you stop here?" and cried, "Get on! Get on!" to the boy riding the leading horse, and then, looking round, seemed for the first time to see the guard there at the gate, with their halberds set against his men outside, and a gentleman of Sir George's who now came out towards the litter.

"Oh!" said he. "It's you, Baynton, is it?"

Master Baynton pulled off his cap. But he said that Sir George had straightly commanded him to admit no one.

"Did he say you should keep out the Constable of the Honour and Castle of Pomfret?"

"No." Master Baynton looked down at his feet, and felt an inclination to shuffle them. "No." But he understood well enough what Sir George's intention had been. The order had been the same for the last three days, but till to-day the guard had been much stronger, for Sir George had expected the old Lord to have been here before this.

"Well," said Darcy pleasantly, but with that in his eyes that Baynton found hard to meet, "it's I now, the Constable, that command you let in my people," and leaning out of the litter he said not very loud, but curt and sharp, "Stand back, fellows!"

The men stood back, and Master Baynton had to skip out of the way pretty quick, for the old Lord's gentlemen knew what they must do, and they and the men-at-arms came on smartly, packed close in line, knee to knee.

So they were all in the first ward, and my Lord's litter going on to the second gate when Sir George came out of that, with his hair and beard not so trim as usual, clutching up his hosen, and with most of the points dangling from under his doublet, for he had just tumbled out of bed, hearing that his father was at the gate.

Lord Darcy beckoned to one of his own gentlemen, and with his help got down from the litter, and stood, taller yet than his son by half a head, all in crimson cloth lined with furs, and an old-fashioned by-cocket hat with a brim of fur pulled on over his hood.

"Son George," said he, leaning on his stick, "who in your fantasy is keeper of this castle? Is it thou, or I?"

George Darcy did not like straight questions; he was a man that found crooked answers easiest. So he said—

"Sir, I have letters from the King."

"And I, His Grace's Commission." Lord Darcy began to go under the gate.

"What preparations have you for the Duke's refreshment?" he asked over his shoulder. "For I hear he comes from Doncaster this day."

The Duke of Norfolk arrived about dinner time, so after he had dined he and my Lord and Sir George went into the Privy Chamber, and there sat down by the fire with wine, wafers, and a dish of late apples. The Duke was just now thawed after a cold ride; he drank, and sighed, and stretched out his feet to the warmth. But though he might have been glad to take his ease he did not forget his duty as the King's Lieutenant, and began to ask shrewd questions as to the state of the North, and how many prisoners had been apprehended in the last troubles, who kept them, and had any yet been judged?

The other two, sitting one on each side of him, answered what he asked; sometimes one held the word, sometimes the other was too quick for him, tripped him up and came in first. Sir George leaned forward to it, very earnest, very eager to have the Duke's favour, for that, he thought, might mean advancement in times to come. Lord Darcy seemed to play it as a game, with dancing sparks, almost of laughter, in his eyes, although he conceived that to have the Duke's good word might, in times to come, mean the difference that lay between life and death.

After they had talked for some time the Duke asked my Lord to give him leave to speak alone with Sir George.

Darcy got up. "Gladly," he said, flipped George's shoulder as he passed him, as though they were the best of friends, and bade the Duke refresh himself well after his journey.

But in the little room over the gate, with Thomas Grice,

his steward, he frowned over the account books which they spread out before them on the desk.

"I have offered," said he, "to keep Pomfret at my own charges, and that, if the Duke consents, will tear the bottom out of my purse. Yet it is most necessary I should keep Pomfret in these days. It'd look ill to hand it over as if I knew myself guilty. And—" he laughed out loud now, "you should ha' seen Sir George's face!"

Sir George, not much later, left the Duke alone to repose himself. He was not so merry as his father, though he had nothing to fear, and though the Duke had expressed great confidence in him, and bade him be ready always with his men to come to Pomfret at an hour's warning.

February 5

The Prioress called from the door of her Chamber:

"Shut the gate. Shut the gate, Jankin! Shut the gate, you whoreson!"

Jankin did shut the gate just in time, and then the wild fellows outside began to pelt it with stones, to beat upon it with their quarterstaves and the butts of their pikes, and to shout, "Open, let us in!" At that the Ladies, who had crowded out of the Cloister, set up such a crying and shrieking as might have been raised in Troy when the Greeks tumbled out of the belly of the wooden horse.

The Prioress came down into the Great Court. She had not screamed, and she turned to shake her fist at those who did, though she would not waste her breath by telling them to stop. She went up to Jankin, who was shoring up the gate with a piece of timber from the pile that was laid ready for sawing. The noise of stones and staves on the door filled the archway, and from the Great Court behind came the screams of the Ladies.

"Who are they?" she shouted in Jankin's ear, and he shouted back that they must be men going to the new muster of the commons at Middleham. There had been bills set up on the church doors the last few days calling out the commons, just as in the first insurrection last October; but these were not like those who had risen then; being poorer, wilder, and more ignorant; some of them came from the savage parts at the head of the Dale; some came even from as far as over Westmorland way.

"What do they want?"

But Jankin, no more than the Prioress, could make anything of the confusion of voices outside.

"I must find out," the Prioress said. "I'll go up to the Guest House Chamber." And leaving Jankin to strengthen the door as best he might, she went to fetch the keys, which hung on the wall in his room; even in this emergency she remained sufficiently nice to nip her nose between two fingers as she went in, so potent were the mingled smells of cheese, garlic, Jankin, leather and mice.

The Guest House Chamber above the gate was rarely entered during the winter, and the lock was stiff to turn, but she got the door open and went in. The room, when there were no strangers upon the road, was apt to be used for lumber, so now besides the settle and stools there were in it a couple of naked bedsteads, an old horse collar with the stuffing coming out of it, a pail of which the wooden strakes had sprung, and a spinning wheel that lacked a treadle. The room was also very dusty, and almost dark, because the tall arched windows at either end were shuttered, and the only light came through a little low window under the eaves on the side facing outwards on the cartway.

The Prioress picked up a sack, and swept a space clean from dust, and the dry, light bodies of last year's wasps and flies. Then she knelt down on the floor, and looked out upon the rabble below. There were perhaps thirty shaggy, dirty fellows; most of them were standing a little back at this moment; only one of them beat on the door with the haft of a rusty pike, and demanded, with plenty of foul words, that the Nuns should open their doors, and give them to eat, "for," said he, "ye Nuns, ye have too much, and we have nothing."

The Prioress put her head out of the window.

"Stop your knocking on my door," she said, "I cannot hear myself speak."

He obeyed, gaping up at her; they all gaped.

She asked them what did they want.

They said again they wanted meat, of which, they knew, the Nuns had store.

She told them, "Who said so, lied. For this long winter has eaten up all that was laid in."

They said let her give them money then, to buy victual withal.

She said, "I have no money," and at that one of them

threw a stone. She pulled her head in. Another stone just missed her, and fell among the stuff on the floor.

She stood clear of the window. Let them shy their stones, she thought, and bawl themselves tired, for so they'll pass on the sooner. But she picked up one stone, and with a tight smile flung it back through the little window, a shrewd throw. Someone outside gave a sort of yelp, as much of surprise as pain, and she laughed.

But then she heard something that was no laughing matter. That was a new outcry, but this time the voices came from the Great Court and cried, "They're in by the stable! They're in by the stable!"

The Prioress beat her hands together as she remembered what she had till now forgotten. When a piece of the stable roof had fallen in last year the Nuns had not mended it, because of all the money that had gone to buy Lord Cromwell's favour, since it was at a corner and no beasts stood just there. She stamped her foot, and went towards the stair. But when she tried to open the door she could not. She shook it, and hammered on it with her fists, but no one came to let her out.

A good deal later Jankin came and opened for her, but he knew not, he said, and stoutly maintained, who had turned the key.

Nor did anyone else know, or would admit to knowing it. By no means could the Prioress discover either who had done it, or their motive—whether of kindness to the Lady, to keep her out of harm's way, or of favour to the rabble who had broken in.

But the damage which these fellows had done was only too easy to ascertain. While the Prioress paced up and down the Guest House Chamber, now stamping on the floor and shouting, now silently biting her nails, they had eaten up the Ladies' dinner, and when they went away they carried with them a pannier full of white sweet cheeses, as well as two sides of bacon, four hams, the whole of one of the Ladies' salted beeves, a firkin of sprats, a dozen hens and the red cock.

February 6

To-day all the gentlemen of Yorkshire were to come to York to take a fresh oath of allegiance to the King, seeing that their first had been so largely broken. Robert Aske left Aughton very early, so early that only ploughmen and ditchers and such were on the roads. He would not wait for Jack, because he knew that while Jack would not have refused that they should ride together, yet he had some qualms about it. As for Mistress Nell, the thought that Jack should appear in York at the side of the chief rebel of all had fretted her almost into a fever.

Inside the gate of York the first man that Aske met was Will Bapthorpe, who came out of his lodging with a frowning brow and important air. He, Aske knew, had gone to the Duke at Doncaster, and followed him since. He waved a hand to Aske, and then walked alongside, and whispered so that Aske had to stoop from the saddle to hear him.

"You got my letter?"

"Yes. And thanks to you for it."

"You understand? The Duke, being the King's Grace's Lieutenant, cannot——" He looked aslant at Aske and gestured with his hands in a way that he meant should be eloquent.

"Cannot what?"

"Sh! Cannot show himself gracious to any—to one—to you who—"

"To me, having the King's pardon?"

"Will you not speak low?"

"No," said Aske, "why should I? But it was kindly in you to write and assure me of the Duke's favour."

Master Bapthorpe had, however, stiffened. He drew up the fur collar of his coat, dipping his chin deep into it, and stepped aside to let Aske and his people pass on.

The next to hail Aske was Rudston, who leaned out of an upper window just above his head, and cried, "Turn in! Turn in, neighbour Aske, and we'll drink together." He was dressed remarkably fine in plum-coloured velvet, and a gilt chain swung out from his breast as he leaned from the window, and shone in the frosty sunlight.

Aske lifted his head and looked him between the eyes.

"Not so early," said he, "but later I'll think of some treasonous words to speak, that you may report on them."

Except for these two no one whom he knew seemed to be pleased to speak with him. Either they avoided his eye, or, at most, gave him a hasty greeting, and turned away. It was so as he went to his lodging that morning, and through the day, and as he waited with the others to take the oath. It was not difficult for him to get the measure of it; only those sure of the Duke's favour, such as Bapthorpe, or nosing about like Nick Rudston for information, the disclosure of which should demonstrate their own loyalty, would willingly consort with him; the others would avoid him as his fellows avoid a man that may carry the plague.

That afternoon, in an early dusk, as he knelt in the Cathedral after Vespers, the singing having died away, and the footsteps of the singers rustled into silence on their way to the Cloister, someone tapped him on the shoulder.

"Master Robert Aske?"

Aske stood up and said he was that same.

"I am one of the Duke of Norfolk's gentlemen. My Lord would have a word with you."

Aske went with him. The Duke's gentleman suggested that it would be well if he hid his face as much as he could in his cloak, and he did so.

The Duke was at Sir George Lawson's house, and sat in that same room, and in that same chair where Aske himself had sat, only last October, and had heard music go through the streets as the people brought the monks back to their Houses.

The Duke did not rise, but, greeting Aske with a kind of high and distant courtesy which became his rank and reputation, waved him to a stool, and then, wrapping himself closer in his fur-lined, black velvet gown, said:

"Mr. Bapthorpe wrote to you that I would open to you in secret the reasons whereby I cannot show you very friendly countenance?"

Aske bowed his head, and replied that he had received the letter.

"But I did not show Master Bapthorpe those reasons, Master Aske."

Aske bowed again, thinking, "Mass! for a breath of fresh air and plain dealing." The room was very hot, as well as sweet with perfume. Sir George Lawson was eager to do all that he could in honour of the King's Lieutenant, and my Lord of Norfolk was known to be of a very chilly humour.

"But with you," said the Duke, "I will be plain. It was because I dared not."

Aske almost gaped at him. Here was plain dealing indeed.

"If, Master Aske, you knew the crafty drifts used here to bring me out of credit, you would say that I am not well handled."

For once Aske was at a loss for words. Craft and intrigue —that had been the very burden of his own thoughts, but the marvel was that the Duke should share it with him. He could only stare into Norfolk's long face, with its sagging flesh, heavy hooked nose, and eyelids drooping over eyes that seemed weary to look out on the world.

"Tell me," the Duke leaned towards him, watching him narrowly, "do men here in the North hold me for one who stands for the old ways, or as one of those who for fear or favour will consent to this New Learning which you call heresy?"

Aske chose his words with care. "When we came to Doncaster, all men, my Lord, thought the first."

"And now?"

"Some still think it."

"And you?"

"I have thought both the one and the other."

"The one then, the other now?"

Aske said, with his eye on the Duke's, "The first then, the second now."

The Duke looked down at his hands, not as if abashed, but considering. At last he smiled. "I like you, Master Aske."

At the Duke's tone, and at his friendly look, Aske felt as if his heart had tripped. What the Duke had said was nothing, he knew, but how he said it—that was a different matter. For the first time since he had come back from the King, a month ago, he saw a gleam of daylight ahead.

"Sir," he said, and in so eager a voice that it was as though another man spoke, "my Lord Darcy told me that, before ever this Pilgrimage was made, fifteen great lords swore together to suppress heresy and its maintainers. If you—"

"Fifteen great lords?" Norfolk had spoken sharply enough to interrupt, but now his tone was slow and reflective—"Who were they then?"

"He never told me their names."

Norfolk leaned back again in his chair. "Well, I can guess their names. Go on."

"My Lord Darcy told me this to put me in comfort not to fear the heretics," Aske explained. "The appointment of those lords took none effect. But if the great nobles are of our part, and if they will come forward in time, then our cause is not lost. But they must come forward in time. They must come forward now, or all will be to do again."

"Master Aske," said the Duke, "will you raise war in the realm as it was in my father's and your grandfather's time?"

"That was different. That was House against House, and King against King. The cause now—I hold it to be of God."

"But you would move war against your Prince, for any cause?"

"My Lord," said Aske steadily, "I have always thought, as did we all, that it were best to get the statutes reformed first by petition, but if we could not so obtain, then to get them reformed by sword and battle."

"Now," he thought, "he must dismiss me." But the silence lengthened. Aske looked beyond the Duke's shoulder to where, pictured on the woven hangings of the room, a dog came out of a lake carrying a duck in its mouth; beside the lake a tree stood, on which a huge hawk perched; the tree bore six leaves as big as trenchers, and three acorns. It was the same hanging that had been here on the night when he sat writing the Oath of the Pilgrims; in the silence now, as then, the Cathedral bells spilled out their notes on the air with the same cool, sweet deliberation.

Because his blind side was towards the Duke he did not know how closely he was being studied, but at last the Duke spoke.

"Master Aske," said he, "what I shall tell you, I should tell few other men. Will you promise me that you will keep my words to yourself?"

Aske promised, and as he did so thought, mistakenly—"None but an honest man would think an honest man's word enough."

"Have you," the Duke said, "ever considered that patience and endurance may better serve than to resist? No. Don't answer me yet. You are a man of the law, they tell me; you will have read in the histories of old time, both of this realm and of others, how some things continue ever, some cease, and some, after mutations, return. And how, above all, there is no man, *no* man, Master Aske, but is mortal."

Now he waited, and Aske said, "You mean—the Cardinal died, and—"

Norfolk held up his hand. "Enough. We understand each other." Then he sighed. "All this that has come upon the realm has come of a wench's black eyes, and I wish, though she were my niece, that she had never been born.

"But consider. For close on a thousand years there have been monks in England, and Holy Church has been one through Christendom. Is it likely that in one day one man, and that man not the King but a lowborn fellow, shall pull down the one, and cleave asunder the other, forever?"

Aske shook his head.

"No!" said the Duke, looking pleased, but he had mistaken Aske's meaning.

"No," said Aske again. "Yet it could be so did none take a hand to stay it, neither in this day, nor in time to come."

"I cannot much fear it," the Duke said loftily. "But even if we fear it, how we should best stay it is the question.

"Take my case." He leaned forward, incredibly gracious and familiar. "Say I let my likings show, what will happen? I know. I can tell you. At the best I shall be at Kenninghall, in the country, speaking my counsel to the ditches and the willows, but never to the King's ear. What can I do then? And that is at the best. At the worst it will be Tower Hill on some threadbare pretext.

"But if I serve loyally my Prince, I may the better also serve Holy Church, since if I serve not my Prince, other men, and worser, will be in my place."

They were silent again then. Aske, though unconvinced, did not, for respect's sake, wish to insist on that which he had already made clear as a line. The Cathedral bells chimed again, and then there came another sound at which the Duke turned his head towards the shuttered windows. The sound grew till the hoofs of the hard-ridden horse rang below them on the cobbles of the street and stopped with a clattering slide. There was some shouting, a door slammed, then another door, so that the house shook. Before even Master Appleyard had tapped, Norfolk cried, "Open there! Open!" Behind Appleyard came in a messenger, booted, and cloaked, with his cap in his hand, but his hood yet on his head.

"From the King's Grace," he said. Norfolk dropped on his knees and took the letter. "Go," he said to Aske, and already his long fingers were picking at the seal.

Aske moved towards the door after the other two who had already gone out. But he lingered, because he had remembered something which, when he came into the room, he would not have believed himself able to forget.

"My Lord," he said, "there is one thing I must speak of, if I have leave."

"I've no leisure now," said the Duke.

"Yet I must," Aske said, and at his voice and his stubborn look the Duke stared, but could not stare Aske down.

"Well, be brief."

"I charged Master Bapthorpe," said Aske, "with a message about one Levening—I do not think he gave it."

"Levening that's a prisoner now? No. He did not."

Aske plunged into it then. Levening was innocent of treason. Bigod had forced him to come out in that last insurrection, and Hallom had threatened to burn his farms if he did not.

The Duke turned his back, and moved away now to the fire. He gave Aske barely time to finish, then said:

"Why do you tell me this?"

"I promised him I would speak for him. He came to me because he feared he would be indicted."

"He was right to fear. I must do justice, Master Aske, and terrible justice."

"It would not be justice to hang Levening."

Norfolk looked at him over his shoulder.

"Master Aske, Bapthorpe knew, but it seems you know not, that it is dangerous to speak so."

"Not to speak so to you, my Lord."

"Well, you have spoken." The Duke turned away again, and Aske knew that he was dismissed.

When he came by the Minster on his way back to his lodging, the moon, not quite full, shone on the East end, making the glass of the windows shine white like ice. He looked up at the great bulk of stone upon which the nearer details showed softly and solemnly, while the shadows of every buttress towered up, densely black.

More than once he walked about the circuit of that huge creature of men's hands, revolving in his mind the Duke's words and looks, and the tones of his voice, recalling to himself that once he had doubted my Lord Darcy, and how needlessly; and once he had doubted the King, yet he had been gracious. At last he stopped walking, and stood with his head bent, not looking up at the height of stone above him, but very conscious of it. "Shall I doubt God?" he asked himself.

February 13

The Prioress found her little greyhound bitch gracefully sprawling upon her new coverlet. The coverlet was of light green verders, embroidered with white butterflies and true lovers' knots, and the little bitch had been rooting in a muddy corner of the Great Court: the Prioress's rebuke was therefore severe, and her attention so absorbed by the damage to the coverlet that she took no notice of an outcry in the Court below. She was indeed used to such outcries, few of which needed her interference any more than those others, not so dissimilar, which arose from rivalries among the Priory poultry.

But now, as she stooped over the fawning apologetic animal, the door opened, and Dame Bess Dalton came in, her face crimson and her voice a squeak.

"They are come," she cried. "They are come to turn us out. And O! Chrissie, to take you away and hang you," and she threw her arms round the Prioress, remembering only the old years when they were Bess and Chrissie, whispering and tittering together behind the Ladies' backs.

The Prioress, who was not thinking of those days at all, disengaged herself decisively. Her mind was wholly on the present, and in that present, no longer ago than yesterday, and no further away than York, nine men, three of whom wore the Monk's cowl, had been condemned to death for their part in the late troubles.

To do her justice, however, her thought was not wholly on this news of hangings which had been served up to the Ladies this morning with their mixtum. "They cannot," she said, and the little greyhound cowered down again at the sound of her voice. "We have licence to continue. They cannot turn us out. Who is come?" she asked sharply.

Dame Bess Dalton did not know who it was. But his men held the gate now, and had shut into the Cloister all the Ladies except herself and Dame Margery. And when she had mentioned the Chambress Dame Bess wrung her hands together.

"Dame Margery laid herself down across the gate. She said the men should come in over her body only."

"And did they?"

Dame Bess mumbled that they did. "They stepped over. And then she sat up."

Even at this moment of crisis the Prioress laughed aloud, then composed her face. She heard voices close outside.

"They are at the door. Open to them," she said.

The gentleman sent by the Duke came in first, with a disdainful look; he was a big man, and in half-armour, so that the floor timbers groaned under him where a joist was weak. Sir Rafe Bulmer came in after him, but patently unwilling. The Prioress, having found time to seat herself in her chair, rose with dignity and welcomed them.

Dame Bess, who had to tell the story many times before

bedtime that night, did full justice to the Prioress's conduct of the interview.

The Duke's gentleman had spoken very high at first of traitors and of naughty papistical persons. "'Therefore,' quod he," so Dame Bess reported the kernel of the conversation—"'Therefore you must come with me, Madame, and for the rest of you, I shall turn you out of doors and leave my men here to take charge,' and thereupon he looked at me, so that I quaked.

"But the Lady, she says, 'The first, and welcome. But the second you may not.'

"'May not?' quod he. 'May not? May not turn forth a nest of traitors that have given shelter and comfort to the King's enemies in this last treasonous disorder?'

"'Sir,' then said the Lady, 'shelter nor comfort we never gave but they broke in on us and spoiled us. But turn out the Ladies of this House you may not, who have the King's own licence to continue. Lord Privy Seal also,' says she, 'being good Lord to us.'"

"Mass!" cried Dame Anne Ladyman triumphantly. "That would give him to think on."

Dame Bess agreed, "Aye, for though he did fret and fume awhile yet he spoke no more of turning us out."

Dame Anne called down a blessing on Lord Privy Seal at that, and even those that in general had little liking for him looked at each other with a sort of covert pride in having such a protector.

"But poor Malle! They will not hurt her, will they? There was never harm in those things she saw. Why did the Lady have her go with them to the Duke? And that poor lubber Wat too?"

For a moment no one answered Dame Margaret Lovechild. Then, "Tush!" cried Dame Anne, "she did not take Wat, but he ran after them. And who cares for a creature like Malle?"

That was further than some of them would have gone, and there was danger of a division arising among them. Yet when Dame Bess explained that the Prioress had taken Malle to the Duke "because the man said that we are evil reported on to him, for the sake of her visions," even the most tender-hearted were impressed.

"And there," said Dame Anne, "is our Prioress given over to the malice of evil men, and some of us think of mad Malle!"

So they ceased to think of her, and returned to their questions about the Prioress.

"Tell us again," said one, "what were her last words before she went away."

"We left her alone for a while," began Dame Bess, "as she commanded us."

"Did she pray when you left her?"

"We could not see. She bade us wait at the foot of the stairs."

"And then?" they prompted.

"She called us up again and said, 'Tell the Ladies I have that shall stand me, and the House, and all of us in good stead.' "

They questioned among themselves what she had meant.

"Surely it was God's help she spoke of," Dame Margery Conyers said, and flushed to the edge of her coif, while her eyes filled with tears.

They all exclaimed that truly it must be so. But some of them would have felt more confidence had they known that the Prioress spoke of the precious little pyx and the bag of gold that had lain hidden in the secret recess, and which she had taken out during those few minutes when she was left alone.

For a long time that evening the Ladies sat around the dying fire in the warming house, discussing the case of the Prioress, and their own case, while the candles guttered and flared unnoticed. At first they were inclined to be hopeful, but as the night deepened round them their spirits sank, and they began to fear not only for the Lady's life, but also the onset of every imaginable enemy, whether of rats in the ceiling, or rough men from the upper dale, or soldiers sent to fetch them after the Prioress, or those ghosts and ghouls that wake when hearts beat weakest. Though at another time they would have revelled in this long, late, garrulous sitting, to-night they would have been only too glad to hear the Prioress's voice, chiding them off to the beds they longed for but did not dare to seek for the perils that thronged on every side of their way upstairs.

February 16

The castle and town of Richmond were crammed with men and horses, and more coming in every hour, for the Duke of Norfolk had called on the gentlemen of Yorkshire to go with him to put down the poor commons in Cumberland, who had risen, and were besieging Carlisle.

This was a sore business for the Duke, who feared to be blamed for it, as he feared to be blamed for anything that went wrong in the North, now he was the King's Lieutenant in those parts. So his temper was frayed and his patience short as he sat by a sea coal fire in a room that led off the great old Norman Hall in the Castle, conning lists of victuals and fodder for beasts, of pikes, of guns, of barrels of arrows, while a couple of clerks wrote busily, a group of gentlemen conversed quietly by one of the windows, and men came and went incessantly with messages and questions and the Duke's orders. Far below the Castle the Swale ran full over its ledges of rock, making in its falls a great noise, which came up to the Duke's ears as a hush, like the sound of wind sifting through dry autumn leaves.

Now and again, when the door into the Great Hall was opened, the noise of men talking there quite drowned the sound of the river. At one time indeed, even with the door shut, the voices outside rose so angrily that the Duke, frowning, sent one of the gentlemen to order the disputants to observe more propriety.

"Who," the Duke snapped, "was brawling?"

"Master Aske," said he who had gone out.

Norfolk looked up sharply, then down. "Ah?" he said, "and of what did he dispute?"

"He maintained that these commons of Cumberland rise not against the King, but to defend their goods and wives against Clifford's horsemen, who, says he, are all strong thieves of the Westlands, and themselves fitter to stretch halters than the poor men of Kirby."

"It might have been thought," said Norfolk acidly, "that one so lately and so deeply dipped in treason would have held his tongue in such a matter as this."

"Yea! Yea!" said they all with great fervour, most of them having been among the Pilgrims of Grace last year, and not liking the memory of it.

But Norfolk stooping again over his papers felt the thought of Aske as unwelcome in his mind as a stone would have been in his shoe. He fairly hated the man, so sure of himself, so glorious even yet as to boast that he would know if there were any stirring in the North and would warn my Lord of it.

And now he spoke openly the truth about this business at

Carlisle and Kirby as he had spoken it privily to the Duke himself. "Yet," the Duke answered his own conscience or else it was his pride which pricked him—"Yet I myself wrote much the same to the King's Grace," and he plumed himself on that for a minute, and then regretted it when he remembered, with a jolt and a sudden qualm, the King's hard, bullying look one day when he had said how men whispered that for favour my Lord of Norfolk had forborne to fight the North Countrymen at Doncaster. That made the Duke glad to remember another letter he had written, this one to Sir Christopher Dacres, ordering him to set on the commons before Carlisle—"and spare not," he had written, "to slay plenty of these false rebels." He had the copy of that letter, and could, if there were need, produce it.

That evening when all preparations were completed, the Duke, having a little leisure before bedtime, consented to see this Prioress of Marrick for whom he had sent, and who, since her coming, had given the officers no rest, importuning them always that she should be brought to my Lord.

When she was brought to him, between two pikemen, he frowned upon her blackly, and then, the more to awe her, said nothing, but looked down at the papers in his hand, or spoke to his clerk, or to one or other of those gentlemen who were with him. But his intention miscarried, for he gave her what she needed—an opportunity to study his face, just as old Andrew had used to study a new buyer of his wool. In her mind she summed him up quickly—he was proud, that of course, since he was first and greatest of the old noble blood; and he was subtle, she knew it by the underlook of his lowered eyes; but was he so sure of himself, or of his footing, as his dignity pretended? "We'll see," she thought.

"Hah!" he said at last, as if he had only now realized her presence— "Another of these naughty papist religious. And I hear that you were instant to be brought to me. I wonder, Madame, that you do not tremble, seeing that I bear the King's sword here for justice on all papists and traitors."

The Prioress went down on her knees, but she kept her chin high. She said in her clear voice that she was no papist, and that she did not tremble since the King's loyal subjects had nothing to fear from His Grace's Lieutenant.

"Nothing to fear?" he scoffed at her, and began to rail upon monks and nuns.

But the Prioress watching him saw that hotly as he spoke,

as if from the heart, yet he kept on looking now at the clerks, now at the gentlemen by the window, with a sort of calculation in his glance, that ill-suited the freedom of his words. So she said to herself, "All this for show!"

"I've a mind," cried the Duke, "to send you and your wench to London, to answer before the King's Grace and his honourable Privy Council—you for your treasons, and she for these pretended visions. For it may be," said he, with a very piercing look, "that as in time past sundry great persons were, with traitorous intent, confederate with that Nun of Kent against the King's person and health, so now once more. And what will ye answer to that?" But he looked triumphantly towards the gentlemen, and not at the Prioress.

"Sir," said she, "that I will go right gladly, and at my own charges."

"What?" he said, and now stared at her, quite taken aback. So serene was her face that he could only think she spoke the truth, as indeed she did.

"Give me licence, my Lord," said she, "to go to London, where I may plead the cause of our poor House, taking with me our poor fool—"

"Fool?" Norfolk was sharp, for this was a new idea. He would look the fool if he sent a poor want-wit all the way to London with a charge founded upon idle tittle-tattle.

The Prioress read him. "The wench," she said, "is a poor thing, but she has this strange manner visions. If there be evil persons who think to use her, of whom I know not, that matter should be bolted out."

She dropped her eyes humbly, but within herself she smiled. If—and she would have wagered Marrick's best crucifix that it was so—if the Duke feared to be ill reported of to the King, and to Lord Privy Seal, now he would hesitate to keep this matter in his own hand.

He crossed one knee over the other, and drummed with his fingers on the arm of the settle on which he sat. She looked no higher than his foot, and saw that fidget and swing. Neatly and quietly she drove in her last nail. "I have," said she, "already sent a letter to my Lord Privy Seal in this matter, seeing that he is so good Lord to us, and as it were our second founder, asking his licence to come to him."

There was no more then to be said. Norfolk dismissed the Prioress, informing her, with a rigid and impressive dignity, that he would take order in her case to send her to the King.

Yet though his dignity might appear to be unimpaired he was conscious that this woman had gone beyond him. Yet he took comfort. He would waste no money over her, since she would go at her own charges. And if she went hardly at all as a prisoner, his own part in it would be, if necessary, the easier to disavow.

He got up at last, yawned, and called for his gentlemen to bring wine and candles. "To-morrow," said he, "we must set out betimes. There's bad roads between us and Cumberland."

February 24

After the trial of the seventy-four rebels of the commons in the Hall of Carlisle Castle the Duke of Norfolk walked awhile on the walls with Sir Rafe Ellerker and Master Robert Bowes. The trial, though briskly conducted, had been, necessarily, because of the number of the accused, a longish business, and the Hall uncomfortably hot, for these last days had been more like early May than February.

Now therefore it was pleasant to walk in the fresh air, and the Duke spoke cheerfully, though with a proper sobriety, of the work they had together been engaged in, Sir Rafe having been Marshal in the late trial, and Master Bowes Attorney for the King.

"Truly," said the Duke, "had I proceeded by jury, rather than by martial law with the King's banner displayed, I think not the fifth man of them would have been condemned."

He looked at Bowes, and Bowes nodded. Knowing him for a silent man the Duke found that enough, and went on:

"For you heard how the poor caitiffs said, 'I came out for fear of my life, or for fear of burning of my houses, and destroying of my wife and children.' And here, in these parts, a small excuse would have been well believed by a jury, where much pity and affection of neighbours doth reign." The Duke looked at each of them again, thinking, "They shall know that I do not fear to speak my mind," and thinking, "There's no disloyalty in that."

They stood for a moment at the turn, feeling the light breeze that touched their faces pleasantly. From within the Castle came sounds of voices and a busy stir, but outside, though knots of men stood about the streets, the town lay strangely quiet; they could hear someone chop wood, and a woman chide a crying child, but otherwise it might have seemed that those who went about walked in their sleep.

The three turned and began to go back again.

"So I hope that His Grace will be content with our doings," said the Duke, "for though the number be nothing so great as their deserts did require to have suffered, seeing that of six thousand I reserved only seventy-four for punishment, yet I think the like number hath not been heard of put to execution at one time."

And again he looked from one to another, and rubbed his hands together.

"Come," said he, "you must be glad to have so well discharged your duty to your Prince."

They said then, Sir Rafe leading, that they were glad.

"And that you shall surely know you have done what shall please His Grace," Norfolk said, "I shall read you a letter." He took it out from his pouch, and spread it out upon the coping of the wall, and ran his finger along the lines to find his place.

" 'Our pleasure,' " he read, " 'is that before ye shall close up our Banner again, you shall in any wise cause such dreadful execution to be done upon a good number of the inhabitants of every town, village and hamlet, that have offended in this rebellion, so well by hanging of them up in trees, as by quartering of them, and setting up their heads and quarters in every town great and small, and in all such other places as they may be a perfect spectacle.' "

He folded up the paper again, and then looked into their faces.

"So," said he, "you see that both you and I have well served the King. Lawyers may say, '*Fiat Justitia, ruat coelum*.' But it is better that these, whom blind Justice might have spared, should suffer, when by the example of such a dreadful severity, many more may be prevented from light doings."

They said, the two Yorkshire gentlemen, that it was better, and that the King was a most gracious, godly and wise Prince.

February 26

The Duke of Norfolk and the muster of gentlemen who had followed him from Richmond to Barnard Castle, and Barnard Castle to Carlisle, came down from the high, bleak moors to the gentle valley of the South Tyne. The sun was low, warm upon their backs, and flashing upon the pikes and halberd blades, when they came within sight of the town of Hexham, sheltered among its orchards. The great bulk of the Priory showed above the walls, piling itself up to the high-ridged roof and tower of the Church itself. From the Priory to-morrow the Canons would be put out, and the King's receiver put in to assess the value of their stuff, and of the stuff in that Church, one of the most ancient in the realm, and for the North perhaps the holiest. So Aske, who rode ahead with those of the Duke's gentlemen who were to prepare for his coming, would look everywhere in the golden green sunset valley, except at the Priory.

After supper, because he did not care to listen to the talk of a parcel of young men who were boasting of the lesson that the saucy commons had received at the Duke's hands, he went out, and wandered aimlessly about the town. It was growing dusk when he came to the place where the brook ran out under the wall of the Canons' garden; the evening air was still and pure, with a deep blue dusk; a thrush sang in one of the taller trees; the stars were coming out and there was a tang of frost as well as the scent of wood smoke from the evening fires. He leaned on the rail of the little foot bridge, listening to the voice of the water with its sweet chucklings and whisperings.

A bell began to ring, uncertainly at first, then steady and insistent. Someone in the Priory had not forgotten that it was time for Compline, even if it were the last time that Compline should be sung. Aske listened for a minute, then began in a great hurry to go round the wall towards the Church.

He reached the Cloister as the bell jangled into silence. Three of the Canons were going into the Church by the door in the northeast corner. He made haste to come up with them, and when he reached the door found that one of them was waiting, who now laid his arm across the open door, barring the way.

Aske stood still. He had come here in haste, because of great need, and for a moment he could find no words. He looked at the Canon, a man of about his own age, but long, lean and already grey. The Canon, bending forward in the gathering dusk, saw a man with one eye. "Who are you?" he said sharply.

Some obscure eddy of discarded habit put the answer into Aske's mouth.

"The Great Captain," he said, and then—"A man desperate."

"Come in, my son," the Canon answered him.

In the silent and darkening Church Aske knelt down beside a pillar, leaning his shoulder and forehead against the stone. Far away in the choir the three Canons began their Vespers; their voices attenuated and deadened by the emptiness around, but answering steadily and promptly, one to another, in the familiar responses. The darkness grew deeper, so that the one candle that they had lit began to cast strong shadows, while the windows turned blank and black with the night outside. Once, when one of the Canons passed between the candle-flame and the wall of the choir, his shadow leapt up, monstrous, to the very clerestory.

When Compline was over Aske heard their footsteps die away and the door into the Cloister clap to. It had seemed to him that one of the Canons lingered, as if expecting him to get up from his knees and come away, but he had not moved, being ashamed of the tears that ran down his face.

At last he got up, stiff and dazed, and groped to the door. He had his hand stretched out to unlatch it when it swung inwards, and he saw, in the swimming light of a number of torches, a small company, and upon the very threshold of the doorway, one man alone. Aske stood still, his eye dazzled and his mind amazed, till he recognized in the gentleman who stood almost foot to foot with him the Duke of Norfolk.

"My Lord!" he said, "My Lord, you must hear me!"

Norfolk had for a second stood staring, almost as startled as the man who had blundered at him out of the dark Church.

Then he saw who it was; he saw the disorder of Aske's face, and along with disgust and quickened dislike came the thought—"In this state that he is in he might speak more freely than he means."

So, leaving the others to begin the business of the inventory of the stuff in the Church, he turned back, and into the Warming House. One of the servants stuck a torch into a bracket and tried to stir up the fire, but the ashes were dead, so he went away, shutting the door upon the Duke and Robert Aske.

The Duke sat down. "Well, what must I hear of you?" After a minute, restraining his impatience, he said in a mild tone, "Come, Mr. Aske."

He did not, however, learn much, or not much to the pur-

pose. At first Mr. Aske clamoured, in a manner almost dis-
traught, that the Duke should have mercy upon the poor
ignorant commons, closing the King's banner, and pardoning
such as had not suffered. When he began to grow calmer,
the Duke put certain questions to him, about Lord Darcy, Sir
Robert Constable and others. But then he would speak only
in their favour, stoutly maintaining that there never had
been any acquaintance between my Lord Darcy and himself
before he came to Pomfret, and that nor the old Lord, nor
Constable, nor he had intended treason, but lawfully to
petition the King.

Yet—as the Duke remarked afterwards to Mr. Appleyard
—such tenderness towards those taken in treason argued little
loyalty to the King's Grace, and that great faithfulness and
kindness that was manifest between Lord Darcy and this
man Aske—he being but a gentleman of no great House—
might in itself be held as worthy of suspicion.

The Duke stopped there, and regarded Mr. Appleyard
closely, though covertly, wondering, "Will he report to the
King my faithful carefulness in His Grace's service?"

March 4

July said, standing beside Mistress Holland at the Vintner's
door: "Hear me while I say it again. Is this right?"

> "Take new cheese and grind it fair
> In mortar with eggs without disware.
> Put powder thereto of sugar I say,
> Colour it with saffron full well thou may.
> Put it in coffins that be fair,
> And bare it forth, I thee pray!"

"Thou hast it, sweet," cried Mistress Holland, patting
July's shoulder. "That is how I make my flawnes."

"But," said July, stepping down into the street, where already Laurence's prentice boy was waiting to see her home,
"it's the pie-crust for the coffins that I cannot make as you
make it, so crumbly and light."

"Lord!" Mistress Holland waved her hand over July's head
to a neighbour going by. "Lord! there are who can make pie-
crust, and who cannot. But chiefly ye must keep it ever dry.
Your wet crust is your hard sad crust."

"Well, I must e'en try," said July, and sighed.

"There!" Mistress Holland leaned down from the step and

kissed her, then whispered in the shelter of July's big white kerchief, "Never fear for thy pie-crust, sweet, to please thy husband. Tell him what thou hast told me. That's how best to please him."

So July went off, with the boy close behind her. She said to herself—"Friday dinner, herrings and flawnes, and ling in that green sauce." She sighed again. She was not averse to pleasing Laurence, since he was always so kind, but she would have preferred to have pleased him by making light crisp crumbly flawnes than in that way which had caused Mistress Holland such delight to hear of. She did not want a child, yet it seemed that she carried one now. She felt as she had felt when Mistress Holland had told her—a little scared, and much more perturbed, but most of all as if she had suddenly become a different person, or two persons—July, whom she had always known, and, as well, this stranger that housed a stranger. Yet, though perturbing, the situation was not, she decided, without its advantages, since she felt herself vastly more important than she had ever been. Looked upon in that light the event should, she thought, be celebrated. She stopped therefore and bought some caraway comfits which she and the boy enjoyed on the way home; July treated him fair; each drew out one at a time and ate till all were gone.

March 6

The Prioress of Marrick, making use of the privilege of a guest and the pretext of an aching tooth to abstain from Terce, went up instead to the Prioress's Chamber in the Priory of St. Helen's, Bishopgate Street, in London. Not for the first time since she came here a fortnight ago, she was struck, as she stood looking round the spacious room, vaulted and painted above, wainscoted and painted below, with the opulence of its design, and the poverty of its garnishings. On the tall carved livery cupboard there was nothing of silver, but wooden bowls and horn cups only; there were no cushions to give ease upon the settle by the hearth; the Prioress's bed stood bare, with naked tester and sparver; when the Prioress of Marrick sat down on it, instead of sinking into the softness of feathers, she heard the harsh rustle of straw.

"God's Passion!" she cried softly to herself, throwing up her clenched hands, and bringing them down upon her knees. It was a relief to be alone, and able to express the impatience that bore hard on her. This waiting of hers upon the pleasure of Lord Privy Seal was made no easier for her by the punctuality and assiduity with which these Ladies of St. Helen's kept their Hours, and she began to move restlessly about the room, remembering how near Privy Seal's house was, almost next door, in Broad Street, yet she had not succeeded in finding a means of coming to his presence. And then she began to reckon what money had been spent already, and what yet remained to spend in the buckskin bag, and to try to fathom the bailiff's report of his efforts to obtain Lord Privy Seal's ear. "Is he cheating me?" she thought, or perhaps it was rather, "How much doth he cheat me?"

In her impatient wanderings she came again to the foot of the Prioress's bed. A big hutch stood there, an old-fashioned but very handsome piece of furniture, carved with foliated circles, and arches traceried like church windows.

To divert her thoughts from trouble the Prioress of Marrick jerked it open, and looked inside; it was full to the top. She laid back the lid upon the bed, and began to go through the stuff there, turning it up carefully at one corner so as to make no disturbance.

There were silk embroidered coverlets, and curtains of fine needlework for the bed; under these she came upon cushions, tasselled, fringed, and worked with roses, butterflies, birds; there were carpets for the cupboard and table, and at the bottom, wrapped separately in soft leather, such silver cups that at the sight Christabel Cowper's eyes widened, and colour came up to her cheekbones as she remembered how she had led the conversation round about till she could boast about her own great cup Edward; but Edward was a poor thing compared with the least of these. There were also, among the silver things, two pairs of very gay shoes, one of red leather, the other of green.

"Mass!" said the Prioress to herself, and, "Why?" Then she laughed aloud. It must be that these things were laid by because it was Lent; such might well be the fashion among these dutiful daughters of St. Benedict. She made all neat again, and shut the lid, lingering only for a second as she considered whether to take out and use one of the cushions. But though the Prioress of St. Helen's was a vague, elderly dame, and timid (Christabel thought) as a sheep, and though Christabel might be on occasion peremptory, contradictory or scornful with her, yet there was that in her (perhaps it came to her by birth and blood) which made the Prioress of Marrick unwilling to take such a liberty as this. So, shutting the hutch with a little slam, she went again restlessly about the room.

There were three arched windows along one side of the room; that side looked out upon the church, which, tall, new and stately, took all the sun, except for a short time at noon. On the other side and at the end farthest from the hearth, was another window, but it was shuttered, and she had never seen it open. This morning, because the Prioress of St. Helen's and the Ladies were so devout, and because, since it was Lent, she must, forsooth, sit without cushions, and because she was sure the bailiff was cheating her, and because she was by no means sure that her long journey here would not end in failure—because of all these vexations, she laid hands on the shutters, unbarred and swung them inwards.

With them came, like a wave pouring into the room, all the noise, stir and colour of a busy street, that was also full of sunshine. "By St. Eustace!" the Prioress murmured, and leaned out, smiling, partly in derision at those who so regarded Lent, and partly from pure pleasure in the lively light, and the moving crowd.

A little way along Bishopgate Street a gentleman and his servants were coming out of the yard of a big hostelry, where was the sign of the Bull hung out over the archway. They came past just below the Prioress, so that she caught the winking flash of the jewel in the gentleman's ear, and got an excellent view of the strong curling black hairs of his clipped beard, and of the gold chain over his shoulder; so fine he was, in scarlet velvet and white hosen, that she must suppose he was on his way to Court; as he went out of sight her heart went with him there.

Then her ear was caught by a run of notes played upon a lute and her eyes were drawn to a window which stood open almost opposite the window in which she stood. A plump, very comely young woman sat there, with half-shut eyes and a half smile, placid as a cat which sits purring in the sunshine. From beyond her shoulder leaned a young man's face that looked hungrily on her, while a boy in the room behind them sang:

> Alone I live, alone,
> And sore I sigh for one.
> No wonder though I mourning make
> For grievous sighs that mine heart doth take,

And all is for my lady's sake.
Alone I live, alone,
And sore I sigh. . . .

The Prioress of Marrick could see how during the song
the young man's hand stole out and was laid upon the
young woman's honey-coloured satin lap; she saw too how
the young woman took it up by the wrist, between two of her
fingers, as though it were a thing she were loth to touch, and
so removed it from her knee. The Prioress smiled, yet sighed;
she liked the young woman's action, which seemed to show
a decision of character such as she must approve; yet she
was grieved for the young man, whose face wore such a look
of loving and longing. She was sorry when, as the song ended,
the two of them went away from the window.

But still there was plenty to watch; a funeral passed, with
candles and torches pale in the sunshine, and many painted
escutcheons, priests in plenty, and a long tail of mourners
following like a black shadow. Then, in the midst of the
street, for a moment empty, a young girl in grey woollen
gown and white coif met a tall prentice lad. The girl put her
hand on the lad's shoulder, and lifted her face, fresh as a
flower, to be kissed. The boy, more shy than she, stooped, a
little awkwardly, and kissed her.

The Prioress laughed at that, so pretty a thing it was, and
so aptly redressing the balance tipped by the proud young
woman in honey-coloured satin, against love and the spring-
time. She heard the door of the room behind her open, and
turned, still smiling.

"When gorse is out of bloom," she said to the Prioress of
St. Helen's, hesitating behind her, "kissing's out of season.
Here have I been watching the prettiest shows as if I were at
a masking."

The Prioress of St. Helen's came closer; she was near-
sighted, with a plain old, wrinkled face and indeterminate
expression. She glanced out of the window, went away, came
again, and said:

"Madame—that window—we keep it shut nowadays." When
the Prioress of Marrick made no reply other than to raise
her eyebrows, the Lady of St. Helen's stepped back, but again
returned and with a very high colour and flustered air,
reached past the guest, and pushed the shutters to.

"Jesu!" said the Prioress of Marrick, "this is indeed to
keep Lent."

"Lent?"

"Why, yes. Is not all this—" Christabel Cowper waved her hand to the bare poles of the bed. "Is it not for Lent?"

The older woman, flushed and confused, dropped her eyes, and muttered that, no, it was not for Lent, and then with a rush of words—"but it is for our sins, that we lived in religion so worldly for a long time, till God's chastisement (I mean the fear we now live in) remembered us of our Rule. So now," she said, her hands picking at her gown, "so now, hoping that God may be merciful, and turn from us His anger, and save us—we—we—"

"I should ha' thought," the Prioress of Marrick broke in, "that a plump purse given to my Lord Privy Seal had been of more service in saving your House."

"Forsooth!" said the other, with great simplicity, "that we have given already, or rather we have given him an annuity."

Christabel Cowper laughed. "Then why not sit on your cushions and look out on the sunshine and the street?" said she, but the other did not answer, except by shaking her head with a troubled air, so that there was silence till the Prioress of St. Helen's asked haltingly whether the Marrick bailiff had sped any better this day.

"No better—yet it cost him four angels—so he says."

"Alas!" The Prioress of St. Helen's sighed and hung her head; then after some fidgeting and clearing of her throat brought out a question.

"And the poor woman you brought from the North, that the sheriff's officers took away to prison in the Fleet— Is she . . . Have you . . . Do you hear of her? And the poor little knave that would not be parted from her?"

The Prioress of Marrick turned. Was she to be questioned by this shrinking creature, and concerning Malle, the crazed fool that had helped to bring Marrick to this pass? She stared hardily into the other's eyes, but this time she could not look them down.

"I hear nothing. The matter lieth not now in my hand." She was at the door before the Prioress of St. Helen's mumbled, "Yet they are of your people. You are . . . you . . ."

"I," said Christabel Cowper, "am a loyal subject of the King's Grace," and on that she opened the door and went out.

March 21

The old lame tailor had come to the Castle at Pomfret to try on Lord Darcy's new gown; black velvet it was, trimmed and lined with black sarcenet. He stood now, reaching up and breathing hard through his nose as he untied the laces at the neck of my Lord's doublet. Darcy, his head turned aside, could see where the gown lay across the coverlet of the great bed, on which an embroidery of swans and cocks, cunningly disposed, made a trelliswise pattern of white, black, and tawny.

The tailor got the laces undone, and the buttons, and Darcy turned, slipping the doublet from his arms, just as one of his gentlemen came in with a look startled and discomposed.

"What now, George?" Darcy hailed him. George Nevill had been in my Lord's Household since his boyhood.

"A letter, Sir."

Darcy took it. When he saw the mark of the King's signet he understood Nevill's look, and moved a few steps away while he opened and read it.

Nevill watched him, though covertly, and when he could discover on my Lord's face no alteration of expression he let out a small sigh. Darcy heard it, turned, caught his eye, and with a lift of the shoulders and a shake of the head gave him a close, hard smile. Meanwhile the tailor, unconscious of all but his craft, stooped over the gown as it lay on the bed, contentedly touching the stuff of the sleeve with the back of his knotted deft fingers.

Darcy dropped the letter down on a stool and came back to where the old man waited; he caught with his fingers the cuffs of his shirt, and so holding them, stretched his arms behind him, while the tailor slipped on the gown. "Ah!" the old man breathed, as it went on, and when he had fastened it at the breast with pins, he stepped back a few paces, and stood, his head slanted, regarding my Lord. Nevill's eyes were on my Lord too, but he was not thinking of the set of the gown.

"Forsooth!" said the tailor, "it fits well. A good gown! A fair gown. But the sleeve there——" He ran forward and began to pull and ease the stuff on one shoulder.

"It is a fair gown," said Darcy, looking down at the tailor's bent head with its thin greying hair. "But you must have it ready for me soon, lest I go up to the King's Grace at Easter time."

Nevill said, "Sir——" and stopped at Darcy's glance. But the tailor lamented aloud.

"Alas! my Lord. If the gown be for a Court gown—— Alas,

[624]

had I known, it should have never been sarcenet but satin at least, or damask. Your Lordship was never wont to wear sarcenet for your gowns at Court. Alas! it will shame me. Suffer me to—"

Darcy interruptd him. "It will serve. It will serve. And"— he spoke now over the little man's head to George Nevill at the door—"it may be the King's Grace will be gracious Lord to me, giving me, in consideration of my infirmities, licence to remain in the North parts."

The tailor, his mouth full of pins, made a little, indefinite humming noise, and then mumbled that in no time he could put satin in place of the sarcenet. "Some say," he added, "that a man may journey more easily by sea than by land."

"Surely," said Darcy, "I should journey more easily by sea," and he laughed, but as if angrily. Then he touched the tailor lightly on the shoulder. "I can see that you would have me go to Court."

"Why, yes," said the old man simply.

When the tailor had finished and gone away with the gown over his arm, still bemoaning the unsuitability of a lining of sarcenet for one of my Lord's station, George Nevill said:

"Sir, have I leave to ask?"

"What do you want to know?"

"Will you go to Court by sea?"

"By sea," said Darcy, "I shall not go. For neither will the King give me leave so to come to him, nor if I could get myself a ship should I go to his Court, but rather to that of the Emperor in Flanders."

"Then . . ."

"I shall wait," said Darcy, "till I am sent for and fetched. And it may be, George, that I shall yet die in my bed." And he laughed and gave George Nevill a buffet on the shoulder.

But when Nevill had gone away he sat long looking through his letter books, weighing in his mind which, out of all those copied there, might be twisted into meaning treason. He read with a very grim face, and afterwards brooded a long time before he took up the pen and wrote—

"For I peremptor feel my broken heart, and great diseases without remedy, to the death of my body, which God not offended I most desire after his pleasure and my soul's health; and he be my judge never lost the King truer servant and subject without any cause but lack of furniture and by false reports of pick-thanks. God save the King; though I be without recover."

What they would make of that, he did not know. But it could do no harm and was as near the truth as he could, or dared to, go.

The old serving woman who had taken the Prioress's money let her into the parlour of Thomas Cromwell's house and slipped away again, furtive as a mouse, behind the carved and gilt screen that stood across the doorway. The Prioress heard the lightest click of the latch, and knew that she was alone, and that now, if her luck held, she would need none other to speak for her, but herself would speak to my Lord Privy Seal.

There was an oriel window at the far end of the room where she would not be seen at once by anyone coming in; so she went and sat down there upon a little gilt stool; sunshine came coloured through the tall window, and brighter and cleaner through a casement which stood open upon a little inner garden.

From the stool the Prioress set herself systematically to observe the furnishings of the noble chamber; she did it partly to calm her breathing, but partly also for genuine curiosity.

There was a tapestry carpet on the floor in the oriel. A greater carpet lay on the floor of the parlour, a very costly thing and such as the Prioress had never seen before, but at once she began to picture her chamber at Marrick with another like it, though of course far smaller. Round the walls there were hangings of red and green say, and on the two carved settles which stood one on either side of the hearth there were cushions of green velvet embroidered each with a rose, the single wild rose which was the King's.

As she sat there waiting, and listening, she could hear not only the noises of the street, dulled by distance, but also the closer, smaller noises of the house; someone in a room above was playing a recorder, and in the kitchen a servant chopped herbs. She heard a bustle begin outside; dogs barked, there were voices, and the sound of footsteps. Then the door opened and from behind the screen came a rather portly gentleman in a well worn coat of russet faced with black lamb. He had a broad, fleshy face, small eyes and a mouth that pouted out full in the middle, but which narrowed to a thin line at each corner, and there turned up, like the mouth of a cat. He was pulling off a hawking glove and now he threw it down on the table; the bell that had been jangling as he tugged at the glove rattled once on the board and then was silent.

"You've lost your wager," said this gentleman to one among those others who followed him. "There's no tercel this side the sea can match my Archangel." Then he saw the Prioress.

"Who is this?" he said, very sharp and quick, to the gentleman behind him; and to the Prioress, "How did you come here?"

She was the first to answer, but not before she had made a reverence of the deepest and humblest that she knew. She said:

"By paying."

"Ho! And paying whom?"

"My Lord, if I told you that, I might not find him—or her —so able or willing to help me to your presence another time."

"No," said Cromwell. "You might not." He looked at her hard, but before he had made up his mind to call the servants and tell them to take her away, she spoke again.

"But it's alone that I should see you."

Her effrontery amused him, and besides he thought she looked too sensible a woman to have come empty-handed.

"Did you pay for that too?" he asked.

She said no; only my Lord himself had that to sell.

"To sell!" Cromwell laughed, and said to the others, "Leave us."

As they went out he came to the window and took the Flanders chair of painted leather that stood there. The Prioress sat down again upon the stool.

"Do you not know," said he, "that a Religious should not be forth of the Cloister? And if she must so, she is bound by her Rule to have two of the Nuns with her."

The Prioress said she knew it well. "Yet when there is sore need—" she said; and then, "As for the Ladies, they would have been afraid to leave our House."

He laughed again. Though her words were of the simplest this woman's tone gave them salt.

"And where is your House?"

"At Marrick on Swale in the County of Yorkshire."

"Marrick," he repeated, and was silent for a minute sucking with his tongue at a hollow tooth. "St. Ambrose—no— St. Andrew of Marrick had licence to continue—last autumn —September." He seemed to reflect again, and then told her the amount they had sent to him as a gift, and reminded her that half their year's rents had also been promised. "And there are other matters," he said, stabbing into her face with his sharp eyes. "Other matters which make me to well remember the name of your House. Is it to speak of these that you have—paid?" and he smiled, but acidly.

She held out the buckskin bag that she had carried clasped in both hands.

"My Lord, there is the rents."

He took the bag, weighing it in his hand before he untied the thongs, and let the gold run out into his palm. "Correct," he said, when he had counted it. "But for those other matters—"

She did not pretend to be ignorant of what he meant, but affirmed, briefly yet categorically, that those men of the Western dales who had raised insurrection had broken into the Priory by force, and by force taken from the Nuns' table and the Nuns' store; she told him precisely what they had taken, even to the red cock and the firkin of sprats, seeing that she could not regard these things as unimportant, and he, listening attentively, seemed to agree with her in that.

"But," he said, when she had finished, "there is, besides all, this woman, your servant, who—"

"Whom I myself, my Lord," she urged, "brought hither, that if there were in her sayings any treason it should be bolted out."

"True." He nodded. "Well, it shall be bolted out." He sat silent, his hands on his knees, his small sharp eyes looking out into the garden. Except for something taut in his stillness he might have been meditating; but she knew that he listened and waited. She knew also that here was her cue.

"My Lord," she said, "I have no fear that you shall find treason, for the woman's but a poor fool."

"I shall know that, when she hath been examined on these matters. If she is innocent she shall be set free."

"As to that," said the Prioress, "I care not, whether or no. But," she got up from her stool now, and did him a reverence; when he turned to look at her, he saw that she held out to him a small thing wrapped in leather.

"What is this?" He took it from her hand and unwrapped it. It was the little pyx, which, as he held it, caught the sun with the pure lustre of gold and the sharper refraction of light from the faceted jewels.

"What we ask," said the Prioress, standing meek and empty-handed before him, "is that the King's Grace and you should know our loyalty. And that we may have and retain your gracious favour, to whom we look as to our second founder, to preserve our House in these unquiet, scrambling times."

He was examining the pyx, turning it round in his fat, strong hands. As she watched it she felt a sharp pang of loss, for the precious, pretty thing.

"Madame, why are you so resolved that even at a great price your House shall continue? Is it because you are one of those false papist Religious who tender more the rags of their outworn corrupt superstitions, than the new light of the true Gospel? Come, why is it?"

If he thought, by the sharpness of his look and tone, to abash the Prioress, he had misread her. She paused for a moment before she answered, but it was for calculation, and not confusion, that she needed time.

"Sir," she said, "I shall tell you. As you would be loth to see this realm invaded by the King of France, or to see the Turk, or any other, triumph here, being yourself not only a member of the Commonwealth, but also, under the King's Grace, the chief ruler of it—so I."

Cromwell did not laugh aloud, but she saw his big body shake as he chuckled. "So you," he said, "being under God, the chief ruler of Marrick—"

He stood up. "Well, Madame, if I find that your wench is, as you say, nothing but a poor crazed thing, your House shall take no hurt." He laid the little golden pyx to his cheek, as though it were a thing he loved, and he nodded to dismiss her.

March 22

Aske sat in the Cross and Martlets Inn at York. He had a book on his knee because if he seemed to read it was easier to keep out of the talk. There were close on a dozen other gentlemen sitting about the room, everyone being indoors this wild evening, and the talk was lively, for now that the Duke's progress of justice was completed, except for the trials and hangings to be done at York, most of these gentlemen expected to have license to return home; they spoke therefore of their stewards, their farms and household affairs.

But a few of them, close to where Aske sat, left such matters for a moment to talk instead of the trial of Master Levening of Acklam, which would be to-morrow.

"He will be hanged," said the most elderly of the three.

"No jury dare acquit." He added quickly, "And that is well." But yet he hung his head down and spoke with a harassed look.

"Ellerker will see that he is cast," said another. "The King has granted Ellerker a parcel of Levening's lands."

"Fie!" the elderly man rebuked him. "The King will grant no man's land before he be attainted."

"It's common knowledge Ellerker is promised it."

"Well," said the elderly man, "whether that be so or no, they'll cast him in an hour."

"No," said an elegant young man with a most assured manner, and a lisp in his speech. "I think otherwise. For they say that Sir Robert Constable has said he would not for a hundred pounds have Levening hung."

"Sir Robert Constable!" someone scoffed. "And how long shall his will weigh with a jury? Know you not that he is sent for, and my Lord Darcy also sent for by the King?"

They began to argue then whether that were true. Some said yes, others no, others that Sir Robert but not my Lord Darcy had been summoned to the King.

"And if it be so," lisped the young man again, "what then?"

"Then let them go, and they shall find that they lie in the Tower," someone answered promptly, "along with Tom Percy and his brother."

"Sh!" said another; and Aske knew, though his eye was on his book, that they looked at him. They began then to talk of other things.

After a few minutes Aske got up and went out. He had thought he needed quiet in which to make up his mind, but when he came on young Ned Acroyd in the way to the kitchens, he found that it was already made.

"Take this book," said he, "and fetch my coat and your own. I'm going out."

While he waited for the boy, Aske stood in the covered way that led from the street to the inn yard. The lantern that hung just over his head sent shadows sliding over the roof timbers as it swung in the gusty wind that fluttered the heavy cobwebs there, and tapped the hanging rope of a bell against the plaster wall. The rain spattered in, and down the gutter outside ran a thin wreathed line of dark water caught here and there by the gleam of the lantern. Now, as he waited, Aske felt his heart knock because of that to which he had, by a simple word to Ned, committed himself.

Ned came back with his coat and a lantern.

"Whither, Master?" he asked.

"To the Duke."

"Then I hope," said Ned, and laughed, "that it's to take leave. They say it's all finished now and that we shall go home. But I would you should take me with you to London, Master, when you go back to Gray's Inn."

Aske told him sharply that he talked too much, so after that Ned held his tongue, and Aske was sorry.

The Duke had supped, said Master Appleyard, his gentleman usher, and he would receive Master Aske. Aske went up the stair, and into the room where he had sat with the Duke in February, and where he had sat alone last October. The only difference seemed to be that to-night there was a posy of daffodils set upon the table.

Aske had had it in mind to move his business at once, but the Duke gave him no time, calling to him in the most friendly way to come in. "Come in, Master Aske, I want your counsel." When he had made Aske sit, and Master Appleyard had been told to send up wine and wafers, the Duke began to talk about the late pacification of the wild lands of Tynedale and Redesdale, and from that slid off to mention Levening and to-morrow's trial, and then began to question Aske straitly—"What think you of this—or this—or that?" Aske gave him the answers, in a mechanical sort of way, since all this was to go over old ground. Not only had they spoken together of these things, but Aske had written down particulars of certain matters at the Duke's request.

And then the Duke said: "It would be well if the King had many servants as honest as you, Master Aske."

"Now!" thought Aske, and again felt his heart knock in his chest. But instead of saying what he had come here to say—"Would His Grace listen?" he asked.

The Duke leaned forward. "I do think he would, did he know one he could entirely trust. For me—I put my life in your hands, Master Aske—for such as me, who am of the great nobles, he has a jealousy. (Why should I fear to say what all have known, both of himself and of the King his father before him?) So he will never trust us. And for the base-born servants he has—well, I'll speak no ill of them. Every man must have his beginning, as my Lord Darcy saith. But it is to you, and gentlemen like you, that the King would listen, if there were one of you that dared to speak the truth."

He stopped there and waited. He wondered if he had said

enough. Master Aske's eye was bent on the ground, his mouth was hard. The Duke thought, "Does he doubt me? Is he taking the measure of his danger? Or does he believe that it is as I say?"

Aske lifted his head. He had hardly heard the Duke's last words. He had indeed been taking the measure—not of the danger, for that he thought he knew—but of his own strength.

He said—"My Lord, do you say that I can serve the King by telling the truth to His Grace, and serve too in clearing unjust suspicions from my Lord Darcy, and Sir Robert Constable and others?"

"I do. I do."

"And that I should, to that end, repair to His Grace?"

"You cannot speak so freely, Master Aske, by letter. It is when you speak to the King as you have spoken to me, face to face, and openly, that His Grace will be convinced of your truth and loyalty."

"Will you—" said Aske, omitting any title of courtesy, because the words that he was about to speak had to be driven out by force—"Will you give me licence to go up to London to the King's Grace?"

"I will, most surely." The Duke clapped him on the shoulder. "And I will write letters in your favour to the King and to my Lord Privy Seal."

Aske thanked him, and when the Duke stood up he knew that he might go away.

As soon as the Duke was alone he called for Master Appleyard.

"It is done, Hal!" he said, most cheerfully. "I have by policy brought him to desire of me licence to ride to London. I shall write him letters, and other letters that will show His Grace and my Lord Privy Seal in what sort to take my commendations of him."

He went away to the table, and lifting the jar of daffodils sniffed at the fresh sweetness of spring in them.

"I shall," he said, "counsel His Grace to use him with fair words, as if he had great trust in him, so that the fellow may cough out all that he knows about those other two traitors, Darcy and Constable." He put down the flowers, and looked at Appleyard, with something like a smile on his face. "So well he loves them he must always be speaking of them, justifying them in their treasons. It will go hard if the King's Grace and my Lord Privy Seal cannot pick out something from it all that will be to the purpose."

The Archbishop's officer and his men started off in the chill of a mist-choked dawn to bring the Marrick Priory serving-woman from the house of the Archbishop, where she had been examined, to the Benedictine Priory of St. Helen's in Bishopgate Street, where her mistress the Prioress lay, and where the woman should be set free.

If, however, on such a raw, nipping morning, a man should meet a friend and turn in to drink with him, it is but nature. And if a man's servant turn in too, it is but nature again, for what's sauce for the goose is sauce for the gander. And if, while they sit drinking, and talking neither of profanity nor wantonness, but of sober and godly matters, the woman and her brat, who had been told to sit still on the bench outside, wander away and are lost, what can a man and his servant do to find them, in all the streets and lanes of London? The Archbishop's officer and his servant spent an hour searching, then gave it up. It was twenty to one that any would inquire what had happened to the wench, who could besides ask her own way, having a tongue in her head, though the lad was dumb.

Later that morning, but still early, Thomas Cromwell, Lord Privy Seal, came to visit Thomas Cranmer, Archbishop of Canterbury, in the Palace of Lambeth.

The remains of the Archbishop's breakfast still lay upon the table with a book open beside the plate; so the two of them stood together in an oriel. Beyond the little leaded quarrels of the window lay the river; the blown glass dipped all the outside world into a dim, watery green, and across its concentric flaws the passing wherries seemed to wriggle and bend like so many caterpillars. The sun was beginning to shine through the mist, though palely, and the tide was at the full.

Cromwell took from his pouch a little silver and enamel box, and offered it to the Archbishop; there were dried French plums in it. The Archbishop would not take one; this was a foreign habit which Privy Seal had picked up abroad; every autumn his agent bought these dried and sugared French plums for him at Antwerp and sent them to London. While Cromwell bent his head over the box, daintily choosing his fruit, and while he popped it into his mouth, the Archbishop continued to hold forth upon the necessity there was for a new Great Bible in English. Cromwell, consuming the plum with pouted lips and critical deliberation, listened, bowing his head from time to time without interrupting the Archbishop's eloquence.

"But," said the Archbishop, "it must be fairly printed, large and plain and not so costly neither that all may not buy."

Cromwell saw that his advice was now required. The Archbishop would concern himself with the spiritual benefits of a new Bible, and judge between the merits of the translations —old versions of Wycliffe, new versions of Master Tyndale and Master Coverdale—but when it came to matters of business, then it was time for Privy Seal.

"Then," said he, "I have the very man for you, one Grafton. And if it shall be well printed, it must be printed abroad. Paris it shall be, for there they have the best printers, and the fairest paper." And he, in turn, favoured the Archbishop with a discourse on that subject.

But, when he had finished, and had opened his little silver box again, and again taken out a plum, he held it between his fingers, looking keenly and yet a little smiling into the Archbishop's face.

"Mass!" said he, "and I had forgotten what brought me here."

Thomas Cranmer shook his head, so that his soft cheeks quivered a little; he too smiled, as if to indicate that he was not so simple as to suppose that there was anything that Privy Seal ever forgot.

"Tell me," said Cromwell, "whether ye have commoned with that woman from Swaledale that I wrote you of?"

"I have."

"Well, is there treason in her sayings?" He was watching the Archbishop, but not now smiling at all.

"There was none."

"None, you mean, that you could discern."

"None at all," said the Archbishop, who could occasionally be obstinate.

"Not when a woman declares she has seen a king in Swaledale, coming to take his kingdom?"

"None."

"Then," Cromwell scoffed, "her visions are from God."

"Nor that neither," said the Archbishop placidly, "but from a distempered wit. Yet that there is nothing unhonest in the poor creature I am assured by certain words she spoke."

Cromwell did not ask what the words were, but, reaching past the Archbishop, opened the window, so letting into the close still room fresh air and many sounds—the voices of men, wailing and laughter of the gulls, the creak of a well-wheel, and through all, the soft, insistent lapping of the tide.

"Those words," said the Archbishop, when his slight pause exacted no question, "were these. 'Of the increase of his government and peace shall be no end.' "

Cromwell, looking out of the window, observed—"Well, that had a loyal sound."

The Archbishop smiled with indulgent superiority. "She spoke not of the King's Grace. But those very words are written in the English scriptures, and therefore I say there is no treason in her. For, surely if any man hath taught the poor creature to speak these things, that man is no papist, but one who knows the New Learning and the very Gospel of Christ."

"That is sure proof of loyalty?"

"Sure proof," the Archbishop said, with the same bland smile.

"Then Sir Francis Bigod is either no traitor or ignorant of the English scriptures."

"Oh!" said the Archbishop, and his smile died.

"I shall," said Cromwell, "myself examine the woman." He put his hand to his cap and moved towards the door.

"I have set her free," the Archbishop told him in a voice that he tried to make confident.

"You—*you* have set her free?"

"Or rather," the Archbishop maintained his dignity with an effort, "or rather by now she is free. For I gave orders to take her this morning to her mistress, the Prioress of Marrick. Who lies," he added, "at the Priory of St. Helen's in Bishopgate Street."

"I know that," Cromwell snapped at him, and went out quickly.

From daybreak to close on noon except when he went down to church to sing Mass, Gib taught the boys that came to the Chantry for their schooling. Except for what small reward he received from Lord Privy Seal for his writings, this Chantry and school were all Gib's living. He owed them to Friar Lawrence's good offices, and knew that he should be grateful. But to teach the children was a hair shirt upon his shoulders.

To-day was no worse for Gib than other days. The red-haired boy he birched three times, and the squinting boy twice. Someone slung ink at someone else, but the offender was not to be discovered, even though Gib threatened to flog all; he began to carry out his threat, but while he dealt with the second victim one behind his back threw his English Testament across the room. He plunged to rescue it, and as he stooped heard a scuffling and giggling behind him. When he stood up he saw that they had all fled—he who had been under the birch went last of all, with his bare behind showing pink between his shirt and the hosen which he huddled up about him as well as he could.

So there was Gib, left standing alone in the little dusty room, hearing their scurrying footsteps, laughter, and derisive hooting die away down the stairs. With raging disgust in his heart he looked round at the empty benches and all the mess and litter of their childish heedlessness. There were some marbles under one bench end; he picked them up and threw them through the window. Sticking out of the pages of Stanbridge's *Accidentia* there was a coloured paper; when he looked closer he saw that it was one of those painted woodcut pictures of saints which devout persons buy at Pilgrimage places, and afterwards give away to their friends. This was a picture of the Rood; angels, with skirts curled up like the tails of mermaids, hovered to receive into a chalice the blood which poured from the wounded side of the Christ. Gib tore the paper into four pieces and stamped on it. Before he shut the book his eye caught sight of the picture on the title page; eight well-groomed docile scholars, disposed in two orderly attentive lines, waited upon the instruction of their master; the effect of serenity and seemliness was a little weakened by a big slobber of dried brown blood which had probably been spilt from someone's nose after combat, but even so it was cruelly far from the truth, and Gib slapped the book down upon the bench. However, when he had for a while gnawed his knuckles, the extremity of his irritation passed, and he decided that he might as well make the most of his freedom. He unlocked a cupboard, took out a packet of writings, pulled on his hood and began to go downstairs; if he went out at this hour he would miss dinner here, but he would be able to hang about the kitchen door of Lord Privy

Seal's house, and in this way he might more than make up for what he lost at home.

When he came down to the lower room he found that the old Kat had been drinking already and was very quarrelsome. She lurched towards him as he went through, and he thought that if she could have lifted from the hook the pot where white puddings were boiling she would have soused him with it. As it was she followed him to the door and stood screeching after him down the street.

But when a couple of hours later, he came away from Lord Privy Seal's house in Throgmorton Street, he had money in his pouch and even a word of commendation from that Chaplain of my Lord who had scanned through his writing against the Papist superstition of pilgrimages. He had also herring, bread, and beer in his belly. So he went more cheerfully; it pleased him that the porter wagged his head as he passed and gave him good-day. "Here," he thought, "I have a place. Here they know me for what I am." It warmed him against the cold east wind that had kept the day huddled in a November-seeming murk. He thought, "Perhaps when my Lord reads more of what I write he will have me into his Household." He saw himself a chaplain there, well fed, warm, with a little room to study in, having in it a curtained bed, a desk, a shelf of books, as that chaplain had before whom he had stood to-day. Then, even as he went through the street, he raised his fist and struck himself on the breast, horrified at himself because, for those writings of his which should have been only to advance God's Kingdom, he hoped to receive worldly reward.

And, in the meantime, he must go back to the Chantry and to old Kat, by now most likely sodden and snoring.

He came to Cornhill and stood hesitating while a dray piled with a brewer's hogsheads went by. He decided not to go home yet, so he crossed the street and went on down Birchin Lane, meaning to fetch a compass and return by Lombard Street.

He had already turned under the low archway leading to St. Edmund's Church, when he found that a crowd filled the way. There was a scaffolding up against the church, and workmen standing on it, not working, but looking down. The crowd too was looking the same way, at a place below the scaffolding.

Gib did not care what they stared at, and walked more

slowly so that he should not have to shoulder his way through them. As he drew near people began to move away.

"Marry!" said a fat woman as she came past Gib, "I marvel the poor wench was not killed."

"That fellow that let so heavy a stone fall into the street should taste of a rope's end," said the man.

"Poor soul!" said another. "It were a charity to bring her to her home, wherever it may be. I myself am in haste, or . . ." and he passed on.

So now Gib had come to that part of the street where the crowd had been, which now had melted away, and there was Malle, the poor foolish wench from Marrick, sitting with her head cast back against the wall of St. Edmund's porch, and Wat, his son, fondling and fumbling at her, and making strange noises in his throat.

Gib thought—"If I had gone the shorter way—" He thought also—"She does not know me," and Wat never looked his way.

Gib went three steps or four, with a skulking glance back over his shoulder. His heart gave a great jump. Malle turned her face towards him. He wrenched his head round, and went on, stepping softly, listening for her voice. At the corner of the street he did not look back.

March 24

There was a northeast wind blowing down the length of Broad Street as Gib went towards Lord Privy Seal's house. He tucked his hands into his sleeves to keep them warm, but, whether he would or no, instead of putting his head down into the wind he must keep it up to peer about, looking for— he would not let himself know what. Instead he muttered under his breath, "Whew! Winter's come again. Early spring is never sure," and he tried to think of fire and supper waiting for him when he went back. Old Kat might natter at him, but she would go out sooner or later to the ale-house, and then he could read by the firelight, or if he chose could go out to one that he knew, and talk with him on the coming reformation of all things—a heartening subject, for not only did New Jerusalem gleam before them, very pleasant and lovely, but also there was the enemy to be thought of, and his downfall, the enemy who was not only Satan, but also such Bishops as Winchester, such nobles as Exeter, as well as the great part of Monks and Nuns, all such in fact as with malicious perversity would not look up to see the heavenly city descending upon them.

He came opposite the gate of a woodyard, and heard a dog begin to bark wildly there. "Some naughty thief," he thought. "There's none honesty in these days." He paused to watch the fellow bolted out, saying to himself that he should, if occasion served, speak a word to him of rebuke and of salvation.

But instead of some rough fellow a woman and a lad came out of the yard and trailed away along the street in front of him. They had not seen Gib. He could easily, by turning back, or simply by waiting a while, avoid their notice.

But when he knew them, after a bump of his heart, and a great perturbation of mind, peace came to him. Like a full bucket dropping back into the well with a dizzy whirring of the winch, and a heavy plop and splash—like that, all in a second, he knew that here was mercy, here was forgiveness, here was his chance of salvation offered to him once more by the unimaginable patience of God.

He overtook the two of them.

"*Pax vobiscum*," he said, standing in their way.

Wat stepped behind Malle; she faced him, but there was no look of recognition in her face.

He said: "You know me."

She only mumbled something about darkness.

"What? Are you blind?"

She shook her head, but said again that it was dark.

"Where do you live?" he asked her.

She said: "We do not know where to go."

"Well," said he, "I shall take you where I live—till I can provide better. Come on." When she did not move he said again, "Come on," and at the sound of his own voice his heart sank and trembled. To attain salvation he must love these two, as the Samaritan loved the traveller. Yet already he heard in his tone sharp exasperation at her stupidity.

March 26

Aske waited till the greyness of the new day was in the room. Then he got up and wakened Ned Acroyd. Ned lit a candle and, stifling huge yawns, began to dress his master. Being so sleepy he was, for once, silent, and Aske was glad of it; like a physical pain this day's departure from Aughton bounded and consumed all his thoughts; he did not so much remember as feel in himself all the other days of summer, winter, spring upon which he had stood in this same room. Those days, and the little room, and all Aughton, were, it

[639]

seemed, lodged somewhere in his body, and they were being plucked away from him with a long, sore wrench. He thought, "If only I were taking Will with me instead of this lad!" And on the thought Will Wall came in.

Aske looked at Will over the top of Ned's bright brown head as the boy stooped to button his doublet. Will's face was grey; he was as thin as a garden rake. Aske thought, "By the Rood! however I needed him, he could not come with me."

"Master," said Will, "send away the lad."

Ned turned round, grinned, stared, then looked up at Aske. He nodded, so Ned went away. Will shut the door upon him, and with his back to his master said, in a wisp of a voice, "You are going to London?"

"Yes."

Will turned, throwing up his hands to clutch his hair with a gesture and look so wild that it startled Aske, who stretched his arm out to catch him if he should fall.

Will took his wrist with both hands.

"Master," he said. "I will not drink. I swear it as I hope for mercy. I will not touch drink but only water, if you will forgive me, and I may come with you."

"It is not that," Aske told him hastily. "You should have come. But you are not fit to ride such a long gate."

Will let go his wrist. He stood there with his head hanging, and said, not wildly now, but so low that Aske could hardly hear, and indistinctly as if he was powerless even to move his lips—"I shall die if I may not go."

"Will!" Aske said, and then, not knowing what he did, went over to the window and flung open the shutters. Outside in a drenched grey dawn a blackbird called nearby, sudden and urgent as a trumpet, but announcing only peace.

"Master, I have always been with you. There never has been a time—never—always—" Will muttered.

"Oh, Will!" Aske began, then stopped short. "If you can ride," he said, "you shall come."

He expected and feared some passionate demonstration of feeling. But Will only stood silent for a moment and then spoke quietly. "You've heard me promise," said he. "If I fail you this time also, may my Maker, when next I receive Him, be my damnation." He opened the door. "I'll see have they a breakfast ready," he said, and went out.

Julian was in the parlour and sat with her uncle while he breakfasted, but they said very little once he had told her that he would leave a servant at Buntingford. "To bring home news how—to bring home news," he said. When he had finished they went out through the Hall and to the Court. Julian looked sharply at her uncle when she saw Will Wall in the saddle instead of Ned Acroyd. But after that glance she made no comment.

Aske mounted, and she stood at his knee with her hand laid on the horse's neck. He had not kissed her, and now they avoided each other's eye as if they were two plotters guilty and unmasked.

He said: "Keep my little coffer for me, niece. You know where it lies."

She nodded. He had charged her with it last night.

"It may be," he said, "that the King's Grace will be persuaded to hear me. Then it will be well that I have made this journey."

She nodded to that too.

"God be with you, niece," he said, touching her head lightly with his hand. She felt the horse move from under her fingers. She looked at him then, meeting his eye.

"God—" she said, and shut her lips tight, and nodded hard.

He did not look back at all. Will Wall and the other men wheeled their horses and followed him. So he was gone, with all that there was to say left unsaid. She went back into the Hall and stood there irresolute what to do now, because there was nothing to be done. She heard little Dickon upstairs calling out, as joyfully ready for the new day as the birds outside.

Gib sat down to supper alone. Old Kat had gone off to the tavern; Wat had snatched what he could get and gone away to eat it in some corner, like an animal; Malle would not stir from where she sat by the hearth. She did not plague him with her chatter now; but he was finding her silence worse.

When he had brought her in the other day old Kat had made a great scene, screaming at him to take away his drab and his bastard, whose presence she seemed to think an insult to her virtuous respectability.

But now, though she still railed on him, when she could find him alone, for bringing these two, it was on a different ground. For this morning she had announced that the wench was bewitched, and the lad a warlock. "Surely," she said, "Satan has them both in his power. For when I speak to her, saying she should fetch or carry for me (and heavy my work is with you all), what will she say but one word over and over. 'There's darkness,' says she, 'darkness, deep, deep darkness.' "

So now, though he despised himself for it, Gib hitched his chair round a little so that he could, out of the corner of his eye, see her if she moved. Yet all he could see was that now and again she would raise her hand, and holding it spread out before her eyes, would strike it up and down a few times; but whether to hide something from herself, or to clear away some obscurity, he could not tell.

Every time she did it, however, the skin of his back seemed to prickle. He even envied Wat's escape, who now seemed to shrink from Malle as much as he had before used to cling to her.

March 27

The baggage was packed, the trussing coffer locked and one of the two saddle-bags corded, and the Prioress of Marrick stood in the midst of the guest chamber at St. Helen's Priory, looking about at the litter of things upon the floor yet to be put in—a girdle, a comb, a little painted box, some shifts, and a pair of shoes. During the last weeks this room had grown familiar, from the painted Passion emblems on its carved ceiling to the worn red brick of the hearth, and the hanging of green verders, paled to the colour of pea soup near the windows where the light caught them. Now, because of the disarray of her packing, and the empty perches where her gown and cloak had hung, it was once more strange. The sun came out with a sudden harsh gleam, filling it with brightness which faded as suddenly as it had shone.

"Tchk!" said the Prioress impatiently. The man who had been sent to fetch more cord, and the woman who had taken the Prioress's riding coat away to brush it—both should have been back by now. She opened the door and listened. Besides the sound of the Ladies of St. Helen's chanting Prime, she could hear voices below. "How they must ever be talking!" she said to herself, and came in again to walk restlessly up and down the room, and at last stand looking down at the trussing coffer, impatience giving way in her to pride and pleasure as she thought of things bought yesterday which were packed inside it.

For the House there was a little silver plate, and skeins of silk enough to last Dame Ladyman through several years of embroidery, besides a reel of wonderful gold thread. There was also a length of sanguine brocade, very rich, very lustrous. But for the Prioress herself there was a small goblet of glass from Venice, almost as clear as water; with bubbles such as rise through water caught and prisoned in it; yet it had been made by the hands of men, and by fire. It had cost nearly all that was left of the money she had so painfully wrung from Marrick lands to save the Priory from suppression. Well, she deserved the pretty thing, for the Priory was saved, and by her doing.

The serving-man came back again; at least he seemed to have made haste at the last, for he was out of breath.

"Come now," she said briskly, "cord it up and then load the beasts and we'll—"

"Madame," he interrupted her, "he says we shall not go till we deliver her up again."

" 'He' says? Who is he? And deliver whom?"

"He says he is a servant of Lord Privy Seal and that we must give up mad Malle."

"*He* is mad!" cried the Prioress courageously, but yet her heart sank. When she came down to the Court she found a tall young gentleman with a loud voice, a heavy gold chain and much assurance; his manner was rough and hectoring but he was certainly not mad.

During their conversation, since the young man would not speak low, quite a number of people collected, at a discreet distance but well within hearing. The Prioress could see, beyond the wide shoulders of Lord Privy Seal's gentleman, a little mob of Nuns jammed in the doorway of the Cloister; they wrung their hands together, and she could hear their voices shrill and shaking, protesting that they were the King's most loyal subjects any day of the week, and that they harboured no such woman, and that she was none of theirs, but the Prioress of Marrick's servant. The Prioress led the young gentleman farther apart, and spoke with him for a long time. He nodded at last; aloud he said, "See to it that you find her," but he winked one eye at the Prioress.

When he had gone away she returned to the chamber which she had thought so soon to leave, but in which she must now endure yet more waiting. Another time she might have taken comfort to herself from the manner in which she had conducted this last negotiation—from her own sagacity, firmness and address—but the blow had been so sharp that she could feel only the bitterness of impotent resentment.

This resentment was not directed against Cromwell, nor against his gentleman, though it was to Cromwell that she had sent, as a humble gift, the little cup of Venice glass, and it was to reward the young gentleman for his good offices in bringing the cup to his master, and word to her again, that the length of sanguine brocade would have to be once more converted to silver pieces.

Christabel Cowper's resentment was aimed rather against Malle, and against the Prioress of St. Helen's, and against something—or perhaps it was someone—behind Malle and the old Prioress, in alliance with, or in support of them. Her thought here became obscure, and she did not try to resolve the obscurity, but she knew that the something or someone was set to gainsay her, as she was set to have her own way, maugre any gainsaying.

Laurence Machyn opened the door of the solar where July sat on the settle beside the fire. As he came in he could see that she did not turn her head, but remained stooping forward, holding out her hands to the flames. She was very idle these days, doleful and tetchy by turns; the child to come seemed nothing to her but an enemy that drained her life.

Laurence knew all that, was sharply wounded by it, and loved her all the more. He came softly behind her now, leaned over the back of the settle, and laid one hand over her eyes. Then, before she could start away, he brought the other hand forward, so that what his fingers held was just under her nose.

"Guess what it is," he said, and dabbed it, soft, faintly fragrant and cool upon her lips.

"Flowers," she said, not striking his hand away. He was so glad at that that he laughed.

"But what flowers?"

She sniffed at the little posy, and cried, "Oh! Sir, primroses!"

He let her go then, feeling himself well paid by the joy in her voice, and almost overpaid when, sitting beside her, he saw her bend over the tight little bunch with its frill of green leaves as she held them cupped in her hands. She looked up at him and they smiled at each other. It was for a minute as though they were very close to each other, and very young together with the young flowers of the year between them.

Very early on this morning Lord Privy Seal's gentleman came once more knocking at the gate of St. Helen's Priory. They told him he might not enter. He said enter he must, and speak with the Prioress of Marrick. He had a letter for the Prioress from his master, telling her that he took in good part her gift, and would be gracious Lord to the Priory (so long as the Ladies should show themselves to deserve it), and would in no wise recall their backslidings, but only their humble supplication and good will to himward. But the young gentleman said nothing of the letter, insisting that he must speak with the Prioress.

So down came Dame Christabel while the bells were ringing for Prime; she had a velvet purse gripped in her hand in which was the price of the sanguine brocade. She received the letter from the young man, and gave him thanks, and the little purse in recompense of his good offices with his master. What she had bought of him was worth the price, and yet she felt a pang when he took the purse from her fingers, and tossed it in the air, before he shoved it in his pouch, kissed her hand and went away.

It was just about that same moment that Malle, coming in suddenly, caught Wat lapping cream from the top of the milk. He thought her hand on his shoulder was Gib's, and he jumped aside as nimbly as a flea. He had his arms up to guard his ears, and when he saw Malle he let them drop, but he edged away from her as far as he might, until the wall stopped him.

Malle said: "Darkness, and God moving nigh-hand in the darkness. The cloud eats up the sky, black cloud, so that the ash trees are white against it as clean bone, and the elms show green. Down there's the Priory. Look, you can see the Nuns' Court and the orchard, and the Church in the midst. And there's Hodge in his red hood carting dung.

"O Jerusalem!" she cried. "If thou hadst known those things that belong unto thy peace. But now are they hid from thine eyes."

She heard Wat's teeth chatter, and stretched out a hand to comfort him. He endured her touch, but only as an animal that stands because it is too terrified to run.

She said: "He has bowed the Heavens down, and their darkness is under His feet, and dark water in the clouds of the air. And now with the wind He winnows snow from the cloud.

"Look, Wat!" she cried, and pointed towards the naked mud and wattle of the wall, but neither of them saw it. "Look! There He comes down the Dale-side with the young bracken uncurling like rams' horns, spreading like wings about His feet. The head of Him and His hairs are as white as white wool, and as snow."

As Wat tried to dive away under her hand she grasped him tighter.

"He's Love," she said, "and that is greedy as a lion, and may not stint till it has ate us to the bare bones.

"For how can He," she said, "give us the whole height of heaven till we come begging to Him with empty pokes? How can He bear us up in His hand while we grovel safe on ground? How can He lap us close and dear in His love when we are girded with housen and cattle, and cloaked about with gold?

"To-day—" she said, "now—we must find the Lady and tell her."

An hour or so later the Prioress of Marrick came into the Cloister to take leave of the Prioress of St. Helen's, just as fourteen old dames, dot-and-carry-one on crutches, twisted with rheumatism, or bent under the mere load of years, went into the Ladies' Frater to eat their breakfast, for it was Maundy Thursday. She heard their clacking yet feeble voices, saw their deformities, and, smelling them also, pinched her nose between her fingers and pulled a disgusted face.

The Prioress of St. Helen's, summoned from the Frater, came out, still wearing the apron patched with damp in which she had knelt to wash the knobbled, twisted feet of an old creature from Portsokenward. She was flustered to see Dame Christabel, because, having been moved by pity and excitement, she had let herself cry, and she guessed that the Prioress of Marrick would not miss the redness of her eyes.

"Will you go, Madame?" she fussed. "Will you not stay with us over the Feast? Why must you ride to-day?"

"Because my business is done," Christabel Cowper said, and no more. She was not going to explain by telling about the visit of Lord Privy Seal's gentleman.

"But hearken!" she said to the Prioress of St. Helen's. "Here comes to me again, this very morning, that same

[646]

serving wench that I brought here, and for whose sake Lord Privy Seal had me in anger. Well, I have had my man send her packing. And if she comes again to your gate do you the same. I tell you friendly. Else she will bring you into trouble with her talk of visions. Even now she would have had me listen to some madness of visions, but I would not hear her."

She snorted through her nose, and gave a derisive laugh. "I gave my man silver to give her, though he's a sad knave and may have put it into his pouch. I cannot help that. Let her fend. I'll have no more to do with her. And now, Madame," she said, in a different smooth tone, proper to one great person speaking ceremoniously with another, "and now, Madame, I am come to take my leave, and to give you thanks for——"

"If she comes again," the Prioress of St. Helen's broke in, speaking breathlessly, "I shall succour her. And I shall hear her visions if she will tell them."

"Ho!" said the Prioress of Marrick, without any affectation of respect, "will you so? Well so you may, if you care not whether your House stand or fall."

"It is better," said the Prioress of St. Helen's, pressing her soft wrinkled hands together, "better it should fall, if thereby shall come peace between us and God. For I think it is for our sins, Madame, that He has chastened us. And if He take from us all we have, it is to make us, who have cleaved to worldly wealth, cleave only to Him, so that He may bless us."

The Prioress of Marrick stared to hear this gentle creature turn upon her. She was even a little impressed; not very much, but enough to make her argue the point.

"But though He bless," she said, "what then?"

"What then?"

"If we——if you shall have lost all, and are turned out and the House fall . . . ? Then it will be too late."

"Too late for what?"

The Prioress of Marrick, thinking in terms of a bargain between buyer and seller, found herself unwilling to use the first words that came to her tongue. "Too late for payment." She would not say that; she even rejected the word "reward." "For His help. For Comfort," she said at last, for once preferring propriety to sincerity.

But the old Prioress answered sincerely, though with a most undignified shaken voice, and a great sniff after she had spoken:

"Let Him alone for that. He will see to our help, and He will know how to comfort."

They stood facing each other a moment longer. From the open door of the Frater came the cackle of the old folks' voices, even, now and again, the smacking sound they made as they ate. Someone belched; someone choked on a draught of beer and began to cough.

The Prioress of Marrick let her lip curl. She had Moses and the Prophets; half an hour ago she had had mad Malle babbling of the insatiable tender love of God. Now she had the old Prioress of St. Helen's. She had not listened to any of these, nor would she have listened though one rose from the dead.

She moved away, not very tall, but in her fur-lined riding cloak bulky and very stately.

"Tush!" she said, and no other word of farewell.

The Chronicle of Christabel Cowper, Prioress of Marrick, ends here.

March 31

Lord Darcy had dined at the house of the Mayor of Pomfret. He came back to the Castle in the afternoon, going slowly on foot, leaning on a silver-knobbed staff, with one of his gentlemen on either side and two servants behind. The boys and girls were coming back from the fields with primroses. Lord Darcy stopped a string of the smallest of them, and asked for a posy. A little girl, all blue eyes, smudged rosy cheeks, and open silly-sweet mouth, gave him her handful, and then backed away, still staring. He kissed the flowers to her, told the servant go give her a penny, and went on, holding the posy under his nose.

When he came into the first ward he found a number of horses standing; evidently they had just come in, for the marks of the saddles and girths were still dark upon them. A stranger came towards him, a broad-faced, freckled, sandy man, who pulled off his cap and held out a letter.

Lord Darcy went on till they were close; then he too uncovered.

"Welcome," he said, "to you in the King's livery, and wearing the King's badge."

Because he smiled, and spoke so lightly, the other conceived that he must talk big.

"I've sufficient force with me—" he began.

"To take me? Why so you shall—when you will." And my Lord went on at his usual slow pace. His two gentlemen and the servants thrust by also, stiff as dogs that square up for a fight.

The King's man looked after them, hesitated, then followed, but at a little distance.

April 2

Aske had waited at Court all day since Mass, standing first on one foot, then on the other, in a kind of blank suspension of feeling. He had handed over to a gentleman of the Bedchamber the letters which the Duke of Norfolk had given him; and now he could only wait. He did not know whether he would wait in vain, to be turned out this evening when the Presence Chamber was cleared, or whether some officer of the Guard would come with a warrant and pikemen, and so he would sleep to-night in prison; or whether the King would send for him, and he would have that opportunity to speak, for which he had come to London. He longed, against his will, that it should be the first, he expected the second; he dared not hope for the last.

When a yeoman usher came to his elbow, and said that the King had sent for him, his heart gave so great a jump that it sent the blood drumming into his ears. If the King would see him on this Easter Sunday evening, when the Court was crowded with all the great nobles and Ambassadors, then perhaps the King would hear him speak, if not to-day, then some other day. At least, he said to himself, following the usher through many passages and up and down stairs, it must mean that all's not lost.

They came to a door in the farther part of the palace; here were the offices in which the Chancellor of the Augmentations and his clerks pursued their business, but Aske did not know that. The usher stopped with his head bent to listen, and knocked. Then he pushed open the door and motioned Aske to enter.

There were five or six persons standing together in the dusty sunshine of the room; their backs were towards him and all looked down at something at their feet. The room was unfurnished except for a big table and a couple of stools, but piles of leather and folded canvas lay about, and against one wall a number of wicker hampers were stacked.

The men standing there turned about, and Aske saw that the King was in their midst, and went down on his knee. He saw also that Cromwell was on one side of the King and Lord Chancellor Rich, Chancellor of the Augmentations, on the other; and what hope he had conceived, died at that sight.

"Well, Mr. Aske?" said the King.

Aske got up from his knees and came nearer; they were watching him, all of them; he knelt down again and asked for leave to kiss the King's hand. The King held it out, white and scented; he kissed it, but the King had already turned away, leaving him kneeling in the midst of them.

It was then that he saw what they had been looking at when he came in. An open hamper stood there half full of hay. Gold gleamed among the hay, and jewels, like small coloured eyes. On the floor in front of the hamper lay tumbled together gold chalices and silver, jewelled and enamelled reliquaries, the crook of an ancient and beautiful crozier, a small image of silver. Aske looked at these, and knew that the others still had their eyes on him.

"Well, Master Aske," said the King again, "you have said that the Act of Suppression of the Abbeys was the greatest cause of the detestable treasons of your North Country men, and that the hearts of the commons most grudged at it. Now tell me again—in your conscience do you think it was so?"

"Surely," said Aske, "it was so."

"And as for you yourself?"

They had to wait for the answer. Then Aske said, "I and all others grudged at it."

"And do you now grudge at it?"

During the still longer pause, the King stretched out his foot, broad-toed as a duck's webbed foot in its yellow velvet shoe. He rested it lightly on the curve of an overturned chalice, rolling the vessel backwards and forwards under the sole of his foot.

"Your Grace," said Aske at last, "has the whole of the North Country altogether at Your mercy."

"I'll have no mercy on traitors, Master Aske," said the King. He gave the chalice a push with his foot so that it rang against the rim of a big alms dish. He waved his hand in Aske's face saying, "Go! You may go!"

So Aske went out of the room. As he found his way back through the Palace he kept his head up, but he was thinking, "Here goes a man that came to London to speak plain, and was afraid to speak." He was aware that he would not have been permitted to speak. Besides that, the outrage of seeing the King tumble the consecrated cup with his foot had strangled every word upon his tongue; but still, he knew that he had been afraid to speak.

When the door had shut behind him Cromwell murmured as if to himself—

"I marvel how such a traitor, seeing his treason utterly defeated, dare speak so stoutly."

"A murrain," cried Rich, "upon so cankered a heart!"

"He is a man much unbroken and rude," said Cromwell.

"As yet unbroken," said the King, moving away from them. They followed him out of the room.

Aske came away from Westminster by water and told the boatman to put him down at Blackfriars' Stairs. This way he could go as easily to Gray's Inn as to the Cardinal's Hat. At Gray's Inn he would find, he knew, men not very ready to be seen in his company; at the Cardinal's Hat, he could guess, he would find Will Wall, sow-drunk.

He had not made up his mind which way he would choose to take when he came to Ludgate, and so hung on his heel a moment under the gate-arch. From the west the setting sun poured into the street a flood of gold; when he looked that way his eye, half blinded, could see only dark shapes of people moving, fringed about with silver. He turned to go back up Bowyer Row towards St. Paul's and heard someone behind him cry, "Sir, Master Aske! O Sir!" and there was little July Savage tugging his arm with one hand, and hauling after her by the other a young, rambling puppy at the end of a scarlet ribbon leash.

He took in first her shining look of joy, then the glance that she threw over her shoulder towards a slight young man with straw-coloured hair, in his Easter Sunday best of tawny doublet and white hosen. If this were July's husband he looked a poor rag of a man, but by his expression a gentle and kindly one.

"Sir," cried July, speaking first to one then to another, and sometimes, it seemed, to both of them. "You must come home with us. He must come home. Sir, I pray you! Sir, ask him! Oh, it must be so!"

Aske laughed. "This little maid and I," said he to Laurence Machyn—"I must still so think of her—we have been friends many a year now."

"Oh, many a year!" cried July.

Laurence said if Master Aske were not pressed—because it was not far to go—he—his wife—they would take it kindly—

"It's but round the corner," said July, "and surely you may not refuse."

As they walked together Laurence was planning that when they reached home he would make an excuse and go out again, and leave them there. Yet when it came to the point he found himself unable to do it. They sat round the fire in the solar upstairs talking little, for it seemed that when July had announced that she and Laurence had been walking in the fields beyond Temple Bar, she thought of nothing else but to sit watching Master Aske, with such a light on her face as would have been proper had he been, thought Laurence, an angel from heaven.

Laurence had sent for wine, and a plate of nuts. He plied Aske with these, and made perfunctory remarks, eyeing his guest furtively most of the time (since he could not endure to look at July), and hating Aske on every count upon which one man may hate another. Aske was a gentleman, and therefore he sat with his chin on his breast in disdainful silence; he was July's leman, fretting that her husband should be gone and leave him to stretch out his hand, to draw her to him, to—Laurence swallowed hard there, and wriggled on the settle so that July flung him a quick, impatient, chiding glance. Master Aske cracked the nuts in his fine white teeth, and Laurence hated him for that. The man was even hateful for his dark hair, though it gave Laurence some comfort to see in it quite a scattering of grey.

During one of the many long silences they all heard someone knock, and knock again on the street door below. Laurence turned, listening. "That boy's run forth again," he said, half to himself. He missed, therefore, how though Aske neither turned nor stirred, the hand that lay on his knee became clenched till the knuckles showed white. But July saw it, and saw how he sat there, stiff as wood, then slowly turned his head towards the open door of the inner room, where a corner of the Machyns' blue and yellow curtained bed showed, and beyond it a window.

Laurence got up and found that July was on her feet.

"No," said he sharply, "I'll answer. It may be some drunken fellow."

He had hardly gone out when July's hand was on the latch.

"Out through the window there," she whispered. "I'll keep them as long as I may."

"No—no," said Aske, but she had gone, and he was left to realize how close fear had followed at his heels, that he should have been even for an instant so unreasonable as to think that the King might have sent to take him here. Yet he sat very still, and must listen with all his ears, and gave a great start when July came in again, shutting the door softly behind her.

"It's only the matter of a corpse to be buried," she said, and then, "What do you fear? What has happened?"

He said shortly, "Nothing." But because at that she looked so miserably chidden he would not leave it there. "Nothing," he said again, "indeed. Yet I think they will take me, in spite of the pardon."

She shut her eyes, leaning back with her arms spread and the palms of her hands pressed against the door. It was apparent as she so stood, though he only later remembered it, that she was with child.

She opened her eyes, and turned her head, listening.

"He's coming back," she said. "Quick. Promise me. If— if they do, find means to send me word."

He said hastily, "If I'm taken, I'll send Will Wall."

Then Laurence came in.

April 6

Aske had not meant to come again to the Machyns' house, since he felt himself to be a man who has detected in his body the unmistakable signs of the plague. But this evening, having vainly waited all day outside the Presence Chamber, as he had waited every day since Easter Sunday, he did, though with compunction, and shame at his own weakness, come to the house in Knightrider Street, and knock. The master was not in, but the mistress, they told him, was in the garden, and they took him through the house, and out under the arched passage into the little pleached garden beyond. The honeysuckle was showing grey-green leaves though the vine and the big old mulberry tree were still stark bare, and there were tufts of primroses flowering in the grass.

But July was not here, so the boy left him to go and find her, and Aske sat down on the built-up grass bank below the honeysuckle. Above, the setting sun caught and glorified the chimneys of a neighbour's house, dyeing them with fiery sanguine, but the small hidden garden was full of shadow, and of peace. As he waited there in the quiet for a little while he almost forgot the blackness of the present.

July, sitting with her face towards the screens at the end

of the servants' table in the hall, had seen him go by to the garden. So had the little grey-haired man, wearing Lord Privy Seal's livery, who sat opposite her, but neither had made any comment. Master John Heath, a cousin of Master Henry Machyn, and so, though distantly, a cousin of Laurence's, was a man of an orderly habit of mind. The sight of Aske in the house had been a surprise to him, and certainly must be looked into, but he would first pursue that enquiry for the sake of which he had come, and only afterwards attend to the other.

"So," said he, "you have had no communication with your sister since you came hither to London?"

"I have told you—none."

"No letters? No messages? Come, sweet cousin, it's not that you are thought to favour her treasons, but if she wrote to you, there might drop a word, to you innocent, but to us disclosing or confirming her guilt."

"I have had no letter, nor message. I never thought to have."

Cousin Heath rooted thoughtfully in his ear, watching her. "Yet," said he, with a cunning look, "you do not ask, 'What treason?' "

"Because," said July, "I do not care. I do not care what she has done. I do not care what she suffers for it."

If she had spoken wildly he might have thought that she lied because she was frightened. But here, he could not but know, was the calm and deadly truth.

He leaned towards her, and began to explain how, hearing that his cousin Laurence's wife was sister to this traitor, he had begged that he himself might question her, rather than another, sure as he was that there was nothing but innocence and loyalty in Mistress July—"as I now hear and can vouch for," he said.

July, thinking of Aske in the garden, looked at him with a blank face.

"But," said Laurence's kinsman, "besides that your sister and her paramour have raised insurrection lately, sending hither and thither to call men out, it was she, we know surely, who set on Bigod to rise, whose detestable conspiracy has given the King's Grace fresh cause to have those of the North Country in his dread displeasure."

"She did that?" July cried, not calmly now. "If she did that—"

"Tut! Tut!" he said, and tried to pat her hands as they tore at each other on her lap, but she took them out of his reach. He began to find her agitation suspicious.

"'If she did that,'" he said, "and so she did, she will die for it. Do you know how?"

July shook her head. She was thinking—"It is her doing. It is her doing that he is endangered."

"She will be burned alive."

"She will deserve to be so," said July, and again he could not but recognize the very accent of truth.

"Well," he said, "I can see that indeed you favour not your sister's doings, so we will let that alone.

"Yet there is another matter."

He hitched his chair nearer to hers, and said, speaking low, "This man Aske, that I saw come in— Will he speak openly to you if you should put questions to him?"

When he had sat in the garden perhaps a quarter of an hour Aske began to suspect that July had been told by her husband to have no more dealings with him. As that was but too probable, the only thing to do was to leave, making some excuse if he saw anyone on his way out.

So he came back to the house, and opened the door leading to the screens passage. The door opposite him was open on the street; July stood there, and with her a small grey-haired man, who leaned close and whispered in her ear. Robert Aske saw Cromwell's livery colour; before he knew what he would do, he had shut the door softly, and gone back a few steps into the garden. He remembered now that July's sister was a whore, and July herself a liar. He thought, "She is to betray me to them."

July found him standing there. She was so glad to see him, for all her fear, that she thought nothing of the sternness of his look, except that for a few minutes she might be able to soften it.

"Come," she said, "come beyond," and went past him towards the further garden. For a moment he thought to turn and go away without a word, yet he followed her.

But when she sat down on the grass bank, patting it to show that he should sit beside her, he would not, and standing in front of her he said, "That man you spoke with—he is one of Cromwell's."

She nodded. "He is a cousin of my husband."

He looked down at her, and now her eyes shrank from his, and she turned her face away.

"And," he said, "when I have talked to you, you shall report my words to him."

She did not look up, or speak, or even shake her head.

Nor could he find any more to say. If it was true there was nothing to be said. But then—how he did not know—but he knew that it was not true, and that he could trust her, if no other. He said suddenly:

"I did not think you would betray me," and, "Nor I do not think it. Surely I know you will not."

She broke down at that, caught his hand and clutched it in both of hers, bowing herself over it, so that he felt her tears fall on his fingers. She told him, so far as he was able to distinguish her words, that indeed she could not—"Oh! do you not know that I could not?"

He sat down by her on the bank, leaving his hand in hers, and hoping that she would become calm; but she did not seem able to stop crying now that she had begun. At last it distressed him too much to be borne longer.

"Sweeting," he said, "let's be merry a little. Will you for my sake?"

She gave a great gulp, and sat still, and apparently without breathing, for a long instant. Then she released his hand, and in silence wiped her eyes, not making any attempt to turn away, but doing it simply, carefully, openly.

The sun had gone down, and a half moon looked into the garden from a sky that was still bright but whose colour was chilling away. With a sudden flurry of wings, a blackbird alighted in the mulberry tree, bowed, swung up his tail, and began his song.

"How sweet he sings," said July, not in the low voice of one who is near to tears, but in a high, clear tone, that brought startlingly to Aske's mind the wild beauty of her sister. "But whether he thinks on the moon or upon worms," said July, "none knoweth." And she laughed.

When Laurence came into the garden, the moon, instead of a thin white flake with the blue showing through, was a well of purest cold light. As he came through the passage he heard voices; at the farther end he stood looking at them.

Aske, stooping down, was playing idly with a pebble, dandling and jumping it in his cupped palm. July sat gazing at him with a little smile and a look of inly bleeding tenderness. This was not that look which a woman bends upon her lover; to Laurence it was something worse than that. It was the look, at last on July's face, of a woman, not of a child; of a woman gazing in her child.

Laurence knew too well in himself the kind of love of which that look came, to mistake it in another. But to see her pour it over the bent head of this man was worse, he thought, than to find them breast to breast.

April 7

Aske heard them driving the nails into his coffin. He braced himself, straining to heave off the lid. He tried to shout, and wakened himself by a groan. It was a dream. He was awake now, but the knocking went on, and someone below shouted, "In the King's name!"

He was out of bed, with his hand on Will's shoulder, shaking him. But Will only rolled over in bed with a snore, and Aske remembered that a few hours ago he had come back to the Cardinal's Hat dead drunk. So there was no help in him.

There was no help anywhere, nor anything to do but dress and be ready. He could hear them opening the doors below. His knees were shaking, and in the dark he could find only shirt, drawers and shoes. By the time he had these on a light shone on the ceiling and slid to the floor, as they came clattering upstairs.

They burst in, half a dozen of them, armed archers of the Guard, and he could hear more outside. They said they had come to apprehend him for new treasons lately discovered, and laid hold of his wrists. Will wakened just at that moment, yawned, stared, and lurched out of bed.

"Will! Stop!" Aske cried, but Will went at the men, clawing and screaming like a maniac, to be knocked down as clean as a skittlepin. Those two who held Aske drove him to the door. He could do nothing, but as they dragged him downstairs he shouted, "Don't hurt the fellow. He's drunk. He means no harm."

Out in the inn-yard, where the sharp night air met him, he remembered that he was not half dressed, and tried to hang back, asking that one would fetch his clothes, or give him time to get them on. They said they were not his body servants, nor his nurse neither, to put on his hosen, and tie his points, and wipe his breach for him.

As they thrust him into the street he experienced for the first time, with rage and fear, the impotence of a prisoner.

April 8

The litter halted, and Lord Darcy in its black interior heard someone beat with the butt end of a pike upon a gate. As the bars rumbled into their sockets, and the gates clattered back upon the walls, the litter moved on, swinging the leather curtains for a second aside, so that a little trickle of the swaying torchlight dodged in, and was blotted again. The litter stopped once more, and just then, from high up above, came the strokes of a great bell, telling the hour. It was ten of the clock, and the great bell of the King's Tower of London had struck it out.

Darcy pulled the curtain aside, and got his foot over the edge of the litter. He was not going to show these fellows any unwillingness to arrive. But for a moment, dazzled by the crowded torches, he could only blink, unable to make out any of the surrounding faces clearly. Then he saw Mr. Lieutenant, Sir Arthur Kingston, lean and tawny brown as a Berkshire hog.

"Good Master Lieutenant," said he, "you give me a kindly welcome."

"Sorry I am, my Lord," replied Kingston stiffly, "to give you any welcome to this place."

"Nor should you," said Darcy, "if honest men were up, and rogues down. Well, show me the way."

They showed him the way to the Beauchamp Tower, and there he found, sitting about the remains of a very meagre fire—but in the Tower that small handful of fuel cost as much as a bushel of sea-coal anywhere else—Sir Thomas and Sir Ingram Percy, strangely pale after their weeks of captivity; and Sir Robert Constable. They had heard of his coming from the guard, and so had saved some of their supper, and made him welcome to it, prizing him not only as a comrade but also, for this night at least, as a novelty, and an event.

So when he had eaten they sat a long while talking, till the two Percys, having wearied themselves out with railing against Cromwell, began to yawn, and lay down under their cloaks. Soon they slept, Thomas with sudden starts, and now and again a sharp cry, and a hand flung out; Ingram with the blank look of death upon his upturned face.

The older men lay down too, but did not sleep. Instead they murmured together of the apparent dangers of their case, or of such slight hopes as they might discern.

Darcy himself had none of these hopes, saying roundly,

"Cromwell is set to pull down all nobles. So I shall go, and those two, yet you may scape."

Sir Robert argued a bit against him; yet was brought to confess that indeed, as a distant kinsman of the Queen, he might, at the worst, find one with power to procure his pardon.

"Yet—" he cried, "Yet—'pardon'! For us who have done no treason since that pardon we were freely given!" Darcy heard him grind his teeth in the darkness, and then mutter, "I do not wonder to hear those two curse and swear."

"Well," said Darcy, speaking slowly after a silence, "I shall not hope but for one thing. Shall I tell you what?"

"What then?"

"That God in His mercy will take my death as if I had died fighting for His Cross."

"Say you so?" muttered Constable, startled and solemnized.

"And may be, in His good time, He will rise up to defend His honour, and Holy Church, and to tumble down," said Darcy, "those heretics and Privy Seals," and he laughed, sharply and angrily.

April 9

Laurence Machyn heard his wife sigh. It was a very small breath, and she was unconscious of it, but to him it was as dreadful as the sound of the passing bell. And again she sat very still, yet with her eyes roving, as though she listened and waited. Laurence groaned within himself, thinking, "She sighs for him."

He laid down his knife beside the ham-bone he was picking and said abruptly:

"They took him to the Tower on Saturday. One told me of it this morning."

He had not meant that there should be the least note of triumph in his voice, and he was ashamed to detect it. Yet it did not matter, since July missed it. The news itself was all she cared for.

She turned her face towards him, and he saw horror quicken it; then, before his eyes it seemed to die, so white and empty did it grow. She said nothing, and her eyes looked past him. After a minute she laid her hands on the table and stood up.

"I have finished," she said, and went out. He heard her climb the stairs, and thought he would hear her footsteps in the room above, which was theirs. But no—she went on to the attics. He knew that she went there so that he should not come in upon her, and he felt as if something had laid a hand upon his heart, squeezing it cruelly.

Upstairs Julian stood in the little closet under the roof, leaning a hand against one of the beams, and looking down, without seeing it, at the old cow-hide trussing coffer. Her thought was not, as yet, precisely of Robert Aske, but rather —"It has come." All her life she had been expecting the worst, and now the worst had come.

April 16

Quite a score of mounted archers, riding close, surrounded the litter in which Lord Darcy was brought from the Tower for examination by the Lords of the Council in Lord Chancellor Audeley's house. They rode into the courtyard, and then the sergeant of them, dismounting, unlaced the leather curtains, and said to my Lord, "Sir, you are to follow me."

The fine new staircase which the Lord Chancellor had lately had built was of an easy and broad tread, but when a gentleman usher opened a door at the top, and beckoned my Lord in, he paused, leaning heavily on his staff. Then he lifted his head and went into the room.

It was a sunny place, and the windows were open upon the tops of the apple trees which showed, among their fresh leaves, round bright pink buds. A small company of gentlemen stood talking together in the pleasant air and sunshine. There was Fitzwilliam, broad and black; Paulet with his smooth look, Edward Seymour the Queen's brother, now Lord Beauchamp, looking, as always, like one who knows himself to be better than his company. Suffolk, who liked to ape the King when he was not by, stood with his fine legs straddled wide, swinging from his fingers a jewel that hung about his neck. At the board's head, apart from all these, sat Cromwell, with a heap of papers before him, licking his thumb and flicking them over as calmly as if they were bills of lading, instead of Articles framed against the King's enemies; as if he were once more a merchant among the merchants of Amsterdam, instead of Lord Privy Seal, presiding over the King's Most Honourable Council.

Darcy stopped inside the door, his eyes snapping bright, and seeming, for all that in these days his great height was bowed, to look down on the whole company. Some of them avoided his glance, some gave him look for look, as they came back from the windows, and settled themselves in the chairs set about the table. Mr. Pollard, the King's Remembrancer, who sat in place of any common clerk at a further small table, dipped his pen in the ink, and held it poised.

"Well," said Darcy, speaking to them all but looking only at Cromwell, "I am here now at your pleasure. Ye may do your pleasure with me. Yet I have read of men that have been in such favour with their Princes as ye be now, that have come at last to the same end that ye would now bring me to. And so may ye come to the same."

"Keep that door!" cried Cromwell, and the gentleman usher, who was one of Norfolk's gentlemen, namely Perce Cresswell, hastily slammed the door and set his shoulders against it, as though that would prevent Lord Darcy's voice, strong still, and still with a sound of youth in it, penetrating the oak of the panelling.

"Outside!" said Cromwell. "Fool!" So Perce went out.

There was an Interrogatory of over a hundred questions, and time wore on as Cromwell put them to Darcy, Darcy answered, and Mr. Pollard wrote his answers down. Now and again one of the other Lords would break in, for Darcy spared none, hitting here and there in his replies, and that was easy for one with such a long memory as his, which could range back, through things done and said in court or camp for twenty, thirty, forty years.

"You," said he, mocking at them all, "you that think you can pull down the walls and leave the thatch standing! His Ribalds and his scribblers," and he pointed his staff right at Cromwell's face, "they go about to teach the commons to grudge and murmur and scoff at Holy Church. Take ye heed that they come not to grudge at us noble men, and when they have pulled down the Church pull down also the whole nobles of the realm, and so rule all, tag-rag."

Cromwell let him finish, and then he smiled, a small thin smile.

"You say the nobility shall be pulled down. God's Bread! but it is you yourself and your fellows who pull it down by treasons against your Prince. Mr. Pollard," he said, turning to the little table at the wall, "put to him that question as to . . ." He ran his finger down the paper. "The one hundred and twentieth," he said.

Mr. Pollard read it out.

" 'If all things had succeeded according to your intention,

what would ye have done, first touching the King's person, and then touching every man of his Council.' "

"Enough!" said Cromwell. "Let him answer so far first."

"Shall I answer?"

"You shall."

Darcy straightened his back. His face was flushed and his eyes a bright frosty blue, so that for all the chills of the Tower, and his age and weakness, for a moment he looked the quick and dangerous fighter he had been.

"For the King," he said, "not a hair of his head should have been touched. For the ancient and noble blood upon the Council, our intent was to preserve it. But the villain blood that is there, that should have been taken and judged."

"Meaning—" Cromwell asked. Now he was not smiling.

"Thee, Master Cromwell." Darcy's look as much as the curt words stripped an upstart of his Privy Seal, and of all his importance.

"For it is thou," he went on, "that art the chief causer of all this rebellion and mischief, and art likewise causer of the apprehension of us that be noble men, and dost daily earnestly travail to bring us to our end, and to strike off our heads. And I trust, before thou die, though thou wouldst procure all the noblemen's heads within the realm to be stricken off, yet shall one head remain that shall strike off thy head."

Cromwell got out of his chair, and began to beat with his fist on the table. "Strike him on the mouth," he cried, but there was no one there would do it for him.

April 20

Lord Privy Seal was among the crowd which waited upon the King as he came out from Chapel. The King waved his hand to put away from him all the others, and went with Cromwell to a window looking upon the gardens.

"Well?"

"From my Lord Darcy," says Cromwell, "nothing but saucy words and high cracks."

"And from Aske?"

"Nothing of moment. Though plenty to hang the man himself," he added.

"You sent to him?"

"I went to him myself. First I told him that his own brother had given information of his treasonous proceedings."

"And he said?"

"Nothing to the purpose. Yet I think it touched him nearly. For he said, 'God help me!' and then, 'Which brother?' I said, 'Your second brother, Christopher Aske.' "

"And then?"

"No more on that head. But I said that he should have pardon for speaking the truth; that if when he comes to trial he should chance to be condemned I should be his intercessor; that no harm was meant to them all, but only to preserve the honour of Your Grace, which would be much touched if rebels should not be judged by law; but that once judged all those shall have mercy that have not offended since the pardon, 'as,' said I, 'His Grace knoweth that you have not. So you may speak freely.' "

"What did he say to that?"

"That for his own part he would always be ready to declare such things as come to his remembrance. But that if he bought his life by condemning other, he would be a thing to be abhorred of all good men, and his life worth naught."

Cromwell dared only to give a slinking glance at the King's face, but it was enough to show him how it had grown red and bloated as Henry stood silent, throttling down his rage. Just then the horns blew for supper, and Cromwell caught a glimpse, beyond the King's shoulder, of the pages and gentlemen of the Chamber, waiting with towel, ewer and basin for the King to wash his hands.

"Tcha!" said the King at last. "He'll speak before long. You shall see. He hath an ill conscience before God for his treasons. He'll not endure."

Cromwell thought of the man he had seen this morning, whose teeth chattered with the cold, but whose look was resolved far beyond defiance. He shook his head. "He answers still very stoutly. And they say at the Tower that though he has had the colic and has moreover a sore cough, yet he will most often be merry when they bring his porridge."

"Merry!" cried the King. "Who sends him help then?"

Cromwell said no one could have sent him anything. "At the foot of his last writing he asks the Lords of the Council for the love of God that he may send for money and clothes, 'for I am not able to live,' says he, 'seeing none of my friends will do nothing for me.' "

"And yet," said the King, "he will not speak! Vile villain!" he said, and there was a kind of incredulity in his anger. "Has he no care for his soul?" he asked.

Cromwell did not undertake to answer that. He said, reflectively, that the fellow might be put down into a straiter place, and a worse. "Or there is the rack."

"No. Not yet." The King brooded. A pleasant strain of music reached them from the Presence Chamber, and a pleasant smell also, of roasted and spiced meat.

"No," said the King again. "Try this." He spread out his hands, and looked down at them, half drew off a sapphire ring, slipped it back into place, and held out to Cromwell a circle of twisted gold, with white enamel and green interlacing tiny pearls.

"If he does not trust you, me he will trust. Say to him that there is his Prince's token to ensure him of pardon, if he will speak the truth."

"Sir," said Cromwell after some hesitation, looking down at the ring upon his palm, "should you pardon this man—"

"He must by some means be induced to tell the names of those others," the King answered in a gentle voice. "But as for pardon—" He turned away, and beckoned for the ewer and basin.

May 12

As July was buying mackerel at the door a man came by who hesitated, turned, and then stood as if uncertain of his way. He was a stranger and yet to July there was that about him which reminded her of someone. She caught his eye and looked hastily down at the fish in the huckster's basket, barred with black ripple marks of the sea, and gleaming with the sea's blue green. She bought half a dozen, had the man lay them on the stone paving of the screens' passage, and was about to shut the door. But as the huckster moved away, that other, who had loitered near, came to her. He had the appearance of a harmless worthy man, and yet there was something in the way he glanced about that made her fear him, though he himself had a look of fright.

"You want my husband?" she said.

"Are you Mistress Machyn?"

She nodded and thought to shut the door. Yet that likeness of his, that she could not account for, made her pause.

"My brother," he said, "made me swear on the Cross I should come to you. He could have no ease till I swore it. I'd have come sooner, but" (he dropped his voice very low) "they had me in Newgate, to question me."

"Come in," said July.

"No. Better not." He glanced about again. "The sooner I'm away, the better for you. But I promised Will—"

"Who is Will?"

"My brother. Will Wall. But Will's dead. He was Mr. Aske's servant."

July could say nothing because of the loudness of that name in her ears, or else it was the blood drumming there.

"Will died a week after they took Master Aske. He came to me at Ware before daylight, for they'd taken his master about midnight. I knew then that Will was a dead man. The moment I saw him I knew it. He raved all that week, clawing and striking at his breast, saying it was he that had brought his master into treason, crying out, 'He was hid, and I brought them to him,' and crying out, 'Oh my master, my master, they will draw him, and hang him, and quarter him!'"

"Stop," cried July, but she had not voice enough to make him hear her.

"He made me swear I should tell you Mr. Aske was taken, for so, he said, he had promised to do. And just before he died he said I should tell you also that his master was taken by night in naught but his shirt and shoes. I'd 'a' come before, but they took me—" He stopped then because the young woman had shut the door in his face.

Laurence came in a while after and shouted for July. She heard him well enough from the kitchen, but did not answer. Then she heard him go upstairs. After a moment he called again, "July! July!" and came to the kitchen door, so she had to go out to him.

"Wife," he said, "I can nowhere find my blue hosen."

July put her hand to her mouth, looking not at him, but out towards the garden. The sun shone through the open door; a bee came in, lingered, and then went off again. There was summer in his humming, and in the silence he left behind him, and in the smell of chopped mint that came from the kitchen. But her mind was frozen; only her heart ached as she felt it beat heavily. The hiss of a pot boiling over, a shriek and a peal of laughter from the maids, made her start, but still she felt that she was not properly awake.

"Why do you want them?" she asked.

"I've torn these on a nail. That fool Nick's no craftsman. I shall turn him off."

"I mended your grey," said July, with a huge effort.

"It is not warm enough yet for them."

"I—I am busy. Can you not find something? You have plenty."

Her voice nearly broke on that. She turned and went away into the kitchen. "Plenty of hosen." So he had, and coats, and doublets, everything. He was warmed, fed, and cared for. She would have been glad, that moment, to do him an injury for being so.

She had forgotten Laurence, because her thoughts clung so tormentedly to the other, when she heard her husband call again, "July, come here."

As she climbed the stairs he went back into their chamber. She found him standing in the midst; the floor was strewn with clothes, tossed here and there, gowns, shifts and shirts, doublets and petticoats.

He said, "My black doublet is gone too, and that red camlet coat, and two of my best shirts."

When she said nothing, and did not even look at him, he asked, "Where are they?" and came nearer to her, to say again, and louder, "Where are they?"

"Master Aske—" she began.

Laurence stepped back. His foot caught in one of her gowns so that he almost fell. Now he could not look at her, any more than she could look at him.

She said in the smallest voice, but it was steady, "He has been there this two months, through all these late frosts and cold, in but his shirt and his shoes."

Stealing a glance at her he saw her whole face shake, and again grow still. She looked straight before her through the window, but she pointed to where the curtains of the bed moved gently in the sweet air. "They are there," she said, "under the bed. I should have sent them to him."

"How?"

She said, "I do not know."

The look of her and her voice so cut him to the heart that he could not endure it. He went past her, downstairs, and out into the street.

Outside the Tower that evening a man hung about till it was almost time for the drawbridge to be lifted and the gates shut. Then, seeing a sour-looking grizzled fellow going in, he seemed to take courage, stepped forward and stopped him.

"Gossip," said he, "there's a gentleman in there called Aske."

"There is," the old fellow agreed.

"Can I . . . How can I get this to him?" With one hand he held out a bundle, and with the other fumbled in his purse.

"Are you a friend of his?"

Laurence dropped the angel that he had between his fingers.

"My wife—" he began, and then stood dumb, his eyes downcast, the very picture of a shamed but acquiescent cuckold.

The old man chuckled softly. "By Cock!" he said, "so it is with these gentlemen, and this one with his filed tongue would be harder for a wench to resist than another. And he mettle. I know something of mettle. I've seen prisoners enough in my day, but this one—" He seemed to recollect himself, and growled, "Saving that he's a pestilent traitor."

Laurence shoved the bundle at him, and said with more violence than so gentle a man could have been thought capable of, "Here. Will you take it or no?"

The old man took it. "Aye. He shall have it to-morrow. A murrain on him for a traitor." He picked up Laurence's angel out of the dust, and stumped away across the bridge.

In bed that night, with the candle blown out, Laurence kept silence a long time. Then he cried out in a harsh, rough voice:

"I took that bundle. The jailer says he shall have it tomorrow."

After that they lay far apart in the wide bed, awake and silent. She could not speak, and he would not.

May 13

The sunshine, which when Aske first came to this place had only touched the stones of the wall and brought its fleeting warmth as low as to his knees, now, unless clouds cheated him, lay for a longer time each day upon the floor, so that he could even warm his feet in it for a little while. He was standing in the precious sunshine, turning himself slowly about when he heard the key rattle in the lock, and old Ned Stringer came in, shut the door, and tossed a bundle on the floor between them.

"There's what you've been asking for," said Ned, with his sourest face.

"What is it?" Aske stared at him, then at the bundle.

"Looks to me like a coat for your back."

Aske stooped. He fumbled at the knot before he could get it open. Then he looked blankly at Ned. "But these are not mine."

Ned cackled at him. "Do them on. Who cares if they're yours? No, they're not yours neither, but they're from your leman, Master, brought by her own husband. (Out on you for a rank seducer!) Though he seemed a poor fellow, yon husband, with his foul teeth, and lank hair; and women's hearts are frail."

Aske, looking down at the open bundle and hearing Ned's words, saw again Laurence Machyn coming across the little twilight garden in this same black doublet with the crimson sleeves; a poor, awkward creature Aske had thought him then.

But now he said: "Hold your tongue, you fool. She's no leman of mine, and may God reward him for his good charity, for he's a truer friend to me than any other."

"Tell me that!" said Ned, and went away sniggering.

May 14

Just before dusk Mr. Kingston, Lieutenant of the Tower, came to inform Lord Darcy that his trial would be to-morrow, at Westminster. Darcy sat over the fire, alone, for to-day the two Percys and Constable had been moved to other quarters, and Kingston, seeing him as if for the first time, said to himself, "He is old. He is ill." He tried to remember how old the old man must be, but could not.

And then Darcy looked up at him with such a quick frosty gleam in his blue eyes that Kingston could not think of him as old at all.

"So Master Cromwell has his false witnesses ready at his tail," said my Lord, and laughed.

"Do you doubt," said Mr. Lieutenant, "that you shall have justice?"

"I doubt it sorely," said Darcy in a friendly, open tone. Kingston shook his head.

"Sir," said he, "I shall show you that you mistake if you think the judgement is foregone, or that my Lord Privy Seal is your enemy."

"Oh! I mistake?"

"Truly you do. As we drank wine but now in my lodging, Beauchamp, Audeley and some others being present, my Lord Privy Seal spoke of your trial. Quod he, 'My Lord's peers may condemn him, for the King's honour's sake, but by God's Passion, I myself will travail to obtain his pardon, the which I am well persuaded the King will not refuse to grant.' "

Darcy had his hands spread out upon his knees and seemed to study them.

"Cromwell said that?" he asked softly.

"He did. He did. I heard him speak so with my own ears."

"I remember," said Darcy, "that the old Cardinal" (he meant Wolsey) "said one day to me that he knew no deeper head than this Cromwell's. And I'd say, 'Nor no blacker heart.'"

"Fie!" cried Master Lieutenant. "How can you so rail on one that would befriend you?" And he began to pace about the chamber till he came to a stand near Darcy, looking down upon him with a reproving frown.

"Well," said Darcy, tilting his head to look up at Kingston, and speaking with a mocking lightness, "I never thought that in these days my peers would do for me what I and others did for my Lord Dacre, maugre the King's and Cromwell's teeth—namely, to acquit me of treason. But now, these words of Cromwell's being known, there is none that may wish me well but will, for the King's honour's sake, cheerfully cast me as guilty, supposing that my life will be spared."

"And then my Lord Privy Seal will get your pardon."

"Master Lieutenant, are you so simple?" He put out a hand, and waved it to move the Lieutenant from his side. "I'll ask you," said he, "as Diogenes the Greek asked King Alexander, to get out of my sunlight, or rather my firelight, for either is very dear to us prisoners."

Master Kingston did not stop after that. Darcy sat on, wrapping himself closer as the fire died down, turning over in his mind all the charges that they might bring against him to-morrow, and his answers; recalling as much as he could of the letters which they might have seized, besides words of his which they might have by report of persons indiscreet or malicious.

"Well," he thought, "it's not from the answers I have given to their interrogations that I shall be charged," and he laughed to himself as he recalled those taunts of his which the clerks had written down word for word, until Privy Seal had cried, "Enough. Enough. Write no more of that." For when they questioned him of his doings he had replied by accusations, and these not against his companions in rebellion, but against those very men who sat at the Council table, and others, not present but in favour, such as my Lord of Norfolk, and his son Surrey.

So he rehearsed his case in his mind, wary as a fox, fierce as an old wild boar. "And we shall see," he said to himself, "when we come to Westminster Hall, whether they will muzzle me so that I cannot speak."

Yet, because he was, for all his spirit, an old man and frail, more and more his thoughts began to slide from what must be to-morrow to what had been, and especially to what had been long ago; so that in his mind he was in the little chapel at Templehurst, which he remembered as far back as he remembered anything. There was the smell of incense, and the fume of snuffed candles hanging in the air; there was the great painted Crucifix above. And at the same time he saw all the candles that stood upon his father's hearse in the chapel blow one way, so that the light slid and rippled over the pall of black and gold tissue. And now, because he himself was little Tom once more, his father stood before his eyes, immensely tall. The servants were dressing him in a gown of rayed cloth that had many gold buttons fastening it all the way down the front from the high collar to the fur-trimmed hem. And little Tom had a pair of wooden knights, carved and painted, and each man jointed on his saddle, that rode at each other as you pulled the strings underneath. They met with a crack, and he woke at a great jerk of his head nodding forward on his breast.

It was time to sleep, since his wits must be keen to-morrow. He got up, and beat on the door to let them know that his servant should come to him.

May 17

July went out shopping very early, with Dickon to carry her basket. She bought a young sucking pig in Newgate Street, and told Dickon to carry it home, saying that she would go on to Goldsmiths' Row because she desired a new silver cup. But when she had watched him out of sight she set off to walk to Westminster.

She found that she should have reached the Great Hall there an hour earlier if she wished to see anything, or even to hear much of this trial of the Northern rebels. All she could do was to press into the crowd that filled the farther end, and there stand wedged, hearing less of the trial itself than of the conversation that went on round about her. For, since all thereabouts must needs miss most of what was going on, they took no pains to listen, but talked, comfortably and pleasantly, among themselves. "And he with the one eye was the traitor Aske?" said a woman. "God put out his other!" "By Cock!" said a big man, "but they'll have their deserts. You shall see that they'll be cast, as Lord Darcy was two days ago, and so they'll hang one and all." "Nay," said another, "but Lords die by the axe." And then they disputed of that, and of the hanging and drawing of lesser traitors. But when July took her hands down from under her veil, unstopping her ears for a minute, they were saying how slow in hatching their goslings were this year. "Ah! That's this long drouth," said a man, and then a thin woman cried, "Chip their shells for them, neighbour, chip their shells."

So July kept her thumbs out of her ears, and strained to hear what was spoken beyond the crowd, where Master Aske was being tried for his life. But someone over there would cough and cough, so that though she listened for his voice she could never be sure that she heard it.

By dint of squeezing and pushing, which brought her black looks from those she pressed against, she managed after a while to draw nearer. But now it was the man with the cough who was answering questions, and what with the huskiness of his voice and his fits of coughing she could make nothing of what he said, and grew almost as impatient with him as the judge was, who would often break in, crying, "Well, I cannot hear you," and to the King's Sergeant-at-law, "Go on to the next point, since he cannot or will not answer."

And Aske, almost voiceless and fighting for his life, felt a rage, and a cramping fear at this malignant injustice which was grappling him down. They were charging him with those things for which the King had granted pardon, and with those things which he had done to keep the country stayed when Bigod rose, only there they twisted his honest deeds and words to treason. For treason they made it that he had not disclosed how Levening had desired his intercession with the Duke of Norfolk; yet to the Duke himself he had disclosed it, when he interceded with him for Levening. And, had he not disclosed it, of what had he then been guilty, seeing that the jury at York had acquitted Levening of treason?

But now it was treason even to have trusted that the King should keep the promises which he made. The blank wrong, he thought, would have kept him dumb, even if his voice had not failed him; and his brain also seemed both blind and bound. Yet, because he was a lawyer, he fought them inch by inch, beating them off from one charge after another; and all to no purpose, for like a sea tide they always came back over the same ground, and if any charge might not in itself amount to treason, "Well," said they at last, "each one plainly showeth your cankered traitorous heart, and together amount to very great treason."

"Jesu!" cried Aske then, finding a little his voice, "now know I what I never learnt before, that ten white pullets make one white swan."

"It shall not profit you," said the judge, "to jest at the King's justice."

At last July realized that the judge's voice, which had spoken so long in a dry, unbroken drone, like a bluebottle shut in a room, had ceased. There was a stir, and the sound of footsteps; far off a door whined, and then shut. A pause followed during which her neighbours in the crowd shuffled their feet and shifted restlessly, telling each other that dinner would be cold if the jurymen were long. This period was broken by the sound of raised voices from the direction of the Court. "What's that? What do they say?" Everyone lent an ear, and then the words came, passed back from mouth to mouth—"They plead guilty."

"Who? Who? All?" So it was questioned, impatiently, for this was a tame ending for a trial. But July only shut her eyes, and shut her lips and waited, almost not breathing, till someone said, "Nay, not all. Only the Percys, Sir John Bulmer, and Hammerton . . ." "And Bulmer's whore," the word came next. That was the first time that July knew that Meg was there among the prisoners. It meant nothing to her.

For a second time a hush spread in a fluttering, whispering way over all the crowd, till they heard the footsteps of the twelve men returning. In the awful quiet the voice of the judge came now quite clearly as he read out the names of the prisoners: Robert Constable, Francis Bigod, George Lumley, John Bulmer, Margaret Cheyne, Robert Aske. To each name the jurors replied with the word "Guilty."

At the end the prisoners were asked had they aught they would say. "Constable?"

"Nothing."

"Bigod?"

"Nothing, except—Nothing."

"Hammerton? Lumley?" Each answered, "No."

"Aske?"

There was a little pause, for Aske was coughing. Then he

said, "Nothing." And at last July knew that she had heard his voice.

The prisoners were brought back through crowded streets where people stared and nudged, whispering together, except where some prentice lads booed at the men, and whistled to make Meg look their way. Just inside Ludgate they were halted for a few moments because a horse was down, and the waggon, loaded with bulging sarplers of wool, blocked the way. The mounted archers' horses came jostling back on the prisoners, and then they all stood, in the open, bland heat of the day, for the sun was now high above the housetops.

In the slight confusion Sir Robert Constable came abreast of Aske. They had not met since they had been together at Templehurst, months ago, but Constable saw that Aske regarded him with as little interest as if they had parted yesterday.

"Heart up, Cousin Aske," said Sir Robert, when Aske turned away a dull, indifferent eye; and then—"Look!"

Aske looked down where the other pointed, and saw, spilt upon the street close beside them, a handful of blue-bells and red campion; some young creatures coming back from the fields this morning must have let them fall, for they were still quite fresh.

Sir Robert stooped quickly and picked them up. He smelt them, and laughed, as if at his own foolishness, and yet for pleasure too.

"So sweet they smell," he said, "and bring to mind sweet things. Take some."

But Aske shook his head as if he were angry, pushing Constable's hand aside, and then the archers moved on, and they were separated.

That evening when Ned Stringer unlocked the door to tell Aske it was time for him to take his turn at the privy, he found the prisoner lying face downward on the straw, his forehead on his crossed arms.

"Come, Master," he said, and turned away, to stand swinging his keys, awkwardly silent.

"Come, Master," he said again, "I never thought I'd see you set down. What then? Do not we all die? And if the pains be sharp, yet they're over before long." He looked round now, and saw that Aske was standing on his feet; he held out one hand towards Ned.

"Here," said he, "take that if you will."

Ned came nearer, and stared at the ring that lay on Aske's palm. It was a very pretty thing, of gold, pearls, and enamel, green and white.

"What's that?" he asked. "I never saw that on your finger."

"I plaited threads from my shirt and hung it round my neck."

"What is it then?"

"It's a token from the King."

"What for? And you'd give it to me! What is it a token for?"

"To promise me pardon for speaking the truth."

Ned cried, "By Cock! You're mad then. You'd give it to me? Why man! there's nothing to fear if you have the King's token."

Aske gave him a look which the old man could not make out; however, he kept the ring and went away down the stairs.

When he came back Ned stared hard at his hands, but there was no ring on any finger.

"What have you done with it?" he cried.

"Cast it down the privy."

"God's Death! You did not!"

"It meant," said Aske, "nothing."

"The King's token—nothing?"

"I am persuaded—nothing. And besides that," said Aske, as he sat down and let his head drop on his clenched fists, "it's justice I want, not mercy. And there's no justice, nor no mercy either. None, I think, under the floor of heaven."

May 18

It was not yet light indoors when the great gross old Doctor of Divinity from the Our Lady Friars in Fleet Street wallowed up the narrow turning stair of the Beauchamp Tower, blowing heavily. The warder stopped, and opened a door. The friar went in past him. Lord Darcy was in the room; he got up, as gaunt as the other was fat, so that they might have passed in a Morality for Gluttony and Abstinence.

"I came betimes—" said the friar, still gasping.

"I thank you for that." Lord Darcy spoke with a very stately courtesy. Then he smiled, and laid his hand a moment on the friar's shoulder; they had known each other for many years, and it was as plain that the friar was moved as that he was unwilling to let it be seen that he was moved. So my Lord went on talking; partly to give him time, partly for sheer delight in talking; for to any captive a listener is as a drink of water to a thirsty man.

"Yesterday," said he, "they told me I should die to-day. Well, 'twas a strange thing, Father. At first I could think of two things only, swinging betwixt them like clock's pendulum. The one was—'I die—*I* die o' Saturday,' and t'other—'It cannot be I.'"

The priest nodded. He might have spoken, but my Lord was not now to be stopped.

"Soon," he said, "why, very soon, in an hour—by the Rood! It was no more—the thing was no longer strange. And then I knew that though I had little time, yet I had to spare for what must be done. For it is indeed a thing remarkable, how few cares trouble a man who is come close to the day of his death."

"There is," said the friar, "one needful care only, and it is that for which I am here."

The old man, with his heavy pouching cheeks and great belly, was one of those whose souls, strenuous and austere, are masked in fat; abstinence bloated him, penance puffed him out. Only if you looked closely at the red, fleshy face, you could see in its grossness, courage, gentleness and a humble spirit. So now, for all his noisy breathing and purpled face, he had put on dignity as if he had put on a vestment.

Darcy went slowly down on his knees to make his last confession.

That was hardly done when there came a knock at the door.

"*Nunc dimittis, Domine, servum tuum in pace,*" murmured my Lord, whose face, purged of passion by the solemnities and mercies of his late concernments, was still as a carved face on a tomb.

The Lieutenant of the Tower came in. Darcy moved towards the door, but Kingston waved him back. He said there was word from the King's Grace that my Lord should not die to-day.

"If not to-day—when?" Darcy asked, sooner than either of the others had thought he would find his voice.

Mr. Kingston did not know.

"Well," said Darcy, and was able to smile, "I may yet die in my bed. And yet I care not, whether it be so or no."

But the two could see that he was still shaken by the stress of not knowing when he should die, though that was the very state in which he had passed all his life until yesterday.

So the fat old friar, disregarding Kingston's gesture towards the door, plumped himself down upon one stool, and my Lord sat upon the other, and when Kingston had gone they were silent for a long time, looking, each of them, at the ashes upon that hearth where Darcy had not expected to see another fire kindled.

Wat had seen the window in the roof change from the coping of a well into which you looked upwards and saw only deep darkness and slowly wheeling stars, to a square of faint grey, and, at last, of pallid light. He got up and crawled along the loft softly so as not to waken Malle. But she was awake, and, though he scowled and shook his head at her, she followed him down the ladder, and when he got into the street she was beside him. So they went together towards the river, Wat walking on the balls of his feet and crabwise, ready to spring away did she try to catch him.

The sky above the houses was invisible, and a cold mist lay close over all; sometimes it moved at a puff of light wind, but for the most part it clung, still and white, to the chimneys and roof-tops, growing thicker and more chilling as they came closer to the Thames.

At the top of the Tower Wharf Steps they met some fishermen going up homewards, bare-legged, bare-footed, with their hoods pushed back on their shoulders, carrying the wet, sharply-reeking nets over their shoulders, and dripping creels of fish.

At the foot of the steps, since the tide had already run far out, there was sand, firm, smooth and clean as though this was the first of days and the world just come new from God's making. Moored beyond the lowest dropping of the tide lay the fishermen's boat, and the track of their feet led up from the water's edge, with here and there a swept patch of sand where a trailing lappet of the nets had dragged behind them. Round about the boat, on the sleek, grey, sleepily swinging water, the gulls sailed, or dozed upon the boat's gunwale.

Malle sat down on a rock beside a little pool. The water in the pool was clear almost as the air; the sand at the bottom was sharply ribbed in the semblance of ripples, one ripple following another, and each smooth, regular, perfect—motion translated into form by the cunning, fingerless hands of the tide, which had worked this craftsmanship during the night.

Wat went on towards the water's edge, following the shallow winding channel which the escaping water had made as it slipped from the brimming pool back to the river. The channel was empty of water now but still marked with the waving lines of its flowing, and edged with tiny cliffs, sharply cut as if built of rock, but all of the cessile sand, and all less than an inch in height.

Down by the water's edge that same bright brown sand was dark with wetness, yet the wetness was bright too, as if it were a shining skin laid over the sand. Wat's footsteps squeezed it dry and pale for an instant, then, as he passed, the water seeped up again so that there was no trace to show where he had trod. Here and there smooth stones broke the gleaming film, clear cold blue, red with a streak of buff, yellow flawed with green; all watery colours brought to life by water. A little farther out the shallowest sliding edge of the receding tide slipped in and out with a hiss, and along this Wat moved slowly, all his life in the soles of his feet to feel the stir of the prawns under the sand, and then to snatch them out and drop them into his canvas pouch for breakfast-time.

Long before he had as many prawns as he wished he heard Malle calling, "Wat! Wat! Come!"

He went to her, lagging, and when he was near would not come within reach of her hands.

She said: "There is darkness, and God moving nigh-hand in the darkness."

Wat made a growling noise in his throat and swung away on one foot. But he could not go. So he stayed to listen, a shoulder hunched between him and her.

Malle said: "All the black night, with not one candle left, not one star, they've dragged Him with them, and now they have Him to judgement before the dawn comes. The fire's lit and burning, and there's a window the blind morning looks through, and another, and that way's the moon; so day and dark may see the light that made them taken in the hands of men."

She turned away and looked up to where above the empty strand and the wharf the great bulk of the Tower loomed, huge and sullen in the mist. High up the King's banner hung dead upon its staff.

"Man," said Malle, "would take swords, bows and bills to save Him. And the angels wait to break Heaven and let burning justice and the naked spirit flake down in flame to heat to scorched souls those men that bear God to die, that so they may know their Maker.

"But He will not. Look, Wat, look! There He is, and holdeth in His hands that glass vessel, clear, precious, brimmed full with clean righteousness. So He hath carried it without spilling, through life and now through death. That shining water's His pure righteousness to wash clean all the world's sins.

"Ah!" she cried, "stay them! Stay them! lest with their swords they shatter the glass and so the water is spilled, for we need it every drop."

She looked at Wat, and he cowered away.

"Sword cannot save righteousness—only spill it for the thirsty ground to drink. And that He knoweth."

She said: "There was the old Lord who came to Marrick saying he was a merchant man. Come and tell him this thing."

But though the two of them managed to come within the Tower by following a young girl who brought in eggs to the house of Master Partridge of the Mint, they did not come to my Lord Darcy. For near the Beauchamp Tower one of Master Kingston's men met and questioned them, and set his pikestaff about their shoulders, and drove them, with blows, and much shouting, out of the place again.

At the distant noise of that commotion Lord Darcy jerked his head round to listen and drew in his breath sharply. When there was silence again he turned back, but now he smiled bitterly.

"They should have had my head this morning. By now I had passed, and I was ready to die."

He brought his fist down on his knee.

"Now," he said, "I am not ready. Now I must hope to live, and yet look to die. Yea, and if I die, I die for the faith of Christ, for which we of that Pilgrimage took arms; yet, if I die, I die because we Northern men were betrayed by the rest," and he began to rail upon the Marquis of Exeter, "a sheep," he called him; and Lord Montague, "that will stumble at any mole-hill, and the other Poles but leaves in the wind.

"So now," he said, "is the King and this Cromwell set higher than ever."

"My son—"

Darcy did not let the friar say further. "My Father!" he

mocked, and shot out his finger at the other's face, "if you, you the spiritual men, had but called upon all the realm, gentlemen, nobles, and commons to rise, they had risen, for Holy Church, and Christ, and for righteousness' sake."

"My son," said the friar, "whether you die to-morrow, or whether you live, put aside from you those thoughts. For I tell you surely, that's not God's way."

"Not—" cried Darcy; and then, while the friar held his eyes, he grumbled angrily, "Is it not then? Well, an' if it be not? Tell me how, then? What other way? How? How? Is it not foolishness to think—"

He did not finish, for the old friar stood up.

" 'Stultitia Dei,' " he said. "It *is* foolishness. It is God's foolishness that is wiser than men."

Darcy did not move nor speak for a long time. At last he raised his head, and the friar saw something that was almost a smile on his face.

"Well," said my Lord lightly, but as men speak lightly before a last, hopeless fight, "I am not of so holy a mind as to be able to take God's way. But," he said, and met the friar's eyes, "I'll not grudge to die. It may be He will accept that for service."

Then he stretched out his hand, and said good-bye.

The Chronicle of Thomas, Lord Darcy, ends here.

May 14

When Gib came to Lord Privy Seal's house in Throgmorton Street, and asked for my Lord's chaplain, he was told that there were orders that he should be brought up to my Lord himself. "Ha!" thought Gib, as he went after the servant through a big hall, and along a passage, "so my Lord has taken note of my writings. He would not have sent for me, but to commend me."

The servant let him into a small, pleasant, sunny room with a big painted mappemonde on the wall, all scarlet and blue, with ships here and there upon the seas, and cities, walled and bristling with towers and spires. At the table sat Lord Privy Seal, and his two hands lay upon a page of writing that Gib knew very well, for it was his own.

"This," said Cromwell, not even waiting till the servant had shut the door, "this will not serve," and he rapped the backs of his fingers on the page.

Gib was so surprised that he fairly gaped.

"No one," said my Lord, "would laugh at this that you call, 'An Interlude of the Seven Deadly Sins.' "

"They are not meant to laugh," cried Gib, angry now.

"If they laugh not, they listen not," said Cromwell, and threw the papers across the table towards Gib. "Mend it," said he, "or I'll not buy."

That was all. He waved his hand, and the big diamond on his forefinger blazed as the sun caught it. Then Gib was outside the door, and raging.

May 28

Until the bent, sour-looking little man's hand furtively twitched her sleeve, July had not realized that this morning, wherever she went, he had been near. Now, as she turned and looked at him, she knew it, and fright seized her; but before she could call out to Mat, who went in front, the man muttered, "Word from him you love." That for July meant one only; she never doubted whom, nor hesitated what she should do.

"Mat," she said, "Mat," and when he turned, "I forgot, at the Cow in Boots, to buy cardamons. Go back quickly and buy two ounces." When Mat had gone—"Now," said she to the old man, "quick!"

But he would not be quick, objecting that the Cheap was too crowded for such privy business as his, so they turned into Milk Street, and there, under a grey white cloud of a flowering cherry tree that branched above them over a wall, he pulled out of his doublet some writings.

"A letter?" cried July. "I can't read writings." But her hand stretched out to take it, for at least his hands had touched the paper.

"Aye," said Ned Stringer, putting her fingers by. "For the King, and for Privy Seal," and he told her, sharply and angrily, as if he hated the whole business, that yon fellow, the traitor Aske, in the Tower, had written to them begging mercy.

"Mercy?" July whispered it. She had never thought of mercy.

"Aye. But he's stiff-necked. I told him, 'Down on your knees to 'em. Confess your fault. Beg! Pray! Howl if you will. What matter so you scape the pains you dread when they cut you down.' " And in July's sight the man made an awful

[680]

pantomime of the executioner's business; and then stared at her, and grinned in her face.

"For he doth dread them. He says, 'If I might but be full dead before I be dismembered—' Oh! I promise you he dreads them well enough, however he may feign. I can see him turning the thought over and over like hay in a wet June. Well—well. So I brought him paper, and 'Write,' I says, 'and none of your pride,' says I. But what will he write? No goodly humbleness, but only 'for the reverence of God and for charity.' "

"Give them to me," said July, through her teeth, and tried to snatch the letters. But again he fended her off.

"Na! Na! Wait till I tell you. There's that one, on the big sheet to the King's Grace, for that was the fairest piece I could come by. And this other is to Privy Seal, and that little bit too goes with it, for at the last he remembered, said he, one in Yorkshire, a poor man whom he had, so he said, defrauded of his land, though unwitting, and now would right him." He held the papers out now to July and she laid her hand on them, but he did not yet let go.

"Will ye swear that ye will take them to the King and Privy Seal?"

"I will take them," said July.

"Well," said the old man, his eyes boring into her face, "I believe you will," and he cackled suddenly as if lovers and their love were a sour jest.

"Did he—" asked July, looking down at the papers which their two hands held. "Did he—at once think of me to carry them? Of me—before all other?"

Ned looked at her. He read, in her averted face and hesitating speech, misgiving and withdrawal. He could not know how July did not dare to look up, desiring so greatly the answer "Yes," knowing that the answer must be "No."

And it was "No." For old Ned began to excuse Aske. " 'Twasn't him thought on you. 'Twas I. He says, 'None will dare take it.' So then I says, 'There's your leman,' says I. 'Try her.' But he was angry with me for that, only at the last he said, 'Tell her then that she shall run into no danger for me. For that,' says he, 'would be worse to me than death, seeing I have been cause of bringing so many into danger. Yet,' he says, 'if she may without danger, tell her I'll pray God bless her for it for ever.' "

He waited a moment, and then made as if to take back the papers. But July snatched them then from him.

"Will ye do it then?" he said, but got no answer from her, as she turned away and left him standing there.

May 31

July met Master John Heath, Laurence's cousin's cousin, the one who was in Lord Privy Seal's Household, as he had appointed at the West end of St. Paul's. It was raining, a soft, misting rain after a great fall during the night, and she was glad of it because she could muffle herself up in her cloak in such a way that none would know her.

From Paul's they went down together to take a boat at the Cranes for Westminster. July was too breathless to talk, seeing that the child was growing a heavy burden, and Master Heath, not liking the business, hurried on always a little ahead of her. Once he pulled up where a pool had swilled out of the blocked kennel and halfway across the road.

"You tell the truth when you say you formerly were affianced to this man?"

"Surely I was," said July, hastening to tell her tale once more, "but then my sister's husband would not pay my dower, and therefore—"

"And," Master Heath continued, without letting her finish, "and it's true also that you came then together, being betrothed."

"It is true."

"Well," said Master Heath, "I've promised you, and so I shall bring you to the Queen. Woman's frail, and if you thought of this fellow Aske as your husband, and if he so used you before you were married to my cousin—"

"He had me in the North Country before I came here to my marriage—just before," said July.

"Well," he looked her up and down with suspicion, "I've never seen a wench carry what must be nigh a nine months' child with as little show as you."

"All women," said July, "are not the same." Then she laughed, as if the matter were a light one and as if she were not desperate with fear lest he should, even now, refuse to help her. "And surely it is I that should know whose is the child."

He laughed too, and leered at her with a familiar, insulting look. But then again he hesitated.

"It's the truth you say? I'll not help you if you've wronged my cousin's bed."

"It's the truth, as God shall judge me. I'll swear it on my Maker at the next church, if you will."

But he said No, he'd believe her, only it went sore against his mind that it should be a rank traitor that had her maidenhead, and he hurried her on again.

By the time they reached Westminster the rain had taken off and the sun shone, so that all the puddles flashed, and the roads steamed; when they came into the Palace Gardens the rose bushes were dressed with diamonds, and the briar rose leaves smelt of sun-warmed apples. As they drew nearer to the Palace there were no rose bushes but tall posts striped white and green, set in puncheons painted with the same colours; the posts had painted and gilded beasts and escutcheons of arms on top. There were too, instead of grass, curious beds of pounded colours set among clipped borders; the gardeners were busy here smoothing away the pock marks which the rain had left in the King's coat of arms, and the Queen's.

The sun was bringing other people out too, besides the gardeners. As July and Master Heath went by the long range of buildings two young men came through a little low doorway; they stooped because they were so tall; and because they were so broad in their puffed sleeves the silks whistled against the stone of the doorway as they came through. They went past laughing, and with only a sliding glance that took in July's pale pinched face and brown stuff gown. July did not look at them at all, but she saw them well enough to hate them for being free and in no danger of the hangman's knife.

She and Master Heath turned into a little paved court, where a dog was busy with a bone; then by an open stairway into a gallery which was bare of tapestries and swept of its strawing herbs. Servants were just then casting down fresh strawings out of big bundles of sacking, and raking them into smooth swathes. As the sweet herbs and rushes tumbled out all the gallery smelt as if the summer fields were come within its four walls.

After that gallery they went on through passages, upstairs, downstairs, through rooms great and small, some empty, some furnished; in some there were ladies, young and old, and children, as well as men reverend and men saucily or grandly young. It was more like going through a whole street of houses than through one house.

At last Master Heath stopped in a gallery where there was a small oriel jutting out, and told July to wait there till he could find out at what hour the Queen would pass by on her way to the Chamber of Presence. July went to the oriel and sat down. She felt the child kick strongly in her body; clutching her hands tight across him, and shutting her eyes, she went over once more the lies that she would tell, not liking them at all since they dishonoured Master Aske, but trying them on her tongue so as to be sure that they were plausible and likely to move another woman, also great with child.

She heard a door open and started up; she had not thought that Master Heath would so soon have returned. But it was not Master Heath. A dozen or so ladies were coming into the room preceded by two elderly persons in black velvet with gold chains, one of whom carried in his hand a white wand. Among the ladies was one young, very fair in complexion, with a pleasant prim face; she wore as many jewels, sewn upon her gown, and loading her neck and fingers, as a May Day Queen wears flowers. Behind her, with one hand on her shoulder, puffed and huge in purple and cloth of gold, came the King, rolling in his walk, and limping a little.

July went out from the shelter of the window, and sank down on her knees, less for reverence than for fear lest she should fall.

"Your Grace . . ." she cried, and dragged Aske's petition from where it lay between her breasts. "Madame, have mercy on an unhappy man, and thereby upon a most wretched woman."

The King took the letter; he read it. July saw the small mouth tighten and sneer. She averted her eyes from his face, and, looking nowhere but at the Queen, began to pour out that same tale she had told to Cousin Heath—all lies, yet the Queen listened, as July harped desperately upon that one string: "the child—the child—his child."

But the King broke in.

"You ask mercy, Mistress, for a traitor, because you carry his bastard," and at that the Queen flushed and turned her head away.

July laid hold of the skirt of her gown and felt the jewels and the gold stitching harsh and crisp under her fingers. The Queen tried to free herself, but July clenched her hands tighter.

She could say no more. To beg mercy for love's sake was impossible, for that would trench upon the truth, huge, inmost, which might not be come at in speech. But she thought —"I'll not let her go. I can't let her go," since to let the Queen go would deliver him to torment.

She heard the King cry, "Off! Pull her off!" But then Queen Jane's eyes met hers again. She said no word, but none was needed.

July loosed her hold, and the Queen laid her hand upon the King's sleeve.

"Sir," she said, "Sir, if I asked mercy for my sake? I do ask it."

"He shall not live."

"Oh!" July cried, repeating the words that Ned Stringer had used, and which had never been silent since in her mind. "Oh! If he could but be full dead before he be dismembered!"

The King's glance, oblique and contemptuous, came back to her face.

"Will that content you? And—him?" He watched her while she nodded. "You think it will? Well then, he shall have that. Tell him that surely he shall hang till he be full dead."

He went away, July had only time to snatch the Queen's hand and kiss it before she too went after the King.

June 15

July, who was alone in the kitchen, the women both being out, heard Laurence come into the house, and go upstairs. After a while, since she must go up sooner or later, she took the dish of honey cakes which she had been baking, and going slowly through the Hall began to climb the stairs. She had her head bent, so that it gave her a start when she saw his feet upon the stair above her; she raised her eyes and found him standing looking down at her.

"Strumpet!" he said, speaking quite softly, and struck at her face with his fist.

It was a wild, swinging blow, and she dodged it easily, but in doing so she lost her footing, tried to grab the rail, and began to fall. As she fell she heard him cry, "July!" and again, again, "Strumpet!"

She picked herself up at the bottom of the stairs, and, dazed and shaken, began to collect the cakes, but then the pains began. He came down to where she leaned against the wall, peering at her and whispering to know what was the matter. Yet really he knew at once what it must be, though July could only shake her head in answer.

So he got her upstairs as best he could and then rushed out to find a woman to help her.

June 30

July sat in Laurence's father's chair, which the journeyman had brought out into the sun for her. Every now and then one of the women would put her head through the open kitchen window and ask if she needed anything. Oftener than that Laurence would come from the workshop, and look at her, and go back again. July answered the maids, because they asked her a question. As Laurence said nothing, but only looked, she did not need to answer him, nor did she turn her head when he came out, though she knew quite well that he was there. She sat staring before her at the bell-flowers, sweet Williams and tall white lilies, and at the washing hung out on the line, men's breeches, women's smocks and sheets and kitchen clouts. Not one of these things, from the lilies to the oldest torn clout, was more lovely to her eyes than any other, or of more significance.

She heard from the house the sound of the women talking, clattering their pails, or churning the clothes in the big tub with the wooden dollypeg. From further away came the noises of the street—grinding of wheels, boy's whistling, sing-song cries of hucksters of lavender, fish, milk, and just now of fine raspberries. She heard, without remarking, one of the women open the street door and begin to haggle over a price. Then the elder of the two came into the garden, and set on her knees an earthen pot full of raspberries.

"There, mistress!" she said. "There's the first of the season." She was a woman with a kind, plain, lined face. "And for the one child that miscarried," she said, "there'll be plenty more in time to come," and before she went away she gave July's shoulder a little pat with her hand, which was pale purple, soft, wet and wrinkled from the wash-tub.

July looked down at the smouldering soft crimson of the raspberries. She did not want them. Nor did she want another child. Nor did she want the one that passed from dark to dark. The one thing she wanted was to know if Master Aske were alive or dead, and here there was no one to tell her, since she could not ask Laurence, and the maids would not know.

Laurence came out of the workshop again, and this time he did not go back, but instead threw down upon the ground a big pair of cloth shears which he had in his hands, and came towards her. There was a little low stool beside her chair, upon which she had set the raspberries. He took them up and sat down on it, looking up at her as she looked down at him. Then each turned away.

He began to take the raspberries one by one and put them into his mouth, as if he were very hungry. But in a moment he spun round on the stool and laid the pot down on the ground, and so turned away from her he said—

"Wife, do you forgive me?"

"Oh! Yes." July was indifferent.

"When I thought you would die I did not care whether —I did not care for anything but that you should live, and should forgive me. You do forgive?"

"Yes," she said again, as evenly.

He was fidgeting with his foot so that he tossed the pot over and the raspberries tumbled out on the ground. He at once began to pick them up as if the matter were one of the greatest moment and urgency. "Yet," he said as he stooped, "if you could tell me truly—if I knew whether—if the child was his— You told the King so."

"Yes. It is. It was. Yes, I told the King," she said, not even wondering how he had come to hear so much, but thinking how she might learn if Master Aske were dead, and safe from pain.

He sat quite still for a moment, then he said, "It makes no difference now. You are all that I love, and that is all I know."

When she heard him say that she was pricked by a thin small shaft of remorse. Yet though she was sorry, she hardened her heart, for she thought, "If I say it was a lie, and the King should hear of it, he might be angry and take a vengeance on *him*." But then, with a quick pang of hope and dread, another thought came— "If I first make him swear to tell no one, I might find out from him whether *he* still lives."

So she asked him, would he swear? "And I'll tell you the truth," she said.

He swore, his eyes on hers, and she told him, and he turned from her once more, "So I killed my son," he said, and after what seemed to her a great while, "But we shall have more. Shall we not?"

"Yes," she said. "Yes," speaking hastily because she could contain herself no longer. She was aware neither that her hands were gripped together on her lap till they shook, nor that he watched them.

"Sir," she whispered, not trusting her voice if she spoke louder, "is he dead?"

He said nothing, and now she dared not look at him. At last he got up. "I will go and find out," he said, and left her.

He went, not knowing clearly why he went at once so far, nor what he should do when he got there, straight through London to the Tower. He had some idea of asking a porter at the gate, or one of the guard, but it turned out to be easier than that. When he came by the foot of the green space to the north of the Tower, he found several men working on a temporary scaffold which had been set up there, and which they were now pulling down. Two others were forking together, and pitching into a cart, straw that was sodden in places with dark brownish red, and one of these was the old fellow to whom Laurence had given the bundle of clothes, and who, it was clear, at once remembered him, and was ready to talk.

There was plenty to talk about, for to-day Lord Darcy had been beheaded on that scaffold, and the old man was full of it. He knew also the latest news of the two last surviving prisoners of the North Country insurrection, Constable and Aske, so that Laurence had not to put a single question.

When he got back July was sitting in the garden where he had left her.

He said, "They took him from the Tower two days ago. It is to be done at York."

"How long will it take them to get to York?"

But Laurence could not tell her.

She said, "I thank you," and after a minute he left her and went back to the workshop.

July 15

July stood by the kitchen table absently fingering the leaves of the rue that lay tumbled on it. There was a bowl of clean water to wash the rue, and an iron pot in which to boil it when washed. Rue boiled long, and strained, was good for the kidneys; Laurence believed much in it, and had asked for it last Christmas when the snow fell, and had lamented the lack of it through the long cold spring. So now she was preparing it against next winter.

Yet if you looked through the kitchen door you might think that there would never be winter again, so gallant was the little space with flowers. The last of the sweet Williams had been overtaken by pinks, carnations, and the first of the snap-dragons; above, in the bright sky, the swifts fled like arrows, and turning, flashed like dark wet gold against the sun. Over all lay the triumphant, open heat of perfect summer weather.

But July was thinking neither of the rue on the table nor of the summer shows outside. She was listening to the bell of St. Andrew in the Wardrobe tolling for a burial. This was not one of Laurence's burials, but July knew all about it, because his cousin Henry Machyn was furnishing it, and Laurence had gone out to help him, and had lent him hangings for the church, and two dozen staff torches; Cousin Henry had on this same day another funeral, almost as great, at St. Martin's, Charing Cross, so he had needed to borrow from Laurence.

When July had listened to the bell for quite a time she suddenly began to bestir herself, bundling the rue into its washing water, and from that, with scant care, into the pot. Calling to one of the women to have an eye on it, she went upstairs for her cloak and hood, and then to the workshop. It was empty except for young Dickon, who had been left behind with plenty to do in cleaning of brushes and grinding of paints. But when July came in he pocketed a pair of dice, and jumped up. "Get the basket," said July, "and come with me."

But she was not going shopping—at least, not yet, and she told Dickon, "I shall go first to church."

"Aye," said the boy, politely though without enthusiasm; but when he understood that she would go to St. Andrew's to see them bring in the corpse of Sir William Laxton, Knight and Grocer and Alderman of London, it was a very different matter.

And even as they came to the church door they could see the procession moving towards them up the street. "Ooh!" cried Dickon, jumping up and down to see better, and then climbing up on the plinth of the church porch, and clinging to the stone like a tomtit to a tree. "Ooh! here they come! See the escutcheons nid-nodding. And the candles, so many!" July looked back from the steps. The crowded escutcheons of arms upon their poles were bright as a garden of flowers, and beyond them the great candles moved close as a thicket, but the flames of these, borne backward as the procession moved, made but a pale show against the sunshine. She gave one glance and then went on into the church.

Here, when the door swung to behind her, there was sudden darkness and quiet, with a sour and solemn smell of old incense, damp, and stale rushes. Two priests moved about in the sanctuary; they looked round as they heard her lift the latch, but she slipped away behind a pillar and knelt down out of sight.

Only when all the train of choirmen and boys, bearers and mourners, had brought the dead Grocer into church and set him down below the painted Rood, did July shuffle out cautiously from where she lurked. Now, in the dimness of the church, the colours of the escutcheons showed only gloomily, but the candle flames, winking and fluttering, were warm gold and very bright. In the midst, where the light was brightest from the clustered candles set on the hearse, she could just see the crimson and cloth of gold pall which covered the coffin.

Requiem aeternam dona eis, Domine; et lux perpetua luceat eis.

The voices rose and fell in the chant, answering each other in words which she did not understand, yet knew, as she knew, mistily, the intent of them.

In diebus illis: Audivi vocem de caelo: dicentem mihi, Scribe. Beati mortui: qui in Domine moriuntur. Amodo jam dicit Spiritus: ut requiescant a laboribus suis . . .
Requiem aeternam dona eis Dominie: et lux perpetua luceat eis . . .

"Give him rest eternal . . . Give him light . . . A voice from heaven saying, 'Blessed are the dead, for they rest . . . Rest, and light.' "

So the words went by in July's mind, yet less akin to words than to musical sounds, disembodied, piercing home beyond the reach of words.

For her it was not the body of that prosperous Knight and Grocer which lay under the crimson, golden-gleaming pall.

It was Robert Aske's body, and it was his spirit that waited now its dismissal among all lovely and loving shows, lights, singing and the presence of friends and lovers. For surely now he must be dead; and if he was dead, then at peace. And perhaps, thought July, death is the best thing, and I need not have feared, because there is always death, and it will not have hurt him long. And surely he must be dead.

She got up from her knees, and was surprised to find Dickon at her elbow, for she had forgotten him.

"Where do we go now, Mistress?" he asked, skipping along beside her, but whispering because of the solemnity of the church.

"To buy some cucumbers," said July.

On that same day, and at about the same time that July was in church, Robert Aske made his confession, and received absolution. He heard Dr. Curwen, the Priest, finish the Office, leave the altar, and come near. Yet he knelt for a moment longer in the little chapel of the Keep at York. When he stood up he must go to the top of the tower to his hanging.

He found himself upon his feet.

"Sir," he said, "I am ready. And I pray God bless the King's Grace for letting me pass without those pains which—"

He stopped, not because Dr. Curwen had said anything, or even moved. Yet he stopped, and waited for the Priest to speak.

Dr. Curwen cleared his throat. He looked at the altar, he looked at the floor. He said: "Aske, it is the King's will, that since you think it a religion to keep hidden between God and you the names of those traitorous persons whom you know of in the South parts—it is his will that you shall hang in chains until you die."

Aske felt his cheek grow cold and his heart begin to jump, before, it seemed, his brain understood what it was that Curwen had said. Then he understood it fully.

"God!" he whispered, and cried again, "God!" so loud that his voice cracked on the word.

Jack Aske, and the other Yorkshire gentlemen bidden to York by the Duke of Norfolk, and now waiting on top of the Keep, heard the cry. More than one of them started, looked aside at his neighbour, and then as quickly away. Jack shut his eyes, and hoped not to fall. In the silence that followed they heard the soft purr of the wind against the battlement, and except for that nothing but the sounds (and they were very slight sounds) of the crowd below. Yet it was a great crowd, York being full for market day, and all the market now deserted for this business of the hanging of the Great Captain of the Pilgrims.

There was a stir at the open door of the stair which came out on the roundway. The Duke's foot soldiers came up, and among them, but alone, the prisoner. Jack shrank back, but even so if he had reached out a hand he could have touched Robin as he passed by with a blank face, and his blank eye socket ("Thank God!" thought Jack) on this side.

Then up came the Duke of Norfolk, whom Jack and all those other gentlemen must salute, as he saluted them with a grave but courteous air. And all the time, as Robin's brother uncovered, and as he received the Duke's greeting, he was in an agony lest Robin should see him there.

He need not have feared. Robert Aske had no wits just now to see anyone. He stood, dumb and still, while they fixed the irons about him, brought him to the ladder, and helped and hauled him up it. He heard Dr. Curwen's voice saying the prayers that he knew, and by some compulsion in him, when the Doctor's voice stopped, he made the necessary responses. But all his mind and will were bent upon one thing only, and that was so to rule his body that when he was cast off it should neither struggle nor scream.

He could not altogether rule it. When he swung out, and the irons bit him, he did struggle, because he must. One of his shoes came off, and it seemed to him a frightful thing that he should have to go short of a shoe, until he remembered that he would not ever again tread upon anything but the empty air.

He was alone now. Close beside him the roundway was empty, but when he glanced down into the sickening depth below his feet, he could see that the green space was full of white faces turned up to him.

With a groaning of iron upon iron, he was turning slowly round. The Minister came into sight just as the bells sounded, tossing out their bubbles of sweet sound upon the air. Still he turned; now he saw Fishergate Bar, half ruinous since it had been blocked up for so long, now the wide country beyond, patched golden with harvest, and far away the low hills beyond Aughton.

The hours wore on, and pain grew. Towards evening he began to suffer from thirst.

July was in Mistress Holland's parlour upstairs when the Vintner brought in another man of his mystery, but a stranger, and not of the London Guild. He was a fine old man, with a handsome, kind, quiet face; his name was Master Oldroyd. He and Master Holland sat down in the window seat, and when they all had wine and wafers and cherries ready to hand, the two men talked of men's affairs in low voices, and it seemed sadly, and Mistress Holland continued her interrupted account of the qualities of a new serving-woman. In a few minutes she got up and went out to fetch a new coif to show July, and July sat, not listening nor looking towards the men till she caught a word that Master Oldroyd spoke:

"York?" she said then. Mr. Oldroyd turned to her.

"Do you know York, Mistress?" said he, leaning forward towards her, because he liked young things.

She nodded, though indeed she knew nothing of York but that she had passed through it, once to go North with Meg, once to come to London to her wedding—that, and a fact that filled the earth—that Master Aske had been hanged there.

Master Holland heaved up his hand, let it fall on his thigh with a great clap, and sighed deeply.

"Alas!" said he. "Tell her what you've told me. It will be sad news for her, for Mistress July knows him, and brought him once here to us, and there he sat."

He pointed, and July followed his finger to the place where Master Aske had sat on a settle beside the hearth which was full now of green boughs for summer. Then her eyes came back to Master Oldroyd's face.

"God have mercy on him," said he, "and send him death soon. I tell you it struck me through the heart the other morning when I came by under the Keep, and saw him move —as, poor soul, he will move yet for many a day."

"Move yet?" said July.

"It was but the day after his hanging, for they hanged him last market day, and men that are hanged in chains live longer, much longer, God help him, than that."

July looked down at her hands as they lay on her lap, but she did not see them or anything else in the room. She only heard the King say, "Surely he shall hang till he be full dead."

Master Oldroyd sighed. "God help him," he said again. "But did you indeed know him, Mistress?"

"Since I was a young child," July said out of a dead body.

She did not leave at once. Mistress Holland came back with the coif, and turned it about to show it off, and July said it was pretty. Master Oldroyd got up, and took his leave, and he and Master Holland went away. Mistress Holland peered at July, patted her hands and said that indeed she looked but poorly yet.

It was then that July said that she must go, and followed Mistress Holland downstairs. It seemed to her to be ages of years after the time that Master Oldroyd had come into the room.

She said good-bye to Mistress Holland, was kissed, was given—and said thanks for—a basket of cherries. There was no hurry. Master Oldroyd had said that he would live a long time yet.

But once she had parted from the Vintner's wife haste devoured her and she fled through the streets, seeing nothing, hearing nothing; needing, before she dared to think, one thing—to be alone.

That morning Malle and Wat had to carry a big pannier of clean, washed linen to the Hostess of the Dolphin. They came back along Bishopgate, Malle going in front and Wat keeping warily off, a few paces after. But just before the gate Malle turned.

"Wat!" she said. "Wat!" and though it was broad day her hands went out as though she felt about for him in a dark place.

He slipped away, so as to put a man with a barrow-load of fresh lettuce between them. Then he made as if to run, yet turned and came again to her, though shrinkingly.

She said: "Darkness, and God moving nigh-hand in the darkness."

Wat seized a handful of her gown and dragged her with him till they were out of the busy street and upon one of the little paths that led, vagrant as sheep tracks, among the thorn bushes in the narrow space between the houses here and the Town Ditch. There was no one about except two old men fishing, a few children, and some tethered goats. Wat pushed Malle down on a little bank where butter-and-eggs and pale vetch grew; he went a little way from her and crouched down, keeping his eyes on her face, as still as a rabbit before a stoat.

Malle said: "Darkness is made over all the earth, deep

as the sea, hissing bitter and black with pain, salted sharp with all men's sins. And He drowns there, hanging from the nails they have stricken through his hands."

Wat moaned and grumbled in his throat, and below them beside the water one of the old men swept up his float and cast it back again with a little plop.

Malle said, "So is He gone down under those waves." She lifted her head and her eyes widened. "Look!" she said. "The Dale's full of light. He has set on fire the sea. Not even the deep waters can quench Him, but He comes again, flaming and shining with the bitter sea itself to be His new coat. Hurt and harm are His coat, and a glory that the young stars didn't know. Light has licked up the dark water. Love has drunk sorrow, rejoicing, and the great Angel of Pain is redeemed."

She stood up.

"Come, little knave," she said, "there's one at the Manor that needs must be told."

But when they found July, hurrying through the streets, and Malle went along with her, telling her what she had seen, and pulling now and again at July's arm to make sure she heard, July only struck her off.

Indeed July marked her no more than one passing through the woods in summer marks the tower of gnats that swims above his head as he goes.

When she came into the house, having slammed the door upon Malle, there was no one in the Hall, so she stood a moment, looking down into the hearth, filled with green boughs for summer, but blackened by fire. She was alone at last; yet now she found that to be alone gave Master Oldroyd's words more room to swell, and swell.

One of the serving maids came in and asked her a question. What the words meant July could not tell. She said, "I do not know. You must see to it," and the answer seemed to fit, because the woman went away. But that had shown July that she could not endure to be found again, and spoken to, especially to be found by Laurence, with his piercing, anxious love.

Then she remembered, as if it had been a thing told her many years ago, that he would be out all this morning, and the men too, preparing a great burial, so that the workshops would be empty. She went out into the yard. The young dog, which was lying in the sun, leapt up, wagging and fawning. He followed her to the door, but she shoved him from it with her foot and shut him out, and stood a moment, staring, but blindly, about the workshop, with its litter of brushes, spilt, powdered colours, and clean cold smell of the lime tempering over all. Yet because she had not gone far enough till she had gone as far as she could, she went on, and climbed the ladder to the loft above, where to-day there was nothing but dust, dust and cobwebs, some odd bits of rope lying about, and one long length hanging from the truss of the roof timbers.

The rope hung dangling before her eyes. It hung.

Laurence found the dog scratching and yelping at the workshop door. It was an eager ratter, so he said to it, "Good dog. Rats!" and let it in. But it rushed to the foot of the ladder, floundered up a few rungs, and when it slipped back, lifted its head and howled.

So he went up and found July. He shouted till one of the men came, and they were able to get her down. Then, in the thick dust, they worked on her. When they had almost given up hope, she breathed.

The first thing July knew was the sparver of the bed above her as she lay on her back. She heard, and seemed for a long time to have heard, a little regular clicking noise. She turned her head with a sudden huge pain, and saw that Laurence sat on a stool beside the bed; he slipped his beads briskly through his fingers but his eyes were on her face.

It was as he got up and leaned over her that she remembered, and she whispered before he could speak—

"He hangs alive in chains. He is not dead."

Laurence sat down again. Now she did not even hear the click of his beads, and again she lay, simply staring upwards.

"Wife," said Laurence suddenly, "we must pray God for him."

She cried, so that it tore her throat—"No. He made pain, He chose it for Himself." That was all she could say, and Laurence must guess the rest. God who had made pain, so that all the universe was corrupt with it, God would do nothing to help one who, hanging in chains, moved yet.

Laurence stood up, and again bent over her. But this time he took her hands in his and held them closely.

"You do not understand," he said. "There's nothing to fear in pain. Love makes it all different. I love you. If I might suffer for you I would be *glad*."

Her eyes came to him, startled, staring wide, and her face changed as she slipped back from him into unconsciousness. Seeing that change he thought she was slipping right away from him into death, and he rushed to the door and shouted for the women.

The Chronicle of Julian Savage ends here.

July 20

Gib had just birched one of the bigger boys, thereby obtaining a silence, sudden, uneasy and charged with rebellion. But at least it was a silence, for which he was thankful, especially when Master Hawkes opened the door and walked in. He was pleased also to see Master Hawkes, who was a Mercer, a man of substance and a great favourer of the Gospel. "He knows me," thought Gib, "for what I am. He sees that I am a man of parts. He is my fellow-Christian, like-minded with me and with all who care for God's honour." That was the second thought which he substituted for the first, yet not so quickly but that he was aware, and ashamed of the other.

"Now," said he to the boys, "con your books," and he brought Master Hawkes away to his own chair, and sitting down there led him into conversation of this Commission that had been set up to determine beliefs. Now and again he had to scowl over his shoulder as the tide of noise began again to flow. At first it was only a rustling. Soon one of the youngsters yelped like a puppy as someone jabbed his seat with a knife point; someone else dropped a book and there was a scuffling of feet and sound of hard breathing and stifled laughter, as they covertly fought over it. That was the worst of children; you could never be free of the care of them as long as they were with you. Shallow-witted, idle and frivolous themselves, so that a man must be always straining to dwarf himself to their littleness, they would never allow him to be at peace to speak with another man. So Gib could have only half his mind upon these Articles of the Bishops, which were to bring all England to a conformity in belief, and of which Master Hawkes was discoursing; it fretted him the more that this was so, because Master Hawkes had private knowledge of what went on behind closed doors, he having a cousin in the Household of Hugh Latimer, Bishop of Worcester.

[697]

"Tunstall and Stokesley," said the Mercer, "gave and took many shrewd raps that day, so I hear."

"Yet they shall not have the better, proud papist prelates that they are," cried Gib, with a tight smile. "That I'll warrant."

The other rubbed his plump, firm jowl with one finger.

"As I see it," said he, "the issue pleases and displeases both them and us. For they have said their own way over their seven sacraments—"

"Fie!" said Gib. "Shall we never be free of this prating of sacraments?"

"Yet Faith is set clear above any sacrament."

"That's well done!"

"And as clear our men have made it that Faith alone justifieth."

"So," said Gib, "that is very well." Yet he did not meet the other's eye, nor did he seem in his appearance at all jubilant, but kept looking down at the floor. For though theologically he was convinced of the truth of that doctrine, he was not able to feel it true in himself. All the Faith which he had, and it seemed to him to burn clear as a great fire, was not enough to enable him to do that simplest first work of all—merely to love his neighbour and receive those little ones, scrabbling and tittering behind him, as if each one were Christ. Without that, should Faith save him?

The Mercer chuckled.

"None will wholly rejoice," said he, "excepting the Bishop of Worcester."

"Why he?" Gib asked quickly.

"By the Mass! Because he is not learned in these subtleties and thinks it's all one, so as pilgrimages and relics and images are brought down, with purgatory, and so as justice be done between high and low; for that last has always been in especial his constant sharp concern."

"I know it has. I have heard it."

Twelve o'clock struck with dilatory halting concurrence from all the steeples near, and from farther off came the faint floating sound of other bells.

"Go! Go!" Gib flung over his shoulder at the lads, and they rushed out. The pounding of their feet on the boards ceased; from the yard outside rose the sharp babble of their voices. He turned to Master Hawkes and asked would he bring him to the Bishop of Worcester.

"Well," said the Mercer slowly, and with a cautious look, "if I could do so, what would you have of him?"

"That he should set me to work. He's a man after mine own heart," cried Gib. "If I could preach or write—" He thought, but did not say—"If I should mightily set forth God's word, that might suffice."

"You write for my Lord Privy Seal."

"He," said Gib, "has done much for the Gospel. Yet he is a worldly man. He minds power and policy, aye, and lucre, more than he minds God's matters."

He looked at Master Hawkes, righteous indignation now contending with the resentment of a rejected author in his face. "Will you bring me to the Bishop?" he urged.

The Mercer, unwilling to meddle further than he need in Gib's affairs, consented, but stiffly. He brought Gib to the Bishop's house and then handed him over to a small, square priest who had the figure and complexion of a ploughman, rather than of a clerk, and whose perfunctory, brief questions made Gib chafe.

Yet within half an hour he found himself sitting at a table opposite Hugh Latimer, Lord Bishop of Worcester, no stately person like Archbishop Lee, but a lean, stooping man, in an old gown and rubbed fur tippet, and with great horse teeth pushing out his lips in the midst of his greying beard.

Before him lay the remains of his dinner—the backbone of a herring on a notched wooden plate, salad, bread, and a horn cup of ale. He made Gib eat and drink too, sending away the square-shouldered chaplain for another fish, another penny loaf and more ale.

So it was easy for Gib to speak to this man, though he were a Bishop, and Latimer sat and listened, only chumbling with his lips in a way he had, as if he could never arrange his teeth quite to his liking.

When Gib had finished both his dinner and his explanation—which was a great deal of the lads at the chantry school, and a little of Lord Privy Seal, and nothing at all of Malle and dumb Wat—Latimer leaned back in his chair.

"As clear as it is to me," said he, "that you are a man who can preach, so clear it is that you are not one made to teach. And as for these massing matters in your chantry, neither you nor I see aught but blind superstition in them. So, if you, having as I can hear heart and will for it too, consent to come with me to my diocese, I will set you to preach God's

[699]

word to those who have not heard it this many a day."

Gib stared at him across the table.

"I—I—I can write," he stammered, and seemed altogether taken aback, and not at all as if this was that very thing he had hoped. "That is no less to advance God's cause than if I preach."

"But I," said the Bishop, "cannot maintain you here for that end. If you will write, you must go to Lord Privy Seal for your reward."

"I could remain at the chantry. It is enough without more reward."

"And the chantry, you tell me, is torment to you."

Gib blundered up, pitching back the stool he sat on.

"It is. It is. If I could come—" He covered his eyes and Latimer saw his throat work.

"Well, Master Dawe," he said coldly, "I can do no more for you than this. I had not done so much, perhaps, but that you sent up word that you were a man poor, and in danger of the judgement."

"Oh!" cried Gib, "shall I have time to think?"

"Humph!" said the Bishop, with some not unnatural impatience. Then he said, "Well, you shall have time. Come again within this week and ask me if you will."

Gib went down the Bishop's stairs knowing that far from escaping the judgement, he had brought himself to it. For once more he must choose whether to bide or to run.

Thunder came after dark and with it rain, a rushing sluice of unseen waters that mashed down great swathes of the tall, head-heavy wheat. Rain beating on his head and neck brought Aske back for a little while out of nightmare into conscious horror. He saw in the scribble of lightning which split black night the sheer drop of the wall beside him; the green far away below.

And as his eye told him of the sickening depth below his body, and as his mind foreknew the lagging endlessness of torment before him, so, as if the lightning had brought an inner illumination also, he knew the greater gulf of despair above which his spirit hung, helpless and aghast.

God did not now, nor would in any furthest future, prevail. Once He had come, and died. If He came again, again He would die, and again, and so for ever, by His own will rendered powerless against the free and evil wills of men.

Then Aske met the full assault of darkness without reprieve of hoped-for light, for God ultimately vanquished was no God at all. But yet, though God was not God, as the head of the dumb worm turns, so his spirit turned, blindly, gropingly, hopelessly loyal, towards that good, that holy, that merciful, which though not God, though vanquished, was still the last dear love of a vanquished and tortured man.

July 22

By this time that which dangled from the top of the Keep at York, moving only as the wind swung it, knew neither day nor night, nor that it had been Robert Aske, nor even that it had been a man.

Even now, however, it was not quite insentient. Drowning yet never drowned, far below the levels of daylight consciousness, it suffered. There was darkness and noise, noise intolerably vast or unendurably near, drilling inward as a screw bites and turns, and the screw was pain. Sometimes noise, pain, darkness and that blind thing that dangled were separate; sometimes they ran together and became one.

That evening Wat came skulking into the chantry chapel to be out of the way while his father and old Kat quarrelled upstairs. Kat had returned from the tavern very drunk and in good fighting trim, so it was likely they would both be at it for some time.

When he had shut the door behind him he was sorry and turned to steal out again; but a stick fallen from one of the jackdaws' nests in the roof snapped under his foot, and Malle, who stood near the altar with her hands over her face, turned, saw him, and called "Wat!"

He went edging towards her, stepping lightly, as if at a word he would run. Yet she did not touch him when he came, but plumped down on the altar steps, and looked up at him standing a little way off.

She said, "Darkness, and God moving nigh-hand in the darkness." Her hands wrenched one against the other, then dropped lax on her knees, and she smiled. In the long silence that followed they could hear the sound of Gib's voice and old Kat's voice, and the bump of something heavy that might have been a bench overturned in the room above.

Then Malle said: "The darkness is done. The sun's risen, just one morning like any other sunshine morning, with folks about their business and wives baking bread, and the mill-wheel turning. It's all light in the churchyard, young new light, the colour of green apples when they're golding over."

Wat crept a little nearer, but he was shaking.

"God 'a mercy!" Malle cried, "God 'a mercy! Here He comes between the graves, out of the grave.

"When He was born a man," she said, "He put on the leaden shroud that's man's dying body. And on the Cross it bore Him down, sore heavy, dragging against the great nails, muffling God, blinding Him to the blindness of a man. But there, darkened within that shroud of mortal lead, beyond the furthest edge of hope, God had courage to trust yet in hopeless, helpless things, in gentle mercy, holiness, love crucified.

"And that courage, Wat, it was too rare and keen and quick a thing for sullen lead to prison, but instead it broke through, thinning lead, fining it to purest shining glass, to be a lamp for God to burn in.

"So men may have courage," she said, and caught Wat by the skirt of his coat as she stood up. "Then they will see how bright God shines.

"Come," she said, dragging Wat towards the door, "and tell him that's been taken far from here to die."

But Robert Aske had gone too far, nor did he need now that Malle should tell him.

For now (yet with no greater fissure between then and now than a man's eyes are aware, where no star was, of the first star of night), now he was aware of One—vanquished God, Saviour who could as little save others as Himself.

But now, beside Him and beyond was nothing, and He was silence and light.

The Chronicle of Robert Aske, Squire, ends here.

November 2

Wat came in late for dinner. He stumbled into the room, leaving the door wide. When Gib cried, "Shut the door!" he turned and lurched towards it, but fell before he reached it. Up jumped Kat, to stare at him as he lay on the floor.

"The Sickness," she said.

There it was, in a word, for they all knew that the Great Sweat was still about in London since the unseasonable warm autumn.

As the disease had struck Wat suddenly, so it worked quickly upon him. By evening Gib could endure the sights and sounds of the lad's malady no longer. He got up, tucked his book under his arm, and said there was an errand he must do, and not to bar the door, for he might be back late.

"Aye, by God's Teeth," said Kat, busy stirring something over the fire. "Go forth if ye're afraid of the Sweat."

Gib was not afraid, and for a moment he hung on his heel, willing to show her that her taunt was unjust. But he cast a look upon Wat, and then he hurried out. He had not thought where he would go, and now did not choose his way with any very clear intention, yet when once he started he went in a great hurry, as if he were late for an appointment. And he was indeed very late. Bishop Latimer had said— "Come to me again next week," but that was months ago. No use to go now. "He'll not see me," thought Gib; and then —"Nor I'll not ask that he shall—only look upon the house when I go by." Yet there lurked in his mind a thought that it was the finger of Providence which had brought the Bishop here to London to preach dead Queen Jane's funeral sermon, just at this very time.

When he came to the house, and saw the broad, brown-faced ploughman of a chaplain even now going in, he was sure that Providence was pointing him in too. And by that sheer conviction he got in, and up to the same small plain room where the Bishop sat reading by the light of a candle, and blowing his nose loudly and frequently, for he had a great cold.

"Well," said Hugh Latimer, when Gib stood before him, glowering at the floor, "what do you want with me this time?"

"Sir," Gib lifted his eyes, and Latimer, though in the throe of a great sneeze, did not miss the meaning of his look; he had known enough men that despaired of salvation to recognize one such when he saw him.

"Sir," said Gib, "is it better that he that knoweth himself to be a castaway should preach or be silent?"

"It is best," Latimer answered, after he had trumpeted into his handkerchief, "that he should by the Grace of God be a man redeemed, and no castaway. But though he hath no assurance of salvation, yet he must preach. For," said he, warming to his subject, "our Bishops and Abbots adulterate the word of God, mingling it with the dreams of men, like taverners who pour good and bad together into one pot.

Purgatory, which they preach, is, forsooth, a fiery furnace, for it has burned away many a poor man's pence. Go you to Canterbury, or even no further than Westminster hereby, and you shall find images covered with gold, and dressed in silks, and lighted with wax candles, yea, even at noon, while Christ's living images are anhungered and thirst. Surely if we who know the light of the true Gospel shall hold our peace, the very stones will cry out against us that let their preaching go unanswered."

Gib, shuffling his feet, listened, but sullenly. All this was true. The Bishop's counsel was also in effect what he wanted to hear. Yet he could not but consider the Bishop's eloquence ill-timed. Shall one preacher preach to another?

However, at the end of it he said, humbly enough, "Then, Sir, if you will, as you offered me before, set me to preach, I will be your bedeman with God for it."

"Good," said the Bishop, and worked his lips a while in silence, snuffling heavily, and at last asked when Gib would be ready.

"I am ready."

"Come then to-morrow. There is a church in Worcester—" and the Bishop began to tell Gib about it; the benefice was no great matter, but there were souls to save, and bitter enmity to meet of papist priests, informers, adversaries of the true light.

November 4

All through the dark morning hours Gib lay waking and wrestling, but whether he wrestled with the devil or with the Angel of the Lord he did not know; nor did he know, when the light came, whether he had won or lost.

The scholars found him by turns absent and savage; yet for once he regretted their going, for he must now return to the room below, where Malle and old Kat watched over the sick lad. There, when they had eaten, he plumped down in a corner, and with fingers stuffed into his ears, and face averted, he tried to read; at least he kept the book open on his knee.

Towards evening, seeing that Wat lay quiet, Kat mumbled that she'd go forth a while, but not for long. She had not been to the tavern either yesterday or to-day, so she went now with eagerness, yet with a backward look. "Not for long," she said again before she shut the door.

When Malle had blown up the fire, and set bread and

bacon and a jug of penny ale on the table for supper she drowsed with her head against the wall. So she did not see Gib wrap the New Testament and *The Prick of Conscience* inside two clean shirts and his best gown with a budge fur tippet, and take his staff in one hand and half the bacon clapped between two pieces of bread in the other, and go softly to the door. He, like old Kat, looked back before he shut it behind him, but he did not speak.

The short afternoon was almost gone when Malle woke. She did not look about her, not even to see whether Wat slept, but sat for a long time without moving, her hands in her lap, staring straight in front of her, with her mouth a little open, and her eyes very wide.

At last she got up and came to Wat. He lay quite still, just as he lay before she fell asleep, his face turned to the wall, and one hand under his cheek. She bent down over him, so that she could whisper in his ear.

She said: "No darkness, no darkness, for God hath come so nigh in the darkness that it tore all to tatters, and now is quite done away."

When he did not stir she stretched out her hand and, touching his neck, found him as cold as any little frog. So she cried over him for a while, but then, without wiping away her tears, she began to talk to him, though, simple as she was, she knew that he could not hear.

"Wat," she said, "listen how the wind blows, as if it were a great water rushing. All the trees in the wood toss their branches, and the leaves hiss and sigh. And though the doors are shut, in church it speaks too, groaning in the tower, for He groans with us. But the candle flames burn bright, lovely fire that we pluck from the empty air, so close He comes to us, for us to lay hold on in our need. So is the triumph of that High One great and peaceable, homely and glorious, and now and forever He sitteth down to His feast, waiting till we sit down with Him, and all the children have come home. But it is He Himself who bringeth us, each one upon His shoulder. We have but to stay still until He lift and carry us."

She leaned her head closer, as if she waited for an answer. Then she said:

"Stay till I come. I must tell your father."

But she could not tell Gib, because he had run away, for

the last time, and would not come back again, and that very hour rode out of London beside one of the Bishop of Worcester's servants, going towards the West.

It was a cheerless evening, and the sun set forlornly in a haze of chill yet tarnished light. Gib hung his head down as he went, and would neither speak nor look up, so beaten to the ground was he by shame, while his soul chawed upon something compared with the bitterness of which the salt smart of penitence would have been sweet as honey.

For now he knew that though God might save every other man, Gib Dawe He could not save. Once he had seen his sin as a thing that clung close as his shadow clung to his heels; now he knew that it was the very stuff of his soul. Never could he, a leaking bucket not to be mended, retain God's saving Grace, however freely outpoured. Never could he, that heavy lump of sin, do any other than sink, and sink again, however often Christ, walking on the waves, should stretch His hands to lift and bring him safe.

He did not know that though the bucket be leaky it matters not at all when it is deep in the deep sea, and the water both without it and within. He did not know, because he was too proud to know, that a man must endure to sink, and sink again, but always crying upon God, never for shame ceasing to cry, until the day when he shall find himself lifted by the bland swell of that power, inward, secret, as little to be known as to be doubted, the power of omnipotent grace in tranquil, irresistible operation.

As they passed Paul's great church it stood up to the south, between them and the drab ending of the day. But the light that smudged the sunset sky so mournfully, glowed warm rose through the clear grisaille of the clerestory, and blazed fire-red in the west window, as though a feast were prepared within, with lights in plenty and flame leaping from the hearth, for the celebration of some high holy days; as if a great King held carousal there, with all his joyful people around Him, with all His children brought safe home.

But because Gib fled, and because he was ashamed that he fled, he did not look up, and he did not see.

The Chronicle of Sir Gilbert Dawe, Priest, ends here.

THE END AND THE BEGINNING

THOUGH Gib did not come back to the chantry, no one else came to turn the two women out, so they stayed where they were. A week before Christmas a priest knocked at the door. He was a little old man who had a face like a mouse, wistful and eager, with very bright yet soft eyes; a tall lad behind him, in the livery of some gentleman, carried a bundle in which the sharp corners of books showed among the softer contours.

Malle came to the door, her arms white with flour, for she was baking, and the old priest told her that his name was Thomas Barker. He seemed to think it natural that he should come in, and the boy came in too and put down the big bundle on the floor. When the priest had given him a groat he went away, but the old man sat down by the hearth where the dough was plumping up and smelling most sweetly.

Malle had retreated into the farthest corner, where Gib's birchrod stood, and was watching him from there. He did not seem dangerous. He looked round the room once, and smiled at her. Then he drew some plain beads from the folds of his gown, and sat with his eyes shut, letting them slide ticking through his fingers. Malle stole from her corner at last, and lifted the cloth from the dough which was ready for baking. He did not glance at her, but when she came near again with the loaves he made the holy sign over them, and said something softly which she knew was a blessing on the bread, before she slid them into the bake-oven.

In a little while old Kat came back from the tavern, swaying and quarrelsome. She did not leave him to sit there without questioning, and soon found out that he was the new chantry priest. When she heard that, she turned from truculent to maudlin, and flopped down on a stool whimpering that, aye, she had always known it, so might she and the poor fool now go packing.

"If you go," said he, "who'll look after the helpless silly old man?"

For quite a time after that Malle expected that another old man, who was helpless and silly, would come to the chantry, but he never came. Only the old priest was there. He slipped as easily into their life as oil into a rusty lock.

Once a big black-bearded gentleman visited him, who seemed, in his high white leather riding boots, and wide-skirted green fustian coat, to fill the room, so that Malle was frightened, especially as he had two dogs with him. But the old priest talked to him with very familiar cheerfulness, calling him Jack, and even Jackanapes, while the large gentleman called him nothing but "Sir," and "my Father."

At supper that night the old man told them that this had been Sir John Uvedale, "whom," said he, "I taught whatsoever latinity could be driven into his thick skull. No scholar—oh, no, no, no—yet a good lad. Surely a very good lad." He went on, in that way he had, nodding and murmuring to himself. At last he looked across at Malle and Kat with bright, gentle eyes:

"I cannot think it right, my daughters, that they pull down the Abbeys, and he is among them that do it. But if it is in him, then I pray God to set against it his goodness to me." He seemed to forget his supper then, because he shut his eyes, and they saw his lips move.

In the spring old Kat died. She fell suddenly to the floor one evening, and lay there twitching and groaning. They got her to bed, but she could neither speak nor move, and her face was puckered horribly as if she snarled at them. In a week she was dead, but Malle stayed on with the old priest, cooking and doing for him in her muddled way. She was not frightened of him now, for he was never angry, and would sit and read, or tell his beads, with his feet under the bench and the skirts of his gown drawn close, while the worst of household disorders weltered around him. Malle talked to him while she worked, chattering as she had used to do with Wat, garrulous as a sparrow, but never about Gib or Wat, or anything that was in the past. Sometimes, though not often, he would check her, saying gently, "Peace, good wench. There are times for silence." Then she would clap her hand over her mouth, and tiptoe about her work, breathing heavily, and overturning or dropping more things than ever in her efforts to be quiet.

One day, nearly two years after he had come to the chantry, she came back from buying pigs' trotters and hocks for making brawn, to find him reading a letter, which, he told her, the carrier had brought him out of Yorkshire. It was from Sir John Uvedale, and he sent, the old priest said, to fetch him back to the North Country—"where I was born," said he. "For I was born a long way from here, at a place called Topcliffe on Swale."

Malle looked out of the window. In the street the rain was falling straight as rods. But she saw a fair early morning when she and Wat had driven Black Thomas, the Ladies' mule, across the river, and he had rubbed the sack of rye off the saddle against a tree.

"The Swale," said she, "was very cold that day and the little knave slipped when the stones rolled under his feet and nearly got a dousing."

"What!" said the old man, "are you also of Topcliffe? No —for I should know if you came from any village in ten miles and more around."

She shook her head, and murmured, as if it were a word she had long forgotten, and must try again on her tongue to know how it sounded "Marrick . . . Marrick."

"God 'a mercy!" said he, "that's stranger still. For Sir John will have me to be parson of Marrick, and if you will come you shall keep my house for me there."

She looked at him in her slow way, and then cried very eagerly—

"Will *He* be there? Shall I find *Him* there?"

He could not get from her the name of him whom she hoped to find at Marrick, but because she grew so wild, at last he took her hand and held it between his own.

"Child," he said, "whomsoever we find there, God's Christ we shall find, if we seek for Him."

"Ah!" she said, with a long sigh. "When shall we go?"

They reached Marrick on the very day that the Ladies went away, and Sir John Uvedale's people at once became very busy setting things to rights against his coming in the evening. The old priest left them to it and went down to the river side, to walk up and down by the Swale in the sweet faint sunshine of November, telling his beads in quietness.

But Malle hunted about both outside and inside the Priory —up to the little gate at the foot of the Nuns' Steps, into the kitchen, the Prioress's Chamber, the Guest Chamber; into the Cloister, where she picked up some of the bravely painted pages of the books which Uvedale's man had torn and scattered there. Then, because two of them shouted at her, she bolted out of the Cloister and went across the Great Court to the dove house and stable. But back she came after a little while to the church, still seeking and peering.

At last she came to the Frater, where, on the table, lay the litter of the Ladies' last meal. Among the crumbled bread and empty egg shells there lay upon one dish what was left of a piece of broiled fish, and upon another half a honeycomb.

She knew then that He had been there, and that they had given Him to eat of these things so short a time before that the comb still oozed into the dish transparent gold from its severed cells.

She hurried away down the steep meadow to the banks of the Swale. The old priest stopped his pacing and smiled at her.

"He *is* here," she said.

He nodded to her, glad that she had found the one she had hoped to find, and then continued to walk up and down.

Malle went and sat down where the grassy bank broke in a low sandy cliff, and set her feet upon the scoured, white, water-rounded stones left dry by the river, which though it was now November was still shrunken by a long autumn drouth. One of these stones she laid carefully upon the painted pages which she had gathered up in the Cloister, so that they should not be blown away. Then she began to fold them, one by one, into the shape of tiny boats.

The old priest drew near to see what she would be at. When he saw, it was in his mind to rebuke her for such a misuse of holy writings. But he did not, for, he thought, she is as innocent as ignorant. And then he thought, "Even so ignorantly, and almost as childishly, do we launch forth our prayers upon the silence and the dark. And to Him they came, and after to us return; but what went out from us as these little boats of paper, He sends again to us, an Argosy, deep-laden." So he only smiled at her when she looked up, and went back to his pacing and to his meditation, which had been of God's love and His great work in the redemption of the world.

For he had been thinking how God's plan had, by sin, been horribly wrested from its high and sweet perfection. It was, he thought, as if number itself had rebelled, forsaking congruity and order, so that not only must the children's sums go awry, but the whole fabric of reason split from crown to base, men's minds founder, and the sun and stars cease to keep due course. "No less a thing," he thought, "no lighter, have we men done with our sins. No less a thing, to make right again of that most monstrous wrong, has God done. To right it God came, and was a man. God did not only send, He came."

He thought—"I must tell her. Even she must learn and know this thing."

Yet when he came close to her again he could find no words to tell her, so sure he was that no words could make her understand so high a matter.

She had taken all the papers from under the stone, and now those which were not yet folded into boats lay in a bright litter at his feet; he looked down and read upon one the words:

It is true, that sin is cause of all this pain; but all shall be well, and all manner of thing shall be well.

On another was written:

See I am God; See I am in all things; See I do all things: See I never left my hands of my works, ne never shall without end: See I lead all things to the end that I ordain it to, from without beginning, by the same might, wisdom, and love, that I made it with. How should anything be amiss?

And on another:

What? wouldest thou wit thy Lord's meaning in this thing? Wit it well: love was his meaning. Who sheweth it thee? Love. Wherefore sheweth he it thee? For love. Hold thee therein, thou shalt wit more in the same. But thou shalt never wit therein other without end.

All those pages had initial letters of blue, or dusky blood-red, painted upon the paper, but there were two which were of parchment, smaller but much more glorious, with borders of twined flowers of all colours and golden letters, plumped up above gesso, and burnished by long rubbing with a bear's tooth.

On one of these was written:

Deum de Deo: lumen de lumine: Deum verum de Deo vero.

And on the other:

Homo factus est.

When Malle had made all the little ships ready to sail, she set them on the water, where it lapped, trembling and bright, close to her feet. They bobbed and curtseyed there, loitering a minute till the strength of the river caught them. Then they went dipping and dancing away towards the sea.

PLAN OF MARRICK PRIORY

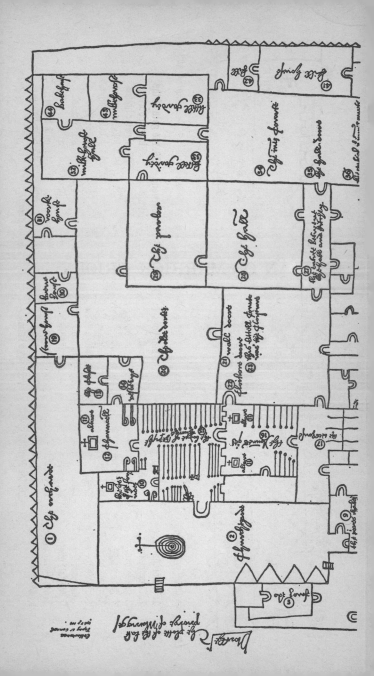

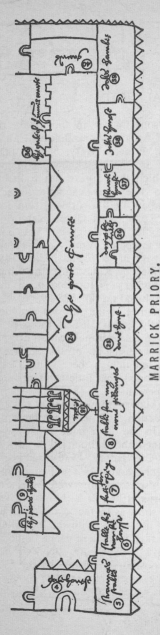

MARRICK PRIORY.

From a plan drawn up probably about fifty years after the Dissolution. (Reproduced from Collectanea Topographica et Genealogica, 1838.)

1. The orcharde.
2. Churchyarde.
3. oxe house.
4. gate house.
5. straungers stable.
6. stable for worke horsse.
7. for fatt oxen.
8. stable for my owne geldinges.
9. the priores chamber.
10. the quier of the founder.
11. altare.
12. Chancell.
13. the Closett.
14. vestereye.
15. the bodye of the paryshe churche.
16. the Nonnes quier.
17. the bell house.
18. stepell.
19. stoore house.
20. The olde dorter.
21. wall doore.
22. Cloistore doore.
23. This littell Courte was the Cloisture.
24. The grate Courte.
25. dove house.
26. dogge kenels.
27. the entree betwene the hall and the kitchen.
28. The hall.
29. The parlor.
30. brewe house.
31. worke house.
32. milk house hall.
33. littell garden.
34. The inner Courte.
35. the hall doore.
36. the gate of the inner courte.
37. slawter house.
38. Joks house.
39. Joks chamber.
40. garners.
41. Still house.
42. Still.
43. milk house.
44. bake house.

HISTORICAL NOTE

A great many historical persons appear in this book, of whom Henry VIII, Katherine of Aragon, Anne Boleyn, Cardinal Wolsey, Thomas Cromwell, Princess Mary, Sir Thomas More and Archbishop Cranmer are the best known. Not all, but many of the episodes in which they appear are founded upon documentary evidence. To take a few examples: much of Foxe's report to the Car nal in 1528 is drawn from the letters of the English agents i. Rome; what Queen Katherine said to Montfalconnet, to the nobles and clergy in 1531, and to Mountjoy was reported to the Emperor by his Ambassador; Anne Boleyn's arrival at the Tower in 1536 and her conversation with Kingston were described by Kingston to the King.

The description of Marrick nunnery is founded upon the late sixteenth century plan, reproduced on pp. 628-29, as well as upon local knowledge. The names of the prioress and her nuns are drawn from the (slightly longer) list of those pensioned at the Dissolution. Owing to delays in publication caused by the war Archbishop Lee's last Visitation of the Nunnery was not available for reference, but though there is little evidence for the character of the Prioress, that little is interesting, and, I think, suggestive of her personality.

Much of Lord Darcy's life is known from documents; these have been used in this reconstruction, and his rather puzzling character inferred from them. On the other hand Julian Savage and Gilbert Dawe are imagined and without any historical foundation. Of Robert Aske's life before 1536 practically nothing is known except his connection with the Percys and his entrance into Gray's Inn; his association with Margaret Cheyne is entirely fictitious. Margaret herself is, however, historical, though it is doubtful if she was in fact a daughter of Buckingham. The events of her life, again with the exception of her relations with Robert Aske, are taken from contemporary documents. From these I had already supposed her character when I found my supposition confirmed by the fact that up to the early years of the nineteenth century she was still remembered in Yorkshire under the name of Madge Wildfire.

For the Pilgrimage of Grace, in which the historical theme of the book culminates, there is a mass of evidence, so that almost all the scenes connected with the rising are founded upon documents. To take some instances: Robert Aske's report to the King gives an account of his own movements during the first few days of his connection with the Lincolnshire rising. Lancaster Herald described his mission to Pontefract in a long document, much of which has been used verbatim; the Duke of Norfolk's dealings with the leaders of the Pilgrimage are revealed in his own letters and in such confessions as that of Cresswell. Aske's replies to examination in the Tower throw much light both on his character and on the motives of the Pilgrims, and I have made use of these, as well as of many other depositions, though unfortunately, again owing to the war, I could not, except in a very few instances, go behind the printed version to the original manuscript.

To indicate to what degree and where this book reproduces authentic history would need, however, far greater space than can be spared in a Note. This is a novel, and much in it is, necessarily, imaginary. But I have been scrupulous to preserve undistorted any fact known to me, with two minor exceptions.* In broad outline the account which I have given of historical events is as correct as I have been able to make it, and there are besides, indistinguishable to the reader among the imaginary scenes and persons, many such intimate yet authentic facts as the devotion of Aske's servant to his master, the dislike of Anne Boleyn for monkeys, or the quarrel of Mr. Patchett's servant with the ostler at Cambridge. The music of the song on p. 546 may be found on page 632, reproduced from the Antiquaries' Journal, vol. XV, 1935, p. 21.

* The name of Robert Aske's servant was Robert Wall, but the name was changed to avoid confusion. The disposition of the buildings of St. Helen's, Bishopsgate, was not that which is here described. In one important particular I have differed from other writers upon the Pilgrimage of Grace. My authority for the King's vengeance upon Robert Aske is Wriothesley's detailed account of the execution of the leaders of the Pilgrimage, in which he mentions the punishment which each received, and distinguishes between the hanging of Sir Robert Constable and that of Robert Aske (Wriothesley I, 65).